Dale Brown

A former US Air Force captain, Dale Brown served as a navigator from 1978 to 1986, logging thousands of hours aboard both B-52 and FB-111 bombers. His bestselling novels include: *Flight of the Old Dog*, *Silver Tower*, *Day of the Cheetah*, *Sky Masters*, *Night of the Hawk*, *Chains of Command*, *Storming Heaven* and, most recently, *Shadows of Steel*. Dale Brown lives in Nevada, where he can often be found in the skies, piloting his own plane.

'Dale Brown is the best military adventure writer in the country today, a master at creating a sweeping epic and making it seem real.'　　　　CLIVE CUSSLER

'Dale Brown is a superb storyteller.'　　*Washington Post*

'When Brown has you in the cockpit, the excitement is hard to beat.'　　*Sunday Oklahoman*

BY DALE BROWN

DALE BROWN

HAMMERHEADS

HarperCollins*Publishers*

HarperCollins*Publishers*
77–85 Fulham Palace Road,
Hammersmith, London W6 8JB

This paperback edition 1993
5 7 9 8 6 4

Previously published in paperback by Grafton 1991
(Special Grafton overseas edition 1991)
Reprinted twice

First published in Great Britain by
Grafton 1990

V-22 Osprey Joint Service Aircraft diagram,
pp x-xi, courtesy of Bell-Boeing

ISBN 0 586 20819 4

Set in Times

Printed and bound in Great Britain by
Caledonian International Book Manufacturing Ltd, Glasgow

To Jean –
yes, you deserve it.
And
to Mayme –
you're the greatest!

Acknowledgments

Hammerheads was conceived in December of 1988 in a quaint old restaurant in London, England, during a relaxing dinner with Jonathan Lloyd, managing director of Grafton Books, and my agents George and Olga Wieser. It was they who planted the idea in my mind to investigate the world of drug trafficking and drug interdiction, an area I previously knew little about, and it is to them that I wish to thank first of all for their ideas, suggestions, and encouragement.

I would like to thank the following individuals, agencies, and companies for their invaluable assistance in the making of *Hammerheads*:

United States Customs Service: To Joe Krokos, Ralph Muser and Ed Perez, for arranging a very enlightening visit to all the south Florida operations; Lt Cmdr Jim Wade and Gene Wilcox at C-3 and C-3-I radar centers in Miami; to all the agents of the Blue Thunder Marine Division for a thrilling ride in their big interceptors; to Inspectors Frank Mullin, Mike Norwood, and Michael Holloway of the Contraband Enforcement Team, who showed me the 'down and dirty' (and 'saucy!') side of drug interdiction; and to Senior Inspector Roger Garland, pilot Dave Sherrey, and the other professionals of the Miami Air Branch, for their hospitality during my visit to the nation's best drug air interdiction unit.

United States Coast Guard: A very special thanks to Lt Jeff Karonis, Chief of Public Affairs, Seventh Coast Guard District in Miami, for arranging a spectacular visit to the Coast Guard's Miami and Ft Lauderdale operations; to Capt Kent Vallantyne, former commander of Coast Guard Air Station Miami, the world's busiest search and rescue operation; to Lt Kevin Rahl and his HU-25C Falcon crew for a spectacular air patrol; to Lt Curry, commander of the Coast Guard patrol boat WPB-1302 *Manitou*; and to Lt Scott Burhoe and the men and women of Coast Guard Station Ft Lauderdale, for their time and helpfulness.

To Terry Arnold and Bob Leder of Bell Helicopter Textron and everyone at the Bell-Boeing Joint Development Team, Arlington, Texas, for their help in providing information on the V-22 Osprey tilt-rotor aircraft;

To my wife, Jean, for legal research into federal agency reorganization regulations and for her valuable advice and help; and to Dennis Hall, for his help in arranging research trips, gathering information, and for his support;

Thanks to Air Force Major Ronald D. Fuchs, Deputy Director and Chief of Media Relations, Western Region, Air Force Office of Public Affairs, for the information he provided that was invaluable in understanding the border security responsibilities of the US Air Force;

To the US Naval Institute Military Database, for information on defense data for nations of the Caribbean and South America; and to the CompuServe Information Service, Columbus, Ohio, for information and assistance in a wide array of topics.

Details on fighter air combat maneuvers in the various chapters provided by Robert L. Shaw's *Fighter Combat, Tactics and Maneuvering* (Naval Institute Press, 1987).

Text from a news briefing by Dick Cheney, US Secretary of Defense, at the Pentagon, 18 September 1989:

'There can be no doubt that international trafficking in drugs is a national security problem for the United States. Therefore, detecting and countering the production and trafficking of illegal drugs is a high-priority, national security mission of the Department of Defense.

'We will work hard to stop the delivery of drugs on their way to the United States and at our borders and ports of entry. Deploying appropriate elements of the armed forces with the primary mission of cutting off the flow of drugs should help reduce the flow of drugs into the country over time. At the very least, it will immediately complicate the challenge of getting illegal drugs into America and increase the cost and risk of drug smuggling.

'. . . The Department of Defense will be the lead agency in performing the interdiction mission.'

(from *Defense 89*, official publication of the US Department of Defense, American Forces Information Service, Alexandria, VA, November–December 1989)

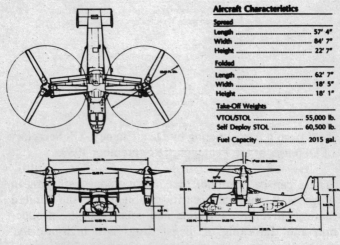

Aircraft Characteristics

Spread	
Length	57' 4"
Width	84' 7"
Height	22' 7"

Folded	
Length	62' 7"
Width	18' 5"
Height	18' 1"

Take-Off Weights	
VTOL/STOL	55,000 lb.
Self Deploy STOL	60,500 lb.
Fuel Capacity	2015 gal.

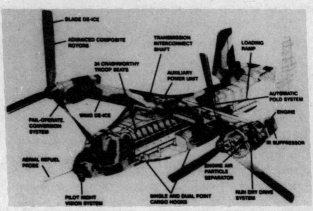

V-22 Osprey Joint Service Aircraft

MISSIONS

U.S. Marine Corps – MV-22

Vertical Assault Transport of troops, equipment and supplies from amphibious assault ships and land bases.

U.S. Navy – HV-22

Strike Rescue, delivery and retrieval of special warfare teams, and logistics transportation in support of the fleet.

U.S. Air Force – CV-22

Long Range special operations missions, insertion and extraction of U.S. Army special forces teams and equipment at mission radii in excess of 500 NM.

U.S. Army – MV-22

Aeromedical evacuation, special operations, long range combat logistics support, combat air assault and low intensity conflict support.

DESCRIPTION

- Two 38 foot rotor systems
- Powered by two Allison T406-AD-400 engines – 6150 SHP each
- Operates as a helicopter when taking off and landing vertically
- Nacelles rotate 90 degrees forward once airborne, converting the aircraft into a turboprop airplane
- Speeds from hover to 300 knots
- Transmission interconnect shaft in case of an engine failure
- Folds for stowage aboard ship
- 70% composite construction
- Crashworthy troop and crew seats
- Two 10,000 lb external cargo hooks
- Rescue hoist
- Cargo winch and pulley system for internal cargo loads
- Aft loading ramp
- Capable of all weather, day/night, low-level, nap-of-the-earth flight
- Continuous operation in moderate icing
- Inflight refueling
- Ballistic tolerant
- Self-deployable world-wide

DEVELOPMENT

First Flight 1988
Service Use 1992

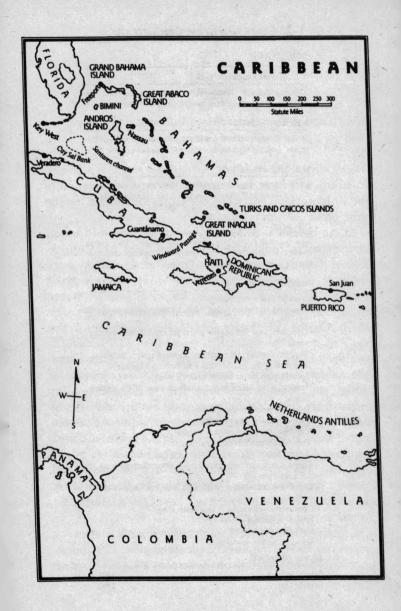

Chapter One

Joint Tactical Drug Interdiction Information Center,
Miami Air Traffic Control Center, Miami, Florida

They called it the 'witching hour,' the time from 8.00 P.M. to 1.00 A.M., when the smugglers seemed to come out of the woodwork. Like cockroaches, they said, when the sun went down the smuggler came out.

In the basement of Miami Air Traffic Control Center, three men were looking for them. These men, two Customs Service agents and one Coast Guard petty officer, were manning the radar screens of the Joint Tactical Drug Interdiction Information Center, known as JTDIIC, where all air traffic in the southeast United States was kept under watch. On the two twenty-four-inch radar screens in the box-like room the JTDIIC, call sign SLINGSHOT, combined radar data from Federal Aviation Administration radars, aerostats – balloon-borne radars located in Florida, the Bahamas and Puerto Rico – and military radar units to form a composite picture of the hundreds of aircraft from North Carolina to New Orleans, including the eastern Gulf of Mexico, the eastern Caribbean and northern Cuba. They could scan aircraft, receive coded identification and flight data information, gain access to flight plans and Customs pre-declarations, talk with air-traffic controllers and vector in Customs Service or Coast Guard interceptor aircraft to trail a suspect aircraft.

In reality SLINGSHOT didn't watch each and every aircraft out there – impossible for three men. Computers processed the information on the screens and squelched or

1

eliminated aircraft not suspected of anything illegal or following suspect flight profiles. So, as far as possible, commercial airliners, local flights, aircraft cleared or talking with air-traffic control or aircraft on established airways and flying at normal route altitudes and airspeeds were electronically removed from the screen.

Theoretically, that left only the bad guys.

Theoretically.

Aircraft from foreign departure points were supposed to inform Customs of their arrival time and destination and to file flight plans when entering the coastal ADIZ, the Air Defense Identification Zones – huge blocks of airspace, some as much as a hundred and fifty miles wide, along the edges of North America's borders that were scanned by the military to warn of any hostile aircraft approaching the continent.

Since it was illegal to fly anywhere in the huge Bahamas island chain at night, aircraft flying to or from the Bahamas after sunset were immediately suspect. Of course, any plane flying very low to the water or obviously trying to skirt the fixed radar sites along the coast was suspect.

Despite this being the witching hour it seemed to be shaping up to be a pretty quiet evening. José Gusman, a Customs Service GS-13 from Hialeah, yawned sleepily as he rolled a cursor across his screen onto a red square on his radar screen. The red indicated that the return was not 'squawking,' transmitting any coded identification signals. He hit a button on his console and a small data block of numerals flashed on the screen: 'UNK TR 4.' The return was an unknown, but from its altitude, airspeed and signal-strength information the computer had assigned it a track reliability of 4, which meant that it probably wasn't an aircraft at all – more likely an isolated thundercloud or a flock of birds.

Gusman turned his attention away from the newcomer but did not forget about it – the computer was known to be wrong, this thundercloud could turn into a real plane. 'Must be a storm brewing out there, I'm getting a lot of fuzz,' he said to his partner, Stan Wexfall.

'I got one that's definitely not fuzz,' Wexfall said. 'Take a look over Santa Clara.'

Gusman, reconfiguring his scope, knew where to look – central Cuba. Santa Clara was the location of a major Cuban airport and, more importantly, an air-navigation checkpoint on the South America to Florida smuggling run. But it was also a major air-traffic corridor, used every day, all day, by dozens of aircraft – but only for airlines friendly with the Castro regime. 'I got him now,' Gusman said. 'No mode four or mode C.'

'Weird. Not transmitting any standard air-traffic control codes,' Wexfall said, zooming his scope in to an area thirty miles around the newcomer, 'but flying right over central Cuba at night. The Cuban Air Force usually gets nervous about night flights – they scream bloody murder when we launch patrols near them at night.' Wexfall looked over at Gusman. 'Military?'

'Gotta be,' Gusman replied. 'The Cubans wouldn't let an unidentified plane just fly around like that. We'll have to call the Air Force or Navy to get a readout on him – we can't display military IFF codes on our sets.' Gusman picked up his coffee cup and went over to a desk that had a computer terminal and printer and logged onto the system. 'I'll ask Navy if they got any codes on this guy.'

A few minutes later they received a response via the computer terminal: 'Bingo. Message from naval intelligence: this guy is squawking military modes and codes.'

'Thought so.'

Wexfall continued to watch the target as it progressed northward. Suddenly: 'Hey, look at this!'

3

The target symbol had changed from red to green as it crossed the northern coastline of Cuba – the aircraft had begun transmitting standard US identification codes. Wexfall said, 'Now he's showing normal modes and codes. Bacchus 204 Delta. Altitude twelve thousand five hundred, airspeed two-forty, dead on the airway.' Gusman turned to the computer terminal again, this time to get a copy of any flight plans the newcomer may have filed.

This guy was smarter than most. A lot of smugglers, either unaware of the extensive surveillance network in south Florida or just willing to take a chance, never activated their IFF radios or attempted to contact anyone by radio. Such activities were prima facie evidence of smuggling and they become fair game for Customs and Coast Guard interceptors.

But smugglers were getting savvy to procedures. It was a simple matter for them to file the proper entry-request forms and use their radios, thereby greatly increasing their chances of safely entering the country. And once over land they could pretty much navigate unmolested.

'Filed for entry yesterday, processed, verified and approved,' Gusman said. 'Departed Santa Marta, Colombia, three hours ago. Destination St Petersburg. Two passengers carrying bank records and accounting materials.'

Heads turned toward Gusman when he read 'Colombia.' Flights from Colombia and Bolivia, the drug producing and export centers of the Western world, were tops on the list of countries watched by Customs.

Gusman returned to the terminal keyboard. 'I'll run a cross-check on the port-of-entry request and the hit list,' he said. He was excited – one of the few things that kept people going at the job was getting involved in a major drug bust.

Gusman entered keywords from the port-of-entry

4

request to cross-check with the hit list – the names of arrests or busted smugglers with the name 'Bacchus' in the database. The system would now try to match those keywords with the files headed 'Bacchus.'

During the search Wexfall kept track on the suspect while he turned over area-wide surveillance to the third Coast Guard specialist. Ten minutes later Gusman called out, 'I got something. Nineteen seventy-two. Damn near identical flight path, except back then the guy didn't file a port-of-entry request. Early evening flight, directly across Cuba, departure Santa Maria, reported as an in-and-out – never landed, just flew in and flew out. Call sign: Bacchus one-seven-three X-ray November.'

'Yeah, but he's got a flight plan this time,' Wexfall said. 'He's cleared to enter. He – '

The printer clattered to life again. 'Another hit. Nineteen eighty. Flights recorded by a Bacchus aircraft, Santa Marta and Cartagena, Colombia, to Saint Pete, Sarasota and Bradenton. Checked out good for several weeks except once for an apparent no-show after reporting in to Miami Center. Flights discontinued soon after.' He read on further, then added: 'Manifest says he was carrying – what else? – accounting materials.'

Wexfall checked his screen. The target had crossed over Cuba and was out into the Strait of Florida on course for St Petersburg, making no attempt to avoid the aerostat site or Navy radar sites at Key West and still transmitting the proper ID codes.

'What now, Stan?' Gusman said. 'Get someone up there to check him out?'

'On what grounds? He's not an unknown. He's been cleared in. Bacchus is a common enough name – you got fifty names like it on that printout. With only two old hits it's pretty weak.'

'But this guy matches up with previous suspects,'

Gusman said. 'His chances of making it to Saint Pete are poor to nil.'

Wexfall still didn't seem convinced.

'We have the authority to launch a chase plane on our own – '

'I know, I know,' Wexfall said. As senior controller at SLINGSHOT, it was his decision. But every launch against a so-called probable suspect, especially night intercepts, was expensive and risky and laid a guy open to criticism – any mistake against a plane attempting to follow the rules could be disastrous. If it was a low-flying unidentified target the decision would be a lot easier. 'The military codes worry me. Maybe we should ask the Air Force to get someone up there to check him out.'

'They'd laugh us right into tomorrow,' Gusman said.

Wexfall nodded – the military was even more squeamish about sending an armed fighter up against a civilian prop-job. 'Who's on deck for this intercept?'

'Coast Guard,' Gusman told him.

Wexfall shrugged – they would have to do. In years past the Customs Service handled intercepts on suspected smugglers like this one, but since the entry of the Coast Guard into drug interdiction in the mid-1980s the job was often split between the two. There was no rhyme or reason to the selection – it depended on who was on deck or whose turn it was to do an intercept. It wasn't exactly the most effective or logical way to go, but that was the way it was.

'Get a Coast Guard Falcon on ten-minute standby,' Wexfall said to the Coast Guardsman seated beside him. 'Then get the air interdiction duty officer on the line. He might mix this intercept but we should have a bird ready to do in case he doesn't.'

* * *

The quarter spun in the air. Lieutenant Commander Kevin Rawlins let it drop into his left hand, turned it over onto the back of his right hand with a slap, then removed his left hand. He peered at the coin with a satisfied grin. 'Heads, I win.' He took the TV remote from his partner's hand, aimed it at the TV and pushed a button. '*Moonlighting*'s on in five minutes.'

'Let me see that quarter,' his copilot, Kelly Sandino, demanded.

'Sore loser.' Rawlins dropped into an armchair and lazily extended his legs across an oak coffee table in front of the television, letting his flight boots dangle over the opposite edge. Rawlins was of average height but had long lanky legs that were sometimes a real hassle. The rest of his thin wiry frame has just refused to grow along with his legs; even his flight suit was custom-made. His fellow Coast Guard HU-25C Falcon pilots always knew when Rawlins was the last to fly the plane because the seat was set all the way back and the rudder pedals set all the way forward.

'And don't forget the microwave popcorn, the one without the salt,' Rawlins said.

'Kiss it,' Sandino told him. Lieutenant, j.g., Kelly 'Grace' Sandino, one of only seventy female pilots in the US Coast Guard, was a dark-eyed beauty from Puerto Rico who somehow managed to tolerate Rawlins' antics and the role of being the only female jet pilot at Opa-Locka, to become one of its best pilots, period.

The crew was in good spirits. They had just begun the last day of a week-long alert cycle – twenty-four hours on, twenty-four hours off; this was their last on day before a two-week leave. Kevin was on his way to Key West for a long fishing trip, as far from a flight line as he could manage.

The alert day had started at 4.00 P.M., nearly five hours earlier, with a routine patrol sortie. This patrol was quick and dirty – actually a flight currency trip for one of the district headquarters staff members, who were required to fly at least six hours every two months to hold their flight status. They had another Falcon up on patrol, and the staffer did a few practice intercepts on him, being directed at first by SLINGSHOT, the joint Coast Guard and Customs Service ground radar controller, and then by the Falcon's own radar intercept officer. A few practice landings and the mission was over.

They were on bravo-ten alert status the rest of the tour, which meant that if they received a call to do an intercept they had to be airborne in ten minutes or less. Miami Air Station, the busiest search-and-rescue station, had Dolphin helicopters and Falcon jets on various levels of alert, from five to thirty minutes depending on the number of air-frames on station, mission requirements and warning time they could expect. Most of the rescue jets, like the search-and-rescue A-model Falcon and the drug interdiction C-model, were usually on ten-minute alert; Dolphin rescue choppers, the sleek, French-built high-tech jet helicopters, were on five-minute alert.

Kelly Sandino had just returned two minutes later with a steaming bag of popcorn when the public address system clicked on: 'Ready, alpha, report to the CQ's office.'

Rawlins threw the remote onto the coffee table, shuffled to his feet and grabbed a handful of popcorn as he found a phone and dialed the Charge of Quarters' office. 'Rawlins here. What's up?'

'SLINGSHOT's putting you on ten-minute alert,' the CQ, one of Rawlins' fellow pilots, replied. 'They got an in-bound north of Cuba they want to take a look at.'

Rawlins turned to Sandino, who was retying the laces on her flight boots. 'Gracie, get the crew together. Let's spin 'em up. I'll do the paperwork.'

Sandino had the crew on board, the auxiliary power unit on and activated and the crew chief ready to supervise the engine start by the time Rawlins came on board. Their Falcon jet was a Dassault-Breguet Falcon 20 jetliner, built in France, a big sexy workhorse of an air machine. Although the official designation was HU-25C Guardian, pilots assigned to drug interdiction kept the unofficial name Falcon on account of the high-tech, combat-fighterlike surveillance equipment and tactics they used chasing drug smugglers.

This version of the Coast Guard's newest rescue-and-patrol jet carried the APG-66 intercept attack radar, the same as on the Air Force's F-16 Fighting Falcon jet fighter, which could detect targets out to sixty miles and track up to six targets simultaneously. The Falcon also carried a high-resolution FLIR, a forward-looking infrared scanner, that was able to track air targets several miles away as well as ground objects as small as a dog from a mile in the sky.

All they needed, Rawlins had thought as he hurried up the airstairs and boarded the plane, were a few Sidewinder missiles on the wings and smugglers might think again about bringing their shit into America.

Sandino had the switches configured, external power on, and was all strapped in ready to go. 'Ready on number one,' Rawlins said as he quickly strapped in. He couldn't help but notice how Sandino's breasts always seemed to strain against the shoulder harness. If there was ever a manpower shortage in the Coast Guard, Rawlins thought, all they had to do was make a recruiting poster starring Gracie – it didn't matter if she was wearing a flight suit. She'd look dynamite in a poncho. Guys would be kicking down the doors to enlist.

Snap out of it, you old letch, Rawlins admonished himself. We've got work to do. 'Crew, stand by for engine start.'

'Radar ready,' from Petty Officer Joe Conklin in the rear end of the Falcon by his sensor console as he moved to a window to act as safety watch during each engine start.

'Clear on the right,' Sandino responded. 'Air, power, radios, lights set. Ready on one.'

Rawlins showed one index finger to Specialist First Class John Choy outside, then twirled it in a tight circle. After a last check around the left-engine area to clear, Choy gave Rawlins a thumbs-up and a twirling index finger.

'Starting one.' Rawlins advanced the throttle a half-inch, engaged the starters and the six-thousand-pound-thrust turbofan screamed to life. Thirty seconds later, as soon as Choy had moved his fire-extinguisher bottle and comm cord to the number-two engine, Sandino had the right engine started. Choy jumped on board, dogged the entry airstair closed and strapped himself in near the big observation window on the port side. A minute later they had taxied the short distance to the end of Opa-Locka's main east–west runway and were ready to go.

The Falcon accelerated smoothly down the nine-thousand-foot runway and soon the scene outside the cockpit windows was filled with the brilliant sprawling lights of Miami as they turned southbound over Miami Beach. 'Pretty romantic, don't you think, Gracie?' Rawlins remarked cross-cockpit as the dazzling panorama swept before them.

Sandino set the newly assigned Miami Center frequency into the number one UHF radio. 'Sure is,' the lady copilot replied. She shot a glance at Rawlins and smiled slyly. 'Present company excluded.'

'Don't you think this is exciting?' Rawlins pressed, sneaking a few more glances at his copilot's stunning profile. 'Even highly stimulating? The lights, the ocean, the speed. Doesn't it make your Latin blood hot?'

'Know what really makes me hot, Rawl?'

'Tell me, baby.'

'Pilots who are only two thousand feet above ground and who start a five hundred foot-per-minute descent instead of climbing. Watch your altitude.' Rawlins pulled back on the control wheel and retrimmed properly for a two-hundred-knot climb.

Five minutes later the Falcon was clear through Miami International's terminal control area. 'Miami Center, Omaha One-One changing to tactical frequency. Good evening.'

The Omaha call sign was a common one for any drug interdiction air unit on an active intercept, and air traffic control agencies knew to clear as much airspace as possible and stay on their toes when they heard that sign. 'Omaha One-One, change to company frequency, contact me on this frequency when returning,' the air traffic controller replied. Sandino switched the radio to SLINGSHOT's scrambled frequency, and both she and Rawlins slid one headphone pad off their ears as a raucous squealing and chirping obliterated all radio sound. Now the chirping sounds subsided until only a faint crackle could be heard as the anti-eavesdropping encryption-synchronization routine matched the built-in codes on the Falcon's radio receiver – only a radio with the built-in codes could lock out the interference.

Rawlins knew the smugglers would soon break the codes on this system, just as they found all the federal frequencies and started intercepting or eavesdropping on them. Incredibly, many of the law-enforcement radio frequencies had been *published*, and it was a relatively simple process to build or steal a descrambler. *They* had all the advantages –especially the money – to fight the drug wars.

Soon the slightly squeaky, distorted voice of Wexfall in the basement of Miami Air Traffic Control came back: 'Omaha One-One, how copy?'

Sandino keyed her mike button. 'Four by.'

'Roger. Stand by for your final controller.' There was a slight pause as Wexfall handed over control to the more experienced Gusman, who had the initial flight vectors set up well before he nodded to Wexfall to accept controller's responsibility. 'One-One, fly heading one-zero-zero and maintain two thousand feet, your bogey is at sixty miles and low.'

Rawlins made a slight right turn and engaged the autopilot. 'Okay, Conk, he's at sixty miles low. Go get 'em.'

'Roger. Stand by,' Joe Conklin replied on interphone. Now Rawlins' digital-display monitor mounted between the pilot and copilot positions in the top center of the instrument panel activated and began pulsing as the radar began its pre-programmed search pattern, sweeping sixty degrees on either side of centerline and twenty degrees up and down. But because the target was only two thousand feet below the Falcon, Conklin narrowed the pre-programmed radar sweep to five degrees vertical and twenty degrees horizontal, putting maximum energy along the range and bearing called out by SLINGSHOT and allowing him to lock onto the target at the greatest distance.

A few moments later the moving radar pips on the screen froze, then began tight oscillations around a square radar-target symbol. A white diamond superimposed itself on the target symbol and RADAR LOCK appeared at the top of the screen. 'Radar lock on a fast-moving aircraft, low, fifty miles at ten-thirty position,' Conklin reported. A few seconds later the radar computed the target's airspeed and altitude and began feeding range-and-bearing data to the crew on the Falcon. 'Left ten degrees, closure rate two hundred thirty knots.'

'Forty-five miles,' Rawlins confirmed as he completed a

12

left turn to move behind the target. 'Ten minutes to intercept.'

'How about giving me the intercept this time, Kevin?' Sandino said over interphone.

Rawlins turned to his copilot. 'You're not checked out in night intercepts – '

'I've had the ground school and one simulator ride.'

'Can't do it until you've had actual rides.'

'How am I ever going to get checked out if I don't *do* actual intercepts? I've been on the upgrade program for a month and haven't had one actual intercept. C'mon, Kev,' Kelly said cross-cockpit. Her voice was different, lower. He looked across at her. 'We'll do it nice and easy,' she added. 'You can take charge whenever you want.'

What the hell, Rawlins decided – he was an instructor so it wouldn't be totally against the rules to let her do the intercept. She was, after all, a good stick.

He nodded and watched as Sandino put her hands on the control column and throttles. 'I've got the aircraft,' she said.

He gave the column a little nudge and felt the acknowledging nudge, then let go. 'You got it,' he said. 'Go get 'em.'

Brickell Plaza Federal Building, Miami, Florida

There seemed to be more of these late-night workdays for Rear Admiral Ian Hardcastle, commander of the Seventh Coast Guard District based in Miami. The solitude of the big empty office was a welcome interlude – and even the paperwork was a welcome diversion from the big, silent, empty bungalow he had to go home to.

The commander of the busiest district in the Coast Guard stood up from his desk, stretched his long stringy muscles and ran a hand through salt-and-pepper hair swept back from his forehead in wavy lines. He caught his reflection in the dark office windows and saw that the blue uniform blouse and navy blue pants hung a bit looser than before – stress, lack of exercise and a few late nights at O'Mally's Tavern . . . His blue eyes were dark in the reflection he studied, and the overhead fluorescent lights accentuated the gaunt face and deepset, narrow eyes. Ghostly, he thought to himself. He could be straight out of one of his grandfather's Scottish ghost stories, the ones that haunted the moors in the dead of night.

The sandwich that had passed for dinner was a cold lump in his stomach. Stretching his aching muscles even more, he felt the occasional twinges of pain in his wrists and knuckles. Arthritis, a reminder of how old he was getting and how close to retirement he really was. Hardcastle pulled on his leather flyer's jacket, a gift from a retired Coast Guard chief petty officer, and headed up to the roof of the eight-story office building.

He might be getting old, but he wasn't ready for a rocking chair. Case in point: the neat little Super Scorpion commuter helicopter parked on the roof was Hardcastle's wheels on all but the worst weather days. The Scorpion could carry two persons from Miami to most of Florida's major cities at twice turnpike speeds and was small enough to fit into a two-car garage. It had taken the better part of a year to get permission from the departments of Transportation and Treasury to land the little beauty on the roof of the Federal Building, but by 'bribing' other higher-ranking persons in the building with offers of free rides he was able to manage it. Rush-hour commuting was now a thing of the past and quick getaways to Orlando or the Keys became possibilities . . .

Except now there was no one to share these getaways with. He just didn't have much desire to go off on the weekends, and late nights at the office precluded any joy rides. Besides, most of his friends were also his ex-wife's friends, and after their separation he saw little of them.

He undid the tiedowns, removed inlet covers and pitot tube covers and stepped into his little eggbeater. Starting the little Super Scorpion was no more complicated than starting an automobile, and soon the engine was at idle power, warmed up and ready to go. He copied a weather report from Miami Flight Service – warm temperatures, clear skies, balmy breezes – then switched frequencies to Miami International's control tower. Since he'd be popping up in the tower's airspace as soon as he lifted off the roof he wanted to get clearance beforehand: 'Miami tower, Scorpion two-five-six X-ray on Victor, departing Brickell Plaza helipad, destination Pompano Beach at one thousand five hundred. Over.'

'Scorpion two-five-six X-ray, Miami Tower, good evening, Admiral.' Hardcastle had been doing this now for three years and was well known to most of the FAA controllers in south Florida. 'Sir, hold your position for zero-two minutes, departing Omaha traffic from Opa-Locka will be turning over the city after takeoff. Looks like one of your boys, Admiral.'

'Two-five-six X-ray, holding position at Brickell Plaza helipad.' Hardcastle shook his head, mildly exasperated at the casual slip of established radio procedures by the tower controller – their short thirty-second conversation could have yielded information to a smuggler. The only admiral that might be leaving Brickell Plaza Federal Building had to be Coast Guard. Now the smuggler would know that Omaha meant a Coast Guard plane was airborne out of Opa-Locka heading southwest over the city. Anyone with a fifty-dollar Radio Shack VHF scanner could provide intelligence information to drug smugglers.

But such thoughts were quickly overshadowed by

15

another – where that Omaha jet from Opa-Locka might be going. He wished he had a descrambler on the Scorpion so he could listen in on SLINGSHOT or BLOC, the maritime radar-patrol center, but not all the brass in Miami could get one of them for a civilian bug-smasher. What was going on? A drug bust? Routine ops? A rescue?

'Two-five-six X-ray, cleared to depart Brickell Plaza helipad, remain clear of the Miami TCA, proceed VFR to Pompano Beach. Over.'

'Tower, I'd like to change that clearance,' Hardcastle radioed back. 'I'd like to head on over to Opa-Locka. Can I get a clearance through the TCA?'

'Stand by, sir.' The Terminal Control Area was a place of high-density air traffic around busy airports where air traffic was tightly controlled. It was asking a lot, Hardcastle knew, to send a small helicopter right through a TCA at night, but things quieted down significantly at Miami International right around nine P.M. and he figured he might get lucky.

'Two-five-six X-ray, Miami tower,' the controller began, 'if you can get your whirlygig off the roof and over to the airport right now, and I mean *now*, you are cleared across the TCA at one thousand feet. You're going to be head-to-head with a very big, very nasty 747 in about five minutes. Over.'

Hardcastle had the rotor clutch engaged on the Scorpion when he made his request, and the blades were spinning up to takeoff speed shortly after the controller issued the new clearance. 'Two-five-six X-ray is off at this time, leaving one-fifty for one thousand feet,' he said as he set power and gently eased up on the collective. 'Thanks, Chuck.'

'Don't mention it, Admiral.' Three minutes later Hardcastle was racing across the brilliantly lit airport, heading north toward Opa-Locka Airport.

* * *

The CQ was completing his duty log when Hardcastle
trotted into the operations center. Flustered, the Coast
Guard lieutenant stumbled to his feet. 'Admiral
Hardcastle . . .'

'Jeff, was that Falcon that just launched on an intercept?'
Hardcastle hurriedly asked the pilot as he studied the duty
board on the wall.

'Yes, sir,' the CQ, Lieutenant Jeff Teichert, replied. He
followed Hardcastle's gaze onto the duty board, pointing at
the relevant line. 'Commander Rawlins and Lieutenant j.g.
Sandino's crew is in alpha alert.' Quickly Teichert filled
Hardcastle in on the sortie's scenario.

'Kev Rawlins is a good stick . . . and Sandino's good too,
but she's green.' Hardcastle paused for a moment, then:
'Squawking military codes, then switching to civilian
codes? What's the word from Air Ops?'

'Continue to track, identify if possible and advise,'
Teichert told him, reading from the log. Not sure if he
should instruct the admiral on something he might already
be aware of, Teichert continued anyway: 'Air Ops won't
decide for at least an hour whether to launch a Customs
Service sortie.'

'Doesn't make sense,' Hardcastle said. 'Did they ask for
a military unit?'

'Nothing on that has come over, sir.'

'Where are they now?'

'I haven't been tracking them,' Teichert said uneasily.
He turned on the descrambler to listen in on the radio
conversations, and Hardcastle went to a map of the
southeastern United States, the Gulf of Mexico and the
Caribbean, ready to plot the Falcon's position as it
continued its pursuit.

'Three miles. One thousand feet above, closure rate twenty knots.' Rawlins' Falcon crew with Sandino at the controls had maneuvered to five miles of the plane with lights off, then circled around behind the quarry and was approaching carefully from the rear and slightly off its left side.

The Falcon's FLIR, its forward-looking infrared scanner slaved to point in the same azimuth and elevation as the APG-66 radar, had locked onto the red-hot plane against the cold winter ocean at ten miles. Cloud cover was minimal and the FLIR maintained a solid auto-track lock on the suspect aircraft.

'This guy's burning up,' Conklin said. 'Range two point eight, one thousand feet below us, closure rate twenty knots. His engines are white hot.'

'He's probably leaned way back to save fuel,' Rawlins said. Reducing the ratio of fuel to air in the carburetor saved on fuel but greatly increased the engine's operating temperature, which caused the striking infrared image on Conklin's screen.

'We need some profile info for the tape, radar,' Sandino said over intercom. Rawlins pulled out a book of aircraft silhouettes. 'Single or twin? Looks like a twin to me.'

'That checks, Lieutenant,' Conklin said. 'Twin. Big sucker – looks like a medium-range commuter plane. High-wing, engine nacelles look like they're under the wing. Big boxy shape. I'm getting it all on tape.'

'Any numbers yet?'

'Still too far,' Conklin said. 'Two miles, closure rate fifteen.'

Rawlins noticed Sandino fidgeting at the controls. Up until now her procedures had been excellent, acknowledging all position calls, making the right corrections, not getting too anxious to close on the target. Now she was tense, alternately squeezing and kneading the throttles and control wheel. The jet began to feel as jittery as Sandino looked. 'Ease up, Gracie.'

'I . . . I got a little dizzy . . .'

Rawlins positioned his hands near the controls but did not grab them. Staring out into a dark sky and focusing in on a tiny spot created a sensation, autorotation, where the spot begins to spiral around by itself. It was very easy to lose one's sense of up and down, so much so that you would begin to steer the jet to follow the images your mind was creating. A lot of planes, he knew, were lost that way.

'Your wings are level, Gracie.' Grabbing the controls would have caused her to go into a panic to regain control, and being only a few hundred feet above water and travelling at four hundred feet per second, going out of control even for a few seconds would be fatal. 'Wings level. Take a look at the horizon, get your bearings, don't fixate on him. Relax.' The jiggling in the jet's flight-path subsided, as she took a deep breath and relaxed her grip on the steering column.

'Thanks, Kev.'

'One point five miles, closure fifteen.'

'Keep it coming, Gracie,' Rawlins said. 'Nice and easy.'

'Range one point two miles, five hundred feet below, closure twenty knots.'

'Ease off,' Rawlins said. 'Keep it under fifteen this close.' Sandino made a barely perceptible throttle change and the big jet settled in to a more comfortable closure rate.

Time seemed to crawl along. The white image of the plane on the screen grew, its two wing-mounted engines glowing brightly. Conklin zoomed the FLIR to its maximum magnification as he studied the image on his screen.

'Look at that nose . . .' Conklin said, comparing the image to his own copy of the aircraft-identification book. 'Commander, I make this guy as a Shorts 330 light cargo

19

plane, like an Air Force Sherpa,' Conklin said, speaking out aloud for the benefit of the running videotape, which also recorded all radio conversations. 'Those suckers can carry over three thousand pounds of cargo. Looks like a false cargo door on the plane's port side as well, maybe styrofoam or cloth.'

The image grew in size, and more details on the plane could be seen. Rawlins stared at the FLIR screen. 'No nav radio antennae visible. No wheel pants. No aft cargo door. These guys ripped out every extraneous piece of metal to save weight.' Rawlins was on the radio to Opa-Locka, relaying the aircraft's description for retransmission to the Customs Service.

'Range three zero hundred feet, one hundred feet below, closure fifteen knots,' Conklin reported. 'You're right, it looks like a smuggler's plane to me . . . hey, it looks also like they spray-painted over their registration numbers . . .'

Sandino checked the radar readouts on the screen. 'C'mon, Conklin,' she said, her fists tight on the controls. 'Read the damn numbers.'

On interphone Rawlins asked, 'Any chance of reading those numbers, Conk?'

'Wait . . . wait . . . yes, I think I can get 'em. There's only a thin coat of paint, and the numbers underneath are warmer than the paint.' As the image on the screen grew larger Conklin punched off the auto-track function of the FLIR, which had locked onto the plane's left-engine nacelle, and slewed the FLIR scanner back along the plane's fuselage.

Sandino was becoming more and more edgy as they moved closer. 'Conk . . .'

'Few more seconds and I'll – '

Suddenly Conklin saw the side of the plane near the cargo door grow dark and a man could be seen inside the plane, moving around. There was a hint of motion . . . then a long tongue of blinding white light lashed out toward the Falcon, obliterating the entire infrared image in a yellow-and-white haze. In the cockpit all Rawlins and Sandino saw was a bright flash of light cutting through the darkness from somewhere on the horizon . . .

'*Gun!*' Conklin called out. 'Port turn.'

Rawlins was barely able to grab the controls, put in full throttle and haul the jet into a left turn before the heavy-caliber bullets from the smuggler's plane found their target. The shells ripped through the heavy Plexiglas canopy on the right side, one shell hitting Kelly Sandino in the face, others tearing across her right shoulder before Rawlins could fully turn away. The shells continued to rip through the fuselage, a few piercing the pressure skin and pinging around inside the cabin, before the fusillade found the starboard turbofan engine. One shell pierced the first and second stage turbine blades, sending shards of metal blasting through the engine and tearing apart fuel lines. The engine exploded as the ruptured fuel lines pumped a gallon of volatile jet fuel onto the growing fire every few seconds.

The loss of the right engine sent the Falcon jet into a wild swing to the right as Rawlins held in the hard left turn. Now the jet was twisting in two directions at once, which combined with the loss of the right engine's thrust bled off precious airspeed needed to keep the thirty-thousand-pound jet flying. As if the jet had been plucked from midair, it hung in a full-stall at ninety degrees of bank, then fell directly downward and crashed into the sea.

Hardcastle stood smoking a cigar in the CQ's office, staring out the window towards the flight line. Teichert was still juggling phones and radios, trying to keep at least three different agencies up on what was going on with the suspected drug smugglers. Hardcastle had considered trying to help the swamped clerk but that would probably just make the guy even more nervous, he decided.

The ground-support crews had just finished towing a HH-65A Dolphin helicopter out of its hangar in preparation for its backup flight, and Hardcastle was watching the ground crew get her ready to fly when another phone rang – but, instead of a friendly jingle this one blew a whistle that sounded like the doomsday trumpets. Teichert lunged for a large red button on his console as he picked up a grease pencil and the receiver.

A warning horn sounded inside the ready room and out on the flight line as Teichert clicked on a microphone. 'Scramble, scramble, helo two, aircraft down over ocean, four souls on board, button one. Repeat, helo two, aircraft down over ocean, four souls on board, vector on button one.' The maintenance men put final touches on their work and moved clear as the flight-and-rescue crews ran out the doors toward the waiting chopper.

'What the hell happened, Teichert?' Hardcastle shouted over the horn.

'SLINGSHOT lost contact with our Falcon. They say the plane may have crashed.'

Hardcastle turned to watch as the HH-65 started engines and made ready for takeoff, then turned angrily toward the CQ. 'Jeff, I want another Dolphin, a flight crew and two armed men on board and ready for takeoff in five minutes.' Teichert wasn't going to second-guess the admiral this time – he called another Dolphin crew together without another word.

When the Dolphin flight crew – two pilots, a crew chief/hoist operator, and rescue specialist – reported to the CQ's office, Hardcastle was the one issuing orders. 'We're going after that smuggler – the first Dolphin will get the Falcon crew. Lieutenant McAlister, get your helo ready to go in

22

five. I'll sign the flight orders – get going.' The pilot, copilot and crew chief hurried off. Hardcastle scanned the paperwork Teichert began putting on the desktop, then told Roosevelt, the rescue man, to go to the armory and check out two M-16s, web gear, body armor and an ammo pack apiece. 'Be on board that Dolphin by the time I get out there. Move.' Teichert tossed Roosevelt the keys to the armory as he rushed off, then put his finger on every place Hardcastle had to sign on the flight orders. He took a deep breath. 'Sir, are you sure you know what you're doing – '

Hardcastle gave the pilot a look. 'Button it, Teichert . . .'

'Sir, I'm responsible for the procedures being followed around this ready room. You have the authority to take a helo, its crew, and rifles, sir, but when they ask me how come I let you do it . . .'

'You did your job,' Hardcastle said, finishing with the paperwork as Roosevelt hurried up to the admiral carrying weapons and combat gear. Hardcastle quickly buckled on a web belt and Velcroed on the body armor. 'You followed orders and you questioned those orders when they didn't make any sense,' he went on to Teichert as he affixed a three-clip ammo pouch to the belt. 'Report my orders and my actions to Area headquarters if you think you have to, or call your commander, Captain Harbaugh.' Hardcastle grabbed an M-16 from Roosevelt and headed out toward the flight line, where the scream of a Dolphin helicopter's turbines could be heard.

Teichert watched the tall figure run out onto the tarmac. The guy had a John Wayne complex, no doubt about it, he thought. A nut case – so the rumors went.

* * *

23

'This is what we got,' Special Agent Rushell Masters said as he slipped on his body-armor vest and secured it against his barrel chest. Six feet tall with curly red hair, two hundred and sixty pounds and built like a professional wrestler, Masters dwarfed his fellow agents, and the bulk of his body armor, utility vest and life jacket only served to enhance his massive frame. 'An unidentified cargo plane from Colombia is going around Key West radar into south Florida. A Coastie jet was chasing it when SLINGSHOT lost contact with it. They think it may have been attacked by the suspects.'

Masters was briefing the five-man operations crew of his UH-60 Black Hawk helicopter in preparation for taking up the chase of the smugglers. In addition to Masters, the crew pilot, the Black Hawk carried a copilot, two armed Customs Service agents and two Bahamian constables. The Bahamian police were carried on-board in case a smuggler tried to evade to the expansive Bahamas island chain – the US Customs Service, with no jurisdiction in the Bahamas, acted as high-tech taxi drivers while the constables made the arrests.

'SLINGSHOT has maintained radar contact on the suspects,' Masters went on, 'and we have been directed to – ' Masters was abruptly distracted by a shapely woman's leg propped up on the sill of the Black Hawk assault helicopter.

'Get on with it, Masters,' the woman's voice cut in. Her words plus the sight of an ankle holster wrapped around her calf holding a Smith and Wesson .380 semi-automatic pistol snapped him out of it and he continued his briefing as she began to put on body armor, utility vest, shoulder holster and life jacket.

24

The diversion was Special Agent Sandra Geffar, in charge of the Customs Service Air Division base at Homestead. Tall, blonde, of German descent, the fifteen-year Customs Service veteran was also a fixed- and rotary-wing pilot, an experienced investigator and Olympic-class marksman. As she sometimes did in emergency cases such as this one, Geffar was personally taking charge as well as acting as copilot of the Black Hawk.

Sandra Geffar was striking enough to make a bear like Masters trip over his tongue, but she had also proved herself in dozens of drug arrests and drug ops. She was more than just one of the boys. Every agent in the place was supposed to be both a pilot and an investigator, but Sandra Geffar genuinely excelled at both. She had cut her teeth in the army as a provost marshal. Where most female GIs in the late sixties and early seventies found themselves behind typewriters, Geffar was volunteering and getting domestic investigations, off-base patrols, law enforcement – building a reputation on jobs no one wanted. When not on duty she spent time at the pistol ranges, where she beat out her eventual first husband as a top army pistol champion. She might even have made the Olympic shooting team except for a messy divorce.

The treatment she received as part of her divorce only spurred her on. She secured a warrant officer's commission and went to army helicopter school to fill an affirmative-action quota that she found insulting not only to herself but to her fellow GIs as well. She used it, though, to become one of the army's best chopper pilots. She flew medevac missions for three years, two of them in Thailand during the evacuation of US and Allied forces from Vietnam, and was twice decorated for bravery in the chaos that followed the American withdrawal from Vietnam.

During the post-Vietnam drawdown she left the army on a Palace Chase option that gave her preferential choice on

25

other government jobs if she would voluntarily leave the army before retirement. Instead of swelling the ranks of the Postal Service or Fish and Wildlife Services as many others did, she joined the Customs Service as an investigator. The GI Bill paid for a commercial pilot's license in rotary and fixed-wing aircraft, and she then joined the Customs Service's Mobile, Alabama, air branch soon after it was opened.

The air branch seemed tailor-made for Sandra Geffar. Drug smuggling in the mid-seventies was booming, and the Customs Service air branch was like the federal marshals in the Old West assigned to clean up a territory. Flying almost every day, planning and executing surveillance and arrest operations, interrelating with the FBI and the DEA, even going undercover – all challenges that she met well and that called attention, however grudging, to herself. After an assignment in Washington as liaison to the Secretary of the Treasury, where she married and divorced her second husband, she returned to flying in Miami.

In the eighties, with drug smuggling an increasingly hot topic, Sandra Geffar was in the center of the action. She fought to expand the size and scope of the air branch and was involved in negotiations between the State Department and the government of the Bahamas for overflight and landing privileges, which greatly increased the Customs Service's area of responsibility. The payoff was almost instantaneous. A joint Customs Service and DEA task force led by Geffar was responsible for the largest single marijuana bust in history, a Mexican freighter off the coast of Bimini carrying seventeen thousand tons of pot. Soon after she was made chief of the Miami air branch and turned that station into the most respected (some said feared) drug-interdiction air unit in the country.

Off in the background now a Customs Service Citation business jet screamed at high speed down the parking ramp toward the Air Force fighter base's main runway. The Citation was configured much like the Coast Guard Falcon, with an APG-66 radar and FLIR scanner; it was, in fact, designed to search, track and identify smugglers' aircraft in all weather, just like the Falcon. The Citation, call sign Omaha Four-Zero, carried a crew much like Masters' Black Hawk with the addition of a radar intercept specialist to operate the scanners. All on board both aircraft, including the RIO and both pilots, carried semi-automatic sidearms, a smaller caliber semi-automatic pistol in an ankle holster and either a pump action shotgun, M-16 automatic rifle or Steyr semi-automatic assault rifle.

'The Citation will pick up the bad guy as soon as he can,' Masters continued, chambering a round in his pistol, lowering the hammer, and holstering the weapon. 'We won't have much time – I'll probably be dropping the ground crew at the landing site fast and hard. Listen up on the radios and stay alert. Questions?' None. 'Sandra?'

Geffar completed her suiting-up. 'We go in and hit them hard. These guys are obviously well armed. The Coasties dropped the ball – now we have to go in and clean up.' She motioned to the Bahamian policemen. 'Edouard, Philip, you two stay in the Black Hawk and cover the ground crew.' The two big constables, armed with M-16s and wearing navy blue windbreakers with 'U.S. CUSTOMS SERVICE' in bright yellow letters, nodded, obviously excited. 'The rest of you, back up your teammate and stay alert. Let's do it.'

The Shorts 330 crossed between Key Largo and Sunset Point on the Florida Keys and skipped across the islands of Florida Bay. Hugging the water only a few dozen feet above the murky water, it turned northwest and headed for the black swamps and thick forests on the southern tip of the Florida peninsula.

27

'Message from SLINGSHOT, Admiral,' Lieutenant McAlister, piloting the Coast Guard Dolphin chopper, radioed back to Hardcastle. 'They've got a Citation airborne tracking the Shorts, Omaha call sign Four-Zero, and they've vectored a Customs Service Black Hawk, Omaha Four-Nine, in on the smuggler. We've got a heading toward them. ETA fifteen minutes.'

'Roger. Keep me advised,' Hardcastle replied. They had cleared the lights of Miami and reached the southern outskirts of the metropolitan area, with traffic lines snarled on the Florida Turnpike. Hardcastle had one of the dropmasters open the sliding cargo hatch on the chopper and fasten a safety strap onto a ring on his combat rig, then he leaned out the door, letting the warm slipstream bathe his face.

Just like Vietnam. Hanging out the door – no safety belts then, just hanging out the door as if no one ever fell out of a Huey before – was one of the small pleasures a man learned to savor in the middle of hell. Hardcastle had been a Marine Corps platoon leader, a cherry first lieutenant in charge of a veteran bomb disposal unit. He had spent most of his time in Nam being bounced from ship to ship and post to post on details ranging from jammed rifles to corroded fuses on huge seventeen-inch rounds on Navy battleships. After two hours of duty and seeing too many buddies lose their lives on BDU missions, hanging out a helicopter door over the South China Sea was tame stuff.

In fact, he had become so casual about life and death back then that, slowly and silently, he did go a little crazy. Which had been the end of one life, and the beginning of his next, his Coast Guard life . . .

He brought his attention back to the radios as the Dolphin helicopter raced over Metro Zoo, following the turnpike south toward the Everglades. McAlister had just keyed the mike on the secure radio channel: 'SLING-SHOT, this is Omaha Seven-O. Request range and bearing to suspect. Over – '

Suddenly they heard, 'Seven-One, this is Omaha Four-Nine.' Hardcastle recognized the voice right away – Rushell Masters, the Customs Service Air Division's operations officer. 'This is an active frequency. Please clear this channel. Over.'

'Four-Nine, this is Admiral Hardcastle, Seventh Coast Guard District commander . . .'

'I copy, sir,' Masters replied. His voice was polite but firm. 'We've got a Black Hawk and a Citation in the area. We won't be able to keep track of all these birds when the fur starts flying. Request you stay clear. Out.'

'Four-Nine,' Hardcastle radioed back, 'we believe that the suspects have shot down a Coast Guard jet. We are over Florida City. Relay your location and location of suspect aircraft and we'll take up a position in support. Over.'

'Ian, I thank you for your offer but it won't be necessary,' a new voice cut in.

'Agent Geffar,' McAlister's copilot said.

'You mean Wonder Woman – '

'Knock it off,' Hardcastle told McAlister.

'Take your helo and stay north of route 27 and clear of the national park,' Masters radioed back. 'We'll call if we need any help. Out.'

'Sandra, dammit, this is no routine smuggling chase. These guys murdered four people on one of my Falcons. Take the collar – all I want is to make sure they don't get away – '

'Then we both want the same thing, Admiral. But you know the drill – once these guys are over land and we have them identified they belong to us.'

'They committed piracy and murder in US waters under Coast Guard jurisdiction . . .' But Hardcastle already knew his arguments were going nowhere. Geffar and Masters had enough on their plates without a Coastie bearing down on them.

McAlister clicked on the interphone: 'What do we do, Admiral?'

Geffar and Masters were right – it was time to back off. The Coast Guard, to be honest, wasn't trained as well as Customs in this kind of combat, and there was little or no integration of tactics and procedures between them. In a ground skirmish his men could get badly hurt . . .

'Can you set us down somewhere close?' Hardcastle radioed to his pilot.

McAlister and his copilot checked their charts. 'There's a deactivated rocket-test site a few miles east – we've done some training there before. I'll set it down there.'

'Do it,' Hardcastle said. 'But I want SLINGSHOT to give us constant updates on the situation out there. Advise them of our position and our status. We won't get in Masters' way but we're going to be looking right over his shoulder in case . . .'

Near the Suspect's Plane, Everglades National Park

Circling three thousand feet overhead, the Customs Service Citation, call sign Omaha Four-Zero, kept watch in the big Shorts transport through the infrared scanner. The green-and-white image on the cockpit screen showed amazing detail. Zooming in on the transport, the Citation's sensor operator studied the image, adjusting bright and contrast, then clicked on his interphone: 'I see flaps, sir. Target velocity decreasing.'

'He's slowing down, Four-Nine,' the Citation's copilot

reported to Masters. 'He might be getting ready to land. We see flaps deployed. Stand by.'

Geffar held up a chart under a small red spotlight. 'Twenty-five miles southwest of Florida City.'

'Mahogany Hammock,' Masters said. 'Blackwater Island. It's the only dry enough place around for a plane that size, unless they got a Shorts with floats on it.'

'A night landing out here is tricky any time,' Geffar said. 'Unless they have a landing zone marked out . . . they might be going for an aerial delivery too.' Geffar switched to her tactical radio. 'SLINGSHOT, this is Omaha Four-Nine. They might be heading for Blackwater Island. Repeat, Mahogany Hammock, Blackwater Island. We are closing to intercept. Have Dade County sheriffs seal off route 27, and I want another Black Hawk airborne to cover any escape routes through the Glades. Break. Omaha Four-Zero, stay on the Shorts. If he makes a break for it, track and identify if possible. Report if he makes a drop, then mark drop position for intercept. Out.'

'Roger, Four-Nine,' the Citation pilot replied.

It did not take long. On board the Citation the sensor operator concentrated on every move, every detail of the target plane. Suddenly a large rectangular object flew out the aft end of the plane. Four more objects, resembling hay bales or steamer trunks roped together, followed in rapid succession. 'Position *mark*,' from the sensor operator.

In the cockpit, the copilot hit a button on her LORAN-Omega navigation set labeled 'FLIR PP.' The navigation computer would combine the Citation's present position and altitude and the computed-sensor angle on the target and compute the exact position of the object in the FLIR sensor at the instant the button was depressed.

The copilot called up the stored set of coordinates, checked them, then keyed his mike button: 'Four-Nine, this is Four-Zero. Drop made. Repeat, drop made. We got it on film. Drop coordinates read: north two-five-three-zero point nine-one, west eight-zero-five-two point seven-three.'

Aboard the US Customs Service Helicopter Omaha Four-Nine

Geffar punched the coordinates into her own Omega set and designated it as the target destination. Immediately the horizontal situation indicator on Masters' instrument panel displayed the direction and range to the target. 'Copy, Four-Zero. We're three miles out. We're moving in.' Masters lowered a pair of night-vision goggles over his eyes, heeled the Black Hawk helicopter hard left to center the HSI bug and began to search for the drop zone.

Seconds later the dull green-and-white image through the night-vision goggles revealed movement in the thick undergrowth. 'I've got airboats,' Masters called out. 'Four . . . no, five airboats.' He scanned the area around the suspects. 'No other clear areas around – I'll have to drop right on top of them. Hang on, crew. We're going in. Stand by on the Night Sun light.'

'I've got you in sight, Four-Nine,' the sensor operator on Omaha Four-Zero reported. 'The Shorts is coming around to your left. He . . . wait, I think he's seen you. He's peeling off – '

'Stay on that Shorts, Four-Zero,' Geffar said. As the Black Hawk got closer to earth Masters flipped the night-vision goggles up out of the way, took a grip on the cyclic and collective and pressed his head back into his headrest to protect his back and neck from the shock of impact. 'Crew, secure for impact, hit the light.'

Masters kept the power high-right until the last second. Suddenly, the whole area lit up like daytime. Five airboats

– flat-bottomed watercraft driven by huge propellers – were ranged around a small clearing less than a hundred feet square. He and Geffar had to marvel at the accuracy of whoever was dropping those bales – they'd put them on a tree-lined secluded area about the size of a baseball diamond at night and traveling almost three hundred feet per second – before the ground rushed up to meet them and the oversized landing wheels of the fifty-thousand-pound helicopter hit the marsh. Spotlights all around the Black Hawk snapped on. The rotor wash had flipped over one airboat, sending its occupants flying, and they had missed another airboat piled high with bales by only a few feet.

'Stay with the bird,' Geffar shouted to Masters, throwing off her shoulder harness. She flung open the door and hit the soggy ground carrying her Steyr assault rifle. One Customs Service agent moved beside her, his M-16 pointed at an airboat, while a Bahamian constable moved into the right gunner's seat trying to cover two more airboats with his M-16.

'Everyone on these airboats,' Masters called over the Black Hawk's loudspeakers. 'This is the US Customs Service. Drop your weapons and raise your hands.'

Men on the airboat closest to Geffar crouched for cover behind bales. Geffar hip-leveled her Steyr, fired three rounds. A smuggler clutched his right shoulder, collapsed, and the other smugglers came to their feet, arms stretched over their heads.

With the Bahamian constables covering the Black Hawk, the agents moved out, gesturing to the smugglers to kneel down and put their hands on their heads. Meanwhile, Masters had moved out of the chopper, shotgun in hand, to help the agent on the left.

If he had stayed a few seconds longer, he would have heard the warning from the Citation overhead. Too late now. The Shorts transport had come back, flying at treetop level over the clearing. Suddenly the heavy pounding of machine-gun fire could be heard – they had opened fire on the Black Hawk helicopter with the fifty-caliber machine gun.

Geffar took three quick shots at the Shorts, shooting blind into the dark sky, then opened fire on the airboats and with her agent took off from the airboats, feet digging into the muddy soil as they ran for cover.

They had managed only a few yards when a brilliant flash of light and a streak of flame erupted from the edge of the clearing, and moments later the Black Hawk exploded in a ball of fire. The body of the agent literally flew into her, and Geffar and what was left of the agent were picked up and tossed thirty feet into a shallow mud pit. Geffar stayed conscious long enough to dig her face out of the mud, then, dazed and bleeding from her wounds, collapsed.

Aboard the Coast Guard Helicopter Omaha Seven-One

Hardcastle heard the warning from the Citation and immediately was on the interphone: 'Let's move it, McAlister. Blackwater Island. Set up an orbit at one thousand feet. As soon as any other air units report in have them move in.' McAlister quickly had the Dolphin airborne, leveled off at a thousand feet, dipped its nose, accelerated and turned sharply left toward the dark Everglades beyond.

Hardcastle chambered a 5.56 millimeter round in his M-16 rifle. Again like Vietnam, he thought – frantic radio messages, air support cautiously moving in, casualties from a sudden, unexpected assault. Even the air smelled the same – a suffocating, cloying mix of dirt, salt air, decay, fear, and death . . .

On SLINGSHOT's tactical frequency they heard,

'Omaha Four-Nine, this is Omaha Four-Seven. We're five miles out. What's your situation? Over.' No reply – the Black Hawk was dead.

'Four-Seven, this is Four-Zero,' the pilot aboard the Citation said. 'Masters and his crew are down. Under heavy fire. Coordinates follow . . .' He read off the coordinates of the smugglers' drop zone. 'We are orbiting overhead. Move in and assist. Over.'

Hardcastle shook himself free of the images of battles past, and as he did he felt the same nervous excitement of years before when the close air support radioed in over a hot LZ in the rice paddies of southeast Asia. 'SLING-SHOT, this is Omaha Seven-One,' Hardcastle called over the radio. 'Vector to the Shorts.'

A confused pause as the controllers back in Miami tried to sort out the situation. 'Dammit, SLINGSHOT, where the hell is he?'

'Roger, Seven-One, fly heading two-niner five, maintain one thousand feet. Your target will be at eleven o'clock position at four miles and two hundred feet. His ground-speed is one-one-zero knots.' The Dolphin swung hard onto its new heading and McAlister opened the throttles to max power.

'Target accelerating, Seven-One. Groundspeed now one-two-five,' the controller reported. 'Five degrees left, three-point-five miles.'

Hardcastle pounded on the bulkhead. 'Damn it, he's bugging out.'

'If he goes over one-sixty before we can catch him,' McAlister said over the howling engines, 'we won't have a chance – '

'Just fly,' Hardcastle shouted.

'Two miles, altitude three hundred feet, groundspeed one-forty.'

'McAlister, take us down to three hundred feet,'

35

Hardcastle said over interphone. 'Put the Shorts on my side of the cabin.' And to the rescue specialist: 'Take a position at the door, strap yourself in and fire on anything that moves down there.'

'You mean shoot at the plane?' the very young drop-master asked.

Hardcastle tried to keep his temper in check. 'Yes, *shoot* the goddamn plane. Those people are murderers. Keep your eyes open and don't cross-fire with me.'

'One point five miles – '

'I got him,' McAlister shouted. 'Eleven o'clock. He's hauling ass.'

The Shorts was close enough to be a dark shape just above the trees. Suddenly the cargo plane heeled left, trying to angle away from the Dolphin.

'Cut him off,' Hardcastle ordered. McAlister threw the Dolphin into a hard left bank, turned inside the Shorts and aimed for a spot ahead of its flight path. The Shorts' turn had cut its speed, and the more agile Dolphin helicopter could move closer to its target.

Now the Shorts was off to the Dolphin's right, and Hardcastle was about to switch over to the right side of the chopper when McAlister's copilot yelled, 'Look out!' and McAlister yanked back on the collective just as a flash of light erupted from the Shorts' left side.

'Put him on the left.' Hardcastle ordered. McAlister banked hard right, looped over the Shorts transport and zoomed back down, using his airspeed to close the short distance between them. Hardcastle leaned out the door, and fighting the wind blast, took aim on the transport and fired.

He had to remind himself to let up on the trigger after a few seconds of automatic fire. The sound of the rotors beating overhead, the ear-shattering noise of the M-16, the target-fixation, the motion of the chopper, the force of the slipstream slapping the rifle muzzle, the excitement, the fear, the anticipation – it was all like a drug, he thought ironically.

McAlister was shouting. 'Cease fire, cease fire!'

Hardcastle ignored him.

Telltale sparks had jumped off the transport's wings as Hardcastle began another volley. He only stopped as the transport moved farther back out of his field of fire and waited for Roosevelt to start shooting.

Roosevelt had looked startled when the admiral had opened fire, but at a dark glance from the admiral he began spraying bullets right and left over the sky. He'd had his finger on the trigger for eight full seconds before Hardcastle stopped him. 'Seaman, watch what the hell you're doing.'

'Sorry, sir,' Roosevelt shouted over the wind blast, not realizing he was screaming into the interphone, 'but I haven't shot an M-16 in almost a year.'

Hardcastle looked at the young man, shook his head. The Shorts transport was in a steep right turn, passing underneath the Dolphin. 'Right turn and come around on him again,' Hardcastle called to McAlister. 'Don't let him get on your right . . .'

McAlister hesitated, and that momentary pause was enough for the Shorts to get around to the right, and for its machine gun to explode into action once again. Heavy pings echoed off the Dolphin's thin aluminum frame before McAlister could dodge away.

'Move away, put him in my door,' Hardcastle shouted. This time McAlister complied, without hesitation or questioning. This time Roosevelt was ready too. As soon as the Shorts popped into view, now less than two hundred yards away, he opened fire directly on the cockpit.

As he did a flash of yellow erupted from the Shorts' right engine, and the transport started a lazy left turn, skimming the treetops. Roosevelt ejected his spent clip and fumbled for another, but Hardcastle waved a hand in his face. 'Hold your fire, you won't need it.' A moment later the Shorts, still in its left turn, lazily flipped over on its left wing and crashed into the thick trees and murky swamps below. A few muffled explosions, a hint of fire – then only the incessant beating of the Dolphin's rotors overhead.

Hardcastle loaded a fresh clip into his rifle. 'Nice shooting, Roosevelt,' he said. The young seaman looked frozen in place, the smoking rifle in his lap, watching the spot where the transport had gone down. On the tactical channel Hardcastle said, 'SLINGSHOT, that Shorts is down near our present location. Mark and record for a search team, then give us a vector back to that drop zone. We'll – '

'Admiral, this is McAlister. We're getting a fluctuating oil-pressure, we may have taken some of that fire from the Shorts. I'm heading toward Homestead to check it out.'

Hardcastle yanked the clip out of his rifle with a frustrated snap. But even as he and Roosevelt safed their weapons he realized they were very, very lucky that they were alive. One look in the young man's eyes and Hardcastle realized that Roosevelt was thinking the same thing.

'What was that gun they had on board, Admiral?' Roosevelt asked. 'I could hear it clear up here.'

'I don't know,' Hardcastle told him, wiping cold sweat from his face. In spite of the wind still coursing through the cabin, he was burning up – the natural amphetamine, his adrenaline, wearing off. He closed the sliding cargo door and locked it. 'Large caliber, maybe a twelve millimeter or even a fifty cal. We'll find out when we get an investigation team in there.'

'A fifty caliber? On a dope smuggler's plane? I thought the smugglers saved every ounce of weight and room on a plane for product. These guys wasted about a hundred pounds on a huge machine gun – I'm no math genius but I figure that's about fifty thousand dollars' worth of uncut cocaine, or damn near a quarter million dollars of street shit.'

Hardcastle stared out the window. 'Heavy weapons – something big enough to take the Black Hawk. Something very bad's going down . . .'

'A drug war? I mean, not just the usual inflow – a real drug war, sir?'

Hardcastle was suddenly aware of the M-16 in his hands, felt the heat of the barrel, the cold metal of the clip. He had carried an M-16 for years through the jungles of Nam, yet the weapon still was as foreign to him as it was to Roosevelt.

More Coast Guard and Customs agents were going to die. Roosevelt was right – drug smuggling was changing, and the men at the front of the escalating war – the Customs Service and the Coast Guard – were going to get killed unless something drastic was done.

On a Yacht off the Coast of Curacao, Netherlands Antilles

The yacht was a floating palace – and fortress. Armed guards with pistols hidden in beach towels or under waiters' jackets strolled each of the massive craft's four decks. Two huge radomes on the upper deck contained satellite transceivers that allowed the ship's master to communicate world-wide – be it a bank in Switzerland or the Cayman Islands or assassins in Washington or Paris – as well as radars that could scan some fifteen miles in all directions for signs of pursuit. Jet propulsion could carry the one-hundred-foot-long yacht at forty miles an hour, faster than most naval vessels and patrol ships.

Above the main salon and behind the master's berth was an office that looked like something in a luxury penthouse suite or Fortune 500 office, complete with mahogany conference table, computer monitors, oak bookcases, liquid-crystal displays of satellite news and video services, paneled walls and crystal service sets. The entire room was secured by sophisticated electronic scramblers as well as round-the-clock guards posted at the salon's two entrances.

It was here that three of the world's most powerful drug smugglers were meeting to divide up the United States of America.

Gonzales Rodriguez Gachez was the oldest of the three at age forty-one. Short, wiry with a thin mustache over thin lips, he seemed never to blink – seemed to stare with the unnerving eyes of a reptile. Pablo Escalante, age thirty-eight, had movie-star perfect white teeth, a tall muscular body, black hair and trim features. Jorge Luiz Pena, the third member of the group, looked thirty years older than his thirty-five years, with a bulging abdomen, a smoker's cough, thin graying hair and the bulbous red nose of a hard drinker.

The three sat now in a circle in the lounge area of the salon, watching each other silently as waiters offered drinks – they had ignored, or chosen to ignore, the sight of bodyguards tasting the drinks. Pena knocked his down as soon as his chubby fingers surrounded the glass, ignoring Escalante's upraised glass. Escalante smiled wearily as Pena's glass was refilled, worried that the little bastard would ignore his host completely.

Escalante turned to Gachez with his glass raised high: 'To our gracious host, may you always sail in calm seas and under bright skies.' Pena mumbled a 'salut' before finishing his second glass of cognac.

'I thank you, Pablo,' Gachez said, sipping his cognac. 'I am pleased you have decided to be with me on this cruise.

You are both my dear friends.' Escalante nodded his thanks; Pena said nothing as he watched more of the amber liquid being poured into his glass. 'Jorge, how is Medellín these days?' Gachez asked the short weasely man, watching as he downed another glass. 'I have been away too long.'

'The same,' Pena told him. 'Hot and boring. The only good thing about it is that my wife is in Rio de Janeiro.'

There was an uncomfortable pause as Pena went back to his glass – his appetite for liquor matched only by his hunger for women. That he found enough to satisfy him was a testimonial to the power of *llaho* and money. 'And how is business?' Pena asked Gachez. 'You've been gone a long time.'

'I would say it goes very well,' Gachez told him. 'At least I am satisfied.' He paused, looking at his two guests with his maddening smile. 'Ah, I see. So that is what this meeting is about? My two close friends from the foothills are not here on a friendly visit? A message from the cartel, perhaps?'

'The other families are well pleased with you, Gonzales, well pleased,' Escalante said quickly. 'We have all been feeling the pressure on us by the Americans and even the leftists in our own government. We have all been forced to cut down shipments and therefore production. But you . . . you do not. You have managed to maintain your production levels far above ours. How do you do this?'

Gachez's smile stayed fixed, but inside he was seething. These are the real cowards, he thought. He said, 'Nonsense, Pablo, I have done nothing special . . .'

'You've shipped six thousand kilos into south Florida in just the past month,' Pena said, with none of the fancy verbiage of Escalante. He took another gulp of cognac. 'At a time when the cartel had thought that south Florida was closed to us you've breached it again. We're sending token shipments in containers and overland by trucks through

41

Mexico while you're sending over a thousand kilos a week right in the Americans' faces. Señor Escalante here prefers his flowery prose and Hollywood smile to charm the info out of you, Gonzales,' Pena bulled on. 'I don't need that. We pay a tribute to the cartel same as you, but you vacation all winter on this floating Taj Mahal while we sweat in the jungles bringing product to port. We have all shared the wealth – now, you must share your knowledge. How are you shipping your product into the heart of the American defenses?'

'There are no secrets between us,' Gachez said, spreading his hands. 'We are a family, I have always told you everything.' He turned to Escalante. 'You remember, my friend. I introduced you to José eight months ago in Havana . . .'

Escalante thought for a moment, then an incredulous expression spread across his chiseled face.

'You mean those *children*?' Pena said. 'You've hired those *escupiros* to fly for you?'

'Yes, I have,' Gachez said, trying not to show his irritation. 'I introduced them to *you* over a year ago and you thumbed your nose at them. I told you they had ideas, plans that could make us *all* rich. You chased them away like an old lady chases away chickens from her back porch.' He stood and began to pace around the conference table. 'Now I am supposed to share their services with you?'

'Keep your Cuban brats,' Pena said. 'I only wanted to know what your secret was. Now that I know . . .' But he was worried.

'They were no more than children,' Escalante said. '*They* are the ones that have penetrated the American Coast Guard's detection network?'

'The Cuchillos are young, smart, resourceful – and loyal,' Gachez said. 'Their services, of course, are at the disposal of any member of the cartel, but they are in my

42

employ. I will be happy to negotiate a fair and equitable price for their services.

'I thought so,' Pena murmured, motioning for more cognac.

Gachez ignored him. 'We can go up on deck and talk business,' he told Escalante, and they left without another word.

Pena accepted another glass of liqueur. So Gachez had hired the Cuchillos. A bold step for Gachez, who usually surrounded himself with blood relatives, like some immigrant Italian mafioso. A bold step . . . but one that seemed to be working. How to argue with success? It would bear additional investigation. There might indeed be more to this than an experiment – this actually might be a move by Gachez to grab the initiative and move up to the head of the Medellín cartel.

In spite of the occasional conflict between the families, the cartel's strength was in part because no family actually ruled over the others. Most large shipments from Colombia included product from each of the families, so if the shipment was lost or intercepted no one family would overly suffer. The coca plantations in Peru and Bolivia were roughly the same size. The distribution networks were accessible to all members of the cartel, and each family head held an equal vote in all cartel matters. They shared the risks and the rewards equally . . .

Crackdowns by the US Customs Service and Coast Guard had put pressure on the families to maintain shipment levels, and in the past several months the families had answered the pressure with smaller shipments of cocaine paste through more risky smuggling routes such as overland through Mexico, and by riskier methods such as containerized cargo. Some shipments were out of the cartel's hands for days, even weeks, which increased the risk of discovery and interception.

43

But, Pena thought, if Gachez could get large shipments into the United States by air or sea drops, in spite of the crackdowns, he was for sure positioned to head the Medellín cartel. And since the cartel had rejected the Cuchillos several months earlier, they belonged to Gachez – he could legally contract their services out to the rest of the cartel. He could actually make a profit on the smuggling business without risking a proportional amount of his own product.

Something like that could *not* be tolerated.

Zaza Airfield, Verrettes, Haiti

It was a short if solemn ceremony executed with military precision. At dawn eighty soldiers marched to the flagpole in the center of the small airfield's headquarters building. With the Cuban national anthem blaring on loudspeakers, the four-man honor guard mounted the colors and, just below the flag, unfurled a small triangular black flag. The two flags were then hoisted and the soldiers saluted the colors until the last notes of the Cuban anthem, *La Bayamesa*, echoed away. The black flag would remain with the standard until dusk, signifying a day of mourning for all those at the small airstrip.

The commander of Zaza Field, Colonel of Aviation Agusto Salazar, dropped his salute and listened to the crisp sound of his soldiers lowering their salutes in unison, then moved forward on the front porch of the concrete-and-stucco headquarters building and came to parade rest position, a signal to his adjutant to order his troops similarly.

Salazar, looking very much the flying hero, favored riding chaps and tall black leather riding boots over a flight suit and flying boots. His shirt was covered with patches

44

and cloth ribbons, crowned by the Soviet-style flying wings over his left breast pocket – Salazar was a graduate of the Soviet Union's premier military flight training school and was qualified in a dozen different fixed- and rotary-wing aircraft, including some of the USSR's newest and most advanced weapons systems – from the MiG-29 fighter to the Antonov 225 heavy cargo transport to the Mil Mi-28 attack helicópter. It helped that Salazar was taller than most of his Latino compatriots by a head, with long dark hair and a thin neat mustache.

Actually he might have been mistaken for a foppish Hollywood-style refugee from Central Casting, trying to look dashing and heroic, and indeed many of the young aviation cadets under his command at the flight training and support base had been known to call him 'Colonel Pepper' or 'Colonal Earhart' behind his back. They were wrong. Salazar's dark eyes had their own message, matched by a black temper.

'We have suffered a tragedy,' Salazar was now saying. 'Loss of comrades is always a tragedy, the greatest for this unit since its inception a year ago. We shall never forget those who died at the hands of the murderous Americans in the service of their country.'

Salazar was also an actor. These were children, he reminded himself. Only children would really accept this nonsense. But they were also skilled and fearless pilots. Extreme youth helped. Live today, for tomorrow we may die, and so forth.

Salazar was the commander of the unit 'Cuchillos,' Spanish for 'knives' or 'blades.' The Cuchillos was a unit of dropouts, men and women dismissed from Cuba's regular flying training units in the Revolutionary Air Force. Because all had compulsory military duties to perform after graduation from high school, the dropouts were usually placed in reserve units close to their hometowns, where they were required to complete their military training – three years on active duty, ten years in the ready reserves and the rest of their lives in the inactive reserves or local militia.

But becoming a pilot in Cuba was often a political decision – it had little to do with flying skills and more to do with who one's parents were or how influential one's family was in Castro's regime. And the favored, well-educated kids were rarely motivated to spend much time in the military, which often meant that the best pilot candidates were discarded while the pampered kids became the pilots more skilled at kicking around enlisted men and going to all-night parties than dogfighting.

But Salazar, although a fervent Communist and harboring an intense hatred for anyone or anything having to do with Americans, eventually found himself a willing member of a large cocaine and marijuana smuggling ring, run by the General of the Revolutionary Army Renaldo Ochoa Sanchez. At first the smugglers had the full cooperation and permission of the Castro regime – as long as Castro was getting his cut of the profits – but when Ochoa's popularity and wealth began to match, then threaten to exceed, those of Castro himself, Ochoa and his loyalists were executed. Salazar himself escaped the purge and fled to nearby Haiti with his secret bank accounts secure.

Using his wealth and power as an ex-Cuban officer, Salazar brought an appointment as a district militia commander of central Haiti and placed in charge of providing air support for the corrupt, quasi-democratic regime. It was the perfect cover for a drug smuggler. With his new official credentials, he was able to procure military hardware from a variety of sources and equip his unit far better than the poor government of Haiti could ever afford. He took the washouts and rejects from the Cuban reserve units and placed them in his secret unit at Zaza Airfield. He trained them in dilapidated old turboprop and jet fighters, broken-down cargo planes and any other flying machine handy. Eventually he hired on experts in other fields like paratroopers, forward combat controllers, air traffic controllers, weapons and even demolition experts. In less than a year he had created an army air wing comprised of men and women who averaged only nineteen years of age.

'Our brave comrades could have escaped with their lives,' Salazar went on. 'They had accomplished their mission, they could have returned to base without further risk to themselves. But they saw that their comrades were under attack from American secret police units. They ignored the risk, turned their aircraft around and attacked, creating a diversion that allowed our freedom fighters to counterattack. They escaped, the mission was a success but our brothers took heavy ground fire and were shot down. I have reports that there were survivors but that they were tortured and then executed.'

Their reaction was better than expected. Even the few doubters in the group, the ones who otherwise recognized propaganda when it was being spoon-fed to them, could not help but be swept up in the tide of anger all around them.

'American Coast Guard and Customs Service have declared open war on the men and women of Cuba, *and* on this organization, *your* family. The Coast Guard pretends to be a life-saving service. Not so. They are just another part of the military that rules the United States. The Customs Service pretends to be a peaceful government agency. In fact it is composed of armed thugs and mercenaries who extort tribute from citizens and collect bribes and payoffs from law-abiding foreigners. They are hired criminals with guns and badges. Remember, however, that they are well armed and tenacious, like hungry mongrels. Do *not* underestimate them. Learn their tactics and their weapons. The memories of our fallen comrades, of the horror of the way they died, must not be forgotten.' Of course, putting the pictures of the dead Shorts crew up in every classroom and hangar in Verrettes would help, too.

'You are the Cuchillos! Be proud and you will defeat your enemies and take control of the skies.'

Salazar saluted the cadets, then turned and walked briskly back into headquarters to his office. He sat down at his desk and propped his jackboots up on the smoothly polished desktop. His paneled office walls were decorated with all manner of weapons from Oriental swords to exotic machine guns – all fully functional – plus an entire wall of throwing knives. The knives, in fact, were his favorite. He withdrew one knife from his boot, hefted it for a moment, then hurled it at the door to the outer office. Right on target, as usual. To celebrate he pulled a nasal atomizer out of a pocket and took a quick snort of cocaine. High-grade. Not too much, he told himself. A tiny bit helped him to forget that he was stationed in the asshole of Haiti, in exile from his beloved Cuba.

There was a quick knock on the door to the outer office. Salazar put the atomizer away. 'Come.'

His adjutant, Field Captain Enrique Hermosa, swung open the door. 'Did you call for me, sir?' Salazar motioned to the back of the door, and watched as Hermosa retrieved his knife from the thick wood and handed it to him. He slipped it back into his right boot as Hermosa poured strong Colombian coffee for the commander.

'Has payment been received for the *llaho*?'

'As planned, *commandante*. Two million American dollars in our Cayman Island account. Señor Gachez also sends his condolences for the loss of our crewmen – '

'Gachez . . .' said with disgust. Salazar drained the steaming hot coffee in a single gulp. Hermosa refilled the china cup, then poured one for himself. 'We delivered four hundred kilos of high-grade to his nose-picking farmers in Florida, cocaine worth ten times what he pays us. We take the risks and he grows richer and fatter. We lose a new cargo plane and a top-notch crew, and all he can say is *sorry*?'

'He sends another message,' Hermosa said. He drank his coffee, relishing the flavor, before finishing the message. He knew his boss' foul moods, there might not be another chance at the rich coffee for who knew how long . . . 'He has been in contact with other members of the cartel. They also seem to want to do business with us.'

'What? Do you think we're some peasant taxi drivers? I'll deliver my reply in a hundred-kilo dynamite letter – '

'If I may, sir,' Hermosa said, 'I would suggest you give this matter some thought. We are not working *for* Señor Gachez . . .'

'You are damned right about that . . .'

'We contracted with Señor Gachez alone, without any other commitments to the other families of his cartel,' Hermosa continued. 'But it is Señor Gachez with the commitment to the cartel – if he has been approached by members of the Medellín families, he has an obligation to provide service to them. On the other hand, we do not. Therefore . . .'

'So we don't let ourselves be tricked the second time,' Salazar said, leaning back and sipping his coffee. 'We were poor starving bush pilots then, we accepted the deal with Gachez because we had little or no choice. Now we are strong, and smarter. We state our new rates for the other members of the cartel – inflation is two, three hundred percent in Cuba, correct? Things are bad all over, eh?'

Hermosa was riding high. Salazar was happy, he was happy. 'The members of the cartel will not allow Gachez to continue to enjoy contract rates better than theirs – he will either have to subsidize the cartel's payments or raise his own contract payments . . .'

49

'Or if he is stupid enough,' Salazar added, 'he will lie about his rates and try to swindle the other families. Then we will have enough leverage on him to dictate our own terms.'

'Sir, I would caution against trying to extort Señor Gachez or any member of the cartel,' Hermosa said. 'They are, after all, powerful men. If we ask for a reasonable mark-up for our services it will be considered nothing more than the price of doing business. There are none better than we. They will pay.'

'You're *right* they will pay.' Salazar resisted the urge to take another shot of *llaho* in front of Hermosa.

Hermosa was silent for a moment as Salazar turned over the plans for sending his bull to the Medellín cartel. Then: 'We do have another option, *commandante*. Perhaps this game has gone on too long. We do Gachez's bidding because he could have destroyed you . . .'

'What are you saying?'

'I am saying that you have more than enough savings to escape Haiti and get out of this business. Gachez can't hold a firing squad or life at hard labor over your head. Not anymore. You can free yourself of this . . .'

Hermosa had hit too close to home, Salazar thought. It was true. Two years earlier he had taken a bribe from Gachez worth thousands of American dollars to fly a load of cocaine on a training mission from Cartagena and drop it north of Cuban waters. He had been offered the typical Colombian bribe, *plomo o plata* – lead or silver, a piece of the action or a bullet in the head – an offer he could not refuse.

He had wanted to make the drop himself but it would have appeared too suspicious for him to take a plane out over Cuba at night. So he had planned an overwater navigation training leg and a practice tactical mine-laying mission for student training. His students performed well, dropping the six bundles of cocaine sealed inside harbor mine canisters dead on target, dead on time.

For accepting this offer he could not refuse, he was paid well, all in untraceable money in numbered accounts. But it was a bitter-sweet pay-off, knowing it put him in Gachez's employ. And there was no way to resign or retire from service with the Medellín cartel. You could take the money and run, but until you tried to spend the money. Then you were dead. The cartel, and in particular Gonzales Gachez, were just too powerful.

But he had reversed that now. Or was about to . . .

'How is it you're so familiar with my savings, field captain?' Hermosa wisely chose not to say what everyone in the cadre knew: Salazar skimmed a percentage of the profits for himself and was not averse to skimming a few kilos off each shipment to sell via his own connections in Haiti, the Bahamas and Mexico. Certainly, Hermosa thought, he could not think that no one, including the cartel, noticed such activities . . .

'I am a *soldier*, field captain. Remember that.'

'Please excuse me, sir,' Hermosa said. 'I did not mean to imply – '

'Get out of here.' The cocaine hit was beginning to affect him. He felt lighter, more powerful. 'Have my helicopter made ready. I will inspect the camp and make an area patrol.'

Hermosa was happy to get out of there and behind the thick wooden door separating himself from Salazar, obviously high, and his throwing knives.

Chapter Two

Gulf of Mexico, South of Marsh Island, Louisiana
0217 CST

'Position fix . . . now.'

Commander Russell Ehrlich, skipper of WMEC 620, the Coast Guard cutter *Resolute*, sipped on a mug of coffee as he tried to relax. The bridge of his cutter was humid with only an occasional breeze drifting through the open steel doors. Outside the slanted anti-reflection windows of the *Resolute*'s bridge was darkness, with just a hint of light visible on the horizon to the north – New Orleans, maybe even a hint of a glow from Galveston or Houston off toward the northwest. It was a clear, beautiful winter night in the Gulf of Mexico.

As he scanned the darkness the navigator's mate centered a set of electronic crosshairs on the center of a radar blip on the bridge's navigation radar set and pressed a button on his control console. Immediately a series of latitude–longitude coordinates, range and bearing, and intercept information zipped across a small computer monitor.

'Got it,' McConahay, the navigator's mate, reported. McConahay was a skinny, bespectacled ensign fresh out of the Coast Guard Academy in New London and sea-navigation training. Ehrlich had to smile – McConahay, an electrical engineer and math whiz out of the academy, looked out of place on the bridge. He was clearly overawed with the hustle of activity on the bridge and seemed to have little desire to look at the ocean at all – content to spend most of his time making lines on his chart and updating his computers. McConahay, it seemed, was trying to lower his rather high squeaky voice when speaking to the captain. Ah, the *new* Coast Guard . . . 'Range thirteen miles, speed perhaps two knots, right on the bow.'

'Does he have any company, Mr McConahay?'

'Radar's showing no other ships, sir,' McConahay replied, checking the fourteen-inch display, 'but we're at extreme radar range now. They may be hard to see or blocked by the freighter.'

'Where's our air cover?' Ehrlich wondered. And to McConahay, 'Fix our position with GPS, then verify with Loran. Plot the target's position. And I want it exact. If we end up hauling this guy into court I want to prove six ways to Sunday that he's in US waters.'

'Aye, sir.' McConahay bent to work – but didn't the skipper know that his position fixes were *always* exact?

The navigator's mate saved the radar target's position data in a memory storage buffer, then punched up the *Resolute*'s position on the GPS computer navigator. The Global Position System used information from a ring of geosynchronous satellites orbiting 22,500 miles above Earth's equator to obtain position, groundspeed and time information with remarkable accuracy – they could record their own position within four feet and get a fix on another radar-identified target within 100 yards.

The *Resolute*, one of sixteen Reliance-class cutters in the Coast Guard inventory, was notable for its advanced electronic suite and computerized automation of almost every task aboard ship. As a result, where most large seagoing cutters needed a crew of well over a hundred, the 210-foot-long, 950-ton *Resolute* and her Reliance-class sisters had a crew complement of only eighty-six – with computers and robots doing much of the scut work. From the start the *Resolute* was designed as a search-and-rescue vessel, only recently being outfitted for law enforcement and drug interdiction. She did carry one radar-guided Mk22 3-inch/50 cannon on her foredeck plus grenade launchers and .50 caliber machine guns that could be brought up on deck from the armory and mounted around the ship. She had a helipad aft of midships large enough to land a single HH-65 Dolphin helicopter rotated in from Coast Guard air stations around the southeast United States; her present Dolphin was borrowed from the Coast Guard air station in Mobile, Alabama.

'. . . Ship's position-information updated and verified,' McConahay reported, using a set of Plexiglas plotters on the board to mark the GPS coordinates on the chart, then making a tiny triangle and logbook entry on the chart. 'GPS position fix on the target verified as well.' He then checked the position readout on the third navigation computer, the Loran, for Long-Range Navigation, a system that used timed signals from synchronized shore-based radio stations to pinpoint their position. 'Loran data recorded. Checks with GPS within a tenth of a mile.' The navigator's mate would update the ship's position and navigation computers with the more accurate GPS and use the radar and Loran to check the GPS.

'I don't need the whole spiel, McConahay,' Ehrlich said wearily, 'just tell me where the hell he *is*.'

'Exactly ten miles south of Marsh Island,' McConahay reported. 'Well inside the twelve mile limit.'

'He got sloppy and drifted into our jurisdiction,' Ehrlich said, now excited. 'All these days of tracking that sonofabitch finally paid off. Mr Ross, find out where our Falcon is.'

Lieutenant Martin Ross, the officer of the deck, nodded and clicked on his intercom to the communications center. A moment later he reported, 'Sir, comm has radio contact with Omaha Six-One out of New Orleans. He says he'll be on station in five minutes.'

'Five minutes? They're already five minutes late.'

Just then on the bridge's speakers a voice blared out, '*Resolute*, this is Omaha Six-One on Uniform. On station in three minutes. Over.'

Ehrlich turned toward the voice as if he had heard a sound from the grave; then turned angrily toward Ross. 'Is he on the scrambler?'

'I'll check, sir.'

'Dammit, he better be.'

'Uh . . . sir?' It was McConahay.

'Hang on, son.' To Ross: 'Well?'

'He's on the scrambler now, sir.'

'Skipper. . . ?'

'What *is* it, McConahay?'

'I . . . I think the target is moving.'

'*What?*' Ehrlich was off his chair to check the radar scope.

'Right after Seven-One checked in, sir. Looks like he's heading out.'

'I knew it! Son of a bitch was monitoring our frequencies.' He swung to Ross. 'Have the duty-crew on deck on the double. Helm, all ahead full. Let's go talk with him before he gets away.'

McConahay stood up from his plotting board on the *Resolute*'s bridge. 'We're going to move in on him? Now? It's . . . it's after 2:00 A.M. – '

'Are we keeping you up, Mr McConahay?' Ehrlich made an entry in the bridge's logbook. 'There's nothing in the book that says we don't work at night. These guys will be out of our waters in ten minutes. It'll take us that long to catch up to them. We move in *now*.'

'My engines are all ahead full, sir,' the helmsman reported. 'Showing twelve knots and increasing.'

'If we lose this guy I'm going to shoot that Falcon crew. We've spent too much time dicking around with this guy to let him go now.'

The *Resolute* crew had indeed been tracking their target – a one-hundred-eighty-foot cargo ship, the *Numestra del Oro*, a Panamanian-registered freighter – for several days. Almost from first contact this freighter had aroused the Coast Guard's suspicion. It had only recently requested a berth at Galveston, but then had waited offshore just outside the twelve-mile limit for the last two days – ostensibly so they could make room for her at Galveston. There was plenty of room in the protected bays and intracoastal waterways around Galveston for the vessel to anchor and for the skipper to grant liberty to his crew, but the skipper could choose to wait wherever he wanted. Then, just when a berth opened up, the *Numestra* skipper had radioed in that he had been ordered by his parent company to take part of his cargo first to Mobile, then turn around and head back for Galveston. True, it was not unheard of for a freighter to wait so far offshore for a berth or suddenly change its port of call, but such moves had alerted the Coast Guard.

Previously the *Numestra* had been inspected by a Coast Guard C-130 patrol plane while it was en route from Panama, orbiting over the freighter long enough to verify its flag and its identification and speak to the skipper by radio about his cargo and destination. It also had been briefly inspected by a Coast Guard Island-class patrol vessel east of Nicaragua, but the inspection of the ship's documents, and cargo, were cursory. The *Numestra*, it seemed, was carrying a mixed cargo – remanufactured engine blocks from Mexico, coffee and rattan furniture from Brazil, scrap metal from Venezuela and the usual ferry mix of cars, busses and a few passengers that made up the bulk of most freighter manifest lists – none of the ferry passengers was of American citizenship. Its decks and holds had been crammed with sealed forty-foot cargo containers, all with the proper seals. The Coast Guard had

56

the authority to open the containers for inspection if permission was granted, but an Island-class boat had only eighteen crewmen – hardly enough to carry out an extensive search of a larger freighter.

After inspection the *Numestra* was released and the Coast Guard had relayed the information to the US Customs Service, which checked with the *Numestra*'s destination ports to verify that the ship was on legitimate business and that the proper manifests had been filed for entry into the United States. Everything checked. The next step would be to send a Customs Service cruiser out to inspect the ship before it reached its port – presumably to expedite clearance through Customs but really to check the ship again for contraband before it had a chance to off-load. But because the *Numestra* stayed so far offshore Customs had not yet checked it over.

It was soon obvious that the *Numestra* had no intention of docking. Any ship so reluctant to pull into an American port immediately came under suspicion, and so the *Resolute* had been sent to shadow the freighter. When the *Resolute* first caught up with *Numestra* well outside the twelve-mile limit it had detected several other ships hovering near the freighter. The smaller ships had immediately scattered when the *Resolute* moved within ten miles of the *Numestra*, which told Ehrlich and his crew that the freighter's surface-scanning radar had at least a ten-mile range and that the freighter was receiving guests that didn't want any run-ins with the Coast Guard.

It also told Ehrlich that the *Numestra* was very probably dealing in a cargo other than scrap metal and coffee – like drugs.

Since the *Resolute*'s HH-65 helicopter had no night-tracking equipment Ehrlich had requested support from Coast Guard air units out of New Orleans as well as a fast patrol boat. The patrol boat, he was told, could not be spared but the C-130 would cruise by twice a day in its patrols, and a scanner-equipped Falcon jet was assigned to operate with the *Resolute* for a few nights while the freighter was in the area.

But the freighter had stayed out of US territorial waters, out of direct Coast Guard jurisdiction. Boarding a foreign freighter was illegal in international waters without clearance from the skipper or the country of registry, so Ehrlich had been obliged to request permission to board the *Numestra* from the Panamanian government. After two days the request was still 'being processed.' Translation: they were being stonewalled. Not a refusal, but a definite stall. And it was a certainty that the skipper wasn't going to give permission to Ehrlich to board his ship a second time, so Ehrlich had decided to stay just outside the freighter's radar range to watch and wait, with the Falcon jet scanning the area for small boats trying to rendezvous with the freighter.

After three days of shadowing the *Numestra*, however, no small boats had been detected returning to the freighter. *Resolute* began to lose the use of their Falcon for longer and longer periods of time when it was called away for other, presumably more urgent jobs. The investigation was going nowhere, and Ehrlich had begun to feel pressure to get on with his patrol when he noted the *Numestra* was beginning to creep toward shore again. A few ships also started to move toward the freighter, gradually at first, then notice-ably closer each day. He would hang in. Something was going down . . .

But if the *Numestra* moved out into international waters there was little Ehrlich could do if the freighter's skipper decided not to stop for inspection. And Ehrlich wasn't about to open fire on the freighter – the Coast Guard couldn't fire on anyone unless they were under attack themselves, and even then firing on a ship on the open seas was politically and diplomatically explosive stuff.

But Ehrlich had a gut feeling this skipper was dirty, and now he was looking for international waters as fast as his old tub could carry him.

Of course the Reliance-class cutters weren't exactly speed demons, either. This intercept was taking forever . . .

'Range, McConahay.'

'Eleven miles and closing, sir. I'm picking up a second vessel, sir, moving away from the freighter at high speed . . . possibly a third target appearing now, sir.'

'Have the Falcon pick up one of the targets and track him,' Ehrlich said. 'Better call in Customs and some more of our boats to round up these turkeys. We're staying on the freighter. I think we've got a live one here . . .'

'Should we get the helo on deck and ready, sir?' Ross asked.

Night helo operations with a cutter going full speed were tricky, but it was a calm night and Ehrlich had some good pilots on board. 'Yes, Mr Ross, see to it. Then get communications on the horn and see if he can get that freighter to heave-to. Broadcast in English and Spanish.' A precaution for a future court appearance. The freighter's skipper could always claim he did not understand the Coast Guard's orders. More than one smuggler had received suspended sentences because of that dodge.

'Communications reports no reply from the freighter on common area or emergency frequencies,' Ross reported. Unless the *Numestra* had lost all its radios – in which case it would be required to heave to and use light signals to call for help – it was definitely ignoring its radios and trying to flee American waters.

'Range, ten miles and closing,' McConahay chimed in. 'Freighter is approaching the twelve-mile limit.'

'Have comm start running through the green book,' Ehrlich ordered. The green book was no longer a book – it was a computerized list of private shipping frequencies that each company was required to turn over to the Coast Guard. The *Resolute*'s computerized radio system would broadcast a warning message on each frequency in the book as further proof that it issued a warning it was in pursuit. 'Then have them report our situation to District headquarters.'

The *Resolute* was closing, but with only about five or six knots' closure rate it was like watching paint dry.

'No response on all green-book frequencies,' Ross reported a few minutes later. 'We've got radio checks from other stations, though. We're definitely going out.'

'Any word from District?'

'They've acknowledged our messages,' Ross said. 'No word yet from State about permission to board.'

'Advise District that I have reason to believe an emergency exists on the *Numestra del Oro* and that I intend to intercept and board her, on my authority,' Ehrlich said. 'I'll need clearance from Area headquarters as soon as possible but advise them that I intend to proceed without delay.'

'Aye, sir.' As he made the orders to the communications room, Ross asked, 'For the record, sir, what emergency did we see on the freighter?'

'Obviously a radio malfunction,' Ehrlich snapped. 'That's a safety of navigation violation for a vessel their size. I'm also concerned with those smaller vessels that were spotted around the freighter – they could have been attackers or there could be a medical emergency on board. We need to investigate immediately. I don't see any running lights, either – definitely a hazard to navigation.' Ross nodded and smiled. The skipper, although fairly young and only a commander, had a veteran's smarts.

'Range four miles,' McConahay reported after several more long quiet moments. 'He's well outside our waters now, sir.'

'I understand, Mr McConahay,' Ehrlich said. 'But the bastard's not getting away so easy. He's either radio-out or ignoring our calls, and both cases give us authority to intercept and board him. Mr Ross, get the helo airborne. Have him flash light signals at the freighter's bridge.'

Ross began monitoring the preparations on the brilliantly lit helipad as the crew made ready to launch. Even though the seas were calm they were using the spear-trap on the helipad – the spear-trap was a device resembling a spearhead attached to the underside of the Dolphin helicopter that helped launch and recover the chopper in bad weather. The spear fitted inside the trap, a large clamplike device in the center of the helipad. When landing in rough seas the spear would be lowered to the helipad and engaged in the trap, the helicopter would take up the slack under power and the trap would winch the helicopter onto even a badly rolling deck.

'Attention on deck. Prepare for spear-trap launch,' Ross called over the PA, then turned to Ehrlich for final approval, which was given with a quick nod. Ross rechecked the area around the ship on radar, gave the helo a once-over with a pair of binoculars and hit a button that changed a bridge-clearance light from yellow to green. 'Clear to launch helo.'

Moments later the Dolphin rescue chopper carrying medics and rescue specialists – each well armed – was ready for liftoff from the helipad. Liftoff was just the opposite of a landing. With the spear engaged in the trap, the Dolphin began to apply power for liftoff; then, simulating that the ship was at the top of a swell, the trap swung open and the Dolphin shot into the air well clear of the cutter and was quickly lost from sight in the still night air, only its red-and-green running lights visible as it raced ahead toward the freighter.

'Three-and-a-half miles,' McConahay reported. The

freighter was barely visible as a moving shape against the horizon, but its engines roaring at full power could be heard clearly.

The Dolphin helicopter reached the freighter quickly, and its powerful three thousand-watt searchlight could easily be seen painting the freighter's entire deck. 'Mama-San, this is Puppy. I am over the target now. Wheelhouse is occupied. I can see men on deck. No sign of emergency, no sign of signals being transmitted. Clear night, no fog. Signals should be easily picked up.'

Ehrlich spoke into the microphone. 'Roger, Puppy, give them the stop signal and stand by.'

The Dolphin searchlight operator shined the light directly into the freighter's wheelhouse, moved the beam out, then swept it across the deck in front of the bridge – the international signal to stop or shut down engines. The freighter did not respond. The Dolphin moved closer to the freighter and swept the beam across the wheelhouse once again. The time the crew clearly saw men inside the wheelhouse shading their eyes and gesturing for the Dolphin to move away.

'Receiving unfriendly response from the crew on the target's bridge, Mama-San,' the Dolphin's pilot reported. 'They show no sign of slowing. They're still going fifteen knots – about full blast for this old tub.'

'Try 'em on your radio,' Ehrlich ordered. 'It's possible they didn't hear us.' To the ship's officer of the deck: 'Mr Ross, signal the crew for intercept procedures. Have the forward 3-inch and the port and starboard .50 cals mounted, manned and standing by. Call Mr Applegate to the bridge.'

Ross' stomach was queasy – the fact that this was not a drill was beginning to sink in. He flipped on the ship-wide address system: 'All hands, general quarters. All hands, general quarters. Man your battle stations. Mr Applegate to the bridge.' The announcement was followed by an electronic gong, the 'law enforcement' signal that reverberated through the ship. Before the blare of the gong had stopped, Lieutenant Commander Richard Applegate, the *Resolute*'s first officer, had rushed onto the bridge wearing a life jacket and blue baseball cap, with 'USCG USS RESOLUTE' on the peak.

'You're relieved, Mr Ross,' Applegate shouted. He grabbed the binoculars from around Ross' neck, checked the radar screen and scanned the dark horizon. 'What's up, Russ?'

'We've got a five-thousand-ton Panamanian freighter out on our nose about three miles, Dick,' Ehrlich told him. 'No response on any radio channels. We've got our Dolphin up flashing him light signals. No reply.'

'We gonna bust him?'

'We caught him inside the limit with ships alongside. He intercepted a radio call between us and the Falcon and booked. Now he's heading for open ocean. Yes, we're going to bust him.'

Just then on the ship's radio speaker they heard, 'Panamanian vessel *Numestra del Oro*, this is Coast Guard Helicopter One-Seven Mike from the United States Coast Guard cutter *Resolute* on Gulf Coast Emergency Channel Nine. You are ordered to stop and prepare for inspection. Acknowledge by radio or light signal.'

Ehrlich took up the mike again. 'Puppy, this is Mama-San. Radio check on GUARD.'

'Loud and clear, Mama-San,' the Dolphin pilot replied.

'Well, we know the radio works,' Ehrlich said, making another log entry. 'This bastard just doesn't want to – '

'Sir, the freighter's slowing down,' McConahay broke in. 'Range two miles and closing rapidly.'

'All *right*,' Ehrlich said. The prospect of a protracted chase and a forced boarding in international waters with an uncooperative – and likely hostile – crew did not sit too well with Ehrlich. The job would be much easier with the freighter stopped. 'The guy turned his lights on, too – he must have just realized we weren't going to let him go.'

Meanwhile the ship's officer reported: 'Skipper, the 3-incher and both .50 cals mounted on the starboard side, manned and ready. Chief Morrison and Patrol Team One boarding crew standing by.'

'Have the boarding crew ready to go on the starboard side. Helm, move us alongside about fifty yards.' Into the ship's intercom he ordered, 'Stand by on the 3-incher. I want it to stay on the lubber line but ready to go at any time. Stand by on the fifty cals.' The cannon on the foredeck of the *Resolute* remained still, but Ehrlich could hear footsteps just behind the bridge as crewmen mounted and manned the .50 caliber machine guns on their swivel turrets.

As spotlights on the *Resolute* now illuminated the freighter *Numestra* Ehrlich saw a vessel a bit longer than the *Resolute*, possibly twice the cutter's age and in the worst condition he had ever seen a large seagoing vessel. Rust seemed to cover every inch of her, paint peeled off the parts that had paint, windows were smashed and whole sections of steel were missing from her sides. The deck was covered with containers of all sizes, some small, others the size of tractor-trailers – but it was obvious the *Numestra*'s broken-down cargo-lading equipment did not load those huge crates onto the deck.

'Would you look at that rust-bucket?' Applegate said, scanning the vessel with his binoculars. 'Who in their right mind would put their cargo on that thing?'

'Depends on the cargo,' Ehrlich mumbled. 'She may look like a garbage scow but she was maintaining nearly fifteen knots for an hour – she's obviously got some horses under the hood. This thing is a lot more than meets the

64

eye.' Ehrlich picked up the microphone and switched his comm panel to the LOUDSPEAKER position. 'Attention on the *Numestra del Oro*. This is the United States Coast Guard. Heave-to and prepare for boarding and inspection.' He turned to McConahay. 'Position, Mr McConahay?'

'Twenty miles out, sir. Technically in international waters . . .'

'Plot our position and mark it for the log as the intercept point,' Ehrlich ordered. 'Mr Applegate, see to it that comm radios our position and situation to District. Tell them to get another cutter out here ASAP.' He thought a moment, then added, 'I want permission from Headquarters to release batteries as well. Inform them I may need an SNO from Panama.'

'Yes, sir.' Applegate put a headset up to his ears and began relaying the message. The SNO, Statement of No Objection, was standard for such intercepts – it was permission from the country of registry to allow the Coast Guard to board a foreign vessel in international waters or, for stateless vessels, a declaration from the Coast Guard commandant that the vessel was under Coast Guard jurisdiction. The release-batteries request was not as standard – it was permission from the commandant to open fire on a vessel attempting to escape.

The port rail of the *Numestra* was beginning to swell with crewmen shading their eyes from the glare of the searchlights and swearing in Spanish. Ehrlich could see a few heavy tools and ropes in the crewmen's hands but so far no weapons. Moments later most of those crewmen were chased away by a fat bearded man in a white shirt carrying a bullhorn who stood on the port rail near amidships and glared at the approaching Coast Guard vessel.

The man raised the bullhorn to his lips: 'You Coast Guard, we do not like you to board,' he said in broken, accented English. 'Why you stop?'

Ehrlich made no reply but gave orders to his own men as the *Resolute* glided in toward the freighter. With Ehrlich on the starboard catwalk giving instructions to the helm, the cutter drifted in to a dozen yards from the rusty sides of the *Numestra*. Thick rubber fenders were attached to chocks, and the crew unstowed boathooks and ropes, ready to lash the two boats together.

Ehrlich put on his life jacket and grabbed his bullhorn. 'McConahay, have comm radio our position and situation again.' And to Applegate: 'Dick, you have the con. I'm going over to talk to the skipper.'

'Shouldn't you wait for another cutter?'

'The way it's going, that could be all night,' he said as he began pulling on a bullet-proof vest, life jacket and utility belt containing a flashlight, walkie-talkie, handcuffs and a steel whip 'impact device' – fancy name for a high-tech billyclub. 'I'll get the captain's name and the master copy of his manifest and be back on board in a few minutes. We'll wait for the inspection until we get some more help. Hang tight.' He turned toward the starboard catwalk exit.

'Skipper?'

Ehrlich turned. Applegate opened a locked bin on the aft bulkhead of the bridge and removed a .45 calibre Colt 1911A2 pistol along with a pouch containing two extra seven-round clips. 'Don't go aboarding without it,' Applegate deadpanned.

'Just checking to see if you were awake.' Ehrlich loaded and chambered a round in the big .45, holstered it, checked the radio and left.

The boarding crew was arranged in standard ready-and-cover formation, with two handlers on the bow and stern lines and two fender handlers, each with sidearms. They were backed up with three riflemen in semi-cover on the port side with weapons at port arms, visible enough for the freighter crew to know they were there but still well covered behind the steel forecastle. Ehrlich glanced up and checked the .50 cal gunner and his mate, both ready with the machine gun barrels pointing toward the freighter but raised high overhead. Two riflemen, one of them Chief Petty Officer Eddie Morrison, Chief of the Boat and head of the boarding and security details, flanked the main starboard gangway just below the bridge, armed with sidearms and slung M-16s.

Ehrlich moved down the side of the forecastle and stepped between Morrison and the other riflemen at the gangway. The two vessels were still separated by about ten feet, with the line tenders holding ropes and hooks ready to catch the freighter's horn cleats. The rusty, scummy sides of the freighter loomed over the polished white hull of the *Resolute*. Crewmen on the freighter hovered in and around the cargo lashed onto the freighter's deck, visible only as long as the searchlights weren't aimed at them.

Ehrlich took up his loudspeakers to his lips: 'I am Commander Ehrlich, captain of the United States Coast Guard cutter *Resolute*. I want to speak with your captain.'

'I am Captain Martinez,' the burly man in the white shirt and wild black beard shouted back. Then he remembered he had his own bullhorn and used it. 'We are in international waters on peaceful business. Why you stop my ship?'

'You did not obey a lawful order to heave-to while you were in American waters, Captain Martinez. You failed to respond on any area or emergency frequencies. That is a violation of safe navigation laws for commercial vessels. I request permission to come aboard your ship and inspect your documents and your cargo.'

'You have no right to search! You cannot come aboard this ship – '

'I am authorized to inspect any vessel transiting American waters if I find they are violating the safe navigation laws of the United States. That includes your logbooks and manifests. If your manifests show you are carrying cargo destined for the United States, I am authorized to inspect that cargo. And according to your port requests of three days ago you are carrying such cargo. Now, you are ordered to heave-to and prepare for inspection – '

'I will not! Not without permission from my owner – '

'I don't need permission from your owner or your government,' Ehrlich said, bluffing. 'If you have a protest you may file it with my government on reaching port. Heave-to immediately.'

'You cannot force me to stop in international waters! This is piracy!'

Ehrlich pulled a walkie-talkie from his holster and keyed the mike. 'Mr Applegate, swing the 3-incher across the freighter's bow and load one blank round. Get Boarding Team Two armed and on deck. Have all hands on deck stay sharp.'

A moment later the loudspeaker on the *Resolute* clicked on and Applegate's voice rang out: 'Team One, cover!' The riflemen at port arms behind the line handlers disappeared into cover positions behind the superstructure, the line-handlers dropped to the deck behind the steel gunwale coaming and drew their sidearms, the riflemen at the gangway moved quickly to port arms and chambered rounds in their M-16s. The turret of the foredeck 3-inch cannon swung to the right, pointing just ahead of the freighter's bow. While the captain of the *Numestra* looked on, six more armed men ran out on deck and took up cover positions, rifles aimed at the freighter.

'Once more, Captain Martinez,' Ehrlich said on the bullhorn, 'stop your ship or we will force you to stop.'

Martinez raised his hands, holding his palms towards Ehrlich. 'We will stop. Hold your men.' Just then a second man in a gray silk suit came out from between some crates on the freighter's deck, stepped up behind Martinez and spoke to him. They appeared to have a brief argument.

'What do you make of that, Chief?' Ehrlich asked Morrison.

'Looks like the real driver of the boat has just been heard from,' the security chief said. 'We should see who's really running the show now.'

The man in the silk suit disappeared behind a crate. The freighter's captain moved up a ladder back to his wheelhouse, and soon after that the rumble of the freighter's engines subsided to a low grumble and Martinez walked out to the catwalk, raised the bullhorn to his lips. 'Permission to board granted.' His English had suddenly improved.

'Assemble your deck crew on the fantail, Captain Martinez,' Ehrlich ordered. He had to repeat it several times before Martinez finally ordered his men away from the rail and back toward the freighter's stern.

Things looked like they might be defusing, Ehrlich thought to himself as he watched the *Numestra*'s crewmen move away. 'Prepare to board,' he now radioed to his men on the starboard rail, who began to holster pistols, sling rifles and pick up their mooring gear. He was about to order the helmsman to move closer when the radio suddenly came to life:

'*Skipper!*' Judging by the background noise, the speaker was probably someone on board the Dolphin helicopter, which had been moving around the *Numestra* during the intercept, shining its searchlight across the freighter's decks. 'I see men carrying heavy weapons, moving to the port side of the freighter. Six of them, fore and aft. Disengage – '

'*Take cover,*' Ehrlich shouted, waving his arms, then turned and called to Applegate on the bridge, 'Vector! Flank speed! *Move . . .*'

Ehrlich had taken about five steps when he heard the raspy, thudding pop-pop-pop of gunfire – even though he knew they were M-16s, they sounded like cheap kid's toys. And then the night erupted into a sheet of fire.

The six men on the foredeck of the *Numestra* spread out along the port railing near the front of the freighter, took quick aim and fired anti-armor bazookas at the *Resolute* – from only a few yards away they could not miss. Two high-explosive projectiles hit the 3-inch cannon, one round hit the foredeck and two rounds hit the bridge. Fire, smoke and red-hot glass showered the men on the forward half of the *Resolute* before they could react. One line-handler and the rifleman on the foredeck died instantly, the second line-handler on the bow was blown overboard by the force of the explosion on the cannon turret.

The surviving Coast Guardsmen providing cover for the boarding crew returned fire but the attack wasn't over. Three more bazooka rounds slammed into the *Resolute*, one hitting close enough to destroy a .50 caliber machine gun mount. Heavy rifle fire from the freighter began to rake the cutter, and the *Numestra*'s engines roared to life as it began to head away from the crippled Coast Guard vessel.

Ensign McConahay had survived on the bridge of the *Resolute* because as the Dolphin pilot's warning echoed through the bridge loudspeakers he had moved behind his plotting table. So there was something solid between him and the freighter. And when the first shot rang out he ducked beind it just before the first LAWS rocket shattered the windows and blew away Applegate and the rest of the bridge crew.

McConahay's ears were ringing, he was dizzy and he tasted blood. He was covered with glass, bits of metal and some gooey stuff. Somehow he had managed to crawl to the aft bulkhead and find one of the auxiliary wall phones.

He opened the phone's cover, retrieved the handset and sank to the floor as another rush of vertigo hit him.

'Bridge, this is Auxiliary,' a voice said. 'Bridge! Respond!'

'We're under attack,' McConahay shouted. He couldn't think of anything else to say.

'McConahay? Is that you?'

'Yeah . . . yeah . . .' Somehow hearing his name helped him think, and slowly a bit of his training began to filter through. 'Radio for help. Call the day crew to the bridge.'

'Where's the captain? Where's Mr Applegate?'

That was the first time McConahay had looked around the bridge, *really* looked around, and the sight brought a massive wave of nausea. The smell of the explosives, the stench of burned flesh, the acid smoke in the air . . . overpowering. It was also then that he noticed the bodies, torn and scattered across the so recently spotless decks.

'They're . . . they're . . .' McConahay couldn't finish the thought. He looked down at the tattered remains of his life vest, covered with glass and red sticky globs. His hands and arms were covered with it . . .

'Can you give us a heading?' the voice in Auxiliary Control shouted. 'Can you give us a course?'

McConahay dropped the phone and staggered to his feet. The Gulf breezes were slowly moving the acidic fumes out of the shattered bridge, and soon he could see the *Numestra* moving off to the right, heading away at growing speed. Then through the broken windows he spotted a few crewmen on the foredeck firing at the escaping freighter – and he saw that the 3-inch gun had taken some hits but its protective steel turret housing, although backward, was still intact.

He found the auxiliary control phone underneath the forward instrument panel – it had been protected by its cradle well under the panel. 'Auxiliary control, report. What's the status of the cannon?'

'The 3-incher is showing functional, ensign,' a voice replied, 'but we're showing a fault in – '

'Come twenty degrees right, make flank speed, and stand by on the forward 3-incher,' McConahay broke in. He leaned as far as he could out the broken windows. 'Clear the foredeck! Clear the foredeck!'

'Ensign, we can't make flank speed. We're sending damage-control to – '

'Then give me whatever you got,' McConahay shouted, 'but get that cannon on line.' The riflemen scurried away from the gun turret as the huge cannon slewed left and lowered its muzzle to near-horizontal.

McConahay now checked the fire-control radar but it was a smoking hole in the instrument panel. Coughing through the acrid stinging smoke that nearly filled the shattered bridge, he found one of the seldom used pieces of navigation equipment intact – the pelorus. This simple device, resembling a surveyor's instrument, had a precision aiming-reticle on a moveable wheel mounted on a compass rose that read bearings from the ship to a distant object. Using the pelorus and a little trigonometry the navigator could compute range and position. The pelorus had been replaced by the more accurate radar and other electronic navigation devices, but McConahay, out of navigation school only a few months, was still familiar with how to use it.

And it came to him that, incredibly, he had what he needed to mount a counter-attack. Maybe . . .

The 3-inch cannon needed range and bearing for an accurate firing solution. Bearing was easy – line up on the freighter and read bearing directly off the pelorus. He knew the approximate height of the freighter's superstructure, and with the pelorus he got the angle to the top of it. He had all the angles and one side of a right triangle – height of the superstructure divided by the tangent of the angle would give the range in feet to the freighter.

The superstructure was about a hundred feet tall – remember to subtract the distance above the waterline, McConahay told himself. He was about twenty feet above water, so that equalled eighty feet. The pelorus measured angles in degrees and mils – degrees for very tall objects and short distances, and mils for more precise measurements. Mils, originally used by Civil War artillery officers to compute distance for cannon fire, were made to order for this situation.

The breeze through the shattered bridge windows was beginning to clear the smoke. Rubbing dirt and soot from his watering eyes, McConahay sighted through the scope at the retreating shape of the *Numestra* – the measurement scales were luminescently lit – and read the angle: twenty-six-and-a-half mils.

He used his fingers like an abacus to make the range calculations. First, mils had to be converted to radians. There were 16 mils in a grad – that came to 1.656 grads. Multiply that by 0.9 to get degrees – that came to 1.49. Multiply . . . *no, divide* that by 57.29 to get radians – that came to 0.26. The tangent of that number was virtually the same – .026. Divide 80 feet – the height of the *Numestra*'s superstructure minus his own height above water – by .026, and moments later, dividing on his fingers, he had the range: 3,054 feet.

'Auxiliary control, range to target three thousand fifty feet, bearing twenty-two degrees, estimated speed of target twelve knots, estimate heading of target . . . one-five-zero degrees magnetic. Deck clear. Report when ready to shoot.'

'Ensign, do you know what the hell – '

'I said *report*.'

Silence, then: 'Ensign, ballistic-mode manual, lead mode manual showing feed fault after eight. Ready up.'

McConahay shook drops of sweat out of his eyes. 'Batteries released. Shoot!'

The 3-inch cannon rang out, a tongue of flame leaping toward the horizon. McConahay, the recent student, probably didn't need all his fancy precise calculations to hit the freighter – it was little more than a half-mile away – but in any case his figures were dead on. The first round hit the freighter just above the waterline and smack in the middle. A mushroom of fire blossomed into the night sky. The cannon fired one high-explosive round every five seconds, and each one hit home. The shells moved aft along the waterline, finally reaching the engine compartment. When the fifth shell hit, it sent a massive ball of fire erupting from the entire aft section of the freighter, and the hulk began to burn fiercely.

'Feed fault on the forward 3-incher,' the officer in auxiliary control reported.

'Auxiliary control, cease fire, cease fire,' McConahay shouted into the phone. The cannon's heavy pounding had felt like hammer-blows to his chest, and the vibration, along with the rush of adrenaline, made his muscles actually quiver with exhaustion. 'Relay to engine room. All stop!' Men were now rushing onto the bridge. McConahay let the phone drop, and found himself slumping to the deck.

'I'll be goddamned, you got the son-of-a-bitch, Mr McConahay,' someone was saying.

'Damage report . . . head count . . . send SOS . . .' McConahay was mumbling. The emergency ship drills at the Academy were jumbling together with geometric shapes and trig tables in his head, and soon everything turned gray, and welcome darkness closed over him.

Coast Guard Station, Mobile, Alabama
The Next Morning

Reporters and camera crews were on hand in boats, in

helicopters and along every dock in the harbor as the *Resolute* was towed into port with the crippled freighter *Numestra del Oro* alongside. A fire tug moved the *Resolute*, with a dozen firemen and engineers on deck studying the rocket-impact points and fire damage on the cutter's starboard side. Another fire tug was covering the *Numestra* on the port side, but this one had as many armed FBI agents and Coast Guardsmen on it as firemen.

Admiral Hardcastle stood on *Resolute*'s helipad just aft of the helicopter's hangar, and was soon joined by Admiral Albert Cronin, Hardcastle's boss and commander of the Coast Guard Atlantic Area. Cronin, just over five feet, had thick meaty hands, a waistline to match and a wrestler's neck. Those friendly referred to him as 'the fire-plug' or just 'Plug,' but Hardcastle never used that nickname even though the two men had known each other for fifteen years.

Now they stood on the edge of the helipad looking over the freighter *Numestra* tied along the port side. Customs, DEA and FBI agents swarmed over its unsteady deck, taking photographs and making notes as if the badly damaged freighter would disappear in a puff of smoke any second.

'I could use a smoke,' Cronin said gruffly. Hardcastle reached inside his jacket, pulled out a cigar, offered it to Cronin, then took one for himself as well. But as the Area Commander was about to light up Hardcastle held up a hand. 'Better not, sir. Diesel fumes.'

In fact, the air was thick with the nauseating kerosene-like smell; the *Numestra* had left a trail of fuel oil in its wake twenty miles long. Cronin's scowl deepened. The two men, unlit stogies clamped between their teeth, continued to look at the *Numestra* as if it were King Kong brought to America on a barge.

'They're going to transfer McConahay,' Cronin told Hardcastle. 'Kid's on the edge of nervous exhaustion.'

'He gave a damn fine account of himself out there last night,' Hardcastle said.

'C'mon, Ian, he was a junior officer on the bridge of a cutter, scared shitless, and he went over the edge. Damn near every other man on the bridge gets blown to hell, he finds himself suddenly in command on a wrecked bridge, under attack, with major damage to the vessel. Now I don't need to tell *you* . . . the first thing to do is alert the crew, take care of the injured and take charge of the damage control detail – *not*, for God's sake, start shooting the damned cannon. Face it, the kid went ballistic, he was out of control – '

'He scored five direct hits on that freighter, at night, without using one piece of electronic fire-control gear,' Hardcastle said, voice tight. 'He made mathematical calculations in his head that you or I couldn't do in a week or a year with a computer – '

'Meanwhile his ship is taking on water and he's thirty minutes away from being on the bottom of the Gulf of Mexico.'

'He made a decision to stop a felon and aggressor from escaping.'

'Escaping? That freighter wasn't going anywhere. We had the patrol cutter *Manitou* only three hours away. We could have run that old tub down – '

'Maybe so. But he couldn't know that.'

'Ian, there were crewmen that didn't even know what was happening up on deck until several minutes after the attack. Just possibly three of the dead might have survived if the proper actions had been taken. McConahay was up there taking pot shots with the 3-incher instead of directing matters on his foredeck.'

He noticed Hardcastle's shocked expression. 'Relax, I'm not going to put that in my report. But this isn't war, when *maybe* such actions might be in order. This is peacetime.

Look it up. Whoever is in charge of a Coast Guard vessel is first responsible for his crew and his ship. One man doesn't keep shooting when his shipmates are lying dead and wounded around him. But I agree, young McConahay's been through enough without laying a review board on him. When the shouting dies down and he gets off convalescent leave I'll recommend that he gets a detailed briefing on the appropriate procedures in such circumstances – including the fact that your crew and your ship comes first. We'll call it counseling or reorientation. His permanent record won't be touched. Satisfied?'

'I agree, his record shouldn't be affected.'

'Admiral, you are a damned hardhead. Which isn't exactly big news.' And then, as though feeling the need to explain himself further: 'Whipping out a gun and shooting at the bad guys isn't always the most appropriate action to take in an emergency. We lost a helluva lot of valuable evidence because you shot down that Shorts 330 instead of trying to force it down or trail it on radar to a landing zone.'

'We've gone over this, sir . . .'

'Well, it's the same with McConahay shooting at the smugglers.'

Hardcastle pointed up to the deck of the *Numestra*, where Customs Service agents were hauling hand trucks full of plastic bags up onto deck. The bags, each the size of a refrigerator, contained cash, American currency in bills no larger than one hundred dollars – most in fives and tens. Customs had already stacked dozens of these bags on deck.

'Look at that. This freighter was a floating smuggler's warehouse,' Hardcastle said. 'I'm told each one of those bags contains one hundred thousand dollars in small bills. They estimate they've got *tons* of cash below decks – not just millions, *tons*. Not to mention hundreds of pounds of cocaine and heroin and another hundred tons of marijuana. Customs says this ship alone could have hauled several such loads of cash out of the country already. Plus, they found automatic weapons, bazookas, LAWS rockets, mines, high explosives, even Stinger anti-aircraft missiles.'

'I know all that – what's your point? What's that got to do with McConahay?' Knowing full well the answer.

'Well, you're saying that the *appropriate* action for McConahay was to disengage, look after his ship and let a smaller, less capable patrol boat like the *Manitou* go after those guys. I say that would have been a mistake. Frankly neither the *Resolute* nor the *Manitou* are well equipped to handle this kind of action, but the *Manitou* would have had *no* chance – these guys could easily have sunk the *Manitou*. I'm saying, Admiral, that maybe McConahay did the right thing by hitting back at those smugglers. If those guys sailed away scot-free and then were chased by other Coast Guard or Customs forces we could have lost a lot more men. McConahay should be recognized as a hero, not as a junior officer who did an "inappropriate" action.'

Cronin privately not exactly disagreeing, but not able to say so, let it pass.

'Anyway, we've got a bad situation on our hands, Admiral,' Hardcastle pressed on. 'This is the second incident – third, if you count the Falcon attack and the attack on Geffar's unit separately – where smugglers have used heavy weapons to attack law-enforcement units in American waters, on American soil or in international waters. These aren't terrorist or military attacks – but they have elements of both. Their primary purpose is to defend their drug smuggling, plain and simple. Except their tactics aren't so simple . . .'

'Well, each Coast Guard station will be briefed in detail about these activities,' Cronin said. 'Priority messages have been sent to each District. We've requested additional personnel for your District and for Admiral Kellerman's

Eighth District as well, along with more air and surface units – '

'Then I'd like to detach a unit and set it up specifically for handling this situation, Admiral. We need a unit that is specially trained and equipped to handle these guys.'

'I don't think that's really necessary, Ian. I can't approve of McConahay's response last night, but at least it showed these smugglers that we're able to respond with force – '

He's talking out of both sides of his mouth, Hardcastle thought. Cronin wasn't a man who did that . . . unless he was less sure of his ground than he sounded . . .

'I disagree, sir. In both situations the smugglers got the best of us, they had a Customs Service assault force and a Coast Guard cutter beaten. They suffered a loss of personnel and equipment because of some . . . unorthodox responses by myself and a green Ensign McConahay who didn't know the rules said not to shoot back.'

'So what the hell are you suggesting, Ian?' Cronin retorted. He chomped down on the cold cigar, then tossed it at the rust-orange side of the *Numestra*. 'We start blasting away at every unidentified aircraft and vessel in American territory? We're the United States Coast Guard, not the old East German Border Guards. It's a damned frustrating job, for sure. There are risks, yes – lots of them. Each man and woman on those ships knows that, but they go out there, it's their duty – '

'But it's crazy to have them go out there unprepared for the – '

'Then we start sending them out better prepared. Better weapons, better training, more backups, a greater show of force . . .'

'I *agree*, sir,' Hardcastle said quickly. 'Yes. Send out a ship or an aircraft better prepared and better armed for such a conflict. *But not a Coast Guard ship.*'

'I don't get it,' Cronin said, shaking his head. 'Who else

79

do we send? The Navy? The Air Force? The Coast Guard has armed vessels, radar planes, trained seamen . . .'

'But do we send out a Coast Guard crew armed and loaded for bear on every mission? Seventh District vessels participated in over fifteen *thousand* law-enforcement missions last year. True, most were routine searches and boardings. We did a few hundred smuggling intercepts, those were in the minority. It's dangerous and impractical to load up essentially a life-saving and search-and-rescue crew with heavy weapons and send them out on routine patrols. They'll be likely to come out shooting when they pull over a fishing boat for a minor infraction. And if they *don't* treat every mission as a dangerous intercept they'll be unprepared when the shooting starts.'

Cronin kept silent. Hardcastle pressed what he hoped was an opening. 'My people are already loaded up with duties, Admiral. We are the only agency in the country that's supposed to enforce international, federal, state *and* local laws all at the same time. The pressure's really on every time they go out on patrol. Now, we give them a new tasking – the next freighter or fishing boat you stop may blow you out of the water with a LAWS rocket. Check him for life jackets, flame arrestors, expired flares, Stinger missiles and, oh yes, drugs, and don't get killed while you're at it.'

'I am familiar with your sortie rate and with the responsibilities of the men under your command. I am also familiar with their duties and the pressures of the job. I don't need a damn lecture.'

'Sorry, sir, I was trying to make a point . . .'

Cronin was looking toward the docks of Coast Guard Station Mobile. Ahead, at the *Resolute*'s berth, the docks and breakwaters were crowded with reporters and on-lookers, all being held back by Coast Guardsmen and Louisiana State Police.

'Who the hell let those reporters on my station?' Cronin said under his breath. 'I'm gonna stretch the sonofabitch who authorized that . . .'

As the *Resolute* approached, Cronin and Hardcastle could see four vehicles moving through the crowd, red lights flashing, cameras swinging in their direction. Slowly the four ambulances made their way to the docks and stopped. The crowd surged toward them to get into position to see into them. The emergency medical technicians swung open the rear doors and awaited their grisly cargos.

At that moment the steel doors leading to the *Resolute*'s helipad opened. Cronin and Hardcastle moved aside, rendered salutes as the bodies of the ten Coast Guardsmen killed in the *Numestra* attack, including those of Commander Ehrlich and Lieutenant Commander Applegate, were wheeled out of the hangar-bay-turned-morgue and brought up to the quarterdeck for transfer to the ambulances. Hardcastle's eyes narrowed as he noted that not all of the dark plastic bodybags were normal man-sized – several were hardly more than shapeless heaps . . .

Cronin dropped his salute as the last gurney was brought past. 'Damn it all to hell,' he said under his breath. He glared at the cameras on the docks, which had begun to zoom in on the bodies, and body parts, being rolled out on deck.

'Sir – '

'*Yes*, Hardcastle?'

'I'm sorry this happened, Admiral. More than I know how to say . . .'

Cronin turned away from the onlookers and reporters and stared at the *Numestra* for a few silent moments. Then: 'I know.' There was a long pause. The tugs maneuvered *Resolute* into its berth, and line handlers began securing the damaged cutter and the disabled freighter.

'Ian, write up your recommendations. Develop your plan for this new security unit you talked about. If I can approve it, I'll make it part of my report to DOT, Coast Guard headquarters and the Joint Chiefs. Hell, maybe it's time for some *real* action. Maybe we'll be able to make a *real* difference.'

Homestead AFB, Florida
Two Days Later

Hardcastle found her at the Homestead Air Force Base shooting range in the early morning sun. Sandra Geffar was at the one-hundred-yard range, with an amazing array of weapons in the gun rack beside her – handguns, including her .45, .389 and nine millimeter automatics; a standard Customs Service issue Browning twelve-gauge full-choke pump shotgun; a Steyr automatic rifle; an M-16 automatic rifle; and an Uzi submachine pistol. Sandbags had been set up to help her sight in each weapon, and she had a set of gunsmith's tools to adjust the sights, trigger pull and safeties of each weapon. Boxes of ammunition lay strewn around her, along with magazine clips. Several more boxes of ammunition had been emptied. She had also been trying several types of holsters and shoulder rigs for each weapon, and a spotting scope was set up on a tiny tripod next to her right elbow.

The array of weapons was dazzling, but Sandra Geffar looked anything but dazzling. She was wearing a neck brace. Her face was bruised and discolored. She had deep black circles under each eye, the result of being caught in the terrific blast when her Black Hawk helicopter was destroyed. She moved with a slight limp. A white elastic shoulder brace she should not have removed was underneath the pile of gunleather.

She either did not notice or chose to ignore Hardcastle as he walked up to the range beside hers to watch. She had just finished sighting in her .45 caliber automatic. She had selected the fifty-yard range, and the man-sized silhouette target automatically moved out to the fifty-yard position, then motored laterally to the left.

'Excuse me, got time to talk?' Hardcastle asked.

Her eyes registered his presence. Without a word she loaded two nine-round ammunition clips, stowed them in the left ammo pouch of her shoulder rig, loaded another clip, shoved it home in the .45, chambered a round, replaced another round in the clip and holstered the big semi-automatic pistol in a right-side holster.

'You're left-handed,' Hardcastle observed, trying to keep it light. 'I never noticed . . .'

No reply. He heard a sudden rattle of paper and turned to see the silhouette moving rapidly across a thin wire from left to right. Quickly Geffar had the .45 out of the shoulder holster, aimed and fired ten rounds at the target. Without lowering her gun hand she ejected the spent magazine, retrieved another, shoved it home and fired off nine rounds. She loaded the third clip but she had gotten only three rounds off before the target disappeared behind a mechanism shield to the right of the range.

'Damn it.' She hit the button to retrieve the moving target, then lowered and safed the smoking pistol. 'My hand's shaking so bad . . . I used to be able to get off all twenty-eight rounds and still have enough time to pull out the .380 before that target went away. Now I can't even shoot straight.'

'Not shooting straight?' What the hell was 'straight,' Hardcastle wondered. Every half-inch-diameter hole except two or three were within the center '5' expert qualifications area on the black silhouette. Twenty-five hits. He would have a tough time, he knew, putting that kind of group into a stationary target at thirty yards – she did it at fifty on a moving target. 'Yeah, a real shame. You're practically a candidate for the gang-that-couldn't-shoot-straight.'

Geffar gave him a look as she reloaded the .45. 'What can I do for you, *Admiral*?'

'I just wanted to see how you were doing. Your office said you were still in the hospital.'

'I checked out this morning. I was going nuts. Air Force doctors are even duller than the civilians.'

'How's the neck?' said seriously.

'I hurt. Okay? I hurt all over. I see stars when I move my head. My hands shake. I can't find a holster I can carry comfortably because my right shoulder feels like it's coming apart. You get the picture?' She finished reloading a magazine for the .45. 'Change the target for me, will you?'

Hardcastle pulled off the battered silhouette target, rolled up a new one and clipped it on the heavy metal clamp. 'I've got a good idea for you.'

'What?'

'Go home and get some rest.' He let the target unroll as Geffar selected the one-hundred-yard range. The target sped away.

'I've been out for a week now and morale at the unit is the worst I've ever seen.'

'Death can do that. The answer isn't to punish yourself.'

'What did you do after you lost your Falcon – throw a party?'

'Forget it. You want to beat yourself up on the target range, fine. But don't drag everyone else down with you – especially when they're trying to help. Even if you do deserve a kick in the rear end.'

She slammed a magazine home in the .45, paused, then ejected it and slammed the weapon down on the bench.

'I'm very sorry,' she said a moment later, 'but I'm not an old ex-Marine ex-Vietnam vet like you. Truth is, I've heard and read about big shootouts with drug dealers, and I've fired a few shots at suspects, but I've never been involved in a deal like the one last week. I've never seen men die like . . . *that* . . .'

'Want to talk about it?'

'No.' She dragged the white shoulder brace out from underneath the pile of holsters on the gun bench. 'Sorry. Yes,' she said quietly as she slipped the brace over her right shoulder and arm. Hardcastle found a Thermos of coffee, retrieved an extra cup from the range security office and poured two cups as they walked out along the grassy area surrounding the range parking lot.

'I think I know what you're feeling,' Hardcastle began. 'A virgin out of Marine Corps Officer Candidate School, I was put in charge of a bomb-disposal unit and sent to Nam. I knew nothing about bomb disposal – hell, I knew nothing about everything. I lost five guys a week, guys I barely knew. I blamed myself every time I got a casualty report.'

Geffar nodded.

'You feel all alone because you're in charge, but you're not. There's people out there waiting to help you, if you let them.'

'What happened to you, then?' Geffar asked. He seemed to be walking slowly. 'I've heard you spent time in a hospital in the Philippines . . .'

'Detox,' Hardcastle said, his voice a monotone. 'They called it "battle injuries" or "physical therapy." I was into everything – grass, booze, uppers, downers, you name it. The Marine Corps cleaned me up, then transferred me to the Coast Guard. That was twenty-two years ago . . .'

'*You* . . . a drug addict?' Geffar said. 'How could they let you . . . I mean . . .'

'Rise up through the ranks? Become an admiral? Things

85

were different during Vietnam. A lot different. Guys looked after one another back then. Marines looked out for one another, because you knew that one day you'd have to rely on someone else to save *your* butt. The Coast Guard was almost the same. No matter who you were or what you did before, the day you set foot on their base or their boats you became one of them. Personnel files, medical records – they meant nothing. You proved yourself by how you worked with the guys in your unit, not by what your personnel records said. That was true for the lowliest grunt or the highest-ranking flag officer.'

'But if you have a history of . . . drug abuse . . . nowadays they bust people for even a minor infraction . . .'

'Back then they needed soldiers more than they needed headlines about drug abuse in the ranks.' He paused, looking at Geffar. 'So you were checking up on me.'

Geffar shrugged, and there was even a hint of a smile. 'It must be going around, Admiral – I discovered that *my* records were pulled the other day. From *your* office.'

'So you checked on me to get even?'

'I asked around, I didn't pull your personnel files.'

'Probably because you couldn't get access, one of the few prerogatives of flag rank. I'll have them sent over to you.'

'Good . . . why are we going round like this, Admiral?'

'Call me Ian.'

'No thanks, Admiral.'

'Suit yourself. I wanted to talk about drug interdiction. Your job and mine.'

'What about it?'

'What's your opinion of our roles in drug interdiction?'

'I think it stinks. We're understaffed, underfunded, we do fewer and fewer investigations and more and more sitting around waiting for stuff to happen. When it does, Customs seems two steps behind, waiting on other people to get their act together or get out of our way.'

'People like the Coast Guard?'

'The Coast Guard, DEA, FBI, SLINGSHOT, BLOC, Justice, Treasury, ATF, the military . . . The Customs Service is supposed to be the primary drug-interdiction force in the United States – that was true even before the so-called Anti-Drug Control Act. But we've taken a back seat to the DEA for the past five years and now we're beginning to get the same ass-end view of your Coast Guard. We can't make a move without half the US government getting involved. Add in state and local cops – we just don't have room to maneuver. A classic no-win situation.'

'So what's your solution?'

'Solution? I'm not sure there is one . . . What are you driving at, Hardcastle? You got a hidden microphone in your wheel hat there?'

'Just tell me your beefs. Compared to you I'm the new boy on the block in this business. I mean, it's been your area for nearly your whole career. I'm just an old jungle pilot.'

She looked at him, still not convinced he didn't have something else in mind beside hearing her gripes, but what the hell . . . she'd had it on her chest a long time . . . 'Customs fights a losing battle by letting the smugglers get onshore,' she began. 'It's obvious – once the stuff hits the shore it can disperse faster and safer than if it was still on a plane or a ship. Customs can't really operate much beyond the twelve-mile limit. Part of the problem is the old 1986 Anti-Drug Abuse Act, which gave your people, the Coast Guard, authority over drug interdiction operations from shore outward – by the time we pick up the smugglers and take control, it's often too late. The druggies get the upper hand.'

'So you try to keep the drugs from getting onshore. The stuff comes in from South and Central America or wherever by plane. The smugglers drop the stuff offshore, and it's picked up by speedboats. How to stop that?'

'Intelligence and presence,' Geffar said quickly, getting caught up in it. 'You've got to try to find out when the stuff is coming in, and you have to have the equipment and manpower to be there waiting for it. You can try to do one without using the other but it's not efficient. Once you find them you hit them. Hard. You can't let them get onshore. You have to get them *before* they scatter, and you've got to nail all of them . . . We have maybe one-tenth of the equipment and manpower we need to do the job. For every one we chase there's five, ten we can't run down. We give ourselves official excuses – the contact is iffy, he's too slow for a big smuggler – but the fact is that we don't chase them all down because we *can't*. I have only three Citations and three Cheyennes here at Homestead that can carry out a night intercept. *You* have only eight C-model Falcon interceptors in the whole Coast Guard – only four here in Florida, the rest in California and Alabama. If we're lucky we can fly half of them at any given time; the rest are down for maintenance, busy or deployed someplace. That's less than half the planes we need to cover all the night smuggling in just south Florida alone . . .'

Hardcastle had actually taken out a notepad and had started taking notes.

'All right, Admiral, just what's going on?' Geffar said.

'I'll come clean. I've been tasked to provide input, like they say, for a project I've had in mind the past few months, and more so since what's happened recently. It's only supposed to go as far as my Atlantic area headquarters, but I'm betting, hoping, it'll go all the way to the top – even to the White House.'

Geffar looked at Hardcastle for a long moment, skeptically at first, then with growing interest. She motioned toward a shady picnic area far from the parking lot. When they got to a table she lowered herself slowly, trying to will away the pain in her aching muscles and joints. 'Okay, Admiral . . .'

'Ian.'

'Okay, Ian. And you can call me Sandra if it'll take that shit-eating grin off your face. So what's this big project of yours?'

'Actually, it's all about what you've just been saying. There are too many fingers in the pie. There's no orderly chain of command, no continuous line of authority throughout what the computer boys call the smuggler's profile. We have no good way to prevent the smugglers from coming onshore, and most important . . . there's not enough *commitment* – political, monetary – to the whole deal. We've got talk, summits and czars coming out of our ears. But real commitment? That takes making tough, maybe politically unpopular decisions to pursue drug smugglers *and* the organizations that finance them all over the world – not just near our own shores.'

'You sound like a politician yourself, Hardcastle. You plan on running for something?'

'I'm not a politician, I'm a Coast Guard officer. No one would vote for me anyway.'

'You got that right.' Geffar paused, shook her head. 'I still don't get where you're coming from, Hardcastle.'

'Look, how much of the drugs entering the US come in by air?'

'One-third, maybe forty percent. The rest by sea or cargo containers – '

'So if we closed down the air route that might result in at least a thirty percent drop-off in available drugs – '

'Wrong,' Geffar interrupted. 'It might result in a *temporary* reduction but that's all. As the price rises more players get involved and they find other ways of getting it into the country. The percentage of air-imported drugs would decrease but other avenues would take up the slack.'

'But if more drugs were coming in by cargo container, and you *anticipated* that, you could head it off, step up inspections of containers – '

'But we're stretched to the limit as it is. There are over three hundred cargo containers entering Florida every day. Every damn day. A real good inspection team, beefed up with National Guard or Reservists, can inspect one container in about two hours. Customs is lucky if it inspects twenty percent of all the cargo containers coming into this country – '

'You're missing the point. Our goal was to close off the air route. Where it drives the smugglers after that – well, we deal with that next. But at least we deny the smugglers the easiest way to get their product into the country – by air.'

'So? You still haven't explained how. How are you going to stop drugs from being smuggled in by air?'

'We have almost complete radar coverage of the southwest U.S. We have computers that can match radar targets with flight plans, integrate data, isolate violators . . .'

'Okay, so you see ten targets that are unidentified, planes that are buzzing around offshore that might be making drops, planes that might be heading north. Out of the dozens, sometimes hundreds of air targets out there, you see maybe two dozen a day that are suspicious. Then what?'

'Go after them.'

'With what?'

'Feel up to a little flying this week?'

'Why?'

'I've arranged for a little demonstration of a new technology that might be able to help us out. I'll meet you here at seven Sunday morning. That'll give you a few days to rest up – '

'What's going on, Hardcastle? You trying to involve me in some stupid plan to get more juice for the Coasties?'

'This isn't a Coast Guard project. Matter of fact, I have my doubts about what exactly the Coast Guard's role *is* in drug interdiction. I've been in the Coast Guard a long time, and frankly I don't think that chasing drug smugglers is a logical part of its job-description. Sure, it'll always have a role in drug interdiction, but I believe it's a waste of time and money to send Coast Guardsmen in Falcon interceptors and Island-class cutters out looking for drug smugglers . . . *We need a drug interdiction organization, specially formed, tasked, and equipped for drug interdiction –* '

'And that's the Customs Service – '

'I don't think so. You said it yourself – Customs doesn't have the juice to do the job. You've got too many restraints. Before Customs can act you're forced to wait until the bad guys get over land or open ocean and drop their load. After that, the odds of you making a clean bust nose-dive.'

'But what if we were to stop every damn vessel entering or heading for American territorial waters? Funnel each vessel through mandatory checkpoints, like border inspection stations? What if we inspect *before* they enter American waters?'

'That's impossible – '

'It's not. How about we require positive identification of each and every aircraft entering US airspace . . . ?'

'We already do.'

'But what if we deny entry of any aircraft that is *not* positively identified?'

'*Deny entry?* What does that mean? If he's unidentified, he's trying to evade Customs or law-enforcement . . .' She looked at him in surprise. 'You mean . . . *shoot him down?*'

'Detect at sixty miles, track at fifty, communicate at

forty, intercept at thirty, communicate at twenty, warn at fifteen, open fire at ten,' Hardcastle said. 'Standardize air-defense-intercept parameters – except air defense doesn't apply the rule to light aircraft on smuggling profiles. Now, *we* apply the rule. We deny the airspace to all unidentified aircraft. Period. If they don't respond to radio, light or visual symbols, they're denied entry. The same for vessels on the high seas. If they fail to stop or fail to identify themselves, they're intercepted and stopped.'

'You say that nice and easy,' Geffar said. 'You're also going to have some innocent people crashing into the ocean if you implement such a plan – '

'What I'm trying to *do* is keep illegal narcotics, weapons, money and other contraband from entering the United States. You know it, I know it . . . our current so-called system isn't working. I'm trying to create a system that *works*. Sure, loss of innocent life would be disastrous, but fear of that shouldn't paralyze us. We'd put safeguards in the system to prevent attack against people who do comply with the rules.'

'You can put all the safeguards in place you want, Admiral, but you and I both know that's not a guarantee. The first family of four you strafe will erase years of work and billions of dollars of manpower and equipment. It could set drug interdiction back twenty years.'

'As I recall, those were *the* same arguments used when the Customs Service Air Branch went operational,' Hardcastle said. 'I know it's the same argument they used when *we* started air-interdiction operations, when we announced that a big three-engine jet plane would fly a few dozen feet behind your plane to read your registration numbers. Families would be splashing into the Caribbean, they said. Well, neither one of us has killed any civilians in almost thirty years and we've done a lot of good. Now it's time to do more, much more . . .'

She didn't seem to be buying it. 'I think I can prove it would work,' Hardcastle said, 'if you're open-minded enough to see for yourself.'

'Hey, I don't have anything to prove to you. I'm doing my job . . .'

'Then what are you afraid of?'

'Nothing that *you* could come up with.'

'Then it's settled. Sunday morning. I'll meet you at your headquarters at seven.'

'I'll be there. But this better be good, Admiral,' Geffar said. 'You can expect zero out of me or my people until I'm convinced that your big idea won't end up a fiasco.' Or a way to ace out Customs, she silently added.

Chapter Three

Brickell Federal Building, Miami
Several Days Later

Under fingers more accustomed to wrestling with helicopter cyclics and aircraft throttles than tiny buttons, things tended to disappear off the computer screen for Hardcastle, never to return. So he relegated the squat, boxy-looking computer with its rodent-looking pointing device to a small desk in a corner and kept the old reliable Selectric on the typing table near his desk.

The sight of Hardcastle hunting and pecking his way through his report would normally have seemed funny to Coast Guard Commander Michael Becker, Hardcastle's aide, except it was now well after nine o'clock in the evening. Becker, who with his horn-rimmed glasses and necktie (a rare sight in humid Miami) looked more like a young ensign than a veteran cutter skipper and station commander, grimace at his boss's painful tapping. Like a Chinese water torture, he thought.

Finally, he could stand it no longer. 'Admiral, I'd be more than happy to do that for you . . .'

'You already offered, Mike. I told you, I can't do dictation. Never have. And it would take you longer to decipher my notes – if I ever bothered to write them out for you. I got to do this part myself. Why don't you head on home?'

'I know you're under some pressure to get this report done,' Becker said, 'and I'd like to help – '

'Then shut up and let me work.'

Becker nodded and slumped back in his chair.

'Has General Brad Elliott called to confirm his arrival time?' Hardcastle asked Becker as he continued his maddening hunt-and-peck. 'We need his equipment for this weekend's presentation. He has to know how important his organization's involvement is.'

'I think he understands, Admiral. He called from Fort Lauderdale. He arrived early this afternoon with his project officer. I met him just after he arrived – '

'He's here already?'

'I knew you were busy so I didn't want to disturb you. He's ready to meet with you as soon as you're free. But in any case he's ready to go.'

It was the first time in a long while that Becker had seen his boss looking optimistic about anything. 'What's Elliott like?'

'Late fifties, thin, kind of hyper. Gutsy and regular Air Force all the way. You'll like him, though. The scoop is he's his own man. His project officer looks young, early thirties max.'

Hardcastle looked up from his work. 'I hear Elliott is an idea man . . . That's good for our side.'

'He also has an artificial right leg. Did you know that?'

Hardcastle didn't.

'He calls it his stump but I hear it's a pure bionic limb, not a prosthesis. Works like a regular leg – ankle, knee, even the ball of the foot fully articulated. He's fully cleared for flight duties, though. I checked. He was the one who flew the V-22 in. Dropped it right on Gorilla One.'

'You know how he lost his leg?'

'I couldn't find out,' Becker said. 'There's a lid on that from the Pentagon to Nevada.'

'The guy gets more interesting every time I hear about him.' Hardcastle turned toward a photograph on the wall of an unusual aircraft, a machine that looked like a cargo

plane but with twin helicopter-like rotors on its wings.
'How's the Sea Lion look?'

'Awesome. You're scheduled for your first flight tomorrow morning. It'll blow your mind.'

'Then I'd better get this report done . . . Oh, the drones? All set to go?'

'Elliott's project officer, a Major McLanahan, has the Seagull and Sky Lion drones ready to go,' Becker reported. 'The Sky Lion's been deployed on Gorilla One, along with the control consoles and data-link equipment. The Seagull will launch from Marathon Airport – there's just not enough time to set up its launch-and-recovery gear on the platform.'

'Well, I'm surprised these guys got it all together, got all this gear in place so fast,' Hardcastle said. 'It was worth all the hassles and hoops we had to jump through to get this mysterious HAWC agency to help us out. The Air Force keeps such a tight lid on HAWC's existence, I'm surprised we got anything.'

Becker got up, waited until Hardcastle rolled another page out of the old Selectric. 'Four hundred and nineteen pages. Think you'll be done soon, sir? This is setting a world's record.'

'Four-fifty, max,' Hardcastle said, rubbing his eyes. 'Not including indexes, glossaries, maps, slides.'

'*Four-fifty*. That'll piss off ATLANTCOM for sure,' Becker said. The draft proposal of the new unit Hardcastle was creating had already gone through ATLANTCOM, the Atlantic Area Commander's office, three times, and had been kicked back with pages of suggestions and directed changes. Once, Admiral Cronin had flown down to Miami unannounced to argue over a particular point that Hardcastle had been adamant about keeping intact. Cronin had also been shocked at the length of the document, saying that the sheer size of the thing would almost guarantee that no one in the White House or Capitol Hill would read it.

'But it's not the length of the thing that the admiral doesn't like,' Hardcastle said. 'He still doesn't know whether or not to back this project.'

'You mean back *you* or not.'

'Maybe. He's already played out a lot of line on this project, but he's also known for supporting his people. Besides, it's only natural that he'd have some reservations about an ambitious project like this. Fact is, I'm damn glad I have an Admiral Cronin around. Another area commander might leak some details of the project to give himself a little advance publicity. This commander won't turn on or undercut his own people.'

Hardcastle had begun his painful typing again when he heard the knock on the door.

'Daniel! C'mon in.'

Daniel Hardcastle, Ian's youngest son and secret favorite, was seventeen years old, blond, tall and wiry and more like his father than Hardcastle's twenty-six-year-old Roger, who was the image of his mother.

'Working late again, huh?' Daniel said and came over to give his father a hug. The Admiral gave Becker a look, one that apparently Becker had been waiting for. 'If you're sure you won't need me, sir, I'll take off,' the aide said. Hardcastle nodded, grateful for Becker's insight.

'How'd you get here?' Hardcastle asked, checking his watch as Becker departed. 'It's pretty late. Did your mother – '

'Hitched.'

'At nine, on a school night?'

'All we have tomorrow is graduation rehearsal,' Daniel said quickly. 'My first class isn't until nine – '

'You're not going to your graduation rehearsal?'

'We went over this, Dad.' Daniel tried to shut it off,

97

staring at a picture of a V-22 Osprey tilt-rotor aircraft on the wall.

'All right, all right,' Hardcastle said, immediately sorry he had brought the whole thing up. Yes, they did discuss it – *argue* about it would be more accurate. Rather than subject either of his estranged parents to the uncomfortable scene of showing up to a graduation ceremony together, Daniel had conveniently arranged an interview with the baseball coach at the University of Miami on his graduation day. That had not helped things between Hardcastle's wife, Jennifer, and himself, but Hardcastle had chosen not to interfere with Daniel's decision. That decision not to interfere had angered his wife even more. 'Hey, no more hitchhiking, all right?' Hardcastle said. 'There are guys out there that'll pop you just because they don't like the shirt you're wearing. Or because they *do* like it. Know what I mean?'

'Sure, Dad. Okay. No more hitching.' Daniel came over to his father's desk and casually peeked at the stack of papers on the desk. Hardcastle slapped a red plastic cover over them. 'Still working on your top secret project?' he asked. 'You've been hitting it awful hard lately, Dad.'

'This is pretty important.'

'What's it about?'

'If I told you it wouldn't be secret.'

'Well, can you at least tell me the unclassified version, or do I face a firing squad if I bug you about it?'

Hardcastle nodded, shook his head. 'It's an anti-drug program. That's about it for now.'

'I figured as much,' Daniel said. 'Why not legalize it?'

Hardcastle rubbed his eyes wearily. 'Can we talk about this some other time?'

'Sure. Sorry to rock the boat, no pun intended.'

'Knock it off, Danny. We've been round and round on this one. Booze and coke *aren't* the same. And marijuana, nobody knows the long-term effects. But hell, you know the arguments.'

'Well, I see you knocking yourself out night and day trying to solve this thing, and the way I see it you're trying to swim up Niagara Falls.' When he got no rise out of his father from that he looked up again at the picture of the Osprey on the wall. 'That V-22 is awesome. You figuring on catching the bad guys with it?'

Smart kid, Hardcastle thought. Especially for one who pulled so many dumb stunts. 'No fishing. Join the Coast Guard, go to the Academy and find out all about it.'

'I'm thinking on it.'

'You're really thinking about the Academy?'

'Sure. How can I *not*?'

Hardcastle, pleased, decided not to push it. He changed the subject. 'How's your mother?'

'Fine.' Hardcastle gave him a questioning look.

'Okay, okay. She's pissed.'

'Because I missed last weekend?' Daniel nodded. 'I want to apologize for that, Daniel. I was swamped . . .'

'You don't need to apologize to me. Mom thinks I'll be scarred for life if I don't interact, as she calls it, with my father every other weekend. Sure, I miss our time together, Dad, but honest to God, I won't be scarred . . .'

Hardcastle stood, collected the stack of papers on his desk and locked them away in an office safe. 'Let's get out of here. Had something to eat?'

'I . . . was hoping . . .'

'Let me guess,' Hardcastle said with a smile. 'A ride in the Scorpion.'

'It's been a long time . . .'

'But the closest airfield to your mother's house is Taimiami. You'd have to walk at least two, three miles.'

'It's worth it, and I'll be careful and not let Mom know.'

Jennifer, Hardcastle didn't need to be reminded, didn't

99

approve of him letting Daniel fly in the Super Scorpion ('You want to kill yourself, fine, but not our son.'). But Hardcastle enjoyed being with his son. He was so full of energy, alive, if also a little wild. Exactly the opposite of his self-controlled, controlling mother, a real estate agent in Miami, not to mention his brother, a third-year medical student at Johns Hopkins. Oh, he was proud of Roger and still had some affection for his wife, but being with Daniel was different, special. When he was with Daniel he felt years younger. You couldn't buy that . . . besides, there was no danger in taking the kid in the helicopter. 'All right, all right,' Hardcastle told him. 'But I'll call the assistant manager of Tiger Air at Taimiami; he should be able to give you a ride home. You're not going to hitchhike in the middle of the night, your mother would really fry my scalp if she found out.'

Hardcastle finished securing his reports and notes, then unreeled the ribbon cassette and fed it into a small shredder mounted on a wastebasket in the outer office.

'Your project must really be secret,' Daniel said. 'You do this every night? What a hassle.'

'That's why they pay me such big bucks.'

'Yeah, right, a whole two thousand nine hundred and eleven dollars and eighty-three cents a month. Before taxes.'

'Afraid you won't get an inheritance?'

'Nothing like that,' Daniel said as they filed out of the office. 'I just hear Mom talking all the time. She says you've gone through hell already and she doesn't understand why you still do it. She says you could have your pick of positions in half the corporations in America if only you'd stop playing sailor-boy.'

'What do you think?'

'I think you do what you do. And I admit I was pretty aced when I heard about that bust at Mahogany Hammock. You really blew away a transport? Right out of mid-air?'

'It's nothing to crow about, Danny. It was something that had to be done.'

'I would've loved to see that baby auger in. Those smugglers must have been thinking they were about to get away when boom, they lose power and plow into the Everglades. Ruined their whole day.'

Hardcastle said nothing as he continued to lock up classified papers, then locked up the office, logged out with building security and they left.

As they emerged onto the roof of the Brickell Plaza Federal Building, the helipad lights automatically snapped on, revealing the sleek, shiny red chopper sitting in the center of the pad. Daniel unlatched the chopper's tie-downs as he had been taught years earlier, Hardcastle was pleased to note, even remembered to look up for the rotors and put his hand on the tail rotor guard for safety as he quickly moved around the fuselage.

They had just climbed aboard the chopper and received weather and traffic advisories when Hardcastle saw a member of Brickell Plaza's security team coming up the stairs to the helipad. 'Damn,' Hardcastle muttered. 'Harrison. The assistant security chief.'

Daniel said nothing. Hardcastle watched the guard for a moment, but he had not yet made any move to wave him down. Sitting back in his seat, checking out the left canopy away from where the guard stood, Daniel finally asked, 'Is he still there?'

'Yes. But he's not saying anything. I don't think I could have left any safes open or doors unlocked . . . starting engines.'

As the engine began cranking up to speed Hardcastle watched Harrison stop near the steps up to the helipad and make a brief comment on his walkie-talkie just before the noise of the engine drowned him out. Now Harrison was moving around to the front of the Scorpion, well away from the rotors but farther left. Suddenly, as Harrison moved in front of the Scorpion, he said something in his walkie-talkie, brought the receiver tight up to his ear to receive a reply, then quickly moved forward toward the Scorpion waving his arms and drawing a thumb across his throat – the shutdown sign.

'What the hell . . .' Hardcastle flashed his landing light to warn the guard away from the spinning rotors, then closed the throttle and killed the magnetos.

'You're shutting down . . . ?' Daniel asked nervously.

'I got to find out what he wants,' Hardcastle said irritably. 'Otherwise I'm liable to slice his head off.'

Harrison was right beside the left door as Hardcastle undogged it. 'All right, Harrison, what's going on?'

Harrison wasn't looking at the admiral, he was looking at his son. 'Sir, I need to ask you and your passenger to step out of the cockpit.' The 'please' he added sounded more like an order.

'What's going on here, Harrison? This is my son, Daniel. You've seen him before. Hell, you must have let him upstairs . . .'

'Your son was not cleared inside, sir. Please step out of there. Now.'

Hardcastle looked over at Daniel, who shrugged and gave him a weak smile. Hardcastle began unbuckling his shoulder harness. 'C'mon, Daniel. This'll only take a second.'

They came out of the chopper, and Harrison led them from the Scorpion to an enclosed corner away from the stairs. 'All right, Harrison. My son didn't check in with you?'

'No, sir,' the guard replied. 'Commander Becker mentioned that he was with you but he didn't come through the front desk or sign in.' Hardcastle realized that that was true; otherwise he would have gotten a call from the downstairs desk telling him that Daniel was on his way up.

'I forgot,' Daniel said, his face now grave. 'I came up to the garage entry door but I forgot it was locked. Someone was coming out and he must've recognized me and let me in.'

'I'm afraid there's more, sir,' Harrison said. 'A boy matching your son's description was seen riding a motorcycle on route 836 toward the city – '

'My son doesn't own a motorcycle.'

'. . . The motorcycle was reported stolen from a residence in Westchester. We found the bike about three blocks from here in a parking garage . . .'

Hardcastle looked at his son – he and his mother lived in Westchester.

'I didn't *steal* anyone's motorcycle – '

'That's enough,' Hardcastle told him. 'Harrison, what's all this got to do with Daniel? He came up here to see me.'

'I'm sorry, sir, you'll have to wait here for the police. They've been notified.'

'Of *what*? Dammit, you need proof before you can accuse someone of something like this, Harrison. What's gotten into you? Daniel didn't steal a motorcycle.' He turned to his son, and when he saw his son's face averted and his hands stuffed into his jeans pockets, he knew something was terribly wrong. 'Daniel . . . ?'

Before he could answer, a Dade County sheriff's deputy trotted up the stairs, followed by another security guard. The cop came over to Hardcastle carrying a large flashlight in one hand and a metal notepad case in his other. 'Admiral Hardcastle? Sergeant Kowalski, Dade County Sheriff's Department. Sorry to disturb you, sir. May we have a word with your son?'

'Go ahead, but I'm sure – '

'In private?'

'No.'

Kowalski nodded, holstered the flashlight, opened the

notepad case and turned to Daniel. 'What's your name, son?'

'Daniel Hardcastle.'

'Address?'

'Five-five-oh-one Ridgecrest . . .'

'Miami?'

He paused, then muttered, 'Westchester.'

Kowalski nodded. 'What time did you leave Westchester tonight?'

'About nine.'

'How did you get downtown?'

'Hitchhiked.'

'Did you get a ride right away?'

'Yes.'

Kowalski looked at Daniel for a moment: 'You sure you hitchhiked into town, Daniel?' Kowalski's radio was now crackling to life. He stepped a few paces away to answer the call, made a reply, then returned.

'We have a set of fingerprints off the motorcycle,' Kowalski said. He turned to Hardcastle. 'An off-duty deputy gave us an exact description of your son on the stolen motorcycle, Admiral. I'm afraid I'll have to ask your son to come with me.'

Kowalski reached out to take Daniel's arm, and Hardcastle was forced to watch his son being led away with his head down like a common criminal.

Dade County Sheriff's Department Headquarters

Hardcastle had been waiting for a half-hour when a detective walked in. 'Admiral Hardcastle? Detective Sergeant Lewis.' Lewis laid two fingerprint cards on the table in front of him and motioned for the admiral to look at them.

Hardcastle was no forensics experts, but even the most casual glance between the two told the obvious – the prints matched. Hardcastle looked back at Lewis, who looked back at Hardcastle to be sure that he understood the obvious.

'Are you the boy's guardian?'

'No, he lives with his mother.'

'Visitation rights?'

'Weekends,' Hardcastle said, his throat dry and raspy.

'How are relations between you and the boy's mother?'

'Fair to poor. She doesn't approve of my choice of career, and especially doesn't think it would be a wise choice for Daniel – '

'I've heard that one before. How about between the boy and his mother?'

'Good, so far as I know.'

Lewis wondered if Hardcastle really knew. 'Well, he seems to think highly of you. Was more afraid of disappointing you than going to jail.' Hardcastle fought a shudder of dread at the word 'jail.'

The detective picked up the fingerprint cards, folded them in half and stuck them in a pocket. Hardcastle looked at him in surprise.

'You're lucky, Admiral. When the owner heard that Daniel's father was the Coast Guard district commander he dropped charges. He has his bike back.'

'I'm grateful,' Hardcastle said.

Lewis nodded. 'Besides,' he said, 'the prints don't quite match the boy.'

'I don't understand . . .'

'Well, I got one set of prints of a motorcycle thief,' Lewis said, 'and I got another set of a pretty decent high-school student, a flying nut, good grades, accepted at the University of Miami, maybe a baseball scholarship. They don't exactly match. What I need to know, Admiral, is this kind of thing going to happen again?'

'I'll do my damnedest – '

Lewis held up his hand. 'I see this every spring, Admiral. The script is pretty much the same. But when I dig a little deeper, what I find are parents that see their son or daughter as a grown-up, someone they don't have to deal with anymore because soon they'll be out of the house and on their own. They slack off. What happens is that the happiest time of their kid's life becomes the saddest. I blame the parents most of the time . . . I can do that because I'm a parent and I see it happening to me too. But it's no excuse.'

Hardcastle stared at the tabletop. He was being lectured at by a cop at least ten, fifteen years his junior – but he also knew he was right.

'Do you hear me, Admiral?' Hardcastle nodded.

'All right, I can't release Daniel to your custody so I've called his mother. She'll be down shortly and I'll have a word with her too. Then Daniel is free to leave. This time.'

'Can I see him?'

'I'll bring him in. Admiral, I'd be real disappointed if I saw either of you in here again. It would mean I was wrong about you . . . and him.'

'I understand . . .'

'I hope so,' Lewis said as he left the room.

His son, arrested for stealing a motorcycle. The kid had always followed his own way, not afraid to take a chance or do something off-beat, but he'd never broken the law. This was a whole different side –

The door swung open and Daniel entered. His eyes were puffy and dark. He looked at his father and swallowed.

'Sit down, Daniel,' Hardcastle said, motioning to a chair across from him. He wanted to take him in his arms, he wanted to give him a shot. Anger, love, all mixed up . . .

'Dad, I'm sorry about this, I didn't mean to embarrass you – '

'I'm not embarrassed,' Hardcastle said. 'I'm angry, upset . . .'

'I know the guy who owns that bike,' Daniel said. 'I know he leaves the keys in a holder under the seat – '

'Bullshit. That doesn't make any difference.'

'I know, I know, it was stupid. I wanted to see you, I was told you were working late, Mom wouldn't let me borrow the car and I didn't want to hitch. The guy's had that bike stolen a half-dozen times. I wasn't going to wreck it or ditch it, I left it in a safe place in that parking garage – '

'Still bullshit, Danny. You're trying to rationalize this? You stole a motorcycle, you could be in juvenile detention for six months. Let's talk about the future. You're still my son, now I got to learn to trust you all over again – '

At that moment the door opened and Jennifer Leslie Wagner-Hardcastle came into the room. Dressed in a light blue dress with matching shoes, a light silk jacket, and carrying a white handbag, she was a striking woman in her late forties, with dark hair touched with silver-gray highlights, a trim body, and deep dark eyes. By now it was after eleven o'clock at night, she was coming to get her son who had been arrested and she looked as if she was ready for a business conference.

Hardcastle rose but said nothing as she squinted with seeming distaste at his thin frame, the deeply etched lines around the eyes and short gray hair. She turned to her son. 'Daniel, wait outside for me.' The boy left quickly.

'I have just been lectured by a policeman about how to raise my son,' she began. 'I have a son old enough to be his brother, and *he* is lecturing *me* on how to raise my son.'

'He knows what he's talking about.'

'Why? Because he blames this whole thing on me?'

'I'm not in the mood for a fight – '

'Why didn't you wait for Vance to come down here?' she asked him. Vance Hargrove was Jennifer's attorney, the one who had handled her divorce. 'It was wrong to say anything to the police until an attorney was present – '

'The police did the talking, Jennifer. They showed me the fingerprints – '

'How do you know they were Daniel's fingerprints? How do you know that the fingerprints they *said* they took off that motorcycle were really – ?'

'Daniel said so. The police got the owner to drop the charges, they kicked Daniel loose. Stop trying to bury this in legalese. Danny screwed up. He broke the law. Now what are we going to do about it?'

Jennifer seemed to straighten her back. 'Well, he must be punished, of course. He'll be restricted to the house, except for school. No more use of the car for I don't know how long – '

'You really don't get it,' Hardcastle broke in. 'He's so tied down now it won't matter if you put a few more temporary little restrictions in place – if he feels the need to sneak out of the house again he'll do it. You already restrict him on weeknights and after ten on Friday and Saturday nights. You won't let him have a job. You don't let him come downtown, he's not allowed to stay overnight at my place . . .'

'*When* you decide you have the time to see him, that is.'

'I know, I've screwed up too,' Hardcastle said. 'It's *us* that have to change.' He paused, then said, 'I want him to spend the weekends with me at my place in Pompano Beach. And I want him to spend the summer with me before he goes off to school – '

'Could we *please* talk about this some other time?' she said.

'You can't duck it, Jennifer. We've got to – '

'I think we've all been through enough for one night. At least Daniel and I have.' She pulled the door open and left without another word.

A few moments later the door opened again and Sergeant Lewis came back in the room.

'How did it go?'

'Bad.'

'It usually does,' Lewis said. 'But don't give up, Admiral. Not on either one of them – '

The door was pushed open farther and Commander Becker came in. He motioned to the door, where Marine Corps Major Pamela Darwin, the District's legal counsel, was standing with a folder of papers in her hand. 'Major Darwin's here to help out but we've been told the charges have been dropped.'

When Lewis turned to leave, Hardcastle thanked him, 'for everything.'

Major Darwin entered the room, closed the door and stood in front of Hardcastle as if making a formal report: 'I've received statements from security personnel at Brickell Plaza, sir. There was a security deficiency on your part. We may have a cause of action against them as well as the sheriff's department for unreasonable search – '

'Forget it, major. I'll file a report with you and Area Headquarters in the morning. Up-channel your comments to my report to Area as soon as possible. That's all.' He turned to Becker. 'Mike, if you wouldn't mind . . .'

'I'd be happy to drive you home, sir.'

Hardcastle took a sideways glance at Darwin as Becker escorted him out of the conference room. She looked back at him with . . . pity? Was she sorry for an old seahorse because he couldn't even keep track of his kid?

Cut it out, he ordered himself. The pity is self-inflicted. And you need all your energy for your *equally* important job of being a drug-buster. Get on with it.

* * *

Customs Air Division, Homestead AFB, Florida
Sunday Morning

Sandra Geffar was standing on the aircraft parking ramp. It was a cool Sunday morning in south Florida, with huge dark thunderheads surrounding the entire area.

Almost as dark and stormy was the mood of Customs Investigator Curtis Long, a Citation interceptor pilot at Homestead and Geffar's chief of enforcement. Long also acted as Geffar's R and D officer, checking out new weapons and evaluating new tactics for possible use by the agency. Long was scarcely five feet tall, broad shoulders tapering to a narrow waist. It was generally acknowledged at Homestead that Agent Long's lack of size was more than compensated by his intelligence and physical strength. He was also one of the most mild-mannered of men, there weren't many things that could wind Curtis Long up . . .

The Coast Guard was one of the things that *could*. 'This deal is going to be a big waste of time,' he was saying.

'You never even met Hardcastle,' Geffar said.

'I know his rep. He's a loose cannon, wants to make points by coming up with flaky ideas. Why did you agree to fly with him?'

'Because . . .' It was a good question. Hardcastle could put her nose out of joint too, but he was also dedicated in his work, intelligent, forceful and not afraid to rock the boat. And right now the guy had something up his sleeve.

'I want to stick close to this man, that's all,' Geffar said coolly. 'He's got his boss's ear on this project, whatever it is, and apparently he's gotten hold of some pretty valuable equipment to play with. If we have any chance of keeping up with whatever the Coast Guard is doing, this is it.'

That wasn't her whole answer. Hardcastle knew that neither Customs nor Coast Guard was really suited for the expanded role being forced on each of them. The Coast

Guard didn't have the skills or the intelligence apparatus to conduct major law-enforcement activities, and the expanded drug-interdiction role was probably unsuited for the Coastie's lifesaving mission. As for Customs, it didn't have the global authority or the firepower. Hardcastle was a guy ready and waiting to break out of the rut. It might just be the time to give him a break . . .

'You're not exactly keeping an open mind about this,' Geffar told Long.

'The Coasties got nothing I want. And neither of us have the time to watch a dog-and-pony show – '

A strange sound interrupted, something that could only be described as a combination of propeller and jet engines. Long and Geffar turned to see what had to be one of the most unusual aircraft in the world make a steep banking turn scarcely two hundred feet overhead. It resembled a twin-turboprop small transport plane, not as big as the Air Force's C-130 cargo plane but still large for a prop job. The plane was about seventy feet long and twenty-five feet wide, with a wing mounted high on the fuselage and a cantilever tail with twin rudders. The turboprop engines were unusual; large and spinning a very large propeller at a remarkably slow speed, and the engine nacelles were mounted directly at the wingtips instead of on pylons nearer the middle of the wings.

As the weird aircraft made a few tight high-speed left turns over the Customs Service parking ramp, Long recovered sufficiently from his initial surprise to say, 'That's gotta be Hardcastle. And this is his big surprise . . . ? A miniature C-130 . . . ?'

'That's not a C-130,' Geffar said. '*Look* at it.'

The strange aircraft completed its last left turn, rolled out, then completed a tight right turn out across Homestead's main runway and rapidly descended to less than fifty feet above ground.

'Great,' Long said. 'That S.O.B.'s going to buzz us . . .'

But the aircraft didn't race overhead as expected. With a sudden roar of engine power, the two engine nacelles at the wingtips swivelled upward until the propeller spinners were pointing vertically, with the propeller blades horizontal, helicopter-like. The plane-turned-helicopter decelerated rapidly, the nose swinging high in the sky, and like a giant eagle it swooped onto the parking ramp and settled in for a landing, the landing gear popping out of the fuselage just in time for a gentle touchdown.

As the twin engines were shut down a smiling Admiral Hardcastle stepped out of the entryway on the right side of the hybrid and walked over to Geffar and Long. 'Nice to see you again, Inspector Geffar,' he said, then turned to Long. 'Agent Long. We've never met but I've heard a lot about you.' Likewise, Long thought. A moment later another man in a flight suit and carrying a helicopter-style flight helmet came up to them. 'Agents Geffar, Long, I'd like you to met Lieutenant-General Bradley Elliott, US Air Force.'

'Air Force?' Geffar heard Long exclaim under his breath.

'I've heard a lot about you, Inspector Geffar,' Elliott said, shaking hands with her and then Long.

'Let me explain what you're thinking but not asking,' Hardcastle said quickly. 'Elliott is the director of an Air Force weapons testing center in Nevada. HAWC. High Technology Aerospace Weapons Center. He and his organization, I'm damned pleased to say, are on long-term loan to me. HAWC has already been helping me with some advanced aircraft design. Brad, why don't you show them your newest toy here?'

Long watched unhappily as Elliott led Geffar toward his aircraft, noting that his boss seemed damn near mesmerized by the strange aircraft.

112

'Officially, folks, this is the V-22C Sea Lion,' Elliott began. 'What we did was take the basic Bell-Boeing V-22 tilt-rotor chassis, lengthened and strengthened the fuselage and added bigger turboprop engines. She can carry, for example, twenty hospital rescue litters plus six crewmen, or ten full-size rescue-raft packs. It has the performance of a small cargo aircraft – top speed of about two-fifty, fully loaded range of about nine hundred miles – but it has the added advantage of helicopter-like vertical flight.'

He moved to the right side of the Sea Lion aircraft. 'The V-22 has two cargo hooks and the capability of lifting over twenty thousand pounds. It's designed for nap-of-the-earth terrain-following flight, all-weather search-and-rescue and long-range surveillance. It also has a stores pod on each side of the fuselage above the sponsons, where we can mount up to two thousand pounds of stores in retractable hardpoints that can be loaded or unloaded from inside the cargo bay. Fuel tanks, cargo pods, sensors, winches, communications gear – '

'Or weapons,' Hardcastle added.

Long stared at Hardcastle. 'Weapons? What weapons?'

'Cannons, guns, anti-ship missiles, rockets, you name it,' Hardcastle said. He motioned to a third crew member who had stayed inside the Sea Lion, and the man now activated a control panel. A panel on the side of the fuselage opened up and a long cylindrical aerodynamic pod motored out from inside the V-22C's cargo bay and locked into position just above the tarmac. 'We're carrying a Sea Stinger rocket pod on the starboard hardpoint; the pod carries six Sea Stinger infrared-guided missiles capable of attacking air or surface targets from a mile away. The pod can be reloaded from inside the aircraft and we can safely carry another eight missiles. The port pod carries an M230 Chain Gun thirty-millimeter cannon. We can carry up to three hundred rounds of thirty-millimeter ammunition, and the

113

weapons are integrated into the fire-control system, which integrates the infrared scanner and weapon computers to locate and attack targets.

'I'd say at this point the Sea Lion is the ultimate maritime reconnaissance and security aircraft,' Hardcastle said as they continued their walkaround. 'We needed a vessel that could get on scene as fast as an airplane, carry plenty of cargo or survivors, defend itself, hover to carry out rescue or law-enforcement ops, and maneuver on land, sea or air. This aircraft is a synthesis of design and function. The Coast Guard has been looking for something like this for a lot longer than I've been around.'

'Pardon me, Admiral,' Long blurted out, 'but what do you want with a tilt-rotor aircraft with weapons in the Coast Guard?'

'This isn't a Coast Guard aircraft. The Coast Guard will get several V-22 Osprey tilt-rotor aircraft by the mid-1990s, and eventually they may get the V-22C model. But we're not talking about new aircraft for the Coast Guard.'

'Then who's this for?'

'For us . . .' was all Hardcastle said, or would say. 'We don't have time, right now. General Elliott and I have a little demonstration for you. Please get on board and we'll begin.'

On board Elliott introduced Major Patrick McLanahan, his project officer and the V-22C's crew chief, to Geffar and Long. McLanahan was the 'baby' of the group – although his rank was the equivalent of Long's and he had authority over the Air Force's involvement in Hardcastle's project. Blond, blue-eyed, the Air Force major could not have been much more than thirty-one or thirty-two, Geffar figured as she began strapping herself into one of the crew's jump-seats. Hardcastle motioned to her to come up to the cockpit.

'Me? I don't know how to fly this thing.'

'Neither did I, two days ago,' Hardcastle told her. 'Brad is a great teacher, and the Sea Lion is a dream to fly.' Elliott was pleased to help Geffar into the right seat and assist her in strapping in. She put up with it.

Elliott pointed inside the cockpit. The interior of the Sea Lion was more like a television control room. The instrument panel was four twelve-inch color monitors, which could display graphic depictions of flight instruments, engine gauges, large-scale numbers as readouts or text and numerals. The data displayed on the screens was changeable by pressing buttons on the edge of the monitors. The function of each button changed depending on the information desired, so each button could perform a multitude of functions.

'All your flight- and engine-monitoring information is set and displayed on these screens,' Elliott said. 'Navigation, radios, flight instruments, engine monitors, performances, autopilot, weaponry – all selectable and monitored through the CRTs and set using these keyboards on the center console.' There were two large monitors on each side of the cockpit plus one smaller CRT just under the glare-shield in the center, two smaller text-only CRTs on the center console and one large text-only monitor on top of the glare-shield in the center of the cockpit. Conventional standby flight instruments surrounded the center monitor for backup.

'It must take weeks to learn these screens,' Geffar said.

'It's really easy,' Hardcastle told her. 'The functions are all displayed on the screen, and you can flip through any one of them in seconds. The copilot – who, in the Sea Lion, sits on the left, by the way, a change left over from Marine Corps aviation – can select functions for the pilot and transfer the selected image to the pilot's monitor. The top center monitor displays navigation and status information and any computer warnings. You'll be using the two center

115

MFDs for most of your flight control, power and navigation information.'

'Pilots familiar with fixed-wing flying usually have no trouble understanding the V-22's control system,' Elliott said, taking over. 'Since you've had both, this should be a piece of cake for you,' he told Geffar. 'You'll notice the controls look like a helicopter's but they operate more like a fixed-wing plane. The cyclic – the center control stick – raises and lowers the nose and banks the aircraft in all flight modes. The lever on the left that looks like the collective is actually a power control – push forward to increase power, pull back to decrease power.

'In helicopter mode forward speed versus altitude control is accomplished by varying the angle of the two engine nacelles, which is done using this wheel switch on the control stick – push the switch forward to move the nacelles down, pull back to rotate the nacelles upward. The computer displays will tell you what the best nacelle-angle range is, and in emergency situations the V-22 will put the nacelles in the proper position to prevent any out-of-tolerance conditions. In extreme emergencies the system will automatically switch to full helicopter mode, and autorotation control is much the same as in any large helicopter. In helicopter mode the cyclic will vary rotor pitch for aircraft control, and the rudder pedals will control yaw just like in a regular helicopter. What at first messes up chopper pilots is that you push forward on the control lever to go up instead of pulling back, but most pilots get used to it in a hurry.

'The system automatically shifts from helicopter-type control to airplane-type based on airspeed and nacelle angle – when the computer decides that you're in airplane mode, it'll activate the ailerons and elevators instead of rotor pitch. The transition will be controlled by computer. You'll hardly notice the change – it'll seem very natural, logical. You'll have X and Y velocity readouts on the instrument panel to help you maneuver; those readouts are on this display.

'You get forward speed by changing the nacelle angle, not by using the control stick – remember, don't push the stick down to pick up forward speed. When switching to forward flight, power will automatically increase slightly when moving the nacelles because you'll be changing the power vector from pure lift to lift-and-thrust combined. Your elevator and rudder-trim controls are here, under the nacelle-angle control, and you'll find you'll be adjusting trim a lot. The on-board computers will automatically compensate for torque. Once lift from the wings builds up you'll find your forward speed increasing rapidly, and the power-control computers will decrease power as the wings provide more and more lift.'

Geffar had to struggle some to keep up with Elliott's rapid-fire tutorial as he now pointed to another of the digital color displays on the forward instrument panel. 'While switching to forward flight the stick and rudder pedals automatically change from cyclics to fixed-wing flight controls, where the ailerons and rudders combine with computer-controlled rotor-pitch commands to help control the aircraft. The computer displays here will prompt you on angle of attack and nacelle angle until the nacelle is horizontal – you'll be a normal airplane after that.'

Elliott looked at Geffar. 'Pretty simple, isn't it?' he said, not knowing how close he was to verbal if not physical barrage. 'Transitioning from forward to vertical flight is just as easy – the computer will prompt you along, although after an hour or two you'll recognize when to start moving the nacelle and adjusting the power so you won't need the computer's help any more.' He pointed out other controls and switches on the control stick. 'Here are – '

'That's enough,' Geffar said. 'I'll watch for the time being.'

'You'll have time to watch later,' Hardcastle said. 'Now, you're making the takeoff. No argument.' Elliott disappeared, reappeared in a jump seat between Hardcastle and Geffar. McLanahan appeared off the nose to act as fire guard and crew chief, and Hardcastle gave him the signal that he was ready to start. 'Starting engines,' he announced to the crew. 'Cranking one.'

The engine-start sequence was remarkably quiet and easy – Hardcastle selected the sequence from a computerized menu on one of the digital readouts, and the computer did the rest. In spite of the huge size of the engine nacelles, their position at the very outer tips of the wings cut noise in the cockpit. Elliott flipped two switches on the overhead engine-control console to engage the rotors, and soon the huge rotor on the port nacelle was turning. Hardcastle showed Geffar the engine-start sequence, and soon the starboard engine was running.

'One important ground check that needs doing,' Hardcastle said over interphone. 'Both rotors can be run off one engine.' He decoupled the port rotor from the port engine, checked to be sure the linkage connecting the starboard engine to the port rotor engaged, then did the same with the starboard engine. 'Cross-coupling check completed.' Hardcastle set up the nav and communications radios, then dialed a specific radial and distance into the autopilot flight-director, setting in a point several miles south of the Florida Keys.

'We going some place in particular?' Geffar asked.

'Patience,' Hardcastle told her. 'It's your aircraft. I'll call for clearance, you make the takeoff.' Hardcastle then called and received permission for takeoff.

'I've got the aircraft,' Geffar acknowledged, holding

tight to the stick-and-throttle quadrant on the center console. 'But what the hell am I doing?'

'Here's your nacelle angle, here's your power, here's your horizontal and vertical vector-velocity displays,' Hardcastle said, pointing to the color monitors. 'Apply power until you get some altitude, then feed in some nacelle angle to get forward velocity. Be careful – it won't take much to get this baby moving.'

Carefully Geffar advanced the throttle. It seemed she had scarcely touched it, but instantly the Sea Lion was twenty feet off the ground. She tested the rudder pedals, and the aircraft nimbly swivelled left and right in response; its agility, she thought, was incredible considering the V-22C's size, and the noise level in the cockpit was so low that she had a hard time believing they were actually airborne.

'You got it,' Hardcastle said. 'Give us a bit more altitude for a safety margin, then feed in a little nacelle angle. You'll feel the bird drop when you move the nacelles, but the computer will increase engine power to compensate so don't try to add power yourself just to hold altitude. Be gentle. Easy power inputs. It won't take much.'

Geffar touched the nacelle-angle control switch, and the tilt-rotor aircraft shot forward, dipping slightly and losing a few feet of altitude. She watched, fascinated, as the power raced in, arresting the slight drop – it was as if the Sea Lion had been reading her mind. The gray-and-black runway at Homestead Air Force Base disappeared as they raced eastward over the forests and coastal swamps.

'Good,' Hardcastle said. 'Combine nacelle angle and power for altitude and airspeed and let the computers take care of flight transitions. Come right a bit so we can stay away from the nuclear power plant.' Geffar eased the control stick to the right and the Sea Lion gracefully banked right, away from the Turkey Point Nuclear Power Station just east of the Air Force base.

'Okay, climb to three thousand feet,' Hardcastle said. They were there moments later, and Geffar expertly lowered the Sea Lion's nose and readjusted power to maintain altitude. 'Now follow the HSI and we'll get the demonstration started.' Geffar checked the Horizontal Situation Indicator, which revealed her desired course and direction, and banked slightly left to center the course-needle on the instrument. 'Great. Now we'll pick up a little speed. Open the throttle to eighty percent and adjust the nacelle angle to maintain at least six alpha. You'll have to apply a little pressure to maintain altitude. Trim it out carefully but be ready to retrim once the wings start generating lift.'

Geffar followed Hardcastle's directions, responding to his unhurried, even voice. As she applied power the upward lift was a force, and it took a large push on the stick to hold altitude. Then, as she lowered the nacelle, she found she had to retrim in the opposite direction to compensate for the loss of lift; then, a few moments later as the forward airspeed started to build, she had to trim away the stick pressure as the wings started to produce lift and the Sea Lion wanted to climb once again.

'You're keeping up with the plane very well,' Hardcastle told her, and meant it.

'It's like holding a rattlesnake with a baseball glove in each hand,' Geffar said, still afraid to look in any direction but straight at her flight controls.

'It's easier than you think. You got it trimmed up?' Geffar nodded tentatively. 'Let go.'

'Let go of the controls?'

'You're not in a chopper any more. Let go.' Slowly Geffar let her hands drop away and was surprised to find the aircraft just as rock-steady as before, with only tiny heading and altitude deviations.

'With this setup, once you've crossed over to airplane mode, you can trim out stick forces and then fly hands-off.'

Clearly impressed, Geffar gently touched the rudder panels and made a few rudder-only turns, keeping her hands off the stick.

Hardcastle checked their progress on the V-22C's navigation instruments, then called Miami Air Traffic Control for overwater flight clearance. 'Take it up to two hundred knots,' Hardcastle said after their clearance to operate in the Air Defense Identification Zone was received. 'It'll take us a while to get where we're going.' Geffar handled the added airspeed expertly, moving the nacelles to almost full horizontal as the forward airspeed increased.

'So your big idea is putting guns on Sea Lion aircraft,' Long radioed up to Hardcastle from the crew seats in the forward cargo bay. 'Pardon my frankness, sir, but I think it's a bad idea.'

'Armed aircraft are part of the project, Agent Long, but they're only a small part,' Hardcastle said. 'The main part of this project I'm proposing is a way to regulate aircraft and vessels entering the United States.'

'We already do that, Admiral,' Long said. 'I believe you know the procedure: Every vessel entering the United States has to provide a manifest of cargo and passengers to Customs at least two days before entry. Aircraft must file flight plans and advise Customs at least one day in advance. On arrival each vessel and aircraft is inspected by Customs or signed off as cleared through Customs.'

'That procedure has a basic flaw,' Hardcastle said. 'It happens to allow smugglers' ships and aircraft to enter U.S. territory. It gives them virtual free access to roam our territorial waters and airspace to make drops or deliveries.'

'But how can legitimate vessels do business if they don't get into port?'

'They get in, all right,' Hardcastle said, 'but *after* they're inspected. My proposal requires identification of all vessels and aircraft *before* they enter American waters or American airspace.'

'Before? You mean inspect a vessel before it reaches a US port? Like the Coast Guard does now?'

'Not exactly,' Hardcastle said. He motioned out the window, and Long strained to look outside the wide forward-cockpit canopy.

Off in the distance was an enormous platform shaped like a huge diamond, each side of which was some six hundred feet long. The main deck was five stories high, with open walkways and glassed-in rooms along the sides. The corners were narrow and pointed. Attached to the sides of the platform was a series of floating docks, where several Coast Guard vessels were moored; catwalks led from the docks up to the lower level of the platform deck. The platform's multiple huge legs could barely be seen extending down into the crystal blue waters.

On the huge deck of the platform were four helicopter landing-pads, along with what appeared to be deck elevators where helicopters might be lowered to maintenance hangars below deck. Communications antennae and surveillance radars could be seen on the far side of the platform's deck beneath an above-deck control building. Positioned along the edge of the upper deck were service cranes, elevators and conveyor belts that led nearly to the ocean's surface.

They were still miles from the platform but it was so large it looked like a massive flat-topped island. 'What the hell is that thing?' Long said.

'It's called Hammerhead One,' Hardcastle told him. 'Rowan Companies of Houston loaned it to us for this project. It's an offshore oil-drilling platform modified as a forward command post, military base, communications center and helipad. The Air Force has been studying using these things as rocket launch-pads – we've just taken the concept a step further.'

'But where did it come from?' Geffar asked. 'We've got patrols out this way every night and we've never received reports about it.'

'It's been docked in Fort Lauderdale for several months,' Hardcastle said, 'ever since we got it from the Air Force last year. Hammerhead One is a registered seagoing vessel – we had it towed out here and set up just yesterday. It has three retractable legs that anchor it to the sea bottom and jack up the platform above water level. Once it's moved into position it can be set up in a matter of hours – you can even leave a full complement of personnel on board while it's being towed into position and keep working while the thing is being moored into place. They've even launched and recovered choppers on it while it was being towed out here.'

Hardcastle turned to the radios. 'Hammerhead One, Lion One-One is five miles out.'

'Lion One-One, Hammerhead One, roger,' a voice responded. 'Radar contact. Clear for visual approach, west helipad one. Winds two-three-zero at ten gusting to fifteen, altimeter two-niner-niner-zero.'

'Lion One-One copies,' Hardcastle replied. 'We'll be orbiting the pad once or twice before landing.'

'Copy that. Hammerhead One out.'

Hardcastle turned to Geffar. 'You've been cleared to land, go for it.'

'Me? Now you want me to *land* this thing? I need a checkout before I fly a plane, Hardcastle. I've already violated my rule once.'

Hardcastle shrugged, moved to put his hands on the controls. 'If you're afraid to give it a try . . .'

She understood what he was doing but still reacted. 'Never mind,' she said quickly, and began transitioning to vertical flight. And feeling very damn good about it. She reduced throttle, feeding in more and more vertical nacelle angle to decrease both vertical descent rate and airspeed at the same time.

'Take it around the platform a few times,' Hardcastle said, 'get a feel for the winds and gusts out here before you land.' Geffar nodded, began a slow orbit of the huge platform, decreasing her range to the main deck on each orbit.

'You know,' Hardcastle said as they completed their first turn around Hammerhead One, 'we can set up full working dock space below to service vessels of almost any size. We can also have fully automated electro-optical, chemical and manual inspection facilities to check containerized cargo or large cargo spaces. A complete inspection can be carried out on two full-sized freighters at once or we can conduct more abbreviated inspections in preparation for thorough Customs inspections in port.'

He pointed out the radar arrays on one corner of the platform. 'With a complement of Sea Lion aircraft, interceptor vessels and other reconnaissance and interceptor assets deployed on these platforms we can control the waters for hundreds of miles in all directions, intercept intruders – '

'Or destroy them?' Long put in.

'Or destroy them,' Hardcastle acknowledged. 'We're talking about *real* security of America's borders. Closing off drug-ingress routes is the best way to begin to get control – '

'Put a Sea Stinger right through them?' Long asked. 'What, sir, if you find a grandfather and his two grandkids in a little fishing boat? What if you blow them to pieces with one of those missiles back there?'

'If that *alleged* grandfather refused to stop, refused to respond to signals from an interceptor vessel or aircraft, yes, right. I'm out to make this project work, Agent Long. How about you? Tough times, tough solutions.' Hardcastle turned back to watch Geffar's approach to the platform. 'Get used to it.'

'How many rounds of thirty-millimeter gunfire does it take to sink a couple of kids, sir . . . ?'

'Knock it off, Curt,' Geffar interjected, although she didn't entirely disagree. She had slowed the Sea Lion to a few knots forward speed and had rotated the nacelles back to the vertical for the descent.

'Hey, that platform sure looks small all of a sudden,' Geffar said as she began her approach descent. A crewman on the platform's deck ran out to helipad number one and held aloft a pair of flags, waiting to help in the landing. 'It's like trying to land on a postage stamp.'

'Relax, you're doing fine,' Hardcastle said. 'Remember, your power controls are very sensitive because the computer augments your inputs. Keep your descent rate under five-per-second – the display will change to feet-per-second when you get down below fifty feet. Keep an eye on the computer monitors. They'll advise you on where to put your throttles and nacelles and compute drift and descent rate for you. Just take it nice and easy.'

As Geffar scanned the edge of the huge platform she noticed the unusual markings on the helicopter parked on the other side of the platform. It was a UH-60 Black Hawk helicopter with Marine Corps markings, but the lower half of the chopper was dark green, the upper half near the engine nacelles white. As she flew closer to touchdown, she made out the words painted on the sides of the UH-60 helicopter . . . ' "United States of Ameri . . ." Hardcastle, that's not a UH-60 Black Hawk helicopter.'

'Thirty feet to go,' he called out, reaching forward and flipping a circular switch full down, checking for three green 'gear down and locked' light indications. 'Gear down and locked. Looking good.'

'Dammit, that's a VH-60. It looked like Marine One . . .'

'Marine Two,' Hardcastle deadpanned. 'I forgot to tell you, that's the Vice President's helicopter. The Veep and Secretary of Defense are both on board Hammerhead One.'

'What?' The Sea Lion did a slight swerve to the left as Geffar stared at Hardcastle. 'I've flown this thing for a grand total of twenty minutes and now I'm supposed to land it on a postage stamp with the Veep watching?'

'Watch your vertical velocity, Inspector,' Hardcastle said. 'Forget Vice President Martindale, concentrate on your deck crew.' Geffar took a firm grip on the throttle control and gave it a power burst to arrest the fast sink rate. 'You've got a ten-knot wind from your right so don't forget to watch the drift, but don't overcompensate. Main trucks first . . . lift the nose a bit . . . a little more . . .' They felt a solid bump as the main gear landed. The deck crewman confirmed the main wheels were down, then guided her in to a gentle nose-wheel touchdown.

'Just excellent,' Hardcastle told her as deck crewmen placed chocks and cable tie-downs on the V-22C Sea Lion. 'I've got the brakes. Throttle to idle – we don't want to blow the Vice President's hat into the water.' Geffar retarded the throttles to idle, and Hardcastle began shutting down the electrical systems and the engines. 'Welcome to Hammerhead One, gang. Doors are clear to open.'

'You S.O.B.,' Geffar said as she pulled off her helmet and stared at Hardcastle. For a moment he was worried she was really sore at him, but it seemed more a sense of relief, and accomplishment, than anger. 'This was a set-up. Why? To embarrass me? Discredit the Customs Service? Get me fired? What the hell?'

'You know it's none of the above,' Hardcastle said. 'If you'd had any trouble landing the aircraft I'd have taken over. I didn't think that would happen and it didn't. I wanted you to fly the Sea Lion so I could get you involved in joining up in this project.'

'You mean you want me to participate in a Coast Guard project to fly armed helicopters and tilt-rotor aircraft off oil platforms – '

'This is *not* a Coast Guard project, damn it. I've tried to tell you that before. I'm trying to create a whole *new* organization, separate from *both* the Coast Guard and Customs. But I want and need your participation, cooperation. We have to create a *united* front . . .'

'Well, I need to know a lot more.'

Unlike the President, who was just over sixty years of age, Vice President Kevin Martindale was a youngster of forty-six. An ex-Congressman, Martindale, unlike a predecessor, turned out to be a bulldog in the White House and on Capitol Hill, more than willing and able to engage in the back-room and cloakroom trench warfare to get the President's proposals, and some of his own, heard by the Congress. One of Martindale's major projects was drug control, and he was an outspoken advocate of tough-line responses to the growing drug problem in the United States.

It was a surprise for Geffar to find him on an oil platform forty miles off the southern coast of Florida, but it was no surprise that he would be involved with something like this.

'Inspector Geffar is our top Air Division officer,' a man standing beside Martindale said, and Geffar realized with a shock that it was Joseph Crandall, Commissioner of the US Customs Service. 'She's been head of the country's number-one drug interdiction unit for two years now.'

'And a pistol champion,' the Vice President added. 'I'm aware of Inspector Geffar's background. You made the landing, right? And this was your first flight in one of those things, right?'

'That's right, sir. Did it show?'

'No. But it's a move that old sea dog Hardcastle would pull.' He turned as Hardcastle came around to greet him.

'When you throw a party, Admiral, you don't mess around. Impressive display, impressive. Inspector Geffar's landing was right on the dot.'

'She's the best pilot on this platform, sir.' They shook hands, and Hardcastle also greeted Commissioner Crandall, Secretary of Defense Thomas Preston, Admiral Cronin and Secretary of Transportation Edward Coultrane. 'I'd also like to introduce Agent Curtis Long, one of Inspector Geffar's deputies, and of course General Brad Elliott, US Air Force, the chief design engineer and consultant on this project, and his project officer, Major Patrick McLanahan.'

'Brad Elliott,' the Vice President said as they shook hands. Geffar was surprised – the Vice President seemed really impressed, respectful, as he shook Elliott's hand. Who *was* this guy . . . ? 'It's good to see you. The President sends his regards.' He turned to McLanahan, and they shook hands as if McLanahan was something special too. 'Major, I want to offer my condolences for the loss of your friend, Lieutenant Luger. We'll have to talk about your . . . your incredible flight. I'd like to hear more about it.'

'Thank you, sir,' McLanahan said. Hardcastle, Geffar and Long looked at the Air Force officers for some answers to all this but got nothing. Who the hell were they? What had Elliott and McLanahan done . . . ?

Finally the Vice President turned to Elliott. 'So, General, you're the one who's responsible for a lot of the toys on this platform, and for this beautiful aircraft here.'

'I'm here to get Admiral Hardcastle's brainstorms off the drawing boards and into action,' Elliott said. 'But I confess the Sea Lion *is* my pride and joy.'

'Then show her to me,' the Vice President said.

'Happy to, sir,' Elliott said.

Hardcastle excused himself and headed off toward the elevators to go below deck, Geffar and Cronin following.

They were met by Commander Mike Becker at the entrance to the elevator, who greeted Hardcastle as they entered the elevator.

'Did you see that?' Long said as they started down. 'Damn, I thought the Vice President was going to kiss McLanahan's ring. What the hell did he do – save the world or something?'

Hardcastle looked at Admiral Cronin, who gave him nothing. He knew what Elliott and McLanahan had done, Hardcastle thought. He's not saying, at least not here, but judging by his expression it must have been pretty awesome.

The flight of the Old Dog was, of course, still top secret. And so, therefore, were the roles Elliott and McLanahan had played in it.

Hardcastle turned to Becker. 'How's it look so far, Mike?'

'So far I'd say they're impressed, Admiral. The platform is in better shape than we'd hoped, and we had time to give it a few coats of paint and a good washing before the choppers showed up.'

'Ready to go to the briefing room?'

'Yes, sir.'

'I'm impressed myself, Ian,' Cronin said, wiping sweat from his forehead as the air-conditioned lower decks began to take effect. 'But Preston, Coultrane and Crandall aren't as wide-eyed about this as the Vice President. What they see is their drug-interdiction appropriations going out the window, out of their budgets and into your hot-shot, high-tech special project here.'

They were on the third floor of the platform, fifty feet above the gentle swells of the Straits of Florida. They could see two Coast Guard cutters about a half-mile away circling the platform and keeping the curious away. Occasionally a Coast Guard Dolphin helicopter could be seen as it continued its security sweep of the waters around Hammerhead One.

The room had been transformed into a radar command-and-control center. Two radar consoles had been set up in the center of the room, with three sixty-inch color projection screens in front of the consoles. Major McLanahan was commanding the consoles.

Hardcastle began his presentation:

'Welcome to Hammerhead One, Mr Vice President, members of the President's Cabinet, ladies and gentlemen,' Hardcastle began. 'We propose to use these huge platforms, suitably modified, as bases for an extensive, bold and far-reaching border security force. Please note, I used the term border security, not only drug interdiction. As I see it, the key to successful drug interdiction is not just routine investigation and arrest but more aggressive, more sweeping tactical operations of a paramilitary organization concentrating on securing America's borders against unidentified vessels and aircraft.'

Hardcastle pressed a button on a remote control device and the left screen snapped on, showing a digital chart of the southeast United States, ranging from South Carolina through Florida to Texas and as far south as South America.

'Why not law-enforcement tactics? Why paramilitary tactics? Because we are talking about the skies and seas surrounding the United States, and the problems associated with controlling our vast frontiers require much more than routine patrol and port-entry efforts. If we take the area three miles from shore out to the twelve-mile limit, we're talking about thirty-six thousand square miles of open ocean in the southeast United States alone. Thirty-six thousand square miles. At present we have approximately one hundred vessels and eighty aircraft, representing both the Coast Guard *and* the Customs Service, to patrol this area. Factor in the airspace and we're talking about over one hundred thousand cubic *miles* of territory.'

The center screen snapped on, showing stock video images of Coast Guard and Customs Service radar installations aircraft and ships. 'The Coast Guard and Customs Service can adequately watch this territory, and the two agencies patrol the major known smuggling routes throughout this entire area. But even though we may detect unidentified aircraft or vessels with our surveillance systems we have no way to intercept all of them. We would need ten times the number of aircraft and ships we now have to accomplish this. The cost would be prohibitive, ranging in the tens of billions of dollars.'

Hardcastle moved over to the right large-screen monitor as it snapped on. 'However, there's another way of securing this tremendous expanse of territory. By changing the rules on how vessels can enter our country.

'Let's talk about ships first.' A spider's web of lines crisscrossed the ocean areas of the chart; most culminated at known port cities such as Miami, Ft Lauderdale, Tampa, and Charleston. 'Vessels entering the United States routinely follow established shipping lanes to American ports. They are not *required* to follow any particular routeing, can freely navigate American coastal waters at will. They may be stopped and boarded by the Coast Guard at any time while inside this area but such boardings are rare – there aren't enough ships to cover this enormous area. Outside of normal shipping lanes, far from normal patrol areas or port areas, unidentified vessels can operate with virtual impunity even though we can usually detect them and may even have them under surveillance.

'Let's get to air traffic.' The computer-sketched chart changed; now the area was much wider. 'This depicts the

Air Defense Identification Zone, the ADIZ. All aircraft entering the United States are required to contact air traffic control before entering the ADIZ. Fewer than fifty percent do it. They know we don't have resources now to respond with. They know that they have only a one in twenty chance of being intercepted. Military air-defense forces key in on very specific flight parameters – high speed, low altitude, military strike flight profiles. Their job is *not* to go after the smugglers, even if they can see them and track them. Understandably, we don't like our military chasing civilians, even if they're criminals.

'In spite of the Customs Air Service's fine record, they don't have the resources to intercept every unidentified aircraft they detect,' Hardcastle said. 'Like air defense, they key on specific flight parameters. They go after big targets, obvious smuggling profiles and intelligence reports – '

Geffar broke in. 'If we had a hundred aircraft, we'd do it the same way – we'd only expand those flight parameters you mentioned. Instead of keying in on aircraft exceeding one hundred and eighty knots, for example, we'd go after planes exceeding one-fifty. You can't pair one law-enforcement aircraft with one inbound aircraft. It can't be done – '

'There's a way it can be done, Inspector,' Hardcastle said. He motioned to the center screen, which showed the territorial waters in orange around the United States, and the right screen, which showed the ADIZ in orange. He pressed a button and ten white lines were drawn across the orange bands leading into the US coastline aimed right at the major port cities of the southeast. The center screen changed, showing an expanded view of the southern tip of Florida, with a blinking dot in the center of the screen. The territorial waters and ADIZ airspace were still outlined in orange. The white line, which in the center screen led from the Gulf of Mexico toward Miami, was now a thin corridor, with the blinking dot at the edge of the territorial waters area.

'This is how we propose to do it. The area in orange, from twelve to two miles out, becomes a positive identification zone for both aircraft and vessels. Neither may transit this area without permission and without positive identification at all times. Our surveillance systems can detect any vessel larger than fifteen feet in length and track it with precision. We've demonstrated capability for detecting and tracking any vessel within two hundred miles of our shores.

'This is how authorized vessels in the positive control area can be tracked and monitored, sir. The computers that operate with our radar systems can monitor hundreds of vessels simultaneously. Anyone operating inside the positive control area can be monitored continuously.'

'But,' Customs Service Commissioner Crandall interjected, 'we can monitor those ships but they can still be smugglers and they can still operate inside our waters. What's different about your system?'

Hardcastle pointed to the blinking dot on the center screen outside the edge of the orange area. 'This dot is our location, sir. Hammerhead One, forty-five miles southeast of Homestead. With this system in full operation all vessels entering our territorial waters must stop at one of these platforms for registration, inspection of documents and cargo and positive identification before proceeding.'

'You're suggesting,' Crandall said, 'that we set up these oil platforms as offshore border-inspection points for *ships*?'

'This's right, sir. Hammerhead One can accommodate several large ships alongside, and we can service others within a few hundred yards. A vessel must stop, have its papers examined, must submit to a Coast Guard or Customs Service inspection; these can be like border-crossing

133

points on land. We can decide to do a documents-only review, a cursory inspection, a more detailed inspection, or a full-vessel search with the crew removed. Once cleared through the entry point it must follow this corridor to its destination unless it is cleared to deviate.'

'It seems you could have some serious bottlenecks at these inspection points,' Crandall said.

'More platforms and extra manpower could be added as traffic increased.'

'What happens to unidentified vessels in the orange zone?' Secretary of Transportation Coultrane challenged.

'They're violating American law and are subject to arrest.'

'Which brings us back to the original question, how do you get the guy that's in violation? You said yourself that detection is not a problem. Interception is. How do you propose doing it?'

'Isolating the target is the primary way to get him. It's easier to intercept if he's all alone in restricted waters. Deploying helicopters or aircraft like the Sea Lion tilt-rotor offshore on oil platforms such as Hammerhead One is the other answer. We *also* propose, as a part of the interdiction mix . . .'

He hit another button on his remote-control device and two of the three screens changed at once, showing two different aerial video images – one focusing on the sky, the other scanning the crystal blue waters below. The aircraft taking the shots were from different altitudes, some very close to the water, some apparently at very high altitude.

'What you're seeing are video shots from two different UAVs, unmanned aerial vehicles – drones. These drones are controlled right from this console in front of you by computer commands radioed to the drones via secure UHF data links – if we have a radar that can see a target we can steer a drone over it.'

Hardcastle moved over to the console in front of the giant screens. 'Older drone-control centers used to look like aircraft cockpits with throttles and control sticks and flight instruments and you had to be a pilot to fly a drone. Now we highlight a target and the computer controlling the drone's autopilot flies it to intercept its target.'

Hardcastle reached over to the console and picked up a large model of what appeared to be a V-22 tilt-rotor aircraft. It had the same twin rotors mounted on the ends of its main wing, a cylindrical fuselage, ski-type landing rigs and ports for bulbous sensors and scanners.

'This is a one-tenth scale model of the Sky Lion, the unmanned drones we're using for today's tests,' Hardcastle said. 'The real UAV is about thirty feet long with a twenty-foot wingspan and carries two five-hundred-shaft-horse-power engines. It has a maximum speed of almost two hundred knots, a minimum speed of zero knots and can stay aloft for about six hours. It can be launched and recovered from a station platform, from shore or from a large cutter-class ship – stowed, each drone can fit in a standard one-car garage. Each carries sensors to help it carry out its mission. Also a small radar to help it guide itself to intercept, and a combined telescopic low-light and infrared camera for visual identification. They can also be outfitted with various payloads . . .' He paused, studying the faces of the Vice President and the others in the room. '. . . Such as weapons.'

The reaction was immediate from Customs Commissioner Crandall. 'You want a fleet of robot planes with guns on board flying around out here with all the other air traffic?'

Martindale held up a hand. 'Let him finish, Commissioner. Go on, Admiral.'

Hardcastle took a deep breath. He'd survived that one. 'To clarify, we would have the option of placing a variety of payloads aboard the Sky Lion drones. Their normal configuration would be with sensors only. As with the Sea Lion aircraft, however, we would maintain armed aircraft and vessels and we would prevent any vessel or aircraft from entering restricted territory, with force if necessary.'

Hardcastle nodded to the console operators, who quickly set up the next presentation. 'We have a Sky Lion drone tracking a Coast Guard vessel at this very moment. Our surveillance radars have detected the target . . . here,' Hardcastle said, using his pointer. 'It's a Coast Guard forty-foot FCI, fast coastal interceptor, heading toward south Florida.'

He motioned to the left screen, which showed a steady crystal-clear picture of the Caribbean. 'Here on the left screen is the bird's-eye view from the Sky Lion drone, along with its flight parameters and status readouts.' At a signal from Hardcastle, McLanahan hit buttons on his console, then turned in his seat to face Martindale and the rest of the Cabinet officials.

'As the Admiral has explained, sir,' McLanahan said, 'the drones are controlled by computer, using sensors both on the drones and by radar and data-link commands from this platform and on shore. I've just commanded the Sky Lion drone to intercept that vessel.'

The scene from the drone tilted sharply and soon it was in a fast descent toward the shimmering blue waters below. 'Ten miles,' Hardcastle said. 'The drone's camera uses slaving signals from the main surveillance radar to aim its camera at the target. We should be picking it up any second.'

Suddenly the screen changed from a standard video image to a black, wavy scene, with several lighter streaks and splotches running through the image. 'I've switched to infrared scan to pick out the boat against the cooler water. The redder the color, the hotter the infrared return . . .

and there it is.' In the center of the image a bright red dot separated from the lighter pinks and yellows of the warm water, and a digital readout said that it had locked onto the suspected target. 'The drone's speed is about two hundred miles an hour in the descent. He'll start slowing as he gets closer.' The infrared hot dot was getting larger. Occasionally McLanahan would switch back and forth from IR to normal video mode until the boat could plainly be seen against the choppy waters.

'The drone is about a half-mile away now,' he said, pointing to the data readouts. 'Its airspeed is now thirty knots – only a tilt-rotor type aircraft could decelerate from two hundred knots to thirty knots so fast, with such a stable platform. As it moves closer you'll be able to make out more and more detail of the boat. In short, we've intercepted and identified a smuggling vessel.'

'Of course, intercepting vessels in American waters is only one part of the process to close down the drug smuggling in this area,' Hardcastle said as McLanahan took his seat. 'Stopping these boats in south Florida may slow drug trafficking nationwide only ten to fifteen percent, and although a ten to fifteen percent hike in the street price of cocaine or marijuana *might* help decrease the drug consumption, it's not a guarantee and it's not enough. The appetite is there. Dealing with it is a very long-range matter. Meanwhile, what isn't available can't be consumed.

'In spite of the best efforts of the Customs Service and Coast Guard, more drugs are still brought in by air than by any other means. Air smuggling is fast, the smugglers retain control of their product longer, and they are relatively assured of success every time if they are organized well enough. If we can stop air smuggling, we can slow the rate of narcotics smuggling into the United States by thirty to forty percent. *That's* significant.'

Hardcastle motioned to the screen, which had changed to show thin white lines similar to previous depictions. 'Our plan would use the same entry corridors for air traffic as with surface vessels. Incoming aircraft would be required to follow these corridors and stay at carefully specified altitudes. Surveillance radars along the corridors would track each aircraft to ensure he doesn't stray from the corridor or from his assigned altitude. Any deviation from his assigned routeing would be a violation and make him subject to interception.

'Notice that these corridors are far from the popular drop sites used by smugglers, the Keys and the Everglades. The Everglades and remote areas of the Florida Keys would become one of the few restricted airspaces over land – areas where all aircraft must receive permission before entering.'

Hardcastle motioned to the left large-screen monitor, where another drone was in flight. 'This scene is from another drone we have orbiting nearby. Air interdiction requires different techniques than sea interdiction, so we're using a different drone for this job.' He held up another model, but of a completely different aircraft than the Sky Lion. 'This is called Seagull, although it hardly looks like a gull. Damned if I know how it got its name. It's a fixed-wing drone, with a big delta main wing, canards – these smaller wings near the nose – for increased maneuverability, a three-hundred-horsepower, constant-speed pusher prop and a payload of almost seven hundred pounds. It can fly at speeds close to four hundred miles an hour down to about eighty and can stay aloft for better than ten hours. The aircraft has a forty-foot wingspan and is twenty feet long. Like the Sky Lion, it can be launched and recovered from the sea platforms, from shore or from special recovery ships.'

'What about general aviation?' Coultrane pressed. 'You'd be forcing non-commercial aircraft into the

138

corridors. They're often the worst-trained pilots but they'd be in the most congested airspace.'

'Mr Secretary, it would be no more dangerous than a civilian plane transiting a terminal control area over a major city or a high-density airway,' Hardcastle told him.

Coultrane shook his head, clearly not convinced.

Hardcastle hurried on. 'The problem of aircraft veering off from their intended landing point at the last minute and evading surveillance radar is at least mitigated with this system. Aircraft are tracked all the way to landing along these corridors – each corridor terminates at a port of entry, such as Miami International, Opa-Locka, Ft Lauderdale or Tampa. If a plane tries to run away he can be tracked and an intercept set up, again using the Seagull drones or manned aircraft.'

Hardcastle received a hand signal from McLanahan. 'We've set up a special demonstration of this capability, Mr Vice President,' McLanahan said. 'At this moment we're tracking a smuggler trying to cross into the United States from the southern Bahamas island chain. We've kept the Seagull drone in the vicinity of the target ever since first detection.' He motioned to the right large-screen TV, which showed the V-22C Sea Lion aircraft lifting off the landing pad four stories overhead.

'With Brad Elliott in command,' Hardcastle picked it up from McLanahan, 'we've scrambled the Sea Lion to pursue. On a normal intercept the Sea Lion would carry a ground assault team, usually two officers armed with rifles and sidearms.' The Sea Lion could briefly be glimpsed out the huge panoramic storm windows as it raced away from Hammerhead One after its quarry, its rotors slowly transitioning from vertical-lift to aircraft configuration as it picked up speed.

The center screen showed an enlargement of the main control-console digital-radar scope. 'Major McLanahan is designating the target now, and the drone will move to intercept and identify.' The scene from the drone, showing on the left screen, suddenly veered sharply right and descended at a tremendous rate as the drone raced after its new target.

'The drone's on-board radar has locked-on at eleven miles,' Hardcastle said. 'It has a two-hundred-forty-knot overtake, which will eat up the distance between them in less than three minutes.'

The target aircraft emerged seconds later in the center of the Seagull drone's camera eye, a beige twin-engined aircraft. Gradually the aircraft loomed larger and larger as the drone closed in.

'Three miles,' Hardcastle said. 'With the telescopic camera, it looks like a Beech Baron, about eight or nine years old. Using its radar, the drone will now automatically move in close enough to read the aircraft's registration number.'

Moments later the drone had pulled in right on the target's right rear quarter; the radar rangefinder indicated it was only a hundred feet away, with zero knots closure. 'The drone is now flying in formation with the target,' Hardcastle said. 'It will match all but the most violent maneuvers and stay within about a hundred feet.'

The scene shifted slowly as McLanahan began manipulating a joystick to scan along the plane's fuselage, and soon the center of the scene was filled with a series of small black letters and numbers.

'You can read the registration numbers now,' McLanahan said, manipulating the camera controls. 'This individual has an N-number, indicating that this is an American-registered aircraft. It has small numbers, which is illegal – they're supposed to be twelve inches high. Notice the number 8 and the letter O. This registration number has been altered; the 8 used to be a 3, and the O used to be a C.

'It's a common trick to confuse agents in the air and on the ground,' Hardcastle said. 'When we do a hot-list check this aircraft will come up with a clean rap sheet. A more intensive registration check will reveal that the number is bogus, but many times an agent will break off a pursuit when the computer reports "no wants, no warrants." '

The scene moved away from the numbers to the entire aircraft, and then slowly the full left side of the aircraft could be seen. 'The drone is now moving around the aircraft off to its left, in full view of the pilot. Notice that the drone has moved out farther away from the suspect. This is because the drone's radar is not being used to track the suspect – the drone is using steering signals from our tracking radars to keep up with the suspect.'

A moment later, the drone was ahead of the aircraft, with its camera focused on the aircraft's cockpit. The pilot could be seen in the shot, wearing a baseball cap, sunglasses, and a thick black mustache. As the camera zoomed in, the Vice President gave a short gasp of surprise.

'Look at that! That plane is full of drugs!' Visible just over the pilot's right shoulder were bales of what appeared to be marijuana.

'This guy is small-time,' Hardcastle said dryly. 'He might be carrying only eight or nine hundred pounds – street value, about a quarter of a million. This might be his second run today. If he made three runs he could make a half-million dollars profit today even if he ditches his airplane in the Everglades at the end of the day.'

The plane suddenly veered out of view.

'What happened?' Martindale asked.

'Major?' Hardcastle turned to McLanahan.

'The guy panicked and broke away,' McLanahan said. 'He thinks he can evade the drone.'

The screen changed briefly to an enlarged picture of the digital-radar screen, showing the closeness of the two aircraft. The Seagull drone was executing a tight left turn to reposition itself in a tail-chase. Outside the area the radar-return and IFF data block of the Sea Lion tilt-rotor moved quickly into view. A moment later the screen shifted again to a telescopic video image of the twin-engine plane. The image was heeling sharply left, then right as the smuggler tried to evade the drone. The sea rushed up into the scene as the smuggler flew his plane lower and lower, trying to escape.

'We're attempting radio contact with the suspect as well,' Hardcastle said. He looked at McLanahan, who shook his head. 'No response. The V-22 Sea Lion is joining up in the chase, he'll take over in a minute.'

'What if your target is having a heart attack and can't respond?' Coultrane asked. 'What if he's on autopilot, trying to save himself?'

Transportation Secretary Coultrane's solicitous concern, Hardcastle couldn't help thinking, had more to do with his perceived threat to *his* space than any humanistic worries over the safety of an innocent. He pushed back the thought and answered with a straight face: 'He has no flight plan, no clearance to cross into our airspace, no Customs-entry report. He's flying off established air routes, at extremely low altitude. Not exactly consistent with innocent, legitimate civil-aviation rules. If he's had the ability to engage an autopilot he's had the chance to set his transponder to squawk emergency – code 7700.'

The scene on the large-screen monitor changed again. The Seagull drone had moved back to a half-mile from the suspect's plane. The scene now showed the V-22C's rotors were in transition-flight position, rotated to a forty-five-degree angle, a position that offered maximum helicopter-like maneuverability along with maximum speed. Both cargo pods on the Sea Lion were deployed, looking like big pontoon outriggers.

'Range to shore, eight miles,' McLanahan reported, monitoring to the large center situation map.

'At this point we have options. The current one is to track this suspect to his destination, see if he drops his load and try to apprehend on the ground or over open waters. Sky Lion or Sea Lion aircraft could survey the cargo dropped over water, vector in patrol boats to try to arrest the smugglers, or even try to intercept from the air. But this would be very risky. A Sea Lion in hover mode is extremely vulnerable to ground fire, especially heavy weapons or shoulder-launched missiles, just like any large helicopter would be. A better option: warn away any boats coming near the drop site and attack anyone who tries to pick up the load.' Hardcastle heard an uncomfortable stir from the audience.

'If the smuggler tried a landing, a Sea Lion with armed men could be dispatched to try to make an arrest, but as we've seen from the Mahogany Hammock disaster, that, to put it mildly, could be dangerous for our people. There's *no* percentage in allowing this smuggler to get any closer to our shores. He has already violated several existing United States laws: he is inside territorial waters and airspace, without clearance or prior report of intention – violation of 5 United States Code 112 point 13, a felony. An unidentified aircraft, evading detection and interception – we would normally try another intercept pass to see if he'd respond and follow the drone, but we won't move the Sea Lion in any closer – we've seen what has happened to aircraft like the Coast Guard Falcon jet that get too close to suspects.' Hardcastle turned to the console operator and nodded.

'This is our response.'

The Sea Lion began a slight decent, leveled off near the suspect's altitude, then heeled to the left. As it did a burst of white light appeared off the right pylon and a streak of black and white erupted from the pylon and homed in on

143

the twin-engine plane. The streak of light wobbled a bit in flight, its smoke-and-fire trail resembling an irregular spiral, but it found its target – the plane's right engine exploded in a sphere of red and orange fire sending a cloud of oily smoke back in its wake. The plane veered sharply to the right, executing almost a full hundred-eighty-degree spin before crashing into the black-and-green sea. Parts of its wings and fuselage bounced off the rock-hard water, and a propeller arced into the air as if tossed like a Frisbee by Neptune himself.

Vice President Martindale had lunged out of his chair. 'Hardcastle, what the hell did you do? *What did you do?*'

Hardcastle took a deep breath – it had been a calculated risk. Was it worth it . . . ? 'Sir, this was a demonstration.' He motioned to the center screen. The image had cleared. When the picture stabilized it showed a wide circle of five Coast Guard vessels surrounding the impact point of the twin-engine plane. 'This was a demonstration . . .'

'Demonstration? That wasn't a real smuggler . . . ?'

'It was a confiscated smuggling plane, outfitted as a remote-piloted drone. We were controlling it from the Coast Guard cutter there on the left in the picture. We had cleared away the impact point for a radius of five miles – '

'Sir, I authorized this demonstration,' Admiral Cronin said, moving past the Secret Service agents to the Vice President. 'I take responsibility.'

'All right, Admiral,' Martindale said, 'what was the point? And this better be good.'

'The station platforms, the air and sea corridors, the surveillance drones, the high-tech aircraft – they're all important, sir, but they won't do the job by themselves. We'll be able to see the intruder, we'll follow him, we'll witness a drug delivery or drop – but we can't stop him from making that delivery, and we can't stop him from turning around and escaping *unless* we make a decision to use force to prevent smugglers from entering or departing American territory . . .

'The Sea Lion aircraft can attack air or surface targets with either the Chain Guns or Sea Stinger missiles, and it has self-protective armor and electronic countermeasures – infrared jammers – to protect it. As I said, the Sky Lion and Seagull *drones* can also carry weapons, typically two Sea Stinger missiles.

'The program can be implemented in stages,' Hardcastle hurried on. 'Notifying the public and others about the airspace and sea navigation restrictions should take at least ninety days after the go-ahead decision . . . During this time the platforms could be put into position and crews assembled to man them. I'm told that six V-22C Sea Lion-class aircraft are available immediately, and flight crew training can begin immediately at the Bell-Boeing flight test facilities in Arlington, Texas. Twenty Seagull and thirty Sky Lion drones can be made available within six months' time. As for personnel, I've made a list of minimum manning levels for the project and I've identified personnel and equipment that can be transferred from specific Coast Guard and Customs Service air-interdiction units and put into service into the new organization – '

' "*New* organization"?' Secretary of Defense Preston said. 'This isn't a Coast Guard/Customs Service joint project?'

'No. This needs to be separate from both organizations. It was my thought to combine the forward drug-interdiction forces of both services into one cohesive, unified command. The organization would not be *under* the Department of Defense,' he added, 'except perhaps it could be federalized, as would the Coast Guard in time of war, under the Navy Maritime Defense Zone concept. But this group would be under *civilian* direction of the new Cabinet-level Department of Border Security – replacing the present so-called drug czar – as a fully authorized executive-level Cabinet position.

'I recommend that the joint-interdiction resources of the Coast Guard and Customs Service, including the joint Command-Control-Communications-Intelligence Centers, the National Narcotics Interdiction Operations Center, the National Narcotics Interdiction Information Center and the Blue Lightning Operations Center be transferred to this new Department. I also recommend that the DEA and the FBI Narcotics Task Force be integrated into the new agency – '

'Disband the DEA?' the Vice President said.

Commissioner Crandall looked at Hardcastle, and if looks could kill . . . 'I wonder who would command this new organization, Admiral? Could it possibly be you?'

Hardcastle decided to ignore the jab. 'The continued operation of these groups outside the command of the new Department of Border Security would only hurt our chances to integrate drug-interdiction.'

Crandall turned to Martindale. 'Admiral Hardcastle is distorting the facts. There's a great deal of coordinated action between Customs and Coast Guard and other drug-interdiction agencies. Adding this new one would just compound the problem – '

'Commissioner, I disagree,' Sandra Geffar finally spoke up. 'I've not been exactly a big advocate of sharing with the Coast Guard. I have to admit that cooperation between Customs and the Coast Guard *is* at an all-time low, and it's been piss-poor for years.'

'So what do you think of this setup, Inspector Geffar?' the Vice President asked. 'Obviously you've gotten your first taste of Admiral Hardcastle's plan this morning, just as we have. But you've been there. You *are* there.'

'I'm impressed.' She was careful not to look directly at Hardcastle. 'I agree with most of the Admiral's approaches. He's come up with ways to control inbound traffic to the United States, and an effective way of stopping uncooperative smugglers. There've been many times, watching a smuggler run away out of reach after dropping off a load of drugs in the Everglades, that I wished I had a Sea Stinger missile that I could put up the bastard's tailpipe. Still, I worry about the military action, much as I'm attracted to it.'

'We both know the problem,' Hardcastle said. 'Narcotics that get within a few miles of our shoreline are nearly impossible to stop. Customs has been active in drug interdiction for decades, but drug use and drug availability in the country is at an all-time high. Is that because Customs isn't doing its job? No and no again. It's because the present system can't stop the flow. I believe my system *can*.

'Drugs that *reach* the shores *are* a law-enforcement issue. The military or the Hammerheads don't belong in the cities or on the streets, and I'm not recommending here that we conduct military anti-drug sweeps of Miami, or New York, or Bogota, or even Medellín. They don't work anyway. We're concerned with one thing: *keeping the unidentified and uninvited ships and planes out of our territorial skies and waters.*'

'So we spend billions on tilt-rotors and drones and oil platforms and radars for the southeast,' Crandall spoke up. 'The smugglers change tactics. They'll step up container-ized shipping, bring the stuff in across the Mexican border and through Europe or Canada. Your project will be obsolete before it's activated.'

'No, sir. We've seen the smugglers try containerized shipping and overland routes through Mexico, and even the United Parcel Service, but they *always* go back to aircraft and vessel smuggling overwater. Why? Because it's the fastest, safest, easiest way. If they put their shipment in containers they lose control of it for days, sometimes weeks, and every hour the drugs are out of their control is another chance for someone to slip up or an informant to squeal or for Customs to move in and seize it. If it goes overland through Mexico the borders can be patrolled better and sealed off faster, and the shipments have to be smaller to avoid detection.

'Air and sea smuggling, whether leap-frogging through the Bahamas or direct flights from South America to Florida, will be the method of choice for sixty to seventy percent of smugglers, and a heavy percentage of those will be brought into the United States through the southeast – half, or twenty billion dollars worth per year, will come through Florida itself. We can tackle the other smuggling routes later on. I propose that we shut off the *main* source of illegal narcotics *now*.'

Downtown Miami
Ten Hours Later

'Hardcastle's a loose cannon,' Customs Service Commissioner Joseph Crandall was saying to Secretary Coultrane. 'We can come up with someone, some*thing* better.' Coultrane didn't disagree.

Vice President Martindale listened. He was waiting for Defense Secretary Thomas Preston to comment, holding back on his own thoughts until the veteran, highly respected statesman and close friend of the President spoke up.

Preston was not a career military man – few secretaries of defense were. He had spent years in the Navy, including two as a liaison officer to the White House representing the Commander of the Pacific Fleet during Vietnam. In those years as a mid-rank but well-respected aide and administrator, Preston began the long series of contacts, introductions, assignments that even now was serving him well after twenty years out of uniform. He had been noted for wearing his Navy uniform clean of ribbons and accouterments. He had cut his teeth in the trenches of Congressional warfare instead of the muddy foxholes of southeast Asia, and unlike many who returned from the wars, internal and external, he had emerged stronger, fiercer, wiser. He knew he had been groomed for his position and maybe something beyond . . .

'Admiral Hardcastle's proposal, backed by Admiral Cronin, is extraordinary, far-reaching, forward-looking.'

'Do I hear a "but" coming?' Martindale asked.

'Not necessarily. I recommend taking it right up to the President. If the President goes for it he should be prepared for some battles, including in Congress. Cost estimates, for example, can be underestimated . . .'

'Four billion dollars,' Coultrane muttered. 'That's equal to the entire Coast Guard budget. That's twice the Customs Service's budget. And all to set up an interdiction network in just the southeast.'

Crandall muttered, 'Let him have the V-22s and the drones – I wasn't that impressed with them anyway. But let him try to take my Black Hawks and Citations and we're gonna tangle.'

Martindale wasn't listening to Crandall. He was studying Preston.

'What about a boss for this Border Security Force,' the Vice-President asked Preston. 'Drug czar Samuel Massey? General Elliott?'

'I doubt Elliott would take it,' Preston said. 'He's on temporary assignment. Air Force is his love and career.' He paused a moment. 'In a way it's a no-win position.' He picked up Hardcastle's thick proposal booklet, where it was open to a color laser drawing of an armed V-22 Sea Lion aircraft, its pylons bristling with missiles, its nose-mounted infrared scanner resembling a hungry wasp's head. 'Whoever it might be will take all of the responsibility and flak and little of the credit, if there's any credit to be taken. He'll be a shuttle between yourself, the President, and the commander of the operational forces – these Hammerheads.'

Martindale nodded. 'Then the commander of the operational forces becomes the main consideration.' Preston nodded. 'Who? Hardcastle?'

'He's your friend, right?' Preston asked Martindale without looking at him.

'We've known each other for a long time, yes,' the Vice President said a bit testily. 'But that won't affect my recommendation. You know it won't.'

Preston nodded. 'Of course.'

Martindale looked at Preston. The Vice President shook his head. 'You're talking ancient history, Mr Secretary.'

'Congress has a long memory, Mr Vice President, when it's convenient.'

Admiral Cronin met Hardcastle, Geffar, Inspector Long, and Commander Becker in the lobby of the Hyatt Brickell Plaza, the hotel right across Second Street from the downtown Federal Building and the Customs Service's canal-side headquarters. Already on hand with Cronin were General Elliott and Major McLanahan.

'The Vice President's just finishing dinner,' Cronin said. 'He should be ready for us in a few minutes.'

Long was staring at Elliott and McLanahan. Finally he leaned forward toward McLanahan and said in a low voice, 'Okay. Who are you guys? Spies? Super heroes?'

McLanahan said nothing.

'The Vice President was talking to you like you walk on water or something. What'd you guys do?'

'We flew planes, we fly planes. Air Force jet jockeys.'

'We're also advisors to Admiral Hardcastle,' Elliott added. 'Leave it at that.' Long did.

Hardcastle lit his cigar. 'So what's on the agenda tonight, sir?' he asked Cronin. 'Good news or bad?'

'I've no idea. But I thought your presentations and organization were top-drawer.'

Geffar spoke up: 'You were going for the shock value, and maybe it backfired. You blew the doors off with that demonstration, but I don't think they like getting their doors blown off.'

'It was meant to shock,' Hardcastle said. 'We've got a shocking problem here.'

'But is putting a missile into some guy's tailpipe the answer?' Long put in. 'I've been flying for Customs for twelve years. Twelve goddamned years. I've got over seven thousand hours in nine different aircraft. We fly seven days a week, we make over four hundred busts a year. We work hard. *Real* hard. Now, it's all going for shit. Now it's not good enough. Yesterday, we were the front line, doing the job. Now, you're trying to tell us, tell the Vice-President, that the answer is a whole new outfit that kills suspects.'

'Good point, Agent Long,' a voice behind them said. Vice President Martindale was a few paces away from the cluster of sofas where they were waiting. 'Don't stop,' he said. An aide brought over a wing-backed leather armchair and the Vice President sat between Geffar and Becker.

'Well, I've gotten feedback from half the President's Cabinet and a few unsolicited comments from some members of Congress who didn't even know what was going on. So, continue. Agent Long has a good point. We have a pretty good program going with the Customs Service in charge of drug interdiction. They make busts and they don't shoot down smugglers – '

'I am *not* proposing a wholesale slaughter of civilians,'

151

Hardcastle shot back. 'I'm trying to design a way to secure this country's borders from intruders. The *main* feature of the program is detection, establishing navigational corridors and restricted-use regions and a system of response, surveillance and interceptor aircraft to patrol the borders and find those who are violating the law. Attacking those intruders who ignore the laws and don't follow the established procedures is the last resort. We don't go into every intercept with fingers on the trigger.

'The suspect is guilty as soon as he crosses the line into restricted airspace,' Hardcastle pressed on. 'The operation begins at that instant, but we don't go in with Sea Stinger missiles in the air. We track the suspect after he deviates from his flight plan or crosses into restricted airspace. We try to make contact with him, get him to follow our aircraft or get back within the designated airspace or routeing. If he ignores our directions, we complete the intercept. We order him to follow. We direct him to land. If he *still* fails to respond, he is resisting arrest and *must be stopped*.'

'Suspects aren't routinely shot for trespassing or for resisting arrest,' Geffar said. 'At least, not by law-enforcement agencies – '

'This is *not* a law-enforcement action, damn it. It's a national-security issue – '

Geffar shook her head. 'Admiral, we're both frustrated about the drug smuggling situation. We see scum float by us every day. We know that for every one we catch, five, six, seven slip by. But at least I realize that the answer is *not* to go extra-legal. This *is* a law-enforcement action, Admiral.

'Sure, I'm frustrated, but the difference is, I'm willing to go an extra step to do something about it. Let's deal with the problem. Let's design a system that catches more of those seven or eight smugglers that get by. If it means that we put missiles and guns on Sea Lion aircraft, *then so be it*.'

The Vice President said, 'I've seen a very impressive display of state-of-the-art hardware, true, but what has impressed me more is the devotion you all have to your jobs. But the disease seems to have spread faster than our capacity or willingness to deal with it. The government has a choice. We can rearm Customs and the Coast Guard, expanding their roles in interdiction at the expense of their primary missions, or we can create a new organization that deals specifically with drug interdiction and interdiction only.

'Admiral Hardcastle, you addressed that question with your report and demonstration today. Frankly I didn't believe it was possible to seal off nearly one-fourth of America's airspace and sea approaches. You've shown me today, and in your report, that it is possible – economically and operationally. I have decided to take this proposal to the President for his review.'

Hardcastle and Becker couldn't help allowing a show of pleasure. Geffar held out her hand and Hardcastle accepted it.

'Congratulations, Admiral.'

The Vice President was gone for a long time. Hardcastle and Geffar stood with Elliott and McLanahan in the Presidential Suite of the Hyatt Brickell Point, drinking coffee poured by an armed White House steward.

'I have to admit, General Elliott – ' Hardcastle began. Elliott held up a hand to interrupt.

'Call me Brad, okay? I don't much go for formality.'

'Okay. Brad. I admit, like Long, I'm curious about you and your organization. It took a month before I even got permission to speak to you. I know you're located in southern Nevada, little else.'

'Unfortunately, I really can't get into it too much, Ian.

We flight-test different weapons systems, that's about all I can say.'

'Flight-test?' Geffar said. 'You must have done some pretty amazing whifferdills. Even Secretary Preston seemed a little in awe of you. Both of you.'

'As Patrick said, we're jet jockeys.'

'Were you by any chance involved with that plane crash in Alaska last year?' Geffar asked. 'The big bomber? I seem to recall – '

'Inspector.' Elliott's tone of voice had changed. More like a warning. 'Leave it alone.'

McLanahan broke the tension: 'Congratulations, Admiral Hardcastle. It looks like you're on your way.'

'You all did a spectacular job.'

'We followed your direction,' Elliott said.

Just then the door of the suite opened, and three Secret Service agents strode quickly into the suite, followed by the Vice President, his press secretary and personal secretary.

'Sorry to take so long. I defy any politician to ignore a shouted question, especially one by a network anchor.' He took off his jacket, loosened his tie. 'Admiral, anything else I should know?'

'Yes . . . after the first few months in operation, our new force might not seem to have a lot to do. But then – '

'Maybe you'd better explain.'

'The smugglers aren't stupid. They're resourceful, and they have damn near unlimited funds – if they can launder the cash they accumulate. Once they discover a force the size of what we are proposing is in place, they'll obviously try to avoid that area. So the initial stage of the unit, with one platform such as Hammerhead One, one shore base unit, six drones, six Sea Lion aircraft and ten fast patrol boats can patrol an area approximately five hundred miles. If that unit is located off Florida's southeast coast, as proposed, it can interdict air and sea traffic for a good part of south Florida. The smugglers will begin to circumnavigate south Florida. The seeming lack of activity with the new unit will no doubt rankle a lot of critics when they try to equate the number of busts made with the amount of money spent on the program.

'The same thing happened when the joint Customs/ Coast Guard unit established the aerostat radar pickets over Arizona and New Mexico, the area where most of the overland air smugglers concentrated. That program cost a billion dollars and netted only six smugglers in six months because the smugglers avoided the area. Two of the four aerostat units were later deactivated after they had been damaged or repaired, *and* smuggling activity promptly resumed full force in that area.

'This can't be allowed to happen to the Hammerheads,' Hardcastle said, fists clenched. 'As I've said, the south Florida area is where the highest concentration of smugglers will be found. They won't keep traveling the area if interdiction forces are stepped up. They'll bide their time, decrease shipment sizes, try other smuggling routes, to wait it out until public or financial pressure forces interdiction efforts to decrease. Then they'll drift back in and set up operations as before. If we go that route.'

'You keep mentioning this name, Hammerheads,' Martindale said. 'Who the hell are the Hammerheads? You make it up?'

'Not exactly. Back in Prohibition days the Coast Guard –then known as the Revenue Cutter Service and part of the Treasury Department, the same as the Customs Service – was given the principal responsibility for liquor interdiction all over the country. The Treasury and Customs agents were known as the "Revenooers" and the Revenue Cutter men were called the Hammerheads because of the big sledgehammers they used to break open rum barrels when they made a seizure.'

'They didn't exactly have a great reputation,' Sandra Geffar added. Hardcastle looked at her with some surprise. 'I had my office check when I first heard you use that term. The name Hammerheads was eventually given to a select Coast Guard unit that used military weapons and tactics to intercept the large mothership of smugglers known as blacks. Apparently they got the name Hammerheads not only because of the rum barrels they busted, but also because of the heads they busted.'

'You're well informed,' Hardcastle said, allowing a slight grin. 'The Hammerheads were rescue and lifesaving men and women that had been given a dirty, unpopular job. They were up against well-armed adversaries, many of them Americans, some even representing military forces of other nations – the British, French and Dutch were notorious liquor smugglers. Most of them had never aimed a gun at another human being until ordered to do it by the government. In a real sense it was kill or be killed for them . . . No matter what size vessel, no matter if it was damaged or on fire or sinking, they had to be ready not only to provide aid but to fight off murderous smugglers – sometimes on the same sinking boat. But what's your point, Inspector Geffar?'

'You're creating another Hammerheads unit, a hundred times stronger and better equipped than their 1926 counterparts – '

'I disagree,' Hardcastle said irritably. 'Strongly disagree.'

The two paused, looked at the Vice President.

'I'm familiar with Admiral Hardcastle's background,' Martindale said, glancing at the Coast Guard officer. 'We go back a ways.'

'How so, sir?' Geffar asked.

'Vietnam. I commanded a Navy patrol squadron, some old plywood boats going up and down the deltas. Death traps. Hardcastle and his squads were frequent passengers. Admiral Hardcastle was in bomb disposal then. We were always finding mines, booby traps, old weapons or bombs – the VC were using stuff left over from the French occupation forces. Pretty dangerous stuff – it would go off it you looked at it wrong.' He paused, remembering back. 'Bomb disposal. Shit detail.' The Vice President turned to Geffar. 'Mahogany Hammock. Both of you lost good agents in that gun battle, right?' Both nodded.

'It was a big surprise to us,' Geffar said. 'I've never seen the smugglers so well armed and organized.'

'It was the . . . incident that sort of seeded my proposal,' Hardcastle added. 'I just felt neither the Coast Guard or Customs was ready to respond to such a display of firepower.'

'And so the Hammerheads,' the Vice President said. 'Control of the skies and sea. Drones and sea platforms and hybrid manned airplanes. Twenty-first-century stuff . . . Look, both of you are strong advocates of your own particular agencies. Both of you are professionals, experts. Both of you are pilots, fixed and rotary wing. Both are veterans in your particular services.' He motioned to Geffar. 'Sandra's a better shot, though.'

'You've never seen me in the horseshoe pits,' Hardcastle said, but he knew Martindale was right.

'There's only one way Admiral Hardcastle's proposal is going to be effective and get over some congressional and public hurdles,' Martindale said, 'and that's if we present a united front. I know cooperation between Customs and Coast Guard hasn't always been the best, but each of you has to be willing to use your considerable influence and authority to show that we can effectively combine our forces to the benefit of our nation's drug-interdiction effort.

'The way I see it, most of the air and sea interdiction

assets of both the Coast Guard and Customs must eventually be unified under this new Department of Border Security. That means the Customs Service Air Branch effectively disappears in five years. How do you feel about that, Sandra?'

'My pilots are just as frustrated by the lack of leadership and the breakdown in cooperation as anyone. But this may be taken as a slap in the face by them. As Agent Long pointed out, they've been doing the job to the best of their ability and with their limited authority for decades. Some will feel this tells them they've failed.'

'Haven't you?' Martindale held up a hand. 'Well, that didn't come out right. My question is, can we convince them to support this new, tougher program? It will involve them more in pure drug interdiction and less in law enforcement. Don't you think they could be happy with that?'

Geffar nodded, a very tentative nod. 'I think so, I hope so, sir.'

'Good.' The Vice President turned to Hardcastle. 'All your Coast Guard C-model Falcons, your fast patrol interceptors, most of your medium-range, Island-class boats, your radar balloons – all get turned over to the Hammerheads, and a lot sooner than five years.'

'That's right. Most are transferred immediately.'

'Unfortunately, the real fight will be with Secretary Coultrane and Crandall, neither of whom like the idea of their budgets being slashed and their assets taken away to build this new drug-interdiction unit. But once the President gets behind the project, as I hope and expect he will . . .'

He glanced at Elliott and McLanahan. 'Whether by hook or by crook, accidental or planned, you've tied up with the hottest group of aviation experimenters and test pilots since the Wright Brothers' bicycle shop. How did you manage that, Admiral?'

'I read about General Elliott in *Air Force Magazine*,' Hardcastle said. 'I've had my eye on the V-22 ever since it rolled out two years ago, and then I heard that some unit called HAWC was flight-testing it. But when I tried to call the general's headquarters in Navada I got a steel door slammed shut in my face. A security lid had been placed on everything to do with HAWC like I've never seen before . . .'

'So that only piqued your interest,' Martindale said. 'You kept on going until you got to talk with someone.'

'Eventually.'

'Your persistence will pay off, I think,' Martindale said . . . 'I want both of you to spearhead this new organization, the Hammerheads,' he said. 'I need both of you. I know Admiral Hardcastle's position.' He turned to Sandra. 'Inspector Geffar? I know you've only been exposed to this for a very short time. You will want to know more and I'll see to it that you get all the information you need. But I need to take your name with me back to Washington as an advocate of this organization. I need to tell the President, Commissioner Crandall, the US Senate, and everyone in America that Inspector Sandra Geffar, the number-one drug buster in the US, is one hundred and fifty percent behind the formation of this new organization. What do you say?'

'How much participation can I expect in planning and organizing the Hammerheads?'

'Full and complete. As I understand it, Admiral Hardcastle's plan initially calls for two of these air-staging platforms, one on Florida's east coast, the other on the west coast in the Gulf. The platform we were on today will be the first one, the prototype of the Hammerheads' new base.

'We are looking at the founding cadre of officers for the Hammerheads right here in this room. I intend to nominate General Elliott as commander, Major McLanahan as his deputy, because of his previous close association with the general, Admiral Hardcastle, because of his extensive knowledge of the weapons, as director of development and strategy, and you, Inspector Geffar, as head of the first Hammerheads air-staging platform, for good and obvious reasons. The Admiral will take over the second platform when it comes on line.'

With that, he made a quick exit, cutting off unwanted flak. He figured he'd done his best by all concerned. Now it was time to get on with the program.

Chapter Four

Valdivia, Colombia
Several Days Later

Seventy miles north of Medellín, Colombia, on the main north–south São Francisco highway running from Santa Maria on Colombia's north coast all the way to Ipiales on the Ecuador border, was the small town of Valdivia. Until some ten years earlier, Valdivia had been known for its freshwater springs, its huge goat population – thirty goats for every man, woman and child within fifty miles – and the shrine to the Mother Mary at the place where she was reported to have visited a peasant family in the late eighteenth century. The shrine still stood, and one could still see crutches abandoned by pilgrims who came to be miraculously healed after tasting the mountain spring waters, as well as the altar that housed Colombia's most prized relic, a rock with the imprint of a human foot that was said to be that of the Mother Mary when she alighted in Valdivia from Heaven.

Now, the secluded grove of the shrine to the Mother Mary was little more than a prominent landmark for mysterious convoys of trucks driving north along the São Francisco highway from Peru and Ecuador. Go past the shrine out of Valdivia, follow the twisting, winding mountain-valley road for four miles, find the barbed-wire fence gate carefully hidden in the edge of the thick forest on the right, stop to open the gate. Whoever was working the gate's latch would find a warning totem – a goat skinned from head to tail, bloody and torn, with a sword through its

161

stomach, hanging from a tree in plain sight. It was usually effective enough to deter curious villagers and pilgrims, but if not, a gunner in a tree blind, armed with a state-of-the-art, Belgian-made 5.56 millimeter FN Minimi automatic machine gun and night-vision goggles would pick off intruders and their vehicles.

Once admitted past the outer perimeter guards and fences, every visitor was tracked electronically and visually every step of the way into the main compound. But once one reached the main compound itself, the exterior of the plant looked much like any other industrial park – a few row-houses for employees, schools for the children, neatly kept facades for administrative centers and manicured employee break-areas. All very normal, all very innocent looking.

All a deceptive facade. In the first few years of business the plant's owners had found it necessary to develop a cover – they had made it into a small paint and varnish manufacturing plant – and many of the props for that cover remained, including barrels of pigments and delivery trucks with the paint factory's logo on the side. But as more and more officials were enticed by *plomo o plata*, lead or silver – a bullet in the head or take the bribe – the cover was found no longer to be necessary except for the rare and often well-announced government sweeps intent on 'eradicating' the cocaine laboratories, mostly to show the United States in particular and the world in general their commitment to stopping drugs.

The narcotics-distribution center at Valdivia was a sophisticated processing and packaging center. Unlike other so-called laboratories, which were usually nothing more than grass huts deep within isolated forests, the Valdivia plant was a full-scale, high-volume operation. Coca paste, or base, processed by peasant farmers from Bolivia and Peru, was shipped or flown to Valdivia usually in the form of dark gray blocks resembling builder's bricks, or dried into a coarse gravel-like mixture and hidden in pigment barrels or cement bags. In the plant the coca paste was mixed with ether and acetone, then dried to form the fine white power, the cocaine. It took one ton of coca paste to make one hundred kilograms of high-grade cocaine, and the plant produced upward of two thousand kilos every month. It was the Medellín drug cartel's number-one processing facility.

Depending on the client's wishes, the prevailing price and the availability, the center prepared various grades of product – from refined near-pharmaceutical-grade cocaine to cocaine cut or diluted with other chemicals, sometimes leaving less than a hundred grams of cocaine in a one-kilogram sample. The cocaine was measured and packaged in airtight bags – usually one-kilo size easy to conceal and transport – and prepared for shipment.

Security at the Valdivia processing center was extra-ordinary. The private Cartel soldiers were better equipped than the Colombian army, or most armies anywhere in South America for that matter – they could even repel air attacks with heavy-caliber, optically aimed machine guns. Helicopters fitted with infrared scanners patrolled the sprawling fifty-thousand-acre facility, with troops especially trained and outfitted to search for any guerrillas trying to infiltrate the outer defenses and sneak inside the compound. The plant's owners and security guards had access to the Colombian government's Customs files and records notifying them who had been admitted across the borders and where they were headed, so as to help them detect any intruders or possible pre-assault operatives, especially from the United States. Even with occasional flurries of activity-for-show, the Cartel barons had little to worry about from the Colombian army. Most high-ranking government officials and military leaders were on the Cartel's payroll.

The well-concealed, ten-thousand-foot reinforced concrete runway at the Valdivia airfield could handle aircraft the size of heavy jet cargo planes, although mostly small planes were used to transport the drugs to other airfields or distribution points in Colombia, Venezuela, Peru, Ecuador, Panama, Nicaragua and Brazil, for eventual shipment to the Cartel's number-one customer – the United States.

It was transportation . . . getting the refined cocaine out of poorly patrolled, lax areas into better-guarded (for all its weaknesses) North America that Gonzales Rodriguez Gachez, the unofficial head of the Medellín drug cartel, was concerned with this morning as he sat in his office in the plant's administrative center. Dressed in motorcycle-racing leathers with tall knee-topping boots, padded elbow and hip protectors – Gachez got his own kicks from racing, not from cocaine – he bent to work adjusting the chain on his newest toy, an Italian eight-hundred-cc cafe racer.

Before the real money began pouring in his father had conducted business out of a hen house, and gauged the character of his men – and, the young Gachez was to learn later, even his children – by watching them watch the trained roosters fight. He could find out which could stomach watching the blood, the violence, the death, which tolerated it and which reveled in it; he could watch the men's drinking, gambling and womanizing habits.

Gachez had never enjoyed the cockfights, had attended them because his father wanted him to, but he always managed to hide behind his father's three-hundred-pound frame just as the feathers started to fly. But he was the youngest, and so not expected to have the intestinal fortitude of his elder siblings.

But Gachez learned well what else went on inside the hen house beside wagers and prize roosters torn apart – deals. Deals of all kinds, from agreements to buy a certain amount of hay for the coming winter months to marriage contracts for a father's unwed eighteen-year-old daughter to the murder of a Brazilian cowboy trying to sell some stolen cattle. No matter how raucous it got, they always seemed able to carry on a conversation between shouts of pain or pleasure. Young Gachez watched them shake hands, pat each other's shoulders and tip a glass of tequila or corn whiskey. Somewhere in among all the noise, a deal had been struck. And the youngest Gachez was fascinated. Along the way he also learned about friendship, loyalty and the value of alliances. He knew who his father's enemies were, who seemed to be his real friends, though the distinctions were not always clear.

When the manufacture and sale of cocaine began to heat up, Gonzales Gachez's older brothers were quick to get into the business, but not very careful in forming their alliances between the other wealthy families. Unlike the early West in the United States, when a rich man could own a huge ranch with little outside interference and seclude himself, owning acreage in tiny Colombia meant forming alliances, like forming tiny states or principalities. Colombian ranchers held onto their power and fortunes by banding together against rivals. The health and welfare of the alliance was important, something to be nurtured. The leader was usually the wealthiest member, but all had to profit or the alliance collapsed.

But the enormous wealth that Gonzales' older brothers brought in from the flourishing drug trade made them think they were beyond the alliance structure. They tried to form their own private armies, bringing in Indian mercenaries from Peru and Ecuador. The outsider's allegiance went to the highest bidder. He was without scruples, pagan, mostly not even Catholic, and Gonzales' older brothers tended to behave more like their hirelings than traditional Colombians. They seemed to feel safer behind the guns and knives of these outsiders than with the alliance, which was many times more powerful than any mercenary army they could raise.

The wars that followed took the lives of Gonzales' older brothers, but before the other landowners could wipe out the entire family Gonzales stepped in. He had attended a European-style university in Rio de Janeiro, could speak three foreign languages and had been in America and Europe. With shotguns literally pointing in his face, the young, handsome, articulate Gonzales Gachez persuaded the alliance to allow his family to rejoin. He did not beg, he did not plead for his life, he did not offer them money or land or anything – except loyalty. He understood that for these men loyalty, along with *machismo*, counted above all else.

This was twenty years ago. Now Gonzales Gachez was just over forty years of age. He had risen from that terrifying moment, standing at the business end of a twelve-gauge shotgun, to leader of the Medellín drug cartel, or so the American press like to call it, stirring up images of strangling monopolies like the OPEC oil cartel, the crime cartels of the Roaring Twenties, the booze-and-gambling gangs of old Chicago. Gachez and his associates considered themselves businessmen, Colombian ranchers. They were patriots, allies, identifying a product, evaluating its market potential, fulfilling that need. Americans were good for half-a-trillion dollars of narcotics yearly – surely it was only smart business to seek to satisfy the market of opportunity. That each of these self-styled ranchers and businessmen conspired to kill judges, lawmen, soldiers, legislators and competitors all over the world, including fellow Colombians, to ship their cargo of death was the cost of doing business. Like having a lawyer, Gachez liked to say.

Gachez now scraped mud off the lower kickplates and

wheel hubs as he inspected the chain on the motorcycle. His father had his roosters; he had his motorbikes. His father used to get bird shit all over the house knowing that someone would immediately clean it up for him – so it was with this mud. The minute he left the office someone would scrub the office. The more things changed, the more they stayed the same. As it should be, he thought.

The intercom on his desk buzzed. Well, his father never had to deal with *that*! Callers were given a glass of wine or strong coffee and asked to wait – the length of time directly proportionate to their rank and status. These days no one seemed to have any conception of that.

'I'm busy,' he called out toward the speakerphone.

'Transmission from Verrantes, Señor Gachez,' the secretary informed him.

'Put it on.' Gachez lit a cigar but kept on tinkering with the chain on the motorcycle. He heard the speakerphone click and snap to life as the scrambled transceivers synchronized themselves, followed by the distorted but intelligible voice of Colonel Augusto Salazar, late of the Cuban Revolutionary Air Force.

'What is it you want, Gachez?'

'I *want* to make a shipment. Tomorrow night. We'll have drop-coordinates available when you arrive. Set it up.'

'That's impossible,' Salazar said, the tension in his voice obvious. 'There are Coast Guard units surrounding this entire region – '

'I am not interested in your problems, Salazar. Get on it.'

'It would be very dangerous. The risks . . . you would stand to lose your entire shipment. Do you have so much you can afford to throw it away, señor?'

'We have no problem with product, Colonel.' And it was true – they had not reduced their production despite the recent impact on the Cuchillos' aircraft by the US Coast Guard. After all, didn't the product still go through?

Gachez's hand-picked distributors working south Florida were magicians, getting a thousand kilos of cocaine out of the Everglades in less than two hours while under attack by the United States Customs Service. The Cuchillo pilots showed some *cojones* too – the whole operation might have been blown had those young pilots not attacked the Customs Service helicopter.

They did, however, suspend air deliveries until the matter had burned itself out in the US press. But ground deliveries from the Valdivia plant couldn't keep pace with production, and they were beginning to develop stockpiles of cocaine – as much as a full month's worth of production for each Cartel member.

'I'm vulnerable as well, Colonel – I can't be caught with large amounts of product at this plant. I have nearly a month's worth of product ready for delivery. I need support immediately.'

The abrupt silence from Salazar's end told Gachez he had just made one of his few mistakes, revealing any vulnerability to Salazar. He knew his hold on the Cuban renegade officer was tenuous, although he pretended otherwise.

When Augusto Salazar was still in the Cuban Air Force, the chief of the Medellín Cartel could just about dictate terms to the Cuban officer. And after Salazar fled to Haiti, escaping the purge of officers that were found to be involved with drug trafficking, he very much needed Gachez's cooperation and money to set himself up on a huge estate in the central highlands of that tiny island country. Salazar and his group of pilots flew for fuel money and little more. There was no specific number of flights or tonnage that Salazar and his pilots had to move to repay the debt with Gachez – but they would know when the debt was paid.

In short order, following some dramatic flights across the

Caribbean Basin and the southeast United States, the ledger book changed from red to black. The debt that Salazar owed had been repaid in full, with interest – the Cuchillos, Salazar's amazing group of flyers, were that good.

Now, it had become strictly business, and that business relied on nothing more than money, planning and careful execution on both sides. Gachez, who knew he had just made a slip, thought he could hear the wheels turning in Salazar's greedy mind. His impression was confirmed when Salazar, his voice no longer strained and angry, said, 'I cannot do it for less than seven thousand American dollars a kilo. Half now, half on delivery, transferred by wire through your banks.'

'We have a contract . . .' Gachez's voice rose, despite efforts to remain cool. 'The firm agreement was five thousand a key, a million now and the rest on delivery. Don't try to renege, Colonel. It's bad business. Bad for one's health.'

'I am paid to take risks for you and your partners, but I will not take such extreme risks without compensation. Six per kilo, four million now, the rest after delivery . . . or you can start hitching your burros to your carts and wheeling your product out of the jungle yourself.'

Gachez was forced to remind himself he was not in a strong position to bargain. Five thousand a kilo was the going rate for a cocky, know-nothing *gringo* pilot with a broken-down, twin-engine plane – even at six thousand a kilo, he was getting a bargain from the Cuchillos, who flew modern planes, even jets, and who were some of the bravest, fiercest fighters he had ever seen. Plus, he needed the cooperation of Salazar's remaining contacts in the Cuban Navy to be sure they were nearby when the drop was made to the Cartel's distribution freighters. Those contacts, those Navy gunboats and Revolutionary Defense

Force patrols that just happened to show up at a drop as the American Coast Guard was moving in to intercept the smugglers, were truly invaluable.

'All *right*, Colonel, I will be generous in the interests of our relationship. Six thousand a key, two when your plane takes off from here, the rest after we are notified the transfer was made successfully.'

In a beat of silence Gachez worried that the bastard would try for more money. Until the distorted voice on the speakerphone replied, '*Cerrado*.'

'I want the transfer made tomorrow night.'

'Be patient, señor,' Salazar said – Gachez thought he could hear the son-of-a-bitch laughing at him through the scrambler's distortion. 'For six thousand dollars a kilo I can provide you with fast, accurate transportation for every gram of your product. How much is ready for shipment?'

'The usual,' Gachez replied. Even over the scrambled satellite transmission he was reluctant to say exact figures. The 'usual' amount shipped by the Cuchillos was around two thousand kilos divided between four to eight twin-engine airplanes. An entire shipment usually took a week or two to leave Valdivia – having a stream of eight King Air airplanes leaving the area would attract too much attention.

'Triple it,' Salazar said. 'Nice to do business with you again, señor.' And the line went dead.

Gachez swore. Triple it? Would Salazar actually try to ship out six thousand kilos? The risks in that were enormous – but the rewards could be even more so.

Of course, using the ex-Cuban military officer was a risk in itself, an even greater one, it seemed, each time. But it was too late to try to find another shipping alternative – the rest of the Cartel had agreed to come in with Gachez in using the Cuchillos. They would be *very* displeased and suspicious if Gachez dropped them now. If the other Cartel members heard that Salazar could ship three times the usual shipment, and that he, Gachez, had refused, it would look very suspicious indeed.

As Gachez began to arrange a conference with the other Cartel members, he could not help but remember the warning planted long about trusted outsiders. His brothers had once fallen into that trap, and they had paid the price for it.

Customs Service Air Branch, Homestead AFB, Florida
The Next Day

Senior Inspector Ronald Gates shook his head in puzzlement at Sandra Geffar's apparent lack of excitement about the new Hammerheads operation and her role in it as sketched by the Vice President. Gates was chief of the Customs Service Air Branch, Geffar's nominal boss. A Harvard Law School graduate, he was thirtyish, tall, distinguished looking, a man who looked dynamite standing in front of a big drug seizure and telling the world how effective his troops were.

A smart front man, but he didn't know the difference between a Cessna-210 and a Cessna Citation business jet, except perhaps their cost. Gates believed all airplanes smaller than a Boeing 727 were alike and would tend to mix them up when explaining, without benefit of script, the details of an interdiction operation to the press or Congress. Luckily, most people listening to him didn't know the difference either, and he always brought along someone who could help him out. Often that someone was Sandra Geffar.

'It sounds like a great opportunity,' Gates was saying. 'You'll be in on the ground floor of a whole new organization. New developments, new challenges.'

171

And more glory for you? she thought but didn't say. It was no secret that Gates aspired to loftier positions than his present one.

'Do you want to be a throttle jockey all your life? This is major, a whole new Cabinet-level agency, and you'll be one of the major players.'

'I didn't say I was against it, I'm just not popping my cork over it. Not yet.'

'Okay, okay. What's on for today?'

Geffar began showing him about the operations in progress, briefing him on what information they were receiving from intelligence sources and informants and how she was planning to respond to each. There were several major projects running, each involving suspected drug shipments from South America or the Bahamas. She showed him a map of the most current operation, an ongoing project that was scheduled to go into operation later that night.

Gates walked over to the map to study the route of flight as she pointed out the assets and manpower she was planning to put into action. She noted the blank face when she mixed 'Black Hawk' with 'Cheyenne' and 'Citation.' Be grateful, she told herself. What if he tried really to run things? And so counting her blessings, she thought of the new one suddenly given to her by the Vice President . . .

She and Hardcastle had left the Sheraton at the same time after the Vice President's surprise announcement about the Border Security Force and who would head its parts. Elliott and McLanahan had stayed behind. They were scarcely noticed as they walked through the lobby and out toward Biscayne Boulevard.

They had not said a word until Geffar began to head toward the hotel's parking garage.

'It's a good mix, Sandra, we'll build Hammerheads

together. It'll take both of us to make it happen. Without either one of us it won't happen. Martindale made that clear.'

She looked at him, nodded slightly but offered only a 'good night, Admiral,' and walked to her car. Her feeling was still jumbled, at least mixed . . .

'Sandy?'

Her attention came back to Gates.

'Something wrong?'

'No . . . I just thought I heard our King Air on final.'

'I see . . . I was wondering what Mayberry here stood for.'

'Yes. Mayberry RFD,' she said, rising and walking over to the large map on the Caribbean on her office wall. 'That's the name we gave this particular operation. One of the Cuban officers involved is named Gomez. One of our guys heard that, nicknamed the guy Gomer and we started using the code-name Mayberry every time someone heard this guy Gomez on the marine band scanner.'

'Cuban officers . . . ?'

'The Cubans are becoming more involved in smuggling operations every year,' Geffar said. 'Never mind all their talk about cracking down on smuggling, unless it gets so obvious it embarrasses them. We believe Gomer is captain of a Cuban Komar-class patrol boat operating out of Veradero military base on Cuba's north coast.'

'I thought the Cubans had cracked down on that. They executed that army general, Arnoldo Ochoa Sanchez, after being convicted for drug smuggling . . .'

'A show trial,' Geffar said. 'He was very popular with the military and with the people – there was talk of him being Castro's successor. That would have bumped Castro's brother Raoul out of the picture. Ochoa had to go, and in a way not to upset the military. Hanging a drug rap on him was the best way.

173

'We also started sharing intelligence data on smugglers, played right into their hands. We told the Cubans where *we* were looking and they used our own intelligence to help *their* smugglers avoid our radar pickets and patrols. Now Cuban gunboats are actually stationed near drug drop points at the edge of their territorial waters. They claim the gunboats keep the smugglers away, but what happens is the gunboat captains are paid to look the other way until we or the Coasties show up. When we try to move in, the gunboats move in too.'

'So what do you do with these Mayberry missions?'

'Follow the smugglers all night, mostly,' Geffar said dryly. She pointed to specks on the map. 'Planes from Colombia, Venezuela, Panama, or Peru drop shipments here, along the Sabana Archipelago on Cuba's north shore. The smugglers pick up the shipments, always in plain view of the Cuban gunboats, then hop around through all these tiny islands and reefs dodging Coastie patrols. They head toward the Bahamas or if they're really brave they'll try to zoom in toward the Keys or the Everglades.

'We watch and wait for one of these bozos to try to make a break for Florida or the Bahamas. We've charted a lot of air and surface activity recently that indicates they'll try a drop some time in the next few days. Nothing definite, but enough to focus in on this area . . . Why don't you come along, Ron? We're putting together a surveillance mission to start in the next few days. You can fly in the Nomad, which stays at high altitude and keeps an eye on everyone on the infrared scanner and the SeaScan radar. Or you can come with me in the Black Hawk.'

'The Black Hawk?'

'If the Nomad reports smugglers are heading north toward Florida or east toward the Bahamas we'll launch the Black Hawk, track them down. If we can we'll vector in a Coast Guard cutter and have them stop them at sea, but mostly we wait until they get closer to land – we usually can't rely on the Coasties to be around when we need them. We get authority to overfly the Bahamas, and we'll carry a couple of Bahamian constables so they can make the bust . . .'

Gates' color was not good. But he managed, 'Fine. I'll ride in the Nomad.'

It was the first time Ron Gates had ever agreed to fly on an actual mission. In fact, it would be his first flight on any Air Branch aircraft where he wasn't escorting a VIP.

'I think it's important for me to get some firsthand knowledge about what's going on. It's about time I got in on the action.'

She kept a straight face, wondering if his courage didn't have something to do with the sudden visibility this unit was getting in the White House.

'Okay,' she said. 'We'll start the mission in two days, running round-the-clock surveillance operations. The Nomad stays up for six hours – that allows plenty of fuel in case it has to begin a chase, so clear your calendar for the whole night. We'll meet here at 6:00 P.M., two days from today. You know where the Air Force enlisted dining hall is on base. You don't need to go to the briefing, but it might be interesting. I need to give you a safety briefing and fit you out with a life jacket' – his eyes narrowed at the words 'life jacket' – 'and we'll do that out by the Nomad on the ramp. That's the big turboprop plane out there. Looks like a little C-130. Big radar on the belly.'

Gates nodded, headed for the door.

Geffar sat alone in her office, clearing up some paper-work that had accumulated in her absence while recovering from the Mahogany Hammock mission and going over details of the mission in her mind. She'd had a little sport with Gates but in reality it was not going to be a laughing matter.

175

With the 250-gallon armored internal fuel tank, which took up all but six of the helicopter's twelve seats in the cabin, the Black Hawk had an operational radius of about 200 nautical miles. That usually allowed a flight of 200 miles at best endurance speed, at least an hour's worth of hovering and maneuvering in the target area and the return flight with almost no reserve fuel. But flying from Homestead to 'Mayberry' was 120 miles alone, and a protracted chase with smugglers from way out near Cuba could draw deeply on fuel reserves. If the chopper had to pursue smugglers to anywhere in the Bahamas Islands chain, it would be even riskier.

Even though the Black Hawk had the fuel to do the job, it was cutting it pretty close. It meant that as long as the smugglers were heading north, the Black Hawk could spend only a half-hour chasing before it would have to return to base – if the smugglers headed south to evade, the Black Hawk would probably have less than ten minutes' loiter time before having to high-tail it back to Homestead or Key West for gas. The Black Hawk was a reliable air machine, with its two huge turboshaft engines, but flying that far away from home ground, at night, was unnerving. Gates was lucky in his ignorance.

The Black Hawk was not ideal for these long overwater missions but it was the only chopper that had the range and capacity for the job – the Nomad, a big turboprop reconnaissance plane built in Australia for radar surveillance of sea targets instead of aerial targets like the Citations or Cheyennes, had good range but needed a long hard-surface runway to land on. The Black Hawk was the only choice. They would have to wait until the smugglers were very close to Florida or Andros Island before launching it.

It was times like this, Geffar thought, that they needed the damned Coast Guard. The Black Hawk could land on one of their big cutters and refuel and a few patrol boats would come in handy if they did observe a drop –

It hit her then . . . Hammerhead One. That huge oil platform was still out there, about forty miles southeast of Key Largo in the Strait of Florida. Its position could not be better: forty miles closer to both Andros Island and Veradero, Cuba, than was Homestead Air Force Base. It had sea-and-sky-surveillance equipment set up on board, and its huge deck could certainly accommodate a Black Hawk helicopter . . .

Or a Sea Lion aircraft. Or both.

She'd better see Hardcastle soon as possible.

The White House, Washington, DC
The Same Day

As Sandra Geffar hurried north toward Miami for her important meeting with her Coast Guard counterpart, another, more fateful meeting was just beginning in the Oval Office.

The President of the United States greeted Senator Robert Edwards, the Senate Republican minority leader, like a long-lost brother, putting one hand over their clasped hands. 'Good to see you, Bob,' the President said. He motioned him to the light brown leather sofa, which was arranged around the walnut coffee table on the south side of the Oval Office along with the President's deep wing-back chair and a few other leather chairs. 'Sandwiches and coffee. Take a load off. Please.' Edwards shook hands with Cabinet secretaries Preston, Coultrane, Secretary of the Treasury Floyd McDonough, Special Advisor on Drug Control Policy Samuel T. Massey, Senator Mitchell Blumfeld, the senior senator from Florida, and finally Vice President Martindale.

Once arranged, the White House photographer came in and, as usual, took photos of the men gathered around the finger sandwiches and china coffee service; although not always publicized, an official photo was taken of each and every meeting in the White House. Coffee was poured for all by a smiling, white-jacketed steward. A few of those having coffee reached for the delicate china creamer with the thin blue ribbon tied on the handle – this, as every guest to the Oval Office knew, was not the cream, not the sugar or the non-dairy lightener, but the pot with the Irish cream liqueur. They poured various amounts of the thick, sweet liqueur in their cups – all but Secretary Preston, who rarely indulged in alcohol at all – as they chatted pleasantries to each other for several minutes. It was all part of the ritual of doing business in the White House; it had been done like this, with a few modifications, ever since there was an Oval Office.

The men were brushing away stray crumbs from the first few seafood sandwiches when the President motioned to his chief of staff, who opened the door to the outer office. Seconds later, a pretty redhead stenographer came in and quickly situated herself a discrete distance away from the coffee table, not too far so she couldn't hear but far enough – a distance directed by the President through his chief of staff – so as to not catch murmured comments between the participants. The arrival of the stenographer signaled the end of lunch, but everyone in the room was astute enough to see what was going on and get ready to get down to business by the time the stenographer's long, rose-colored fingernails were poised over her keyboard. At a nod from the President, Vice President Martindale sat up straight in his chair across from the President, cleared his throat quietly, and set his coffee cup down on the table. The delicate 'CLICK' of the china cup on its saucer immediately silenced the low murmur of voices around the table; in the stately confines of the historic Oval Office, that tiny sound was more effective than the loudest gavel.

'Thank you, Mr President, gentlemen,' Martindale began. 'As coordinator for the President's narcotics control policy I wanted to review the progress of the ongoing program with you and see if we can come up with a united policy for the future. Drug abuse is on the rise. The rise of drug shipments into the United States indicates a rise in the offensive nature of drug smugglers, witness the attacks on Coast Guard and Customs Service interdiction forces.

'Intercepting and stopping aircraft and vessels suspected of carrying illegal contraband is a big problem. Measures *must* be taken.' Some previously fixed-in-place happy smiles disappeared. Especially those of the Secretaries of Treasury and Transportation, McDonough and Coultrane.

'Our drug-interdiction effort has two major faults: not enough resources – aircraft, ships, and manpower – to do the job; and most important, not enough coordination between the federal agencies to do the job – specifically the Coast Guard and the Customs Service. Recently I have received a lengthy, detailed proposal from a Coast Guard Admiral on how the drug-interdiction assets of the Coast Guard and the Customs Service can be combined into one new and different unit that would take over all drug-interdiction responsibilities from the coastline and borders out to the United States' legal boundaries, its territorial limits. I asked for a demonstration to view this organization in operation and talk with the author of the proposal, Rear Admiral Ian Hardcastle, commander of the Coast Guard Seventh District in Miami. I also had a chance to speak with Inspector Sandra A. Geffar, commander of the Customs Service Air Branch in Miami. Air Force General Bradley Elliott and Major Patrick McLanahan were also there. In fact, it was Elliott's organization that supplied most of the hardware in Admiral Hardcastle's test. You're all aware of

General Elliott, Major McLanahan and their recent . . . operations.' There were a few surprised glances around the table – most had heard of General Elliott and his remarkable mission, knocking out a Soviet laser installation, the Old Dog, or some such – by rumor only.

'I've told you my feelings about Admiral Hardcastle's project and I've discussed them with the President. He agrees that such an organization dedicated exclusively to drug interdiction and border security operations is necessary and should be implemented as soon as possible.'

In answer to expected concerns about shooting down civilians and so forth, mostly masking bureaucratic turf-protection, Martindale went on: 'I've *seen* Admiral Hardcastle's forces in action,' the Vice President said. 'They can read aircraft tail numbers, follow aircraft by remote control, measure course and altitude with precision. Yes, mistakes could happen, but I'm very impressed with the technology *and* its application. I really think they can do it. And it's not just the hardware, but the restricted airspace plans he's devised – simple and straightforward. He wants to corral all air and sea traffic into specific corridors and past radar and platform-based checkpoints, like cattle being led through chutes to their pens. If someone goes outside the corridor without permission they chase the guy down and intercept him.'

'And that's when he gets shot down?' the President asked.

'Only if the guy refuses or fails to respond to signals given him by the intercepting aircraft or vessel. Unless they find a reason to believe he's not a smuggler, Hardcastle proposes that they will *not* allow any unidentified aircraft or vessel to cross the borders . . .'

Secretary of Transportation Coultrane complained that the procedures would be too difficult to spell out. Defense

Secretary Preston said he'd prefer not to become involved in drug interdiction, the military should not be involved.

'No problem,' Samuel Massey, the 'drug czar,' said. 'It's time to try an all-out interdiction program. If the stuff starts getting scarce or expensive, if they can't buy it or sell it so easily, maybe our other programs will kick in and become more effective.'

The President cut it off. 'I want this program put into action. I'm encouraged by what's been reported to me by Mr Martindale and I think we have the ability and the resources to do the job.'

'Where are we going to get the money?' Secretary McDonough protested.

'The proposal drawn up by Admiral Hardcastle spells out where the money comes from,' the Vice President said. 'And you know it, Mr McDonough – initial investment of two hundred million from the Defense Contingency Fund to activate the unit in the southeast and place three platforms in operation; eight hundred million per year from Defense to procure the V-22s, drones and radar gear; three hundred million per year from Treasury, mostly in the form of aircraft, vessels and manpower from the Customs Service' – McDonough groaned aloud at that – 'and seven hundred million per year from Transportation for aircraft, vessels and manpower, mostly from the Coast Guard. These funding levels would continue until all drug interdiction operations are transferred from Treasury, Transportation and Defense.'

'Defense can afford those kinds of assets,' McDonough argued. 'Treasury can't.'

'After nearly thirty years trying to stop drug trafficking,' the Vice President said, 'along comes a man who puts together a demonstration of a new organization that *works*. I believe it deserves full support.'

'Any other comments?' the President asked. No replies,

only a few empty stares and a couple of shaking heads. 'Very well, I will draft a memo to all departments outlining the Administration's plan to put this proposal into action.'

The President turned to the Senate Republican leader from Texas. 'Senator Edwards, Justice is drafting a bill to amend Title 53 and create the Department of Border Security. Senator Blumfeld has already pledged his support for the measure and as the senior senator from Florida, will sponsor it in the Senate. But I would appreciate your co-sponsorship.'

Edwards nodded, but his face was impassive.

'I still have reservations, Mr President,' McDonough said. 'Give me and my staff some time to draft a counter-proposal, one that would be far less disruptive of the existing system – '

'Floyd, let's get on with this, all right?' the President said, rubbing his eyes. 'I like this proposal. It sends a very clear message to the smugglers that we mean business. It does away with a lot of the bureaucratic crap floating around everything we try to do, especially in drug interdiction. Legal says it can fly. The Senate minority leader is willing to back it on the floor, and I think a lot of the majority will too if they know what's good for them. I know it takes something away from your people but last I heard we're all on the same damn team. I need a united showing on this one.'

'I urge the Vice President to reconsider the proposal, re-evaluate it,' McDonough said quickly, ignoring the look of anger on the President's face, 'and resubmit it at the earliest possible time. If this is not done I wish to go on record opposing the proposal in its present form.'

'Thank you very much for your candid opinion, Mr McDonough,' the President said, snapping off each word like an alligator chewing a mackerel. 'Any other comments?' He didn't wait long for a reply. 'This meeting is adjourned. Thank you all very much.'

The President got to his feet and took a step toward McDonough. 'You signed on with me in the good times – I expect loyalty at *all* times. I heard your opinions, I considered them. I made my decision based on *all* the recommendations from my advisors. Now, I expect you to do your job. All clear, Floyd?'

'I'm sorry, sir. I can't support this proposal. My resignation will be on your desk within the hour.' He turned, squeezed past the other Cabinet members and the Senator minority leader, and strode out of the Oval Office.

Good, the President thought, now I don't have to fire the son-of-a-bitch.

Hammerhead One Staging Platform
Two Days Later

A light, warm rain was falling as Customs Agent Rushell Masters maneuvered his Black Hawk helicopters over the north landing pad on the huge Hammerhead One platform. A good breeze was blowing from the southwest but Masters had been landing on oil platforms, small helipads, jungle clearings and rooftops for twenty years.

To mask its presence, except for required anchor and anti-collision lights, Hammerhead One had been dark until Masters approached the platform. When he was three miles out, following the platform's navigational radio beacon, the lights were suddenly turned on.

'Mother of God,' Masters exclaimed over his interphone. 'That's the biggest damned oil platform I've ever seen.'

Geffar said, 'The company that built Hammerhead One has a bigger one called King, and the Saudis have an even bigger one in the Persian Gulf.'

Nevertheless, the sight was remarkable, as if Times

Square in New York or Fremont Street in Las Vegas had been transplanted out into the Straits of Florida. The platform's four landing pads were illuminated, and bright red-and-white warning strobes indicated the location of Hammerhead One's radar, radio, satellite and data-link antennae cluster. The six-story engineering, maintenance, and living spaces beneath the roof were clearly visible now. The designated landing pad was rimmed with a bright strobe, blue circumference lights and a triangle-shaped illuminated azimuth and drift indicator that was plainly visible even from several hundred feet in the air.

Masters brought the chopper gently in for a touchdown, the chopper was secured by Coast Guard plane captains with quick-release cables, and Masters began shutting down the big helicopter. The huge searchlights were extinguished just as Masters, Geffar and their crew began exiting from the helicopter; only half-height 'ballpark' lights were used to illuminate the Black Hawk's landing pad for the benefit of the chopper's crew chiefs servicing the machine. Masters, Geffar, two Customs Service agents and two Bahamian constables were led to the elevators to be taken below by Admiral Hardcastle wearing a bright yellow raincoat and yellow baseball cap with a strange emblem on it.

'I can't get over this facility, Admiral,' Masters remarked as he took off his Customs Service baseball cap and shook the rain from it. It wasn't until then that Hardcastle noticed the burn scars that creased almost the entire right side of Masters' face, neck and shoulders – the remnants of the attack at Mahogany Hammock. Masters noticed Hardcastle's expression. 'To coin a phrase, sir, it only hurts when I laugh.'

Hardcastle nodded. 'I'm glad you're up and around. You handled that Black Hawk as if you've been landing out here for years.'

They exited the elevator, hung up wet raingear on hooks in the corridor and headed toward the converted conference room.

'Well, we've had our first casualties by the Hammerheads,' Geffar said to Hardcastle as they were led through an office where coffee and sandwiches were ready.

'I heard,' Hardcastle replied, taking a mug of coffee. 'The Secretary of the Treasury *and* the Customs Commissioner resigned. Who's going to take their place?'

'Last word I got was Geraldine Rivera, the OMB director, was going to be nominated for Treasury,' Geffar said, 'and Ron Gates was first choice for Customs commissioner. I talked him into riding along with us one of these nights – he'll be aboard the Nomad tailing anyone heading north out of Cuba. It'll be his first real mission with us – it's like he suddenly got religion.'

As they were hanging up their coats, Geffar picked up Hardcastle's cap and examined the insignia on it. The peak had a vertical profile of a hammerhead shark on it in black, with the large eye stalks on the head at the bottom and the large fins at the top. Extending horizontally from the shark was a pair of wings.

'Someone's been doodling, I see,' Geffar said.

'Just an idea I had,' Hardcastle said.

Hardcastle reached up into an overhead cupboard and removed another cap – this one bore the gold scrambled-eggs oak leaf on the brim signifying a vessel commander. He handed it to Geffar. 'This one's yours.'

Sandra took the cap, examined it, then without a word hung her blue Customs Service cap on a hook, put her back-pocket crush on the brim of her new cap and slipped it on.

Hardcastle motioned the newcomers up five steps onto a higher tier. 'As you can see, and for the benefit of you who haven't been on board before, we've done a little remodeling in this control center. The primary operations and UAV control consoles are down there. We've got two Coast Guard technicians manning the consoles now. The screens we'll use to get pictures from the scene are newer and larger high-definition monitors, with better resolution and higher quality than the regular big-screen TVs we had before. Up here are the commander's and deputy's seats . . .'

'Where's General Elliott and Major McLanahan?' Geffar interrupted.

'Called to Washington,' Hardcastle told her. 'None of the HAWC people are here. They gave my people a quick lesson in how to use this gear – most of it is computerized and highly automatic, thank God. The Sky Lion drone is on board but we won't use it unless absolutely necessary . . .'

He punched a button on the commander's console, and the left large-screen monitors changed to show a well-lit hangar. In the center of the hangar floor was the V-22C Sea Lion tilt-rotor aircraft. 'As you can see, we have the V-22 on board as well, and we can have it on deck in five minutes.'

'Is it armed?'

Hardcastle nodded.

Masters looked at Geffar. 'Armed? That V-22 is *armed*?'

'The V-22 carries heat-seeking missiles,' Hardcastle said, 'capable against either aerial, ground or sea targets. It also carries a M230 Hughes Chain Gun.' Even Rushell Masters raised an eyebrow at that.

Geffar quickly added, 'We won't be using the V-22 tonight.' Masters looked at the image of the V-22 with a mixture of amazement and delight – obviously the thought of using an armed aircraft against smugglers appealed to him. And as Geffar and Hardcastle watched him, with his horrible burns and scars, they could understand why.

'On the right-hand screen is the radar display from

Diamond,' Hardcastle said, 'a Coast Guard cutter-based aerostat unit. We have him stationed just east of Cay Sal Bank in the Santaren Channel, about fifty miles southeast of our position. Diamond has been reprogrammed to scan for both sea and air targets, so we have no E-2 or E-3 radar planes in on this operation – the weather's a bit marginal anyway, and I think the Air Force is a little skittish about putting an E-3 in the area after that Coast Guard Falcon was attacked. We can keep Diamond on station for four days – after that it's scheduled to go back to Miami Beach.'

Hardcastle motioned to the commander's high-backed seat, similar to the chairs found on the bridge of Navy warships. 'Yours, Sandra. Want to take over now?'

Geffar looked at him. 'Jumping the gun, aren't you? As of the moment I'm the Customs Service task force commander, and this is a Customs surveillance and interdiction operation with Coast Guard support. The difference is we're fifty miles closer to the action, thanks to this platform. We're not Hammerheads yet . . .' But we're getting there fast, she thought.

'We have Omaha Three-Four, the Nomad radar plane, heading south to take up a position north of Veradero, Cuba. He'll be leap-frogging with Omaha Three-Five as his fuel status changes. We're the forward unit, Omaha Three-One. We have one backup chopper, Omaha Three-Two, but he's also scheduled for another ongoing mission so he may or may not be available.' Geffar turned to Hardcastle. 'Do you have a map of the area?'

He entered commands on the commander's console keyboard and instantly a full-color map of the south Florida and Caribbean region snapped onto the left HDTV monitor. Hardcastle handed Geffar what looked like a small pen and showed her how to use it. She touched the fourteen-inch screen on the commander's console with the soft tip of the pen, and an arrow appeared on the left screen pointing to the spot she touched on her screen.

Geffar shook her head. 'Okay. Mayberry point is right . . . here.' She hit a button that allowed her to draw a spot where drug drops were usually made. 'Ten miles northeast of Veradero military base, just inside Cuban waters.' She drew a line across the Nicholas Channel, through Cay Sal Bank and across the Santaren Channel and the Great Bahama Bank toward Andros Island. Hardcastle hit a button and the computer drew the present position of the Coast Guard aerostat cutter Diamond just a few miles north of where Geffar had drawn her line.

'This is the usual track intelligence says these boats take after rendezvousing at Mayberry. They usually divert a little south, down along Anguilla Cays at Cay Sal Bank, then in a zigzag pattern toward Andros Island. We're not sure where they're headed until they're well into the island. This time, though, we're going to find the bastards and nail 'em.

'They *could* move north, up Cay Sal to Elbow Cay, then in toward the Keys,' Geffar went on. 'It looks like Diamond may not be in position to track them if they move north or if they try to send some decoys – they won't move further west toward Key West, we know that . . .'

'Send the Nomad after anything moving north,' the deep voice of Rushell Masters suggested. 'The aerostat can help us track whatever, moving toward the Bahamas. We have a FLIR on the Black Hawk – that'll help us too.'

'Agreed,' Geffar said. 'We'll commit the Nomad to track anything heading northbound. If they use more boats – well, we'll just have to do the best we can.' She glanced at Hardcastle.

'The Sky Lion drones easily track any stragglers or decoys,' he said.

'We're not authorized to use the Sky Lion, Admiral . . .'

'We can data-link through the Nomad and run an automatic intercept,' he said. 'If we lose the Nomad we can run the Sky Lion out on a data-link from Diamond until the drone's sensors pick up.'

'Admiral, you gave me the cap. We'll use our assets, period . . . That's the plan, then. We'll be on for the next twenty hours, and then rotate with Curt's crew. Now we wait until the Nomad gets something for us. You can look around the platform but be ready to go when we page you.'

Hardcastle and Geffar sat at the command console and watched Diamond's radar display on the right-hand HDTV.

'How do I talk with the Nomad crew?'

'Comm screen is here,' Hardcastle told her, pointing to a smaller ten-inch screen to the left of the main monitor. The screen had four columns of rectangles with a label and frequency for each box. Hardcastle handed Geffar a lightweight headset. 'All the channelized freqs for this mission are displayed on this screen. You just touch the screen to talk. Touch this button in the lower right corner to call up more frequencies – air traffic control, NORAD, the sheriff's department – we've got five hundred different UHF, VHF, HF, CB and FM frequencies programmed into the computer.'

Geffar touched the rectangle labeled 'NOMAD OMAHA 34.' She watched as the rectangle blinked a few times and a message on the top of the screen flashed, 'SECURE SYNC,' indicating that the secure frequency circuits were locking in to the other receiver. When it changed to a solid white, she spoke: 'Three-Four, this is Three-One.'

She heard the soft squeal and hiss as the other transmitter completed its own security synchronization, then: 'Three-One, this is Three-Four. Go.'

Geffar was about to ask for their position, but one glance

at the left HDTV told the story – when the Nomad crew keyed their microphone a tiny green square and data block on the area map blinked on showing the Nomad's location to be about twenty miles north of Veradero, Cuba – along with its altitude, airspeed, and heading. 'Say status,' she said instead.

'In the green,' the Nomad's pilot reported. 'Preparing to enter orbit now.'

'Move farther north out to the edge of your scanning radius,' Geffar said. 'If Gomer shows up he'll be able to pick you up on his radar. We've got a pretty good eyeball on Mayberry.'

'Okay. Three-One. We'll move up to BRONCO and set up shop there.' Point BRONCO was Elbow Cay. It was a perfect position – the Nomad's SeaScan radar would fill in gaps between Hammerhead One's limited radar to the northeast, the Coast Guard aerostat Diamond to the east and southwest, and the aerostat unit at Key West to the west, and it could still watch Cuba's northern coast for signs of any activity.

Geffar sat back and studied the display as the Nomad aircraft moved north to its new orbit. She then hit the comm button labeled SLINGSHOT. 'SLINGSHOT, this is Omaha Three-One, radio check.'

'Three-One, this is SLINGSHOT.' A data block appeared over Miami on the map. 'Read you loud and clear. Ident and say position.'

'Three-One is not airborne,' Geffar replied. 'We are presently secure at Hammerhead One awaiting traffic.'

'Say again, Three-One?' the controller at SLINGSHOT radioed back. 'You're *where*?'

'Hammerhead One.' There was a long pause on the radio. 'Those turkeys,' Geffar murmured to Hardcastle. 'They were briefed on this platform . . .'

'Three-One, authenticate Whiskey for me.'

'For God's sake.' Geffar sighed, touched the screen. 'Three-One authenticates one-niner-niner-five. Get with it, guys – you were briefed this morning.'

The pause was a bit shorter this time: 'Good authentication, Three-One. My mistake.' He still didn't sound too sure but was willing to trust anyone who gave him the Air Branch commander's coded reply. 'Negative traffic at this time. Will advise. Over.'

'Roger. Three-One out.' Geffar then checked in with Diamond. Everything seemed to be working well.

'Anything we've overlooked?' Hardcastle asked as he and Geffar settled in front of their electronic 'eyes.'

'I don't think so. We could always use more choppers out here but we're committing all of the Miami Air Branch's Black Hawks on this one operation. We're maxed out.' She took a sip of coffee. 'Everything's in place. Now we sit and wait.'

Valdivia, Colombia
The Next Morning

Salazar's arrival in Valdivia the previous evening created a stir anything but pleasing to Gachez and the other Cartel representatives. Instead of the usual flight of three or four small- to medium-sized cargo planes that usually touched down on Gachez's private runway, only one arrived this time – but it was by far the largest aircraft that had ever landed in Valdivia.

It was an Antonov-12 cargo plane, the largest Soviet-made turboprop aircraft available for export to other countries. It had been repainted in dark camouflage green with a small Cuban flag on its vertical stabilizer. The huge cargo plane made a picture-perfect touchdown on the Valdivia runway, stopped short of midfield and taxied into a large parking area at the edge of the secluded airfield.

Gachez watched in silence as Salazar and his aide Hermosa exited the plane. Salazar, wearing his typical riding outfit, all but swaggered over to where Gachez and his bodyguard were standing and waved the Cartel chief a casual salute with a leather riding crop.

'What's this, Salazar? What in hell is *that*?'

'That, señor, is your salvation.' Salazar motioned toward it just as a group of his soldiers deplaned carrying dark green camouflage netting and erector poles. They began stringing the netting over and across the plane. 'My pride and joy and the solution to your problems. A recent acquisition from my former colleagues in the People's Republic of Cuba. We will deliver as much product as you like on board and deliver it anywhere within fifteen hundred kilometers.'

'That monstrosity can be detected on radar hundreds of kilometers away,' Gachez said. 'It's an easy target – '

'It is also the only way you will get any product delivered in the near future. The American Coast Guard has established a picket across the Straits of Florida and the western Bahamas – '

'That's why you make the drop in Cuban waters,' Gachez said. 'We enjoy protection in Cuban waters – '

'But your product will go nowhere,' Salazar said. 'They can concentrate firepower in one area, possibly two or three different areas. The best chance we have to beat their cordon is to make several drops in numerous locations at the same time, and the only aircraft that can haul the quantities you need and make the trip is *this* one.'

Gachez was still fuming – Salazar seemed out of control. Out of *his* control, anyway . . . A car drove up to take Gachez and the others to the administration center, but it was clear that the drug kingpin wasn't ready to leave. 'What do you mean, several drops? You don't make the plans here, Salazar. *I* do.'

'But it is *my* men that fly the planes,' Salazar said. 'It is *my* men who will suffer if they are caught. I bring you the best way to do the job, Señor Gachez. If you do not want my help, I will take my soldiers and my plane and leave.'

It was true, Gachez thought grimly. Salazar clearly was tired of playing messenger boy and was trying to take control. But at least for the moment he felt he still had the upper hand. 'All right, tell me your grand idea.'

'Very simple, señor,' Salazar said, and motioned to Hermosa, who took out a chart from a briefcase and spread it on the hood of the car, then shined a flashlight on it. 'Instead of one drop at the usual point in the Archipelago de Sabana, we stage several drops.' He indicated the marked points on the map. 'First, we make the usual drops along the Camaguey and the Sabana, as planned. This may draw off any Coast Guard patrols waiting for us along the north coast of Cuba. I then take the shipment toward Cay Sal Bank. We set up three drop points there. After that, drops along Andros Island, Ragged Island Range, Mayaguana Passage, Great Inagua Island and Silver Bank Passage. When the shipment is depleted I recover in Verrettes.'

'Ten drops?' Gachez said. 'All in *one* night?'

'The Coast Guard will be confused,' Salazar said, waving a hand at Hermosa to take the chart away. 'Even if they have the ability to catch one or two of your men, the rest will slip away. Instead of the measly twenty- or fifty-kilo containers we normally carry on the smaller planes, you divide your shipment into ten loads and divide each load into one-hundred-kilo parcels with flotation and recovery gear – '

'One hundred kilos!'

'Your men should be able to handle that size container even in a small racer,' Salazar said. 'In a larger vessel, a freighter, it will be a simple matter. Our plane will not circle any area to make drops. We make one run in the designated area and leave.'

Gachez's anger was slowly running out. The idea had merit. 'I will need to contact my men and position them for the drops. It may take several days.'

Salazar shrugged. 'Take your time. The longer you wait, the more likely that the Americans will relax their pickets.' He laced his fingers behind his head and put his feet up on Gachez's desk. 'I would also investigate your organization for an intelligence leak or informant, señor. The Americans have obviously received information that a drop was imminent.'

'*My* organization!' Gachez told the infuriating ex-Cuban officer. 'If there is a leak, colonel, it is in *your* organization.'

'My men are totally loyal to me,' Salazar said. 'They are the best pilots in the world and proud Cuban soldiers. They would never betray their loyalty to me or their country.'

'I have heard how you enforce your loyalty,' Gachez said. 'A mock trial, a knife in the back by so-called outraged patriots. Yours is a gang of terrorists, señor, and you prey on your own just as you do on others. But that is of no concern to me as long as our contracts are followed and security is maintained. Look elsewhere, however, for security leaks. It may be coincidence that the Coast Guard has a patrol in the Caribbean at this particular time. In any case, no one knows where the drops will be made at the time of takeoff except me. I alert the entire network on the day of the drop but I advise no one that a drop will be made at their location until *minutes* before the drop is made.'

'You can still have a serious breach – '

'Perhaps so, colonel,' Gachez interrupted. 'Yet *I* did not devise a complicated plan for a massive twenty-thousand-kilo delivery – *you* did. I never draw charts or carry maps – *you* do. Tell me – how long ago was this mission of yours planned, and how closely does that coincide with the arrival of the American patrols?'

Salazar's smile faded. There was really no way to put the blame on either side without finding the informant himself, of course. Gachez's words, however, made sense. But a spy in the Cuchillos? Impossible . . .

'The mission must be cancelled,' Field Captain Enrique Hermosa decided. 'It is our only option.'

Salazar shook his head as he ran a short, thin throwing knife across an oiled gray-green whetstone. Hermosa stared at his superior, then once again went over to the chart. 'Our latest reconnaissance flight shows the Coast Guard cutter between the eastern edge of Cay Sal Bank and Mangrove Cay on Andros Island. The cutter carries an aerostat radar balloon that has a radar range of nearly two hundred kilometers . . .'

'I heard you, captain,' Salazar said, wiping the blade clean and replacing it in its sheath in his right riding boot. They were meeting with the Antonov-12 cargo plane's crew of three pilots, flight engineer, senior loadmaster, two assistant loadmasters, two armed soldiers and gunner for the plane's 23-millimeter anti-aircraft gun mounted in the tail blister. The crew was sipping tequila and whiskey provided by Gachez as they examined the proposed route.

'I also heard you report the transmissions we were able to intercept between this vessel and an aircraft,' Salazar continued, 'which you presume to be a Customs Service or Coast Guard tracking plane also operating in the vicinity.' Hermosa nodded. 'You have surmised therefore that this plane is working in conjunction with the cutter.'

Hermosa was about to speak but Salazar raised a hand. 'Hermosa, if the US Customs Service and Coast Guard both are operating in this area they must have received intelligence about our operation. It is also strange that our

195

agent in Florida City chooses this particular time to go incommunicado on precisely the day I need to know the aircraft status at Homestead Air Force Base.'

'Our agent went to ground the day the American Vice President came to Miami, sir. There were Secret Service agents at every toll booth from Fort Lauderdale to Homestead. His forged green card would not have held up to close scrutiny by federal authorities.'

Salazar shook his head. 'The Americans still haven't forgotten the downing of their patrol aircraft and Customs assault team. If they've received any word on our activities they will be out in force. This delivery is worth one hundred and twenty million dollars to us. I want a way to make sure it gets through.'

'We can't insure something like that,' the Antonov-12 pilot, Major Jose Trujillo said, 'especially with a plane like the Antonov-12 – it's too large and too cumbersome to fly at low altitudes and try to sneak under radar – '

'Not that it will do us any good,' his flight engineer added. 'Not with those aerostat units that can track us every kilometer we fly all across the route, no matter what altitude.'

Trujillo downed a shot of tequila and chased it with cold beer. 'We fly the mission, stay out of American airspace and hope they don't shoot us down. What we need is air cover of our own . . .'

Salazar's eyes widened at the pilot's words. 'What did you say, Jose?'

'I was just remembering back to Angola, sir,' Trujillo said. 'Flying escort missions for Luanda's government, such as it was. All we had were MiG-17s and a couple of MiG-23s, but it was the best flying we've ever done. Wide open skies, easy ground targets – '

'Fighter escort . . .' Salazar said. 'Send a fighter to accompany a drug shipment?'

Trujillo's eyes sparkled with anticipation. 'It would be easy to plan. We have our two training MiG-21s. But we have no external fuel tanks and no weapons for them except a few hundred rounds of ammunition for the cannons – '

'We can get weapons, spare parts and fuel tanks through the Haitian government,' Salazar said. 'As military commander of the central district I have the authority – and with our offshore accounts, the transactions will be untraceable . . . Yes, you have given me the answer. I think I now have a way our shipment can be made with safety . . .'

Hermosa had been ignored, overlooked in the exchange that followed, standing inconspicuously nearby, waiting for orders, pouring beer and tequila for the group. But his ear was tuned, and his busy mind was taking it all in . . . Use fighter planes as escorts for drug shipments? Shoot down Customs planes? Colonel Salazar was becoming obsessed with power. The integrity of the organization was threatened . . .

What to do? Save him from himself. Tip off the Coast Guard and Customs . . . ?

Hammerhead One Staging Platform
Later That Evening

Geffar settled into her seat and activated the communications monitor. It was getting easier to operate the system now after three days working with it. On the screens before her were aircraft and ships with tiny highlighted data blocks belonging to Customs Service and Coast Guard aircraft operating in their region. Three days ago it was confusing; now her fingers danced across the console keyboard, retrieving bits of information and swapping screens between the high-definition monitors and the regular screens to give herself the best possible view.

197

'Omaha Three-Four is airborne,' Mike Drury, the pilot aboard the Australian-built sea surveillance airplane, radioed in. Geffar checked that his data block was transmitting – isolated thunderstorms in the area were interfering with some transmissions.

'He's thirty minutes late,' Hardcastle said.

'Gates must've been delayed,' Geffar told him. Gates, the new Customs Service Commissioner, had been sworn in earlier that morning. He had decided to fly on the night's mission anyway.

Geffar shook her head in amazement, Coast Guard and Customs working together. 'Why can't we work like this all the time?'

'That's what we're trying to get Congress to buy off on – '

Hardcastle said, 'You've got to have one commander, one person with the authority to move all the vessels, aircraft and men under his command to support an operation. I don't have the authority to launch your Nomad or your Black Hawks, and you don't have the authority to position my aerostats. Only a federally mandated unit with one commander in charge of all drug-interdiction assets can get this kind of support. McDonough didn't understand that.'

Geffar nodded, feeling more than before that the Hammerheads would work and Hardcastle was right.

She called up the main SLINGSHOT composite radar screen of the whole south Florida/Florida Straits/Bahamas region. As she touched the transmit button on the touch-screen monitor, the data block belonging to Customs' Nomad surveillance aircraft highlighted itself, and an additional data printout reported its exact position, flight parameters and estimated fuel endurance. 'Three-Four, status check.'

'Three-Four in the green,' Agent Mike Drury aboard the

Nomad cargo plane replied. 'We've got a VIP on board tonight.'

Geffar smiled and nodded to Hardcastle, who was in the seat beside her. She clicked the channel open. 'Roger that, Three-Four. Pass my congratulations to Commissioner Gates.'

'Thank you, Sandra,' the new commissioner said over the radio.

In the dark interior of the Nomad, Gates could be seen under the glare of subdued cabin lights. His life jacket was askew, his headset was pushed too far forward on his head, but his hair was neat and undisturbed. He was wearing a blue nylon windbreaker with a large Customs Air Branch patch over the right breast. The Nomad's two sensor operators – Jacqueline Hoey, working the SeaScan radar, and 'Buffalo Bill' Lamont, operating the Westinghouse WF-360 infrared scanner – were bathed in the greenish glare of their sea-mapping scopes.

Hardcastle was staring at the Diamond-towed aerostat unit's radar display. The controllers aboard the cutter had highlighted a target several times in the last few minutes. The target, represented by a red square, was just off the northern coast of Cuba heading northwest at almost six miles per minute according to the aerostat radar's read-outs. Hardcastle touched Geffar's shoulder. 'We might have something here.'

Geffar checked the HDTV displays. 'Fast-moving, flying right on the edge of the Cuban waters – he's going over three hundred fifty knots . . .'

'Altitude five hundred feet,' Long reported, now on one of the lower-deck consoles. 'A military flight?'

'Could be.' Hardcastle punched commands into the keyboard, telling the computer to display any military

199

air-traffic-control radio beacons from any aircraft. The radar display flickered once as the computer quickly redrew the screen, but there was no change. 'No squawking military codes. He might be military but I doubt it.'

'One of ours?'

'No way,' Geffar said, 'unless I don't know about it. Could it be a Coast Guard Falcon?'

'We'd be picking up his beacon if it was,' Hardcastle said. He punched in more instructions, displaying a short list. 'Aircraft, Seventh District, Flight Status.' A map of the southeast United States came on one of the large screens, and flashing data blocks indicated the location of each aircraft.

'Three Seventh District aircraft are up, and one is operating near the Bahamas,' Hardcastle reported, 'but no one is anywhere near Cuba. It could be a bizjet from Puerto Rico or the eastern Caribbean hot-dogging around Cuba – some pilots like to stay as close to shore as they can in case they get an engine problem. It could be a military flight with an inop transponder. Or . . .'

'Or it could be a new player,' Geffar said. 'Making a drop.' She magnified the view of northern Cuba. The image showed only a few sea targets sailing along the coast in the path of the plane. 'Altitude down to three hundred feet,' Geffar said. 'He's making a drop, I know it.'

'But he's a fast-mover, not a bug-smasher,' Long said. 'Doesn't make sense . . .'

'Sense or not, the guy's heading for Mayberry.' The fast-moving target was on a direct course for the yellow-highlighted area where drops had been made in recent weeks. Two vessels were inside that area, another a few miles away. 'He's down to one hundred feet and slowing – now down to two hundred knots and decelerating. He's making a drop for sure.' She turned to Hardcastle. 'We have any planes in the area?'

He rechecked but he knew the answer. 'The Nomad is the closest airborne. The Black Hawk is the only other that's closer . . . unless . . . the Sea Lion can make the intercept faster than the Black Hawk.'

'We're not authorized to use it. Not yet, anyway. Launch a plane from Homestead and put him on the guy. We'll keep the Nomad in place in case any vessels head north toward the Keys.' Hardcastle called up his own communications screen and contacted the Customs Service Air Branch to launch a Citation chase plane.

Geffar opened the secure channel to the Nomad. 'Three-Four, this is Hammerhead One. We think a drop is going down at Mayberry. We're watching a fast-moving aircraft on a drop profile. Stand by.'

'Roger, Hammerhead,' Drury replied. 'We've catalogued four vessels on station at Cay Sal Bank. They might be players too.' Geffar put a magnified view of the Cay Sal Bank on a monitor. There were four vessels within a mile of each other. The computer reported each target had remained in the same relative position since first catalogued by the preceding Nomad flight earlier in the day.

'Hammerhead One, this is SLINGSHOT,' the joint Customs Service–Coast Guard radar ground controllers radioed. 'Be advised, Omaha Four-Zero airborne.' A blinking indicator over Homestead AFB in southern Florida on the larger scale map confirmed the call.

'Hammerhead, this is Three-Four.' It was Jacqueline Hoey, the SeaScan radar controller on board Nomad. 'Target coming off Mayberry, turning north. Projecting flight path directly toward Cal Say Bank area, ETA six minutes.'

Geffar touched her light pen on the digital blip representing the Citation Hardcastle had just ordered be launched from Homestead and drew a line between it and the radar target of the fast-moving newcomer heading north. 'If that guy continues north we should catch him. If he turns tail and runs we might not.'

'He's heading right for the four vessels that have been sitting on Cay Sal Bank all afternoon,' Hardcastle said. 'He's a player, all right. Whoever's in charge of this one, they got some serious wings on their side now.'

Customs Service Air Branch Headquarters, Homestead AFB, Florida

The duty officer heard the ringing and picked up the phone on the intra-agency direct line from Miami headquarters. 'Homestead. Davidson.'

'Chuck, this is Willy at Brickell Plaza. I received an anonymous call. Claims Commissioner Gates is in danger and should leave the drug-drop area near Cuba soonest possible.'

Davidson responded with the universal cop's first line of any investigation: 'Say that again.'

'I said, guy claims that the Commissioner is in danger on that Nomad flight. He was on the horn for only about five seconds but he said Commissioner Gates' plane may come under attack.'

'Where? When . . . ?'

'Nothing else. Can you get hold of Geffar and let her know?'

'Sounds like a crank to me,' Davidson said. But he had been in the Service long enough to know never to ignore even the most far-out calls. 'I'll pass it along. Do you have a tape of the call or a tracer?'

'It came through the switchboard. I'll ask. And I didn't make a tape. I just came in for a minute, thought the call was from my old lady.'

'Give me a call if you got a tape or a trace.'

Davidson put in a call to the Air Division to set up a call to the platform where Geffar and her people were staging. It would take several minutes to put the call through; communications out to the platform were shaky at best. Never mind, it smelled bogus anyway.

Hammerhead One Platform

'They've got a fast-moving jet making a drop to four vessels in Cay Sal Bank – sounds like a taxi dance to me.'

Hardcastle called up snapshots of past area maps – the computer could store several days' worth of images in its memory. He went back as early as when the four vessels appeared at Cay Sal, then backtracked those four vessels as they made their way north. 'Those guys first appeared from South America. Can't see a positive origin but definitely South America. Not Cuba. Not west of Panama, either.'

He studied the four ships as they passed through the Yucatan Channel between Mexico and Cuba. 'Look – there's more than four ships here. There's six, maybe eight. All traveling together.' He forwarded the screens one at a time, using computer-generated markers to keep track of each vessel. 'Here – breaking off, going past Cay Sal. Dropping off four. These guys heading toward the Archipelago de Sabana . . .'

'Mayberry,' Geffar said. 'Four smugglers station themselves at Mayberry, four more at Cay Sal.'

'There's lots of other clusters of boats out there,' Long observed. 'Too many to get an accurate fix.'

'Accurate enough,' Geffar said. 'Eight smugglers deployed in organized clusters, stationing themselves and waiting for a drop by a high-speed plane. It's enough to order more aircraft.'

'I'll get some Coast Guard vessels underway too,' Hardcastle said. 'It looks like a party tonight.'

'Don't have them converge on Cay Sal,' Geffar told him. 'Have them report in to us. We'll try to position them in the path of that plane near some of the boats sitting out there and see if they can get within range of a drop. We'll pick the ones that scatter after the plane passes overhead and try to intercept them.'

'Omaha Four-Zero is three minutes away from intercept,' Long reported. 'Target still proceeding north. Almost to Elbow Cay. Target showing three hundred feet and descending. He's coming up on that cluster of boats.'

'I've got a Navy Pegasus hydrofoil from Key West on the line,' Hardcastle said. 'We're putting a Coast Guard crew on board. The Pegasus can be in the area in ninety minutes. I suggest we put the Pegasus unit between the Keys and Elbow Cay. If those guys in the boats make a break for the Keys, we can try to intercept.'

'Three-Four should be able to keep an eye on them.' Geffar turned to her communications console and touched the screen. 'Three-Four, this is Hammerhead. What have you got?'

On Board Omaha Three-Four

'Hammerhead, this is Three-Four,' Hoey reported. 'We're taking up an orbit position near Mayberry. We have radar contact with suspects. We are descending to get a clear infrared picture of the suspects. Out.'

Ron Gates was clutching onto the armrest of his seat as the Nomad's motion took hold of him. Was this trip necessary?

They were in a descent and turning. Not just the plane but his stomach too. Hoey had announced a high-speed plane that seemed to have just made a drop very close to their position – below them actually. She kept the telescopic infrared camera on the plane while at ten thousand feet above the water. There were four boats. Several large boxes were spotted in the water, and boats waiting for the delivery were hauling them on board their vessels. The plane that made the drop was heading southeast, not doubt to make more drops to prepositioned boats up and down the Bahamas. It was a very major delivery . . .

Hoey was excited and understandably so. She could hardly sit still in her seat. 'Hammerhead, this is damned amazing. They're making a major delivery – we're going to need all the boats and choppers you can get out here – '

'We copy all, Three-Four. Stay with them as long as you can. Keep feeding up position updates after they break off and run.'

'Copy, Hammerhead.'

'Be advised, Hammerhead,' a specialist reported as he finally began to get a clearer picture on his infrared scanner, 'we see at *least* fifteen big cases being dropped in the water, cases large enough to be two-hundred-pounders. Can't get an accurate count yet but there's at least fifteen . . . my God . . .'

'Keep those reports coming, Buff.' Geffar turned to Hardcastle. 'You guys airborne?'

'Three Falcons and two Island-class boats out of Miami Beach. I'm getting more. We've got Customs units assembling. They'll be ready to deploy as soon as we get a clear picture on where these guys go.'

'Admiral Hardcastle,' one of the young Coast Guard techs reported, 'Diamond has picked up another air target. Sixty miles southeast of Mayberry, another fast-mover – preliminary velocity estimate says five hundred knots.'

'Five *hundred*?' Hardcastle switched to that screen and found the highlighted radar return. The radar aboard the

Coast Guard aerostat vessel had assigned the new target a confidence of 1, the highest factor – this was no stray return. 'Got an origin on this guy?'

'Negative. Appeared on radar well offshore, though. Not out of Holguin or Camaguey.' Those two areas were large Cuban Air Force bases with sophisticated air-defense units at both locations.

'This better not be the Cuban Air Force moving in on this.'

'They've launched fighters at us before,' Geffar said, 'but never from the interior bases – it's always been from Havana . . .'

'Sandra,' one of the Customs investigators manning the phones called out, 'message from Homestead. Intelligence got an anonymous tip about Gates . . .'

'Hammerhead, this is Three-Four.' It was Drury on the radio a few minutes later. Sweat was pouring from his neck, his gloved hands were hot and damp. 'Where is that guy? What's his position? Talk to me . . .'

'Three-Four, turn right thirty degrees, vector for traffic at your nine o'clock, ten miles,' a controller on the Hammerhead One platform ordered. 'Advise when you have visual on him . . .'

'Negative visual, Hammerhead,' Drury said. The strain in his voice was palpable. 'I don't see any lights. Flight visibility is about five miles. He must not have his lights on. I'm in a right turn.' They could hear Drury's copilot broadcasting a warning on the GUARD emergency channels, trying to order the intruder to stay away.

'Definitely a pickup, Hammerhead,' Specialist Buff LaMont reported from the Nomad. 'We count at least eight strings of large boxes with flotation gear being picked up, at least three big boxes on each string. All the boxes are roped together. Estimate each box to weigh around two hundred pounds, maybe more.' The image from the infrared scanner showed the scene below with graphic clarity. 'It takes two guys to lift each box. Wait . . . I count four boxes altogether. Four boxes, over two hundred pounds each on each string.'

'I still don't see that plane, Hammerhead,' Drury yelled over the radio. 'Where in hell do I go now, dammit?'

'Three-Four, turn left, maintain your altitude,' the controller replied to Drury. 'Target is at your twelve o'clock and above you . . . roll out, maintain heading and altitude . . . target passing off your nine o'clock, two miles.'

'It has to be the Cubans – who else would have a plane that can go so fast and who'd be harassing American Customs Service planes?' Geffar said.

'Almost a thousand pounds of drugs for each boat,' Hardcastle said. 'A big drop. If they made a drop that size over Mayberry – '

'And if they make more drops near those other places near Andros Island and Exuma Cays where we saw those other boats sitting,' Geffar said, 'this guy is carrying a huge load. *Much* bigger than a little prop job.' She paused, then looked at Hardcastle with a startled expression. 'A fast transport, faster than the Shorts you shot down . . . flying all the way from South America to the Bahamas with a huge load. A big civil transport . . . or a *military* flight . . . ?'

'Military . . . If that's a *military* cargo plane' – they stared at the magnified view around the Nomad, which was still trying to maneuver away from the unidentified newcomer – 'then that guy might be military, too . . . a military jet . . . *fighter*. . . ?'

Geffar scrambled for the touch-screen. 'Three-Four, break off from your surveillance. Head for Marathon or Key West at best possible speed . . .'

'The boats are heading west, Hammerhead,' Drury told her. 'If we're clear of that traffic we'll continue our surveillance – '

'Never mind the surveillance, break off and head north *now*.'

'Tell him to stay low,' Hardcastle said. 'Maybe the guy will leave him alone. Keep broadcasting on all emergency frequencies. I'll try to get my headquarters to raise the State Department.'

'Target at Three-Four's six o'clock, three miles,' Long reported. 'What the hell is he doing? Playing tag? Is he one of your guys, Hardcastle?' Still suspicious of the Coast Guard, like a good old Customs true-believer.

'Crew, we're breaking off surveillance,' Drury announced. 'We got some plane chasing us out of the area – '

He never finished the sentence.

A loud, animal-like screech erupted from the radios, followed by a hiss of static and muffled bangs. Geffar grabbed onto the console, thinking that something had hit the platform. Hoping that . . .

'Fire!' someone shouted in the command center of the Hammerhead One platform. 'There's a fire on board the Nomad! . . .'

A column of flame leapt out from underneath the radar console in the Nomad, spreading directly into Jacqueline Hoey's lap. Her scream was nearly drowned out by shouts from inside the cabin. Lamont was there with a fire extinguisher but seemed unable to keep his balance – he seemed to be floating around in the cabin as if weightless. Suddenly both he and Hoey were thrown against the ceiling.

Ronald Gates, newly installed commissioner, opened his

mouth to scream but nothing could be heard over the roaring sound of wind and explosions. His body was straining against his seat belt, the upper half pinned against the radar-control console. His hands shot up to his face, covering his death's mask.

'Contact lost with Three-Four!' Long shouted. 'It disappeared off radar!'

Geffar got to her feet, tore off her headset. 'Get the Black Hawk ready for takeoff. Broadcast the Nomad's last position on all emergency channels. Track that unknown and find out where he goes. Tactical crew armed and on deck in two minutes.'

Hardcastle clicked on the platform's intercom. 'Helipad one, helipad one, prepare to launch helo. All hands, stand by to launch helo. Customs tactical crew to your helo immediately. Repeat, Black Hawk tactical crew, report to your helo immediately.' As Geffar ran outside he punched up the intercom to the lower hangar deck. 'Deck three, this is Admiral Hardcastle. Get the Sea Lion up on deck and get her ready for takeoff . . . no, I want it up *now*. Spare two plane captains from the Black Hawk launch and get that Sea Lion on deck *now*!' He threw off his headset, turned to Curtis Long, who was trying to reach the Navy Pegasus hydrofoil ship by radio. 'Can you handle things here?'

'What . . . ?'

'I'm taking the Sea Lion airborne to – '

'That's not authorized, we've got a plane down and two more in the area. It's dark, we've got lousy weather. I'm not sure if I can work all of this stuff in a rescue situation. Taking that thing up there, *sir*, can just screw things up – '

'I've been notified of a disaster at sea and I'm launching to investigate and assist.' He headed for the exit, ignoring Long's following complaints.

The rain was coming down in driving sheets now as

Hardcastle reached the upper flight desk and went to the elevator from where the Sea Lion tilt-rotor aircraft would be raised. The Sea Lion came on deck a few minutes later. The aircraft, designed to be stowed on board an aircraft carrier or Marine Corps landing assault ship, was in its below-decks stowed configuration – the rotors on both engines were folded along the engine nacelles, the nacelles raised horizontally, and the wing was swiveled around so that the starboard nacelle was nestled between the Sea Lion's twin tails and the port nacelle was suspended out off the plane's nose. In this configuration the Sea Lion could almost squeeze inside a space equivalent to a two-car garage but within sixty seconds reconfigure itself with the flip of a switch into takeoff configuration.

As the plane captains began towing it over to helipad number two Hardcastle jumped inside and began pulling the safing pins from the Sea Stinger missile pod on the starboard side and the Chain Gun pod on the port side. By the time the aircraft was moved onto its helipad, Hardcastle was beginning to strap into the pilot's seat. As he did, three men, two Coast Guardsmen and a Customs Service agent, got in with him.

'We heard you and Long talking in the command center, Admiral,' one of the Coast Guardsmen said. 'Seaman Toby Morton, sir. We figured you might like some help.'

Hardcastle didn't argue. 'Strap in and get ready,' he said as he put on a helmet. 'Who else is with you?'

The three were pulling on headsets they found on the seats and strapping themselves in. 'Seaman First Bill Petraglia and some junior G-man we grabbed on the way.'

'Anyone armed?'

'I got one M-16 and a coupla clips. The Customs guy has a sidearm.'

A moment later the Customs Service agent moved beside Morton. 'Agent Jim Coates, Admiral. Could you use some help in the cockpit? I'm fixed and spin-wing qualified.'

'You just signed up for a free flying lesson, Agent Coates. Get up here.' As Coates maneuvered over the center console and jumped into the left side copilot's seat, Hardcastle activated the Sea Lion's battery and internal power switches. Full fuel, full oil and hydraulics, good battery. No time for a complete preflight. Fortunately the Sea Lion needed no tools or crew chief intervention to prepare itself for takeoff, also no external power cart to start engines.

Once the helipad was clear of ground personnel Hardcastle turned on battery and internal power and started the Sea Lion's auxiliary power unit, which supplied electrical, pneumatic and hydraulic power. That small engine was powerful enough to swing the wings back to their conventional position, rotate the engine nacelles to the vertical, move the rotors back into place and spin the turbine on the port engine up to engine-start speed. Two minutes later both engines were started, the drift lights and perimeter lights in the helipad were illuminated and the Sea Lion reconnaissance attack plane was ready for takeoff. Without waiting for clearance, Hardcastle made a vertical takeoff and immediately headed toward the Nomad radar plane's impact area.

'Omaha Three-One, this is Hammerhead Four-Nine,' Hardcastle radioed. 'I'm airborne, southwestbound.'

'Four-nine, this is Three-One. Dammit, Hardcastle,' Geffar was saying, 'you are not authorized to fly the Sea Lion on a Customs mission – '

'I called to ask if there was any assistance I could render Three-Four,' Hardcastle interrupted. 'What's your status?'

A pause, then: 'All right, all right, I knew you were going to launch anyway – nothing I could've done to stop you. We're over Three-Four's impact area. No sign of the aircraft or of survivors yet. We have a commercial fisherman twenty, thirty minutes away, and the Pegasus hydrofoil is about an hour out. We observe two- to four-foot seas out there. You might be able to set the Sea Lion down and pick up any . . . survivors.'

'Copy that, Three-One,' Hardcastle replied. 'We can handle the search for survivors. Instruct the hydrofoil and Omaha Four-Zero to intercept those boats involved with the drop.'

'This's no time to be thinking of that,' Geffar said. 'We need to concentrate on rescue – '

'Dammit, Sandra, I want them – don't let them get away!' He didn't say please.

Actually Geffar wanted an excuse to change her mind. She understood where he was coming from. The noise on the radios had gotten almost unbearable, even on the Customs Service discrete-operations frequency – units were calling in from all over the area asking what the hell was happening. 'All stations other than designated Omaha and Hammerhead units, *clear this channel*. Break. Hammerhead One, this is Three-One. Vector the Pegasus unit to intercept those boats leaving this area. See if Four-Zero can intercept target one. Continue to dispatch any available units to intercept vessels that might be picking up drops along target one's flight path.'

Hardcastle was over the Nomad radar plane's impact point a few minutes later. 'The controls for the FLIR scanner are by your right elbow,' Hardcastle told Agent Coates. 'Plug the cables into your helmet and power your IR visor.' He demonstrated for Coates as they both lowered the infrared-scanner visors over their eyes. 'All right. Can you see the status indicators?' Coates nodded. 'Okay. I'll activate your helmet. The FLIR scanner will send the infrared images to your visor. As you move your head the scanner will look in the same direction. You can zoom in and out and switch from normal to reverse-image with the controls on your cyclic. If you want to stop, just raise your visor.'

It was as Hardcastle described. Coates could look in any direction outside the Sea Lion's cockpit – even behind him or in a direction that would normally be blocked by the fuselage – and the scene he saw through the electronic visors appeared well lit. As he moved his head the heat-sensitive image moved with him. Tiny electronic numerals told him the aircraft's heading, altitude and airspeed as well as the relative bearing of whatever he was looking at. Several times he stopped his sweep and used switches on the control stick to zoom in and get a better look.

What he found were bits and pieces of the Nomad, spread out over an area the size of four football fields. The heat-seeking scanner registered several warm objects but none were distinguishable as human forms. Pools of fire were everywhere, obscuring their view. Finally they found what was left of the strongest section of the plane, the wing-connecting box that joined the wings to the fuselage.

'The right side of the connecting box looks sheared off, probably from the impact with the water,' Coates was saying. 'The left side looks . . . looks blown off. There's a big semicircular hole in the box just inboard of where the engine nacelle would be.'

Coates touched the scanner's zoom controls to get a better look. 'Oh, Jesus . . .'

'What is it?'

'I'm not positive,' Coates said, 'but . . . Jesus, I think those are bullet holes along the top of that connecting box, Admiral. My God, I think someone strafed the Nomad and shot him down.'

The Oval Office, Washington, DC
The Next Morning

The President seemed exhausted. Dressed in a somber

213

dark suit and tie, he wore his silver-rimmed eyeglasses instead of the contact lenses that he had just removed after several irritating hours. Not having the time to rehearse the hastily written statement, he sat at his desk with his speech in his hands instead of reading off the TelePrompTer. He received his cue from the stage director, straightened his broad athlete's shoulders and began:

'My fellow Americans, by now you may have heard about the horrible incident that occurred over the waters off the southern coast of Florida last night. I will summarize the events as we know them at this hour, and then announce our response to this atrocity:

'At eleven forty-six eastern time last night a United States Customs Service reconnaissance plane with seven persons on board was attacked and destroyed during an anti-drug surveillance operation in the Straits of Florida approximately one hundred miles south-south-east of Miami. The plane was involved in an operation tracking boats strongly suspected of carrying drugs into south Florida. Shortly after four boats were observed picking up several objects that Customs investigators believed were drugs, a high-speed aircraft appeared and before the Customs aircraft could take evasive action, attacked the reconnaissance plane with large-caliber machine-gun fire. The plane crashed and was destroyed.

'There were no survivors.

'Along with the five Customs Service crewpersons on board, casualties included Commissioner of the Customs Service Ronald Gates, whom I had just sworn in that same day. The other fatalities were Customs Service pilot Michael Drury, copilot Jeffrey Crawford, radar officer Jacqueline Hoey, sensor officer William LaMont and flight engineer George Bolan.

'Using recorded analysis provided by a joint Coast Guard–Customs Service unit on the scene, we have determined that the Customs Service reconnaissance plane was attacked by a fighter-type aircraft working in concert with the drug smugglers. We believe the fighter was actually providing air cover for the drug smugglers as they made several drops to waiting speedboats all across the western Bahamas and eastern Caribbean. When the smugglers found that our radar aircraft was vectoring in Coast Guard vessels to make arrests, the smugglers ordered the Customs plane destroyed.

'This tragic incident follows two other similar attacks by well-armed and well-organized smugglers that have used extraordinary military-like power to kill Customs Service agents and Coast Guard patrols. In recent weeks twenty-one men and women have been killed by these terrorists in their attempts to bring illegal narcotics into the United States. *I am determined that these attacks shall not continue.*

'Under current law I am unable to direct our military forces to attack aircraft outside the territorial limits of the United States without a declaration of war, or to strike at suspected drug smugglers in the role as law enforcers. I agree with and respect those laws. I do not believe tactical military forces should be involved in drug interdiction. They are not authorized or trained in law enforcement, and the involvement of military forces trained for war offers fewer options – they are trained to destroy when destruction may not be warranted.

'Instead . . . I am issuing a presidential reorganization order, effective this date, that creates a new agency that will officially and temporarily be placed under the Department of Defense. This new agency will be composed of air and sea interdiction elements of the Coast Guard and Customs Service, and will retain full authority to make arrests, conduct investigations, make searches and perform air intercepts and arrests in international airspace and on the high seas as well as within the United States. They will exist to secure the borders of the United States. As an agency of the Department of Defense they will also have authority to employ military weapons and tactics against anyone considered a threat to this nation, such authority to include attacking and destroying aircraft or vessels that penetrate or transit American territorial boundaries without permission, or commit a crime within American coastal territories.

'This new agency will be called the Border Security Force.'

The President paused to turn a page, and to cope with the anger and frustration that had weighed so heavily on him. This was it, he thought. He had worried – *agonized* – over this decision for weeks. The public formation of a paramilitary organization, a unit with the powers of both the FBI, the Coast Guard and the Air Force all rolled into one. No President had gone this far since the Civil War. But he felt as though a tremendous weight had been lifted off his broad shoulders. He had acted. And just as with the Russian *Kavaznya* laser incident a year earlier, he found that action, decisive *action*, was the best response. The only sure failure was the failure to act . . .

'This new agency,' he went on, 'will legally exist for the next ninety days under limited authority from me as commander-in-chief. Later today we will present a presidential reorganization plan to Congress authorizing permanent reorganization and creation of the Border Security Force. This measure must be approved by a simple majority of both houses of Congress. At the same time a bill will be presented on the floor of the Senate that will create a permanent Cabinet-level Secretary of Border Security Forces, making it a separate government department with authority in its area equal to the Department of Defense. This measure already has the support of the Senate minority leadership and key congressional leaders. I urge and expect swift passage of this measure.'

The President paused, looked up from his papers directly into the camera. 'In plain English, my fellow Americans, this means that the United States will no longer tolerate smugglers, terrorists, armed aggressors or any other unidentified or uninvited vessels or aircraft to cross our borders or airspace. Actually we've had laws on the books for years, but we have never believed we could enforce them because our borders were so vast, not to mention our bureaucracies. Well, as of today we will begin to enforce those laws.

'If you are a smuggler, if you are a terrorist, if you attempt to enter this country without permission, we will find you, and we will intercept you. You can expect to be taken into custody and placed under arrest until your identity is verified. If you attempt to evade our patrols or ignore our warnings, you will be attacked and you will be destroyed before you cross our shores.

'Some of you might be concerned about accidents, of our patrols attacking innocent persons, especially Americans traveling by air. I have shared that concern, so much so that I delayed implementing this program for several weeks. I am sorry it took the death of Commissioner Ronald Gates and five brave Customs Service agents before I acted. I have carefully reviewed the regulations to be put into effect, and I believe that this program will minimally impact on law-abiding persons who follow the rules and who are not trying to evade the law. I feel confident that this plan will work. It *must* work.

'We have dealt with the situation as a law-enforcement matter. No longer. We will now use the full power of the American government and all the resources at our disposal to control access to our shores and apprehend anyone trying to escape our justice. With your support, we can make this plan work. Thank you very much, and God bless you.' And God help me, he silently added.

Hammerhead One
Border Security Force
Air Operations Staging Platform

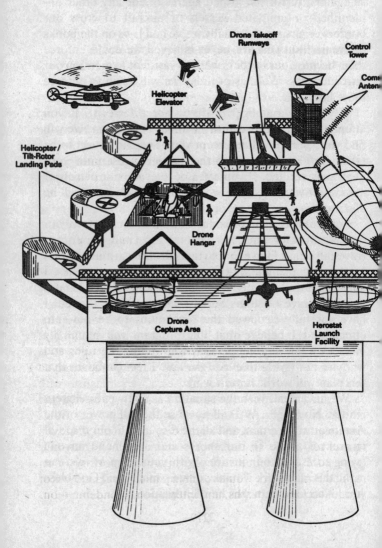

Helicopter Elevator

Drone Takeoff Runways

Control Tower

Comm Antenna

Helicopter / Tilt-Rotor Landing Pads

Drone Hangar

Drone Capture Area

Herostat Launch Facility

Chapter Five

Hammerhead One Staging Platform, 0700 Hours
Six Months Later

The huge converted oil platform had undergone an amazing rejuvenation. Hardcastle was on his way to his first inspection of the platform in weeks, flying out from the Border Security Force's new headquarters center at Aladdin City, Florida, to the platform sixty miles to the southeast in the Straits of Florida. Although the new Border Security Force's commander of the first air-operations base had been receiving daily briefings on the progress of the new base, he was told she'd be amazed at the platform's refurbishment.

A huge thunderstorm was sitting on the horizon in front of him, but it was dwarfed for the moment by his thoughts of the breakneck days after the President's historic announcement of the formation of the Border Security Force when the country seemed about to split itself apart, or rather the noisier opposition forces made it seem that way.

It was a miracle that the Border Security Force survived the first ninety days. It seemed every organization with access to a microphone or camera was telling America that the Border Security Force was a bad idea. Civil rights groups, aviation lobbies, commerce organizations, even travel and trade groups were going on record with their very vocal opposition. They felt that the presence of an armed border force would result in panic, a dramatic loss of trade, accidental deaths, and international condemnation.

It was instantly compared to Communist internal security police and Russia's Border Guards, paramilitary groups that were in place as much to keep their population *in* as to keep enemies out.

The personal attacks were even worse. Hardcastle's divorce was fair game for nightly news broadcasts and the so-called 'tabloid' news shows, and even the fact that Sandra Geffar was a national pistol champion seemed to be a negative as reporters portrayed her as an ultra right-wing survivalist gunslinger. Geffar, Hardcastle, Elliott, even young McLanahan, who had only appeared with Elliott once before Congress, were all carefully scrutinized by the press. The rumors were especially wild as the press quoted several 'reports from unnamed sources' that Elliott and McLanahan had almost single-handedly started World War Three.

But despite the initial furor, overall public opinion about the need and usefulness of the Border Security Force was generally positive. There was little sympathy for persons who flew regularly from the Bahamas or Central America to Florida – most persons believed they were rich folks complaining, that the government was interfering with their playtime. The press, assisted by numerous and frequent interviews by Hardcastle, Elliott, and Geffar, picked up on reports that smugglers were going to bypass the southeast and import their drugs elsewhere – it simply meant that the program, at least in their estimation, was working already.

Of course, Geffar and Hardcastle played a few tricks as well. The Sea Lion tilt-rotor aircraft with the missiles and machine guns on board was carefully hidden away, and they had explained that putting weapons on board Border Security Force aircraft was still 'a ways off.' The Sky Lion drone with its benign bug-like appearance was demonstrated frequently flying over friendly fishermen and happy families on Sunday outings, wagging its wings and buzzing around good-naturedly like a friendly hummingbird; while the sinister, deadly-looking Seagull drone was also carefully left out of the news reports.

Most importantly, however, no one had died since the group was formed. All of the complaints that the Border Security Force was going to cause hundreds of deaths, millions of dollars in damage and billions of dollars in lost revenues and lawsuits against the government began to fall on deaf ears. The polls said that most Americans favored the existence of the Hammerheads – a name that was also not too widely publicized at first – and everyone involved with the Border Security Force trotted those polls through every office on Capitol Hill.

The Senate Committee on Governmental Affairs, at the gentle but insistent urging of the Vice President, sent the measure to the Senate Subcommittee on Military Affairs. Many believed this was the beginning of the end of the Hammerheads – they were sure the plan would get bogged down in rhetoric and pork-barrel add-ons by the subcommittee's members. Instead, it was a ploy by the White House to gather more high-powered support for the measure. The plan was greeted with enthusiasm by the prestigious subcommittee, which praised it lavishly before voting in the affirmative and sending it back to Governmental Affairs. It eventually went back to the full Senate, which passed the President's Border Security Force reorganization plan on the first vote.

The House, which looked more carefully at the program's five-billion-dollar price tag, and the opposition party in particular, which wanted to keep the White House from scoring such a dramatic victory, kept the measure in the House Committee on Government Operations right up to the maximum seventy-five day limit, then allowed it to be sent back automatically to the House floor without a vote. The opposition tried to kill the plan right then, or at least delay it past the maximum ninety-day time limit, but the provisions of Title Five, chapter 9, paragraph 911, were clear – committee *approval* was not necessary before presentation to Congress, only committee *review*. Committee discharge was not grounds for disapproval.

The full House debate on the measure then went far over the maximum ten-hour time limit – in fact, it went a full fourteen days past the debate time limit – but finally the question was called. The Speaker of the House tried one last tactic to kill the measure – a voice vote, where the Speaker's ear would decide whether the 'ayes' or 'nays' carried. At the very least, the outcry that usually followed such a blatant device of the Rules of Order would push the session past the fast-approaching ninety-day limit. But the roll-call vote was quickly proposed, seconded and accomplished by a weary and frayed House of Representatives.

It was not a resounding affirmation, but it did pass. The Hammerheads became an official reality. Now, it was up to Elliott, Geffar and the rest of the Hammerheads to make the new organization a success.

That day was happening.

Hardcastle was at the controls of a former Coast Guard Dolphin helicopter. Its distinctive Coast Guard red diagonal stripes had been removed and replaced with the Hammerheads' insignia – a hammerhead shark with wings, the same one Hardcastle had made up – on the helicopter's nose, along with electroluminescent strip lights on the sides that highlighted the sixteen-inch-high words: FOLLOW ME.

'Shark, this is Hammerhead Two-Five,' Hardcastle called in. 'Request one trip around the base, then landing on main elevator. Over.'

'Zero-Five, this is Shark. Request approved. Remain clear of southeast side. Report when ready for landing.'

222

The platform looked larger than before. The west side now had a row of three circular landing pads that projected out over the edge of the platform, which helped preserve deck space; each pad was large enough for a Sea Lion tilt-rotor aircraft and all other helicopters in the active military or civilian inventory. A ramp led from each pad onto the main deck. On the west side of the main deck inboard of the center landing pad was a large aircraft elevator that moved aircraft from the main deck down to the hangars and maintenance shops directly below. Ballpark lights, huge banks of high-powered sodium lights on tall poles, were arranged around the elevator and parking areas for night operations and could be raised, lowered or aimed.

In the center of the platform was the launch-and-recovery facility for the Sky Lion and Seagull drones. The Sky Lion drones, being tilt-rotor aircraft like their larger cousins, could be launched and recovered automatically just like any other chopper.

The above-deck operations building was in the center of the platform, a two-story steel-and-glass structure that served as the maintenance operations headquarters, crew lounge and pre-launch hangar for the drones. Hardcastle noticed that the Hammerhead insignia had been painted on both the north and south sides of the building, and the biggest American flag he had ever seen was flapping lazily on a roof-mounted mast.

At the apex next to the maintenance center was the electronic-landing-system transmitter. The ELS provided a side radio beam that guided the Seagull drones to the platform; once locked onto the beam the drones would follow it right into the recovery corral, where arresting cables on the deck and a large nylon mesh backstop net snared the drone.

The northeast side of the platform had a four-story air-traffic-control and security tower. This was also where most of the station's radio, radar, data-link and sensor antennae were located. The central and southeast sides of the platform carried the most unusual part of the entire facility – HIGHBAL, Hammerhead Initial Balloon, the aerostat radar balloon launch-and-recovery area. One hundred and fifty feet long and seventy feet at its widest, it carried an RCA AN/APS-128 sea- and air-scanning radar that could search for surface and low-flying air targets out to almost two hundred miles, and for higher-flying targets out to three hundred miles. HIGHBAL also carried data-link communications equipment for the Hammerheads' fleet of remote-controlled drones. Using the aerostat alone, the drones could operate at patrol altitudes out to two hundred miles from the platform; if a data-link could be established between the platform and other ground- or sea-based radars, the drone's operating range was limited only by the drone's own fuel supplies.

HIGHBAL was flying this morning up to its maximum altitude of fourteen thousand feet – nearly three miles up. At that altitude it had a sea-scanning range of about one hundred-fifty miles and an air-target scanning range of up to two-hundred miles. Of course, the dark, towering thunderstorms off to the south and west reduced that range but most smugglers didn't want to fly through a Caribbean thunderstorm.

'Shark, this is Two-Five,' Hardcastle called in. 'I've completed my orientation. Ready for landing.'

'Two-Five, this is Shark,' the controller aboard the platform replied. 'Cleared to land on center deck.'

'Roger. Center deck for Two-Five.'

Geffar opened the cockpit door for him as the Dolphin helicopter's rotors spun down after landing. 'Welcome aboard.'

They rode down with the Dolphin helicopter to the main hangar deck, where crewmen immediately wheeled the helicopter off the elevator and began to unload the supplies she had brought. The hangar occupied one-fourth of the entire volume of the platform – three stories high and nearly an acre in total area. Three V-22C Sea Lion aircraft or four Black Hawk helicopters could be parked below. The drone shop was also there, where the small chase-and-reconnaissance planes were serviced – the drones were stored in shelves that rose all the way to the top of the three-story ceiling, and were moved with forklifts.

They found Major Patrick McLanahan in the drone repair shop manning a control console. A Seagull drone was on a test stand, looking like some giant prehistoric flying reptile on a perch. Its large infrared TV camera swiveled around to stare at Geffar and Hardcastle as they entered.

'What happened the other night?' Geffar asked.

'The data-link between the Seagulls and the platform is weak at the extreme range of HIGHBAL,' McLanahan told them. 'Bahamas Route six-four is seventy miles north of us. Both us and Caribbean Balloon were operating at max range and performance, the drone should have locked on easy.' CARABAL, the Caribbean Balloon, was a former Coast Guard aerostat located on Grand Bahama Island forty miles east of Freeport. The whole aerostat network, including the one at Cape Canaveral, the Navy's KEYSTONE unit at Key West and the future Hammerhead Two site off the west Florida coast near Sarasota, were to allow the Hammerheads to fly Seagull or Sky Lion drones anywhere from Jacksonville, Florida, in the north, to Governors Harbor in the Bahamas to the east, and to the very edge of Cuban airspace to the south. 'I've finished a test of the drone and it seems okay. We'll start looking at the data-link system next. Meantime I'd limit the range of an intercept to, say, sixty miles from this platform, or to the maximum range of the aerostat. Let the system work, it might be a transient fault.'

'Sixty miles won't cover much,' Hardcastle added. 'We'll have to fill in our coverage with manned aircraft.'

Geffar and Hardcastle then went to the elevator for a ride up to the control center. Behind the rows of consoles was the senior controller, Hardcastle's former aide, Michael Becker, who had transferred his commission to the Border Security Force along with his boss. The place was a smaller version of the command-and-control centers for such as the Strategic Air Command and the North American Air Defense Command.

Geffar and Hardcastle put on headsets and logged into the computer. Immediately one of the monitors began to scroll a list of messages, a few flagged for Geffar's attention by Rushell Masters, the Hammerhead's chief of air operations based at Homestead Air Force Base. She called up the communications screen on her main console monitor and dialed his office.

'Glad you called,' Masters said. 'The FBI just arrested one of the cleaning women that works on the base. Said they caught her near the flight line with a VHF radio. She had a forged green card, too. They think she might have been spying on us out here and may have been relaying flight information for some time. FBI's got her in Miami.'

'Spying for who? Colombians?'

'That's their speculation.'

'Can we get someone over there to question her?'

An uncomfortable pause, then: 'I tried. They said I don't have clearance to interrogate one of their prisoners.'

'But you've done that before – '

'As a Customs investigator,' Masters said. 'They said they've got no guidance on the status of Border Security Force people. A crock if you ask me.'

'We'll get right on it, Rush. Anything else?'

'The boys can't wait to get their hands on some Sea Lions. Are they on their way?'

226

'You'll be getting six of them. As soon as they get repainted and reconfigured for fuel and weapons we qualify everyone on platform landings. After that we'll be putting four of them here on Hammerhead One and keeping the other two at Homestead for training. I understand we've gotten a dozen more applicants for pilot, too – things are lookin' up.'

'I've got a call into Brad Elliott about intelligence clearances,' Hardcastle said as Geffar closed the channel to Homestead. 'That's good news about getting more pilots. It's about time.'

'I'm glad to see we're finally getting the V-22s,' Geffar said. 'We have the pilots but no aircraft. We've got to qualify everyone on platform landings, day and night, then get the scheduling worked out. And don't worry about budgets. Let Elliott fight those battles. That's his job. He knows what he's doing. He's supposed to be buddy-buddy with half of Congress, and the other half is in awe of him for whatever the hell he was involved with last year from his base in Nevada – '

He was interrupted by a call from Becker. 'Traffic alert. An unknown, origin possible from Nassau. Not on any airways. Low altitude, slow mover. If he stays on course he'll cross the FIR in five minutes.'

'We're on, gang,' Geffar said, turning back on her console. 'Check the computer logs, begin radio warnings on all frequencies.'

'Computer log enabled and running,' Becker acknowledged.

'Attention all aircraft, attention all aircraft,' the controllers began, 'this is the United States Border Security Force. Unknown aircraft on the one-five-five-degree radial, four-zero miles southwest of South Bimini VOR-TAC, six-five miles east of Biscayne Bay VORTAC, you are about to enter United States restricted airspace without

227

authorization. Contact me on frequency one-two-one point five or reverse course. All aircraft on this frequency, check your position and report to your inbound controller.' The warning was repeated several times, on over a dozen frequencies and in Spanish. That broadcast was a warning to all other aircraft and vessels within a hundred miles of America's shorelines – the Hammerheads are watching, we can see you, and we will intercept if you do not respond.

'No response,' one of the controllers reported to Geffar and Hardcastle. 'Crossing the FIR now.' The FIR, Flight Information Region, was a boundary of airspace where different nations or different air traffic control procedures went into effect. In the airspace east of Miami, where the distances between Bahamian, Cuban and US airspace were very short, the Border Security Force controllers began broadcasting warning messages when aircraft crossed the FIR instead of the Air Defense Identification Zone, even though the Hammerheads' authority did not legally begin until an aircraft crossed the ADIZ. 'Estimating ten minutes to ADIZ penetration.'

'He's altering course farther south,' Becker said. 'He'll fly right over us. His altitude is one thousand feet.' Becker had put the HIGHBAL's radar display on the center screen. The computer, which constantly displayed the target's flight data, had also predicted the aircraft's course and time of arrival at a variety of different airports in the area. 'This might explain things – the computer predicts this guy's heading for the Sunrise Beach Club.'

Geffar shook her head in exasperation. That explained a lot. The Sunrise Beach Club on the northern tip of Key Largo was one of the most exclusive residential communities in Florida. Sunrise Beach residents returning from a weekend in Nassau or Freeport – many of whom were politicians, corporation chairmen, or retired bigwigs – frequently assumed that they were allowed to cruise any time into Sunrise Beach without prior notice.

But Geffar and Hardcastle weren't about to let anyone go. 'Let's get Customs moving towards Sunrise Beach,' she told Becker. 'Bring a Seagull up on deck and prepare for launch. Let's get an ID on this guy.'

Hardcastle said, 'Why don't we take this one? We deserve it.'

'In a Sea Lion?' Hardcastle nodded. 'I haven't flown that hybrid since the demonstration flight with the Vice President,' Geffar said. 'I don't think so . . .'

'You've been working hard,' Hardcastle said. 'You need a refresher flight. I'm current in the V-22. This looks like a pretty simple intercept – some retired doctor who forgot to turn his radio on. What do you say?'

Geffar hesitated, but only for a moment. She logged off the commander's computer console, tossed her headset on the desk. 'Okay, Hardcastle. Let's go flying.'

They waited for the plane, a single-engine Cessna 210, to fly over the platform, then took off directly behind it. They were a few miles from the inside boundary of the ADIZ when they pulled up alongside the plane and made themselves visible to the pilot.

'Cessna Three-Victor-November, this is the United States Border Security Force,' Geffar radioed as they tucked in off the Cessna's left side, about fifty feet away. 'You are in restricted airspace and are in violation of United States law. We will direct you to a landing area. Follow this aircraft or you will be considered hostile.' The pilot clearly saw the Sea Lion but sat there and stared at it. He wore a headset but made no reply.

'Cessna Three-Victor-November, acknowledge instructions. Over.' This time, as Geffar edged closer to the Cessna, she could see the pilot gesturing at something. 'Three-Victor-November, I am not receiving any reply. If you can hear me, wave your hand or wag your wings.' The man in the pilot's seat waved casually, actually managed a smile.

'I don't believe this, the guy can hear me . . . I think I recognize this guy, too.' She clicked on her microphone. 'Cessna Three-Victor-November, wave if you can*not* respond on the radio.' Again, another quick wave.

'Radio-out,' Hardcastle said. 'He can hear but he can't talk back.'

'I *do* recognize him,' Geffar said. 'He's some hotshot attorney . . . wait a minute. Three-Victor-November? Max Van Nuys, I think his name is. He represents real estate developers and investors all over the Caribbean.'

'A spoiled playboy, you mean,' Hardcastle added. 'I've heard of him. He owns most of Miami Beach, or at least acts like he does. Anyone with a custom-airplane registration has got to be a prima donna.'

'If he has a radio malfunction and if he's lost his navigation equipment, flying over the platform makes sense,' Geffar said. 'He can use that as a visual checkpoint, then fly west and he'll find the Sunrise Beach Club airport.'

'But that doesn't explain why he's up here, flying from Nassau or somewhere in the Bahamas to Florida without a flight plan or Customs clearance,' Hardcastle said. 'I don't give a damn who he is. We either divert him to Opa-Locka or bust him at Sunrise Beach.'

'Cessna Three-Victor-November, wave if your destination is Sunrise Beach Airport.' The wave could be seen. 'Be advised Sunrise Beach is not an airport of entry. Without prior permission from Customs you must land at an airport of entry. We will escort you to Opa-Locka Airport for inspection.'

Van Nuys nodded his head to signal that he understood, then suddenly Van Nuys seemed very agitated, snapping his head back and forth, looking down, up at the Sea Lion every now and then, fear in his expression.

'Smoke!' Hardcastle shouted. 'I see smoke coming out from under his cowling.'

'In the cockpit, too,' Geffar said. She clicked open the channel. 'Cessna Three-Victor-November, we see smoke coming from under your engine compartment and in your cockpit. Disregard intercept instructions. We will proceed to Sunrise Beach airport. Follow us. Do not acknowledge.' Geffar could see Van Nuys frantically nodding his head. The smoke directly in front of the windshield was being cleared away by window defroster vents and by overhead cabin vents, but the smoke in the cockpit was getting worse.

'Mayday, Mayday, Shark Two-Zero,' Hardcastle called out on the emergency channel. 'Position twenty-five miles southeast of Biscayne Bay, heading two-zero-zero, altitude one thousand feet, airspeed one hundred twenty knots. We are in formation with Cessna Three-Victor-November, type Cessna 210, one soul on board. The Cessna appears to have smoke in the cockpit and he is partial radio-out. We are enroute for emergency formation landing at Sunrise Beach airport.'

'Cessna Three-Victor-November, lower your landing gear,' Geffar said. 'Maintain this airspeed until we get closer to touchdown.' The long, spindly landing gear began to drop down, but abruptly stopped in mid-extension.

'Three-Victor-November, recycle your landing gear.' Nothing. Van Nuys was maintaining altitude with the V-22 but seemed to be having trouble staying on a straight course. Geffar moved out to about eighty feet to stay away from the Cessna's widening swings but crept back in so Van Nuys would not lose sight of her.

'Three-Victor-November, we are ten miles from landing. We will start a gradual descent and slow to ninety knots indicated airspeed. Lower one notch of flaps and begin slowing to ninety knots.' No flaps came out. The Cessna was slowing but things seemed to be getting worse.

231

'It may be an electrical failure or alternator fire,' Hardcastle said. 'He'll have to shut his alternator before he starts a bigger fire in his engine compartment.' Geffar relayed the instructions but the smoke continued.

'Three-Victor-November, we are five miles out. Recycle your landing gear once more, or try manual extension.' Still no movement – they were stuck fast. 'Okay, Three-Victor-November, you'll have to prepare for a gear-up landing. If you can't move your flaps, leave the flap switch in the intermediate position. We'll give you a shallow approach at ninety knots. When we see you over the threshold, set your mixture switch to cutoff, shut off your fuel system and turn your battery switch and magnetos off to reduce the chance of a fire. Good luck.'

Van Nuys was a little wilder in his approach as they got closer to the runway but he hung in there as they got closer to touchdown. At the end of the runway they were about twenty feet off the ground. The Cessna's landing gear looked as if it had moved down another foot – the wheels were exposed and clear of the fuselage but the gear was still unsafe. And still no flaps. 'Crossing the threshold . . . now!' Geffar and Hardcastle could see the propeller spin down and finally stop. Van Nuys was keeping his cool – he even had the presence of mind to crank the engine's starter a few times to angle the propeller blades so they would not strike the ground on impact.

Touchdown. The man was obviously a skilled pilot. He let the back end of the fuselage skid in first, then as if doing it all by feel, slowly nestled the plane down on the partially extended wheels. The gear wasn't locked down so it did not support the Cessna's weight, but Van Nuys kept on flying the plane, gliding the belly in. Suddenly the Cessna spun sharply to the left, skidded on its nose, and swerved across the the runway and into a shallow ditch on the west side of the field.

Geffar swung the Sea Lion off to the north end of the runway about a hundred yards from the Cessna and brought the tilt-rotor aircraft to an abrupt landing, then ran toward the crippled Cessna. Suddenly fire trucks and rescue vehicles came out of nowhere, nearly sideswiping her, and screeched to a halt in front of the Cessna. A fireman with a captain's white helmet went out toward Geffar and told her to stop and stay clear.

Geffar nodded. 'We're equipped to medevac Mr Van Nuys if necessary,' she said.

The fire chief looked at her with surprise and suspicion. 'How did you know it was Van Nuys?'

'We tracked him in from the Bahamas. We intercepted him near our platform and followed him here. We got a pretty good look at him.'

The fire chief looked over Geffar's shoulder at the Sea Lion tilt-rotor aircraft, then back at her. 'You were close enough to get a look at Van Nuys' face – flying *that*?'

'So it *is* Van Nuys . . .'

'That's who owns the plane here at Sunrise Beach and that's who filed the flight plan.'

'Border Security didn't receive a flight plan. He violated Customs entry procedures. We'll have to talk to him – '

'Stay here.' The fire chief then headed back toward the trucks encircling the plane, speaking into his walkie-talkie. At that instant, a loud hissing sound could be heard and mountains of white, foul-smelling chemical foam began spraying over what they could see of the aircraft.

'How is he?' Hardcastle asked as he came up to Geffar.

'I don't know, they won't let me any closer. The chief said it was Van Nuys, said he had filed a flight plan.'

'We sure as hell didn't get it. Neither did FAA or Customs.'

An ambulance raced onto the runway, and a stretcher was brought out.

'We should secure that airplane,' Hardcastle said. 'Even though we know who the pilot is and now know his destination he's still in violation. That plane has to be secured.' Geffar nodded but her mind was somewhere else. 'I'll radio Homestead and tell them to send an investigation team.'

'I'll take some statements and secure the plane,' she said and walked over to the crash site.

Van Nuys was just being hoisted onto the stretcher when she got to the plane. He was strapped securely onto the plywood backboard, heavy straps under his chin and across his forehead securing his head and neck onto the board. Van Nuys was dark and athletic, big hands crossed on his midsection. It took four paramedics to raise his large frame onto the stretcher and carry him into the ambulance. Geffar stepped over to the rear door of the ambulance and watched Van Nuys being wheeled inside. Out of the corner of his eye he spotted Geffar and raised a hand to the men carrying him.

'You're the one who intercepted me?' The words came out raspy and hoarse. 'You were the pilot of that . . . amazing machine out there?'

Geffar nodded. 'Sandra Geffar, Border Security Force, Mr Van Nuys – '

'Max.'

Geffar was only human. Here was a man in obvious pain, about to take an ambulance ride, somehow able to be not only friendly but interested . . . in the V-22, of course . . . 'You saved my life. Thank you.'

He tried to stretch out a hand toward her, but the movement sent a shock of pain through him. The paramedics hustled him inside the ambulance and drove off, and the fire trucks left shortly afterward.

Hardcastle was inspecting the wreckage of the Cessna when Geffar returned. The plane lay on its right side, right wingtips crumpled into the sandy soil between the runway and the taxiway, the fuselage sitting on the ground, the landing gear sprawled out underneath like the legs of a newborn colt. It was covered with at least twelve inches of gooey chemical foam that smelled like formaldehyde and sawdust. The fuselage was crumpled a bit in the middle, but it was remarkably intact, with no sign of explosion or fire . . . Well, Hardcastle thought, Van Nuys had sure kept his cool. 'Investigation unit's on the way,' he told Geffar as she stood beside him. 'They're going to need a shovel and protective gear to clear that gunk out. It's weird, though, no sign of fire, only minor wing fuel-tank damage.'

One of the fire trucks drove over to Hardcastle and Geffar, and two firemen stepped out of the truck carrying chains and thick nylon towing straps. A moment later the fire chief walked over to them from the crash site.

'I'm Police Chief Joseph Hokum. I've received a call from UNICOM. They'd like you to move your . . . whatever that thing is at the end of the runway. They have inbound traffic.'

'The runway's closed until further notice,' Geffar told him. 'Since this is an uncontrolled field we're leaving the V-22 there for now as a reminder. You can't move the Cessna yet either. We have an investigation team on the way – they'll advise you when you can move the plane – '

'An investigation team?'

'This plane was involved with a Customs and Defense Department violation,' Hardcastle told him. 'The area will be sealed off until the investigators are done. You'll have to divert any inbounds somewhere else.'

'Hey, you don't have jurisdiction here. Sunrise Beach is private and I'm the security department here. I've got to clear the damage and reopen this runway.' He turned and jabbed a finger at his men, ordering them to continue working.

Geffar, the adrenaline still pumping through her from the excitement of the pursuit and crash, shocked everybody, including herself. She took three quick steps toward Hokum, grabbed him by the back of his jacket and yanked him backward.

'Why, you – ' He reached inside his coat and Hardcastle saw an under-the-arm holster with the butt end of a very large gun.

Hardcastle was on the case fast. He clipped the man under his jaw, hard, knelt down on the man's chest, pulled a nine-millimeter automatic from the chief's holster and tossed it aside, then rolled the man over on his stomach and yanked his coat back down over his arms.

'What the *hell*?'

'He tried to pull a gun on you,' Hardcastle said, drew his own nine-millimeter SIG Sauer automatic and used it to motion toward the firemen. 'Move away from the plane. Now.' They did. 'Take off your coats.' They did. All of them were wearing guns. 'Drop those holsters on the ramp.'

They looked once at their chief on the ground, slowly unfastened their holsters and let them slide off.

Hardcastle pulled out his walkie-talkie and thumbed the mike. 'Shark, this is Two-Zero.'

'Go ahead, Two-Zero,' Becker replied from the Hammerhead One platform.

'We have a situation here at Sunrise Beach, Mike. Send a chopper with a couple of officers out from Homestead or Shark to our location.'

'We'll divert the Dolphin heading back to headquarters, ETA, about two minutes.'

'Why are you wearing guns?' Hardcastle asked.

'We're the *police*!' the chief shouted, wincing at the pain.

'What are *firemen* doing with guns?' Geffar asked. 'That's dangerous and stupid – '

236

'Not half as stupid as what you two are doing. This is private property, you can't come to this airport without permission – '

'We have authority to go to any airport in the country . . .'

'Not without probable cause you don't.'

'Van Nuys entered the country without Customs clearance. He was flying in restricted airspace without permission. We have authority to pursue any airspace violators.'

'Van Nuys had clearance and a flight plan filed and executed,' the chief said. 'I verified it with the FAA myself when he called it in from Freeport. As for crossing restricted airspace – well, he was radio-out, an emergency aircraft can deviate in an emergency. Besides, all this Border Security Force is a crock . . . you people have no authority over land.'

A white-haired mustachioed man appeared from the crowd that had gathered. 'I'm Fred Weintraub, chairman of the homeowner's association. What's going on?'

'We're from the United States Border Security Force,' Hardcastle told him. 'Your fire chief, or police chief, whichever, was uncooperative, he's being detained – '

'Detained? Assaulted, you mean.'

'He was reaching for a weapon – '

Just then they heard the sound of a Dolphin helicopter approaching. The yellow chopper sped overhead, completed an orientation circle over the center of the runway, then landed a few dozen yards from the growing knot of people at the edge of the runway. Two Border Security Force personnel hopped out of the right-side door wearing sidearms and carrying fire extinguishers.

'Margaret, Jack, keep everyone away from the Cessna here,' Geffar told them. 'No one go near it until Customs arrives. When they get here give me a buzz on the radio.'

They nodded and placed themselves between the airplane and the crowd. 'Looks like we stirred up a hornet's nest,' Geffar said as an aside to Hardcastle.

'Something's strange here,' he said, holstering his sidearm. 'All this local security, all this crap about us invading them . . . Why?'

Border Security Force Area Headquarters, Aladdin City, Florida
Four Hours Later

The new Border Security Force headquarters was located in Aladdin City, about fifteen miles southwest of Miami. It was located on a US Coast Guard communications reservation, where a huge labyrinth of antennas had been erected over several dozen square miles to allow Coast Guard vessels across the southeast United States and the Caribbean region to link up with their Miami headquarters.

It was also the location of the former joint Coast Guard and Customs Service surveillance and command and control center known as C-3-I, an abbreviation for Command, Control, Communications, and Intelligence. C-3-I was the nation's most sophisticated command post, an electronic hub that combined radar data from several different sources – civil, federal, local, military, and intelligence sources – plus worldwide communications facilities into one building. When the Border Security Force was established, control of C-3-I transferred immediately to the new organization; with its sophisticated security setup, remote yet accessible location, and the nearby New Taimiami Airport, which was large enough to handle military aircraft, it was the logical place to set up a base of operations for the Hammerheads.

The facility was quickly expanded to handle the Border

Security Force, with administrative facilities, even more advanced security and communications setup, and expanded access and capacity near Taimiami Airport to handle the unit's manned and unmanned tactical aircraft. The new base was soon nicknamed the 'Zoo,' because of the headquarter's location – the Border Security Force's headquarters was less than a mile from the Miami Metro Zoo.

'Your little episode at the Sunrise Beach Club was about as well-received as a stripper at a funeral,' Brad Elliott said with a weak smile. He was meeting with Hardcastle and Geffar at the Border Security Force's headquarters later that same day. They were in the intelligence operations center, an enclosed, electronically sealed room just off the master control center. Beyond the one-way windows in the front of the room, they could see the three twenty-foot square computer monitors from where the entire southeast United States, and soon the entire nation, was kept under constant watch by the Border Security Force. Those three screens displayed combined radar and sensor images from dozens of different sources, and so complete was the picture on those screens that virtually every aircraft and vessel flying within two hundred miles of America's shoreline was constantly being plotted and tracked by the Hammerheads.

Geffar was pacing around near the office's windows, her flight suit clinging to her body. Hardcastle sat on one of the sofas.

Hardcastle protested. 'We were doing what we're supposed to be doing . . .'

Elliott held up a hand. 'I know, I know, and you were right . . . well, dropping the police chief wasn't such a hot idea . . .'

'I saw his gun and reacted,' Hardcastle said. 'He was reaching for it, had his hand right on it . . .'

239

'Dammit, Ian, no one's accusing you. The chief will get a very detailed explanation of the authority and responsibility of the Border Security Force. But you know the press and the investigators will focus in on what *you* did, not on what he did to promote it.'

'He didn't even seem like a *fire* chief to me,' Hardcastle went on angrily.

'We pulled his files. He was voted in three years running. Ex-Dade Country deputy sheriff.'

'Ex?'

'Resigned after eight years on the force. No explanation given, none required. Most likely a BBD.'

'What's that? Bad Boy Discharge?'

'Bigger and Better Deal.'

Hardcastle shook his head. 'He just . . . hell, I don't know. He seemed wrong, that's all. Everything seemed wrong. What was with all that foam? They covered everything on that plane.'

'He said he saw smoke and ordered the foam applied,' Elliott said, flipping through a folder with Hokum's accident reports. 'He says he was concerned with the safety of the eminent Maxwell Van Nuys, wasn't thinking about any investigations. He thought the foam was the best and most immediate option – '

'Well, who the hell uses foam any more?'

'Just because the military doesn't use it doesn't mean it's not effective,' Elliott replied. 'He says his responsibility is to the residents who – '

'Still doesn't wash,' Hardcastle muttered.

'What did Customs find on Van Nuys' plane?' Geffar asked.

'Plans for a new hotel on Grand Bahama Island, souvenirs, a case of Diamond Plantation rum. It looks like a shortcircuit in his alternator caused the radio blackouts and the smoke in the cockpit.'

'What about his flight plan and Customs clearance?'

'We found it in the system,' Elliott said. 'He had a defense VFR flight plan from Freeport to Sunrise Beach, including a Customs advisory and declaration. There's some question about when it was filed – the chief logged it in one hour before takeoff, but our records didn't show it in the system until he crossed into American airspace. Someone slipped up in there somewhere. We're investigating. And, yes, he declared the rum.' He paused, then added, 'It was a good sortie. Completely justified and authorized. If anyone's to blame for what happened it's Hokum, he should have backed off – '

'What about Van Nuys?'

'He claims exactly what Sandra suspected,' Elliott told them. 'He lost his navigation radios, found the platform and used it as a landmark to find Key Largo.'

'But what about entering the country without a flight plan or permission to enter?'

'He had a flight plan . . .'

'Not a valid one,' Hardcastle said. 'Not one filed before takeoff or approved by us.'

'He did request a waiver of normal Customs inspection procedures for this trip along with the flight plan, but again, the request was never processed.'

'So he skates, is that it?' Hardcastle said.

'Well,' Elliott said, 'the man loses his radio and can't communicate – '

'Funny thing about that. He can hear but can't talk. His IFF goes out, too. Pretty damned convenient. Enough to claim he was lost but not enough to risk getting his ass shot down.'

'We'll backtrack to see if Van Nuys tried to enter the country without filing a flight plan,' Elliott said, 'or maybe tried to file one after the incident, when he got caught. But I can't promise a lot even if we find out he tried to enter

241

without permission. Van Nuys cuts a popular figure in Florida, is well respected. He's already donated the salvageable parts of the wrecked Cessna to the Customs Service – that's worth almost thirty grand right there. Besides, the man's in the hospital with neck injuries. I agree it's a little fishy, Ian, but actually, we've got bigger fish to fry. Like getting the Border Security Force to be a Cabinet-level department. There's opposition, as we knew there would be. See if we earn it, the opposition keeps saying. Hell, if we don't have Cabinet status we won't have some of the clout we need to show our stuff.'

'Wonderful,' Geffar said. 'Politics. If we're successful, they'll be shoving to get their mug-shots with us. If we fail they'll be shoving to be the first to pull the plug.'

'There's another interesting topic being circulated – decriminalization. Rumor has it a measure might be proposed that would virtually legalize marijuana and mandate only rehabilitation for possession of amounts of cocaine less than fifty grams.'

'That's incredible!' Geffar said, shaking her head in disbelief. 'That's just perfect. Here we are, risking our butts like this, and it all might go for nothing.'

'Equally incredible, the congressional leadership has decided not to comment on the rumor as of yet,' Elliott continued.

'There's a strong precedent to decriminalize certain drugs, Sandra,' Hardcastle said. He smiled, knotting his fingers together. 'It's amazing how history repeats itself sometimes. Back during Prohibition, it took the advent of groups such as the first Hammerheads before most persons started to think that maybe alcohol wasn't so bad and the amendment should be repealed. They found out then that if the people want alcohol, they can get it. No amount of strong-arm tactics were going to stop them.'

'Narcotics are different,' Geffar said. 'The drug problem

is affecting the youth of this country. Entire cities are under siege by gangs trafficking in drugs . . .'

'It was no different back then,' Hardcastle insisted. 'There were lots of alcoholic kids, infants born alcoholic, gangs running liquor, shoot-outs in the streets between gangs vying for the black market liquor trade – remember Capone? Bathtub gin? Speakeasies? Alcohol was liquid poison back then, just as drugs are considered now. But Prohibition was still repealed, and alcohol was legalized. They found that society can police itself better than the government can police society.'

'You surprise me every damn day, Hardcastle,' she said. 'Here I thought you were some kind of one-man crusader, launching off in your whirlybird to fight the forces of evil. Hey, my main reason for getting up in the morning is to see what the hell you'll do or say next . . . Anything else for me, Brad?'

'I guess not . . .'

She nodded and headed for the door. 'I'm going down to the Sunrise Beach Community Hospital to have a talk with Van Nuys.'

Hardcastle got to his feet. 'I'll fly you – '

'I have a car. I'll drive. When I'm done I'll go over to Homestead and catch a ride back to the platform.'

After she left there was silence in the office for a long moment. Then, Elliott said: 'How are you two? Things going okay?'

Hardcastle shrugged. 'Fine . . . we really haven't been working together much until today. And we don't always see eye to eye on everything. But you've known that since the beginning. I disagree with her wanting to limit the operational radius of Seagull drones until the data-transmission problem is solved. I'm not interested in how the public feels about seeing a drone parachute into the water. She is, and I understand why. I still . . .'

Elliott nodded. 'Good. Well, I'm going to spend the weekend in Key West, then head back to Washington. If you need to reach me . . .'

'I understand,' Hardcastle said. 'Don't.'

Sunrise Beach Community Hospital, Key Largo, Florida
Two Hours Later

Sandra Geffar had taken just enough time to change into slacks and a linen jacket – which was loose enough to hide her .45 caliber automatic in its shoulder rig – before leaving her headquarters building and starting the drive to Key Largo.

At the hospital she found Van Nuys on his feet, pacing around the room near the window. A neck brace sat on top of broad shoulders, and his movements were very stiff.

'Mr Van Nuys, I'm sorry to disturb you but – '

'Miss Geffar, what a surprise.' Van Nuys moved toward her. Geffar extended a hand but he took both of hers. 'A very pleasant surprise. Please, come in.' He tried to settle in the chair but an obvious spark of pain caused him to sit upright.

Geffar, without thinking, took a pillow from the bed and placed it behind him. 'Much better, thank you. You'll make some man very happy. Or are you – '

'Divorced.' Personal biographies weren't why she was here, she tried to remind herself. 'I need to ask you some questions about this morning.'

'Of course,' all affably. 'I thank the Customs Service investigators for being brief with their questions. I'm afraid I wasn't very helpful. My doctor pumped me full of painkillers.'

'I understand you didn't have your shoulder harness on.'

He looked at her in some surprise. Which hardly

244

matched hers that she'd said it. 'How did you know that?' he asked.

'. . . Your injuries are common for people who are unrestrained and try to brace themselves against the force of an impact. I've been there.'

'I'm sure you have,' smiling, smiling.

'Yes, well, I understand you filed your flight plan by phone to Chief Hokum here at Sunrise Beach. Why? Why not file directly with the FAA?'

'By speaking directly with the Chief I was able to accomplish several things. I not only transmitted my flight plan to him but he was notified of my ETA and other messages I had him deliver for me. Chief Hokum co-operates nicely in such matters.'

That all checked with her information from past FAA records, which showed Hokum had filed flight plans for Van Nuys and other Sunrise Beach tenants at various times. It seemed a strange way of filing a flight plan, but on the other hand trying to file a flight plan through Bahamian air traffic control or long distance to Miami Flight Service could result in lost plans.

'Am I going to be charged with a crime?'

'Technically, you're in violation. The Border Security Force's fine is a minimum of ten thousand dollars and confiscation of your aircraft, unless there are mitigating circumstances. Next trip I'd suggest contacting the FAA directly instead of going through Hokum. If he loses your flight plan you're still responsible. Turning over the salvageable parts of your plane to Customs, well, I doubt Hammerheads will levy a fine, this time. But the decision will come from Washington.'

'The 210 was old and not my favorite plane for overwater trips . . . You mentioned the Hammerheads. Exactly who are the Hammerheads?'

'It's our nickname for the Border Security Force. We're

not very big yet, but we can secure the whole southeast United States from unauthorized intrusion and we'll soon be able to cover the entire southern flank.'

'Hammerheads . . . Like the shark, eh? Sounds very military. What's a beautiful woman like you doing – ?'

'Just lucky, I guess.' She didn't add a 'thanks' for the compliment, but she had to admit it registered. 'Let's talk about why you didn't fly the entry corridor after discovering you were radio-out.'

'What?'

'According to your flight plan you were filed VFR from Freeport to Opa-Locka, stopover for inspection, and then VFR to Sunrise Beach. Yet when you lost communications just before entering the ADIZ you were detected flying several miles off course directly for Sunrise Beach. Why?'

Van Nuys shrugged. 'I suppose I panicked a bit . . . I thought I was on course but I found myself drifting south of the corridor. When I saw your platform I knew where I was and decided to go directly back to Sunrise Beach instead of going through the Miami terminal control area radio-out.'

Geffar nodded. He was smart. It was the correct reply – the *only* correct reply. Flight through a terminal control area as busy as Miami's was never recommended for radio-out aircraft unless he was on instrument flight rules. Unless it was the only option, the preferred course would have been to land at an airport not inside a TCA, and since Sunrise Beach was his final destination it was the logical choice . . .

'Since you had deviated from your flight plan,' Geffar went on, 'rescuers would have had a hard time finding you if you had gone down in the ocean . . . And making an approach at an uncontrolled airport with no radios isn't a good idea. *But* under the circumstances, your decision did make sense . . .' Was she being turned around easy? No, she didn't think so. Come on, Geffar, stop the two-bit self-analysis . . .

'I'm afraid I wasn't too concerned about Customs at that particular moment,' Van Nuys said, looking earnest, 'and Hokum did know I was arriving. One pass over the field without a call to UNICOM would have alerted him that I was having difficulty. But I take your points, there were other options that I no doubt should have considered. But I never expected what greeted me. You made a very impressive show in your flying machine out there, Sandra Geffar. Was that a V-22 you were flying?' She nodded. 'The one with the missiles and guns on board?' A half nod. The smile was back. 'Well, I'm very glad you people didn't open fire, but I'm also glad I did what I did – it got me a chance to meet *you*.'

Compliments again. They made her suspicious or nervous . . . As she stood to leave he struggled to his feet, towering over her. 'I'm sorry if I made you feel uncomfortable,' he said.

'You didn't.' But he did.

'May I see you again?'

She had been half-steeling herself for that question but it still startled her. 'This incident needs to be cleared up . . . Take care of yourself, Mr Van Nuys,' she said, and left.

She headed for the exit, but at a last-minute thought she turned up the hallway and found the room adjacent to Van Nuys', belonging to Joseph Hokum. Before knocking she patted the .45 underneath her jacket, knocked on the door, waited a few seconds, then entered.

Several of the chief's deputies and firemen were clustered around the bed. They had a chart spread out on Hokum's lap – of what Geffer could not tell – and several papers and what appeared to be fax or telex message sheets on the bedstand. As soon as she came through the door one of the deputies moved quickly toward her and she could see another pushing the nurse's call button.

'You're not allowed in here . . .'

Geffar moved closer to the bed as the deputies scrambled to put away the chart and papers. Hokum's face was badly swollen – Hardcastle would have been proud, she thought. He was also sputtering to his people to remove her. 'Just wanted to check on you, Chief – '

She was grabbed tight around the forearms and shoved backward.

'What a big gun you have there,' the deputy said as he pulled her .45 out of her holster and tossed it to one of the men behind him.

She was considering a judo move when she heard, 'Get your hands off her, Buck.' Standing in the hallway, half-leaning against the wall for support, was Maxwell Van Nuys.

'Everything's under control, Mr Van – '

Van Nuys reached over and grabbed the deputy's left wrist, encircling it in his left hand. 'I *said*, get your hands off her.' The deputy's knees began to buckle under Van Nuys' grip before he finally released Geffar. 'Give her the gun back.' The fireman did. She had to wonder at the sheer power of Maxwell Van Nuys even in his obviously weakened condition.

'Get out of my sight,' Van Nuys said. His voice was weak with the pain shooting through his back but the message was clear. They both retreated into the chief's room and the door closed behind them.

Van Nuys groaned and held himself up, his back flat against the wall. A nurse came by to help him back into bed, where he lay flat and motionless.

'What did you think you were doing?' Geffar said.

'I might ask you the same question,' glancing at her out the corner of his eye. 'Stay away from them. Hokum may be the police chief of a conservative peaceful Sunrise Beach but he runs the place like the marshal of an Old West town. The residents like his tough-guy act.'

'This is the man who files your flight plans for you?'

Van Nuys smiled and gave her a nod. 'All right, all right. Message received. I'll do like everybody else and file directly with the feds. But I'm serious about Hokum. He has the law and a lot of powerful, influential citizens behind him . . . So . . . how about it? Can I see you again?'

'I told you, there are serious questions that need to be cleared up with your affairs.' And mine, she silently added as she turned and left without another word.

Van Nuys lay flat in bed, savoring the thought of Geffar, until he heard a knock at the door and it swung open. One of Hokum's men poked his head through the door. 'Sir?'

'Get out.'

'Sir, the Chief would like to speak.'

'Tell him to go piss up a rope.'

'I'm afraid he . . . insists, sir.'

Van Nuys sat up in bed, stood, adjusted his bathrobe and without a hint of the discomfort he'd shown Sandra Geffar pushed past the man and stepped through the door connecting their two rooms.

Chief Hokum was lying in bed surrounded by senior deputies and assistants. He had just downed a shot of tequila. His face was puffy. 'That Hardcastle sure did a number on you, didn't he? Okay, now what the hell do you want?'

'I want to know what *she* was doing here.'

'Visiting me.'

'Then why was she in my room?'

'Maybe she stopped by to admire her partner's handiwork.'

'Very funny . . . You'd better not see her anymore.'

Van Nuys, his patented smile in place, stepped over to Hokum's bedside, nodding – then suddenly reached over and grabbed Hokum's neck with his right hand. The chief yelled in pain. Van Nuys gave a quick glance at the deputies but none raised a hand.

Van Nuys leaned forward and moved his face within an inch of Hokum's, maintaining his grip. 'You listen to me, scum bag, *I* run this operation. I say what goes down and what doesn't. Now I'm telling *you*. You stay away from Geffar and Border Security. Clear?' Van Nuys released his neck with a snap of his wrist. 'I'm interested in what happened to my flight plan and my airplane. If I had a suspicious nature I'd say you sabotaged my plane and didn't file the flight plan so Border Security would catch me – '

'That's crazy, Mr Van Nuys,' Hokum managed through the pain in his face. 'You were carrying five million dollars worth of blow. Why would I want anything else but to see that shipment arrive safe and sound?'

'Maybe I wasn't supposed to make it. Maybe you want to take over my operation. You let me get caught with the drugs – '

'No, no, Mr Van Nuys. If you get caught I'm implicated right away. They'll come down on me harder than you. I want to do everything I could to make sure you're covered. That's why I kept Border Security away from your plane and foamed it. I wouldn't do anything to jeopardize our operation – '

'*My* operation,' Van Nuys said, not entirely convinced, although Hokum seemed panicked enough to be telling the truth. 'What happened with my flight plan and Customs clearance? Why was Border Security alerted?'

'I *swear* I don't know. I filed the flight plan as you directed. We had it all worked out how we were going to delay the Customs inspector at the front gate until we offloaded the drugs. We had the proper cargo seals with the copied numbers all ready to go. They must've lost the flight plan in the system – '

'Very convenient – for you. You screw up once more, Hokum, and you'll find yourself part of a concrete foundation in my new gallery mall on Grand Bahama. And you make very damn sure that plane is sanitized before it's turned over to Customs.'

'He's crazy,' one of the deputies murmured after Van Nuys had gone and they helped Hokum settle back into bed and poured him a shot of tequila. 'He's going to blow this whole deal over that bitch – '

'Like hell he is,' Hokum said. He turned to his senior deputy, David Frye. 'What happened? Why *didn't* that plane go down?'

'The charge must've been defective,' Frye told him. 'Instead of detonating it burned through some wiring and shorted out his alternator. We're damned lucky he made it back here instead of being forced to land at Opa-Locka or Miami . . . But if you wanted Van Nuys to get caught with the coke we had hidden on his plane why did you order us to foam his plane and take the stuff off?'

'Use your head,' Hokum said. 'I wanted Van Nuys dead *and* the coke found in his plane. If he's alive he can talk, and if he can talk and explain that he had nothing to do with the stuff being in his plane, the attention focuses on us again. The weapons-smuggling operation I've spent years organizing inside Van Nuys' drug smuggling almost went down the tubes because of your bungling. You get one more chance – that's it.'

Hokum lay silent a moment, then tossed back a mouthful of tequila and jabbed a finger at Frye. 'I want to know all there is to know about this Sandra Geffar. I want to know where she lives, where she goes, what she does and who she does it with. Use our contacts in the Dade County Sheriff's office and DMV. And keep it quiet.'

* * *

25!

Hammerhead One Air Staging Platform
Two Weeks Later

Geffar and Hardcastle were, officially, off duty, having finished a twelve-hour day shift, but both were in uniform. They were sitting near the bay windows watching a Customs inspection of a Costa Rican freighter tied alongside the platform's east docks below the aerostat-balloon-launching area. The ballpark lights that rimmed the platform's top level were bathing the freighter in stark white light.

Michael Becker, his earset looped around his neck, cord dangling from a pocket, walked up to their table with his dinner. 'Mind if I join you?'

Geffar stood. 'I've got to get ready for tonight's . . . interview. Excuse me.' She looked embarrassed and she was.

'She's got a "Nightline" interview in a couple of hours,' Hardcastle told him.

'I know . . . I heard. She makes a great spokesperson for the Hammerheads.'

'She's lost, burning it at both ends,' Hardcastle said, staring down at the freighter.

'You've been spending an awful lot of time out here yourself, Admiral. I've noticed you missing the chopper back to shore more and more. Why don't you take some time off? Go see Daniel.'

'I should . . . hell, I'll give him a call . . . You know, Mike,' he said, jabbing a finger at Becker, 'after more than six months we've only got four fully operational Sea Lion aircraft and only five platform-qualified crews.'

'We have two Sea Lions on the platform and one at Homestead, plus one for training. Congress has been screwing around with our funding from the very start. They delayed the next six Sea Lions for two months, waiting for public reaction, according to Elliott, who's doing his best. Also, having this big shot Van Nuys testify on how effective and how heroic the Hammerheads are was a good move – '

'Yeah. Van Nuys,' Hardcastle said, shaking his head. 'Our new buddy, our very own socialite-playboy-spokesman for the Hammerheads. I could do without it, without *him* . . .'

Becker said nothing, but understood Hardcastle was less than pleased by the apparent friendship between Geffar and Van Nuys.

'Mike, we should be flying the hell out of the crews, the Sea Lions and the drones. We should be making our presence *felt*. We've got to get this station on the damned track.'

Again, Becker kept his mouth shut. Because this was between his boss and Geffar. And because he believed his boss was right.

The camera's lights created a spot of daylight at the edge of the platform, even brighter than the illumination of the ballpark lights on the east side of the huge facility. A camera crew was set up on the Hammerhead One upper deck, positioned so that the camera could swing freely from Geffar on deck down to photograph the activity on the deck of the Costa Rican coastal freighter moored alongside the platform.

Geffar, with one finger covering her right ear and another holding the earpiece secure in her left ear, strained to listen to the question from the TV interviewer. 'Miss Geffar, thank you very much for joining us tonight.'

'My pleasure. Beautiful night out here. Glad you could join us.'

Hardcastle, in his office beside the command center on the third deck, shook his head as he half-listened. Talking

253

about the Hammerheads' main operations platform as if it were a white sandy beach in the Virgin Islands . . . ?

The intercom on his desk buzzed, and he touched the button without taking his eyes from a TV screen. 'Yes?'

'Dolphin's ready to head on back to shore,' Becker said. 'They're waiting for you.'

Some people think they've got time, he kept thinking. When the smugglers start coming in force . . . damn it, we've got to make sure they don't succeed when they begin to make their move . . . 'I'll catch the morning chopper, Mike.'

'You've been hitting it pretty hard.'

'I'll catch the next one out,' he said, clicked off the intercom and went back to watching the interview.

'What's happening out there tonight?' the interviewer was asking.

The camera slowly swung out over the railing and down toward the freighter as Geffar said: 'We're helping the Customs Service on a special vessel search. In this case, apparently intelligence was received that this freighter might be carrying a large amount of contraband, so the ship's crew was directed to stop at our Border Security Force platform for a search before entering US waters. The Customs Service comes on board the platform, we take the crew off the freighter and Customs conducts a compartment-by-compartment search. They use fiber optic probes, dogs, electronic sniffers, ultrasound detectors and thermal-neutron analysis to search each cargo container.'

'Isn't it rather unusual to conduct a search such as this?'

'No, the Coast Guard conducts dozens all over the world. Here on this Hammerhead platform we have *better* facilities and can keep better control of a situation than conducting a search on the high seas. It adds a new dimension to controlling our borders. We have the facilities out here, we use them.'

'Has anything been found on this freighter?'

'Nothing yet . . .'

'Does that mean your intelligence is faulty?'

'Intelligence isn't an exact science. If the smugglers found out that *we* knew, they may have arranged to pay off or procure another vessel, or cancel the shipment altogether. Maybe they threw it overboard when we ordered them to stop at the platform. Either way, just by *having* this facility here we've stopped another suspected shipment of drugs from entering the country. And every time we force them to change their plans, it's one in the plus column.'

'Explain, please.'

'Let's say there was a thousand-kilo shipment of drugs coming in – over a ton of cocaine. They take that ton of cocaine and, say, pack it in creosote or stuff it into vegetables or sink it in barrels of tomato sauce. That one ton of coke packed in three tons of stuff. Now they get word that we found out which vessel they're going to try to smuggle the stuff in. The smugglers have to unload it or dump it, unravel the mess they made and then repack it to send it out some other way. It costs them time and money. And if they try to ship it anyway, we'll be waiting for it.'

'So instead of shipping it through the Caribbean they truck it overland through Mexico or Texas or Arizona?'

'Maybe, but what we've done is force them to spend time and energy in their operation. And by increasing our vigilance, establishing tight control in the Caribbean and south Florida frees up more agents in the south and southwest. Soon the Border Security Force will establish control over the south and eventually move into the southwest itself – '

'Are you saying that one of your major objectives was to force the smugglers to go somewhere else?'

'No, that's putting it in the worst light and oversimplifying.' She tried to swallow the anger rising in her throat. 'The FBI reports that the street price of cocaine is up near fifty percent since the Border Security Force was activated only six months ago. And since over half of the cocaine that comes into this country comes through the southeast, I'd say we are making a *real* impact.'

'You see that reported price increase as a victory?'

'I *do*. A fifty-percent increase begins to make cocaine too expensive for a lot of users. Someone who six months ago may have been able to find a hundred-dollar vial of coke easily now finds his or her supply drying up, or finds he can't afford it anymore – '

'So he robs another liquor store or snatches another purse or embezzles more money from the till to get the extra money – '

'*Or*, sir, he does without. Or he finds a treatment program because use is too expensive. Or he does something stupid, something he's not accustomed to, and gets caught. Or he does drugs less often, or shares less of it, or dilutes it more. The fact that our new operation here is chasing a lot of the rats out of their holes and into the open where we can better get at them is in itself an accomplishment. We *are* making a difference. And we've only just begun to fight . . .'

Valdivia, Colombia

Gonzales Gachez picked a slice of lime from a cup on the bar and hurled it at the wide-screen television set.

He had been sitting at his bar in his oak-paneled office at his ranch in central Colombia watching the interview program via a hacked satellite descrambler – any announcement of an interview with any American official involved with drug interdiction or drug policy got his close attention these days. With him were officers and foremen in charge of various aspects of his drug trade.

The TV program cut to a commercial, but because Gachez was receiving the satellite broadcast live as it was being transmitted from the Hammerhead One platform they still saw Geffar standing in front of the camera, taking a message on a walkie-talkie.

'Does she really believe she can have such an effect on our operation?' Gachez said aloud. 'We ship a thousand kilos a day right under their nose, all their fancy helicopters and drones can't stop – '

'She's gotta say that on TV,' Luis Cerredo, Gachez's chief of staff, said.

Instead of calming Gachez, as they should have if believed, Cerredo's words had the opposite effect. 'Just for TV, Luis? Then why are we not getting paid? Why are our buyers saying we are not delivering as promised? We distribute drugs all over the Bahamas, all over Mexico, and we get only *half* our money and no product in return. Why?'

'The cowards on the receiving end see helicopters coming and they run. They say that the Cuchillos' planes attract too much attention, that they draw the *federales* to the drop point and they cannot pick up the product – '

'And are they attracting attention?' Gachez asked. 'Are the Cuchillos becoming sloppy?'

'Not in my opinion, sir,' Cerredo told him. 'They take precautions. They have analyzed the weaknesses of this Border Security Force and have managed to take advantage of their deficiencies – '

'How have they done *that*? Making drops in the middle of the mountains in Mexico? Making fifty-kilo shipments? *That* is their idea of taking advantage of weaknesses?'

'We agreed it would not be wise to send the Cuchillos up against these Border Security Force troops right away,'

Cerredo said. 'The only way to bypass them was to stay away from the usual drop points near Florida. We shifted more to overland transport and our distribution routes in southern California – '

'Yet we send the same amount of product but have more of it confiscated by the authorities. We need much more reliable means of getting our product into the United States. Every shipment we successfully make is worth its weight in gold – we can command nearly twice the price as before.'

'I still think we should continue to improve our other import methods, rather than trying to reopen our usual routes,' one of the brasher lieutenants said. 'My men have made several test runs into south Florida, and one of those Border Security Force planes always seem nearby. We constantly hear their warnings on the radio – '

'But have you actually tried to penetrate their defenses?' Gachez asked. 'Have you ever continued, to see what would happen?'

The lieutenant looked uneasy. 'Why . . . no, we stay outside American waters – '

'Why? We have heard warnings on the radio before . . .'

'Because, sir, we can see their . . . whatever those small helicopter-planes are. They buzz around like flies. They fly one way, then suddenly stop and hover in place like a helicopter. It stays for a while, then flies off. Soon a larger plane appears and does the same, and soon one of their high-speed patrol boats comes.'

Gachez was silent, pacing in front of the long bar, tapping on its polished surface. 'We need to reestablish our intelligence base with this Border Security Force. I want to know exactly how these . . . these Hammerheads operate, who they are, what are their weaknesses. These drones, their special new aircraft – I want to know what their range is, their performance, how many they have operating in the area.'

'We can do that immediately,' one of the officers said.
'We can send several boats and planes in to test their
surveillance. So far they have not fired on us if we have
turned away from shore or are farther than twelve miles
from shore – '

'Wait,' Gachez said, raising a hand, straining to listen to
the television interview again:

'I think it's interesting,' the interviewer was saying, 'that
one of your biggest supporters is a man that you arrested
not too long ago – Maxwell Van Nuys . . .'

'Mr Van Nuys flew into south Florida without a properly
filed flight plan. He was fined twenty thousand dollars, his
aircraft was confiscated, his pilot's license was suspended
for thirty days. There were mitigating circumstances –
including serious equipment malfunctions at the time and
his useful cooperation with the Border Security Force.'

'You of course know that an important vote on the
Department of Border Security Act is coming up shortly.
Any thoughts on that?'

'No. The Hammerheads is an *operational* entity with or
without a new box on the White House organizational
chart. Our work will continue and grow . . .'

'*Find him*,' Gachez said. He turned to his men in the room.
'I want to know everything about this Van Nuys. Perhaps
we can get to her by getting to him.'

'Van Nuys is a jet-setter, a playboy,' Cerredo said. 'Why
don't we deal with her directly?'

'Because she is government. If we put pressure on this
friend of hers, whatever he is, we may create an opening to
her. Do it.

'And I want to find the weaknesses in this Border
Security Force. I am not convinced they can control access
to the whole southeast coast of the United States. Find me a

weakness I can exploit. I want to know exactly how and when this Border Security Force goes into action, I want to find a sure way to beat them . . .'

'You mean draw them out?'

'I don't care *how* you do it, but I want it done. The Hammerheads charge ten thousand dollars and confiscate the airplane or vessel? I will pay the fine *plus* five thousand dollars and provide a boat for anyone with the courage to try it.' Still no takers – except for one hand raised in a corner of the office. The Cartel leader walked up to him. 'What's your name?'

'Carlos,' a very young man answered. 'Carlos Canseco.'

'How old are you, Carlos?'

'Nineteen, Señor Gachez.'

'Nineteen.' He gave the boy an affectionate slap on the cheek, wrapped an arm around his shoulders and led him to the front of the room. '*Here* is a man. His bravery puts you all to shame. He will receive *ten* thousand dollars and a house for his courageous behaviour.' He turned to the young man. '*Bueno*. We will have a Puerto Rican registered speedboat ready for you in Freeport tomorrow night. And if you make it to shore, as I am confident you will, I will give you an extra five-thousand-dollar bonus.'

Canseco looked as if he might explode with pride. If Gachez had been wearing a ring the boy might have knelt and kissed it, Cerredo thought glumly.

Hammerhead One Staging Platform
The Next Morning

Becker found Hardcastle asleep at his desk. 'Morning, sir. Figured I'd find you here.'

'What time is it?' Hardcastle asked, massaging his neck.

'Six-thirty. The morning chopper will be landing any

minute. I made sure there was room for you on it for the return trip.'

'Hell, Mike, I go on duty in twelve hours. I might as well stay.' He turned toward his window and stared wordlessly out into the gray morning skies.

'You're *off* duty. I logged you off for the next two days.'

'I appreciate the thought, Mike, but I can't – '

'It's official.'

Hardcastle turned and saw that the leave form Becker was holding up had his own name on it.

'The Jay Hawk will wait until you're on board. You've been hitting it harder than ever, sir,' Becker told him. 'The Inspector and you . . . well, sir, pardon me, but I think you need to step back a little . . .'

'Dammit, Becker, I don't need you to – ' Hardcastle stopped himself, ran a hand over his eyes and across the night's stubble on his face – 'all right, all right, yes, I feel frustrated because I think we're not doing enough, so I stay on board this platform and the more I stay on board the more frustrated I get.'

Becker nodded. 'It's a matter of time, sir. You know that. Meanwhile, Sandra's in charge of operations here. But you're head of plans, weapons . . . I mean, the Vice President said it . . . you two have to make it work. It's your baby, sir. She's never denied that. Hey, if I'm out of line, sir . . .' Hardcastle half-smiled and waved him off. 'I'll be up on deck waiting. And I know Daniel would sure like to see you.'

'Becker? Thanks, buddy. See you on deck.'

It was a Saturday, and Hardcastle and his son took advantage of it.

Hardcastle was the guest of the University of Miami's baseball team at a pre-game breakfast before the first game of the season. Although a freshman and still mostly a benchwarmer or utility player, Daniel was considered an up-and-coming infielder with an impressive batting average and better than average fielding skills. Hardcastle put on a warm-up suit and jogging shoes and participated with the team in a two-mile run, then led them in a few calisthenics and warm-up drills later that morning. Afterward he stood with the coaches in the tower to watch batting and fielding practice and later was invited into the dugout to watch the game against the University of Georgia.

Daniel was put in the game in the sixth inning after a minor injury to the Hurricanes' second baseman and played well. His range around second base was excellent and he went one-for-two at bat with a double and a long fly-out before being rotated out of the lineup during a late-inning pitching change. For Hardcastle, it was hard to believe how fast his son had grown up . . .

Over dinner they talked like long-lost best friends or brothers, not as father and son. Daniel held nothing back, including fellow-students' reactions to him as the son of the creator and a chief officer of the Hammerheads. Over coffee Daniel asked his father if they could go out to Key Biscayne and see a V-22 Sea Lion and Hardcastle readily said yes.

'This thing is *amazing*,' Daniel Hardcastle said as they walked around the huge aircraft in its hangar just outside the Hammerheads' operational headquarters. The Sea Lion at Aladdin City was one of the non-platform-based alert aircraft configured to take off within minutes and loaded with extra fuel tanks, a Hughes Chain Gun in the port pod and six Sea Stinger missiles in the reloadable starboard pod. 'What's her top speed?'

'About two hundred and fifty knots in airplane mode,' his father told him. 'About one hundred knots in helicopter mode. It can even go about forty knots in reverse.'

Daniel walked quickly around the strange aircraft, pointing out things he recognized and asking about what he did not: 'Looks like an FLIR turret, right? Infrared TV, steerable intercept ID lights . . . a radar? *Is* that a radar?'

'Multi-mode APG-176,' Hardcastle said. 'Sea scan, air targets, ground mapping, navigation and terrain avoidance. It even picks up things like power lines, flocks of birds and even large wind shifts to warn of dangerous wind shear conditions near thunderstorms. The guns and missiles use the TADS/PNVS system. Translation: Target Acquisition and Sight, Pilot Night Vision Sensor. It's the same fire-control system used onthe Apache attack helicopter.'

'Radical,' Daniel said, then stopped, as Hardcastle knew he would, at the sleek aerodynamic Chain Gun pod, which looked something like a a baby albino whale strapped on the Sea Lion's port side. 'You really put guns on this sucker, huh?' Hardcastle did not reply. Daniel turned toward him, a more somber expression on his young face. 'Shoot anyone yet?'

'No.'

'Would you? If you found someone trying to – '

He never got to finish the sentence. A horn blared outside the hangar where the Sea Lion was parked. Lights outside on the ramp snapped on. Hardcastle was about to head into the operations building when several crewmen walked into the hangar and began to climb inside the V-22.

'They don't seem to be in so much of a hurry,' Daniel said, expecting a fire house rush of men to their stations.

'The Aladdin City crew is the third response crew. If the drones and Sea Lions out on the platform are busy they'll send a drone from Marathon or aircraft from Homestead. If they need more support, they'll launch aircraft from here.' He moved across to the right side of the V-22 to the pilot's side. 'What's up, Adam?' he asked the Sea Lion

263

pilot, Adam Fontaine, as he began to activate external power to monitor the radios.

'CARABAL has picked up a fast-moving boat coming out of Bimini, heading somewhere north of Fort Lauderdale. They're not launching any drones from Hammerhead One – they said it's too far away for reliable data-link control – so they want aircraft on standby. We're in better position to respond than Marathon or Homestead so we've been moved up in backup priority.'

'Is he following the entry corridor?'

'No. They said the guy was usually inside the corridor – between Alice Town and Fort Lauderdale you can't help but be in the entry corridor – but it's SLINGSHOT's guess that the guy's not following any corridor routeing.'

'No Customs clearance notification?'

'That's what triggered the alert,' Fontaine said. 'He went through Customs in the harbor at Alice Town, but when they backsearched his registration the make and the model didn't jive.'

'What's his destination?'

'Some rinkydink marina along the inland waterway. I wouldn't expect him to show up there, though. Sounds like a runner to me – not a very smart one, but still a runner.'

Hardcastle's eyes narrowed with anger and some frustration. 'We should go get this guy right now. I wonder what the problem is on the platform?'

'Geffar apparently wants to leave it to Customs,' Fontaine said. 'They're saying small potatoes, not worth a Sea Lion sortie – '

'What? The whole damned idea behind the Hammerheads is to prevent slugs like that from even entering our waters. If he's not challenged before he gets to shore we might never catch him without a large-scale hunt – and then it'll *really* cost.' The pressure inside was building. 'Who's on the duty console?'

'Geffar's on board the platform,' Fontaine said, 'but I think Annette Fields is on the desk.' A former Drug Enforcement Agency regional director, she was one of the first non-Coast Guard or Customs Service officers to join the Hammerheads. And because of her skill and expertise at commanding urban-scale enforcement operations she was immediately trained as a shift commander for a Hammerheads air-staging platform. She was in line to be the deputy of Hammerhead Two when it was completed.

Hardcastle impatiently motioned to Fontaine to trade places, and moments later Hardcastle was sitting in the Sea Lion's cockpit with a headset on. 'Shark, this is Bravo. How copy?'

'Bravo, this is Shark,' the controller aboard Hammerhead One replied immediately. 'Copy five-by. Stand by for Kitty.' A few moments later Fields came on the channel. 'Bravo, this is Kitty. How are you, tiger? Are you at headquarters?'

'I'm with Shark Two-Three,' Hardcastle told her. 'I want to put together an air sortie against the target heading north of your position. Do you have a machine out there ready to go?'

A slight pause, then: 'Not really, tiger. The target's outside HIGHBAL's drone-range restriction and we only have one Victor-22 available – the other went down this morning. Alpha wants to keep it on deck unless we get an air target and let Customs have the northbound target. We've got an SES from Fort Lauderdale, call-sign Five-One, preparing to get underway to intercept, ETA twenty minutes.'

'Twenty minutes?' Hardcastle muttered to no one in particular. 'It'll take an hour for him to get in position. The *idea* here is to stop the sons-of-bitches *before* they get in, not after.' On the radio Hardcastle said, 'We're going to launch Two-Three after him, Shark.'

'Roger,' Field replied from Hammerhead One. 'Will you be on board, tiger?'

'Negative. There's a crew here.'

'Uh . . . we're not night-intercept qualified, sir,' Fontaine said.

'What? I thought you were checked out – '

'I was signed off when the number was five,' Fontaine said. 'The number's fifteen now; I've only got eleven. And a half.'

Hardcastle rolled his eyes in frustration. 'Well what the hell are you doing on night alert?' he asked, suddenly aware of his son standing nearby. 'What's the use in having you out here if you can't run a night intercept?'

'Surveillance, support, rescue – and toga,' Fontaine said quietly.

'Toga? What does *that* mean?'

'T-O-G-A. The Only Guy Available.' He noted Hardcastle was not amused. 'Sir, the commander knew my rundown, she put me out here.'

Hardcastle tried to control himself. 'Well, you're going to get your night intercepts tonight. We're going to get that guy before he reaches the three-mile line.' He turned to the Sea Lion's plane captain. 'Get her towed out to the ramp and ready for launch.' He looked at Daniel. 'If you're game you can ride along.'

Daniel was clearly surprised. Fontaine looked even more surprised. 'Uh, sir, do you think that's a good idea . . . ?'

Hardcastle slapped his hands eagerly. 'We've given TV interviews, brought reporters and politicians on Sea Lion night sorties – '

'But on a night-training mission?'

Hardcastle didn't seem to hear him. 'Get him body armor and a life jacket and let's get rolling. I'll file flight orders and get us a clearance.' Hardcastle trotted into the operations center to change into a flight suit as the V-22's

266

plane captain attached a motorized tow cart to the Sea Lion's nose gear and prepared to tow it out of its hangar for takeoff.

When Hardcastle returned, he found his son in the starboard aft-facing jump seat right behind the pilot. Hardcastle could see him easily by looking over his shoulder from the left-side copilot's seat. Daniel was securely strapped into a thinly padded metal tube seat with thick web belts, but the straps would allow him movement to turn in his seat or look out the rectangular observation window beside him. Bundled in a light shirt underneath the heavy, inch-thick bulletproof body armor, an orange Hammerheads windbreaker, and a CLU-93 twin-bladder underarm inflatable life preserver strapped on over it, plus a helmet with built-in headphone and night-vision goggles, Daniel's normally athletic frame looked stuffed and trussed.

'All set?' Hardcastle yelled back to Daniel as the Sea Lion's auxiliary power unit revved up. Daniel gave him a thumbs up.

Daniel's seat provided a dramatic view of the configuration of the V-22 Sea Lion from stowed to takeoff positions. Slowly the wings swiveled around from their stowed position along the fuselage until they were locked in their normal position. The engine nacelles swiveled to vertical and the rotor blades motored up from their stowed positions down along the nacelles to their normal positions. It was like watching a giant transformer toy unfolding by itself. Less than three minutes after the wings and engines were back in their more conventional positions they were ready for takeoff.

The Hammerheads headquarters area at Aladdin City had a five-thousand-foot runway, but the Sea Lion needed only a fraction of that distance for takeoff. Fontaine made it with a gentle stream of instructions from Hardcastle. As the engine nacelles cocked just a few degrees down from the vertical and the wing flaps extended, Daniel heard the engines wind up to full power. They rolled only what seemed like a few short yards down the runway and then, with a powerful leap that drove Daniel right down into his seat, the V-22 jumped into the air. But unlike any of the helicopter rides Daniel had ever taken, the Sea Lion gained forward velocity with breathtaking speed. Soon the nacelles were fully horizontal, the wing flaps retracted and the Sea Lion was hurtling through the dark skies over the east coast of Florida.

'Shark, this is Shark Two-Three, airborne headquarters, passing two thousand feet for three thousand five hundred.'

'Two-Three, this is Shark, radar contact,' the controller aboard the Hammerhead One platform replied. 'Surface target is at your twelve o'clock, forty miles. His speed is approximately twenty-eight knots, occasionally thirty-three in light to medium seas. Your ETA is eight minutes.'

'Have you tried him on the radio?' Hardcastle asked.

'Affirmative, Two-Three. No response on any frequencies.'

'Well, the turkey's making thirty knots in light to medium seas,' Hardcastle mused on interphone, 'so it's obvious he's not in distress. He's obviously ducking us.' He turned around to glance into the V-22's cabin. 'I'd like all warning flares loaded in the starboard pod,' he said. He caught Daniel's eyes just then – round with both excitement and a little fear. Daniel turned to watch as the rocket-launcher pod was motored back inside the cabin and three of the six missiles were unloaded and replaced by three four-foot-long missiles with yellow markings. The three missiles that were removed carried fluorescent red markings: FIM-93 RMP LIVE HE – live high-explosive Sea Stinger missiles. For Daniel it was like watching the old newsreel-type videos of news reporters in combat in Vietnam – except this was real and now.

Hardcastle lowered his FLIR visor down over his eyes and activated the system. 'Night intercepts are no different than night-rescue or night-support missions,' he told Fontaine. 'Let the copilot take the FLIR and the radios until you get within a few miles of your target, then switch the FLIR image back and forth until you get yourself orientated. Use the ID light within one hundred meters or so. Flying the aircraft is job one – don't get fixated looking at the target and forget about the plane. Use your crew. If you feel yourself getting overwhelmed get some safe altitude, hover out of ground effect and get it together before continuing.'

'The main difference is integrating the weapons solutions with everything else?' Fontaine said.

'You use the weapons just like every other sensor on board,' Hardcastle said. 'I'll bring the guns on line and safe – check it out.' Hardcastle activated the port-gun turret and Fontaine lowered the sensor visor into place. In the center of his field of view was a tiny set of crosshairs projected onto the green-and-white infrared scene. As he moved his head side to side and up and down, the crosshairs moved as well, staying centered at all times. But as he looked to the left toward the nose, the crosshairs stopped moving. 'That's the limit of the gun turret,' Hardcastle told him. 'It won't let you shoot in front of the Sea Lion's flight path, even in tight turns. The system computes the impact point using altitude and airspeed information, so the more straight, level and unaccelerated you are, the more accurate your shots will be.

'Here's the Sea Stinger sight.' Hardcastle deactivated the Chain Gun and turned on the missile-weapon system. The crosshairs were replaced by a thick yellow circle, the 'doughnut' that represents the approximate seeker head's field of view. 'It's not a steerable circle like the Chain Gun turret, so you have to be a bit more skillful in maneuvering the aircraft to place the target inside the doughnut. Once you have the target in the doughnut, hit the missile-select switch on your cyclic. That will power-up a missile, run a self-test and uncover its seeker head to give the missile a look at the target. Once the missile is locked on, the doughnut will change from yellow to flashing green and you'll get a tone in your headset. Clear your area of fire, choose your direction to maneuver after missile launch – usually to the left, but it can be in any direction, even in reverse – uncover the launch button and let 'er rip.'

'Two-Three, distance to last known target position, fifteen miles,' the controller aboard Hammerhead One reported. 'Be advised, contact is intermittent from HIGHBAL. Attempting to relocate via CARABAL.' Hardcastle thought back to a Geffar warning about using a Sky Lion drone with the poor reception at the extreme ranges of the platform's aerostat radar – maybe she was right. He lowered his FLIR visor and began scanning the sea ahead of the aircraft, trying to find a bright yellow object that might be the boat they were seeking.

Hammerhead One Air Staging Platform

The intercom system was shut off in Geffar's cabin, but the sounds of increased activity and the muted announcements out in the hallway finally woke her. She got to her feet and glanced at the repeater of the master monitor in the command center, but she had shut it off hours earlier. Muttering to herself, she flicked on the monitor and went to get a glass of water as the large twenty-four-inch repeater came to life.

When she returned she studied the display through weary eyes. The coastline was on the left, and two Hammerheads machines were highlighted by their encoded data blocks – Two-Three, a V-22 tilt-rotor from Aladdin City, and Five-One, a ninety-five-foot surface-effect patrol ship from Fort Lauderdale. An area in front of both vessels was highlighted by the computer but it showed nothing – no data blocks, no radar returns.

She went to her desk and hit the intercom button: 'Annette, what's up?'

Fields replied from the command center: 'We have a surface operation in progress. We have an unidentified fast-moving vessel from Bimini crossing in and out of restricted waters heading for shore. We have a V-22 and a SES in pursuit.'

'No Customs clearance?'

'Falsified registration. Just came through.'

'When did you launch the Sea Lion, then?'

'I didn't launch it. The Admiral did . . .'

'Hardcastle? Where is he? Headquarters . . . ?' Geffar closed her eyes. She knew damn well where Hardcastle would be . . .

'He's on the Sea Lion.'

I *knew* it, Geffar said to herself. To Fields: 'I'll be right up,' and clicked off the intercom.

Aboard the V-22 Sea Lion Aircraft

'Three miles to computer-projected position, Two-Three,' the controller reported. 'No contact from CARABAL.'

Only three miles away – a fast-moving vessel of any size should be a huge target on the infrared scanner, Hardcastle was thinking. Several times he had steered Fontaine toward what he thought was the boat, only to have it disappear or be something else – a northbound whale, an oil slick, a trail of garbage jettisoned by some cruise ship or freighter.

271

'Two-Three, this is Alpha,' he heard on the radio.

'Go ahead, Alpha.'

'We're all surprised to see you airborne, Bravo,' Geffar said. 'Cut your vacation short?'

'Trying to combine a little training with an actual intercept, Alpha.' He didn't miss the edge in Geffar's voice. 'We'll get this crew checked out soon as possible.'

'Just find the guy, steer the SES in on him and RTB,' Geffar said. 'We have a training program – no real need to freelance on an actual intercept. Vector in the SES and bring it on home.'

'We got it wired, Alpha,' Hardcastle said. 'We should be coming up on him any second.'

Geffar shook her head. That was not an acknowledgment. It was a direct challenge. Hardcastle was going to take an inexperienced crew and perform an actual intercept.

Should she tell him to return? This was not the time to start an argument on the radio – less than three miles from an intercept, low altitude, a nervous crew chasing an evasive target. And she knew she'd get one from him. No. He was an experienced pilot, and he was at the controls and on the scene. It was Hardcastle's sortie.

Less than two miles to go. Fontaine had slowed to less than one hundred knots, the Sea Lion's rotating nacelles at twenty degrees below the vertical. As they approached the computer's estimated intercept point – determined by taking the last known position, speed and direction and dead-reckoning it out over time – he reduced speed and brought the nacelles full vertical, slowing to ninety knots so Hardcastle would have a better chance of spotting him.

'Nothing,' Hardcastle muttered. 'Damn it, he should be right off our nose.'

'This guy's no dummy,' Fontaine said. 'Most of them

272

would make a dash for shore – this guy's evading us and so far doing a good job of it.'

With its anti-collision and position lights on, the low-flying aircraft was easy to see as it came closer. When it was about a half mile away, Carlos Canseco turned sharply left perpendicular to the aircraft's flight path, traveled a few hundred yards, turned a full one-eighty so his bow was pointed at the approach aircraft, and brought his engines to idle. Canseco had been told how military aircraft searched for sea targets. Present a low visual cross-section, keep the engines hidden as much as possible, don't stay on the same course and don't move when it was in close – that was the way to avoid detection, especially at night. As the Cigarette ocean-racing yacht came to a halt, Canseco threw a dark blanket over the thin, sloping windshield to neutralize any reflection.

The man riding with Canseco, a Puerto Rican gun for hire, raised up an AK-47 assault rifle with a fifty-round banana clip and muzzle-flash suppressor and pointed it at the oncoming noise. 'Sounds like a big one,' the gunman said to Canseco. 'It'll be like shooting ducks . . .'

'I didn't bring you along to shoot at airplanes,' Canseco said. 'I hired you because you know these waters and you know English. You had better be ready to throw that thing overboard if they find us.'

'These American Coast Guards don't worry me . . .' The deep-throated hiss of the approaching aircraft became louder. '. . . I have done it many times before. Fire a few shots at them and they run for cover and yell for help – '

Canseco was younger and smarter. 'If you want your money, you do as I say.' He knew that although many military aircraft had some capability of scanning astern, he was safer by far so long as he stayed behind the search aircraft. 'Now hold on.' Canseco yanked the blanket off the windshield, gunned the engine and headed toward shore.

The gunman slung the rifle over his shoulder just as the aircraft zoomed past. What a weird job this was turning out to be, he thought. This kid from Colombia, a stupid snotnosed kid with a hundred-thousand-dollar boat, says he's going to race to Florida and back. He's not carrying weight, he's not on the run – he even clears through Customs. Another spoiled rich kid. He was offering a couple thousand for a credentialed English-speaking pilot, someone who had tried to make the run recently . . .

Of course he had brought his own shipment – five kilos of blow in a duffel bag weighted down with a half-dozen bricks. This kid just wanted company, nothing more. He didn't need a pilot or throttle-man – he was doing just fine by himself. Now he says he doesn't need a gunner. Well, he's got one anyway.

Canseco caught a glimpse of the strange-looking aircraft ahead – this was not a regular Coast Guard plane. It had twin rotor blades like a helicopter, but it was far quieter and much larger than a standard search helicopter. Even more unusual were the large words on the side of the plane – FOLLOW ME, highlighted in big bright letters that could clearly be seen even several hundred feet away, plus rotating lights all over the plane's fuselage just like a police car. If that plane found them, they were going nowhere.

He had been told about the strange new aircraft the new American Coast Guard troops were using, unusual aircraft that could fly like planes and hover like helicopters and carried bombs and missiles. Was this one of those machines? He was not sure, but better assume that it was and get to shore as fast as possible . . .

'Dammit,' Hardcastle said over the interphone. 'The bastard's just disappeared.' He clicked open the radio channel. 'Shark, any readout from CARABAL on this target?'

'Negative,' the contoller replied. 'They're picking up false targets at their extreme range capability. Low confidence in all targets right now.'

'The FLIR is doing us no good at low altitude like this,' Hardcastle said. 'We'll have to climb up and start a search over this area. Damn, I *know* he's around here . . .'

'Uh . . . Dad?' It was Daniel calling on interphone from his aft-facing jump seat.

'Go ahead, Daniel.'

'Can you start a left turn out here? I thought I saw something back behind us.'

'You sure?'

There was a pause. 'No. There are a lot of waves and they all look the same. But I thought I saw a reflection.'

'Of what?'

'I don't know, maybe nothing.'

It was worth a try. 'Give me a slow turn to the left,' he told Fontaine. He lowered his FLIR visor and turned around in his seat facing aft and to port, which would slew around the seeker turret in that same direction, and slowly began a side-to-side scan of the choppy waters.

Daniel only saw his father staring directly at him with dark visors on, which made him nervous. When he saw his father slowly shaking his head, Daniel shouted to him, 'I'm sorry, Dad . . .'

'No, you did good. I'm looking outside with the FLIR, not at you.'

'It's like you're Darth Vader shaking your head at me befoe putting me into a Jedi throat-lock – '

'Contact,' Hardcastle called out. 'I got him.' He hit a switch on his cyclic's control panel, which locked the infrared image in the center of the FLIR's scan and provided steering signals for Fontaine. 'Target's locked on, Adam. We got him.'

* * *

As the rotating lights suddenly stopped retreating and began a lazy left turn, Canseco began a correction to the right to place himself farther off the plane's tail. But suddenly the plane began a tighter left turn and a rapid descent to just a few meters above the water, and he knew they had found him.

'We're only a few miles from shore,' he said in Spanish to the gunman riding with him. 'We'll try to make a run to shore.' He gunned the throttles and made a beeline for the lights just popping over the horizon. The racing yacht began pounding over the choppy waves, sending a rooster's-tail of water flying twenty feet high behind it. With the throttles at full power Canseco wedged himself in as tight as he could into the padded seat, grabbed on tight to a handhold on the padded dashboard, and concentrated on controlling the boat as best he could.

He was not able to see the near-gleeful face of the gunman in the bench seat behind him. The man shook his fist at the approaching plane, unslung the AK-47 assault rifle, chambered a round, braced himself against the pounding of the yacht under his feet, and wrapped the shoulder sling around his hands to steady his aim . . .

'It looks like a forty-two foot Cigarette racer,' Hardcastle reported over the radio. 'No registration numbers yet. Jet powered, racing cockpit. Looks like two males aboard. I think we might have one with a weapon. Stand by.'

'Two-Three, this is Shark Five-One. We're ten miles from your position, ETA one-eight minutes,' Thomas Petraglia, the skipper aboard the SES *Sea Hawk*, radioed in. WSES-2 *Sea Hawk*, an ex-Coast Guard SES, a surface effect ship, was a twin-hulled fast patrol boat, very much like the 110 foot Island-class cutter in size, crew and armament with a much greater top speed and a much shallower draft for inland and shallowwater operations; the*Sea Hawk* had two 900 horsepower engines that powered huge fans under its bottom to pump air through the catamaran channels in its hull, which in turn allowed the vessel to ride a cushion of air at speeds approaching fifty miles an hour. Along with six of the Coast Guard's eight WFCI ocean interceptors and ten of its sixteen WPB Island-class cutters, four WSES cutters had been transferred to the Hammerheads for drug-interdiction duties.

'Roger. Five-One,' Hardcastle replied. 'He's heading just north of Pompano Beach, directly for shore – he might be able to see the Boca Raton Inlet harbor light and might be aiming for it. His estimated speed is three-six knots. Be advised we may see one weapon on board. Use caution. Over.'

'We copy, Two-Three,' Thomas Petraglia replied from the *Sea Hawk*. 'Negative radar contact yet on surface target. Will advise. Out.'

Hardcastle switched his radio channel to the pre-set emergency channel. 'Unidentified racing vessel east of Pompano Beach, Florida, this is the United States Border Security Force. You have entered restricted waters without clearance. Shut down your engines or we will open fire. Repeat, shut down your engines or we will open fire. Acknowledge on any frequency. Over.' He repeated that warning over several emergency channels and set the V-22's radio to scan them once every three seconds.

There was no reply.

'What is he saying?' Canseco yelled to the gunman behind him. There was no reply. He risked a quick turn and saw the man pointing his AK-47 at the oncoming aircraft.

'*No*, don't shoot . . .'

'Why? It'll scare them off.'

'You idiot, they'll kill us if you shoot. We're not here to shoot at Coast Guard planes!'

'So why else are we here?'

Canseco did not reply. He picked up the radio's microphone and said quickly in Spanish, 'Our position is ten miles north-northeast of Pompano Beach harbor light R-5, heading west. We have been intercepted by a large aircraft with twin rotors, but it is not a helicopter. I cannot see more details. They are warning us in English but I cannot understand them and this Cuban is an idiot. He understands less English than I thought, or is pretending to . . . Repeat. We are ten miles north-northeast of Pompano Beach. They have found us. They are chasing us with a very large twin-rotor aircraft. We will be caught within minutes.' He dropped the microphone and held on as his Cigarette yacht careened off yet another swell and hurled itself into the air.

Near Delray Beach, Florida, about fifteen miles north of where the chase was beginning its final leg, a fifty-foot cabin cruiser motored slowly, traveling right at the edge of the recognized three-mile limit of unrestricted coastal waters. It carried several high-powered transceiver antennae arranged all along its deck plus a small satellite transceiver located in a protective fiberglass 'golf ball' on top of the main cabin.

Down below in the main galley a pair of dividers walked across a chart of Florida's eastern coast. Several penciled marks on the chart depicted the course of Canseco's rakehell dash from Bimini to Florida. The marks on the chart were made with the practiced skill of an experienced sailor and navigator – small, precise and as neat as a draftsman.

'They are still not using their secure radios,' someone said to the man with the navigator's dividers. The second man, the cruiser's master, popped open a can of beer and poured half of it down his throat before continuing: 'There must be something wrong with their radios.'

'The secure system is limited in range and effectiveness,' the first man told him in Spanish. 'Besides, Canseco knows they have found him, and they know that their target has spotted *them*. Secrecy is no longer necessary.' He plotted Canseco's last position and penciled in the point at which the chase aircraft had made contact.

'What sort of aircraft is out there?' the second man asked.

'They call it a Sea Lion,' the first man replied. 'A sophisticated aircraft, faster and larger than a helicopter but able to hover like a helicopter.'

'It carries weapons?'

'Oh, yes,' the first man replied. 'The Hammerheads will use them, too – this *bravo*, Admiral Hardcastle, has an itchy trigger finger. Canseco must be prepared to stop if they press the intercept. They will open fire if he does not respond.' He tapped on the chart. 'The Sea Lion had trouble finding Canseco . . . Both the platform radars and CARABAL must be ineffective at this range.'

'What was that you said?' the second man asked.

'It doesn't matter. Canseco has earned his twenty thousand dollars tonight. I think he may have found the Hammerheads' vulnerable spot.'

'Okay, Adam,' Hardcastle said to Fontaine. 'The SES is still pretty far out, and this guy ahead of us might be able to get around him – he's hitting forty knots now. We've got to get him slowed down so the *Sea Hawk* can move in. I'm worried about that rifle I *think* I see, we've got to do this carefully. We'll close our range gradually on him and move in to about one hundred yards' range, then hit him with the ID light. If it doesn't slow him down, back off and we'll reevaluate.'

'What the hell does that mean? Reevaluate?'

'That *means*,' Hardcastle told him, 'that we begin getting lined up for a shot across his bow if he decides not to stop.' Fontaine did not reply; he only gripped the collective tighter.

'Two-Three, this is Five-One,' the skipper of the *Sea Hawk* reported, 'we have radar contact on you at this time. We should be in position to see your target shortly. What's his position?'

'He's about three hundred yards in front of us, heading west at almost forty knots. We're going to move in to try to slow him down.'

'We'll be in position in five minutes,' Petraglia reported. 'Be advised, we now have positive radar contact on your surface target. You can break off close pursuit at this time, Two-Three.'

Fontaine seemed to relax at that last transmission, but Hardcastle replied, 'Negative, Five-One. We're moving in. Stand by.'

Sandra Geffar tensed as she listened to that last interchange. She knew Hardcastle would move in, knew he would press the engagement no matter where the surface-effect ship was.

Annette Fields was thinking the same thing as she turned and looked up at Geffar. 'He's the on-scene commander,' Geffar told her. 'It's his action. If the target gets by the SES he's in the best position to take over.'

Fields paused for a moment, then said, 'He's got a civilian on board.'

'What? Who?'

'His son Daniel. He brought him on board when – '

'He's bringing his own son into a firefight?' She calmed herself down as the others in the platform's command center turned to watch her, told Fields, 'I want him to recover that plane as soon as possible,' she said in carefully

280

controlled words. 'That passenger is my responsibility too
. . . he must be protected as much as possible . . .'

By then Fontaine had taken the Sea Lion to within a
hundred yards of the speeding yacht and down to fifty feet
above the ocean. Hardcastle retracted his FLIR visor and,
with the infrared tracker still locked on, activated the
NightSun identification light.

The five-thousand-watt searchlight flooded the area
around the yacht with brilliant white light, and for the first
time they had a good eyeball on their target. The two men on
the yacht were clearly in view, as was, in stark clarity, the
huge automatic rifle one of the suspects had aimed at them.

'Shark, this is Two-Three,' Hardcastle radioed. 'We
have visual contact on the evading target vessel. We have
two male Latinos on board the target vessel. One is
carrying a military-style rifle, probably an AK-47. Five-
One, how do you copy?'

'Five-One copies,' Petraglia replied. 'We see your ID
light and we have a visual on the target. We can take over
from here, Bravo.'

'Shark copies all, Two-Three,' Fields radioed from
Hammerhead One. 'Alpha requests you take all efforts to
protect passenger and RTB. Acknowledge.'

Hardcastle looked at Fontaine, then back over his right
shoulder at Daniel. He hit the mike button: 'Say again,
Shark?'

'In consideration of passenger safety, Alpha requests
you RTB.'

Hardcastle shook his head but nodded at Fontaine. 'You
heard, Adam. Give me a thousand feet. We'll keep the
light on this bozo from high altitude until Petraglia catches
him, *then* head on back.' On the radio channel he said,
'Roger, Shark. Two-Three will monitor the intercept from
high altitude, then RTB. Over.'

'Copy, Two-Three. Will advise when situation under control. Out.'

Aboard WSES-2 Sea Hawk

'All hands report to LE stage-two stations,' Petraglia announced over the ship's intercom from the bridge of the *Sea Hawk*. 'This is not a drill.' Four miles ahead of them, just visible in the glare of the Sea Lion's searchlight, was their quarry thundering through the swells and heading for the shore at full speed.

'Port and starboard M-60s manned and ready,' the officer of the deck, Janet Cirillo, reported to Petraglia. Under law-enforcement readiness conditions, everyone on board – including the cook – had deck duties. Cirillo picked up a phone on the aft bulkhead of the bridge, listened for a few moments, then dropped it back into its holder. 'Crew reports ready at LE two, sir.' Although the vessel and her crew were officially with the Border Security Force and technically had no military rank, the former Coast Guard vessel and her crew automatically reverted to their military training and experience in such situations. Their life jackets and body armor displayed the 'flying shark' insignia of the Hammerheads, but right underneath the stick-on patches they read 'US Coast Guard.' It would take time for allegiances to shift completely.

'Range three miles now and closing slowly,' the radar operator on the bridge reported. 'Recommend heading three-three-zero to intercept in three point four miles.'

'Make it so,' Petraglia ordered. He scanned both sides of his bridge to check on his crew. Surface-effect ships were much more stable at high speeds than the Cigarette racing yachts – while their target was being pounded by the short choppy waves the *Sea Hawk* was gliding on a thick bubble of air with amazing stability for such a large craft. Even so, Petraglia checked his people to make sure they were moving about on deck and ready to engage the target.

'Sir, we might have a problem,' the radar operator said. 'We're approaching five miles to the shoreline and we're on course to intercept in three and a half. We've got a cut-off, but it's not much. He could reach shore before we catch up to him if he doesn't slow down. If he turns farther north, we might lose him.'

'He's got to slow down,' Cirillo said. 'There are boats all over the place along the shore – '

'I don't think this guy gives a rat's ass who's in his way,' Petraglia said. 'This guy just wants to reach shore, period. If he gets close to shore or cuts into the Intracoastal Waterway through the Boca Raton inlet, he could kill a lot of people damn quick.' He reached up and grabbed the radio microphone. 'Two-Three, this is Five-One.'

'Go ahead.'

'Bravo, our radar tells us we're going to intercept in a little under four miles at this speed,' Petraglia told Hardcastle. 'This could turn into a tail chase, and then we'll be out of position. If you could get him turned or slowed down, we could catch him farther out from shore. Please advise. Over.'

'Copy that, Five-One,' Hardcastle replied. He had seen the developing chase and had come to the same conclusion as Petraglia – they might catch the guy but not before he blasted very close into shore. 'We're maneuvering to intercept. Stand by.' He turned to Fontaine. 'Take us back down to one hundred feet and move in to one hundred yards. Crew, stand by for intercept.' His adrenaline was really pumping.

Daniel found his breath was short, he felt frozen. The two gunners in the cargo bay of the V-22 Sea Lion had reloaded the starboard rocket pod with four live Sea Stinger missiles, leaving two warning flares in place. They had double-checked the feed mechanism of the Chain Gun in the port-side pod and prepared a second hundred-round magazine. Out the starboard windscreen Daniel could see the starboard pod with its deadly load motored back out into the slipstream. When it was locked into place the crewmen adjusted body armor and strapped themselves into their seats. They did not speak to Daniel, but one of them reached over to touch his holster pistol. He did not look too reassured.

Hardcastle was running down the checklist with Fontaine, whose attention seemed fixed on the brilliantly lit speedboat ahead of him. Then, as if jerking himself out of a trance, he forced his eyes to scan his instruments and around the cockpit. Hardcastle performed the checklist functions he could do and notified Fontaine of items that only the pilot in command could handle.

'Crew notified,' Hardcastle read. 'Fuel quantity and feed, checked on AUTO, looks like another two hours' worth. Fuel pressurization to AUTO. Generators checked, warning lights out. Hydraulics, primary and secondary, checked, warning lights out. Seat straps, shoulder harnesses, emergency equipment, checked and set. Flight controls checked pilot and copilot.' Fontaine had again focused on the racing yacht. 'Adam, bring your power back a notch.' No reply. 'Adam?' Fontaine snapped his head, nodded and complied. He leveled off at one hundred feet as the radar altimeter warning light blinked at him, but he was still reluctant to decrease the range. 'Move in another sixty yards,' Hardcastle prodded.

'He's still got that rifle on us . . .'

'He's also bouncing around. The first shot he takes, we'll be all over him. Fly the aircraft.' Hardcastle clicked on the external loudspeaker and said into his microphone:

'Attention racing vessel, this is the United States Border Security Force. Stop your engines and prepare for boarding.' In hesitant Spanish he repeated: '*Atención marinos. Esto es* Border Security Force, *Estados Unidos. Pare. Alto. Cuidado.*' No reply – the racing yacht continued on the same course, as fast as ever.

'Let's try to maneuver to his right side,' Hardcastle said. 'See if you can turn him farther south into the SES.'

Still keeping the nose pointed at and slightly ahead of the yacht, Fontaine sideslipped the V-22 around and off the yacht's right side, keeping the ID light focused on the boat.

Still no response.

'Three miles from the shore,' Fontaine said, glancing at his DME distance readouts. 'I can see the harbor entrance lights.' He had pulled slightly ahead and to the right of the yacht, flying sideways so he could keep it in view and so the speedboat's crew could see the Sea Lion's illuminated FOLLOW ME sign on its left side. The speedboat made zero turn to the left. 'Either he knows the SES is coming onto him or he wants to get into the harbor real bad,' he told Hardcastle.

'I think it's time to stop screwing with him,' Hardcastle said. 'Crew, arm warning flare.' On the radio, he reported: 'Shark, be advised, we are firing a warning rocket at this time.' To Fontaine he said, 'All right, Adam. With a warning flare armed, you still center the doughnut on the target – the fire control system will automatically compute a fifty-yard lead point and fire the missile ahead of him. Center the doughnut, don't worry about where the nose of the plane is.'

Fontaine made a small correction to the left. 'Got it,' he muttered into the interphone between tight-clenched teeth.

'Batteries released. One warning rocket ready. Clear to shoot.' Fontaine unguarded the missile-launch button on his cyclic, took a deep breath, and pressed the button. They heard a sharp hiss from the right side, and suddenly a brilliant flash of light streaked by the canopy. The sudden glare startled Daniel so that he did not open his eyes for several seconds after the rocket was gone.

The rocket trailed a long bright yellow plume of fire and sparks as it sailed across the dark waters in front of the yacht. Even in the brilliance of the searchlight, the glare of the warning rocket was unmistakable.

The suspect's reaction was just as unmistakable – the man carrying the AK-47 rifle could be seen raising his rifle toward the Sea Lion and although no muzzle flashes could be seen, the violent backward jerking motion on the gunman's shoulder made it clear what was happening.

'Vector!' Hardcastle called out, but Fontaine had already banked the V-22 hard right away from the racing yacht. He had made almost a full 180-degree turn and had gained five-hundred feet of altitude in his escape maneuver before Hardcastle put his hands back on the controls. 'I've got the aircraft.' It was then he saw that Fontaine's side of the front canopy window had been starred by a bullet. 'Report, everybody all right?'

'Aft end's clear,' one of the gunnery techs in the cargo section reported.

Fontaine was brushing glass and plastic from his flight suit. 'You okay, Adam?' Hardcastle said cross-cockpit.

'I'm okay,' but it was obvious he was not. Although he was hit by only a few pieces of debris, he had seemed to forget about the aircraft, the controls, his crew and didn't stop wiping debris from his flight suit. Hardcastle gained a few hundred feet more altitude, put on the autopilot and checked Fontaine's head under his helmet. It was a one in a million chance, but a heavy-caliber bullet from the AK-47 had found its way into the Sea Lion's cockpit, and had gone right between Fontaine's head and the side of his helmet – it missed killing the pilot by millimeters . . .

'Get up here and help Fontaine out of his seat,' Hardcastle ordered. Fontaine was already dazedly un-buckling his shoulder harness as he continued to track down pieces of glass scattered all across his chest. The gunnery techs lifted him out of his seat and over the control console in the center aisle and back to a clear space on the cargo-bay deck. Daniel looked on as the semi-conscious man, his face a mask of blood, his eyes fluttering, was laid out before him.

'Looks like he got creased across the left temple,' one of the gunnery techs reported. 'He's conscious but he looks like he's going into shock.'

'Shark, this is Two-Three,' from Hardcastle. 'Be advised, we have come under fire from this target. One injury, minor aircraft damage.'

'Roger, Two-Three,' from the controller on Hammer-head One. 'We will get clearance for you to land at Boca Raton or Fort Lauderdale Executive. We will have emer-gency vehicles standing by.'

'Roger – ' But just then Hardcastle saw the yacht speed past underneath him, still going full speed directly north-west toward Boca Raton. The gunman in the yacht's cockpit was still taking shots at the Sea Lion, shaking a fist at the retreating aircraft. That was a sight that made something too long controlled inside Hardcastle snap. The injured pilot, his son, everything except getting that yacht and its gunman was blocked out. He heeled the Sea Lion over hard right, sent it swooping down on the speedboat, selected the Chain Gun with the arming switch on his control panel. The searchlight immediately caged forward and the aiming crosshairs appeared in his elec-tronic visor precisely in the center of the searchlight beam. Now a slight move of his head centered the crosshairs on the speedboat. He opened the safety guard on the trigger, and fired.

Less than twenty feet from where Daniel sat, the sudden activation of the Chain Gun and its thunderous, booming rattle made him nearly jump out of his seat. The entire port-side windscreen was filled with the bright orange-and-blue flashes from the thirty-millimeter cannon as three armor-piercing rounds per second hurtled toward the target.

Hardcastle saw smoke and a puff of fire erupt from the speedboat, but from two hundred feet up the results were not too satisfying – nothing short of total destruction would be. Hardcastle selected the Sea Stinger rocket pod, armed a missile and waited for the aiming doughnut to appear in his visor. When it did he found that his descent rate and altitude were both too high, but instead of easing his descent rate with the collective and improving his firing solution, he pitched the nose forward to center the doughnut on the racing yacht. At the first flash of the doughnut, signaling that a missile's seeker head had locked onto the target, he fired.

The Sea Stinger with its eight-pound high-explosive warhead struck the engine compartment dead on target, but because of Hardcastle's steep descent and velocity the Sea Lion aircraft was right behind it. The missile detonated on impact, turning the left engine in the yacht into scrap and exploding the remaining gallons of fuel – as Hardcastle pulled the V-22 out of its dive and banked sharply left, the fuel-tank explosion was just fifty feet away.

The Sea Lion felt as if it had been hit by a giant fly swatter. The right engine raced, its power controls torn apart. The concussion shattered the pilot's right-side windscreen, sending a shower of glass into the cockpit and buffeting Hardcastle with one-hundred-mile winds. The Sea Lion felt as if it was doing an aileron roll with the right wing jerked violently up and straight overhead. Hardcastle pushed the power to full and cut back pressure on the cyclic, reducing the system torque seconds before the tremendous stress on the drive system would have snapped the left rotors clean off the nacelle. With less counter-torque driving the wing over, Hardcastle was just able to bring the Sea Lion under control a few scant yards above the dark waters of the Atlantic.

But the right engine was not responding to control inputs, and pressure readings indicated it was losing oil. Hardcastle quickly switched the system to cross-over power, which would use the left engine to power both rotors, then pulled the fuel cut-off control to the right engine to shut it down before the loss of oil pressure completely seized it.

'Shark, this is Two-Three,' Hardcastle radioed. 'We've sustained damage to the cockpit and right engine. Right engine is shut down and we are in emergency cross-over mode. We are declaring an emergency. We will attempt recovery at Aladdin City and keep you advised. Over.'

Geffar's was the next voice on the channel: 'Copy all, Two-Three. We will notify ATC of your emergency and your intentions.' She was about to ask how the Sea Lion could be so badly damaged after she had just said to bring the Sea Lion back, but no good to press it now. 'Break. Five-One, what's your situation?'

'Five-One is in the green, approaching the suspect vessel now,' Petraglia replied. 'We have Two-Three visually. He is currently heading south just off the shoreline, estimated altitude five thousand feet. We see no smoke or fire on board but he was very close to the target just before . . . he encountered damage.'

'Is this an open channel?' Geffar asked Fields on intercom.

'Yes, the secure channel is unreliable. We've been on the open VHF aerostat relay all night.'

That was the reason for Petraglia's cryptic replies. Geffar

realized – half the state of Florida must be listening in on this. 'Understand, Five-One. What's the status of the target?'

'We are in sight of the target. He is dead in the water, possibly with a small fire in his midsection and is listing by the stern. We are three hundred yards away and closing. I see one person in the cockpit waving his arms. I see no weapons but we are proceeding with caution under LE two.'

'Roger, Five-One. Stand by.' To Fields, Geffar said, 'Launch a Sea Lion to support Five-One. I want a Dolphin on deck with a rescue crew to escort Hardcastle and assist in emergency recovery. I'll be riding along with the Dolphin.' Geffar logged off her computer console and headed to the hangar deck.

They caught up with Hardcastle's Sea Lion just over Virginia Key five miles before landing at the Border Security Force's headquarters area. It was creeping along at only forty miles an hour on account of the shattered right windscreen and because it reduced the strain on the left engine. By flying in close formation on the right side Geffar could see the missing right cockpit glass panel and the streaks of oil and other evidence of blast damage on the right engine nacelle.

'How's it handling, Ian?' Geffar radioed over on the secure radio frequency.

'It's fine. I've locked the system in full vertical flight mode to keep the nacelles and wings from shifting. I get overspeed warnings past eighty-five percent power but no unusual vibrations and no control problems.'

'All right,' Geffar told him. 'If you won't have any trouble landing bring it in at headquarters. If you think you might have trouble take it over the Rickenbacker Highway to Key Biscayne and land it in the Crandon Park golf course. We have rescue vehicles standing by. You can follow their truck lights to the touchdown point.'

The landing at the headquarters landing pad went smoothly except for a bit of uneasiness a few seconds before touchdown. Ambulances, rescue trucks and crewmen from Geffar's helicopter rushed to the Sea Lion when they heard the engine begin to wind down, and within moments an unconscious Fontaine was on a stretcher and being loaded into the ambulance. Hardcastle's crewmen had stopped the bleeding and treated his wound. Geffar briefly checked on Fontaine then returned to the Sea Lion's starboard side door as Hardcastle was helping Daniel down out of the plane. They were staring silently at a large tear in the back padding of the seat Daniel had just vacated – a spot where the bullet that had entered the cockpit had come through, inches above Daniel's head. The bullet that had almost killed Fontaine had also almost killed Daniel Hardcastle.

Daniel looked ashen. He was staring at the jagged hole in the seat. Hardcastle appeared drained; his hair was matted down, his flight suit soaked with sweat. Daniel looked chilled right down to the bone in spite of the layers of life jacket, body armor and clothing. 'I'll drive you two and the other crewmen over to the clinic in Key Biscayne to get you checked over,' Geffar said.

Hardcastle nodded, realized the two had never met. A helluva way to make introductions, he thought as he put an arm around his son's shoulder and led him to a waiting van for the ride to the hospital.

As they went to the van Geffar grabbed a flashlight from its holder beside the starboard cargo door of the Sea Lion and inspected the right wing. The blast damage was severe – Hardcastle had taken a chance bringing the aircraft all the way from Boca Raton overwater to Aladdin City. The drive train running through the wing was intact but badly

291

damaged – even with the cross-connect mechanism working, the drive could have failed, which would have meant a water landing at night. It was a risky decision to make, especially with live weapons and a passenger – his son, no less – on board . . .

At Key Biscayne Community Hospital a team of doctors and nurses checked over each man, and each was found fit for duty. Except, of course, Fontaine, who had suffered a concussion along with traumatic shock and would be hospitalized for several days.

Geffar brought the crew back to the headquarters building, where they met up with Brad Elliott and Patrick McLanahan. The Hammerheads' commander let them make phone calls and talk to their families, ordered them hot meals from a local restaurant, then separated them into individual offices and had them prepare statements on what had occurred from their point of view. Daniel was given the same.

When the crew members were settled and working, Elliott brought Hardcastle into his office. 'This is a little unusual, isn't it, Brad?' Hardcastle said after the door was closed. 'Reports are usually filled out as a crew, not separately. This begins to look like an inquisition.'

'Hardly that, but it won't be SOP, either. This is the first time we've fired on a vessel. Since we didn't have a very good tactical picture of the incident I want individual statements from the crew. We'll also debrief you as a crew.' Hardcastle nodded, but didn't like it. Elliott noticed electronic messages were queued up on his computer terminal, several marked IMPORTANT. As he read the electronic messages he asked, 'Why did you go on this flight tonight, Ian? You were off-duty, in civilian clothes, and had your son with you. Not exactly what I'd call mission-ready.'

'Daniel and I were out at the hangar. I was showing him

around. When the crew responded on standby I learned that Sandra wasn't going to launch aircraft to chase down that Cigarette boat – '

'That's right,' Geffar said. 'That guy cleared Customs in Freeport. We tracked him as soon as CARABAL picked him up. He was clean when he left the Bahamas and according to the radar no other vessels rendezvoused with him. We didn't have the qualified crews or the assets to do an intercept so I turned it over to Customs.'

'If he was inspected in Freeport where'd he get the automatic rifle?' Elliott pressed.

Geffar spread her hands. 'Who knows? Maybe he bribed some inspectors, maybe he sneaked it on board. The point was that we knew the boat was clean and we knew it wasn't involved with any major smuggling – '

'So, why not send a unit to intercept him? We're a border security unit, we don't selectively stop some and allow others to pass – '

'That's not what we did, sir. We didn't have the air assets to do a full intercept, the crew here, Fontaine's crew, wasn't qualified to – '

Hardcastle interrupted. 'Then why are we putting un-qualified crews on alert like this? We should be flying them every night to get them qualified – '

'We've been flying them,' Elliott told him. 'Fontaine and his crew flew this afternoon, just before their shift.'

'You know what the training schedule is like, for God's sake,' Geffar added. 'We barely have enough crews to go around as it is. It takes time to qualify in a complex aircraft like the Sea Lion. And lowering the sortie count to qualify more crews in my opinion is *not* the answer. We need to be more selective about which targets we intercept, involve seaborne assets more instead of unqualified air assets. That means Customs, the Coast Guard and our shore-based patrols. That's who I had on the intercept and that's all I wanted . . . Ian, I understand, developed this whole deal, but I'm operations here . . .'

'Sandra, I heard the report on the target. I'm qualified on night intercepts. I made the decision to do the intercept . . .'

'Maybe not such a hot idea, Ian,' Elliott said.

Hardcastle frowned. 'It was my decision as the senior officer . . .'

'A reporter contacted the switchboard just after the intercept began,' Elliott said quietly. 'Since all the radio transmissions were generally in the clear and reporters seem to be adept at tracking our movements, the press has a pretty good picture of what happened tonight . . . This reporter *says* he saw you at a restaurant this evening, and that you had a drink at the bar before dinner and wine at dinner. Any comment?'

'Sure, it's true. I won't deny it – I don't *have* to deny it. It sure as hell didn't impair my abilities or judgement – '

'Would you submit a blood test?'

'*What?* Are you asking me to?'

'Yes.'

'Then I'll do it. You didn't think I would, did you?'

'Come on, Ian, when you think about it you'll realize I'm asking this for the good of us all, for *your* Hammerheads. I don't like the PR stuff but it's my job, at least for now . . .'

Hardcastle hated the idea but knew he was right. He also still thought he had taken the proper action and said so.

'What happened after I said to disengage from the intercept?' Geffar asked him.

'Hey, what is this, tag team interrogation?'

'Please answer it,' Elliott said.

The sudden edge in Elliott's voice surprised Hardcastle. He took a deep breath, choking down his anger. 'I disengaged. We climbed to a thousand feet and kept the light on the target. But Five-One radioed us and said he didn't think they'd catch him before he reached the Boca inlet. We responded by descending back down and flying north of him, trying to get him to turn towards the SES. He maintained his course. When he didn't respond we launched a warning rocket across his bow. He opened fire. A few shots hit us, and one damn near killed Fontaine. I took the aircraft and climbed to three thousand feet.'

'How did you get so much damage?'

'I was ready to return to Ford Lauderdale to get attention for Adam but then I saw that son of a bitch right underneath me, speeding along like nothing happened. The guy was shaking a fist at me. I knew Petraglia would turn to assist and that this guy would get away. I admit, it was too much to accept. I turned, descended and attacked with the Chain Gun and a Sea Stinger. I got a little too close after the rocket attack and took some collateral damage. Then I headed south to recover.'

Elliott shook his head. 'I understand, but I also think you should have left it to Petraglia on the SES and Customs – '

'I disagree. I was in a position to assist, Fontaine's wounds weren't critical – '

'He has a concussion – ' Geffar broke in.

'We're supposed to be out there keeping these people away from our shores. We're *supposed* to be using our assets, not withholding them or turning the job over to Customs. That's what Hammerheads is about. What if the guy got away? More, what if he killed someone in the harbor? What if he was carrying explosives – '

'Ian, you launched when you should have stayed on the ground,' Elliott said, interrupting. 'You attacked when you should have stayed away. You pressed the attack when you should have withdrawn. You exposed your crew, your aircraft and a civilian to unnecessary danger, and the

Hammerheads to a lot of potential lousy publicity – bad for you, for all of us.'

'Not true! I did it because it's my *job*.'

'Not for the next forty-eight hours, it isn't. You're off-duty. Someone will take you to the Coast Guard clinic on Miami Beach and we'll get a blood test. After that he'll take you home. Tomorrow morning you report here for duty. Stay incommunicado until I say otherwise.'

'This is crazy, Brad, we don't have time to – '

'Dammit, I can make it an order. Is that what you want?'

Hardcastle shut up, pounded a fist on his desktop, turned and went out of the office.

He met Daniel in the crew lounge, sitting on a sofa, staring at the report form he had been told to fill out. When he saw his father, there was a new look in his eyes. It made Hardcastle very uneasy. Was this the same young man he'd seen only hours earlier on the baseball diamond and in the restaurant, exchanging confidences man-to-man?

A pilot was standing in the hallway waiting for Hardcastle. 'We're taking my son home first.'

'My orders are – '

'Screw your orders.' He led Daniel to the door. Behind him, Geffar watched as Hardcastle shoved past the pilot and stormed away. It was a bad scene.

Outside at least a half-dozen news cameras and a dozen reporters crowded around the other gate that surrounded the Hammerheads headquarters building, pushing and shoving each other to get a better shot. Hardcastle pulled his son quickly along, shielding him as best he could from the crowd of cameras only a few feet away.

'Admiral Hardcastle, can you tell us what happened tonight?' one reporter called out. 'We understand one of your pilots is dead – '

'*No one is dead.*'

That short answer only intensified the reporter's efforts. 'Who is that with you, Admiral? Is that a suspect?'

'Were you drinking before shooting at that boat tonight, Admiral? Were you drunk?'

The babble was shut off as they got into the sedan and closed and locked the doors, but Hardcastle knew that the nightmare had just begun.

Chapter Six

Zaza Airfield, Verrettes, Haiti
Two Weeks Later

The room broke out into applause as young Carlos Canseco entered the main briefing room.

Salazar joined in as Canseco limped up to the stage, stood before him and saluted. Most of Canseco's handsome face had been badly burned in the attack and the fire, and he had suffered more burns on his back and legs. Doctors in Miami had treated his burns and had even performed skin grafts to repair some of the damage. Considering his condition, he had been placed under light guard in the hospital, which allowed him to slip out a third-story window and make his escape. He had stolen a boat and sailed it to Andros Island, where he arranged for a pick-up.

Salazar returned the young man's salute, then carefully wrapped his arms around him. Actually, Salazar wished Canseco was still in American custody – he would not betray the Cuchillos, and that way he would be a useful martyr to invoke. Still, his escape was a morale booster for the Cuchillos.

'The actions of Canseco deserve the highest praise. Attention to orders.' The crewmen came to attention. 'As of this day Private Canseco will be promoted to the rank of lieutenant of aviation. His deeds made in the name of the Cuchillos should inspire us all.'

Canseco saluted again with a bandaged right hand, then limped off the stage.

'Thank you for the honor you gave young Canseco, sir,'

298

Trujillo told Salazar as they began their meeting. 'It means a lot to all your pilots, especially the young ones.'

'He showed guts,' Salazar said idly. 'Still, what did he tell us? What did we learn from this?'

'We have plotted out the effective ranges and the response times of much of the Border Security Force's assets in southeastern Florida, sir. Their strength is formidable, they have significant firepower and are able to use it.'

'Canseco almost made it,' another senior pilot said. 'He came very close . . .'

'But his boat was destroyed by a Sea Lion tilt-rotor aircraft,' Trujillo said. 'He could have opened fire much earlier. A slower vessel might not have gotten as far.' Trujillo turned to Salazar. 'In my opinion, we should stay away from south Florida as much as possible. The Border Security Force has concentrated most of their efforts in this area. After this incident it will be even greater.'

'But most of the Cartel's distribution network operates out of that region,' Salazar said. 'The Cartel will pay less for shipments directed anywhere else.'

'Perhaps so, sir, but we run significant risk by operating in that area. The Cartel should be advised of this. We should exploit new openings in Mexico and in the southwest United States as soon as possible before the Border Security Force closes in on these areas as well.'

Valdivia, Colombia
Later That Day

'It was a stupid plan, Salazar,' Gonzales Gachez was saying over the phone in his office at his main production plane. He got to his feet, squeezing an autographed baseball in one fist. 'Why are you telling me this? What are you saying?'

299

'I am saying that I cannot risk my people trying to deliver your product into your established drop points. If you want your shipments brought into Florida or the northern Bahamas area it will cost you extra – ten thousand dollars a kilo. Half up front, half on delivery – '

'Ten thousand? Are you insane? This is almost the full retail price of a kilo of cocaine – '

'Then the price goes up, señor,' Salazar said. 'The Border Security Force is real, Gachez. This is no paper tiger. It will cost you ten thousand dollars a kilo. End of negotiations.' And the line went dead.

Gachez slammed the phone down. 'Damn him, I should have him killed.' He turned to one of his lieutenants. 'Salazar wants ten thousand dollars a kilo to deliver product to Florida. He says the Hammerheads are so strong it is too risky.'

'He is trying to blackmail you, Señor Gachez,' his assistant said. 'Don't deal with him. Let him come to us.'

'And what do you suggest I do with two thousand kilos of cocaine in our warehouses? Not to mention the rest of the Cartel. This threatens my position in the Cartel, Juan. The Cartel might even negotiate with Salazar directly.'

'Sir, you are the richest and most powerful of the Medellín families . . .'

But Gachez was obviously worried. Now Juan held out his hand. 'Perhaps this will solve your problem, sir.'

Gachez put his autographed Yankees baseball back on its stand on his desk and took the object from his assistant. It was a jar of clear liquid, of the consistency of mineral oil or turpentine. Gachez opened the jar; it was odorless. 'What is it?'

'That is a half a kilo of cocaine,' Juan said. 'Dissolved in water with some hydrochloric acid to reduce crystallization and precipitation. It is colorless, odorless and tasteless. It cannot be detected by X-rays or visual inspection. To bring it back you simply put it into a pot and boil out the water – and you are left with pure concaine. Or it can be sold and marketed as a liquid.' He took the jar back from Gachez, tightly resealed the jar, then walked over to an aquarium in a corner of the office. He lifted the aquarium's lid and dropped the jar in . . . and it promptly vanished. There was no trace of it except for the metal lid. 'We can pack it in shipments of tropical fish, or seafood, or tanks of gasoline – we can even make blocks of ice out of it.

'This is even better.' Juan held up a grocery bag and extracted several grapefruit. 'Each one of these has been injected with liquid cocaine,' he said. 'They carry a quarter-kilo's worth. A standard fifty-pound bag of fruit holds about twenty kilos. Even if it is cut open by inspectors they will find nothing – they look only for powdered cocaine hidden in the fruit itself. Unless they test the juice itself, it is undetectable.'

'Ingenious,' Gachez mumbled. 'So you are saying we should forgo air and sea deliveries? Ship product in fruit and tropical fish containers?'

'Containerized shipment is a safe alternative, sir. Thousands of sealed containers pass through American ports every day. Customs inspects only a fraction of them. If we mix up our shipments between carriers and ports and don't try to flood the market we can maintain deliveries without having to submit to Salazar's blackmail.'

Gachez nodded. 'It is no substitute for air-and-sea deliveries, but as you say, it is an alternative for the time being. And it should take some of the air out of this pirate Salazar's sails.'

At least so he hoped.

'Forget Salazar and his pirates, eh? I like it, Juan. See to the new process immediately.'

* * *

Miami, Florida
Three Days Later

Maxwell Van Nuys rose to his feet at the head table in the banquet room of the Gusman Heritage Center in downtown Miami, chock full of major players. He was about to introduce the evening's guest speaker.

Even though Van Nuys was now the ex-officio chairman of the Miami Chamber of Commerce he remained a popular and admired figure in south Florida affairs.

'While the coffee and brandy is being served, it gives me great pleasure to introduce our honored guest for the annual Chamber of Commerce awards banquet. She has become one of this country's most dynamic leaders. With her colleagues she has taken on the most difficult and important tasks this nation could assign – securing the borders from those who would impose their death crops on the people of our country, our state and our proud city. She has been doing this job with intelligence, determination and professionalism for years.

'She is a former Army security officer, former commander of the United States Customs Service Air Branch drug-interdiction unit at Homestead Air Force Base, a former United States pistol champion as well as a commercial and military pilot. *And* she is presently an airoperations commander of the new United States Border Security Force, also known as the Hammerheads. This organization, in just a few months' time, has captured over two hundred aircraft, dozens of large vessels and nearly a half-billion dollars worth of illegal narcotics. I give you Sandra M. Geffar of the Hammerheads.'

Sandra Geffar, not liking it but doing it as a duty, had become a different person in public. However she felt inside, she could be, could seem, self-assured on the outside.

302

'Thank you very much, ladies and gentlemen . . .' and graciously named all the important ones. 'I want to express my gratitude to the members of the Chamber of Commerce for their support of the Border Security Force in recent months. I know it hasn't been easy, but with your support, the ominous predictions that tourism, commerce, shipping and the lifestyles of south Florida somehow would all be ruined by stricter border-security measures has not come true. We work as a team, and as I applaud your efforts I also ask for your continued support in the future.'

It was a smart move. The Chamber of Commerce had at first denounced the Hammerheads and called for their headquarters to be moved out of south Florida, but her public relations and apparent friendship with Van Nuys had paid off.

'Let me tell you something of what we've accomplished together. We can see the shift in air and sea drug deliveries dropping off dramatically in the southeast. Drug-smuggling activity is spreading to other parts of the south and southwest United States, which, of course, is why we need your *continued* support and the support of our representaives in Washington so we can continue to expand our operations. Within the next three years I truly believe we can stop ninety percent of all narcotics smuggled across our borders. That is more than a conviction, it is a pledge I make to you tonight.

'Border security means working to keep the supply of illegal narcotics down, but we must do something about the demand too, and that means getting more involved with our children's education, their lives. We need to tell them straight about the incredible danger of becoming hooked on drugs – the physical dependence, the emotional enslave-ment, the pain and suffering it inflicts on families. We all know about co-dependency. That's a fancy term for the innocents' being destroyed. I have urged that proceeds from fines and confiscated-property auctions collected by the Hammerheads over and above our non-appropriated funding levels be added to the Drug Education Trust Fund to support drug and alcohol abuse education for school-age children . . .'

The rest of the speech went by flawlessly and successfully, and Geffar received her fifth standing ovation at its conclusion. That applause was only intensified when Van Nuys joined her at the podium. There was no doubt about it – Geffar and Van Nuys were the hit of the evening.

Later, in the back of the limousine provided for her and Van Nuys, Geffar kicked off her shoes. 'I am *exhausted*,' she said. 'I feel like I've been on my feet all day.'

'Your day starts at five A.M.,' Van Nuys summarized for her. 'You fly two or three hours a day, back and forth to that platform out there, and then you come ashore, spend half the evening in your office, and *then* give a speech in front of the Chamber of Commerce. I don't know where you find the energy.'

'Sometimes I don't know, either,' Geffar replied. She snuggled closer and wrapped his arms around herself. 'Right now, I don't have any.'

He moved his hands around and cupped her breasts in his big hands. 'No energy at all?'

'Well, enough energy for *that*.' But she shook her head. 'As intriguing as that sounds, doing it in the back of a limo driving down an interstate is not my idea of romantic. Or maybe you just can't control yourself, Mr Big-Shot attorney.'

He grasped her breasts firmly with both hands and encircled her nipples with his forefingers. 'I can if *you* can, Miss Hammerhead drugbuster.' She sat back in his arms and stared out the dark windows in silence.

'Quite a speech you gave about that education funding proposal, Sandra,' Van Nuys said. 'You usually talk only

304

about the Hammerheads. Tonight it was different. Impassioned.'

'That's how I feel,' Geffar replied. 'Children are the most important natural resource we have. It sounds clichéd, but I happen to believe it.'

'It doesn't sound clichéd coming from you.' He paused a bit, then asked, 'Do you want children yourself?'

He felt her entire body relax. 'Oh, yes,' she replied.

'Really?'

She looked up at him with surprise. 'You don't believe me?'

'You don't really seem the settling-down type.'

'Another sexist remark, eh?' she admonished him with a humorous lilt in her voice. 'You think that just because I'm the commander of a paramilitary organization, that I carry a gun and fly planes, that I'm not the motherly type. God, spare me from men with tiny minds . . .'

'Hey, give me a break, lady,' Van Nuys said. 'It was an honest question.'

She responded by wrapping his arms tighter around her body. 'I've just never *found* the settling-down type,' she said. 'Successful, established men who want families are hard to find. Besides, career has always come first.'

'Now? Always?'

He felt her shrug in his arms. 'Children . . . perhaps. With the right man. Children would be lovely.'

'That's good,' Van Nuys said, nuzzling her neck, 'because we can go back to my house and practice making a few.'

Geffar sighed with pleasure as his hands roamed over her breasts once again, but he felt her suddenly stiffen. She had spotted his Rolex under the cuff of his tuxedo and had seen the time. 'The invitation sounds superb, Max, but I can't. I have a staff meeting in seven hours, and I've still got to prepare for it.'

He let his head hit the back of the seat with a frustrated *thud*. 'You can't be serious, Sandra,' he said with a twinge of agonized humor in his voice. 'You've got me so hard I can't walk straight, and now you tell me you have to work . . . ?'

'I'm sorry,' Geffar said. 'Give me a rain check for tomorrow night, will you? I take over the evening shift in two days, so I have the day after tomorrow off.' She gave him a conciliatory kiss. 'We can do something about your walking problem then.'

He let out another exasperated groan and a muttered, 'Women . . . ,' then reached over and clicked on the intercom. 'Edward, turn around and head for Miss Geffar's residence.'

An hour later, Van Nuys arrived back at his luxurious estate at Sunrise Beach. As the driver opened his door and let him out, Van Nuys told him, 'Thank you, Edward. Looks like our first meeting in the city isn't until eleven-thirty. Have the car ready by eleven.' The driver nodded and hurried away to park the limo.

Van Nuys loosened his tie as he started up the brick steps of his house. Damn Geffar, he thought to himself. What a bitch. No wonder she doesn't have any children at nearly age forty – she won't sit still long enough for anyone to get a poke at her. She could be a very sexy bitch and a ravenous lover, but she was too easily distracted by her work to pay total attention to something as inconsequential as a man.

Well, she wasn't worth losing any sleep over, he decided. He had dozens of bitches of all ages hanging around that would crawl over broken glass all the way up his driveway just to suck his kneecaps. He was with Geffar only to learn as much as he could about the Hammerheads, not because he was going to father any of her damned offspring. For all

306

he knew, the little brats would be born wearing fatigues and jack-boots . . .

Near the top of the steps leading to his front door he suddenly felt uneasy. His big Indian-born butler, Salman, would have heard the announcing buzzer at the front gate and have greeted his employer at the front door by now. The light was on and the lock on the front door was still secured, as evidenced by the blinkering red light on the keypad next to the doorway . . .

He stooped a bit, lifted his right pants leg and removed a palm-sized Beretta 21A .22-caliber automatic pistol from an ankle holster. His hand completely engulfed the tiny weapon. He entered the code to unlock the front door, pushed the latch, quickly swung the door open and stepped back. Nothing. No movement, no sound.

'Salman. Get over here.' No reply. 'Salman?'

Something was definitely weird – Salman would have left a note if he had to leave in an emergency. Van Nuys hurried down the steps and around the semicircular driveway to the garage. His driver, Edward, was also an experienced bodyguard – if he was going to go through any doors, he was going to increase his own odds of survival if he brought someone else with him.

The lights in the garage were already out, but the car was still parked in its place beside the garage. He tried the side door, it was locked. No way Edward would have gone home so soon. Whoever was in the house now had Edward as well as Salman. Which meant they had muscle and firepower. Neither of his people was easy to bring down.

No way in hell he was going through that front door. He thought about calling Hokum, but the only phone outside the house was on the back patio, and it was too exposed – whoever was in the house could easily spot him on the patio. There was a spiral staircase leading from the patio to the second-floor bedroom, but they could be covering that entrance too. Run for a neighbor's house? How far would he get?

One option left. The garage was detached from the main house but connected via a second-story breezeway linking the spare storeroom over the garage with the game room. The breezeway had a half-height roof with access on both ends and was big enough to crawl through. He might be able to get into the house through the breezeway without setting off any other alarms.

He climbed the steps to the second floor of the garage, used his keys to unlock the door, slipped inside. He made his way to the hidden doorway that connected into the breezeway, hoisted himself through the tiny door and into the breezeway roof. This space was only intended as access to phone lines and as extra storage space, hardly big enough for his large frame, but it was the only way. He low-crawled across the breezeway eaves to the house, then found the door that led to the storage room. Prying open the door, he slid through and crawled inside. He removed his shoes, picked his way in the darkness past boxes and old pieces of furniture and found the door leading to the short stairway. Slowly, carefully to avoid making any sounds, he moved down the narrow stairs that led to the game room. The door was unlocked. He cracked it a few inches, saw that the game room was dark and quiet, crouched low, slowly opened the door and went inside.

At least for a few seconds he might have the element of surprise over whoever had broken in. Trying not to cause any creaking sounds in the hardwood floor, he stepped carefully around the pool table and made his way to the door to the upstairs hallway.

He was a few yards from the door when the lights snapped on. Two men were crouched down in the corners of the game room, Uzi submachine guns in hand. Behind him was the sound of derisive clapping.

'Very good, very good, Mr Van Nuys. You have the markings of a master spy, or at least a second-story man. Perhaps you should forget the drug-smuggling business and take up espionage or house-breaking, no?'

The two men in the corner moved quickly forward, one placing the barrel of his Uzi against Van Nuys' right temple, the other taking the Beretta out of his hand. They grabbed his hands, put them on top of his head and spun him around to face back inside the room – to face a man in his mid-to-late forties, with dark hair, a moustache to match and a dark suit with a flowered tropical shirt underneath. Seated on a barstool in front of the bar, he twirled a pair of sunglasses in one hand while his other rested on the handle of a cellular phone sitting on the counter. He was smiling at the dirty, insulation-covered frame of the usually elegant Maxwell Van Nuys.

Flattened against one wall, hands on their heads, were Edward and Salman, both prevented from turning by the shotgun barrels in their faces. Salman showed trails of dark dried blood down the side of his face. Edward showed enough anger to chew off the barrel of the shotgun covering him from behind.

But the biggest surprise was the man seated beside the gunnery stranger – none other than Fire Chief, Police Chief, Chief of Community Services Joseph Hokum. He did not have his hands on his head like Edward or Salman, though he too was being covered by a gunman. 'What the hell is going on in here, Joe? Who are these people – ?'

'Silence,' the man in the flowered shirt told him in Spanish. 'Not say a word.'

'What's going on – '

Van Nuys was instantly slumped over the billiards table, his head ringing, his vision blurred from a blow from one of the gunmen behind him. He felt as if he were going to black out.

'Hervé will crack your skull open next time,' the man said. 'I will not warn you again. It is only because I am intrigued with you and your little operation here that you are still alive – I was told to come here, cut you up into little pieces and scatter you across your front lawn for the pleasure of your fine neighbors.'

'Bullshit,' Van Nuys said. 'Whoever sent you wants something.' He heard a rustle of movement behind and prepared for another shot to his head, but the man in the flowered shirt raised a hand.

'I have killed men for less than calling me a liar, Van Nuys – '

He doubted it. 'You're a messenger boy. Now let's cut the gangster crap and tell me why you broke into my house.'

'I do indeed have a message for you, but if I shot you and yours right here and now I wouldn't be blamed for anything but making a mess. Do you understand me?' He said it quietly.

Van Nuys' face was pushed hard into the green velvet of the pool table, but he managed to look up enough to say, 'If you're going to shoot me, goddamn it, then do it. Otherwise, give me the message and get out.' Bravado, of course, but he'd lived by the bluff his whole life.

He heard the metallic *snik* of a safety being removed from a weapon, and he closed his eyes and prepared himself. But instead of a bullet crashing into his brain he heard the man in the flowered shirt laugh, then was hauled upright, the gunmen backed away and the guy sat back in his chair by the wall and smiled at Van Nuys.

'How did you get in my house?' Van Nuys said, continuing his own show of *machismo* and with more confidence now – whoever had sent the men didn't want

310

him dead or he would have been. He could challenge them, so long as he didn't overdo it . . . He glanced at Hokum, who seemed to withdraw under his gaze.

'You are right to be displeased,' he was told. 'It was the chief of police here who told us about your secret corridor from the garage. I would have that deficiency corrected, if I were you.' Hokum sat motionless in his chair.

'You got *cojones*, I'll say that for you, mister,' the man in the flowered shirt continued. 'But I also know they're in your mouth right now . . . yes, I was sent here to check on you, Mr Van Nuys. My associates and I learned about your apparent association with both Sandra Geffar of the Border Security Force and Hokum, the chief of police here. But imagine my *surprise*, Mr Van Nuys, when my informants tell me *you* are running a million-dollar-a-month smuggling operation. Truly I was shocked, impressed. Importing cocaine right under the lady's lily-white nose.'

'I don't know what you're talking about – '

'Now it is you who are lying. That is no way to do business, señor. We know you have managed to fly as much as a hundred kilos a month from Grand Bahama Island right to this place. Señor Hokum here has been most cooperative with us. He has told us how his men have unloaded the drugs just before Customs arrives to inspect your plane, and how he alters the records to hide your money. Ingenious, I must say.'

Van Nuys gave Hokum a look that amused the man in the flowered shirt. 'Do not be angry at Señor Hokum. He has managed to keep your operation a secret from us for all these months even while he was working for us, helping us transport weapons and money into and out of south Florida. At first he was most reluctant to tell us anything about you. We are generous, but it took a surprising amount of money to convince him to talk. After that,

311

however, I must admit he could not have been more cooperative. That was good for him, it kept him alive.'

'What do you want? Money? Drugs? I don't have either. Go ahead and kill us – '

'I have *never* met a man so willing to die, Señor Van Nuys. A gratifying change. No, as you know by now, what we want from you is information. We want you to tell us everything there is to know about Commander Geffar, and we would like you to distribute a few of these.' He held out a black plastic case, then tossed it onto the pool table in front of Van Nuys. 'Open it.' Van Nuys did and found several items that looked like stick-pins and small thick buttons with thin wires trailing.

'You want *me* to bug her house?'

'Her house, her cars, her office, the Hammerheads platform, *everything*. Our agents cannot penetrate the Border Security Force's security screen at this time. But you seem to be in the enviable position of having access – to Geffar. You are such friends. We would also like you to report any unusual movements, projects, special activities, operations.'

'You're crazy. I don't have that kind of access to her. I see her occasionally, mostly at public events. I haven't even been on her damned platform.'

'Then we expect you to turn on your noted charm and get closer to her, Mr Van Nuys. After all, she *is* still a woman. If you provide her with companionship and trust, surely even she will let you into her world.' He patted the cellular telephone on the bar. 'We will even provide you with a telephone, Mr Van Nuys – untraceable, unbuggable, and no cost to you. As a businessman you should appreciate this offer.'

'Offer? What do I get if I go along with you? A bullet in the head?'

'There you go, so melodramatic, sir. You will find that

312

my employers can be very generous. Ask the chief here. Cooperate, live, and prosper. My employers could always use another shipping and distribution outlet. Even a small one such as yours.' He examined his sunglasses, deliberately put them back on. 'My employers are not pleasant with those who disappoint them, or cheat them. You seem to be a man with a good deal to lose, Mr Van Nuys – nice house, reputation, business. A shame if you were obliged to spend the rest of your life in prison. Perhaps if you asked for death then, someone would be kind enough to give it to you.'

Van Nuys knew he had no choice. He might avoid prison by going to the Hammerheads or Customs, but how long would he live then? 'What if I can't get you any information? What if she won't confide in me?'

'I have more faith in you than that, Mr Van Nuys.' He stood. 'You have a reputation with the ladies – I feel you will want to uphold it. If for some reason you do not, we will be back to visit you. And we will proceed to cut off your balls. We will ruin your career, your reputation, and your sex life all in one visit. And then we will kill you.

'Now, tell me a story, Mr Van Nuys. Tell me what you know about this Sandra Geffar.'

San Diego, California
The Next Afternoon

Customs Service Chief Inspector Roger Bolan had to acknowledge the effect the Hammerheads were having on his own agency – something he did not like to admit – all the press the Hammerheads were getting, good and bad, caused a surge in applicants for the new agency, and the overflow meant more good men and women for Customs. The resulting manpower made possible increased inspections, which were finding more drugs than ever before. This, in turn, bolstered morale, which made the whole process run more smoothly. Things were snowballing in a very big way – a development even Hardcastle hadn't anticipated.

Bolan was the commander of the Port of San Diego CET, or Contraband Enforcement Team. The CET was responsible for finding contraband – narcotics, stolen goods, cash, and any other illegal or non-declared items – in cargo containers or vessels entering the huge port at San Diego. Bolan was a thirty-eight-year-old fifteen-year veteran of the Customs Service who had taken command of the San Diego CET three years earlier as one of the youngest chief inspectors in the country. The reason why he was placed in command was obvious – he took his job very, very seriously, and he expected all those assigned to him to do the same. As an ex-Army officer, he ran his CET with military-like enthusiasm.

In the past few months, the number of inspectors assigned to him had nearly doubled, allowing him to do much more with his operation than ever before. Because of his increased manpower, they could inspect more ships in port, and (partly because of the effectiveness of the Hammerheads, something Bolan did not often admit) because of those increased inspections, they were finding more drugs than ever before. Their success in finding huge caches of drugs increased morale, and subsequently increased his manning and increased his detection rate. Things were snowballing, and in a very promising direction.

Bolan put his feet up on his cluttered but (he told himself) organized desk, shifted the bulk of his .44 Magnun revolver under his left armpit, and looked over a Customs Form 1302, a cargo declaration of an American freighter due in port in a few hours. Bolan was short but wiry, with short brown hair and dark brown eyes. His wife had complained about his moustache and he had shaved it off at her gentle persistence, which only made the CET chief look even younger. Like most of the CET members, who had at one time or another worked the docks and warehouses as inspectors, he had a trim, muscular build from carrying crates and lifting barrels, with thick, veined forearms, big biceps, and thick, powerful thighs. His attention to more mundane desk duties, however, had resulted in the inevitable 'executive spread' and spare tire. His wife had already started bugging him about *those* as well.

The cargo declaration he read was about thirty pages long, so he grabbed a cup of coffee from the outer office before retaking his position and looking it over. It was a typical 'milk run' freighter cargo, with a cargo manifest as varied and unusual as you could get. The freighter, the *Maria Star Kelly*, the largest freighter of the Kelly Steamship Company of Alameda, California, had made six ports of call in the past three weeks: Valparaiso, Chile, loading tomato products, grape juice, lumber, wine, furniture, and fish; Callao, Peru, loading personal effects, cars, copper wire, and lead shot; Guayaquil, Ecuador, loading glass bottles, balsa wood, coffee, frozen shrimp, and banana puree; Buenaventura, Colombia, loading coffee and automobile tires; Balboa, Panama, loading ceramic bricks, melons, and electronic goods; and Puntarenas, Costa Rica, loading bamboo furniture and ceramic pottery. The *Maria Star* had all this packed into fifty-two twenty-foot containers resembling the big cargo boxes on interstate tractor-trailer rigs, and fifty-six forty-foot containers, some refrigerated, all with registered steel seals on the locks with the seal numbers logged onto these manifests.

The manifests also showed the ship's master's name, the date of each port call, the shipper's name, the consignee's name, and the NF name, or the person to be notified of the cargo's arrival if it was to be picked up by an agent. It described the contents of each shipping container, how the goods were packaged, what state they were in (if the tomatoes were whole, crushed, sauce, puree, etc.), if the goods required refrigeration, and the total weight of each container.

Not long ago, inspecting a freighter like this would be a nightmare. Perishable cargos needed immediate attention – they couldn't afford to let these shipments sit around on the hot, steamy docks awaiting the next CET team – and the Customs inspectors always had to be careful going through fragile cargo like personal effects, pottery, or glassware. It was risky sending a young kid with a two-ton forklift through a container with two thousand glass bottles – very often, Customs would end up buying thousands of pounds of accidentally destroyed goods on top of the items that were routinely destroyed during most inspections.

But this type of shipment needed the attention – it fairly cried out for an inspection. There was something about it, something that spelled 'strike.' Bolan and the other CET members called it 'getting a hard-on.' when a shipment or freighter just *seemed* to be suspect. Of course, having ports of call in Peru, Colombia, and Panama – three major cocaine production and distribution nations – only fed those suspicions. Bolan was getting a raging hard-on about the *Maria Star*.

He picked up the phone and dialed the harbormaster of the Port of San Diego, a Greek-born bear of a man named Danerkouros. 'Hello, Inspector Bolan for Mr Danerkouros . . . Hello, sir, Inspector Bolan. We've got a manifest on the *Maria Star Kelly* due in this morning . . . yes, sir, that's the one . . . you've read my mind, Mr Danerkouros. Dock it at the "carnival" for us, please . . . I don't know when we'll be done, sir. My manifest shows one hundred and eight containers altogether, which is a lot, and I have no count on how many double-enders they have. I can give you a more accurate estimate about an hour after the *Maria* pulls in . . . thank you, sir, I appreciate it . . . no, I don't know which one will be next. I'll let you know as soon as I do . . . thanks again.' Bolan then finished his coffee, made a few phone calls to his family and to his headquarters downtown, hit the head, then headed for his unit's small computer center, where he picked up the intelligence report printouts on the *Maria Star* that had been compiled for him as soon as the Form 1302 had been received by the shipping company. One last cup of coffee, a check of his portable phone, and Bolan headed out the door towards the docks and the area known as the 'carnival.'

The 'carnival' was a specialized area of the port that had been created only a few months earlier, as a result of the same funding measures that created the Border Security Force. It had been argued that the Hammerheads would not be involved with more routine narcotics interdiction jobs such as inspecting freighters and aircraft once they arrived at American ports of entry, so the Customs Service was provided with much more sophisticated and powerful tools for carrying out inspections of large seaborne cargo shipments such as this. These CAI, or Cargo Automated Inspection, systems were installed at several large American ports of entry in the south to allow inspectors to quickly and accurately inspect an entire freighter's cargo in just a matter of hours. Located inside a tall chain-link security fence, the chambers, buildings, container rails, docks, cranes, slides, and transporter arms reminded someone of a cheap amusement park; hence the nickname 'carnival' – except at a hundred million dollars a copy, this amusement park was definitely not cheap.

The place was empty at the moment; the last ship had

unloaded its cargo and had been inspected earlier in the day. Bolan went to the operations center at the CAI and met with the inspection team chief, Ed Bartolo. The inspection team chief of each eight-hour shift usually ran all three divisions at the CAI: the inspection, warehouse, and security divisions. 'We got another one coming in soon, Ed,' Bolan told the shift chief. 'The *Maria Star*, the South American milk run I told you about.'

Bartolo nodded and retrieved his copy of the customs declaration form while stuffing the last of his lunch into his mouth. 'Yeah,' Bartolo said after studying the Form 1302, except his reply sounded more like a muffled 'ughk.' 'Figured you'd be sending this one through the carnival. Well, the boys are ready.'

They found the warehouse and inspection crews in the dining hall eating lunch, so Bolan briefed them as they ate: 'We got a good one for you this afternoon, boys and girls,' he began. '*Maria Star*, American registry, six hundred footer. One hundred and eight containers total, fifty-two twenty-footers and fifty-six forty-footers. Thirty refrigerated. No count on double-enders.'

Bolan opened the intelligence printout on the freighter: 'This vessel was involved with a very small marijuana smuggling incident three years ago on a run to New Orleans,' he said. 'The company and master were not charged, although they did get a hefty fine. No other reports on the company, this vessel, or the master; in general, US-registered vessels are not major targets for smugglers. They know our security is a little tighter and our foreign officials a lot less accessible. This vessel last underwent a complete top-down compartments search nine months ago and a complete cargo inspection six months ago, without the carnival of course, with no hits recorded.

'Let's go over its cargo and our actions. Starting from the

top of the heap: Empty container goes to ultrasound mapping; see if we have this container's electronic profile on file in the computer, but map it anyway for a cross-check. Household goods, pottery, and bamboo furniture can go through the sniffer chamber; I have a signed statement from the owners of the military household goods saying that there are no pressurized bottles inside. Fresh fruit have to be hand-checked; we have honeydew melons, tomatoes, and bananas. Watch for tarantulas, guys and gals.' A humorless moan went up from the audience; the hairy spiders were sometimes present in even the best-inspected boxes of fruit, and although they were not deadly and little more than a nuisance, they were not welcome guests.

'Electronics goods can go through the sniffer,' Bolan continued. 'Melons . . . more melons . . . ceramic bricks go through the sniffer, but I want each container random checked if they are not double-doored.' Double-doored containers had doors at each end, which facilitated inspecting a container. Although shippers were not required to have them, those that did were usually given preferential treatment by Customs, and those who did not retrofit their containers with extra doors usually attracted attention. It was much easier to hide contraband in the old-style containers with a single set of doors, which were exactly the ones that Customs kept an eye out for.

'Coffee – lots of coffee,' Bolan went on. There were a few 'ooh' and 'aahhs' from the inspection force – there was nothing in the world like the smell of a forty-foot container full of Colombian coffee beans, even from those few who didn't drink coffee. 'These can go through the sniffer. We have . . .' Bolan made a quick count of the containers that held sacks of coffee beans, '. . . twenty-four containers from Colombia with coffee beans. I want at least six of these hand-inspected after they come out of the sniffer.

'What else? Balsa wood can go in the sniffer. Cigarettes in the sniffer. More coffee beans, Ecuador – sniffer. Frozen shrimp, ten containers: sorry, boys, hand inspect. It says eighteen degrees Celsius, so you'll need parkas and mittens.' More displeased moaning. 'Drums of banana puree can get ultrasound. Household effects: aha. A special handling request.' Bolan nodded thoughtfully. Special handling requests were common with dependents of foreign diplomats returning home; they usually brought back expensive items that they wanted protected from damage.

'What are you going to do, boss?' Bartolo asked.

Bolan looked at the 'special handling' request again, then shook his head. 'I haven't done a hand inspection in a long time,' he said. 'I'll take this one.'

That seemed to please a lot of the inspectors in the room – Bolan got a lot of approving nods and sly smiles, happy that their boss treated the big-shot diplomats – and himself – like everyone else. 'Well, I'll help out to make sure you do it right, then, sir,' Bartolo offered.

'I would've insisted on it,' Bolan said with a smile. He continued down the list, assigning each container to a particular area or system in the CAI, then read off a list of Customs briefing notes compiled from reports from around the country, advising inspectors on things to look out for or things that other inspectors had found. He also read off the latest intelligence summaries, outlining any information received by the FBI, DEA, or Border Security on drug shipments or activity.

'We've received an alert on household goods again,' Bolan read off. 'Seems we get one of these every other month, but it's still a popular way to smuggle in small quantities. DEA says to watch out for military and government household goods shipments in particular, since packing jobs for government employees overseas are now being contracted to local moving companies, often the lowest bidders. This means that any smuggling operation can front itself as a moving company and load a shipment down with product relatively easy, during several stages of the moving process. Stay on your toes. The sniffer should catch most jobs, but as we've learned, it isn't foolproof.

'We've received a status briefing from the FBI on narcotics sales nationwide: they're supposed to be down ten percent from this time last year, with cocaine prices now averaging twenty-three thousand dollars a kilo for street grade. That's almost a hundred percent more than last year.'

'This almost sounds like a commodities report on the Financial News Network,' somebody quipped.

'Well, here's the difference, Duncan,' Bolan told him. 'The FBI says they blame rising cocaine prices for increases in violent urban crime, gang-related violence, and a rise in the felony crime rate. Stick that up your portfolio. This FBI report is supposed to highlight the enormous tension these price increases are causing, and the turf wars and crime it's causing. The pressure to import a kilo of coke is really getting bad. It's also supposed to highlight the security question, guys and girls – the bad guys will be pulling out the stops to get their product. They haven't called for increased security measures yet, but they might be implementing tighter restrictions and added security soon. That line about a commodities report might be a good analogy, Duncan – the higher the price of street drugs rise, the greater the profit margin becomes and the more players want to get into the action. When the price gets really high and the quantity goes down, things really might get tense.

'Along with that FBI report, we're also getting an alert from Border Security about increased activity from aircraft trying to break through the air cordons. It's hard to believe, children, but smugglers are still trying to go right through

321

the cordons instead of around them. Activity is picking up along the Mexico border and in the southwest, and Border Security predicts that our area will become the new Caribbean very soon. Border Security isn't planning on expanding into the southwest for a few years, so the bad boys will take advantage of a relative gap in offensive border coverage.' He closed the briefing folders and set them down on a table. 'Okay. Questions?' No reply. 'Everyone fat and happy? Good. The *Maria* will be in shortly, so let's get to work.'

Processing an incoming freighter, even a medium-sized one like the *Maria Star*, was a monstrous task for the Customs Service. Because the *Maria* was making its first port call in the United States, the crew had to process through the port of entry before anything else for passport, baggage, and records checks. The ship's records would be checked, and the Coast Guard would conduct a safety inspection before the ship would be allowed to navigate American waters. Bolan's Contraband Enforcement Team was responsible for inspecting the vessel and its cargo for illegal or undeclared goods being brought into the United States. As soon as the in-processing and standard port of entry inspections were finished, a huge overhead rolling crane was wheeled into position and the Cargo Automated Inspection process began.

Each container was hoisted off the freighter and onto a trailer mounted on a railway inside the 'carnival,' and the container would be automatically towed to its programmed stops inside the inspection facility. The first stop for the container, the CAI routing clerk, logged the container in and checked the number and integrity of the steel strap seals that secured the locks on each container, to be sure there was no tampering – any seal that was broken, missing, or if the seal numbers did not match or appeared to have been altered meant that the container was suspect and would immediately be confiscated. The clerk would then issue computer commands to direct the container for processing to one or more of three areas of inspection – the 'sniffer,' the ultrasound/radar chamber, or the manual inspection docks.

At least half of all goods could be directed into the Atmosphere Analysis Chamber, the 'sniffer,' a sealed chamber large enough for a container to be wheeled inside. Once inside, the chamber was closed off and the air pumped out. As the air was evacuated it was analyzed by high-speed computers and compounds in the air were catalogued. Compounds found in narcotics, explosives or any specified item could be scanned and if found would sound a warning and alert Bolan's inspectors.

The sniffer was not perfect. Smugglers could seal drugs so firmly in airtight bags or deeply within thick heavy products that the sniffer couldn't find them.

For items the sniffer couldn't sniff, the US/EM chamber, Ultrasound/Electromagnetic Chamber, a.k.a. the 'buzz box,' was used. The buzz box could take an electronic photograph of the interior of almost any container, from huge fuel tanks down to small aerosol bottles. If the reflections became distorted or different from other similar containers, it signaled that there was something foreign inside deflecting the beams. The largest and busiest area was the manual inspection facility. The most high-tech piece of equipment here was a good old fork lift and strong backs to lift the pallets out of the containers. Bolan had help here from National Guard troops – a dramatic result of the relaxing of the post-Civil War Posse Comitatus Act, which normally prevented the military from participating in civil law enforcement.

Each box, crate, piece of furniture of the freighter was unloaded onto the warehouse floor, catalogued and opened. Sniffer probes were run through boxes of clothing, cookware, papers. Canine sniffers were used on furniture and some of the boxes. They found several crates of what appeared to be large pieces of South American pottery wrapped in thick sheets of liquid-filled shock absorbers.

'Let's run 'em through the ultrasound and X-ray to see if they're hollow. After that I think we can pass them,' Bolan said. The pottery and statues were unwrapped from their high-tech packaging, placed on fiberglass charts and taken to the ultrasound/X-ray chamber for analysis.

An hour later, nothing, inside or out.

'Well, I thought for sure there might be something here,' Bolan told Bartolo, as a phone call came in on his portable.

'Inspector Bolan, this is Deputy Simpson's office,' a secretary told him. 'I am inquiring for the Deputy Consul on the status of his household goods. I've been told by the shipping company that you have the shipment.'

'That's correct. I – '

'Please hold, Inspector.' A few moments later another voice came on the line, definitely much more agitated than the first. 'This is Deputy Consul Simpson. Bolan? You have my household goods?'

'Yes, sir. I – '

'I *specifically* received assurances from Customs through State that we'd receive priority treatment for the delivery of our goods. We've been living in a hotel at three hundred dollars a night for nearly three weeks. Our things were supposed to be shipped to Washington – what in God's name they're doing in San Diego, I have no idea. Now I want those things released and I want it done now.'

Bolan hadn't heard of Simpson before, but at three hundred dollars a night he didn't feel too sorry for him. Most diplomatic people in the administration were appointed because of their financial support for the President and his political party. Simpson must have been one of those fat cats. 'The inspection on your shipment has been completed,' Bolan told him. 'When the entire shipment has cleared you can arrange for – '

'Well, when will *that* be?'

'Late this afternoon or first thing in the morning.'

'As soon as *my* shipment is inspected I want it picked up. I'll have the movers there in two hours.'

'We can't release it unless the entire – '

'Inspector Bolan, you'll be hearing from your superiors. I advise you to have my things ready to go in two hours.'

'All this stuff belongs to some political pencil-pusher,' Bolan told Bartolo. 'He's pissed because the only place he can stay costs three hundred dollars a night.'

Bartolo shook his head. 'Poor baby.' He motioned toward the National Guardsmen, who were drifting back from the break area preparing to move the shipment back into the container.

Bolan glanced at the stuff lying around the dock. 'I was so *sure* about this one, it seemed so . . . wrong.' He paused. 'How's the rest of the inspection going?'

'Clean as a whistle,' Bartolo said. 'Thought we had a positive on some of the lumber containers but it was a false alarm from the resin that set off the sniffer. They've checked eight containers of coffee, all clean.'

Bolan nodded toward the National Guardsmen rewrapping the pottery and statues with the special anti-shock material. 'I would've bet a month's salary that the junk was in those statues.'

'They checked out clean,' Bartolo told him.

Bolan didn't seem to be listening as he stared at the National Guardsmen, who finished covering the biggest statue. There was a cotton sheet that first covered the statue, then the liquid-filled padding was placed over the statue, suspended by an iron frame. The entire mass was then secured to the frame by rubber cords and the wooden crate reassembled around it. The first statue was just being completed and work starting on the second when Bolan noticed one of the Guardsmen wiping his hands on his camouflaged BDU pants. He went quickly over to the man. 'What's that on your pants?'

The Guardsman shrugged as he wrestled with another anti-shock blanket. 'You got me, Inspector. A leak in one of these shock absorber things?'

Bolan grabbed the guy's hand and smelled it. 'Sergeant, you ever smell cocaine before?'

The Guardsman smelled his hand. 'No, sir, I don't do that shit.'

'That's the first thing we ought to do with you guys,' Bolan said. 'Give you a class in what cocaine *smells* like. Break down that statue you just wrapped. Find the leak in the blanket. Bartolo . . . seal off the warehouse and alert security.'

As the shift chief went to alert the rest of the area, Bolan began to direct the National Guardsmen in taking apart the protective wrapping around the first statue. After the wooden crate and rubber cords had been removed he carefully searched the cotton cover around the statue. After a few moments he found a softball-sized wet spot near the bottom.

'Building and compound secure,' Bartolo reported. Bolan grunted and got down on his hands and knees around the bottom of the anti-shock blanket, where he found a small rivulet of moisture and a few drops of liquid. He reached into a breast pocket and extracted a thin plastic vial of cobalt thiocyanate. By tapping on the blanket he got one drop of the clear liquid into the vial to break a tiny glass capsule inside and shook it to mix the chemicals. When he held it up to the light, the liquid in the vial was blue.

'*Liquid cocaine*,' Bartolo said. 'I heard about it but I never seen it until now.'

Bolan nodded, 'Supersaturated solution. Hard to detect

on X-rays – a container filled with this stuff will still look empty in X-rays – and sometimes even the sniffer can't pick it up. One kilo of coke in every gallon of fluid in these blankets – that could account for a hundred pounds of weight alone.' He looked at the National Guardsman. 'Fifty kilos of coke, and you had your hands all over it.' He turned and gave Bartolo a very pleased smile. 'Notify Brad Elliott at Aladdin City. I think our antsy Deputy Consul will have a few other things to worry about than his hotel bill.'

Office of the Assistant Secretary of State, Washington, DC
That Same Day

The Assistant Secretary of State for Latin America, Wilson Riley, stood as Geoffrey Simpson, the former deputy chief of mission at the American Embassy in Peru, entered the office. 'Good to see you again, Geoffrey. Sit down, sit down.'

'Thank you, sir . . .'

Riley returned to his desk and folded his hands on his desk. 'They miss you in Lima already, Geoffrey,' he said. 'You seemed to have found a home down there. Made some real strong bonds to the people.'

'I thank you, but of course I shouldn't take all the credit – '

'Well, the evaluations I've received from the Peruvian government and from the ambassador look good.'

'Thank you, sir.'

The phone buzzed, and Riley picked up the receiver. 'Give me a minute,' he said, and hung up. To Simpson: 'Well, when your evaluation comes through you have to be ready to get down to work here in Washington – I'm sure you'll be slated for a job in this section, or perhaps on the European side. That's what you wanted, right? I'd hate to lose you, Geoffrey, but someone else with more juice than me will undoubtedly snatch you up.' Simpson was beginning to relax, smiling and nodding, nodding and smiling. 'Anything I can help you with? You found a place in Williamburg, I heard.'

'Sure did,' Simpson said. 'Just signed the papers yesterday. We should get our goods today or tomorrow and I'll be all settled in.'

Suddenly Riley's face seemed to drain of its good humor. 'Yes . . .' There was a knock at the door and a new somber-faced Riley said, 'Come.' Simpson turned in his seat to see none other than General Brad Elliott come in, followed by a man he did not recognize. Simpson got to his feet when he recognized Elliott. 'General Elliott, this is Geoffrey Simpson, formerly deputy consul in Peru. Geoffrey, General Elliott, Border Security Force, and Special Agent Michael Farmer, FBI.'

Simpson broke into a sweat when he heard the words 'Border Security Force,' but his sweat turned to ice when he heard FBI. Elliott found a chair beside the assistant secretary's desk; Farmer went to the other side of the room, facing Simpson but far enough away so Simpson couldn't see him without turning toward him.

Riley said, 'Geoffrey, it seems Customs found some contraband in your household goods shipment.'

'Oh, my God . . .'

'Listen to me, Mr Simpson,' Farmer said. 'We're not placing you under arrest at this time, but I am going to read you your rights so we can question you. We're expecting, of course, to get your full cooperation.'

'I want an attorney,' Simpson said.

'Mr Simpson, if you do not cooperate we'll have to detain you.'

'I thought you said you wouldn't have to arrest him,' Riley said.

'He's a flight risk, sir. He has friends in Peru and Bolivia, overseas bank accounts, contacts . . . I can't take the chance. I assumed he would cooperate.'

Knowing the Department would hate the bad publicity, Riley turned to Simpson. 'Dammit, Simpson, you've *got* to cooperate . . .'

'I want to speak with an attorney first, sir,' he said in a toneless voice. His hands were beginning to shake.

'Get him out of here,' Riley said. Farmer moved over to the door, opened it, and two plainclothes investigators entered the room. Simpson got to his feet as one of the agents grasped him firmly by an upper arm. While the other agent read a Miranda statement from a laminated card, the first agent placed Simpson's arms behind him, handcuffed him and searched him. 'Do you really have to cuff him like that?' Riley said. 'The whole damn building will see him.'

Farmer looked at Riley, nodded and instructed his agents to remove Simpson's jacket and cuff Simpson in front of his body. Then they draped Simpson's jacket over his wrists just before leading him out of the office. 'We'll contact the section counsel and your wife, Geoffrey. Don't worry, we'll get this cleared up in no time . . .' He wasn't sure if Simpson had heard him. He also would have liked to strangle Elliott.

When they had left, Riley went back to his desk and got on the phone: 'Anna, get Bob Turnbull in here on the double.' Then he turned on Brad Elliott: 'We handle things in-house around here. We don't go off to the FBI – '

'I had no choice.'

'You could have come to me first, before getting the FBI involved. We have a very good investigative unit here. We would have turned over everything to the FBI and Border Security when our investigation was complete. Besides, maybe he's got an explanation . . .'

'Sure, Mr Riley,' Elliott said, heading for the door. 'It

329

may turn out that Simpson knew nothing about the shock absorbers, that he's an innocent babe. I'm not doing the investigation. My job in this is to find out everything I can about whoever made those shock absorbers and put them around an ambassador's personal articles.'

'Why are you getting involved in this, General Elliott? I thought Border Security was only in charge of securing the borders. This doesn't seem like it's exactly your beat.'

'Border Security is the agency in charge of the Drug Enforcement Administration, Mr Riley. DEA is our intelligence and investigative arm. Customs turns all drug-related incidents concerning border crossings over to us; once the matter involves other government agencies or moves further inland we *have* to turn it over to the FBI.'

'Sounds like bureaucratic mumbo-jumbo.' Coming from State, that was almost funny, Elliott thought. 'I heard you were the President's fair-haired boy – looks like you got yourself a real sweet billet. But let me tell you, you start using your leverage to get one of my officers shit-canned without solid evidence and I'll come down on you like a ton of bricks.'

Elliott stepped up to Riley's desk, leaned forward.

'As long as we're getting personal here, let me make some observations,' Elliott said in a soft but rumbling voice. 'Speaking of bureaucrats, I see one who's more concerned with his own butt instead of finding out the truth. Your section doesn't have an investigative unit. I checked. I'm sure you would have come up with one in an instant, but their main focus would have been to lessen the impact on you, not to get at the facts.

'You're more shook up about adverse publicity than about what happens to Simpson. You wanted him to talk, knowing that it was the worst possible advice you could have given him – he could have blood all over his hands or a gold halo over his head, but you know he should have his

330

lawyer present before questioning begins. I don't know a helluva lot about the law or about investigative procedure, Riley, but I do know that having your boss tell you to cooperate and talk is a sell-out.

'I think *you* think he's guilty. You wanted the State Department lawyer here to advise *you* on what to do. You wanted to hear what Simpson had to say so you could start your own damage control . . .'

'Get out, damn you,' Riley said. 'Just get the hell out of my office.'

'My pleasure,' Elliott said.

Later That Day

The Geoffrey Simpson that walked through the door of Wilson Riley's office twelve hours later was a different man. His jacket was crooked and rumpled, as if he had slept in it.

Riley let Simpson stand in front of his desk a few moments as he pretended to write something into a folder, then motioned toward a chair with his eyes. Simpson dropped into it as if his legs had just refused to support his weight any longer. Riley continued his doodling until he saw Simpson begin to fidget in his seat. 'I received a call from the FBI. They are releasing you. No charges are being filed.'

Simpson let out a sigh. 'Thank God . . .'

'But you're not out of it, Simpson, not by a damned long shot. All they told me was that, in their opinion, you had nothing to do with packing your household goods.'

'Of course I didn't have anything to do with it! I was staying in the ambassador's residence when my goods were being packed – '

'But you hired *this* company to move your things,

331

bypassing the State Department guidelines for selecting a moving company . . .'

Simpson rubbed his eyes wearily, then held up a hand. 'If you don't mind, sir, I'd rather not go over all this again . . .'

'You had better talk to me, Simpson . . .'

'My attorney said – '

'Don't *give* me that lawyer crap. I don't care what your lawyer says. You're a State Department official and a part of *my* section. All of this could have been avoided if you had cooperated with the FBI and told them what you know. Legal says the FBI would not have arrested you if you'd cooperated. But you waved the Constitution around like some sleaze Mafia boss, they put handcuffs on you and marched you through the building – *my* building. You are a major goddamn embarrassment, Simpson, and right now you are way beyond this "remain silent" Miranda stuff. Now, when I tell you to talk, you talk and keep talking. When I tell you to shut up, you shut up. All clear on that?' Simpson nodded. 'Okay, why did you hire that moving company to pack your stuff? You read the advisory from Border Security that said drug smugglers often front as moving companies to ship drugs. Why did you ignore that advisory and go outside department regulations?'

'The moving company was owned by the nephew of one of the district Conservative Party chiefs,' Simpson said quietly. 'He helped us establish the new free-trade-zone regulations a few months ago. It was a personal favor – '

'It was also, at best, a damned stupid thing to do,' Riley said. 'He was probably on the smuggler's payroll. The whole free-trade-zone agreement was probably part of the smuggling operation, and you, bright boy, fell right into it. But why did you call Customs and complain about the handling your goods were getting? Why did you call the Customs commissioner's office? You sounded like a pusher who couldn't wait to go back into business.'

'Because we're paying three hundred dollars a night for a hotel room,' Simpson said. 'Our goods have been in transit for almost a month – '

'And that's another thing. Why the hell are you staying at a suite at the Madison, living it up like some damned Arab sheik? The FBI was sure someone had lined your pockets with a little cash. It looked suspicious as hell.'

Simpson's head bowed a bit. 'Tina . . . my wife, Tina . . . she was so happy to get out of Peru, to get back to the States . . . she always wanted to stay at the Madison. We were only going to stay for a week, sort of . . . sort of as a holiday. We just . . . never checked out . . .'

'And you paid *cash* for your room?'

'We . . . we had cashed in a lot of pesos . . .'

Riley turned away from Simpson in disgust, shaking his head. 'Stupid,' he muttered. He stared out the window for a few moments, letting Simpson squirm in the hard, thinly padded armless chair. Then: 'You've been reassigned to Frank Melvin's section. My secretary has your assignment folder outside.'

Simpson looked ashen. 'Melvin . . . I've been assigned to Africa? Why? I don't understand . . .'

'The consul general in Lubumbashi has a request in for a replacement,' Riley said. 'They need someone right away. You're what the doctor ordered.'

'Lubumbashi? You mean Zaire? You're sending me to *Zaire* because of this?'

'Have a nice trip, Simpson.'

'But I'm *innocent*.' Simpson half-rose from the chair. 'I didn't know about the damn cocaine. I didn't know about my household-goods shipment being used to transport drugs. I can account for every penny I've spent – '

'Simpson, the Department takes care of its own, if they cooperate. I gave you a chance to take advantage of that when the FBI and Border Security people stormed into my office. You thought you'd hide behind some outside lawyer and your *rights* – well, now I've got FBI agents and Border Security I-Team investigators rummaging through my files, and I had to put up with a gimp prima donna Air Force general lecturing me on how to run my shop. You embarrassed this entire section. I can't help you any more. Good luck, Mr Simpson. Have a ball in the Congo.'

Zaza Airfield, Verrettes, Haiti
One Day Later

'Señor Gachez. What a surprise,' Salazar said over the scrambled phone. He was at his desk in his office, getting a shoe shine from a young peasant boy. With Salazar was his chief pilot, Major Trujillo, and his aide, Field Captain Hermosa. They had all been expecting the call.

'We heard about the unfortunate incident in San Diego the other day,' Salazar continued. 'One hundred kilos. A small shipment but an incident of large consequences.'

'Don't gloat, Salazar,' Gachez said. 'That was one small shipment. Others have been making it through . . .'

'Liquid cocaine? Frozen cocaine? Very imaginative, señor. Except it took only two weeks for the Hammerheads to discover it. Now the whole southwest is closed up tight. Radar balloons are flying everywhere – Arizona, New Mexico, Texas – and Customs has doubled their investigators at every inspection station. All because of one hundred kilos.'

'Let me know when we can talk some business.'

'You tried to cut me out, Señor Gachez. You tried to renege on our contract . . .'

'You were the one who reneged. We had a deal for six thousand dollars a kilo – '

'And because of you the price has again gone up,' Salazar

334

interrupted. 'With the entire American border on full alert, it will cost extra for every shipment.' He paused, considering his thoughts, then decided: 'It will now cost you twelve thousand dollars a kilo for delivery, anywhere. Half upfront, half on delivery to the place specified by your ground crew.'

'Twelve . . . thousand . . . dollars . . . I will never pay. I will see that you are executed instead – '

'For that amount, I will guarantee delivery to any place in the United States,' Salazar said. 'No matter what the Hammerheads do, you have my guarantee. And it will not be for a few measly kilos – we will ship every kilo you and the rest of the Cartel has ready.'

There was a long pause on the line; Salazar thought Gachez had hung up on him again. Then: 'Ten thousand a kilo.'

'Twelve, *señor*. The price and the terms are not negotiable.'

Another long pause, then: 'Done.' And the line went dead.

Salazar leaned back in his chair. The boy had scurried around to the other side of the desk to do the other boot. 'We're back in business, gentlemen,' he said, 'at twelve thousand dollars a kilogram.'

Hermosa was silent, his face grave as it usually was of late. Trujillo nodded his approval. 'Good news, Colonel, but what I said about the Border Security Force is true. Their detection and interception systems are accurate and reliable. It will be very difficult to defeat them, even with fighter escort.'

'We multiply our assets, spread the shipments out over more territory, move farther north and west . . .'

'That depends on where Gachez wants the deliveries made, sir,' Trujillo said. 'If he insists on the southwest again, we may not be successful unless we devise another tactic.'

'You will think of something, Major. I have confidence in you.' Salazar glanced down at the youngster busily running two soft-bristled brushes across his boots.

'I think I may have an idea, Major,' Salazar said. 'Yes . . .' And he reached down to pat the boy's head.

Hermosa saw the cold look on Salazar's face, and his heart felt as if it had dropped to his feet. No, he screamed to himself. Not even Salazar could possibly be considering *that* . . .

Hammerhead One Air Staging Platform, 0715
Two Days Later

'Attention on deck. Prepare for drone launch, prepare for drone launch.'

Geffar was in the Seagull drone launch area as the drone-deck crew wheeled a delta-winged black Seagull drone out from the elevator near the center maintenance building to the catapult launch pits. Standing alongside her was Patrick McLanahan, now a full deputy commander of the Hammerheads, in charge of drone operations. He was monitoring reports from the flight-operations tower on a wireless headset. 'They sounded the alert at five past the hour,' he said, checking his watch. 'They should have this baby airborne within five minutes.'

'Where's the target?'

'One hundred fifty miles off the west coast of Florida,' McLanahan said. 'No flight plan, no Customs clearance, smuggler's profile. The Seagull will nail him in thirty minutes.' He listened for a moment, then added, 'A Sea Lion tilt-rotor bird is reporting ready to go at Homestead for the follow-on.'

The deck crew was like an Indy race-car crew prepping a racer in the pits. The Seagull drone was pushed and pulled

336

into the launch-catapult area and lined up with the left launch rail, a fifty-foot-long channel in the deck, where a large hook was set. A bar on the Seagull's front landing gear was set into the hook and tested for position, then raised out of the hook. 'Drone in place, catapult checked and set, one minute gone,' McLanahan said, copying the times and a few notes on a clipboard. The deck crew secured the drone with a chain leading to tiedown bolts under each broad wing.

'Why don't you leave the gear bar in place?' Geffar asked him.

'In case the catapult accidentally fires we don't want our guys flying off along with the drone. We also put the bar in place just before launch, when everyone's clear, the engine's running, and the data-link is active. We learn these things the hard way,' McLanahan told her. 'We were preflighting a truck-launched model when the catapult accidentally went off. The wings nearly took a guy's head off. The front gear got modified the way it is now.'

Four technicians now moved around the machine. The multi-sensor cameras, the engine, propeller, fuel supply, antennae and overall condition of the bird were checked and a thumbs-up given to the safety officer. 'Power-off preflight completed. Two minutes gone,' McLanahan said.

The technicians scrambled and the safety fence at the end of the launch rail leading to the edge of the deck was lowered out of the way. 'They're activating the data-link,' McLanahan told Geffar. The safety officer made one last check around the aft end of the drone, then signaled to the command center via his own headset. A moment later the engine coughed to life, the propeller snapped around, stopped, spun around, caught and roared to life. 'Engine started, beginning power-on preflight,' McLanahan said. 'Three minutes gone.'

The controllers in the command center now performed a

preflight on the Seagull, checking its flight control, recovery, backup, emergency and sensor equipment. The wing ailerons and wingtip rudders moved, the sensor ball could be seen swiveling around in its turret, and lights popped on and off all around. The lone whine of the propeller oscillated up and down as the engine power and propeller pitch were changed – the drone danced on its wheels as the power was increased to full, despite the chains holding it securely to the deck.

Moments later the power eased back to idle. 'Power-on preflight completed, thirty seconds to go,' McLanahan said. 'Pre-launch and launch checklists.' The tiedown chains were removed, the launch deck was cleared and safety nets were erected around the launch deck in case a brisk breeze blew the bird off course at launch. A holdback bar was placed on a bracket at the rear of the craft to keep it in place just before launch. The rudders were cocked to the left to compensate for a slight breeze from the left; at launch, its nose would then swing into the wind and prevent it from skidding back into the platform. The last step was the safety officer going out and engaging the catapult bar on the front landing gear of the Seagull.

'Ready for launch, deck clear. Clear for launch.' The Seagull's engine revved up to full power, creating a small whirlwind against the backstop net. It shook on its holdback bar, as if asking to be let free. Suddenly the holdback bar popped out of the landing-gear bracket and the Seagull shot forward out toward the edge of the deck. The left wing dipped, and in response the nose angled upward and the bird rode on its rear landing-gear wheels as it cleared the platform. When it dipped several feet after leaving the deck, even with its nose high in the air, Geffar was afraid it would stall and crash into the ocean. But a few seconds later its nose-high descent subsided, it leveled off, shot into the sky and was quickly lost from sight.

'Good data-link being received from the Seagull,' McLanahan reported. 'It's already tying in with the KEYSTONE aerostat and receiving intercept data on the target.'

For backup, just in case, a second Seagull was wheeled off the elevator and over to the launch area as they headed toward the maintenance building to the elevator that would take them down to the command center.

Hardcastle was in the commander's seat, studying the central radar display that showed the west coast of Florida within one hundred miles of the target they had just launched the Seagull against. Geffar logged into the commander's terminal, and Hardcastle made room for her at the console. 'KEYSTONE has contact with Seagull, on course and approaching Plantation Key,' he said. 'We have radar contact on several vessels west of Cape Romano and Ten Thousand Islands that might be pickups.'

'Any of our boats in the area?'

'Nothing in the immediate area. Closest would be an SES out of Key West, about two hours cruising time. We should get a Sea Lion airborne and cover the target's flight path.'

'Right. Launch one out of Aladdin City.'

McLanahan glanced at Hardcastle. The veteran ex-Coast Guard officer looked less than ecstatic when Geffar suggested launching an aircraft out of the Hammerheads' Everglades air base – no doubt he was hoping to fly a Sea Lion off the platform himself, McLanahan thought. Except for instructional and ferry flights, Hardcastle had been virtually grounded by Elliott since his so-called incident near Boca Raton – no operational flights. It had taken its obvious toll on him. Not to mention the snide shots taken at him by some in the media about his alleged drinking. And his son Daniel, part of the same story . . . All of these because of the death of one of the smugglers? He had done

339

what the Hammerheads were authorized to do, what he had envisioned would be the solution to the drug problem in the United States. And instead of being recognized for his actions he was being condemned. Damned unfair, McLanahan felt, and he wasn't alone. Many of the line people in the Hammerheads agreed, and their morale was being affected.

After he had issued the orders to launch the Sea Lion tilt-rotor aircraft from Alladin City, Hardcastle stood and headed out to the elevators. McLanahan followed.

He found Hardcastle leaning on the safety fence between the maintenance building and the aircraft elevator. A Sea Lion was just being raised up to the main deck in preparation as backup to the ongoing chase operation in west Florida. He leaned up against the fence alongside him.

'Hey, Admiral, how's she going?'

Hardcastle looked at him, offered a wary smile. 'All right. Watched the launch on the monitors. Your crew is really humming. Got it off under five minutes this time.'

'Yeah. Thanks. Remember just a few weeks ago when we thought launching one under ten minutes would be impossible? Now we do one under five and they think it's no big deal.'

'You've done a great job with the drones and the crew,' Hardcastle said.

'For an Air Force jock, you mean?'

'You'd make a pretty good sea dog, too.'

A few beats of silence, then McLanahan said, 'How are things really going with you?'

Hardcastle stared straight ahead, his lips taught, his eyes hard. 'You know they changed the designation of the Sea Lion, don't you? It's officially an AV-22, an *attack* plane.' McLanahan had indeed heard – it had come up in Congressional testimony about the offensive way this 'rescue' aircraft had been used.

340

'I don't know why you're beating yourself up like this,' McLanahan said. 'It was a good bust, a good intercept. Bringing Daniel on the flight, flying after drinking – '

'I was *not* drunk.'

'I *know* you weren't. I'm just saying maybe that peripheral stuff wasn't so hot, but damn it, you did the job, just the way she wrote . . . the way *you* wrote it.'

'I was disappointed in Elliott, I thought he – '

'Admiral, let me tell you something about Brad Elliott. You know him on a higher level than I do, but I think I maybe know him better than you do. We've done some flying together, and I can tell you that, like you, Brad would rather be up there flying than in this big-deal executive job. But he took it on because the Hammerheads are on the cutting edge of something, and that's what he likes. Me too. Frankly, I guess we'll both be happier when we get back where we came from, to Dreamland and Brad's toys. Meanwhile, though, I guarantee you that inside he's really on your side. But he has to do some of this PR stuff to keep the wolves from the door and he's doing it. Sorry, sir, end of speech, but I thought I should – '

Hardcastle looked at him, half-smiled. 'You make a pretty good case, Patrick, and I appreciate it, but damn it, I still hate this inaction, and I feel left out.'

'Admiral, you *can't* be left out. Sandra Geffar is the commander of this platform, and she does a real good job, but everybody knows you're the heart and soul of the Hammerheads. You made all this happen. You took on the big shots and the old-line people in Customs and Coast Guard. We all got in this because of the challenge and excitement that you gave it. We believe in what you believe in. So, if you don't mind, sir, please keep that in mind when you're feeling all low and lonely.'

'They say I screwed up, that – '

'That's bull too. We know that kid in the racing yacht

wasn't going to turn around for nobody, especially Fontaine. You stopped him from getting through. You took it by the balls and got the job done. As far as having Daniel on board, well, maybe not such a hot idea, but it's no big deal. They bring reporters and politicians within a thousand miles on actual intercepts.'

'What am I *supposed* to do, Patrick?' Hardcastle asked, turning and pounding a fist on the railing. 'Hey. I screwed up. I gotta take my lumps . . .'

'That's bullshit too, Ian, and you know it,' Patrick told him. 'We know that kid in the Cigarette racing yacht wasn't going to turn around for nobody, especially Fontaine. You stopped him from getting through. You took the initiative and got the job done. As far as having Daniel on board, it's no big deal. You Coast Guard guys bring reporters and politicians and every bigwig within a thousand miles on actual intercepts, and I know Customs does it as well.' Patrick studied Hardcastle for a moment. 'What else is bugging you, man? There's something else on your mind.' He waited, watching the pain twist through Hardcastle's face; then, he said, 'Daniel. Something's wrong with Daniel . . . ?'

Hardcastle's face turned stormy and dark, and he turned away from McLanahan. 'He won't talk to me, he won't listen to me any more,' Hardcastle said. 'He doesn't return any of my calls. His mother tells me he's quit the baseball team. It's like he freaked out or something.' McLanahan had no reply. Hardcastle continued: 'It started when we left the headquarters building, surrounded by all those damned reporters. He was shaking so hard after I got him into the car, I thought he was injured. He said he felt like a criminal, like I murdered that kid on the boat and he was a witness to it. His mother said he stayed home from school after he heard his name on the news the next morning. I haven't seen him that scared in fifteen years.'

'Hey, Ian, try not to worry,' McLanahan said, trying his best to console him. 'He went through quite an ordeal, but he'll snap out of it . . .'

'Patrick, that was *three weeks* ago,' Hardcastle said. 'I haven't seen my son in three weeks. Either I get a message from him or a message from my ex-wife, telling me he can't make it for a weekend or for a holiday. I know his grades have slipped, and I know he either hangs out in his room by himself or stays out late at night, but I can't help him. He won't let me get close to him again.'

McLanahan reached out and put a hand on Hardcastle's shoulder. 'I know you're going through hell right now, Ian,' he said. 'My dad was a police officer back in California. He worked his butt off for years, first on the force and then at his tavern. It was hard to get close to him because he worked so hard, but I didn't learn until later that he worked so hard because he cared for us and wanted us to have everything possible. I didn't understand that until too late. It's not too late for you, Ian.'

The PA system on the upper deck crackled to life: 'Mr Hardcastle, Mr McLanahan, to the command center, please.' McLanahan stepped towards the elevators, but Hardcastle caught his arm as he walked past.

'Thanks for listening, Patrick. You're all right . . . for an Air Force puke.'

At the command center they found the image of a twin-engined plane in the main high-definition monitor. 'There's our boy,' Geffar said as Hardcastle logged back onto his terminals. 'Cruising right along. No reply to any of our calls.'

Hardcastle put up a chart of west Florida and then placed the target's data block on it. 'Seventy miles from shore – about thirty minutes till he reaches landfall. Well inside the ADIZ. And he's staying low. This guy must have been out of town for the past ten months – like Antarctica.'

Meanwhile McLanahan had moved over to the drone-control panel and called up the Seagull's status readouts. 'Seagull Six-One in the green,' he reported. 'Four hours of fuel left at this speed. Good data-link signal from KEYSTONE.'

'We're plotting seven vessels in his flight path that he could be setting up for a drop,' a controller reported. 'He's only ten minutes away from the first target.'

'Let's launch the Sea Lion from Homestead, then. And have a Sky Lion from Aladdin City airborne as soon as possible to assist in case he tries a multiple drop.'

'He won't have time,' Hardcastle said. 'The first bale that goes out the door, he's ours.' A few of the controllers in the command center nodded their pleasure at that ominous prediction.

'Six-One is two miles from the target,' McLanahan reported. 'Closure rate forty-five miles per hour. Intercept in three minutes.'

'Continue broadcasts on all frequencies,' Geffar coached her controllers. 'Get that guy to turn around, at least.' The warning messages were transmitted through the aerostat transceiver unit, KEYSTONE, and through the Seagull drone. No response. The twin-engined aircraft continued on as before, staying only a few hundred feet above the water and well off any mandatory entry corridors. No attempt was ever made to contact Border Security or air traffic control.

'One minute to intercept,' McLanahan announced. 'Six-One's in the green. Auto switchover to high sensitivity intercept autopilot. Auto breakaway enabled.'

'He's staying where he is,' Hardcastle said.

'Thirty seconds to intercept. Looks like a Piper Cheyenne in cargo configuration. Pretty good deflection on his horizontal stabilizer – it might mean he has long-range fuel tanks or he's loaded down pretty heavy. I think I can pick out a few letters of his registration number – nope, disregard. He's painted over them.'

'He's dirty for sure,' Hardcastle said. 'Definite smuggler's profile.'

'He's five miles from passing overhead the first sea target,' a controller reported. 'He's altered course toward it. I think he's going for the first sea target. Designating as target two.' The right monitor that had been scanning the area for surface targets now merged with the main display showing only the twin-engine plane, so that both targets were on the main screen at once. Data columns showed the distance and time between the two targets and how far the Hammerheads assets were to each.

'I agree,' Geffar said. 'Have Shark Two-Five stay on target number two. Get an SES headed north to intercept, but the Sea Lion may have to launch a boat.' Until the Hammerheads had more seagoing vessels in their active inventory they were now carrying RHIBs, Rigid Hull Inflatable Boats, on every AV-22 Sea Lion aircraft sortie. In calm seas the Sea Lion aircraft would land on the water and the RHIB would be launched off the rear cargo ramp. The twenty-foot-long boats had a sixty-horsepower out-board motor that could drive three to five intercept officers across to a vessel at nearly thirty miles an hour. Along with the AV-22 hovering or floating nearby with its weapons at the ready, the intercept crew could keep small- to medium-sized vessels under surveillance or arrest for several hours until more help arrived.

'Coming up on the intercept,' McLanahan announced. 'No registration numbers visible but we're running down the configuration through EPIC' – the El Paso Intelligence Center, which was the central information center on all drug-related activities.

'Move out and let's get a look at the pilot, and let him see us,' Geffar said.

'Moving out,' McLanahan acknowledged. His controller issued the commands and the Seagull's autopilot commanded a slight left jog, a turn back to course and an acceleration past the target's nose. As it made its side-step maneuver its TV camera widened its field of view and began to sweep along the entire fuselage, letting the tense but excited crewmembers in the Hammerhead One command center get a good look at the smugglers and their cargo.

'Three minutes to contact with target two,' the controller reported.

The camera swept across to the first set of windows on the left side of the twin-engined plane, and found the window blocked off by what appeared to be cases or boxes made of fiberglass or smooth wood. 'Looks like floating drop cases to me,' Hardcastle said. 'They're definitely making a drop.' The camera continued to pan forward a few feet until it came to the plane's cargo door, unlatched and partially open, flapping in the slipstream.

'Not being too subtle about it, are they?' Hardcastle said.

'Let's fry these turkeys,' one of the seagull drone controllers said.

'Hold your positions,' Geffar ordered. 'We make sure the pilot knows we're here and we give him a chance to bug out. We don't open fire until I give the word.'

Now under manual control the camera continued to pan forward to the first set of windows forward of the left cargo door. What they saw in the window amazed them all.

There, framed in the small oval window, *waving* at the Seagull drone, was a young girl – no more than three or four years old. They could see her in detail . . . dark hair, big dark eyes, a wide happy grin. She continued to wave at the drone as it cruised on ahead of the plane.

'Sweet Mother of God,' Geffar breathed, 'they brought a *child* . . . a little girl.' She reached over to the communications screen and punched up the AV-22 aircraft that was in pursuit. 'Shark Two-Five, this is Alpha. Acknowledge this transmission. Do not lock weapons on target one. Over.'

'Two-Five copies, do not lock weapons on target one. Acknowledged. What's the problem?'

'Never mind, ensure weapons on safe and stand by.'

The camera moved toward the cockpit windshield and they saw the pilot, a Latino about twenty years of age wearing 'aviator' glasses and laughing at the camera on the Seagull. With him was a young boy ten or twelve years old. The boy, too, laughed at the drone, even gave the camera the finger.

'What are we going to do?' a controller asked.

'We can't just sit here and do nothing,' Hardcastle said.

'We'll send the Sea Lion after any boats they make drops onto. We'll keep the Seagull on the plane and track it back to its home base.'

'*Track* it?'

'What do you suggest, Admiral?'

'Drop in progress,' a controller broke in. Several of the fiberglass cases were flung out the partially opened entry door on the left side of the plane, each with lifejackets tied to them.

'Mark and record drop coordinates and transmit to the AV-22.' The controllers called up the smuggler's exact location as plotted by the aerostat's radars, which coordinates would be transmitted to the AV-22 Sea Lion's navigation system for the intercept.

'We can launch a Sea Lion and intercept the plane,' Hardcastle said. 'The Chain Gun can be targeted accurately enough to hit *non-critical* parts of the plane – '

'We're not shooting at him with a Chain Gun – '

'Then put someone with an M-16 in the cargo door of the AV-22 and have him shoot at the rudder or at the nose. He doesn't have to try to disable it. A few bad holes in him might convince the pilot to surrender – '

'We can't direct any kind of fire on a plane with children on board – '

'If we don't do *something* that same pilot is going to be back tomorrow with a bigger plane and another load and more kids. If they know they can get away with this they'll do it again and again until we act. We need some kind of response now – '

'Two-Five is two minutes to the drop point,' the controller reported. 'Target one has not reversed course. He's continuing toward shore.'

'He's making multiple drops,' Hardcastle said. 'A couple more over the ocean, a few on land – we won't be able to cover all of them.'

'Launch the Sky Lion from Aladdin City to cover any other sea drops. Have them get a Customs enforcement team airborne to intercept any ground targets. Get another Sea Lion airborne from Homestead.'

Hardcastle got to his feet, reached up to remove his headset. 'I'll take one of our Sea Lions – '

'*No*.' It was as if Geffar's word had sucked the air out of the whole command center – the place went abruptly silent.

'There's a major delivery going down in west Florida, Sandra,' Hardcastle said, trying to keep his voice under control. 'It's happening a hundred fifty miles from here. We're chatting on the radios, slinging orders, launching aircraft in several different directions at once with no on-scene commanders. It's no way to run an operation – '

'I *know* that . . .'

'We're wasting valuable time. I say you get on that aircraft and take charge of this mission, or I will.' He lowered his voice as he said those last words.

Geffar slammed a fist down on the commander's console, got to her feet and logged off her computer terminal. '*I'll* do it. Take command of the platform. Prepare to launch support aircraft as necessary.'

Hardcastle moved to the commander's chair and entered his password into the computer terminal, logging on as commander of Hammerhead One. 'I've got command of the platform,' he announced as Geffar ran for the exit.

As she went through the door to the elevator she heard Hardcastle say, 'All right, people, we're behind enough as it is. Prepare Shark Two-Eight on deck ASAP. Get me a tactical display of the area. Get a line open to Customs, ask them where their Black Hawk crew is. Move it. I want this leak plugged right *now*.'

Geffar continued out through the door and toward the life-support shop to get suited up for her flight. How do you tell a twenty-year Coast Guard veteran, who at least was every bit as qualified to take action as she was, *not* to do anything?

Shark Two-Five was in the drug-drop area five minutes later. 'Shark base, this is Two-Five. We've made contact with target two. We have a thirty-foot Chris Craft sport fisher departing the area. Name on the stern removed but we might be able to read the outline of the removed letters. It has a flying bridge, color white, no flags, estimated speed twenty knots, heading east toward Ten Thousand Islands. Four persons in sight on board. We'll try to get a registration number. Stand by.'

The AV-22 tilt-rotor swooped lower toward the retreating vessel, flashing its intercept lights and NightSun spotlights to get the attention of the vessel's master. With the engine nacelles in full vertical position the Sea Lion smoothly nestled down to one hundred feet above the water and maintained a distance of about three hundred feet astern and to the left of the vessel. From that distance the Sea Lion crew could see three crewmen on the boat cutting the rope that tied the four fiberglass cases together. They didn't seem worried about discovery – they opened the cases right out on deck in full view of the Border Security crew.

'Shark, they have opened the fiberglass cases on deck . . . I see . . . Shark, there are several packages inside the cases that sure look like narcotics . . . brown shapes wrapped in plastic. They opened the cases right up on deck and – '

The copilot making the report stopped, lowering his binoculars, and looked at his pilot in stark disbelief. He raised them again and stared hard to confirm his own shocking observation: 'Shark, they're unloading those cases and giving the drugs to a bunch of *kids*. They have children on board that boat helping them unload . . .'

On board Hammerhead One Hardcastle could hardly believe what he had just heard. 'Target two has kids on board too? So they figure they've found the perfect way to keep us from attacking – give us a target we can't shoot at . . .'

'Shark, this is Two-Six. Beginning engine-start sequence.'

Hardcastle hit his transmit button on the communications screen. 'Roger, Two-Six. Be advised, Two-Five reports that target two is also carrying children on board. How copy?'

Silence for a long moment, then just before Hardcastle was going to repeat his message Geffar replied: 'Copy, Shark. Break. Two-Five, this is Alpha. Do not lock weapons on target two. Track and monitor. Acknowledge.'

'Two-Five acknowledges. Target two heading toward shore. We are in pursuit.'

'Two-Six,' Hardcastle radioed, 'we have no sea or shore assets in position. We must use the air assets to stop these targets or they'll get away – '

'Get assistance from Customs to handle the shore

350

targets,' Geffar said from the AV-22. 'Continue to track and monitor the sea targets but do not open fire on them. Broadcast those orders to all Hammerhead units.'

Hardcastle paused, the anger swelling up. On the intercom, he said, 'Ed, broadcast to all air units, do not open fire on the sea targets. Track and monitor.'

' "Track and monitor",' the pilot of Shark Two-Five, Eric Whipple, muttered on interphone. 'What a waste.' He was flying his AV-22 Sea Lion several hundred yards behind the speeding Chris Craft sport-fisher, maintaining an altitude of two hundred feet. He was flashing the NightSun searchlight at the vessel, trying anything to get the boat to stop. Nothing was working. The vessel continued its steady trek eastbound for the Everglades.

'This is bullshit,' Whipple's copilot, an older pilot named Hardy, added. 'This is supposed to be a *war*. In war innocents get hurt . . . including my in-laws in Naples. These druggies will be cruising right by my nieces and nephews. They get a pass, then they push their drugs to *my* relatives and kill *them*. We got the stuff to stop these people, and they won't let us.'

Whipple nodded, clicked on the radio channel. 'Shark, this is Two-Five. We're right on these turkeys. What the hell are we supposed to do now?'

Hardcastle looked at the right large-screen monitor, which was focused on the launch pad as Shark Two-Six, Geffar aboard, was just lifting off. He stabbed at the transmit button on the communications screen. 'Two-Five, this is Shark. Maintain radio discipline. That's an order.'

'Fine, fine, I'll talk nice and pretty for you if you tell me what we're supposed to be doing. I have these guys only six miles from shore. We got any backup on the way?'

'Customs is. ETA to the shore position, twenty minutes.'

351

That was only an estimate – in fact, the Customs tactical team, which were supposed to make arrests on land or in port, had not yet left Homestead. It would take them twenty minutes at max speed just to reach the general area where the smugglers would go ashore; then, they had to find the smugglers and get in position to drop in on them. The bottom line – these smugglers were going to get away if the Hammerheads didn't stop them.

This pointed out a very serious deficiency in the border security program. The Hammerheads were the front line, the main defense against illegal smugglers and intruders. They *had* to act decisively – the ripple effect of any problems they encountered would create a major gap in border coverage. If the Sea Lion aircraft or Seagull drones couldn't force a smuggler to turn around or stop, other support units had to be called into action immediately. They – the Hammerheads, and especially the person logged in as commander – was responsible for calling on those support units when a problem developed. Customs was out of position, and it was all because they didn't act fast enough when it was discovered they could not attack the smugglers.

Hardcastle knew he had to do something. He stood up, paused for a few moments, then touched the communication screen's transmit button. 'Two-Five, this is Shark. Do not lock weapons on target – *but find a way to stop that vessel.*'

'Copy that, Shark,' Two-Five responded.

Geffar had just completed the transition from vertical to forward flight mode. It took her a few moments of concentration to readjust herself as the controls switched from helicopter to airplane configuration and she let her altitude drop off almost a hundred feet as she compensated for the change. Her copilot, Maryann Herndon, was coaching her along over interphone: 'Still a little low, Sandra . . . there, you got it. You might need more nacelle angle . . . that's it. Fifty degrees is good until you get our airspeed over two hundred . . .'

Geffar raised a hand as she caught a bit of conversation between the platform and Shark Two-Five. Herndon stopped talking, but by then the radios were silent. Geffar keyed her mike button: 'Shark, this is Two-Six. Status of Shark units?'

'All in the green,' Hardcastle replied. 'Target two about six miles from shore. Two-Five still in pursuit.'

'Did all Shark units acknowledge not to lock weapons on manned targets?'

'Affirmative . . . Two-Five, acknowledge.'

'Two-Five acknowledges.'

Geffar continued her transition to full forward flight. What had Hardcastle said to Two-Five? Well, it would do no good to badger him on the radios. She would get a better idea of the situation soon enough . . .

'Crew, stand by. We're moving closer to the target.'

Whipple added power and zoomed the twenty-five-ton aircraft down and across the front of the smuggler's vessel, less than ten feet above his flying bridge superstructure and not more than thirty feet alongside. The Sea Lion's rotors whipped the ocean into a white froth, the thick vapor streaming all around the aircraft and its prey. The Sea Lion wheeled around and flew backward, not more than fifty feet directly in front of the smuggler's boat, directly in the smuggler's path.

'Hey, Whip,' Hardy said cross-cockpit. 'You think this is a good idea?' The smugglers tried to evade the Sea Lion, zigzagging back and forth to get away from the rotor wash and noise of the aircraft directly ahead, but Whipple

353

matched each turn and stayed directly in front of them. 'If they got guns, they can hose us real easy here.'

'Well, I got guns too.' He hit the switches on his control panel and deployed both the Sea Stinger missile pylon and the M230 Chain Gun pod, then selected head-pointing control of the Chain Gun and armed the pod.

'You can't do that, Eric – '

'I was ordered not to lock weapons on this target,' Whipple said. 'Well, I'm not locking them on target.' He waited until the sport fisher made another cut across the Sea Lion's left side, aimed the cannon just ahead of the vessel, and squeezed the trigger. The pounding of the machine gun could be heard both over the roar of the Sea Lion and the vessel's engines, and the sharp columns of water erupting ahead of the vessel were unmistakable. The Chris Craft dodged to its left away from the stream of thirty-millimeter shells hitting the water.

If Hardy had been apprehensive before, he was not any longer. He shouted every time the smugglers made a wild turn to escape the shooting. 'Look at them run!' he shouted. 'Maybe they'll run out of gas before they reach the shore – '

'They haven't seen anything yet.' Whipple deactivated the Chain Gun and allowed the smugglers to return to a steady course, which they promptly did. As soon as they stopped weaving back and forth Whipple began to move closer to the vessel. Still flying backward, Whipple closed the range between them to a few yards, then slowly eased in closer until the right wing was directly over the bow of the sport fisher.

The water around the vessel was so whipped up by the Sea Lion's rotor wash that it looked as if the boat was sailing through a typhoon. The vessel was being shaken back and forth, and looked as though it might even capsize. But the vessel refused to slow down, kept at full power trying to outrun the Sea Lion.

The smugglers had been aiming for the Cape Romano lighted marker just southwest of Gullivan Bay in the western Everglades; once past the light and in the mass of tiny islands that stretched out west of the Collier-Seminole State Park, a shallow-draft boat could easily be lost in the low trees and saltwater marshes. But in his evasive maneuvering, the pilot of the Chris Craft had lost track of the Cape Romano light. Actually the light was no more than a half-dozen thick wooden poles driven into the ocean bottom and lashed together at the top into a tepee-shaped structure, plus a solar-powered strobelight system installed at the top. It was an obstruction no more than fifteen feet wide, and against hundreds of acres of open ocean the likelihood of hitting it was remote. But as the smugglers tried to get away from the maelstrom all around them, the Cape Romano light suddenly appeared directly in front of them. As the pilot tried to veer away, the stern of his boat clipped the light poles . . .

A tremendous flash of light appeared directly underneath Whipple's right cockpit window. 'We're being fired on,' he called out over interphone, and immediately raised his collective up to the stops and zoomed skyward, gaining a thousand feet in a few seconds, then entered a tentative hover. 'Station check!' he said to Hardy. 'Crew, station check!' He looked over his flight and engine-readout monitors – all appeared normal . . .

He found the Chris Craft a few moments later . . . a thin trail of smoke rising from somewhere in the engine-access compartments, and it appeared to be listing to starboard. Whipple keyed his radio mike. 'Sharp, this is Two-Five. Target two appears dead in the water and listing slightly. I'm going to launch the RHIB and investigate.' On interphone: 'Prepare to launch the boat. Four-man response team.'

The RHIB occupied most of the aft portion of the Sea Lion's cargo bay. It was lowered from its storage rack on the upper bulkhead and checked for full inflation. It was like a big fourteen-person inflatable river raft, but it had been fitted with a light metal floor, a pilot's control console with steering wheel, throttle quadrant, compass and radio panel, and storage lockers fore and aft. A helmsman's padded seat behind the control console covered two five-gallon fuel tanks.

The intercept and boarding team wore body armor, life jackets and visored helmets with miniature two-way voice-actuated radios installed in the helmets. Each man carried a sidearm, usually a SIG Sauer nine-millimeter semi-automatic pistol with a fifteen-round clip, and except for the RHIB helmsman, each carried an M-16 rifle.

The group appeared uneasy. Two of the four men on the team were graduates of the Coast Guard's Maritime Law Enforcement School, an intensive four-*week* class. Actually, a four-*year*-long school could never prepare any of them for what might happen next. Every intercept or boarding was different. The most benign scene could erupt any moment into pluperfect hell. This smuggler was cornered, a Hammerheads gunship was hovering over him and armed men were coming to board his boat . . .

Whipple brought the AV-22 down to the surface of the ocean and hovered a few feet above the gentle waves, about a hundred yards from the sport fisher. 'She's gonna roll any minute,' Whipple said on interphone. 'Let's move it.'

'Ready on the ramp,' came the reply. Hardy activated the switch, and the rear cargo ramp that formed the aft end of the AV-22 slowly motored down into position. Whipple eased the Sea Lion down until the aircraft settled on the ocean's surface. 'Ramp awash,' one of the crewmen told Whipple as the outboard end of the ramp dipped into the water. The Sea Lion was afloat. Whipple kept the power up on the rotors for stability during the launch.

The RHIB was slid down the ramp far enough so the outboard motor's propeller could be lowered into the water and the RHIB's helmsman climbed on board and started the engine. After the helmsman checked the systems on board and made a radio check with the Sea Lion and the three intercept crewmen, the other crewmen climbed aboard, slid the RHIB off the ramp and into the water. Once Whipple could see that the RHIB was clear of the rotors, he raised the cargo ramp and lifted off from the surface, flying a few feet above the water and paralleling the RHIB's course. As he moved forward, Whipple deployed both the Chain Gun and Sea Stinger rocket pods and readied them for action.

'I can't see the driver of that boat,' Scott, one of the boarding crewmen said as he trained mini-binoculars on the Chris Craft speedboat. 'Two-Five, see if you can swing around the other side and spot him.'

'Roger,' Whipple replied, and eased the Sea Lion left around the stern of the sport fisher and slowly circled it. 'He's nowhere in sight,' he reported. 'I'm moving closer.'

He had come to within a hundred feet when suddenly a tall dark-skinned man rushed up on deck carrying a young girl in one arm and a pistol in his other. Slung across his shoulder was a bulging nylon bag.

'Scott, I see someone,' Whipple called. 'He's got a kid, a hostage, *he's holding a gun to her head*.'

The man swept his right arm over the girl's head, then pointed the muzzle at her.

'I think he's telling me to move off or he'll kill her.'

Scott motioned to the helmsman of the RHIB to cut right toward the bow out of sight of the smuggler. He took off his communications helmet and began to unlace his boots.

'What the hell are you doing?' Randolph, the helmsman of the RHIB, asked him.

357

'Going over the side,' Scott told him, 'before he sees us.'

'That's nuts, Scotty,' one of the other crewmen said. 'This guy's going nowhere, he's got no choice but to surrender –'

'Yeah, right, but what if he starts killing those kids in the meantime? We've got the drop on him, now's the time to act.' The intercept crewmen had no answer for that. 'After you drop me off swing back to the left and show yourself. Make sure he keeps his eyes on you and the Sea Lion.' Scott took off his gun belt, clasped the webbing in his teeth near the holster to keep the weapon out of the salt water and edged over the side of the inflatable tubes of the RHIB. When they were about a hundred feet away he slipped into the cold water and began to swim for the sport fisher. The RHIB helmsman immediately veered away, and was soon in sight of the smuggler on deck and took up a position ninety degrees to the right of the Sea Lion and about a hundred feet away, threatening but holding position.

The water was much colder than Scott had thought, and the deep chill seemed to turn his arms and legs to lead. He was a strong, well-trained swimmer, but it seemed he had to fight to keep his head above water. He choked down the panic rising in his throat and kept pushing it, the butt of his pistol slapping his face at every stroke . . .

His situation had gone to hell in ten short seconds. Alberto Runoz saw the bristling guns on the strange warplane, aimed right for him. The rubber boat filled with Border Security troops had, it seemed, come out of nowhere.

The young ones were his only way out – if he had one. The little Haitians had been easy to lure into the boat; fifty cents' worth of food could buy a half dozen in that impoverished country. Even with no place to run, they still might be of value. Still holding the young girl in one arm, he shifted the bag full of twenty kilos of cocaine over to another shoulder, grasped the Tokarev TL-8 pistol in his left hand, and reached for the radio on the control console. He thought the radio was set to the oceanic emergency channel but it didn't really matter – the Hammerheads were sure to be monitoring them all.

Runoz had been told by Colonel Salazar that the children were the key, which was turning out to be true, he thought, as he knelt down to hide himself from the M-16 rifles as best he could and keyed the mike:

'You Border Security guards, this is the captain of the disabled boat in front of you. I will kill these children if you do not cooperate, and then I will kill myself. Their deaths will be on your head.

'I want that rubber raft and free passage to shore. All of you but one will return to the helicopter. The one soldier will remove all his weapons and bring the raft to me. I will get on the raft with three of the youngest children to make sure of my escape. You will comply immediately. Or else . . .'

'Where's Scott?' Whipple radioed to the helmsman of the RHIB. 'I don't see him.'

'He looked like he might be in trouble,' Randolph said. 'I don't see him. He was swimming pretty slow. He may not have reached the boat, or he might be hurt.'

'Well, he gave it a try, I just hope we can get back to him in time,' Whipple said. 'Hold your position. Two-Six should be here in minutes. When this nut sees two Sea Lions on top of him maybe he'll surrender . . .'

Both the strange airplane and the raft with the three armed men held their positions, nobody making a move. Runoz, furious and frightened, grabbed the microphone again. 'I will not play your waiting game. I want that raft *now*!' He dropped the microphone and transferred the Tokarev back to his right hand.

Maybe the skinny kid he'd picked out did not deserve to live, but the boat was sinking faster now . . . Runoz thumbed the hammer back on the Tokarev –

'Freeze . . . Hammerheads . . . freeze . . .' The voice was weak, strained, almost a whisper. Nonetheless, Runoz jumped at the sound of it, then looked over the port side of the boat. There, lying in the water supported by his life jacket, was a Border Security Force crewman, the insignia clear and recognizable. His face was deathly white, his lips purple. He clutched a black automatic pistol in his left hand, but his arm was shaking, and it didn't look as though he'd last many more minutes.

Runoz picked up the radio microphone. 'Hey, Border Security Force. I found one of your men here. Now bring that raft over here and move that airplane at least a mile out of my sight or I'll blow this sad asshole's face off.' He stood at the edge of the boat, still using the little girl as a shield, his Tokarev pointed over the side at Scott. He checked to be sure the soldiers weren't moving closer, then checked the man gasping and heaving in the water, his gun hand shaking badly. Runoz yelled over the side: 'Hey, you in the water, drop your gun or I'll finish you right away . . .'

Suddenly the gun steadied itself, the man in the water made a leg kick that lifted his shoulders three feet above the surface, and the gun fired and bucked once, twice, three times. Runoz was instantly flung backward across the deck, one bullet in his chest, another in his right shoulder.

He dropped the girl and grabbed at his bloody shoulder with his free left hand. But by this time Scott had reached the sinking stern of the sport fisher and had just begun to climb over the transom when Runoz saw him and raised his pistol. Scott was no more than ten feet away – even a dying Runoz could not miss.

Scott faced Runoz with the huge, murderous-looking pistol aimed squarely at him. There was no time either to jump away or get at Runoz. Shots rang out, Scott's body convulsed with the sound, his pistol went overboard, and he fell backward into the icy water to wait for expected death's darkness to close over him . . .

It did not. His response had been a reflex to what he was sure was coming. But as his head broke the surface, to his amazement he found himself alive. He climbed back up over the transom and over the edge. The smuggler was slumped over the port railing of the boat, his head and neck sliced by two dozen high-powered M-16 slugs from the Hammerheads in the RHIB. Only one hundred feet away, the Hammerheads could not miss either.

By the time Scott had managed to crawl on board the sport fisher, the RHIB had pulled alongside and its crew boarded the stricken vessel. Quickly they found life jackets or flotation devices for the children, and several were loaded into the RHIB for transfer to the Sea Lion. Meanwhile Scott had gone below and emerged a few moments later with a blanket wrapped around his shoulders and two large brown packages in his hands. Randolph met him on deck. 'You okay, Scotty?'

'I'm freezing but I'll be okay. Look here, there's a hundred more stuffed in the V-bunks, and two more fiberglass cases still full of stuff. Three hundred kilos of cocaine – four and a half million dollars' worth.'

'We'll bring a portable pump over from the Sea Lion and try to keep this thing afloat until the SES or the Coast Guard comes to offload the stuff,' Randolph said. They looked out on deck and watched the children getting ready to be transferred to the RHIB for the ride to the Sea Lion. 'My God, what kind of scumbags use *kids* on their drug runs?'

'A new mutation,' Scott said. 'We got lucky. We probably wouldn't have gotten this guy if he hadn't hit the light. What about next time . . .'

* * *

The Seagull had been recovered from McLanahan's crew. Shark Two-Six, with Sandra Geffar piloting the AV-22, had taken over the chase.

Since taking over for the drone, they had marked and identified three other sea drops made by the smugglers. Being intercepted by Geffar's aircraft made no difference at all to the smugglers in the plane. Geffar saw children in the port-side window, *waving*.

Geffar tried everything to get the pilot of the plane to stop. Warning shots with both the Chain Gun and Sea Stingers, close formation flight, putting men in the cargo doors with M-16s. The smuggler made a few evasive turns when the aircraft got very close but immediately turned back to course and could not be diverted from shore . . .

Almost as if he were reading Geffar's thoughts and doubts, Hardcastle called on the secure channel: 'Two-Six, what's your status?'

'Still in close formation with target one.'

'He's about three miles from shore,' Hardcastle reported. 'Customs is ten minutes out to assist in intercepting ground pickups. Two-Five is RTB with the children from the target two intercept. Two-Seven is launching to intercept targets three, four or five depending on which is easiest for him. We've got an unarmed Sky Lion airborne to assist with the surface targets.'

'Thanks for the update,' Geffar said. 'Continue to monitor. Get two Seagulls ready to track target one after he comes off his land drops. Two-Six will prosecute any shore targets we see – we'll have a better chance of making the intercept on land.'

'Say again, Two-Six? You want Seagulls to take over for you on the Cheyenne?'

'Affirmative. I'm not doing any good up here. We'll have the Seagulls track this guy as far as they can back to wherever he came from.'

There was a noticeable hesitation from Hardcastle – he still felt that the airborne smugglers should be dealt with *before* they had a chance to get over land. But he gave her a 'Roger' and kept his thoughts to himself . . .

Gullivan Bay was approaching rapidly. This had been a favorite spot for smugglers for several centuries, with almost four hundred square miles of tiny islands, inlets, marshes, bogs and invisible beaches, and limited access to the few inhabitable places. Airboats were usually needed in the area – there were few places to land a helicopter, much less a monster like a Sea Lion tilt-rotor, and any boats with propellers might quickly find themselves caught in shallow weed-choked waters. The smuggler's plane swooped low, only a few yards above the water, so low that even the aged bent willows and cypress trees towered over the plane.

'He's throttled back to about eighty knots,' Geffar radioed back to Hardcastle on Hammerhead One. 'Looks like he's getting ready to make a drop.'

'Roger,' Hardcastle replied. 'We're launching a Seagull drone to intercept him on the way out. We read your altitude as less than thirty feet. Do you confirm that?'

'That's confirmed,' Geffar replied. 'He's low and slow.'

'This might be a good chance to try a shot at his rudder or one engine,' Hardcastle said. 'Even if he loses control he won't fall very far and he'll land in the marshes. The damage should be minor, to everybody. I recommend giving it a try.'

'No . . . I want no other Hammerhead units even to deploy weapons if children are nearby. We can't risk it.'

Hearing only silence, Geffar returned her concentration on the Cheyenne as it approached its drop point.

Down below at least six airboats suddenly popped out from under the trees. 'Airboats beneath me,' she radioed. 'Six . . . drop in progress. Mark and record drop point.'

Their operation was done with military-like precision.

The airboats were just a few feet away from the impact point as the fiberglass cases hit the marshy water. The agile, speedy propeller-driven boats did not seem to slow down at all as the cases were scooped up and secured at the front of each flat-bottomed craft. As Geffar peeled away to the left and began circling the drop point, the Cheyenne made a hard right turn and headed back out to sea at low altitude.

Each airboat had one fiberglass case on board, so Geffar picked the slowest boat and began tracking it. 'Shark, do you have a radar plot on any of these surface targets?' Geffar radioed.

'Negative,' from Hardcastle. 'We're trying to tune out the foliage and we get intermittent targets, but nothing the system can lock onto, and you're at the northern edge of coverage by KEYSTONE radar. The Customs chopper is five minutes away, and we have one Sky Lion on the way.'

'I suggest they try infrared to pick out the airboats among the trees. Also that Collier County sheriffs block off routes 961 across Big Marco Pass, route 92 out of Gullivan Bay and route 41 through the state park. These guys are still a few miles from shore – we may be able to get some of them.' She focused in on the airboat she was pursuing and groaned. 'On my surface target . . . they've got a child on board there too. Don't fire on them . . .'

Geffar felt sick as she began her pursuit. The young boy on the airboat, who, unlike the other kids, looked Caucasian, was clutching the airboat's raised pilot's chair as the boat sped across the murky water. The man in the front of the airboat, also a Caucasian, held a shotgun cradled in one arm while hanging on tight. The kid could have been kidnapped, or an innocent relative of one of the smugglers who had gone out for a ride with his uncle or father, not knowing that he was to be a living shield against the Hammerheads.

The course the smugglers decided to take was relatively

clear of foliage for a mile or so, so Geffar brought her Sea Lion down closer to the water, just ten feet above the airboat. The airboat became more unstable, swishing now left, now right, as the airflow through the boat's directional rudders and fan was disrupted by its rotors. The pilot yelled something at the gunman, and the gunman promptly raised the shotgun, took quick aim, and fired at the Sea Lion –

'*No*,' Geffar yelled, and yanked the cyclic hard left, dodging away just as the gunman fired. She felt a sharp impact somewhere on the right side of the AV-22 just behind the cockpit, and immediately climbed a hundred feet and checked the engine instruments. 'Check for damage on the right wing,' she called back on interphone. 'I think we took a hit.' One of her four tactical crewmen low-crawled over the sliding cargo door on the right side and peered out through the wide window, keeping his head clear in case another blast came through. 'I see a few large black spots on the underside of the wing and right flap,' the crewmen reported, 'but the nacelle looks okay and I don't see any fuel or fluid leaks . . .'

'All right, the plane feels okay . . . we're going back in.' She banked right, started searching for the airboat, found it and began a gradual descent back toward it. When she was about a hundred feet above it, she called out over the interphone: '*Hey*, I don't see the boy on the airboat! He was standing on the left side of the airboat holding onto the seat, I don't see him anymore. He must have fallen off . . .' Geffar started an immediate hover, stopping her forward momentum so abruptly her copilot's shoulder-harness reel locked as his body was thrust forward. 'Prepare to launch the RHIB. Two-man team. I want that boy found.' Gradually she brought the Sea Lion down to the surface of the saltwater march and lowered the cargo ramp. A moment later the RHIB was in the water and Geffar was immediately airborne again as soon as the inflatable boat was clear. It took less than five minutes for Geffar to relocate the airboat and take up the pursuit again.

'Do you see him anywhere on that airboat?' she called out to her copilot.

'Negative.' The copilot had lowered the telescopic scanner goggles and was searching the airboat as it rushed in and out of sight beneath huge magnolias and drooping trees. 'I don't see anything . . .'

'I have to know,' Geffar muttered.

'Two-Six, this is boat one,' a crewman on the RHIB radioed. 'We found him, seems okay . . .'

Geffar clicked on the Chain Gun pod, waiting a few seconds until the stowed pod had motored out of the fuselage and locked into position, then armed the cannon and transferred control of the TADS/PNVS nose sensor to her targeting goggles. She flipped the WARNING/TARGET shot mode switch, centered the aiming reticle on the airboat and locked on the sensor so she could concentrate more on flying the Sea Lion at low altitude. After gaining another fifty feet to be sure she cleared a few of the larger trees, she pulled the trigger on the Chain Gun.

Perhaps there was a glitch in the fire-control computer, the electronic system that linked range and azimuth information from the nose sensor and air data from the Sea Lion's flight-control system to train the Chain Gun in its intended target; or perhaps the gun system somehow mirrored its crew's thoughts and feelings of anger and revenge. But however it happened, there was no eruption of waterspouts fifty yards *ahead* of the airboat as designed – instead each thirty-millimeter shell hit directly in the center of the boat. The engine exploded in a bright yellow ball of flame, the airboat skidded sideways and flipped end-over-end, throwing the fiberglass case and one of the smugglers through the air. The pilot, who was strapped into his seat, was literally ripped apart by the exploding engine and slammed into the water as the airboat spun away in flames.

'Shark, this is Two-Six,' Geffar radioed back to the Hammerhead One platform, 'mark and record present position coordinates for Customs investigators. Surface target struck and destroyed.' She flipped the Chain Gun switches to safe and found that the WARNING/TARGET mode switch had been left in TARGET. She swallowed hard, moved the switch to WARNING, and continued: 'I am returning to pick up one survivor and my RHIB. Out.'

An ambulance met Geffar at the Hammerheads base at the Aladdin City headquarters ramp, but the boy that had been tossed from the airboat and picked up in the salt marshes was able to walk over to the ambulance. Geffar met up with Whipple and Hardy, who had landed a half hour earlier with a cargo hold full of six children. Whipple was lying on the open cargo ramp, letting the sun dry the perspiration off his flight suit. Hardy was a few yards away from the Sea Lion. The rest of the crew was helping the ground crews service the RHIB and reload the weapons pods. 'You okay, Whip?' she asked.

'Yeah. God, what a day.'

'How's Scott?'

'I sent him to the hospital to get checked out,' Whipple said, 'but I think he'll be okay. So what's the score so far? I've been lying here ever since the Admiral told me he didn't need us.'

'I got one airboat, Customs got one and the sheriff's department got two,' Geffar told him. 'One boat is still being tracked by a Sky Lion and we've got Shark Two-Eight moving in on him to make the intercept. We lost two airboats and two boats. The Cheyenne is halfway back to South America by now, but we still have a Seagull on him.'

'It was a first-class operation,' Whipple said, staring up at the tail of his Sea Lion from the cargo ramp. 'They moved a huge amount of dope with precision and organization . . .'

'Almost military, wouldn't you say?'

'I would.'

'It fits with what we've seen before,' Geffar said. 'Cargo-sized aircraft, fighters, heavy artillery, sophisticated weapons, close timing. Not your garden-variety smugglers.'

'They're smart, powerful and . . .' Whipple said, shaking his head, 'those kids I brought back said they came along for a *pack of cookies*. Pathetic.'

'The boy I picked up was kidnapped,' Geffar said, 'picked him up in Everglades City. Just asked him if he'd like to go for a ride.'

'What the hell do we do?' Hardy asked. 'We can't protect every kid from being kidnapped or coaxed into riding with drug smugglers. The smugglers have taken the guns right out of our hands . . .'

'No they haven't, Will,' Geffar told Hardy. 'They didn't stop us today. We got some of them – '

'Well, we only got our guy because the idiot ran into the Cape Romano light,' Hardy said. 'Even so, if Scotty hadn't had the guts to slip over the side of the RHIB and jump this guy we'd still be out there in a stand-off. We'd have had no choice but to give the guy what he wanted – let him take the RHIB and escape.'

Geffar looked hard at Hardy and Whipple. 'You really figure it would've been better to attack that Cheyenne? Look, we came out of this thing pretty good. No dead kids, hundreds of kilos of cocaine seized and a bunch of prisoners. We did good.'

'Hey, I'm not a cold-blooded creep,' Hardy said, 'but what's to stop the next joker from trying the same damn thing? Is every smuggler gonna have kids on board? Snatch a kid off the street and stick him in the plane or the boat with him – '

'Maybe they won't try it the next time,' Whipple said. 'If they know their slime-ball buddies still get their butts shot down even with kids on board, maybe they won't make a trip . . .'

'Nobody in this country would buy it. What if it was your kid that got snatched? How would you feel then?'

'I wouldn't blame the Hammerheads,' Hardy said quickly. 'I thought we were here to do a job. They give us guns and planes to *stop* those scum. We committed ourselves to the job, we've got to do it . . .'

'You guys are tired, you're not thinking straight,' Geffar said, shaking her head. 'We'll talk about it later.'

Hardy and Whipple looked at Geffar, then at each other, decided to shut up, for now. They felt painted into a corner, between the old rock and a hard place.

They weren't the only ones. Geffar was a silent member of the club. She told herself she ought to feel good about the outcome . . . after all, the smugglers had tried to use the children to get their drugs past the Hammerheads and they'd failed. Wasn't that the bottom line? But what about the ones that got away? They'd be back to dump their poison another day . . .

On Board the Smuggler's Plane, Heading Southeast Toward Haiti

'It went off without a hitch, Colonel,' the pilot of the Cheyenne reported. He glanced out his window again to check if the black batlike drone was still off his left wingtip – and there it was, flying in ridiculously perfect formation, with its huge bug-eye camera squarely fixed on him. 'The Border Security aircraft were right on top of us and they did nothing. We ignored their warnings and their attempts to divert us, just as you said, and it worked to perfection.'

369

'I am pleased,' Colonel Agusto Salazar replied over the scrambled telephone hookup to the plane. 'Unfortunately the performances of some of your comrades was less pleasing. Several of our ground forces were intercepted by the Border Security forces, and several deaths resulted . . .'

'I'm sorry to hear that, sir,' the pilot said. 'We may have a similar problem ourselves.'

'What? Fuel reserves? Malfunction?'

'No malfunction, sir,' the pilot replied. 'But our fuel is dangerously low.'

'Climb to a higher altitude, reduce power to best range. You have clearance to overfly Cuba. Plot as direct a course as possible.'

'We have done all that, sir, but with all these brats we brought on board, plus the empty fuel bladders in the rear, we are too heavy to continue step-climbing to a more fuel-efficient altitude. We are slightly below the fuel curve without reserves. Our computations show we may be forced to land as much as a hundred kilometers short of the base. Can't we get permission to land in Cuba?'

'As I told you, that is *impossible*,' Salazar told him. 'Castro's politicians are trying to make it seem they are *cooperating* with the Americans. They will not allow a known drug-smuggling plane to land. If you land in Cuba you will be arrested and possibly even extradited to the United States. That should encourage you *to bring that plane back intact*.'

Hammerhead One Air Staging Platform

McLanahan was in his high-backed seat beside the drone control center when Hardcastle came over to him. McLanahan was intently peering at an old Air Force E-6B

370

flight computer, the old aluminum 'whiz wheel' circular slide rule used for making mathematical and navigational calculations. After making a few notes and spinning another calculation, he stared at the monitor showing the image of the Piper Cheyenne carrying the smugglers, apparently back to safety.

'Drone statues, Patrick?'

'In the green. Looks like he's about twenty minutes from Cuban airspace. We can send the drone around Cuba as planned and pick him up on the other side.'

'Okay. I've already notified Elliott about the overflight. He'll contact the State Department and have them issue an official protest to the Cuban government for allowing an overflight by a known drug smuggler. They let a drug smuggler overfly but won't clear our drone or Sea Lions through. So much for their so-called cooperation.'

McLanahan nodded, obviously preoccupied. 'Something wrong? What are you working on?'

'Just running a bunch of range calculations on that Cheyenne,' McLanahan told him, and punched up the computer's track of the aircraft, which included the plane's previous sorties into American airspace as well as a prediction of where the plane might likely go next. Most of the lines indicated that the plane would land in one of several Cuban airbases on its northern coast. A few other predictions, not very heavily weighed, had the plane crash landing off Haiti or ditching in the shallow waters near Cay Sal Bank. 'You figure the Cubans will let that plane land in Cuba?' McLanahan asked.

'Who knows? The Cubans, talking the good-neighbor line lately, haven't said a word today except about overflight restrictions. My guess is they'll let this guy overfly, and they may let him land if he declares an emergency. We have the hot line working to Havana. If we notify the Cubans far enough in advance and feed them some of our radar data on this guy, we *might* be able to convince them at least to allow extradition if he's captured. They're feeling pretty isolated these days.'

'Well, I expect he'll be declaring an emergency any second, then,' McLanahan said. 'Look here, the computer predicts the flight path and arrival point of an aircraft based on unloaded weight plus thirty percent over authorized added internal ferry fuel. This guy dropped fifteen one-hundred-kilo cases of cocaine – that's well over three thousand pounds of cargo. Add twelve hundred pounds of extra fuel in internal bladders, plus the weight of the five kids we counted on board that plane – this guy was at *least* a thousand pounds overweight just before he made those drops. He's gotta be running on fumes.'

'That could be why he's stayed at fourteen thousand feet all this time instead of heading for twenty-five thousand,' Hardcastle said. 'Maybe he can't climb any higher.'

'More accurately, the trade-off would be unacceptable,' McLanahan told him. 'He would burn more gas climbing to a best-range altitude than he would save at the higher altitude.'

'So . . . maybe there's a real *downside* to using kids on smuggling runs,' Hardcastle said. 'Every kid they put on board is that much less product they can haul into the country. Plus the added weight is a drag on fuel.'

'Plus the kids are a liability throughout the flight. The drugs are dumped overboard – the kids stay. They're a range and weight liability from start to finish.' McLanahan scowled at his computer, then tossed it on the table. 'I'd say get an SES or Coast Guard vessel out to that vicinity and get under that Cheyenne, because he's coming down any – '

'We got something going down on target one,' the senior controller reported. Hardcastle and McLanahan glanced up at the image of the Cheyenne on the TV monitor. 'He's slowed way down, under one-fifty. Thought I saw a hatch open . . . there it goes . . .'

The short airstair hatch and curved upper hatch on the plane had popped open. Both door sections vibrated violently in the plane's slipstream, threatening to break off the fuselage at any moment.

'They're still at fourteen thousand feet? That's strange. Are they making a drop?' Hardcastle was saying. 'Are there any boats in the . . . *Holy Mother of God* . . .'

Hardcastle and McLanahan were on their feet, jaws gone slack as they watched without believing what they were seeing . . . One of the children had just been thrown from the open hatch of the Cheyenne.

It got worse. One of the girls, her long hair pulled straight back in the slipstream, was clutching frantically at the cable that held the bottom half of the airstair. Her fight only lasted a few moments, and suddenly she was gone.

'*Mark and record position, mark and record . . .* oh God, cut off broadcast to shore!' Hardcastle knew that sometimes it was possible for people with satellite dishes to intercept their video signals from the platform, and it was very possible that politicians or other visitors at the Alladin City base might be watching the Seagull drone's transmissions. 'Get all available Sea Lion units airborne immediately, I want – ' His last order was cut off in a near-shout as another youngster went plummeting to his death, thrust out the open hatch of the plane like the fiberglass cases of drugs that had already been tossed out. The last child, older and bigger than the others – the one in the cockpit, the one they first saw with the Seagull's camera – was not thrown far enough away from the plane and hit the fuselage and horizontal stabilizer – each sickening impact clearly seen by those in the command center. The Cheyenne swung hard left after the last impact on the leftstabilizer, and the Seagull initiated an automatic breakaway and veered hard left away from the Cheyenne. The video picture was, thankfully, lost from view.

Hardcastle barely made it back to the commander's console and quickly sat down, feeling strength wash out of him. He had to take a deep breath to force his words out: 'Instruct the Seagull drone to begin an orbit over that position,' he said in a shaky voice. 'Infrared scan at five hundred feet. Get every available Coast Guard unit out to that area immediately. Get . . . get . . .' His words faded like an old phonograph winding down, and he could do nothing else but stare in utter disbelief at the computer monitor before him.

Chapter Seven

The Swamps South of Dulac, Terrebonne County, Louisiana
One Week Later

Scattered through the swamps and bayous between the small town of Dulac and the northern part of Lake Boudreaux, Louisiana, a hundred armed men, most with shotguns and hunting rifles, sat motionless in flat-bottomed bass boats. They seemed rather tolerant of the heavy downpour they were experiencing, a thunderstorm with the biggest, fattest raindrops anyone had ever seen. The thunderstorm seemed to provide them some sense of relief, as if believing that only they would ever be out on a night like this, that only *they* could take the worst Mother Nature could dish out. These men of Dulac and this backwoods area of Terrebonne County used the bad weather, and their knowledge of the southern Louisiana swamps, to protect themselves from those who would take advantage of them as well as those who would dare to come to the swamps and try to arrest them.

The locals' small bass boats surrounded a large, fast airboat – a flat-bottomed craft propelled with a large aircraftlike propeller and steered with aircraftlike control surfaces – which served as the command vessel for this operation. The leader of the group, a smuggler named Girelli, flicked his cigarette at a dark, slithery shape gliding across the murky water. 'Jesus,' he murmured, his Staten Island accent as strange to the locals as a Martian's. 'This place gives me the creeps.'

Girelli turned to a man beside him who had a radio headset pressed to one ear. The radio itself, big as an ice chest, was in a waterproof canvas bag in the middle of the airboat, with a rigid rubber antenna extending far above the airboat's fan; it had a navigational beacon in it as well as a powerful descrambling radio receiver. 'What's the story, Mario?'

'I can't hear anythin',' the guy said. 'I ain't heard anythin' for hours.' The radio was a tactical backpack radio transmitter used in Vietnam by Air Force and Army combat air controllers who parachuted behind enemy lines on WET SNOW missions and set up the beacon at presurveyed points. Air Force and Navy bombers would use the beacon signals as navigational and bombing checkpoints and offset aimpoints to strike their targets – the beacon would appear as thick and thin lines now on a radar scope, corresponding to the agreed-on code used for each mission . . . now the radio could be had at almost any surplus store for practically nothing. Mario was selected for this smuggling run because of his familiarity with the beacon system as a combat air controller in Vietnam. But instead of directing air raids along the Ho Chi Minh Trail, they were going to use the war surplus beacon system to precision-drop Colombian cocaine to waiting smugglers . . .

'How do we know these guys took us to the right place, eh?' Girelli asked. One of 'these guys,' a man named George Debeauchalet, assigned as the smuggler's escort, ignored the two outsiders' remarks. 'We could be miles from the drop point.'

'These guys ain't dumb, Tony,' Mario said. 'They're getting paid good money to cooperate. We don't show with this stuff, these guys are gator food.'

Girelli looked uneasily around him, trying not to look as apprehensive as he felt. The locals, mostly Cajun-speaking, burly fishermen and trappers, came out of nowhere when Debeauchalet took the two smugglers alone to this section of the Lake Boudreaux swamps of south Louisiana. How these guys could navigate through the endless swamps, islands, overhanging mangroves and unmarked mud trails Girelli could never figure out. But they had met precisely on time, two or three men per boat, without either Mario and Girelli knowing they were nearby. Fortunately the Yankee smugglers were assured that the cops, local FBI or local DEA boys didn't possess the same skill.

Each boat had one of Girelli's heavily armed men on board, both to ensure the locals' cooperation and to add to the considerable firepower as well as to help disperse the shipment as fast as possible after the drop. Each man carried either an AR-15 rifle modified for fully automatic fire or a Uzi or some other small automatic weapon. It would be much tougher to catch twenty escaping smugglers than one or two. But the presence of Girelli's soldiers alongside the scruffy locals didn't help ease his apprehension. 'These guys could probably toss us over the side, take the stuff and disappear.'

'Hey. They know the score,' Mario said. 'The cartels and the Cuchillos own these guys. And their families, too. They do their thing, they get paid big bucks. We don't show, all these bozos swallow swamp scum. Now shut up. I'm trying to listen.'

The group fell silent. After a few moments Mario removed the headphones and looped them over his neck. 'Nothin' yet. It's still early. A few more minutes, we should hear.' He switched a level on the radio to VOX and picked up a microphone: 'Duncan, this is Mario. Radio check.'

'Yo mama,' came the reply. Mario laughed and set the microphone back on its clip. Duncan was another member of the smuggling gang stationed fifteen miles south of the drop zone, along the path of the inbound plane. He would watch and listen for any signs of pursuit as the drop went down, and warn the drop-zone crew.

'Pretty good thinking, the cartel movin' the drop site over to Louisiana,' Girelli said. 'Just think: three million dollars' worth of blow. Three *million*. And we make three hundred grand for a couple days' work.'

'A hundred of which we fork over to these good ol' boys, remember.'

Girelli spat overboard. 'These inbreeds do the job, they can have the dough. It's their own fault they bring half the county – we only asked for twenty guys.'

'I just wonder how those flyboys – what do they call 'em, the Blades or something? – how will they get past the Hammerheads?' Mario said. 'The Heads got this whole area closed off, don't they?'

'You butthole,' Girelli said. 'What do you think we're sitting in this swamp for? The Heads don't have the whole Gulf closed off. They just do Florida and the Caribbean and over that way. They don't have none of them oil platforms out this way. The nearest place they got to land is seventy miles away.'

'I *know* that, dickbrain' – he didn't know any of that but he didn't want to admit it – 'I mean, they got those radar planes too, you know, the prop-jobs with the radar flyin' saucers on them. They can see planes comin' for a hundred miles. I heard it on TV.'

'*That's* why we're sittin' here in a damned thunderstorm, Mario,' Girelli said. 'Those radars can't see through thunderstorms.'

'They can't? How do you know that?'

'Radar can't see through water. Didn't you pay no attention in school? All's a radar sees in a thunderstorm is a big white cloud. And the planes stay away from thunderstorms, too. Too much bouncin' around in a thunderstorm.'

378

'So how are the Blades gonna make a drop in this shit then?'

'How is, the Blades got brass balls. Also, they know the Heads can't fly in this stuff, so that's when they come. These Cuchillos, they ain't afraid of nothin'. Besides, the Heads don't come out here. Most of the dope goes through Florida, so that's where the Hammerheads operate.' He had to laugh. 'Them Heads are good against spicks and wetbacks but they don't wanna take on good ol' *American* runners.'

Girelli nudged Mario. 'You know what else I heard? In case the Blades do get caught, you know what they've done to keep from gettin' shot down? Carry *kids* on their planes. You believe that?' If Girelli could have seen Mario's face, he would have seen that his partner didn't think too much of that. 'And that ain't the half of it. In case they run low of fuel and don't think they can make it back, you know what they do?'

'You . . . you're not – ?'

'They toss the little ones right outta the plane.' Girelli made a whistling sound, stomped a foot in the water pooling up in the bottom of the airboat. 'You believe that?'

'That ain't funny,' Mario said. 'I got kids. Anybody that uses kids like – '

'Business, pal. It's business.'

'I guess that's how the Blades fly in shitty weather like this – they got no sense except gettin' the job done,' Mario said, changing the subject.

'You think about makin' the big score, you can do anything.'

The two became silent again, then Mario put the headphones back on, listening intently. He turned to Girelli. 'I think I hear somethin'.' He reached for the top flap on the transmitter case.

'Wait,' Girelli reminded him. 'Get a definite code first.'

'I know, I know, let me listen.'

The signal seemed to fade out, then disappear. Mario was only slightly worried – he was told the loss of signal was part of the search routine as the incoming plane lined up on the right course. A few moments later the signal returned, this time stronger. Mario counted the clear, sharp pulses he heard. 'I got it. It's the right code.' He lifted the top flap of the radio and pressed a rubber-covered button. This time when the signal returned it illuminated a yellow light on top of the transmitter. He turned a key on the radio that locked the navigational beacon in the ON position. The yellow light came on once more, then was out.

'They're comin',' he announced. 'First contact is about fifty miles out, they said in the briefing. This means a rendezvous in about ten minutes.'

'And that radio does it all? We don't need to set up flares for a drop zone or nothin'?'

'This baby does everything,' Mario replied, recovering the transmitter with its protective canvas top. 'These Cuchillos will drop the stuff right in our laps. I watched these guys work on another drop – these guys are good. They go balls to the wall and they can still drop a dime from a hundred feet in the air. They use the beacon as an offset aimpoint – '

'What?'

'An offset aimpoint,' nearly preening. 'They don't fly at the beacon but they use it to line up on the drop area.' Mario pointed to a long, weed-covered bog about fifty yards away. 'That's the drop zone. They see the beacon, they can hit the island. Then we cruise on over and pick it up.'

'Well, they better. I'm not sticking my hand in that water, and I don't care how much dope is floatin' around.' He remembered the size of the snakes he'd seen while cruising out to the drop site – they looked like huge tree branches, with heads big as a man's fist.

'Don't worry,' Mario said. 'The Cuchillos are pros. We just hold out our hands, and they'll drop the shit in like ol' Warren Moon throwin' the bomb to a wide receiver. Relax. It's in the bag. We're good as home free.'

Border Security Force Headquarters, Aladdin City, Florida

'Data connection in progress, sir,' one of the controllers reported. Everyone looked up at the center main-viewing monitor, one of three twenty-foot monitors that dominated the Hammerheads' command-and-control center in south Miami.

The center screen usually showed a picture of the southeast United States, focusing in on the busy drug trade routes through Florida, the Bahamas and throughout the Caribbean – areas where the Border Security Force operated balloon-borne radars and tied in with FAA and military radars to get a composite radar picture of the region. This time, though, the center screen showed the southern United States between Mobile, Alabama, and Houston, Texas.

There was not too much to see. Brad Elliott, seated at one of the controller's consoles, studied the picture as information from radar sites all along the south coast was assembled by the Hammerheads' computers and displayed. Samuel T. Massey, the President's Special Advisor on Drug Control Policy, a.k.a. the 'drug czar,' shook his head. 'Not a very good picture, is it, Brad?'

'The Houston Center radar tie-in is pretty marginal,' Brad Elliott replied. 'I'm told we're improving the data flow, but it'll be a few weeks off before we can test it. There's also a big thunderstorm over the target area that's causing a lot of trouble with reception.' He turned to one of the controllers to his right. 'Plug in ROTH.'

Instantly the picture changed, the screen came alive with streams of data, pinpointing several aircraft in and around the New Orleans area, smaller aircraft flitting around the edges of the thunderstorms; it even registered movement-information on some vessels in the Gulf of Mexico. 'That's the ROTH information?' Massey said. 'It really sums up the situation in that area – it's even picking up ships out in the Gulf. Where's the radar located? New Orleans? Baton Rouge? Or is it an airborne?'

'How about Bull Shoals, Arkansas,' Elliott said.

'Arkansas? That's got to be hundreds of miles from the coastline – '

'Exactly five hundred ten miles from the southern Louisiana coastline. In fact, the location was specifically chosen to be at least five hundred miles from the coast – the *minimum* range of ROTH-B.' He tapped instructions into a keyboard at the console, which expanded the view on the center monitor to the entire south-central United States. He then entered commands to display a red curved wedge that extended all the way from Bermuda to the east to Los Angeles to the west, and as far south as the Yucatán Peninsula of Mexico and the Lesser Antilles of the north coast of South America.

'This is the scan area of ROTH-B,' Elliott said. 'ROTH-B, you know' – doubting that Massey did – 'stands for relocatable over-the-horizon backscatter – they call it relocation even though the main antenna array is nine *thousand* feet long. ROTH is a radar system that bounces radar energy off the ionosphere to detect targets hundreds of miles away over the horizon, up to sixteen hundred miles.'

'Isn't that ten times greater than a normal radar? I thought radar was always line-of-sight – how can it look out sixteen hundred miles when there's all these mountains in the way? Hell, the curvature of the Earth should be enough to block out the energy.'

'In a typical radar system it would,' Elliott said. 'The ROTH transmitter unit in Bull Shoals shoots the energy well above the horizon and it doesn't read the reflected energy signals until it computes a specific time delay from the reflected energy. It's like a gigantic air hockey game – we shoot radar energy out at various angles, getting it to scan all altitudes at longer ranges by bouncing the radar beams off the ionosphere at different angles. The computer picks out the reflected energy returns based on its computations of how long that reflected energy should take to return to the receiver site. It doesn't work at ranges shorter than five hundred miles because you run out of angles – no matter how you try to shoot the energy out it'll never return to the receiver site.'

'But doesn't this system obsolete your aerostats and radar sites? With a couple more of these you could keep track of every mile of borders.'

'I wish we could,' Elliott said. 'But ROTH is new and not completely reliable yet. It needs data on the electrical nature of the ionosphere, and fine-tuning the radar signals to match the electrical surface of the ionosphere is tricky, far from perfected. Plus, when there's a disturbance in the ionsophere like a solar flare, ROTH is all but useless. And because the time and duration of solar flare activity is published everywhere, the smugglers know when ROTH is off the air anyway.

'The other problem is we've just now begun to develop fast enough computers to compute target altitudes. Our altitude readouts are only good within one or two thousand feet.'

'This should be looked at right away,' Massey said. 'Air-and-fleet defense is a top priority, but in peacetime our security against border intrusion, and especially against smugglers, is more important. And that's you guys. But what you're talking about is a lot more money . . .'

'I agree one hundred percent, Mr Secretary,' Elliott said. In fact, that was one of the reasons he had brought Massey to Aladdin City – it was much easier to fight for such a costly, far-ranging proposal such as this with the top people on your side.

'I appreciate your decision, Brad, to let Customs in on this drug bust.'

Elliott inwardly hated this PR ploy, but what the hell, if it helped the Hammerheads . . . 'We've got intelligence that a drop will take place in a specific area. We're acting on it as a law-enforcement action.' Elliott knew, like ex-Treasury Secretary McDonough and ex-Customs Commissioner Crandall, that Massey still believed in non-military drug interdiction organizations like the old Customs Service.

'Zoom in on the target area and let's see what's up,' Elliott told the controller running the ROTH radar data.

The radar information was reduced to a few dozen miles on a side, centered around the delta swamps southwest of New Orleans. Aircraft were highlighted by the computers, including one directly in the center of the display. 'There he is,' Elliott said. 'We picked him up an hour ago flying over Cuba. He was flying the airways until crossing our Air Defense Identification Zone, then dropped down to low altitude and is making a beeline for the drop zone. He's got nerve, I'll say that for him – winds at his altitude are gusting to fifty knots, with severe up- and down-drafts in the thunderstorms, and he's only a thousand feet above the water.'

'And New Orleans radar can't see him coming?'

Elliott told the controller to switch off the ROTH radar data. A few of the air targets remained, including a target in the center of the screen that seemed to disappear for several seconds, then reappear. When it came back, it was marked with a TR 5 symbol.

'This is what Houston Center radar sees,' Elliott said. 'A target does show up, intermittently, but it's marked with that symbol. Which means the Center radar's computer thinks it's not an aircraft – or at least there's a low probability that it's a plane, given its speed, position and radar signal. As it moves closer or when it's picked up by New Orleans Approach radar, it may eventually be identified as an intruder, but by then it would be too late to stop it. Most controllers squelch TR 5 targets to unclutter their scopes.' Elliott ordered the ROTH radar data replaced, and the scene changed to highlight the target aircraft.

'So where are your planes?' Massey asked.

'We have two AV-22s and three Black Hawks on the ground at a small airfield, South Lafourche, about forty miles south of the drop zone. They're under camouflage netting in case the target overflies the airport, but our guess is he'll stay in the clouds until just before the drop. We also had an AV-22 trying to trail him offshore in case he made any overwater drops but our plane couldn't handle the weather. When the target flies past South Lafourche our birds will launch and begin the chase, staying as far back as they can and still keep him in contact. They'll be using infrared trackers to follow him, since we've received word that these guys might have radar detectors in their planes that could pick up our plane's tracking radar.'

'Don't the smugglers usually use ground observers that watch for trailing planes and can warn the drop crew?'

'They sure do. We plan on trailing the target high and as far back as we can to avoid being spotted, but remember, we're going after the smugglers on the ground – if we want to have a chance to make an arrest on the ground we have to move double-time after the drop is made. It doesn't take long for these guys to grab the cargo and disappear after a drop. And if the plane sees us and breaks off before making its drop, we trail the plane. At the worst we stop a big shipment from making it into the country. But we're out to do much more than that . . .'

'Should only be a few more minutes,' Mario said. He was watching the yellow interrogation light on the beacon unit – it had begun flashing more during the last few minutes, indicating that the drop plane was using it to fine-tune its position in preparation for the drop.

'I can't hear him,' Girelli said. 'Shouldn't we hear him by now?'

'He'll be outta here and gone before you know it,' Mario said. 'These Cuchillos don't come in slow – they haul ass all the way.' He was watching the yellow light when he heard a voice on the radio call out, 'Mario, this is Duncan. Mario, come in.'

Mario picked up the small microphone and clicked the button: 'You got problems, Dunc?'

'I hear choppers,' the voice on the other end reported. The trailing lookout sounded nervous. 'Maybe two, maybe more.'

'Are they following the plane?'

'I don't know, I can't tell. I'd bug out if I were you.' The connection went dead. Mario and Girelli knew that that was what Duncan was doing right now.

'Some lookout,' Girelli said. 'The fucker's worthless.'

'So what do we do?'

'We stay,' Girelli said. He raised his rifle, an M-16 with an M-203 grenade launcher attached, buckled a bag full of ammunition clips and forty-millimeter grenades onto his belt. Mario had his own M-16 slung over his shoulder ready to go. Two choppers, we can handle. He turned to Debeauchalet. 'Tell your boys to get ready.' The old Cajun

386

guide turned and made a motion to the nearest bass boat, and the message was quickly, wordlessly passed along. Most of Girelli's soldiers had small wireless radios and had already heard the brief warning message from Duncan.

The drop seemed to come out of nowhere. The smugglers heard a dull roar of engines at high speed, then a huge, dark green shape seemed to crash out of the dark stormy sky directly at them. They caught a glimpse of two huge propellers and a large squat fuselage before the plane screamed overhead, barely thirty feet above the swamp. They felt a blast of warm air, heard a loud snapping of trees and a rush of sound – at first they thought the plane might have crashed. But then they saw an object hit the murky water right at the very edge of the target island, skip twice onto the bog and flip end-over-end until it came to rest on the island. The object had a dim flashing strobe light and a long orange streamer attached to it, but they weren't needed – the drop was dead solid perfect, almost in the exact center of the island. The huge plane pulled up steeply just before hitting a grove of trees, the tree branches whipping and snapping, and then it disappeared into the turbulent skies. Seconds later the drop was over.

'They did it!' Girelli said. 'They hit the island dead on. Get the boys movin', Mario.'

Mario was already in action . . . 'Move,' he ordered into the microphone, then shut down the radio. Girelli motioned with his rifle toward the island, and Debeauchalet started the airboat engine up and steered the craft over to the island.

The fiberglass case was cracked but intact. Mario used a KA-Bar assault knife, a leftover souvenir from his Vietnam days, to cut open the steel bands around the case. Not bothering to count the heavily taped bags of white powder inside, he quickly tossed two bags to Girelli, who stowed them in a gym bag in the airboat. As men quickly moved in toward the tiny island, Mario began tossing bags out to them.

'We *did* it.' Girelli was laughing. He felt a rush, almost like a cocaine high itself. The first few bass boats skittered off into the downpour and the darkness, moving off to prearranged hiding places until the rendezvous time. Girelli was shouting orders, laughing, oblivious to the rain pouring down on them . . .

. . . And to the sound of heavy rotors moving closer until they were only a few hundred yards away. Suddenly several five-thousand-watt searchlights stabbed out of the maelstrom and illuminated the tiny island.

'Hammerheads. All of you, stay exactly where you are.' The voice came over a loudspeaker. A huge white-and-orange aircraft resembling a cargo plane but with helicopter rotors hung over the island just fifty feet above, the rotor downwash beginning to stir the swamp water up into a froth. And now the entire area was filled with rotor-craft, a few black conventional-looking choppers with US CUSTOMS SERVICE emblazoned on the side, others with US BORDER SECURITY FORCE and illuminated FOLLOW ME lights on the sides. Two choppers veered off and roared into the swamps, tracking some of the bass boats that had already picked up their loads and where trying to make a quick getaway.

A searchlight from one of the weird-looking choppers was on the airboat and another was sweeping around the island – for a moment, Girelli was in total darkness. He was stunned, amazed that the Hammerheads had moved in so quickly, so silently, that they had surrounded the island so fast. One chopper was moving closer, getting ready to land on the island – if he let that happen they'd be overrun by agents. He dropped a forty-millimeter grenade into the breech of his grenade-launcher and cocked the action.

'You with the rifle,' the loudspeaker barked. 'Drop it and stand up. Hands on your head. Now.'

These guys didn't need searchlights – they must have had cameras that could see in the dark.

For a moment he sat frozen with indecision. He couldn't let that chopper land . . . All right, they could see him, but could they stop him. . . ?

Girelli leveled the M-16 at the chopper and squeezed the trigger . . .

Aboard Lion Two-Six, the Lead Hammerheads AV-22

Rushell Masters had been switching back and forth between the infrared scanner's view on his helmet visor screen and the regular view – every time the Customs' NightSun searchlight swept across his line of sight it wiped out his vision. But when the Black Hawk moved further down the island to find a landing spot he was able to use the scanner without interference. He swept the area with the infrared scanner and found the load of drugs and a couple of smugglers crouched near it. Both men were armed, but only one of them had raised his rifle.

'I've got the cannon,' he told his copilot as he selected control of the M-230 Chain Gun and slaved it to his infrared scanner. He zoomed in on the tense body of the smuggler centering the crosshairs on the largest heat mass in the picture – the man's chest. The man was facing the Black Hawk helicopter watching it as it eased in for landing. Then Masters saw him drop a cartridge into a breech on the bottom part of this M-16 rifle and cock the knurled handgrip pump action.

'You with the rifle,' Masters called over the loudspeaker. 'Drop it, stand up with your hands on your head. Now.'

Masters could see him look toward the AV-22 Sea Lion, the rifle still upraised toward the Black Hawk. Masters changed from the loudspeaker switch to the command radio button: 'Omaha One-Seven, one suspect at your two o'clock, sixty yards, with a rifle and what looks like a small grenade launcher. Shut off your light and move clear . . .'

The warning blared in Masters' mind when he saw the smuggler with the rifle twist one shoulder toward the Black Hawk – he was going to fire . . . He spared a few seconds to shout, 'Omaha, move *clear*,' on the radio, then reached down with his thumb to lift the safety guard on the control stick-mounted trigger button and mashed the Chain Gun's trigger.

But Masters was a moment too late. Just as he lifted the safety-guard lever off the trigger, the smuggler pulled the trigger on his rifle's grenade launcher. There was a bright flash of light and a round cloud of white smoke as the weapon fired – a split second before the first thirty-millimeter shell from Masters' Chain Gun drilled through the smuggler's chest.

The grenade hit squarely on the nose of the Black Hawk helicopter, exploding on contact and blowing the whole cockpit section into a cloud of fire. The chopper pitched upward and to the right, flipping over backward in an impossibly tight looping arc until the main rotor knifed into the bog on the opposite side of the island, and the helicopter exploded.

Masters fought the abrupt overpressure and concussion from the exploding helicopter but was pushed down and away from the island by the blast. He managed to keep the Sea Lion out of the swamp but his right nacelle hit a clump of trees and the big forty-foot diameter rotor sliced through the rain-soaked branches. Masters applied full power, tried to swing the nacelle away from the trees, but his twin-boom tails were also looping through some nearby branches. He managed to stabilize, hovering only a few feet above the murky water, then slowly nudged the AV-22 clear of the trees and out into the open.

'All Omaha and Lion units, this is Lion Two-Six,' Masters called over the command radio. 'Omaha One-Seven is down. Repeat, One-Seven is down. Two-Six is beginning rescue efforts. Suspects in the area, armed and dangerous. Out.'

Now hovering several dozen yards away from the island, Masters activated the searchlight and scanned the area for survivors, but it was obvious that even if some of the Customs agents on board had managed to jump clear, they would be engulfed in flames that now covered almost the entire bog. He gained a bit more altitude and began to move closer, searching the edges of the island for survivors.

One smuggler had pushed the body of the rifleman off the cargo case and was dragging it to the edge of the bog, trying to get it on board an airboat floating nearby. Masters hit him with the searchlight and slaved the Chain Gun sights to his helmet visor sight-pointing system. As soon as the searchlight beam hit the man he rolled over to his right side facing the Sea Lion and raised his hands in surrender. But Masters also saw the rifle looped over his shoulder, and was not going to hesitate again – he pulled the trigger, sending a hundred rounds of metal-piercing shells into the man, letting loose until his frustration was vented, his copilot yelling at him to stop, and the smuggler an unrecognizable lump of flesh mixing with the mud. A dozen bags of white powder could be seen ripped open and scattered about, covering the bloody corpse with a fine white dust.

Masters, totally exhausted, managed to withhold his fire and allow the other survivors to crawl onto the mud island. The fires had all but died out from the destroyed Black Hawk helicopter, and it appeared that no oil or fuel had spread on the water. 'Prepare to launch the RHIB,' Masters said, and stowed the scanner ball and lowered the Sea Lion to the water's surface. The rigid-hull inflatable boat along with two Border Security Force I-Team members and three Customs Service investigators was launched off the aft cargo ramp and a detailed search for more survivors began.

As Masters looked out over the devastation on that tiny island he thought back to before the Hammerheads were formed, back to the incident that sparked the creation of the Border Security Force. This was the second lethal firefight that Masters had been involved in during the last few years, he thought wryly, and even with the added firepower of the Hammerheads working for them, death always seemed to hover over them . . .

The first group of I-Team investigators moved up to the cargo case where Masters had shot the two smugglers. The Customs agents had four men lying on their stomachs, using plastic binders to tie their wrists. He could see the I-Team member kick the rifles away from the bodies, as if the corpses would somehow reform themselves and pick them up. 'Two dead here,' the I-Team investigators radioed back to Masters on his helmet communicator. Under the glare of the AV-22's searchlights the investigator scooped a bit of the white powder up from the shattered cargo case into a vial of cobalt cyanimide, broke the capsule inside, shook the contents and held it up to the light.

'Cocaine, all right. Low purity. Maybe thirty percent. Looks like they had about twenty to thirty kilos here.'

'Twenty to thirty kilos? That's all?' Masters looked over to the other side of the island, where Customs and Hammerheads investigators were dragging battered and burned corpses from the wreckage of the Black Hawk helicopter.

'This stuff's like gold nowadays, Rush,' the I-Team member said. 'There's probably a couple million bucks' worth lying here.'

'Take the stick,' Masters told his copilot, then put his

head back in his seat and stared up into space, trying to fight back frustration. When he looked out toward the island again six bodies had been lined up on the edge of the bog, so badly ravaged by the crash that they merged with the mud all around them. He recognized a few orange life vests, a few gnarled fingers or helmeted heads blackened by the fires, but mostly . . .

'Goddamn,' he muttered, squeezing his eyes closed to shut out the sight. 'Goddamn . . .'

Over the Gulf of Mexico
Twenty Minutes Later

'Unidentified twin-engine cargo plane, this is the United States Border Security Force on GUARD. Reverse course and follow. Respond. Over.'

The escaping smuggler's cargo plane, an old Soviet-made Antonov-24 twin-engine cargo plane, had made it through the thunderstorm on its way out and was now at eighteen thousand feet heading southeast across the Gulf of Mexico. Right beside it, less than fifty yards away, was a Hammerheads AV-22 Sea Lion, call-sign Lion Two-Two. Lion Two-Two had tried to intercept the cargo plane as it came into the US, but the turbulence and lightning inside the thunderstorm drove the AV-22 away. It had returned, though, as soon as the smugglers moved south. The chase was on again.

The Sea Lion pilot, Hank McCauley, checked his navigation display against a moving-map diagram on one of his cockpit displays. 'Just east of Alpha-321 and approaching Alpha-39,' he said. He turned to his copilot, Janice Hudkins. 'Try the BSF frequency again, the aerostat on that new platform, Hammerhead Two, might pick us up.'

Hudkins had been trying for several minutes but with no

success. There were no bases within radio range. The Border Security Force aerostat radar balloon at Mobile had been lowered and stowed because of the thunderstorm winding through the Gulf states, and the storm was disrupting high-frequency communications. The only other possibility was the newest Hammerheads air-staging platform off Florida's west coast, NAPALM, fifty miles west of Naples. With its aerostat operating, they might move within radio range at any moment.

'NAPALM, this is Lion Two-Two on ten-ten,' Hudkins radioed. 'If you read me go ten-ten. Over.' No response.

'What are we going to do, Mick?' Hudkins said. 'We don't have the gas for a long overwater chase like this. We go bingo in five minutes and we're three hundred miles from a non-liquid runway.'

'Masters said these guys shot up one of their choppers,' McCauley said. 'We've got a bead on them – I'm not going to let him go. These guys are smugglers. Their buddies on the ground *shot down* a Black Hawk helicopter, a Customs chopper. You were in Customs, Hudkins . . .'

'What if they're carrying children – '

'They'll kill them anyway. We're *not* responsible for what they do. *They* committed the crime. I'll chase this guy until we got to turn back.'

Hudkins kept trying to reach someone on the radios. As she did, she watched as McCauley deployed the Sea Stinger missile pod. 'Hank . . .'

'I'm going to fire a warning shot,' McCauley said. 'Keep trying to reach someone.' As he talked she could see him slowly moving in position to align the port-side-mounted missile pod with the cargo plane's starboard engine nacelle. He had not yet selected any missiles or armed the fire-control system.

Once he was in position, he again punched up the navigational display. They were almost equidistant from

394

the Yucatán Peninsula of Mexico, Florida, Cuba and the Mississippi Delta; at least three-hundred miles separated them from any sizeable landfall. They were at least forty miles off the nearest trans-Gulf airway and well out of UHF and VHF radio range of any shore stations.

'We're bingo, Hank,' Hudkins said. 'We should start heading back. The weather's pretty bad north of us. Let's head east toward St Petersburg or Miami. We'll have a little tailwind that way.' McCauley continued on course, directly behind the cargo plane. 'Hank . . . ?'

McCauley looked at Hudkins, then back at the cargo plane. 'Get me the approach plate for St Petersburg out of the FLIP bag. It's in the lower storage compartment behind my seat.'

'Hank . . .'

'We could all use a cup of coffee, too . . .'

'Hank – '

'Cream and sugar for me.' He turned, lowered the targeting-and-attack visor over his eyes and powered up the targeting-and-attack display system with the pilot's night vision sensor computer and the Sea Stinger missile pod.

Border Security Force Headquarters, Aladdin City

The ROTH radar had been tracking the chase every moment. Elliott and Drug Czar Massey were watching the center computer monitor, waiting for contact with the pursuing Sea Lion aircraft.

'No response yet, Brad,' the controller reported. 'The NAPALM aerostat's been lowered to five thousand feet because of high winds. Two-Two's at NAPALM's extreme range now.'

'You can't talk with your crew up there?' Massey asked.

'The high-frequency radio was our only hope, but there seems to be a lot of interference,' Elliott said. 'He's in the radio dead zone of the Gulf right now – out of range of just about all our line-of-sight radio stations. The new air-staging platform west of Naples can't reach him.'

'Will the AV-22 follow that plane all the way to its landing base?'

'He's got to be low on fuel,' Elliott said. 'He might hang on for a couple more minutes but then he's got to break off.'

'So . . .' Massey said unhappily. 'One helicopter destroyed, six dead and the smugglers get away. . . ?'

'We got the drugs, we got several of the smugglers. This isn't a matter of an eye for an eye, not yet, anyway. It's – '

Suddenly the data block surrounding the escaping smuggler's radar icon began to blink. The controller called out, 'Altitude alert on target one, sir,' he told Elliott. 'Groundspeed zero, altitude . . . rapidly decreasing altitude . . . contact lost, sir. Contact lost with the target.'

'What about Two-Two?'

But they could see for themselves – Lion Two-Two, which had been within a mile of the suspect only a few seconds earlier, was now turning eastbound and heading for Florida. 'Dammit, what *happened*?' Elliott demanded, although he already knew.

Massey studied the big screen for a moment, then turned to Elliott. 'I think it's obvious,' he said in a low voice. 'It appears your pilot decided not to let this one get away.'

Hammerhead Two Air Staging Platform
Two Weeks Later

Sixty miles southwest of Sarasota the green Black Hawk helicopter with the distinctive white top called Marine

Two, escorted by two AV-22 tilt-rotor aircraft belonging to the Border Security Force, churned the still morning air with their cacophony. The low, sleek chopper flew at high speed directly to its destination, a huge flat-topped sea platform that resembled an iron-covered island surrounded by a sea of blue.

Marine Two stayed at eight thousand feet until just three miles from the platform, then swooped in, flared a few feet above the landing area and hit the steel deck of the platform hard – because of terrorist threats surrounding the visit to the platform by the Vice President of the United States they were not bothering to perform a slow leisurely approach to landing, nor would there be any orientation orbits of the huge facility.

'Welcome aboard, Mr Martindale,' Elliott greeted the Vice President.

'From what little I've seen, Brad, this platform is amazing.'

'Mostly what's different from Hammerhead One is the size. She's a beauty though, I agree.'

Martindale noticed Sandra Geffar and Ian Hardcastle nearby and greeted them. He shook hands with Hardcastle. 'How are you, Ian? Excited about this? You're seeing your plan swing into full throttle today.'

'I think it's great, sir,' Hardcastle said. The interchange was short, rehearsed, and a bit strained. Martindale then took Geffar's hand warmly.

'I want to let all of you know right away that the President sends his best on the opening of your second air operations facility. He recognizes what you've all done and what you're going through, and he sends his congratulations on this next important step in the building of the Border Security Force as a major national defense and law-enforcement unit.'

Elliott smiled appropriately. 'The platform crew is assembled in the briefing room on the third level. Please follow me.'

'The opening of Hammerhead Two, the Border Security Force's newest air operations platform,' the Vice President told the audience assembled in the platform's briefing theater, 'is a time of celebration. The American people are proud of you, of the Hammerheads. Because of your efforts, we are really beginning to win the war on drugs. The opening of this base, and the opening three months from now of platform number three off the coast of Mobile, Alabama, is an endorsement of you and your efforts.

'Your unique mission and reaction to the challenges you face were outlined in reports when the idea of this unit was conceived nearly two years ago. Ian Hardcastle predicted some opposition, distrust, even animosity. Some of it exists today. But Hardcastle and Geffar have had and have an answer. Remember why you are here . . . to protect the United States from intruders, to control access to America's frontiers, to seek out, identify, and intercept suspected criminals and terrorists, and to defend those frontiers with military force if necessary. Remember that America's borders were once weak, virtually defenseless, wide open to smugglers and murderers. Drugs flowed across our borders, in spite of the efforts of those of you who were once Coast Guardsmen or Customs Service investigators or Drug Enforcement Agency agents. Because of *your* efforts, that's no longer true. America is in your debt . . .'

There was a programmed pause in the speech, planned for applause, but there was nothing but a few murmurs from the audience. The Vice President pushed his speech aside and moved to the front of the podium.

'Well, that's the official word. Now let me just talk with

398

you. First, I want to extend my condolences to the family and friends of the men lost in the battle in Louisiana. It was the first major head-to-head between law-enforcement agents and smugglers in two years. It highlighted what these smugglers are feeling. They're still testing our resolve, arming themselves like regular armies, and still willing to shoot at us.

'Are you making a difference out here? Damn right. The drugs found in the Louisiana raid amounted to less than thirty kilograms, but according to the FBI the street value of that shipment alone was three million dollars – that's one hundred thousand dollars per kilo. The DEA analysts told me that the cocaine found in that raid was no better than forty percent pure. The users are paying more and getting less. The cartels are importing garbage and, for the moment, getting top dollar for it. But the market, even in drugs, can take its revenge on bad supplies. For example, on the upside is the increase in attendance at drug rehab programs, public and private, and a greater public awareness of drug therapy versus incarceration. Judges are taking the users who want or need help out of the jails and prisons, putting them in hospitals and treatment programs, and handing out community service sentences rather than jail time in jails that don't exist. One gram of cocaine, equal to half the weight of a paper clip, costs one hundred dollars on the street. It's far less expensive to attend a drug rehabilitation clinic than it is to buy cocaine. This new attitude of helping the user rather than punishing him at huge costs to society has made more room in our prisons for the *really* hard-core dealers and suppliers. Several states have adopted life sentences and even death penalties for *violent habitual* dealers and suppliers.

'America is in a state of transition. In a way, we're going through a sort of drug-dependency withdrawal. There's pain and fingerpointing, and some of it is directed against you

. . . but let me tell you something, what's happening in the country, *including* these gang wars and complaints and crowded jails and treatment centers, shows that you are doing your job. You're fighting and I believe you're winning this fight.

'More than any other organization, the Hammerheads have proved their worth. Let the politicians fight each other – you fight the smugglers. If illegal activity is taking place, the government expects the Border Security Force units on the scene to take appropriate action – including the use of deadly force . . . Look, the bottom line is this: do whatever you can to avoid killing innocent persons. *Try* not to kill anybody. But if you're positive that the suspects understand your orders and are deliberately disobeying them, *and* you've done all you can to warn them, then remember that you do have the authority to act with, as I say, deadly force if necessary. Stay within your guidelines, use a generous amount of common sense and what I believe you call situational awareness, and I guarantee that the White House will support your actions. I hope that's clear enough.' The applause from the crewmen showed that it was.

Hardcastle's office on Hammerhead Two was on a new third floor of the central maintenance facility. From there he had a spectacular, commanding, three-hundred-sixty-degree view of the entire flight deck of the platform. The only building taller than the three-story office was the platform control tower to the south and the thick steel-and-nylon tether for the aerostat radar balloon, which stretched skyward like Jack's beanstalk. The Vice President tried to look up the cable and spot the aerostat balloon itself but could not – it was flying at almost fourteen thousand feet and all but blended in with the brilliant blue sky.

'Very nice, Ian,' the Vice President said. 'A real sea

dog's roost . . . Three months ago you wouldn't have had an office. Congress was ready to feed you to the lions – '

'I know that, sir.'

'I told the President that everybody was overreacting to what you did. You don't deserve a dog house, you deserve a command of your own. The President agreed. The downing of that Customs helicopter in Louisiana a couple of weeks ago and the atrocities of the smugglers have stirred up the public in support of the Hammerheads. The President might even have approved an air strike against the smugglers' base, if we were sure where it was – '

'We *know* where it is, sir.' McLanahan couldn't let it go by. 'Both smugglers' planes headed for the same place after making their drops – Haiti. Their base of operations is in central Haiti – '

'The report I read said the smuggler's plane that carried the children crashed just across the coast,' the Vice President said irritably. 'It didn't land at any airfield.' He glanced at Elliott. 'And we all know that the second plane never made it even *close* to any airfield . . .'

'That's true, sir,' McLanahan said, 'but we assumed that both planes were taking a direct course to their destinations when they crashed. Extending their projected flight path, we've found several possible landing sites – none was in Cuba. *Both planes were heading to Haiti.* I checked our records for possible landing sites large enough to accommodate planes the size of the cargo plane that was detected out of Louisiana and came up with only one real possibility. It's a place called Verrettes, a deactivated World War II military installation, deserted and now in private hands. This data matches up with radar-data records I pulled from the computer – '

'That's not enough to go on,' he said. 'It's not enough for a DEA or CIA investigation, let alone some kind of a fullscale military operation – '

'Then let us expand our surveillance in this area,' Elliott said. 'I think Patrick's right, but we also need more information. Our radar coverage of Haiti and the Dominican Republic is spotty because of the unreliability and occasional interference of our aerostat unit at Guantanamo by the Cuban government. If we could get permission to station an aerostat unit on Haiti or the DR, or station an aerostat vessel in the Windway Passage, we would know for sure.'

'Haiti, Cuba, and the Turks and Caicos Islands claim our radar balloons interfere with commercial aviation, communications, television reception, military flights, free passage, commercial fishing, even tourism, for God's sake,' the Vice President said. 'They're saying we can't allow our radar energy to cross their precious borders without their permission. It's bull, of course, but we've got to play along until we can come up with a bigger bargaining chip.'

'It's garbage,' Elliott said. 'The poorest and still the most corrupt country in the hemisphere lets smugglers use them and we can't do anything?'

'It's the way it is, for the moment. We're working on it, State is. That's it. And in case you've forgotten, people, I've managed to keep a lid on the . . . incident over the Gulf of Mexico.'

'Pilot McCauley still denies hitting the cargo plane, sir,' Elliott said. 'He says he made repeated radio calls, made his presence known by direct visual contact and fired a single warning shot – '

'Don't try to con me, Brad. I've seen the tapes of the ROTH radar data. There's no question what really happened up there.' He paused, staring out the windows. 'McCauley and Hudkins are out, I'm sorry to say. Hammerheads can't afford . . . mistakes like this, Brad. Plenty of old-timers in Congress are waiting for such an

402

incident to shit-can this organization. You make your friends look bad, including the President and me. Anyway, here's the new poop . . . The President wants you to develop procedures for dealing with suspect aircraft that have already entered the country legally, or have been allowed to enter the country. I want a defined set of rules for intercept crews to follow if they're in pursuit of an aircraft that has entered US airspace but is believed to be involved with a drug-smuggling operation. You follow me, Brad?'

'But we'll still have authority to intercept and attack aircraft or vessels observed to be involved in a drug operation?'

'Yes – under careful guidelines. The intercept or attack, for now, has to be in American territory or airspace, not in open ocean or international airspace. The suspect has to be observed and recorded dropping or delivering drugs. You have to verify that the object dropped from the suspect plane was in fact the same object recovered, and it has to be found that that object contained illegal substances.'

'And all this has to be done before the guy leaves US airspace?' Hardcastle said.

'That's it. The Cabinet and some Congressional leaders really got upset over the recent . . . incident. They say they don't want the Hammerheads ranging all over the northern hemisphere shooting down planes or blowing up boats in international territory . . . The pressure's on, my friends. I grant you, it's a hell of a way to do business, but that's the way it is. Follow the rules or we'll all be out of a job. Hang in there.'

Elliott, Hardcastle and Geffar followed along as the Vice President headed for the exit, but just before leaving, he turned to Elliott and McLanahan. 'Take a ride with me, you two.'

* * *

403

Aboard Marine Two, the converted UH-60 Black Hawk helicopter, Martindale crushed a few pork rinds, washed them down with juice and looked at McLanahan and Elliott. 'What about this base in Haiti, Patrick?'

'Verrettes. I need detailed intelligence on what's going on there. I know it's an old World War II British commando base, and it was used by various branches of the military for years before being sold to a private corporation. There's a lot of air activity out of that base, some of it fast and heavy. I need to know who's there, what they've got and what they're doing.'

'It's not the Haitian military?'

'From everything I can find out it's an inactive militia training base, but Haiti has no air force except for a few single-engine jobs and a few cargo planes.'

'You really think this is some kind of smuggling ring?'

'I think this is *the* smuggling ring. I also think they're the ones responsible for killing those children . . .'

The Vice President looked at Elliott. 'Brad?'

'I agree. They could be behind the ring that shot down the Customs helicopter in Louisiana. We shouldn't wait.'

Martindale stared out the observation window. 'Relations with Central America and the Caribbean basin are pretty sour these days. They act like the Border Security Force is a smokescreen to cover US ambitions for hemispheric military domination. Can you believe it? Well, we retain access to most of the ports in the Caribbean but only because most are still British crown colonies or commonwealths – the rest of them are *reducing* cooperation, denying port access and even restricting passage. We're being asked for hands off until things calm down some.' He looked at Elliott. 'The President went to you through JCS Chairman General Curtis about that *Kavaznya* thing, didn't he?'

Elliott's eyes narrowed as he remembered 'that

Kavaznya thing,' the flight of the B-52 bomber they called the Old Dog . . . never mind what it did to him personally, it had turned US–Soviet relations to dead ugly . . . Now in just two short years it was some nebulous 'thing.'

The Vice President seemed to understand Elliott's silence. 'It was a remarkably incredible feat, Brad, amazing – even more amazing was how the whole thing was kept so quiet. Do you think you can come up with something to find out what's going on in Haiti *quietly*, without attracting attention?'

'I don't think that's a job for this outfit,' Elliott said. 'We've got a lot on our plate, the CIA and DEA should run an operation like that – '

'And the Strategic Air Command should have conducted that bombing raid into the Soviet Union. Instead you and Patrick and a group of engineers and lab types did it. Not only did you accomplish the mission but to this day the public doesn't know what happened, except by rumor and innuendo.'

'That was different,' Elliott said. 'We'd been testing gear for the B-1 bombers. We knew all there was to know about the mission . . .' He paused when he saw McLanahan's expression. Patrick looked like he was already at the computers and chart table drawing up this mission.

'An AV-22 Sea Lion could make it in and back using a ferry-fuel configuration,' McLanahan said. 'Otherwise we'd have to get landing rights in the Bahamas or the Dominican Republic – '

'That would be very, very tough,' the Vice President said. 'It would take several days and we'd have to go through channels. State Department channels.'

It was obvious the Vice President wanted to handle this mission himself, with as little interference from outside as possible.

'I agree with you, Brad, up to a point. I don't want any

Border Security assets used in this operation. If something goes wrong I don't want Haiti or anybody else pointing fingers and saying we're trying to bully the Caribbean countries – '

'So what assets are we supposed – ?' Finally the light dawned and Elliott understood. So did McLanahan, who grinned at him. 'You mean, use aircraft from Dreamland?'

'Yes . . . No one knows what the guys have out there,' the Vice President said, 'hell, *I* don't even know. But stage the mission from there, get in, get out and return to Dreamland. Nobody would know what the hell happened. It has to be dead-bang classified and totally deniable. If this leaks out the smugglers will go underground and the bad publicity could wipe out the Hammerheads and maybe Dreamland too. You've got to shelter the White House from all . . . involvement.'

Elliott sat back in his seat, wearing a pained expression, then shook his head. 'To tell you the truth, sir, I'm a little tired of *sheltering* the White House. If you want to stage an operation out of Dreamland, fine, but let's document the . . . thing. I don't want to end up like North and Poindexter.'

'North got in trouble because he exceeded his authority and used bad judgement,' Martindale said. 'I trust *your* judgement, Brad. So does the President. He's authorized me to get things moving in the Border Security Force, to do everything we can to make this unit more effective and head off any negative sentiment. If there's a smuggling ring operating out of Haiti that's responsible for killing those kids and bringing drugs into Florida we need to know about it. Okay, I'll even put this in writing and copy your office with a classified memo, but you don't want to wait for all the damn Ts to be crossed. I want results, and I want them right away. I figure you and yours do too. Find out all you can about this private airfield, do it without attracting attention and involving the Hammerheads. That's it, that's the job.'

The atmosphere had chilled. Martindale had always shown Elliott and McLanahan a huge amount of respect, even deference, on account of what they had done during the *Kavaznya* 'incident' with the Soviet Union. The Vice President had been virtually cut out of the decision-making process on that one. Now, when he wanted the same kind of action, he wasn't about to let Elliott pull in his horns.

McLanahan couldn't believe what he now heard from his boss. 'When I receive your classified memo I'll run it through my staff, formulate a plan and advise you of it. When I receive final authorization to act I'll execute the plan – '

'General, there will be no goddamn plan, no authorization, no staff, no exchange between you and me. Just do the operation and get it over with.'

Elliott snapped back. 'Sir, you may think this is exciting, going out there, being the behind-closed-doors maverick with the bombers and missiles and guns. You may think you have the authority to call up some super-secret spy plan to bust in and get the pictures and to hell with the consequences but that's not the way it works and it's not the way I work. I get my orders direct from the President on everything my Dreamland group does, which is the way it was with the *Kavaznya* mission. I'm not running a bunch of damned mercenaries. If you want me to set up this operation for *you*, Mr Vice President, put it in writing and I'll staff it. I can get an answer for you in twelve hours.'

'Don't get big-headed about your importance to the White House, Brad . . .'

'That goes for you as well, sir.'

Martindale's eyes blazed. 'You are still in *my* chain of command – '

'True, and I'll do what you want, and I'll do it right. I'll plan a helluva mission, but I want the right authorization first. For me, yes, and for my people. If I don't get it we tangle and the whole thing gets backburnered. You can fire me if you want, but we both lose out – and I think we're both working toward the same objective.'

The Vice President gripped the armrests of his seat, his jaw muscles tight. He hit a call button on his right armrest. 'Todd, get in here. Bring a notebook.'

His aide appeared, closed the curtain behind him, braced himself on the bulkhead against the gentle sway of the Black Hawk and got ready to take dictation. 'Classification: secret, my office as OPR. Date, place, time, persons present. Subject: Special reconnaissance mission. The Vice President of the United States hereby authorizes Bradley J. Elliott, chief, Border Security Forces, add office and identification number, to undertake covert operation to collect information vital to border security operations. Objective: information on possible narcotics smuggling operations by unknown individuals in or near town of Verrettes, nation of Haiti. Funding through NSC file one-one-nine dash J, limits as specified in file. Time limit, none. Coordination through my office only in accordance with contingency operations master regulations special use section eleven – research the proper ones and add applicable paragraphs. Add my name. Copy through distribution list Echo. Print that out on the teletype, send it out on the satellite right away, get me all the acknowledgements, make three copies and bring them to me.' The aide added the names of the three men present, glanced at his watch to note the time, turned and departed.

'Distribution Echo,' the Vice President told Elliott, 'the NSC, Joint Chiefs . . .'

'Departments of Defense, State, CIA, and DIA,' Elliott finished for him. 'All more or less directly accountable to the President of the United States.'

'You sound like you disapprove. You want me to get on the radio and broadcast it on your AM dial?'

'No.'

'My NSC action file specifies no more than twelve hours before I brief the President, and seventy-two hours before I brief the rest of his staff. Once I get approval from the President he can authorize immediate execution. That's what I expect. I expect you, Brad, to be airborne ten minutes after that. Which means I want a plan on my desk in eight hours.'

'It'll be ready.'

They flew on in silence. Several minutes before landing at Miami International Airport the Vice President's aide entered the tiny office and handed him a red-covered folder with several sheets of paper in it. He gave one to Elliott. 'Satisfied? Orders, funding, distribution records, receipts. Paper trail.'

'Thank you,' Elliott said, and handed his copy to McLanahan without looking at it. McLanahan held onto the classified document as if it would leap out of his hand.

After Marine Two landed in Miami, Elliott and McLanahan were told to stay in their seats until the Vice President left and the press had been cleared from the ramp area. The Vice President shook hands with them both, telling Elliott, 'I'll contact you soon through your office here in Florida. I assume you'll direct the operation from there.'

'Right, and if I'm not there my office will patch the call through to Dreamland or wherever in between.'

'Good.' He allowed a smile. 'We're counting on you, Brad. Do it.'

* * *

409

Border Security Force Headquarters, Aladdin City
Two Hours Later

Two hours after the Vice President's departure from
Hammerhead Two, Maxwell Van Nuys met Sandra Geffar
outside the Aladdin City headquarters of the Hammerheads in his Jaguar XJ-7. He looked very much what he
intended . . . the sophisticated Italian race car driver. He
greeted her and settled her into the passenger seat. He
moved into the sedan and roared out of the Border Security
Force parking lot.

They drove along in silence until reaching the Florida
Turnpike, where the pace improved on the open highway.
'So how was the visit to the new platform?' he asked once
they were established in the fast lane. 'Was the Vice
President impressed?'

Geffar had resisted meeting him, but also argued with
herself that she was entitled to some life outside the service
. . . 'I think so,' she said. 'I just really wish Congress would
make up its mind to support the Border Security Force all
the way.'

'What do you mean? Sounds like they're supporting you
all the way. A new platform, new aerostat units. Are they
deactivating some of your installations?'

'No, they've even recently activated a new radar
installation.'

'That's great,' Van Nuys said. Be careful, now, he told
himself. Be cool . . . 'I think I heard about that proposal
from someone at a Customs party a few weeks ago. The
base in Arizona, right?'

'No, Arkansas. Someplace . . .' She paused, thinking
twice and thrice about saying any more. 'Someplace you
never heard of.'

Arkansas? He had heard nothing about a radar site in
Arkansas. But it wouldn't do to push for more right now.

She's smart enough to be suspicious about being pumped for information. 'In any case, it sounds promising. Congress won't give up on you now . . .'

'Especially not if the smugglers keep using children to try to protect themselves from attack. It was the most obscene thing I've ever seen . . .'

'I couldn't believe it either,' Van Nuys said. Which was the truth – until Hokum and the other gangsters had given him his so-called options – go along or go down. They were capable of anything.

'Well, I don't think that will work again,' Geffar went on. 'Hardcastle was always in favor of attacking the smugglers, and he very well may get what he wants. The Vice President has more or less left it to the discretion of the on-scene commander . . .'

At Geffar's request they drove into Key Biscayne to her apartment so she could change out of her uniform overalls into a dinner outfit for the evening. She left to take a shower and get dressed.

When he heard the water running and the shower door open and close he went to the cabinet where she kept her service pistols, unlocked the door with her keys, retrieved her Smith and Wesson .45 and ejected the seven-round magazine with a push of a button.

He had taken a major risk, but of all the things she wore or took with her regularly, her .45 automatic was the only thing he could recognize that she had with her most of the time. Some women wore the same bracelets, or earrings, or the same shoes most of the time or at work – not Geffar. Her pistol was the only accouterment she consistently brought along, so it was the obvious – if the most dangerous – thing to be bugged.

She used to take frequent trips to the shooting range at Homestead Air Force Base to hone her already consider-able marksmanship skills but rarely had time to do that any more. Her work on the Hammerheads' first air staging platform gave her little time for any actual field work, so the risk of her actually using her weapon was low.

He flipped out the first three bullets and inspected them. The top bullet was a powerful miniaturized antenna-and-transceiver unit, tuned to a precise high-frequency, low-power setting; the second bullet was a battery that powered both the receiver and the third bullet, which was a digital microchip recording unit. The transceiver unit picked up impulses from a remote microphone – in this case, one of several tiny buttons and bugs attached to Geffar's flying boots, clothes, telephones, office furniture and around her apartment – encoded the impulses into scrambled digital bits and recorded them on the microchips in the third bullet.

The bugs were the latest sleeper technology units, activated only by voice; othewise they were shut off so as to be undetectable by conventional bug-sweepers. The information recorded by the bugs would be stored and transmitted to the receiver in short bursts whenever they were in close proximity to each other, which significantly reduced the chance of anti-eavesdropping or bug-sweeper devices from detecting them.

Van Nuys quickly retrieved all three bullets, replaced them with real shells, quietly snapped the magazine in place, and put everything back exactly the way he had found them. He knew very well that ultimately this was the wrong way to play this. He would, after all, be on the hook to the drug-smuggling ring no matter how useful his information was, would be exposed or killed at any time it suited his blackmailers. Sooner or later he would be caught or compromised . . . He knew that his only real chance to recoup from this disaster and save his skin would be to cut a deal with Geffar, the Border Security Force, the Feds. In exchange for immunity from prosecution and protection in the federal witness-protection program he could let them in on any meets, inform them of what the smugglers were going to do and help set up an arrest. He didn't know much about the smugglers that had him against the wall – not yet, anyway – but he should find out more while he got his affairs in order before going to the Feds, which meant playing this game a bit longer. After carefully and quietly relocating his assets in offshore banks, he could afford to go underground.

For now, though, he had no choice but to continue spying on Geffar for these Colombian animals.

Verrettes, Haiti
Two Days Later

'They have almost succeeded in closing off all of Florida to air and sea traffic,' Field Captain Enrique Hermosa said. He used a large chart of the Caribbean basin as he spoke, indicating points on the chart with a wooden pointer.

It was Salazar's weekly situation briefing, a carry-over from his days as an operational Cuban Air Force squadron commander, when he insisted on an overview of force deployments, order of battle, command setup, and intelligence updates. The atmosphere was deadly serious. For the first time in the Cuchillos' short life they were facing an enemy that, it seemed, had more firepower than themselves.

One of the flight commanders asked, 'What parts do they control in Florida? Are you saying they control the entire southeast side of Florida?'

'No, lieutenant,' Hermosa told him, 'they control *all* of Florida. The coastline of the entire state. In fact, they may control most of the southeast United States itself.'

Colonel Agusto Salazar wreathed himself in a cloud of

Cuban cigar smoke, not pleased with what was being presented to him, and ten of Salazar's Cuchillo flight commanders uneasily studied the chart. Salazar told Hermosa, 'It is impossible to completely control such vast territory. There has to be a weakness.'

'Sir, I am giving you information passed along by our intelligence operatives and by our informants in Florida, including information from Maxwell Van Nuys,' Hermosa said. 'It is not my analysis. Would you like me to continue?' The chief of the exiled Cuban smuggling ring waved a hand impatiently to indicate that he did.

'They have activated the new landing platform off the coast of Sarasota,' Hermosa went on. 'The aerostat radar unit had been active at that location for several months, but now it is capable of launching their Sea Lion aircraft, unmanned drones and standard helicopters. This new platform is only fifty miles from our new ingress route to the Ten Thousand Islands area of Florida. Many of our carriers and agents in that area were killed or arrested during our last drop there. It is inadvisable to use that corridor for deliveries for the next few months. This Border Security Force, Hammerhead, has reinforced its small base at Key West, taking over interdiction duties from the Coast Guard, and our informants tell us that their aircraft have staged out of Freeport on Grand Bahama Island. Of course they have had an operational aerostat unit on Grand Bahama Island for years.'

He motioned to his chart and placed a clear plastic sheet over it, which laid colored circles around each Hammerheads base in the southeast United States. 'In summary, sir, American Border Security now has the capability of electronically patrolling the entire southeast United States,' Hermosa said. 'They have tied together radar sites from Wilmington in the state of North Carolina all the way to Brownsville, Texas. This means they can fly one of their

414

drones from takeoff points in Florida all the way to one of these places, and they can maintain contact with their forces. Also, Van Nuys reports to us something about a new radar installation, a long-range radar located within the United States. We have no more details on this.'

Another angry burst of blue smoke from Salazar. Hermosa hurried on. 'Their air fleet is small but building. They can launch drones from only four Florida bases – the new platform near Sarasota, Key West, the platform south of Miami, and their headquarters in south Florida. But once launched the drones can fly for several hours and can be controlled from long distances through their radar network. Both of their model drones can be armed with air-to-air and air-to-surface weapons but they usually aren't because of their unreliability – '

'Where is the command point for these drones?' Salazar said.

'On the first air-staging platform, Hammerheads One. Although we believe any launch base can control them at any time, and that they may even be controllable from other aircraft, our intelligence indicates that the drones are controlled strictly from Hammerhead One and that the other installations are used as command relay points. The aerostat radar units act as radio command relay stations.

'But their most dangerous weapon is the Sea Lion tilt-rotor aircraft,' Hermosa went on. 'The Border Security Force has deployed armed Sea Lions into bases from Savannah, Georgia, to Mobile, Alabama, and they have been reported to be seen at military and civilian bases all across the United States. The two platform bases regularly carry four Sea Lion aircraft each, and the ground bases usually have one or two. The Sea Lion aircraft carry eight multi-purpose heat-seeking missiles, capable against both air and surface targets, and three hundred rounds of thirty-millimeter ammunition, also multi-purpose. They are as fast as our turboprops but have the added advantage of vertical flight – '

'We *know* that, Hermosa,' Salazar said. He also disliked hearing it.

'In summary, sir, all of our southeast air operations are in jeopardy. Chances of success in continued air operations into this entire region are low – the probability of one of our large aircraft making it all the way through restricted American airspace for a successful drop is . . . perhaps one in fifty – '

'One in fifty!' a senior pilot broke in. 'That's a lie. I can take any aircraft in our inventory straight to any location in Florida. Just give me a chance, Colonel Salazar.' A number of pilots agreed out loud.

Hermosa held up his hand. 'According to information from Van Nuys, the Border Security Force may not even withhold fire from aircraft or vessels carrying the children. Anyway, they have orders to use force if intruders do not respond – '

'It doesn't matter what the orders are,' Salazar said. 'None of those spineless pilots will fire on an airplane or vessel carrying those urchins.' He shrugged. 'They are dead anyway. If the Americans don't kill them they will die of starvation in this damned country – '

'They take up space on the plane that could be used for cargo – '

'Pick skinnier ones next time. They're also weaker, easier to get into our plane, take up less space and weight . . .'

And easier to throw out, thought Hermosa, who thought he was going to be sick. His hands holding his briefing notes trembled, beads of sweat glistened on his forehead. The Cuchillos had turned into mindless robots, capable of anything, it seemed. Salazar could probably convince them to tie their own mothers to the planes' wings if that's what it took to complete the mission.

'Our unit's best pilots flew in the worst possible weather and they were intercepted by the Hammerheads,' Hermosa said. 'We lost a shipment and the distribution network in Louisiana was breached. Our plane was followed back to this area, which threatens security . . .'

Salazar gave him a head-shake warning and he hurried on. 'I have compiled information from all intelligence reports and the conclusions are these: to avoid losses we should stop sorties into the American southeast and concentrate on finding and developing new routes over land in Texas, New Mexico and Arizona, sparsely monitored and not yet patrolled by the Border Security Forces. Southern California may be another possibility, since our distribution routes are better developed there – '

'You say avoid the confusion and run?' Salazar said. 'Run and hide, eh?'

'Not run and hide, sir. Withdraw and use our resources to find more secure ingress routes. We risk our manpower if we – '

'But we also make *no money*, Hermosa.' A knife had appeared in Salazar's hand, and just as suddenly it was quivering in the wooden molding around the chart – missing Hermosa's left ear by a hair. 'Get out of my sight, idiot!' Hermosa did, praying that a knife wasn't on its way to the middle of his back as he retreated.

Salazar now came to the front of the room and faced his flight commanders and pilots. His eyes blazed with theatrical intensity. He was good, and he knew it. 'Forget all talk about retreat and hiding. You are the *Cuchillos*, the elite, the best pilots in the entire western hemisphere – no, the best in the *world*. We do not run and hide from the enemy. We challenge them. We *defeat* them . . .

'I will tell you what we will do. The platform called Hammerhead One is the Border Security Force's main base, the center of operations for their long-range drones and the main radar monitoring our most lucrative ingress routes and distribution points. The platform protects the coast, but *nothing* protects the platform. I want an operation to attack this platform, to render it useless for at least the next several months or destroy it completely. During that time, we can boost our deliveries to our best distribution points in Florida. The American appetite for cocaine has not dropped an ounce in the past year – the cartels will pay us hugely for our deliveries . . . Major Trujillo!'

A tall, powerfully built pilot with burn scars on the left side of his face and a slump in his left shoulder shot to his feet.

'You are my best flight commander, my oldest and most experienced pilot. I want you to plan an operation against the Hammerhead One platform, with a secondary attack target against the aerostat unit on Grand Bahama Island. I want this attack to begin at the earliest opportunity and I want the damage to be severe. Can you do it?'

'It's as good as scrap metal, Colonel. My staff and myself thank you for this opportunity.'

'All of you make me proud,' Salazar said to the rest of the crewmen. 'You have demonstrated time and again that there is no challenge, no obstacle, that you cannot overcome. But the enemy we face now is stronger than ever. That's why we must use all of our courage, all of our skill, to crush the opposition and complete the mission. You men are the Cuchillos. You cannot fail – '

At that moment a loudspeaker blared: 'Attention. Attention. Unidentified high-speed aircraft inbound to base. All air defense units to condition red.'

The pilots ran outside as the air-attack sirens began their shrill warning. Salazar began to follow behind his men, then decided to head instead for the underground command post, probably the safest place in the Caribbean outside of Fidel Castro's own Havana command bunker.

He found two terrified operators on duty in the dank, musty command center – it was used as a survivable alternate command center and usually manned only by a skeleton crew. 'Report,' Salazar ordered.

The old-style American-made TPS-17G airport surveillance radar had just completed its warm-up cycle and was being retuned by one of the operators. 'Sir, we have a report of a high-speed aircraft, identification and origin unknown, heading toward the base from the south at high speed.'

'I heard the warning, I want details.'

Luckily for the operator, the radar set had finished warming up and he quickly acquired the target. The short-range radar reported four hundred knots . . . altitude decreasing, now at one hundred feet. Range eight miles and closing fast – '

'Air attack,' Salazar called out. Inside he was thanking his stars he had not run outside with the rest of his brave pilots – even a lone fighter or attack plane such as an Ameican F-111 or British Jaguar could carry enough ordnance to decimate their flight line. 'Order air defense ground units to engage the target at maximum range.'

'Should we wait for visual identification . . . ?'

'It's not one of ours, and Haiti has nothing that flies at four hundred knots,' Salazar said. 'Everything else that has not reported its arrival to me is an enemy. Destroy it.'

'Yes, sir.'

The base at Verrettes was capable of fending off everything but a sustained aerial attack. Salazar had invested mostly in older-model Soviet-made SA-7 shoulder-fired heat-seeking missiles, which had been mounted on Jeeps and other small personnel carriers for better mobility around the base. He also had acquired air-to-air artillery pieces, mortars, assault weapons and armored vehicles. But his prize piece was a small surplus

UH-1 Huey helicopter parked within easy running distance of the bunker and command center. The Huey, fueled, serviced and ready to go, could take him to Jamaica, the Cayman Islands, the Turks and Caicos Islands or the Bahamas. Once in hiding, he could gain access to his private Caribbean and European bank accounts.

He thought now about the Huey and when the best time to make his escape would be as the reports began to filter in from his deployed forces:

'Range four miles,' the radar operator reported. 'Still at one hundred feet, slowing to just above three hundred knots. He's aligning himself with the main runway, just inside the runway boundaries along the main taxiway . . .'

'Standard anti-runway operation,' Salazar said. 'Side-step between taxiway and runway while delivering ordnance, and you can put a crater in both surfaces every two thousand feet. One aircraft can shut down the base's flight operations in seconds. The aircraft should not be allowed to cross the perimeter. Are the SA-7 crews in position?'

'No report yet. Sir . . . the south crew says they have visual confirmation of the target. They say . . . they report it is a Soviet fighter . . . a Sukhoi-27 – '

A *Soviet* plane? 'What the hell . . . ? Order the south crew to hold their fire. All units, track but do not engage. But if the fighter attacks our positions, order all units to open fire.'

Salazar thought about this new development for a moment before heading for the exits to make his way to the flight line. A *Soviet* plane overflying Haiti and his base? Could it be a visit by some of his old buddies? Although he knew the Russians had the advanced long-range Sukhoi-27 fighter based in Cuba, to his knowledge none were flown by Cuban pilots, except perhaps for training or to show off for a Cuban politician. But why was a Russian pilot taking an advanced fighter to an outlaw base in Haiti? Was he defecting? In Haiti? Did he want to sell his plane to Salazar and the Cuchillos? A Sukhoi-27 would be a valuable asset, of course, but it would attract far too much attention from the wrong people – about ten thousand very angry Russian soldiers only a hundred miles away, who would not look kindly on the loss of their plane . . .

A Jeep with a rifleman and driver, waiting for him outside the command bunker, drove him quickly to the flight line – Salazar carefully directing the driver away from potential targets such as hangars and the control tower in case it *was* an air attack. They parked under one of the few trees near the flight line and watched as the Sukhoi-27 crossed the airfield's perimeter fence and began its pass.

To his and everyone else's surprise, the fighter began a series of remarkably agile turns, twists, aileron rolls and high-speed passes, all no more than a hundred meters above ground. The Sukhoi-27, combining the best features of the American F-15 Eagle and Navy F-14 Tomcat fighters, was without question one of the world's premier fighter-interceptors, and it was putting on an amazing aerial display right in front of the astonished rebel Cuban troops. Even if the gunners with their SA-7 missiles or thirty-seven-millimeter cannons could keep up with the plane's moves, it was unlikely that a shell or missile would even come close to the aircraft.

The fighter's last maneuver was its most unbelievable . . . The Sukhoi-27 raced down the runway, again at no more than a hundred meters off the ground and well over three hundred nautical miles per hour, when it heeled sharply upward, its nose rising rapidly as if it was going to do another high-performance climb-out – but this time its altitude did not change. The nose kept on rotating upward and backward until it reached, then passed the vertical – and suddenly the Sukhoi-27 fighter was flying *tail-first* straight down the runway, with its nose inverted and pointing backward, and its twin tails upside-down but pointed forward. The fighter held this flip-flop maneuver for several seconds, its engines screaming, until the air-speed decreased to well below normal landing speed; then the fighter seemed to relax as it rotated forward, righted itself and accelerated quickly away by the end of the runway.

Salazar shook his head. 'I've never seen anything like it in my life . . .'

The Russian fighter now began a lazy left turn on the downward side of the runway, ready for another pass, when Salazar's walkie-talkie crackled to life: 'Control, Squad One taxiing, ready for release.'

Salazar glanced down at the far end of the runway. Two of the Cuchillos' four Mikoyan-Gurevich-21 'Fishbed' fighters were taxiing out of their semi-underground concrete shelters and racing down the alert taxiway toward the runway. Part of any base-wide emergency was the launch of Verrettes' tiny alert force of late-model Soviet MiG-21 and French Dassault-Breguet Mirage F1C fighters, as well as turboprop Argentinian FMA Pucara and jet-powered Aero L-39 Albatros bombers to help repel invasion; as necessary, the Cuchillos' fleet of transports and civil aircraft would be evacuated as soon as possible.

Salazar keyed the microphone button on his walkie-talkie. 'All units, hold your positions. Repeat, hold your positions.'

Field Captain Hermosa came running up to Salazar's Jeep a few moments later. 'This guy appears to be putting on an air show,' Salazar said. 'Why? Who is he?' He turned and looked at Hermosa, who was breathing heavily from his running. 'Where have *you* been, Hermosa? Hiding?'

'No, sir. I have contacted the Cuban Air Force district headquarters at Camaguey, your old unit . . .' Salazar gave him an evil glare when Hermosa mentioned Camaguey, the location of the unit that in effect sold him out to the government because of his smuggling activities. Hermosa swallowed, then continued: 'They will not confirm or deny the activities of any Sukhoi-27 fighters operating from there.'

'The standard response,' Salazar said. 'But you should have gotten that information out of them. Did you say who you were, that you were calling in my behalf?'

'I believe they are as confused about this as are we, sir.'

Salazar gave Hermosa a disdainful wave and continued to watch the Russian fighter. It had obviously spotted the MiG-21s at the end of the runway and had probably seen the other aircraft hidden in bluffs and bunkers all across the field; it had also stopped its airshow and was flying parallel to the main runway, maintaining a safe distance. He set the channel-select thumbwheels on his walkie-talkie at 121.5, the international VHF emergency frequency, and keyed the mike: 'Unknown Sukhoi aircraft over the town of Verrettes,' he said in Spanish, 'you are ordered to identify yourself. Over.'

'*Kto tahm?*' came the reply on the radio. The voice was young, energetic, and spoke Russian. '*Shto ehtah znahchyet?*'

'Unknown Sukhoi, speak Spanish if you can.' He rubbed his forehead, trying to remember some of the Russian he had learned ten years earlier during his training in the Allied Air Training Command Center in Moscow. '*Vi gahvahreye pah espahnske? Ahngleyske?*'

'I speak Spanish,' the young voice replied in hesitant, heavily accented Spanish.

'This is Colonel Agusto Salazar, commander of the airfield you are orbiting. Identify yourself and declare your intentions.'

There was a long pause, then in English: 'I speak English better than Spanish. Please repeat.'

Salazar shook his head in exasperation. In English he said, 'You fool, do you understand me now?'

'Yes, I understand you.' The Sukhoi pilot's English was excellent, almost without an accent. 'Nice place you have down there. Are those MiGs all yours, or are you renting them by the hour?'

'Do not mock me. This is Colonel of Aviation Agusto Salazar, commander of the base you are orbiting. You have violated sovereign airspace. We are authorized to fire on all aircraft without warning. State your home base, intentions and armaments, or depart this area immediately . . .'

The man in the rear cockpit of the Sukhoi-27 Flanker fighter was typing on a small ten-by-four-inch keyboard with an eight-line LED readout. His compact, husky frame seemed almost too big for the tiny aft cockpit, which had originally been designed as a two-seat trainer; this model, however, had almost all of the flight and power controls removed from the rear and was used simply as a way to bring a crew chief on long deployments, along with a little baggage and a few toolkits.

Instead of baggage, however, this aft cockpit was packed with specialized radio gear and photographic equipment, including a satellite transceiver that could send video images as well as data from the keyboard. Pictures were taken with a digital-imaging camera, a unit that saved images on a computer disk instead of on photographic film. The computer disk was then inserted into the satellite transmitter, which would send the digital information via UHF radio to a military geostationary satellite twenty-two thousand miles away in space. The satellite would then relay the information to earth-station receivers, where the data was decoded and reassembled on computer monitors to be studied and analyzed. The crew on the Sukhoi fighter had already sent dozens of pictures back to their home base.

'Salazar . . . Salazar . . . never heard of him. I don't remember him mentioned as commander of any Haitian military units in any of our situation briefings.' US Air Force Major Patrick McLanahan finished typing in the information on Salazar, along with a few other observations on the MiG-21s and other aircraft at Verrettes. 'Ring a bell with you, Lieutenant Powell?'

'Nope,' First Lieutenant Roland (a.k.a. 'J.C.') Powell muttered. McLanahan almost missed the terse reply in the steady whine of the Sukhoi's twin engines. McLanahan paused, waiting for more, then realized he wasn't going to get anything else. The young pilot of the Sukhoi-27 wasn't much of a talker.

The Sukhoi-27 was a recent addition to the US Air Force's High Technology Aerospace Weapons Center, or Dreamland research complex in the southern Nevada desert, turned over to General Elliott after a defecting Soviet fighter pilot flew it from Khabarovsk in the Far East military district of Russia to Japan in exchange for asylum. It had been used for classified difference, identification and adversary training for crew members assigned to secret reconnaissance or espionage missions close to Russian airspace where the advanced fighters might be encountered.

Its newest pilot, and by far the most skilled American ever to touch its controls, was Air Force First Lieutenant Roland Q. Powell, a flight instructor at Williams Air Force Base in Arizona. The twenty-two-year-old pilot, an engineering major, seemed unconcerned with the danger of flying such a complex, inherently unstable aircraft and always seemed to push the edge of the envelope, even in an aircraft that did not have one English word or marking on it. Still officially assigned to the Air Training Command, Powell was frequently sent on temporary duty to Dreamland and asked to fly the Sukhoi-27 on special missions, and his reaction to any situation always seemed to be one of complete ease, of *sangfroid*, no matter how tight the numbers were running. Powell was a perfect future selection as a Dreamland test pilot – if they managed to get out of this one alive.

'Tell him that we can't tell him where we're from or what we're doing, *and* assure him we're not armed,' McLanahan said. 'Keep on orbiting the base. I need a few more pictures and I want to check out how and where they've deployed any air-defense equipment.'

Powell, on the radio, said, 'I am not authorized to tell you my home base, my destination or my weapons status, friend. I can assure you, however, that I am presently in contact with my regional headquarters, and I have proper authorization – they are not in the habit of letting the best fighter in the world stray too far from mother's nest. I am no threat to you. We are up here for a little ride on a beautiful day . . .'

'This man sounds crazy,' Salazar said to no one in particular. Hermosa was just as perplexed. 'What does he think he's doing so far from Cuba, and stunting like that?'

'He must be a high-ranking officer of the Russian Air Force in Cuba,' Hermosa said. 'I've heard the Russian pilots are normally not allowed to even fly overwater on training missions. Only a very important officer could get authorization to fly all the way to Haiti – '

'A high-ranking officer? He must be the commander of all the Russian air forces in Cuba,' Salazar said. 'But this one sounds so young, he must be one of their new aces.'

'But what is he doing over Haiti?'

'Perhaps testing air-defense units, or on a reconnaissance mission for Cuba . . .' Salazar said, but not convinced by the reach of his speculations.

'Or the prelude to an attack?' Hermosa added. 'This could be an advance scouting sortie – '

'Ridiculous. One plane? A fighter? And all those stunts? It makes no sense . . . .' Salazar thought for a few moments, then: 'But because of its unusualness it makes the best sense of all. We must prepare our units as if an attack is imminent.' He switched frequency on the walkie-talkie. 'Alert units one and two, ensure weapons on safe. Remain within ten miles of the base and stay between one hundred and two thousand meters altitude. I want that Sukhoi shadowed but do not engage unless I give the command. Clear for takeoff. Show him what the Cuchillos are made of.'

The MiG-21 pilots replied enthusiastically, and moments later the two older Soviet fighters were airborne, with the Sukhoi-27 fighter waiting patiently overhead.

Not so patient was McLanahan, suddenly feeling trapped like a rat in the back seat of this same Soviet fighter. 'They're launching those two MiGs from the shelters on the east side of the field,' he shouted. 'Better get out of here.'

Instead Powell made a turn directly for the MiGs as they arced over the west end of the runway and began their climb over the base. 'Too late,' he said. 'They'll be all over us if we run. We've got to stick with them,' and as he said it he angled in on the oncoming fighters.

'What the hell do you think you're doing, Powell?' McLanahan said, ripping off his face mask. 'You're not going to dogfight with those MiGs – '

'Don't worry, Major,' Powell said in his soft, almost sleepy monotone. 'This'll be real interesting . . .'

'We're trying to conduct a reconnaissance mission on these guys down below, not get *interesting* with a couple of MiGs – '

'He caught us dead to rights,' Powell said, watching as the MiG-21s began their initial turn toward him after takeoff. 'If we tried to bluff our way out he'd be suspicious.

He'd sure try to trace our flight path or trail number and he'd start running into dead ends. Too many unanswered questions. He and the rest of them down there would pack up and leave Haiti and we'd have to find them all over again. This way we make him think we really *are* Russians.'

Powell shoved the throttles forward, gaining speed to engage the two MiG-21s and activated his radio: 'I see your fighters airborne, Colonel Salazar. If you're up for a little exercise, I'm ready for you.'

The first pass was a simple identification run, head-to-head, with the second Fishbed fighter in extended-trail formation directly behind the leader, which allowed both the leader and the wingman to get a clear look at the Sukhoi fighter and to avoid telegraphing any moves.

'Fishbed-Js,' Powell announced, and reeled off specifications like a manual. 'They've got the old Tumansky turbojets instead of the newer R-33D turbofans, and they don't have the dorsal spine fuel tanks. They've three external fuel tanks, two air-to-air missiles – standard K-13AA infrared – and two fifty-seven-millimeter ground-attack rocket-pods. These guys are ready. Hold on, Major.'

Powell yanked back on the control stick, the G-forces slamming McLanahan back in his seat as if a boulder had fallen on his chest. His arms and legs, every part of his body, even his nose and fingers, suddenly felt as if they weighed hundreds of pounds.

'See them out there, sir?'

'What?'

'Look for the MiGs, sir. Find them for me.'

McLanahan tried to arch up to look up through the top of the cockpit, but it was almost impossible to move his head – he could hardly even lift his eyelids. 'I can't,' McLanahan grunted, forcing the words out in strained coughs. 'I can hardly move . . .'

'Look behind us,' Powell said. His voice was a bit huskier but it was still quiet, even, despite the G-forces. 'Search between the tails. See if he climbed with us.'

'Can't you unload a little. . . ?'

'Find them yet, sir?' When McLanahan didn't answer, Powell grabbed handholds on the canopy sill and pushed and pulled himself around so he could look behind him – McLanahan couldn't figure out how Powell, who couldn't have weighed more than one-fifty soaking wet, could fight past the tremendous G-forces and move around so easily. 'Like I thought. One tried to climb with us. He forgot about all that gas and drag he's got.' Powell took the Sukhoi inverted, then aimed the nose straight down at the first MiG. By then, the MiG that had tried to climb after the Sukhoi had slowed down, appearing to be almost frozen in the sky.

'He's running out of airspeed,' McLanahan said, and as he did the MiG flopped over, lolling, skidded sideways, exposing his entire right side to the descending Sukhoi fighter. 'You got him . . .'

'Where's the other MiG?' Powell said, emotion now in his voice.

McLanahan searched the sky, spotting the second MiG a few seconds later. A tiny dot was rising off the horizon, slightly higher than the Sukhoi, then beginning to lower its nose to cut off the angle and intercept Powell. 'I see him, three o'clock high . . .' And over the radio they heard something in Spanish – a loud shout of victory?

'These guys are good,' Powell said, and rolled hard right, checked his altitude, shoved the nose down to build up some speed, then yanked it back up to try to put his guns on the second MiG. But for a brief moment the higher MiG-21 had the speed and position advantage and Powell had no choice but to roll under the MiG and escape before the second MiG locked him in his gunsights.

McLanahan, who found himself sucking in volumes of oxygen, snapped off his oxygen mask to avoid breathing any more pure oxygen until he got his hyperventilation under control. The dogfight with these Haitian MiGs was bringing back some scary images of another dogfighter over eastern Russia – images he'd hoped had been buried forever. Damn Powell, he's having a good ol' time playing with these guys. He could easily see the blazing guns and the missile launch from the second MiG – he could easily see himself getting shot down in a huge fireball. He'd seen it before, seen what those things do, the devastation . . . For all his skill, Powell didn't realize that this was a damned serious business. He needed to be bloodied . . .

'These guys are aggressive, downright hot shit,' Powell said. McLanahan could hear rising excitement in Powell's voice as well as a few heavy sighs as he fought to control his own racing pulse and breathing. 'Classic loose-deuce engagement – one guy plays dead while the other peels away, then comes back and goes in for the kill – and they pulled it off. Did you keep the first fighter in sight, Major?'

McLanahan felt his lower lip trembling slightly and hated himself and Powell for it. 'I can hardly see straight. You want me to keep a damn speck in sight after all that rolling around?'

'Sir, you've got to help me out here,' Powell said, his cool back. 'When I go for one guy you have to keep the other one in sight. If I switch or extend you need to keep both in sight until I reengage. We don't have an operable radar or search-and-track system in this beast, so our eyes are our only sensors . . . How's our fuel?'

McLanahan strained to look at the standby gauge in the aft cockpit instrument panel. 'Reading ten thousand five hundred liters.'

'We've got another few minutes before we need to head back. We'll . . . I got one of them,' he called out suddenly.

'Nine o'clock low. Now keep on searching for number two, Major. Don't fixate on any one object until you find the second fighter.' Powell threw the Sukhoi-27 fighter into a hard-left banking dive and began to line up on the MiG. The MiG below them suddenly turned sharply right.

'He's seen us,' Powell said. To McLanahan's surprise, he did not turn right to chase the first MiG.

'He's getting away – '

'Look up over your left shoulder, eight o'clock, our altitude or slightly higher,' Powell interrupted. He paused for a second, then asked, 'See him?'

McLanahan scanned the sky, then shouted, 'I see him, eight-thirty to nine o'clock, our altitude.'

'Half-split maneuver,' Powell said. 'Another classic, right out of the textbooks. These guys could be teaching our pilots a thing or two. Sir, watch the guy peeling off to our right. Keep an eye on him. What's he doing?'

'High-tailing it out of here.'

'Good.' Powell watched the second MiG off to their left – he stayed there, not maneuvering.

'I see smoke from the first MiG,' McLanahan called out. 'Looks like he's slowing down, too.'

'He wants us to chase him,' Powell said. 'Wait . . . wait . . . *now.*'

Powell made a hard turn right, jinking toward the first MiG escaping to the north but keeping an eye on the second MiG off to their left. As soon as the second MiG began its right turn to pursue, Powell yanked the control stick up and left toward the pursuing MiG. As he did, McLanahan's helmet slammed against the right cockpit railing, and he grunted loudly as the G-forces began their pressure once again.

'Powell!' McLanahan heard himself yell. The MiG-21 was all around them – it seemed only a few feet away, close enough to touch . . .

Powell's Sukhoi-27 executed a fast, wide barrel roll over

the second MiG, continued into a second full roll, and emerged several moments later direcly behind and to the right of the second MiG, in firing position. 'Splash one MiG,' Powell announced over the radio. Simultaneously he threw the Sukhoi fighter into full afterburner and accelerated out past the MiG just as it started a defeated right turn back to base. 'Where's the first MiG, sir?'

'Turning left, one o'clock, below us.'

'Got him. The first MiG should be coming back to help his buddy,' Powell predicted. 'He extended a little too far . . . here he comes.' The first MiG that had tried to draw Powell into attacking was now in a left turn and picking up speed, but it was turning directly in front of the Sukhoi-27 now. Powell tracked it through its turn, keeping the Russian fighter's nose on it for several seconds. 'Missile, missile, bang, bang,' Powell radioed to Salazar. 'Switching to guns.' The MiG tried to dive and twist away, but the damage had already been done.

McLanahan fought to relax his tensed-up thighs and toes. A game to Powell. Sure, he was very, very good at it. But one day it would not be just for pictures but for real . . .

Salazar and Hermosa were still amazed by the maneuver the Sukhoi-27 had made to get around and behind the second MiG-21 when they suddenly realized that the first MiG was under attack as well. In a few seconds, both Cuchillos had been beaten by the seat-of-the-pants flying of the young pilot in control of the Su-27. 'Lieutenant Miguel extended five seconds too far,' Hermosa said. 'They had this stranger in a perfect rolling pincer – '

'The Sukhoi is much more maneuverable than the MiG-21,' Salazar interrupted. 'It's not difficult for such a plane to outmaneuver a less capable adversary. The MiGs are carrying extra fuel tanks, which would normally have been jettisoned before the flight, so their drag ratio was much higher than normal. Still, Thomas had the Sukhoi dead after the loose-deuce engagement . . .'

'He did not call that he was locked on or firing . . .'

'It doesn't matter,' Salazar said. 'They executed properly and sucked the Russian in with precision – the contest was over before it began – '

'Knock it off, gents,' Salazar heard the pilot of the Sukhoi-27 call over the radio in Russian. He waited until he was sure both planes weren't going to try another run at him, then turned the Sukhoi-27 westward toward Jamaica and their planned recovery base. 'I'd love to hang around, boys, but I'm getting low on fuel. Time to go home. Thanks for the action, Colonel.'

The mocking tone in the Sukhoi pilot's voice was too much for Salazar. On the Cuchillos' command radio net he ordered, 'Alert units one and two, I want that plane to land here. Force them back to the base. Use your guns to get his attention, but do not lock weapons on him.' The last said reluctantly.

The Cuchillo pilots reacted quickly. When Powell and McLanahan last fixed the MiGS' position, the two Soviet-made fighters had completely turned away from the Sukhoi-27 and joined on each other in preparation to land; the next moment they had expertly boxed in the Sukhoi, surrounding Powell's Russian jet.

'Talk about sore losers,' Powell deadpanned. 'I think we may have pissed these guys off a little.'

'I've got a message out to headquarters,' McLanahan said, checking the receipt messages on the satellite-terminal keyboard on his lap. 'We've got an F-111 bomber and a Special Operations Black Hawk helicopter at Hurlburt Field on the way to help if they force us down.'

'I think we can evade these guys,' Powell said. 'It'll be risky. We don't have any weapons, these guys are loaded for bear. And they're good. But I figure this jet can outrun those older MiGs . . .'

'I don't think we have any choice, Lieutenant,' McLanahan said after a short, strained pause. 'We're going to have to land.'

McLanahan could see Powell's head shake and his shoulders stiffen. 'You can't be serious. You actually want to *land* on this guy's base?'

'As long as he thinks we're Russians, this Salazar character will be afraid of retaliation if he does anything to us. This will be a great opportunity to check out this guy's operation. I can get more pictures and – '

'What am I supposed to do? Ask this guy if he's a smuggler? Ask to see his cargo? We're wearing American flight suits, American boots and carrying American charts. You don't think he'll be a little suspicious?'

'Our flight suits have no rank or insignia, they're civilian cut, not military. All flight suits look the same anyway. And everyone flying in the western hemisphere uses American charts – the Russians are probably one of the biggest subscribers to US National Oceanographic Service government charts – '

'My Russian's lousy. Yours is worse. We'll never pull this off.'

'Come on, where's the old can-do? Besides, English is the flyer's universal language. My Russian is good . . . or bad . . . enough to pass myself off as someone else, like a Pole or a Czech. I can be a crew chief or a security guard and just follow orders and keep quiet. You humor the guy, show him around the cockpit.'

'Well, what if it doesn't work? What if they lock us up or shoot us and take our plane?'

'Then it's up to the F-111 raid and the Black Hawk. This was a risky mission from the start. But I'd say we'd have no chance if we're forced to shoot it out . . .'

They both knew the odds were long, but the options were bad and lousy. 'If we act like indignant pissed-off Russians we might be able to get away with it – '

'This is crazy, sir, it'll never work.'

McLanahan could see Powell check his instrument panel. The MiGs were already nudging him to the right, and Powell could do nothing else but follow. 'I guess we *might* be able to pull it off, but I'll be mighty happy when that F-111 shows up.'

'All right, Roland, go ahead and follow them.' McLanahan began typing on the keyboard, relaying their situation to headquarters.

'By the way, sir, I don't use the name Roland. I go by J.C.'

'J. C.? What's that stand for?'

As if in reply Powell suddenly heeled sharply up and over to the left and executed another tight combination aileron/ barrel roll over the MiG that had been on his left wing. In the blink of an eye Powell was now flying in perfect formation with the Russian-made fighters, just off the left wing of the second MiG. The pilot of the second MiG gave Powell an appreciative wave, which Powell quickly returned.

McLanahan's reaction was: 'Jesus Christ, Powell . . .'

And, so saying, realized that he had answered his own question.

The Cuchillo pilots executed a Navy-like overhead pattern before landing. They and Powell's aircraft flew straight down the main runway at five hundred feet altitude, but instead of using timing to gain aircraft separation, each plane in the formation executed a tight left mid-way down Verrettes' main runway at the same moment, using only the severity of their turn to gain separation. The first plane pitched out at six Gs, turning so hard that the pilot's heart,

435

which normally weighed about five pounds, now weighed *thirty*; the second plane pitched out at four Gs, and Powell pitched out at two. The result of the variable left pitch-out turn was that each aircraft was separated by about six seconds after completing a hundred-eighty-degree turn. As they crossed parallel to the approach-end of the runway, each lowered his landing gear and flaps, then made another left turn and landed, one behind the other.

Powell used the Sukhoi-27's unusual ability for high angle-of-attack flight and low maneuvering speed to land at the very end of Verrettes' eight-thousand-foot-long runway, stopping the forty-thousand-pound fighter in less than two thousand feet. He taxied to the nearest perpendicular exit but did not taxi off the runway – the smugglers would have to block both the runway and the taxiway to prevent his Sukhoi-27 from departing . . .

Which they promptly did. Two Jeeps screeched to a halt directly in front of the fighter, both carrying three soldiers armed with AK-47 and AK-74 automatic rifles, and a fuel truck pulled up behind. A third Jeep drove up the taxiway and parked in the middle of the narrow roadway. Powell's Sukhoi was surrounded.

Salazar climbed out of the Jeep parked on the taxiway and put his fists on his hips like Il Duce, waiting as the Sukhoi-27's engines were shut down, then moved toward the Sukhoi. As he did the canopy swung open and the man in the rear cockpit, still wearing a camouflaged flight helmet with his visor down, aimed a Uzi submachine gun at the ex-Cuban Air Force officer. Guns were immediately drawn and cocked all around him, but Salazar realized that the Russian crewman in the back seat would get him before any of his men could return fire. Moving out in the open was a bad idea, Salazar realized after the fact, but who would have expected these Russian pilots to carry such weapons?

436

'*Prerodigh*,' the Sukhoi pilot called out, removed his helmet, set it on the canopy still in front of him and hopped out onto the canopy rail. This time in English he said, 'At ease, everybody. I'm coming down.' The young pilot climbed down off the Sukhoi-27 and trotted over to Salazar, extending a hand to him. '*Buenos días, señor*. That about exhausts my Spanish, sir. You must be Colonel Salazar. I am Flight Captain Viktor Peytorvich Charbakov.'

After a long moment, Salazar took the pilot's hand. He was studying the man's eyes, his uniform, his mannerisms. He saw the pistol holster on the pilot's survival harness – it looked European or even American, not Russian. 'You are a pilot in the Soviet Air Force, Captain Charbakov? What unit?'

'I'm afraid I can't tell you, sir,' Powell told him. 'I am assigned to the Revolutionary Air Forces in Cuba. Beyond that, I cannot answer your questions.'

'You fly a Russian fighter but you do not wear a Russian flight suit or use a Russian flight helmet. Very unusual. It will be necessary to hold you and your crewman until we receive verification of your identity.'

'That's not very hospitable, Colonel.'

'You are on my base. I make the rules here.'

Powell shrugged, turning toward McLanahan in the Sukhoi, who still had his Uzi aimed at Salazar. 'That's fine, Colonel. You do what you like. But if Boris back there doesn't make a radio call in five minutes, my squadron comes looking for me. There's my wingman in another Sukhoi-27 and two Sukhoi-24 bombers airborne right now from Santa Clara, and a helicopter ground assault team will be airborne behind them.' Powell folded his arms casually, looking at the growing circle of pilots and soldiers around Salazar's Jeep. 'Now, you people are good, Colonel. Very good. But do you really want to mix it up with the

Pedyesyaht-Ahdyen Sukhoputnyye Voyska and my squadron?'

Salazar nodded at that last question. He did indeed recognize the name of the Fifty-First Shock Troops, the elite Russian marine expeditionary unit assigned to Havana. The strategic mission of the Fifty-First, apart from its 'public' mission as training advisors to the Cuban Army, was to decimate coastal American defenses and base in case of a conflict, and to continue on to destroy communications and transportation lines within the United States. Salazar knew them as the toughest, best-trained, and best-equipped military unit in the world – they could sweep through Verrettes' defenses with their eyes closed.

The Russian pilot noticed that Salazar had indeed recognized the name and importance – and the threat – of the ground-assault unit designated to come to his rescue, and he put an arm around Salazar's shoulder, turned him, and gently steered the exiled Cuban commander to his Jeep. 'Now, Colonel, I'd appreciate it if you moved all those Jeeps off the runway and away from my plane. I'd also appreciate it if you would sell me a few thousand liters of gas – fully reimbursable, at whatever price you determine, by the full faith and credit of the Soviet Union, of course.' He could see Salazar's faint smile – obviously Salazar wouldn't be averse to making a fat profit from the Russian military. 'Then I'd like to look around your fine base here. In exchange, I will show you my Sukhoi fighter, and I will debrief your pilots on our exercise this afternoon. And I trust we may dispense with all this mistrust and suspicion now.'

Salazar swallowed hard. 'Of course, Captain. Invite your crewman to come along as well.'

'Unfortunately he has his own tasks to perform. He will remain with the plane. He would have little appreciation for what we have to discuss in any case.'

438

'Why is that?'

'He is a Special Forces security officer,' Powell said. 'His job is to see to it that his plane does not fall into the wrong hands. He knows how to operate that machine gun, the radios and the ejection handles, and little else. If he even suspected me of defecting or escaping inflight he would shoot me and eject. If any of your men took one step toward the Sukhoi he would hold you off long enough to push the button on a destruct mechanism in the plane. The marines would then have destroyed your base in a follow-up attack.' Powell smiled. 'I may be able to walk away from that plane, Colonel, but my leash is very real. And now it encircles you and your men as well. I suggest you do as I say.'

Salazar, knowing more than a little about the Russian elite force and security people from his days before exile, tried hard to swallow his earlier doubt. Never mind *glasnost*, the old guard was far from impotent or defeated. Especially in Cuba. And the Soviet Air Force would never allow an aircraft such as a Sukhoi-27 to fall into enemy hands. They would destroy everyone and everything around to see that no unfriendly forces got too close.

The ex-Cuban officer turned and waved a hand at the Jeeps and trucks bracketing the Sukhoi-27, and they rolled away immediately. The gun in the hands of the man in the back seat of the Sukhoi did not waver.

'Thank you, Colonel,' Powell told him. 'I would like to supervise the refueling and hear about your base here, and then, as promised, I would be happy to show you my jet.'

Salazar picked up his walkie-talkie and ordered the fuel tank to refuel the Sukhoi-27. Powell did not understand the words, but the fuel tank parked in back of the Sukhoi moved quickly to the left side of the advanced Soviet fighter near the refueling/ground-service panel. Powell directed the ground crew on where the single-point refueling port and fuel-tank valves were located, then began a walk around of the jet with Salazar while it was being refueled. The man in the aft cockpit stayed put even during the refueling. 'He does not care that the plane could explode any second if there is an accident?' Salazar asked, motioning to McLanahan.

'He doesn't understand about accidents and refueling. He understands his orders, that's all.' Powell paused, then asked, 'So. You have two MiGs and a couple of other planes. Is this a detachment of the Haitian Air Force or . . . something else?'

'You understand the need for security on my part as well as your own, Captain. We are indeed part of the Haitian reserve militia. Their government is very unstable, as you know, but more than that I cannot tell you. We too have our orders. We are a very well-equipped unit, fortunate enough to have acquired considerable aircraft and weapons. We are not, I assure you, any threat to Cuba. Cuba is my birthplace. It is sacred to me.'

'I understand. But how does a militia in Haiti get such weapons when the standing Haitian military does not have them?'

'We have need for skilled, fearless pilots, such as yourself, Captain Charbakov,' Salazar said, a forced smile appearing. 'Your skills are impressive. Your questions, however, show a certain lack of . . . discipline. What was that last maneuver you accomplished over the runway? I have never seen it before.'

'The tail-first flying maneuver? It is called Pougachev's Cobra,' Powell said. 'An emergency deceleration technique. The alpha limiters on the Sukhoi-27 are deactivated to allow flight at up to one hundred twenty degrees angle-of-attack for brief moments.'

'Have you ever considered a flying career in Haiti, Captain? We are very well paid by our clients – our

440

government. You would command our training unit, second in command to myself and my aide, Field Captain Hermosa there.'

'It is a tempting offer, Colonel.' They watched as the refueling lines were disconnected and the fuel truck moved off the runway. 'I thank you for the fuel. Now, I would like to meet with your pilots, if I may.'

Salazar nodded, then motioned to Hermosa. 'Stay with the fighter.'

Powell glanced at McLanahan in the Sukhoi's cockpit. He was still standing there, the Uzi in his right hand now aimed upward away from Salazar. It appeared he had not moved, but Powell immediately saw that McLanahan was holding onto the headrest on the forward seat with three fingers of his left hand visible in a prearranged signal. Three minutes until the F-111 showed up. Ten minutes after that, if they weren't airborne, the MH-60 Black Hawk helicopter from Hurlburt Field in Florida with a dozen Air Force Special Operations troops would attack the base in an attempt to rescue them. At least that was the plan.

Powell didn't want to stray too far from the flight line, but Salazar was already motioning him to a seat in his Jeep and he had no choice but to follow. He took a seat in the front, Salazar and another soldier in the back seat.

He had climbed into the Jeep and they had started away from the flight line when Powell noticed a covered truck screech to a halt at the far end of the aircraft parking ramp. Several armed soldiers jumped out and began taking positions behind the truck, concealing themselves from McLanahan in the Sukhoi. Powell put a hand on the doorway of the Jeep to help himself jump free, but he felt a hard object placed roughly on the back of his head.

'Relax, Captain Charbakov, if that is who you really are,' Salazar said. 'We will take good care of your plane. Now

441

put your hands on the dashboard. Do not move or we will be forced to – '

Powell did not wait for the rest of it. He reared back with his left foot and kicked the gear-shift lever between the two front seats, slamming the transmission from second gear into reverse. The Jeep screeched to a halt and the soldier in the back seat flew forward up against the driver. His rifle muzzle scraped along the left side of Powell's head and was only a few inches in front of his face when the rifle went off.

Propelled partly by the concussion of the rifle, Powell threw himself out of the stalled Jeep. He landed on his right shoulder, rolled and tried to get to his feet. But the blast from the rifle had turned his vision into yellow-and-white stars of panic. He could not make his legs and feet respond. He heard loud shouts in Spanish, a shuffle of heavy-booted feet, and the sound of a gun being cocked behind him . . .

Shots and screams, the sound of bullets plowing into metal and concrete, but he was still alive. McLanahan had opened fire on the Jeep from the Sukhoi-27. 'Powell, goddammit, *run!*'

The ringing in his head was still disorienting, but McLanahan's warning came through. Powell tugged his pistol from his holster and, moving sideways, headed for the Sukhoi-27 – the rifleman in the Jeep beside Salazar raised his rifle but Powell took quick aim and got off a shot. The soldier, uninjured but surprised at the return fire, jumped out the other side of the Jeep away from Powell and McLanahan's fire and took cover.

Salazar, disgusted, muttered his feelings to the soldier, climbed out of the Jeep and stood facing Powell, who was about twenty meters away, half the distance to the Sukhoi, popping off random shots in Salazar's direction. Salazar reached into his right riding boot, extracted a long, thin throwing knife, and like a baseball pitcher winding up for a fastball, threw the knife at Powell with all his skill and force . . .

Almost there, Powell thought. The rifleman from the Jeep was gone, Salazar appeared to be unarmed and McLanahan had pinned down the riflemen in the truck. 'Major,' Powell shouted. 'Start the APU. Get her ready to – '

Powell heard a thin, whispering hiss, like a bumblebee flying near his head. A thin piece of steel had imbedded itself into his left arm just above his elbow. Blood spurted through his flight suit's sleeve, staining the fabric with inky black circles. He dropped the pistol, grabbed at the knife with his right hand – and the pain hit him with full force. He felt the point of the stiletto scrape against bone and half stumbled as his face flushed and the fingers of his left hand grew numb. The pain traveled up his left arm, sending a jolt through his spine to his brain. His feet felt like concrete weights, and he couldn't seem to make them do what he wanted any more.

'Powell, quick, this way . . .'

Thank God McLanahan was still calling out. Powell regained his balance, headed toward the sound of the Sukhoi's high-pitch whining auxiliary power unit – and ran headlong into the Sukhoi-27's fuselage. He crawled under the nose, found the built-in handholds and toeholds on the left side of the Russian fighter and began to crawl into the cockpit. He had almost reached the safety of the cockpit when he felt a hand tug at his right leg.

Strength washed out of his body, his energy spent. His left arm felt dead. 'Major, help,' Powell muttered.

McLanahan aimed the muzzle of the Uzi over the edge at Field Captain Hermosa, who now had his hands high over his head. A slip of paper was in one hand.

McLanahan kept a careful watch on the soldiers off the

right side of the Sukhoi, but kept the Uzi pointed at Hermosa. 'What the hell do you want?'

Hermosa tossed the slip of paper into the cockpit. 'I know who you are,' he said. 'I have seen you on television, you are one of the Hammerheads of the Border Security Force . . .'

The whine of the Sukhoi's number-one engine grew louder, threatening to drown out Hermosa's voice. Yelling, he continued, 'I have pulled the wheel chocks on your jet. You must return that list to your headquarters. It is very – '

A shot rang out, and Hermosa collapsed onto the runway. McLanahan took aim and fired at soldiers who had gotten around to the left side of the plane. One fell, the other scurried away and jumped down the slight embankment on the left side of the runway.

'*Hit it*, Powell,' McLanahan called as Powell dragged himself into his seat and wearily began preparing his systems for takeoff.

The right engine had just started and was winding up to full power when Powell put on his helmet, released brakes and shoved the left throttle forward. McLanahan emptied the Uzi's last clip at soldiers near the truck who were moving toward them, tossed the weapon clear of the rolling fighter, sat in his seat and motored the canopy closed. The thick glass-plastic laminated canopy had already been starred by several bullet holes.

'Look,' Powell shouted, his head clearing. Out ahead of them, nearly at the end of the runway, sat trucks blocking the departure end of the runway. Soldiers had already fanned out along the runway with weapons aimed at the Sukhoi. Powell slammed on the brakes and brought the throttles of the big Russian fighter to idle.

'Can you get over them?'

'I think so . . . they're parked nearly at the end of the

runway, which leaves us about four thousand feet. But they'll hose us for sure when we go overhead . . .'

'It's our only chance,' McLanahan said. 'This thing has some armor around it – maybe we'll get high enough to survive it – '

McLanahan stopped abruptly as they saw two soldiers raising what appeared to be bazookas or a shoulder-launched heat-seeking or wire-guide missile launcher down the runway. 'They're not going to wait for us to surrender,' McLanahan said. 'They're going to blow us away right now . . .'

Two large puffs of smoke erupted from the large man-carried weapons in front of them, and two yellow streaks of fire arced away – but the missiles didn't hit the Sukhoi-27. The two missiles, fired from SA-7 infrared anti-aircraft weapons, roared overhead and down the runway behind them.

'By God, they missed,' Powell said, not believing it. He painfully reached for the latch mechanism to the canopy, preparing to fling it open. 'Let's get out of here – '

'*No*, they didn't fire at us . . .'

McLanahan, it seemed, was right. As the smoke from the SA-7s cleared they could see the soldiers in the barricade beginning to scatter. Suddenly the trucks in the barricade exploded into flame. Smoky streaks flashed overhead into the inferno. In moments the entire line of trucks blocking the runway was burning fiercely. And then they saw a lone jet aircraft flash through the smoke and disappear.

'The F-111, they were firing at the 111 . . . now, let's get the hell outta here.'

Powell brought both engines to military power, waited a few seconds for them to stabilize, clicked them into min afterburner, released brakes and slowly brought them to full afterburner. Unlike American fighters, the Sukhoi banged into each afterburner stage with a loud explosion, but the power advanced quickly. Powell held the control stick back as the speed increased, lifted the nose gear off the ground at ninety knots, then fed in a little forward stick as the main gear lifted off. He raised the landing gear with a flick of the switch, allowed the Sukhoi to accelerate to one hundred-eighty knots with the fighter only a few feet off the ground, then flipped another switch to turn off the alpha limiter on the flight-control computer.

The Sukhoi-27 at full power in level flight had accelerated to nearly three hundred knots – five miles per minute – in only a few seconds. When the wall of smoke was five hundred feet away, Powell yanked the nose skyward. With the alpha limiter off, Powell was able to move the fighter's nose nearly vertical, and the fighter raced skyward like a rocket. It was over five hundred feet in altitude by the time it crossed the line of burning trucks, and almost a thousand feet when it crossed the departure end of the runway.

'Get out of afterburner and get the nose down, J.C.,' McLanahan urged his young pilot. 'They might have other anti-aircraft weapons on us. It's better to stay at low altitude and keep the hot engines away from them.' Powell did as he said, and several minutes later they were over water and clear of both Haitian and Cuban airspace.

Even though the damaged canopy threatened to shatter and disintegrate at any moment, Powell kept the power at full thrust, and McLanahan watched the skies behind them until they were within radar range of the Hammerhead One aerostat unit – better for the canopy to come loose than for one of Verrettes' MiGs to find them. But the canopy somehow held together, and after ten minutes of flying near the speed of sound Powell brought power back to two hundred knots, climbed back up to normal VFR air-traffic altitudes and set a special frequency on the radio unit installed for this mission.

446

'Hammerhead One, this is Pinko,' Powell radioed on the pearranged scrambled tactical frequency. 'How copy?'

'Loud and clear, Pinko,' Elliott aboard the Border Security Force's platform replied. 'Say status.'

'The machine is code one, the pilot is code two and the back-seater is scared as hell but code one,' McLanahan told them. 'You got a place for us to set down? We shouldn't risk flying it all the way to the planned recovery base.' That landing spot was one of the many hard-surface auxiliary runways at Eglin Air Force Base in the Florida panhandle, the largest and one of the most desolate military bases in the country – a perfect place to hide the illegally obtained Sukhoi-27 fighter.

'Bring it in to Aladdin City,' Elliott told him. 'We've got a recovery team standing by and we'll get an ambulance rolling for J.C. Can you make it?'

McLanahan saw Powell's head nodding in the affirmative, and he did seem to have pretty good control of the plane in spite of the wicked-looking blade still protruding from his upraised left arm. 'Affirmative, Hammerhead. We will recover at Aladdin City. Have rescue and medical personnel standing by.'

'Roger, Pinky. We're ready for you.'

'How did the pictures turn out?'

'Better than we expected, Pinko. We think we found our boys, all right. Well done.'

McLanahan for the first time was able to look at the note that Hermosa had thrown into the cockpit. As he read his eyes widened. He attached the note to the back of Powell's seat, then photographed it with the digital camera, slipped the camera's recording disk into the transceiver and hit the XMIT button.

'I've got one more picture for you, Hammerhead,' McLanahan said. 'This one you're not going to believe.'

* * *

447

The bullet from a soldier's rifle had sliced Hermosa's spinal cord in two. One hand had been crushed as the left wheel of the escaping Sukhoi-27 had rolled over it, and he had been tumbled down the runway for several meters by the hot, oily jet blast of the Russian fighter. But somehow the ex-Cuban military aide was still alive.

Salazar found him in a twisted heap on the side of the runway, his eyes full of pain. Kneeling down in front of Hermosa's face, he turned to the soldier standing behind him who had shot Hermosa: 'You said it was a note he passed to that crewman of the Sukhoi?'

'Yes, Colonel, I first saw him pull the wheel chocks so I moved across to warn him that your orders were to try to keep the plane from taking off. When I saw him throw the note into the cockpit, I suspected something . . .'

Salazar nodded, then looking at Hermosa, said, 'You probably shot an informer. Is that *right*, Field Captain?'

Hermosa attempted a feeble reply. Salazar bent down to listen. 'This . . . is for the children you murdered . . .' and he managed to spit into Salazar's face.

Salazar didn't flinch. He showed the blade of a stiletto to Hermosa, then drew the razor-sharp blade across Hermosa's throat.

'Bury him with the other trash,' Salazar ordered. 'I want his office and belongings searched. I want to know why he passed a note to a Russian fighter crew – *if* they were Russians . . . Russians . . . ? The only thing really Russian about them was their aircraft. Without that Sukhoi-27 they could have been Americano . . .'

Salazar had his UHF walkie-talkie in hand. 'Control, this is Salazar. I want all flight commanders and squadron chiefs to meet in the briefing room in five minutes. See to it that it is set up for an operational strike briefing. Do not call Field Captain Hermosa – he will not be joining us.'

The huge Indian aide, Salman, filled the doorway as he looked unsmiling at Sandra Geffar, one hand on the open door, the other on the door frame.

'Hello, Salman,' Geffar said, removing her sunglasses and placing them in her flight-jacket pocket. She wore a flight suit and flying boots, and despite the growing heat of the day she had kept her lightweight jacket on during the ride from the Hammerheads' base to the quiet seaside community. 'How are you today?'

So saying, she tried to step through the door but Salman was immobile as a tree.

'Is something wrong?'

'I am sorry, Miss Geffar, but Mr Van Nuys is engaged in a business meeting and has asked that he not be disturbed. He instructed me to show you to the sun garden, where he will meet you for lunch.'

Geffar turned toward the walkway, then suddenly reached over her shoulder, grabbed Salman's arm, twisted her hip away and executed a classic judo throw. The three-hundred-pound Indian butler spun over Geffar's right hip and down the stairs, landing like a pallet of bricks on the slate flagstones below.

But he was also a trained bodyguard, and he knew how to take a fall. He landed hard but was back on his feet in an instant, his left hand reaching inside his coat for the gun. Geffar was expecting that, and her .45 caliber Smith and Wesson automatic was in her hand and leveled at Salman's chest before he could regain his balance.

'Don't move or you're dead.' Salman raised his hands clear of his coat. Immediately two Border Security Drug Enforcement agents, with Monroe County sheriffs as backup, surrounded Salman, handcuffed him and led him away.

449

'Nice throw,' one of the agents said. He handed Geffar a Kevlar body-armor jacket and a Hammerheads operations helmet – bullet-proof, with built-in radios, lights and face protectors.

Geffar nodded as she strapped on the helmet, replaced her flight jacket with the body armor, and activated the communications link in the helmet. 'I'll go through first, see if I can draw Van Nuys into the open,' she told the agents and deputies. 'He's got this place wired for sound and video and I'm sure he's been alerted, so be careful.' She pointed at the four deputies, who had on communications headsets so they could monitor the Hammerheads' tactical frequency. 'Go to the back but stay behind cover. You people' – she pointed at two of the DEA agents, adjusting their own body armor – 'follow me in, then take the upstairs. You others, check the office and bedrooms on the east side. There's a doorway that leads to the basement at the end of the hallway through the utility room. This place has a huge cellar and he might be down there.

'There's a driver, and he's bigger than Salman, so watch for him. There might be others. They obviously know we're here and they're not coming out. Don't hesitate.' She hefted the .45 and stepped back through the doorway.

Geffar looked in through the doorway, scanning for any movement inside. Nothing. She pushed the door open wider, moved the helmet's microphone away from her lips. 'Occupants, US Border Security, search warrant.' She waited a few seconds for any sign of movement, heard nothing, moved inside.

As she moved across the threshold she withdrew a folded set of papers and held it up to one of the far corners of the room, where she knew a wide-angle security camera was hidden – with that system Van Nuys could monitor his estate inside and outside from several places in the house.

'Max, this is Sandra Geffar,' she called out – if he was

450

anywhere in the house he would hear her. 'This is a search warrant.' She held it up, then dropped it behind the door and resumed her two-handed grip on the pistol. 'The place is surrounded, the airport is closed and a Hammerheads vessel is blocking the marina. We've got Salman in custody. If you run you'll be shot. Give yourself up.'

Nothing. She moved the microphone back to her lips. 'Deputies, move to the back. Watch the second-floor balconies.' Geffar reached up to her helmet and clicked a button that activated a microphone that would amplify sounds in the rooms around her. She could, among other things, hear the hum of the refrigerator in the kitchen, ice cubes clattering into a bucket from the icemaker behind the bar in the great room, and seagulls outside on the back lawn.

The basement of Van Nuys' huge house was Geffar's main concern – he could hide an army down there. She walked through the kitchen, carefully checking the pantry and storage closets, and stood in front of the door that led to the basement suites. Centering the helmet's microphone on the door, Geffar held her breath and listened.

The faint creak of wood, breathing, a hard swallow – someone behind the door.

'Border Security, anyone behind that basement door come out hands up.'

'I'm coming out, coming out . . .' It was Bullock, Van Nuys' driver. The door was pushed open a few inches, nobody appeared.

'Bullock, toss your gun out – '

Through the directional mike she heard the too-familiar *snik* of a hammer being cocked into position, followed by a sharp intake of air into lungs, and she dived for the floor just as six holes erupted out of the wooden door, the subsonic rounds sounding like hammer blows as they crashed through the door. From her position, Geffar traced

451

a figure-eight pattern of .45 caliber slugs around the center of the holes Bullock had made in the door. She heard a short cry of pain, then the sound of a body falling, thumping down the stairs.

Two DEA agents and two sheriff's deputies with M-16 rifles appeared beside her. As one deputy covered the door, the other inched it open, turned to his partner. 'Cover me.'

'Don't try it,' Geffar said after one of the DEA agents helped her up. 'The basement goes on forever. Tear gas the basement and call for a K-9 unit and more backup.' One deputy went off to relay the request.

'We're upstairs,' one of the other agents announced to her over the radio. 'Bedrooms, bathrooms, den, attic all secure.'

'Get a team up there and search the place,' she radioed back. 'Breezeway connects to the driver's office in the garage – check that out, too.'

'Roger. I-team is moving in.'

Geffar suddenly felt very tired. After seeing the note that the Cuban drug smuggler had passed to McLanahan, the note with Van Nuys' name on it, she had felt a chill, and a shock she had thought she had long ago insulated herself against. For a while she had almost let herself believe something might be possible with this man . . . and then the weariness gave way to the anger that had replaced the hope . . .

She got to her feet and went to the back patio, reloading her .45 with a fresh clip as she made her way out into the hazy sun. One of the Hammerheads' Cigarette ocean interceptor yachts was patrolling the area just outside the marina, ready to chase down any suspect, and three small Florida Marine Patrol vessels cruised through the marina itself searching for Van Nuys. A Sky Lion tilt-rotor drone with its large bug-eyed surveillance dome on its belly hovered a few hundred feet over the Sunrise Beach Club, electronically scanning for a sign of Van Nuys or his car.

Geffar could hear the progress reports on the helmet radio, including one that did not surprise her – Van Nuys' Jaguar was at the airport, and one of his planes was missing. It appeared that he had managed to escape just before the Hammerheads could close in on him.

'Did you copy that report?' one of the DEA agents queried over the radio. 'Van Nuys skipped.'

'Get a report from Hammerhead One,' she replied, 'and see if they got a radar plot on any aircraft leaving Sunrise Beach. Continue the search.'

Geffar walked to the edge of the immaculately groomed lawn off the back of the estate on the marina side of the spit of land on which the estate was located. To the right was the pool, the garages. Beyond was the marina and the narrow channel that led to Old Rhodes Key. To the left was the main driveway from the development to the house, a drainage ditch under the road, patches of trees and bushes that bordered Van Nuys' property, and beyond, a narrow beach and the Atlantic Ocean. This northern tip of Key Largo had been coveted for decades by the rich and famous; and although the main house had been redecorated and expanded several times it was in essence the same mansion that had stood on this property for almost a hundred years . . . including Prohibition years when this coastal part of south Florida was a haven for whiskey smugglers . . .

Geffar now drew her pistol and followed the driveway out toward the drainage ditch that emptied into the ocean. Although the brush and debris appeared near-impenetrable, the ditch itself was wide and deep – and there was a small rubber raft bobbing in the shallow water, partially hidden in the darkness of the aqueduct . . .

'Hello there,' Maxwell Van Nuys said as he appeared

453

from under the drainage pipe beside the raft, his expensive suit smudged from where he had had to squeeze through the drainage system to the hidden escape point.

She leveled her pistol on him. 'You almost made it,' she said. 'They found your car and the missing plane – they were ready to call it off.'

'An old bootlegger's escape-and-supply system,' he said with studied calmness, motioning inside the aqueduct. 'The house has several levels of basements. Most are underwater or caving in but there's one level where they had this nifty escape corridor from the house to the ocean.'

'Bullock tried to kill me.'

'I told him to surrender. He's a three-time loser – probably afraid to go to prison.'

'Bullock does what you tell him to do – '

'No, I could never hurt you, never order someone to . . . I was trying to get away before my mistakes ruined any chances I had with you – '

'Tell me you had nothing to do with the military smuggling ring in Haiti.' Van Nuys glanced at the gun – it did not waver.

'Look' – his cool was slipping – 'they found out I had a little business of my own, they made me an offer I couldn't refuse, if I wanted to go on living. But I always intended to turn myself in – '

'Who is "they"?'

'A Colombian drug family. Very rich, powerful, well equipped. They run a bunch of ex-military pilots that make their deliveries. That's all I know about them.' He took a few steps towards her, sloshing through the brackish seawater. 'I played along until I liquidated enough assets to set myself up in South America. I own a ranch in Brazil now. I'll give you and your people everything I have on these guys if you'll let me go. I've got radio frequencies, maps, names, contacts, safe houses they use in Florida and the Bahamas. But it's got to be kept quiet. If the cartels even suspect I've double-crossed them I'm dead. I'll turn over everything I have to the Hammerheads. But only in exchange for the right to insure my own protection.'

'Put your hands on your head and come out of there slowly,' Geffar ordered him, shaking her head. 'You're under arrest.'

Van Nuys moved noisily toward the embankment, used his hands to help him crawl up the muddy, weed-choked ditch to the road. 'Please listen to me – '

A voice from behind Van Nuys: '*Move*.' Van Nuys hit the ground. Hokum, the security chief for the Sunrise Beach Club community, was standing in the shadows of the drainage tunnel with a rifle in hand – and before Geffar could move, Hokum pulled the trigger.

The impact of the .30-06 round on Geffar was like an overhanded sledgehammer blow, but because of the Kevlar material and the steel shock-attenuator plate inserted into the body armor the bullet did not penetrate. Geffar was, though, driven ten feet backward, unable to take a breath. She could hear the rustle of water and the slide and click of a gun being cocked – Hokum was coming out of the ditch to finish the job.

Fighting off waves of pain, Geffar reached down to her right boot for the .38 caliber automatic in its ankle holster.

'Are you okay?' someone was calling out to her on the helmet radio. 'Come in. Answer.'

She tried to speak but Van Nuys crawled over to her and removed the helmet. Gathering her strength, she tried to bring her .38 around, but it was like trying to lift a truck.

Van Nuys scrambled to his feet, down the muddy sides of the ditch and back toward the escape tunnel, trying to grab Hokum and take him along.

Geffar raised the .38 with both hands and shakily aimed. 'Max, stop . . .'

'I got a score to settle with this one first.' Hokum shrugged out of Van Nuys' grasp, came up out of the ditch and raised the hunting rifle at Geffar's head. 'I told you you'd be sorry for the day you clobbered me. Say good-bye to her, Van Nuys . . .'

Geffar reflexed at the sound of three gunshots, dropped her .38 and waited for darkness to take her over. It never came. When she opened her eyes she saw Hokum's body lying at the edge of the ditch, and Van Nuys standing in the knee-deep water, a smoking .45 in his hand.

'It's over,' he said flatly, and disappeared into the tunnel as a wave of intense pain blotted Geffar's senses and drove her into unconsciousness.

Border Security Force Headquarters, Aladdin City, Florida
Two Hours Later

The monitor showed in stark detail a profile view of the main part of the Verrettes airbase. It appeared to those in the closed-door session at the Hammerheads' headquarters like a typical military installation in the United States or anywhere else – and that was frightening. A serpent's den, a scorpion's lair – so deadly, and so close to home.

The room was filled with energy. For the first time they had a fix on a major smuggling ring. Hardcastle and Michael Becker were especially on edge, itching to get their forces together to counter the obvious target so close to them – and get back at the ones that had struck at Geffar. The secret mission to Haiti was also the first real indication by the Administration that they were willing to back the Hammerheads with substantially more than rhetoric, and they were anxious to follow up on its success. Even Brad

Elliott appeared excited – finally they had a target, possibly the heart of a major smuggling ring.

'Armed, organized and skilled,' McLanahan summarized for his audience. 'It's not like any other smuggling operation that the Border Security Force normally faces. They have *military combat-capable aircraft and weapons*, and they know how to use them.' He turned up the lights in the small conference room, low enough so they could still see the screen, high enough so they could see one another. 'Question: what do we do about it?'

'They're obviously a major threat to us and the entire region,' Brad Elliott spoke up. 'A force that size, that well armed, with no political organization or control, is an obvious direct threat to our *security*. Whether or not they're involved in drug smuggling is almost immaterial – *any* such force so close to our borders would be considered a threat and should be disarmed and broken up. What we've got here is a well-equipped terrorist organization operating less than two hundred miles from our shores.

'I will take these tapes to the Vice President, along with Lieutenant Powell's statement. I'll recommend that, in cooperation with the so-called Haitian government, we send in a strike force to disable their aircraft and airfield facilities, then move in a ground-assault unit to disarm and secure the base.' He turned to McLanahan. 'You and Powell did a super job. You took an enormous risk and you got the information and somehow made it out alive.'

McLanahan looked serious. 'This Colonel Salazar isn't exactly a wimp, and his pilots will follow him into hell. J. C. Powell is one hell of a pilot. He flies better with one good arm than a lot of two-armed jocks.'

'J.C.? What's that stand for?'

'If you flew with the guy you'd know.'

Elliott smiled knowingly – he was accustomed to flying with hotdog pilots, as was McLanahan in the short year he

457

had been with him at the secret Air Force research center in Nevada. If McLanahan said so, young Powell must be one crazy stick . . . 'Well, I hope he understands that his days as an ATC instructor are numbered,' Elliott said. 'After flying a mission like this into Haiti with a stolen Russian fighter, we can't just send him back into the field.'

'Knows too much?'

'Something like that. He'll be reporting to Dreamland as soon as he's back on flying status. He might just be wild enough to handle the Cheetah project.'

McLanahan nodded at that bit of news. 'You bet he is. He's asked for another shot at Salazar's people, too. This time in an American fighter with real missiles and bullets.'

'He may get his chance . . .'

'Well, while we're standing around jawing like good ol' boys about Cheetahs and Dreamland and hot-shot pilots,' Hardcastle said, 'Salazar and his pilots may well be heading for the hills. They could have heard about Van Nuys and they must suspect by now that we were on a recon mission to their base. There's got to be something we can do to keep them from packing up and leaving right now.'

'When I reported to Washington the preliminary results of Powell's mission, the Vice President agreed to take the matter up with the President, but he also said not to try anything more until he gives the word. Overflying an isolated part of Haiti without permission was one thing – and we might catch a ration of shit for doing that, if they find out for sure it was an American crew in that Sukhoi-27 fighter – but sending in an armed strike team to destroy a military base is another.'

'So it might be politically unpopular, even create an international incident,' Hardcastle said angrily. 'What's going to happen? Haiti breaks off diplomatic relations with the United States? Big deal. We pay them off and apologize like we always end up doing and it's gone with the wind.

Meanwhile we get rid of a major smuggling ring in our own damned backyard . . .'

'I hear you, but I can't authorize it – '

Michael Becker spoke up now as he motioned to the HDTV monitor, which was auto-replaying the intelligence photos he had taken over Verrettes. 'Look at those pictures. They've got at least two MiG-21s and two Mirage FIC fighters, and the MiGs we saw were loaded down with heavy air-to-air and air-to-ground weapons. Real missiles and bombs, not decoys or retreads. If they had even half of those planes armed and fueled, they could probably defeat a dozen V-22 aircraft from long range. It would be suicide to send in a V-22 to Verrettes without first destroying or disarming those fighters. They've also got SA-7 missiles and air-defense artillery, in case some of our planes or choppers *did* make it through . . . Once we got on the ground – if we did – they've got at least three Pucara light bombers and two Aero L-39 Albatross jet bombers for close air support and tactical suppression. Which means we counter with ground-to-air missiles or anti-air artillery of our own or we're sunk. And all that is before we encounter their ground forces. McLanahan reported some thirty armed soldiers on that ramp, with automatic weapons. That tells me that we'd better have at least a hundred soldiers before we even consider taking that base – '

'I don't want to take the damn base, Mike,' Hardcastle said. 'I want to knock out this outfit's ability to smuggle drugs into the country before they leave and set up shop someplace else.' He turned to McLanahan and Elliott. 'Hell, send in that F-111 bomber again – send in three or four of them. Target the hangars and destroy that runway. Knock out as many planes as possible. If we can't kill them, at least cripple them enough to put them out of action for a while.'

'I'll take your recommendations to the Vice President,'

459

Elliott said, 'but I want a plan of action, not just some shouting for blood. Ian, give me something concrete I can take to the White House and I'll get in there and pitch for you.'

'I'll fax my report to your plane,' Hardcastle said abruptly. 'You'll have them before you land in Washington. But emphasize that *this* is our backyard, our area of responsibility ever since we had the sea power to patrol it. The United States is responsible for ensuring the safety and security of this entire region, and that includes Haiti, never mind the rhetoric about the big bad Yankee colonies of the north. This unit in Verrettes is a major destabilizing force. It's our responsibility to go in and clean it up.'

'All right,' Elliott said, 'put it in your report, along with a plan on how to deal with Salazar and his flyers and I'll take it directly to the Vice President. But no Lone Ranger operation against Salazar or Verrettes until we get the word. We'd be defeating ourselves and the Hammerheads if we go off without documented authorization. He paused, then asked, 'How's Sandra?'

'Hurting, but I think she's okay,' Hardcastle said. 'The bullet didn't penetrate the Kevlar, and the steel shock plate minimized the impact injuries. She's going to have a bruise the size of Pittsburgh, but otherwise they say she'll be fit for duty in a couple of days.'

'I wish I had time to see her but I want to get this information to Washington soonest. Give her my best.' And he limped out the door to his waiting plane.

Hardcastle pounded a fist on the desktop and slumped in his chair. 'What's his problem? When I first met the man he was all fire and gung-ho. Now, it seems he's so cautious about everything we do – '

'Not so,' McLanahan said. 'He believes in this organization. He knows he'd be responsible if something he did undermined or destroyed – '

'But he put together this Russian fighter routine in just a few hours . . .'

'After he got the okay from the Vice President to execute. Believe me, he wants to get these guys as badly as you do. But he doesn't think with his gut, he thinks with his brain – '

'Unless the Veep blows in his ear,' Hardcastle murmured.

'Right. And be glad of it. You saw the directive, the classified replies – you were in on the paper trail, the planning and recovery operations. You think that was just coincidence? Believe me, with his organization and resources he could have destroyed Haiti and plenty more. He does it by the book, at least until the fight starts.' McLanahan paused, a half-grin on his face. 'After that he's been known to shake some people up.'

Hardcastle still looked skeptical. 'Well, Brad will be landing in Washington in about three hours,' he said. 'By then I need a plan to deal with this Salazar character. I've some ideas, now I just have to flesh them out – '

'Let me show you something I've come up with,' McLanahan said. 'It will be tough and risky, but I've seen too much amazing stuff in the past year to say anything is impossible. J. C. Powell and I came up with some ideas flying back to the Zoo. I told you, Powell can't wait to get back at Salazar for that pig-sticker in his arm. Anyway, I think we've hit on a way to take care of the fighters and the air defense units so we can get a few AV-22s in. After that we attack any aircraft on the ground and get out of Dodge. I transcribed our notes into the computer, we can access it – '

'Well, what are we waiting for?' Hardcastle broke in. 'Let's do it.'

The intelligence-operations center at Aladdin City was a separate, smaller facility than the master command-and-control center in which it was located, although the tall, wide viewing windows with the one-way glass gave people in the center a clear view of the three wall-sized computer monitors in the master command center while those outside could not look in. Here in the soundproofed, electronically sealed room, information from federal, military and worldwide police intelligence-gathering units was assembled, analyzed, and presented to tactical commanders and field units. The room had space to brief several dozens persons – even benches and weapons lockers for military personnel. It was *the* place to plan a strike mission.

McLanahan double-checked the security of the center's doors and windows, then activated the computer database and unlocked his data-storage area. 'As I said,' he began, 'those fighters at Verrettes are our biggest worry. We assumed that they had four MiGs and four Mirages there. With four missiles and three hundred rounds of ammo per fighter, and all dead-eye shots, each fighter could destroy up to eighty aircraft . . .'

'So we'd need at least sixty-four aircraft to counter their fighters?' Michael Becker asked. 'We don't have that many AV-22s . . .'

'No we don't, but we do have that many Seagull drones.'

'You're going to send in *drones*?'

'It's what the drones were designed for in the first place,' McLanahan said. 'High-speed surveillance, reconnaissance and attack against heavily defended targets. We've got the means of controlling an entire flight of Seagull drones from a single Hawkeye radar plane or from an aerostat radar-data link towed from a Hammerheads cutter. We send in the Seagulls to lure the fighters out, and then engage them. They'll waste a lot of their fuel and weapons on the drones, I hope. When they go back to refuel we hit them on the ground. We use the drones,

Seagulls or Sky Lions, to make out where their air-defense units are deployed, then take them out with small, mobile ground troops or tactical air attacks. Once we offset their fighters' effectiveness and take out their air-defense systems, we or whatever unit we link up with should be able to move in on Verrettes.'

They put the file material into one encrypted data file, formatted for high-speed transmission, and less than two hours after locking themselves into the Zoo's intelligence center Hardcastle hit the XMIT button on the electronic computer-data transceiver and sent the document, complete with computer-generated maps and estimates, to the facsimile machine on board Elliott's Border Security Force jet heading to Andrews Air Force Base near Washington, DC.

'It's a risky plan,' Hardcastle admitted, 'but it might just work. It depends on how fired-up these pilots of Salazar's get when they see us coming.'

McLanahan nodded. 'Their alert birds, the two MiGs and probably the two Mirages will be airborne and gunning for us when we get inside of fifty miles of their base. Those pilots are good – I can attest to that. They might have put their planes on round-the-clock alert after our little visit today, in which case they'll launch when they see us heading toward them . . . It'll be no picnic.'

Becker reported to the duty controller that he was on his way to the Hammerhead One platform for the start of his twelve-hour shift – which because of the attack on Geffar would probably grow to a full-day shift. Hardcastle logged off-duty on the computer terminal and punched in his pocket phone's number for the computerized message center. Like McLanahan he had been on duty for well over twenty-four hours; he was bone-tired and was going 'home' – in this case, out to the Hammerhead Two platform – to get some rest before . . . before the next crisis. 'I hope they do come for us,' Hardcastle said as he left the office with the young navigator.

'They will – they won't be able to stop themselves,' McLanahan said, then added, 'of course, the first person to shoot us down may very well be the President of the United States.'

It was nearly dark outside when the evening AV-22 shuttle flight arrived from the Hammerhead Two platform. Hardcastle watched the off-going crew exit the plane, the ground crew refuel and service the big tilt-rotor aircraft, and watched the night-shift flight crews change over, all the time eyeballing the amazing Sea Lion aircraft with undisguised awe. This particular bird was used mainly as a crew shuttle and cargo carrier – its Sea Stinger missile and thirty-millimeter cannon pods had been removed to make room for more airliner-style seats and cargo – but, Hardcastle thought, it was still a deadly yet beautiful work of flying art. Even with the ominous-looking FOLLOW ME signs, the infrared scanner ball under the nose and the steerable searchlights poking out in every direction, it was still beautiful.

At a PA announcement from the crew chief, the on-going crew began filing into the Sea Lion and Hardcastle followed along, noting the surprised expressions on the crewmen's faces at seeing the platform commander riding along with them. The Sea Lion could carry twenty-four passengers in relative comfort in the thinly padded seats, plus a three- or four-person flight crew and a few thousand pounds of cargo in the rear; at times the Sea Lions would also sling a ten-thousand-pound pallet of supplies or fuel bladders underneath on the cargo hooks along with full interior cargo. The cargo bay's insulation and soundproofing – plus the fact that the engines and rotors were way out on the wingtips instead of directly overhead as on a regular helicopter – made the interior noise level easily tolerable.

The night crew on both platforms were usually the most upbeat, high-spirited group of the two shifts, since this was when most of the serious no-shit intercepts occurred. Despite the stringent crackdowns by the Hammerheads, a few daredevil smugglers still tried to sneak past the sophisticated radar cordons – at night when they believed their chances were better – and were usually apprehended by night crews. Crews were, therefore, rotated about once every three or four weeks to give everyone a chance to prosecute an intercept. This night shift was in particularly good spirits, and Hardcastle worked to try to make himself as inconspicuous as possible during the flight.

He was offered one of the front starboard side-seats, coveted most by the passengers because of the big observation window on the right entranceway door and because it was close to the galley and the coffee pot; but he gave it up to one of the newcomers on the night shift and took one of the backseats near the aft-cargo ramp. He wadded up a spare jacket as a pillow and quickly fell asleep. It was one of the few times he had ever sat in the back of a Sea Lion; usually, by right of rank or position, he claimed at least the instructor pilot's jump seat and usually managed to get in some stick time. He didn't waste one minute of the forty-minute flight out to the platform – he pulled his seat belt tight, turned off the overhead light and was sound asleep before the hybrid airplane-chopper leveled off at eight thousand feet five minutes later.

Dozing off, he had an intimation that his dreams would be disturbing, and he was right on target. He dreamed that he and not J. C. Powell had gone on that mission to Verrettes, and worse, that he couldn't keep his cool as well as the young Air Force pilot had. He'd been shot down by Salazar's men, and McLanahan had been taken out of the

465

rear cockpit of the Sukhoi-27 and shot after he, Hardcastle, spoke English to him and gave him away. He saw this Salazar as a giant skull-headed figure with blazing red eyes, bony fingers and a black cloak who recognized Hardcastle right away and ordered his execution. He tried to make a run for the Sukhoi, to get out and warn the Hammerheads, but no matter how hard he tried, Salazar was right there, eyes blazing red, a huge knife clutched in his fleshless hand. His feet moved in slow motion, bogged down by sticky globs of blood from McLanahan's battered body. The skull-faced apparition hurled his knife, and it imbedded itself deep into his left arm, making it go numb. He tried to pull the knife free but it stuck there – the tighter he grasped the hilt the more it held on, threatening to saw off his whole arm . . . Suddenly the sky was filled with fighters and bombers and transports strafing and bombing the Hammerhead Two platform. Some of his crewmen were running around the platform pointing to the sky and calling out to him to stop the attacking planes but he could do nothing except try to pull the stiletto from his arm. The skull-faced Salazar was close, in his face, telling him to die like a man, let go of his miserable life, let go, let go . . .

'Let go, Admiral. C'mon, sir, wake up.'

Hardcastle's eyes snapped open. Lee Tanner, the on-coming duty controller on the Hammerhead Two platform, had one hand around Hardcastle's left arm, trying to shake him awake, and Hardcastle had a tight grip around Tanner's hand trying to pull it off. Hardcastle was huddled down in his seat. He quickly uncoiled himself and straightened up. 'What the hell is it, Lee?'

'Sorry, sir, you were having a bad dream.'

'Sorry, it's been one long damned day. What's going on?'

Tanner held out a hand to ask for quiet as he listened intently on his headset. 'Tanner, what the hell is going on?'

'No . . .' Tanner paused again and Hardcastle was about

466

to rip the headset from the controller when Tanner rolled his eyes skyward and shook his head with exaggerated exasperation. 'Those damned Dolphins,' he said, 'they're getting hosed – '

'One of *our* Dolphins? We lost a chopper? Who . . . ?'

'No, sir. The Miami Dolphins. The Buffalo Bills are kicking their butts all up and down Joe Robby Stadium – '

Hardcastle wanted to kill him. 'That's what you got me up for?'

'Well, I . . . you were having a bad dream, sir, and I thought . . .' He paused, looked at Hardcastle's murderous expression, muttered an apology, then made his way to the front of the cabin. The amused expressions of crewmembers around Hardcastle had disappeared as well.

A few minutes later Hardcastle made his way forward to accept a cup of coffee from a contrite Lee Tanner. But as he returned to his seat he had the same feeling he'd had before he dreamed off into a nightmare. Only now the bad feeling was about a reality yet to come . . .

Miami Air Route Traffic Control Center, Miami, Florida

'Miami Center, this is Sun and Sand three-fifty-one, with you at one-two thousand. Good evening.'

The air traffic controller in charge of frequency 127.30, the southern sector of Miami Air Route Traffic Control, hit the frequency-control button. 'Sundstrand Air Three-Five One, ident.' The controller, who had already received the flight's overwater flight plan filed several hours earlier from Willemstad Airport on the island of Curacao in the Netherlands Antilles, had already picked out the newcomer's radar blip as it inched its way across the Santaren Channel, now one hundred fifty miles south of Miami and heading toward Fort Lauderdale. He watched the blip with the altitude readout and the code for an unknown target light up with a bright yellow box around the data block, indicating that the pilot had hit his ident button. There he was, dead on time, dead on course.

'Sundstrand Three-Five-One, radar contact at one-two thousand. Good evening to you.'

The pilot replied by two friendly clicks on his transmitter. These pilots liked to call themselves 'Sun and Sand' instead of Sundstrand – they were the principal air-shuttle service from Florida, Georgia and Texas to the Netherlands Antilles with their casinos and beaches. Lucky devils. They spent their off days either in the casinos in Curacao or the beaches in Miami. Real tough life.

An outside network radio channel suddenly beeped to life with an insistently flashing button on the main keyboard channel. The controller knew that call was from the Zoo – the Border Security Force controllers in south Miami. The Hammerheads – or as the air traffic controllers sometimes called them, the Hammer*brains* – had a direct line with every agency with a radar scope in the entire southeast United States, and they used it a lot, too much, the controllers felt, with questions and orders for the pilots under FAA control.

FAA air-traffic controllers might be responsible for traffic separation and sequencing, but the new air-traffic regulations said that the Border Security Force had final authority over who was allowed into American airspace at all times. And they used their authority frequently and sometimes at the most inopportune moments. Usually seconds after assigning a pilot a certain altitude or heading to clear traffic the Hammerbrains would call and ask the controllers to check the guy's identification and flight plan, tell the controllers to issue a different heading or altitude, even make the guy orbit or divert to a different destination. It didn't matter that there were a dozen jets lined up behind the guy waiting to get in, or that the guy was low on fuel or didn't speak English that well. The Hammerbrains didn't have to deal with the pilots. No. It was the Miami Center controllers who got the complaints about clearance changes and deviations, not Border Security.

And their machines . . . It was not unusual for the Hammerbrains to send out a half-dozen planes into a crowded approach-corridor or intersection without a word of coordination or acknowledgement. And the unmanned planes, the ones controlled from dozens, sometimes hundreds, of miles away, were the scariest. One day one of those ten-thousand-pound remote-controlled mosquitos was going to fly through the cockpit of a 747 for sure.

Border Security planes also would soon stop acknowledging calls from anyone other than their own controllers when the action was getting hot. The FAA controllers would then have to get on the direct phone line and relay critical traffic advisories and warnings to the Border Security controllers. Even that broke down sometimes, and the FAA controllers had no choice but to clear the airspace for a hundred miles around a Border Security furball intercept to avoid collision alerts with civil traffic.

The Miami Center controller, Kravitz, put down his coffee cup. If he waited too long, he thought, the damned Hammerbrains would ring his supervisor. He hit the flashing button. 'Kravitz, southeast seven. Good evening, Aladdin,' Aladdin being the call-sign of the Border Security Force headquarters unit located in south Miami near, very appropriately, he thought, the Miami Zoo.

'I need a verification on Sierra-Alpha three-five-one,' a no-nonsense female voice said.

No 'hello,' no 'good evening,' no nothing. Typical Hammerbrain. 'What exactly do you need, *ma'am*?'

'We show his altitude as one-two thousand. Does that check?'

'Yes, it does. One-two-point zero-five – he's fifty feet off his altitude. Want me to bust him for you?' That was not wise, he told himself. The brass on both sides reviewed these running transcript tapes. Stop with the humor, Kravitz.

No appreciative reaction, though, from the lady. 'That's a bit low for a commercial plane so far offshore. We need to know why he's flying at twelve thousand and if he's going to stay at that altitude.'

Kravitz wondered what the big deal was. 'I'll ask him, if you really need the information. May I ask why the inquiry?'

'Our records show the Sundstrand planes are normally higher until crossing the ADIZ. They're equipped with speed brakes, so their pattern has been to fly high and do a steep idle-power descent in the terminal area. He is not following the profile.'

Kravitz shook his head. Border Security bitches with their super-powered computers could be a real bite in the ass. 'You want me to quiz this pilot because he's flying a few thousand feet lower than normal?'

'He's flying within three thousand feet of HIGHBAL's altitude,' she said, as if that explained everything.

'He'll be passing forty miles west of restricted airspace, ma'am,' Kravitz said. 'I think your beautiful blue balloon is safe.' The HIGHBAL radar balloon was flying near its maximum altitude tonight, protected by thirty miles of restricted airspace and by routes that were at least twenty miles outside that restricted zone. Besides, it was lit up like a sausage-shaped Christmas tree. No one ever went near it and its nearly two-mile-long tether – hitting them could ruin a pilot's whole day real fast.

'I need to know the reason, Mr Kravitz.' Boy, this one really had a stick up her ass.

'Stand by, please, ma'am,' Kravitz said with exaggerated

politeness. He hit the ground-to-air frequency button. 'Three-five-one, Miami Center with a request.'

'Go ahead.'

'State the reason for your present altitude, sir.'

'Say again?'

'Border Security requests the reason for your present altitude and how long you intend on staying at one-two zero, sir.' Mention Border Security this time, so maybe *they'll* take the heat.

'I didn't know I needed a reason to stay at this altitude, Center,' came the confused reply.

'You don't need a reason to stay at one-two-zero, sir. You're clear of traffic. Border Security requests a reason why you decided to fly at that altitude and how long you intend on staying there. Over.'

'I intend on staying there until it's time to land,' came the reply that Kravitz was expecting. The pilot's raised voice emphasized a much stronger Latino accent this time – no doubt the guy was a Latino pilot who worked at masking his normally accented English, a common practice, since a lot of controllers, employers and customers were prejudiced against Latino pilots, believing them to be not as well trained as Anglos.

'I copy, three-five-one. Any reason why you chose this particular altitude, sir?'

'What is this, Center? I pick an altitude, and you tell me if I'm cleared to fly that altitude. That's how it always goes. Would you like me at a different altitude?'

'Negative, three-five-one. You're cleared on course at one-two thousand. This request originated from US Border Security Force controllers in Miami. If you wish you can speak with them on frequency one-one-two point five-five.'

'I don't wanna talk to no goddamn Border Security. I'm following the rules. Why I bein' hassled?' The Latino accent was very strong now, and for the first time Kravitz felt a touch of apprehension. This pilot seemed to be losing it. There was a slight pause, then: 'Sorry about that, Center. I lost my head. We'll flip over to one-one two point five-five.'

'Three-five-one, cleared off Center frequency, monitor GUARD, report back up on my frequency,' Kravitz said.

'Three-five-one.'

Kravitz immediately dialed up the Border Security's flight common frequency and put it on his headset, loud enough to hear the transmissions but not loud enough so his assigned calls would be drowned out; then he leaned over and told the controllers near him about the interchange that was about to take place. Boy, this, he thought, is going to be good . . .

Hammerhead One Air Staging Platform

'Border Security, this is Sundstrand Air three-fifty-one on one-one-two point five-five.'

Angela 'Angel' Mink – a name she had tried to live down by joining the Coast Guard ten years earlier before transferring to Border Security – was the controller in charge of the southern sector of Hammerhead One's area of responsibility. Her sector extended from Puerto Rico to the center of Cuba and as far south as Hispaniola. Although the Hammerheads could only engage targets inside the boundaries of the Air Defense Identification Zone, which was very narrow in Mink's sector, she routinely tracked and studied radar targets throughout her area.

With her long blonde hair, sculptured face and athletic figure, Angel Mink looked like her name sounded. Both her name and appearance were the opposite of her

472

personality – shy, introverted, intellectual and all business on the platform. Her specialty, as Kravitz had guessed, was using the extraordinary power of the Border Security Force's computer network on nearly every radar target on sea or air within her sector.

The altitude readout of Sundstrand Air Flight 351 got the computer database's attention right away, and she had put it up on the duty controller's attention-list. With Geffar still on the beach recovering from her injuries, Michael Becker was in command of Hammerhead One; Becker had a trainee, Ricardo Motoika, in the duty controller's seat and was giving him a continuing lesson on how to keep track of the three main screens and the dozens of other messages and events going on in the command center.

Becker stepped away now from the raised commander's platform over to Angel Mink's station, moved his headset's microphone away to prevent eavesdropping over the command center's interphone and leaned over behind her left shoulder. 'What's so interesting?' he asked.

'Sun and Sand flight coming back from Curacao,' Mink told him, swiveling her microphone out of the way and wetting her lips with a sip of water. 'I think that's where you should take me when we go on leave together next month.'

'We're going on leave together? Since when?'

'Since I just fantasized it,' she replied. 'You and me, on the white sand beaches, skinny-dipping at midnight with a bottle of champagne.'

'All this time, I thought you were working over here.'

'I am a woman, Commander Becker . . .'

'Prove it, Technician Mink.'

'. . . We women can recall mountains of information on a suspected smuggler or terrorist, plan a romantic vacation and fantasize about a wildly passionate night with a gorgeous tight-assed hunk all at once. Two bad you men can think of only one thing at a time.'

473

'Then think about this, woman,' Becker told her. 'The beaches in Curacao have pink sand, not white. You fall asleep after one glass of champagne. And I already made reservations for us at the Barra Palace in the Barra da Tijuca. Look that up on your computer when you get some free time, Technician.' He moved his microphone back to his lips. 'Tell Ricardo what you got, Angel.'

'Ricardo, I've got Sundstrand three-five-one on flight common,' Mink reported. He nodded an acknowledgement as he searched the three high-definition screens for the plane's data block.

'Use your console screen to get the story on the event you want first,' Becker told him. He demonstrated how to call up Mink's screen onto the duty-controller's console and how to dial in the proper radio frequencies. 'Some other things you should be thinking about: notifying the commander if he or she is around, ascertaining the status of your flight deck and aircraft and thinking about how much time you have from the target's present position to when you need to make an intercept. That means thinking about the Seagull's performance factors, available crew, maintenance status of your Sea Lion planes – '

'All that just because Angel buzzed me about a scheduled inbound?' Ricardo Motoika interrupted. 'Nothing's happened yet and you're saying that I should be planning to take the guy down.'

'C'mon, Ricardo, you've been a radar controller for the Navy,' Becker said. 'When you buzzed the CIC deck officer with a target that looked flaky, what was his usual reaction?'

Motoika nodded, remembering back to his eight years as a combat air controller aboard the now-decommissioned USS *Coral Sea*. 'You're right. He got the flight boss or the OOD on the horn and got the word on the status of the flight deck and alert lines.'

'Your controllers here are the same breed. They see so many targets that when one really stands out it's usually serious. Okay. On your other screens you should have the video of the drone-catapult area called up, maybe with the ready status of the Seagulls superimposed on the same screen, and on the other you might want the flight status of the Sea Lion crews or deployed vessels in the area. Be able to brief the platform commanders on the situation when they check in. You buzzed Angel, you better be able to explain why. Meanwhile, have your controller talk to the target and find out what his story is.' Becker nodded to Mink, who turned to her radios:

'Sundstrand Air three-five-one, this is the Border Security Force, radar contact, one-zero-five miles south of Miami at one-two-thousand feet. Sir, verify your intentions to stay at your present altitude. Over.'

'Yes, ma'am, three-five-one would like to stay at twelve thousand until cleared to descend into Fort Lauderdale. I'm in an entry corridor, I'm at the minimum enroute altitude, I've got a flight plan and I've got clearance. Is there a problem?'

'We thought you might be having difficulty maintaining your normal cruise altitude, three-fifty-one,' Mink replied. She was making this up as she went along. *Something* was wrong there, but so far everything the guy was doing was legal. 'Are you encountering any problems, adverse flight conditions?'

'Negative, we're fine . . . We heard reports about rougher air higher so we decided to stay down here and enjoy the view. Over.'

'Bingo,' Mink said half-aloud. She called up the National Weather Service's upper-air weather charts for south Florida and the Caribbean. High pressure dominated the entire region, with a southerly flow of air. She clicked on her interphone to the duty controller: 'NWS says negative turbulence at his normal cruise altitude, and no pilot reports of any turbulence all night, Ricardo. He'd have a thirty-five-knot tailwind at his normal cruise altitude. Where he is, he's got a twelve-knot tailwind.'

Ricardo paused, then shook his head. 'So he's not flying at the most economical altitude. He's dead on course, dead on time, and he's following all the rules. What do we have on him? Nothing.' He turned to Becker. 'Right?'

Becker said nothing. Technically the guy was legit – but if he had a controller who was suspicious it was best not to drop things until everyone was satisfied. 'Play it out, Ricardo. You're the duty controller.' He motioned to Mink, who had turned around in her seat watching their exchange. 'Work with your controllers.'

Ricardo nodded, then said, 'Angel, I want you to piss this guy off again. Tell him we're going to divert him. Get his passenger list, home base, cargo, all that stuff and compare it with the flight plan he filed.'

Mink nodded and turned back to her radios: 'Copy all, three-fifty-one. Sir, we're having difficulty verifying your Customs clearance request. We must instruct you to divert to Opa-Locka Airport for inspection. Please acknowledge. Over.'

'Say *again*, Border Security?' came the thick Latino accent once again, louder and angrier than ever. 'You want me to go *where*?'

'Opa-Locka Airport,' Mink repeated. 'Sundstrand Air three-fifty-one, by order of the deputy chief of Border Security Forces unit one you are directed to proceed immediately by the most direct route, avoiding known restricted areas, and land at Opa-Locka Airport, Miami, and report immediately to the Customs Service inspection station there for records and aircraft inspection. This order is directive in nature, and deadly force is authorized to enforce compliance.

'Opa-Locka is currently VFR, landing runway two-seven right, visual or ILS approach in use. We will advise Miami Center of your new destination. Maintain heading and altitude and remain on this frequency. I will provide further traffic separation and flight routing. Sundstrand Air three-five one, acknowledge new clearance.'

The pilot was already responding . . . when Mink released her mike button they heard '. . . Can't do this . . . I have clearance to Fort Lauderdale, I am gonna hang you by your titties, *puta sucia* . . . I demand to speak with your supervisor right now. Over.'

'Three-fifty-one, I've notified my supervisor, please stand by,' Mink said. She didn't mind him sounding off on the open channel – this guy was going to get clobbered when he landed. The Hammerheads I-Team and the Customs Service CET at Miami International Airport, who would by now be rolling toward Opa-Locka Airport, would be listening in and would not take kindly to this guy's popping off.

'You had better get him on the line, lady,' the pilot retorted. 'You guys are crazy. I don't have no passengers on board. You can do your inspection at Fort Lauderdale. They got facilities there. Why don't you do your damned inspection there?'

Mink was typing on her keyboard, then sat waiting on the computer to retrieve the information she requested. 'I'm calling up his Customs clearance form to be sure,' she told Ricardo. 'But I think he's supposed to have passengers.'

'What?'

'Excuse me, Ricardo,' another controller cut in. 'Just a notice. Looks like CARABAL has dropped off the line.' He was referring to the aerostat radar balloon facility at the Hammerheads' land base on Grand Bahama Island one hundred twenty miles east of Palm Beach. Michael Becker moved back to his commander's console to check out the report himself.

'Make sure it's logged in to our system, then give them a call and see what's up.'

'You got it.'

'I'm not getting anything from Grand Bahama on the radio,' Becker said. 'I'll give them a try on the phone.'

'Got it, Ricardo,' Angel Mink suddenly chimed in. 'His Customs declaration form says eight passengers, all Americans. Social Security numbers, drivers' license numbers, the works.'

'Yet he tells us he doesn't have passengers,' Ricardo said. 'Ask him to verify.'

Suddenly the platform's emergency buzzer sounded three times and Becker promptly got on the address system: 'Attention on the platform, this is the command center. We have received notification that the aerostat radar unit on Grand Bahama Island has just come under attack and has been destroyed by hostile aircraft. I am placing this platform on yellow alert. Clear the flight deck and prepare for aircraft launch and recovery. Off-duty crew, report to emergency stations. Repeat, this platform is on yellow alert.' He turned to Ricardo. 'Broadcast an alert warning on all Border Security, Coast Guard and military channels, and clear the airspace for fifty miles around this platform.'

Most of the controllers and crewmen were watching the activity up on the commander's podium. 'Take your seats and watch your sectors,' Becker told them. 'Get your life jackets on but continue monitoring your sectors. Do it.'

One person did not get to her feet. Angel Mink only pressed her headphones tighter on her head against the noise in the control center and repeated into her radio, 'Sundstrand three-fifty-one, acknowledge. You are exiting the entry corridor and approaching restricted airspace. Turn left to heading three-five-zero immediately.' No reply. On interphone she called out, 'Mike, Sundstrand three-fifty-one has left the entry corridor and is heading for us. No response. His speed has increased to two-eighty. He's thirty-eight miles southwest, ETA eight minutes.'

Aboard Lion Two-Nine Heading Toward Hammerhead Two Platform

Hardcastle was making his way back to his seat in the rear of the V-22 shuttle with a cup of coffee – decaffeinated this time – when Lee Tanner touched his shoulder. 'Excuse me, sir . . .'

'Tanner, aren't you ever going to let me sleep?' But Tanner's face was serious this time. 'What is it? The Bills score again?'

'Broadcast on all freqs from Hammerhead One,' the controller said. 'They are at yellow alert. They said CARABAL was just attacked from the air – '

Hardcastle nearly took off Tanner's ears as he grabbed the headphones. 'Ken, what's going on?' he called up to the cockpit.

'No contact with CARABAL,' the pilot, Ken Sherry, replied. 'Platforms one and two are at yellow alert. Key West and the Zoo have been alerted.'

'What was that about an air attack?'

'Unconfirmed, sir,' Sherry told him. 'But Hammerhead One said something about an air attack on CARABAL.'

Hardcastle looked out the observation window on the starboard-side entry-hatch but it was pitch black outside. The crew in the back of the Sea Lion started to rustle uneasily, sensing the tension in Hardcastle's voice. 'Where are we?'

'Twenty miles west of the coast. Hammerhead Two is off the nose at twenty-five miles.'

'Turn us around and land us somewhere,' Hardcastle

ordered. 'Somewhere close – Naples or Southwest Regional . . .'

'But what about Hammerhead Two?'

'If they come under attack I don't want twenty-five more crewmembers on that platform. We can evacuate crewmembers better with an empty plane. Turn us around and get us on the ground pronto.'

The White House, Washington, DC

The President was in his familiar, blue, red and white nylon warm-up suit, a reminder of his former football years – when he met in the White House Situation Room with Vice President Martindale, Secretary of Defense Thomas Preston, the Chairman of the Joint Chiefs, Army General Randolph McKyer, the newly promoted White House Chief of Staff Jack Pledgeman, CIA Director Kenneth Mitchell and the just appointed National Security Advisor, Air Force General Wilbur Curtis. Other NSA and Cabinet officials were represented by top aides or deputies. Along with the top White House brass and their aides were Brad Elliott and Patrick McLanahan, sitting away from the group with their briefing boards and notes.

'With all due respect, General Elliott,' the President began irritably, 'what I see are a bunch of ifs and maybes here.' He turned to Vice President Martindale. 'What about it, Kevin? You send McLanahan and a kid pilot over Haiti in a' – he stopped, disbelieving what he was about to say – 'a Russian fighter plane. They're forced to land and are damn near taken into custody. Or worse. Now you're claiming that this military unit is a drug-smuggling ring?'

'The evidence may appear circumstantial but it's documented and verified, sir,' Martindale said. 'This base has been under surveillance by Border Security for some time.'

480

He was stretching the truth a bit, McLanahan thought, but it was necessary for now. 'Major McLanahan has evidence that the smugglers that killed those children, *threw* them out of their aircraft, landed at the base in question. I did therefore authorize General Elliott to use whatever assets at his disposal to investigate, and do it in a timely manner.'

'With a *Russian fighter plane*? Why did you use a Russian fighter?'

'It was the only aircraft available that could do the job, Mr President,' Elliott put in. 'We needed a plane that was fast and maneuverable for self-defense, but we were also trying not to spook the smugglers into running and hiding, which we felt would happen if we sent an American fighter or bomber. There are Cuban fighter bases with Russian planes near Haiti . . . a Russian plane seemed the logical choice – '

'And if they got caught or killed? We'd have a hell of a lot of explaining to do.'

'General Elliott's group is deniable and highly classified, Mr President,' Martindale said. 'White House or US government involvement would have been difficult if not impossible to prove.'

The President looked at Secretary of Defense Thomas Preston, who gave a slight nod. 'Even I was not aware that we had a flyable Sukhoi-27 fighter being flown by American pilots, Mr President,' Preston said. 'Although I would have preferred the use of a more . . . conventional aircraft for this mission, I am impressed with the results. However, I am still not entirely convinced that this group discovered by McLanahan here is a drug smuggling ring, and I am even less convinced that we should do anything about the situation at this time – '

'I *disagree*,' Martindale said. 'We need to go in there, with the Haitian government, such as it is, and break down that bunch right now. If we wait they escape and set up shop somewhere else and we have to find them all over again.'

Assistant Secretary of State for Central America Janet Johnson said: 'I checked on the legal status of this Colonel Agusto Salazar that Lieutenant Powell discovered in Haiti. It turned out Colonel Salazar is a district militia commander – '

'A *what*? You mean the guy's legitimate?'

'Salazar is a dual-national, a citizen of both Haiti and Panama, although he was born in Cuba and was a colonel in the Cuban Revolutionary Air Force,' Johnson said. 'He serves without compensation except for the right to establish a local militia in the west-central region of Haiti. He is under nominal command of the Haitian military and is authorized to arm and equip a fighting force in Verrettes.'

'The man is also an ex-Cuban military officer, tried and convicted of drug smuggling in Cuba,' CIA chief Kenneth Mitchell put in. 'His supporters, probably most of the soldiers and pilots there at Verrettes, broke him out of prison days before he was to be executed. My sources say he lives under the good graces of the Cuban regime by some big payoffs to the Cuban government. In exchange, his men and planes have virtually unrestricted access to Cuban airspace and waters for their activities, although they would never admit it, of course. After all, he operates out of Haiti.'

'So what's the bottom line, people?' the President cut in. 'Can we get this guy or what?'

'We can ask the Haitian government to turn him over to us,' Johnson replied. 'Salazar is a lot like Manual Noriega was in Panama – a military leader, a strongman, enjoying full protection and immunity of a government official. He's richer and more powerful than anyone else in Haiti . . .'

'Once we get permission from the Haitian government we can have him out of there in no time,' General McKyer said.

'Another invasion force?' the President said. 'We looked like bullies to the hemisphere when Bush invaded Panama.'

'But the operation worked, sir,' McKyer said. 'We got Noriega. The man is serving time – '

'If we move into Haiti we'll lock in the condemnation of the entire world,' Johnson said. 'They're already calling us empire-building bullies, invading neighboring states whenever we feel we need to. I'd recommend against that course of action.'

'I must agree,' Thomas Preston said. Martindale's shoulders slumped – he knew how important Preston's voice was in all of the President's decisions. 'The situation with this Salazar character is much different from that with Noriega. Noriega took control of Panama by trying to kill off the opposition and by nullifying the free elections. *And* he declared war on the United States and threatened to destroy the Panama Canal. The decision to invade Panama was a necessary one, a defensible one. Besides, we already had a sizeable force in place. We would have no such advantage in Haiti. We're not at war with the government there, no one in Haiti has declared war on us, and this Salazar doesn't threaten the security of either Haiti or the United States . . .'

'I agree, Thomas,' the President said to Preston. He turned to Martindale. 'We can begin actions against Salazar that will show our displeasure at his actions – maybe even indict him for drug trafficking the way we did Noriega, and we can get the cooperation of the Haitian government in monitoring his activities. But nothing I've heard justifies a *military* action against this guy. It's out of the question. We can't possibly identify *anything* he's done.'

'Except, of course, for his drug smuggling,' Elliott said quietly, the tension nonetheless loud and clear in his voice.

'His *alleged* drug smuggling,' Johnson corrected. 'If we're going to indict him we might as well start thinking legally.'

'If we *can* indict him,' McKyer said. He looked at Elliott – it was obvious that McKyer did not think highly of the White House's esteemed trouble-shooter. 'Our best evidence that this Salazar is in Haiti was obtained from American servicemen flying a Russian plane uninvited into Haitian airspace. Not exactly prime evidence for a grand jury. Fruit of the poison tree, I think is the legal expression.'

'That mission was an authorized government secret operation, general,' Martindale said quickly. 'We can protect our sources and methods, and the evidence is still admissible in any court in this country.'

'We have to do this thing right,' the President said. His tone signaled that this meeting was definitely coming to an end. 'If we don't have a solid footing, unless the guy does something stupid like . . . I don't know, like attack the United States or one of our ships in the Caribbean, we can't move against him – '

'I believe he already has, sir,' Elliott said. 'We're analyzing the photos we took over Verrettes to see if we could possibly match a plane there with the wreckage of the plane shot down over the Everglades two years ago, as well as some of the other drug planes seized or destroyed since. I think we can find enough evidence to prove that one of Salazar's planes attacked and destroyed our Coast Guard patrol plane.' Elliott stood. 'But I can't emphasize enough, Mr President – that base at Verrettes is a major threat to our national security.'

'It won't fly, Brad,' the President replied. 'Analyzing those photos is a positive step, and if you find something that we can go on, then we'll take it up then. Otherwise we'll continue with what we're doing.' The President stood and straightened his warm-up jacket. 'Thank you all for coming. Sorry to keep you up at such a late hour.'

A few of the Cabinet sidled up to the President to speak with him privately. Pledgeman began herding Elliott, McLanahan and the others out of the Situation Room when a silenced phone began flashing its ringer-light on the table in the center of the room. Simultaneously, beepers on the belts of several persons in the room went off, including those of Preston, Curtis and Elliott.

Preston's aide answered the phone as the men cut off their beepers. 'Message from the communications center, sir,' the aide said. As Preston moved to the phone the aide motioned to Elliott. 'Call for you, sir, from your head-quarters. The comm center says it's an urgent.'

Elliott took the receiver, listened, then in a loud voice to get the others' attention, said, 'Say that again.' A moment later he said, 'I'll be in touch,' and hung up.

'The aerostat radar balloon site in the Bahamas has been destroyed by an air attack, Mr President,' Elliott said in a loud voice. The announcement silenced every voice in the room. 'Both Border Security Force air-staging platforms are now believed to be under attack by light aircraft.'

Hammerhead One Air Staging Platform

Angel Mink's digital color display was in a ten-mile range, configured so as to show both Lion Two-One, the AV-22 tilt-rotor launched from the Hammerhead One platform only moments before, and the Sundstrand Air target aircraft. The two aircraft were on opposite sides of the rectangular screen, like knights at opposite sides of the lists ready to charge.

And, virtually superimposed over the computer symbol representing the Hammerheads' aircraft, was the symbol representing the Hammerhead One platform. Less than ten miles away – about two more minutes – and the plane, whatever its intention, would be right on top of them.

'Two-One, your target is at eleven o'clock, nine miles,' she reported. 'You are clear to engage. Suggest left turns to evade. Seagull One is at your four o'clock, five miles, on auto intercept.'

'Roger.' The AV-22's pilot sounded even more worried than Mink. Then: 'Two-One has a judy. Two-One has radar contact, maneuvering to intercept.'

'Negative,' Michael Becker cut in. 'You're not doing a tail chase, Two-One. We don't have the time. Engage at long range, then pivot and engage again. Use your aircraft's capabilities and stay behind him.' On interphone Becker directed, 'Keep broadcasting warning messages, dammit.' There was still a glimmer of hope, remote now, that this guy was lost or disorientated and had started flying off course and toward the platform at the same moment that CARABAL went off the air.

'Target altitude now one thousand and descending,' Mink reported to the command-center crew. 'Seven miles from Two-One and closing, twelve o'clock, now five miles.'

'Mike, Homestead is launching alert fighters in support,' one of the controllers reported. 'We've got one F-16, designation Trap One, thirty miles out and closing at Mach one point two. Two are heading toward Key West and one toward Hammerhead Two.' Mink expanded her scope to include the Air Force F-16.

'Two-One, missiles away,' the pilot on the AV-22 reported. He was shooting at the Sea Stinger missile's extreme range-limit, at a head-on propeller-driven target at low altitude – the odds of a hit were not good. A controller began broadcasting navigation-warning messages to alert aircraft and vessels in the area.

The result was not long in coming. 'Miss,' the pilot

aboard the AV-22 reported, 'I didn't have a solid lock-on. I'm lining up on him again.'

'The F-16 is at twenty miles, now at Mach one point two,' Mink reported. 'He says he has a radar lock on both aircraft and he wants the V-22 to move away.'

'What's his ETA?'

'Ninety seconds to intercept,' Mink said. 'Same as the target's ETA to the platform.'

Becker hesitated. The AV-22 was only miles away from the intruder but it would take him precious seconds to maneuver for a high probability of a hit – the AV-22's weapons were not designed for long-range attacks but for rear-quarter attacks within visual range. By the time the AV-22 had a chance to really get into position to stop the intruder it could be too late.

The F-16 had a long-range radar-guided missile – it was probably ready to strike right now at twenty miles' range. It could also close in quickly and finish the job with its murderous twenty-millimeter multibarrel air-to-air cannon. But if it missed on its high-speed head-on pass it would be too late to stop the intruder – an F-16 travelling at Mach one had a turn-radius of over thirty miles, especially with its restrictive fuel tanks, fuel load, and weapons load that prevented the pilot from pulling high-g turns. It could not reattack in time before the target reached the platform.

And there was another problem nagging at his brain – what if this guy *wasn't* an attacker at all? His records didn't check out and he was certainly doing some very suspicious things, and it was happening at the same time their radar post in the Bahamas was apparently under attack. But records were known to be wrong, pilots often did weird and unexplainable things (especially at night, overwater and during confusing incidents such as this), and the attack (if it *was* an attack) in the Bahamas and this incident *could* be a monstrous coincidence . . .

'Are there any responses to our warning calls?' Becker asked.

'Nothing, Mike.'

'I need clearance for the F-16 to move in, Mike,' Mink said. 'Sixty seconds to intercept. He's decelerated just above the Mach for weapons release but he's coming in hot.'

'Damn it,' Becker muttered, 'keep making warning calls. Tell him he's about to be blown out of the sky.' He knew he had just been paralyzed into indecision but he had no choice but to take the time to think this one through . . .

The Border Security Force wasn't supposed to strike at a target without visual identification and communication – that had been a Hardcastle concern when he was drawing up the Hammerheads' lethal-intercept concept. They had always waited until they positively communicated with an intruder with visual hand or light signals before even considering an attack. Usually the sight of a Seagull drone flying off your wing, or a Sea Lion tilt-rotor airplane with guns and missiles was enough to scare most intruders into submission. Not all, but most. The one common denominator in all this was that they gave the intruder ample time to comply with warning signals before attacking – and that always meant positive visual signals. Without relying on radios, the intruders always knew they had been caught, and the ones that chose to ignore the warnings were the ones that got smoked . . .

'Michael . . .'

But, damn it, this time was different, wasn't it? The situation with the terrorist group in Haiti, the attack in the Bahamas, the increased tension . . . he couldn't let anything happen to the platform. Fifty people on his platform were counting on him. He had a responsibility . . . to protect the *public*, not just the Hammerheads. A wrongful death would destroy everything that Ian Hardcastle had worked so long to achieve. He couldn't attack this guy without positive ID no matter what he was doing, no matter what the potential threat. He had to be sure . . .

'Tell Two-One to intercept and identify that bastard,' Becker ordered. 'Tell the F-16 to break off the attack and stand by.'

'Trap One, Trap One, disengage and clear,' Mink called over the radio. On interphone she said, 'F-16 is climbing . . . he's clear.' Seconds later they heard a rolling rush of sound, then a sharp BOOM that rattled the windows of the command center as the sonic wave swept over the platform.

'I want a standard intercept, light signals and warning flares,' Becker shouted. 'Get on his ass, get a light in his cockpit but don't attack until he sees your FOLLOW ME lights. Is that clear?'

'Two-One copies. I'm turning and moving into position. My lights are on him and he's not responding.'

'Thirty seconds to arrival.'

'Two-One has radar lock . . . Two-One has missile lock. Am I clear to engage?'

'Get beside him, Two-One,' Becker ordered. 'Close to gun range. Try a warning shot . . .'

'I can see the platform, Becker,' the pilot called out. 'He's heading right for the platform. He's too close, I've got a missile lock. Am I clear to engage?'

'Hold your fire. Get beside him. Make him turn away . . .'

'It's too late for that, Mike. He's going to hit. *Am I clear to engage?*'

'Sound the platform alarm,' Becker ordered. 'Remain on yellow alert but warn the crew of – '

Suddenly, booming over the controller's headphones, they heard: 'Border Security, this is Sundstrand three-five-one.' The voice was high-pitched, almost a screech. Becker had never heard such terror in a man's voice since Vietnam.

489

'Don't shoot, don't shoot, can you hear me, *don't kill me* . . .'

'Get him turned away from the platform, Angel,' Becker shouted.

'Sundstrand three-five-one, this is the Border Security Force. If you can hear me, turn right immediately. Turn right forty degrees or you will be attacked . . .'

The reaction was instantaneous. The target-aircraft veered at what appeared to be a tight hard bank angle and headed away from the platform. Mink took a breath as if it was her first in several minutes. 'Target turning right, heading zero-four-zero, climbing. Well clear of the platform.' Several crewmembers allowed groans of relief. Becker found he had gotten to his feet and was leaning over the front edge of his commander's console, then dropped back into his seat, removed his headphones and rubbed his eyes.

'Have Two-One escort that sonofabitch Sundstrand Air flight to the Zoo,' Becker ordered. 'I'd like personally to bust that guy right in the face. Tell the F-16 thanks for the assist and send him home.'

'Roger,' Mink said. On the tactical frequency she announced, 'Trap One, this is Hammerhead One. Our target is clear and responding. Thanks for the assist.' Mink reconfigured her scope back to its standard fifty-mile display and checked the traffic between the F-16 and Homestead Air Force Base to the northwest. 'Clear on heading three-five-zero, take ten thousand feet, contact Homestead Approach on one-one-eight point one. Good night.'

Mink saw the newcomers just as the pilot of the F-16 responded, 'Stand by, Hammerhead One. I've got a – '

On interphone, Mink called out, 'I've got two targets bearing zero-seven-zero, ten miles, altitude five hundred feet, speed four hundred knots. Closing on us fast. One more up high, near the F-16.' On the radio, she called out: 'Trap One, I have traffic at your six o'clock, eight miles. His indicated air speed is – '

Suddenly on the emergency GUARD channel they heard, 'Mayday, mayday, mayday, Trap One, five miles southwest of the Hammerhead One platform. I am under attack. I am hit. I am hit.' The GUARD channel broadcasts overrode all others, and the pilot's calls got more and more frantic – until they cut off completely.

'I'm picking up an emergency locator beacon,' Mink said. 'The F-16 . . . I think the F-16 is down.'

'What the hell is going *on*, Angel?' Becker said.

'Three planes . . . no, I count four, four planes just appeared out of nowhere. I was in short range and never saw them. Two are up high around the F-16. Two more are off to the northeast, coming at us at high speed. No identification, no flight plans.'

'Launch all available Sea Lions,' Becker shouted. 'Broadcast warning messages on all frequencies.' He looked up at the faces of the command-center crew, then, his attention directed at several who were standing at their consoles, he told them, 'Sound the emergency alarm. Report to the rescue stations.' He motioned for Angel Mink to run for the exits, but she only turned in her seat, took off her headphones and watched . . .

A few of those crewmembers, the younger and less experienced ones, bolted for the emergency slide that would get them to the lifeboats on the lower level. Most stayed by their consoles, continuing to issue advisories and warnings as two AV-22 Sea Lion aircraft lifted off, followed by a third; the last AV-22 was being raised up onto the flight deck on the central elevator when the planes struck.

'Splash one,' the radio message reported.

'Very good, fangs, very good,' Agusto Salazar radioed to

his wingmen from the lead fighter. 'Claws engaging. Fangs, take the high CAP and be ready to run.'

Because they were so close to the air-defense units of the United States, all four jet fighters of the Cuchillos' strike team were heavily armed for air-to-air combat, even though that one F-16 would be the only fighter they would encounter. One MiG-21 carried two fuel tanks, two radar-guided missiles, two heat-seeking missiles and a twenty-three-millimeter cannon. One Dassault-Breguet Mirage F1C needed only one fuel tank for the strike mission; it carried two thirty-millimeter cannons and four missiles. These were the fangs, the Cuchillos' fighters reserved for air cover for the other two jets.

The other MiG-21 and Mirage F1C were also equipped for self-defense, each carrying two medium-range radar-guided missiles along with their external fuel tanks in case a wave of air-defense fighters jumped the Cuchillos' planes, which left room for only two air-to-ground strike weapons apiece. Salazar equipped these strike planes, the claws, with a single six-hundred-pound BL755 clusterbomb unit to strike the Hammerheads' aerostat radar site in the Bahamas. Each British-built BL755 CBU carried one hundred and forty smaller two-pound submunitions, which scattered all across the aerostat site and control center and devastated the entire area. That had left room for only one relatively small, lightweight weapon with which to strike the Hammerhead One platform itself.

The Argentinian-made Martin Pescador, the Kingfisher antiship missile, was the most devastating strike weapon in the Cuchillos' arsenal. It weighed only three hundred pounds but it could fly for two or three miles at a speed of well over Mach one, and even without its eighty-eight-pound high-explosive warhead, its destructive power was enormous. Thanks to the large numbers of Kingfisher missiles put on the international arms market after the Falklands War, when the world discovered the awesome power of the Exocet missile, the Kingfisher was a relative bargain by the time Salazar went shopping for weapons. The MiG and Mirage fighters designated for the strike each carried one Kingfisher missile.

'Claws engaging, lead's in first. Good hunting.' Salazar's MiG-21 and the other Mirage F1C fighter slowed to below Mach 0.5 for weapons release, and launched missiles in a shallow dive when just outside two miles from the platform. The Kingfisher missiles were radio-controlled, and even at night from two miles out and with the platform blacked out it was a simple target. The fighters had to continue flying toward the platform to aim the missiles all the way to impact, so, unlike the cluster bomb attack, they got the opportunity to watch the fireworks from start to finish . . .

Both missiles hit the flight deck of the Hammerhead One platform at almost the same instant, one hitting near the aerostat-recovery pad and the other directly on the central elevator with the Sea Lion aircraft still on it. The nose of the Kingfisher missile was actually a titanium projectile designed to split open the skin of a vessel and allow the high-explosive warhead to penetrate inside the ship before exploding. That was exactly what occurred.

The first missile ripped through the second level easily, the warhead piercing the roof of the second-story command center before detonating. The explosion shelled out the command center and most of the east half of the second and third levels of the platform, killing everyone remaining in the command center and buckling the flight deck on the east side. The control tower on the northeast corner collapsed into the crater, and the aerostat mooring and control systems ruptured from the blast, releasing the aerostat balloon and sending the two-mile long, four-thousand-pound mooring cable crashing back on deck.

'Dead center, dead center!' Salazar announced over the radio.

The second missile powered through the flight deck, sending the explosive warhead into the three-story maintenance hangar before detonating. One AV-22 aircraft and one Dolphin helicopter were destroyed in the blast and fire. Twenty people were killed instantly. The overpressure from the fuel explosion blew out the entire west side of the platform, shearing loose the connecting points of two of the four massive legs supporting the platform.

Weakened and wracked by secondary explosions, the entire west side of the platform collapsed into the sea, and the two legs buckled, sagged, and toppled over. Four of the six legs did hold, but not enough to keep the entire platform from rolling onto its destroyed side. The remaining legs kept the structure from capsizing, but all of the lower decks and half of the flight deck hit the water and flooded. Fires burned out of control, and leaking fuel and oil spread across the ocean surface, setting the water on fire for a mile in every direction.

In sixty seconds, the first Border Security Force air staging platform was destroyed, and the four fighters were at maximum speed heading south to safety. The AV-22 aircraft that were airborne at the time of the attack began rescue operations, but they would soon learn the grisly details – forty-one men and women on the platform had lost their lives, including Michael Becker, Angel Mink and Ricardo Motoika.

Chapter Eight

Aboard the AV-22 Aircraft Lion Two-Nine, in West Florida

'Attention all aircraft, attention all aircraft, this is an air defense emergency warning message from the United States Border Security Force,' the radio transmission began. 'Be advised, SCATANA is implemented immediately in the Jacksonville, Miami and eastern Houston air traffic control regions. Repeat, SCATANA procedures will be implemented immediately. All aircraft in receipt of this message stand by for emergency air-travel instructions.'

Hardcastle felt a shudder through the V-22C Sea Lion aircraft as the pilots heard the warning message and accidentally nudged the controls, as if the airplane was expressing the fear the pilots felt at that moment, the fear that something you once thought was invulnerable and strong – namely, the continental United States itself – had been breached and attacked by an unseen, unknown enemy. SCATANA, the mouthful acronym for Security Control of Air Traffic and Air Navigation Aids, was the plan developed to control inbound and coastal traffic in the United States and to deny the use of U.S. radio navigation aids to enemy aircraft in the event of a wartime emergency. Except for infrequent exercises this was the first time SCATANA had been implemented in the continental United States since its inception during the Cuban Missile Crisis.

'All IFR and VFR aircraft entering or transiting the

United States on approved flight plans on all Alpha and Bravo corridors and on Victor routes 157, 539 and 225, stand by for divert instructions,' the message, broadcast on UHF and VHF GUARD emergency radio stations, continued. The message was also being broadcast on marine radio channels, high-frequency and short-wave stations and on satellite and TV networks that provided weather and information services to mariners and commercial pilots. 'Be prepared for radio navigation aid interruption. All IFR aircraft, divert, and emergency instructions will be issued by your controller. All other aircraft, exit American airspace immediately or you may be fired on without warning. Contact the United States Border Security Force on VHF frequency 121.5 or UHF frequency 243.0 for assistance.' The message began to repeat, both in English and Spanish, and then instructions for aircraft in specific sectors or destinations began air.

Hardcastle felt a knot tighten in his stomach as he listened to the broadcasts. SCATANA procedures were designed way back in the early sixties to deny enemy bombers the use of America's extensive air-navigation system during an attack. Under SCATANA, the Border Security Force and the military could shut down all radio transmitters that could be used as navigation or location markers – including commercial and private radio and TV stations located within a hundred miles of the coastline, as well as federal air-navigation facilities – and all for an indefinite period of time. In an age of diminished military budgets, nuclear disarmament and worldwide *perestroika*, SCATANA was considered by many to be almost an anachronism, a relic of the disappearing Cold War. An air attack against the United States was considered a fantasy.

But someone had actually dared to do it. Someone had targeted the Hammerheads' radar network for precise, coordinated air attacks . . .

Agusto Salazar, Hardcastle thought immediately. It had to be. The high-tech Cuban drug smuggler, the so-called district military commander of Haiti that commanded more concentrated firepower than several Caribbean nations combined, had actually dared attack the United States' offshore drug-interdiction facilities.

Salazar might be a fanatic, even crazy, but right now this man had the upper hand. Somehow, the attacking aircraft had sneaked through the radar coverage in the confusion over the report of an attack on the CARABAL aerostat station, and they had destroyed or disabled HIGHBAL. No transmissions and no radar data were available from that station. No messages except for the SCATANA warning messages had been received. The KEYSTONE, NAPALM (nickname for the Hammerhead Two aerostat unit located off the coast from Naples, Florida) and even the Navy radar sites at Guantanamo Bay in Cuba and the Border Security Force sites in Puerto Rico and the Turks and Caicos Islands might be in imminent danger.

Hardcastle and his AV-22 shuttle were now on the ground at Naples Municipal Airport on the west coast of Florida about fifty miles east of the Hammerhead Two platform. They had just pulled up near the small Airport Authority general aviation terminal, to the wide-eyed shock of the teenagers in their golf carts who usually met the small single-engine airplanes, washed the windows and checked the fuel and oil. He undogged and opened the starboard-side hatch and was greeted by a teenage girl in yellow shorts and a blue satin jacket carrying a bucket with windshield cleaning supplies and another with cold soft drinks and a Thermos of coffee.

'Welcome to Naples Airport Executive Terminal, sir,' the obviously confused but determined young woman began. 'I'm Jennifer. Can I . . . check your oil or some-thing?' Jennifer was going to do her job, whether it was a

497

rag-wing biplane or a Concorde jet that pulled up to her terminal. Hardcastle told her to stay away from the engine nacelles and the rear cargo ramp and ran to the executive terminal building.

The evening airport manager at the terminal, less stunned by the Sea Lion's arrival, had the phone out on the countertop and did not say a word as Hardcastle ran inside and dialed the line to the duty-controller's desk at Border Security Force headquarters at Aladdin City.

As Annette Fields answered the phone, Hardcastle could hear a confusion of voices in the background, the excited, tense voices of controllers talking with uncharacteristically loud voices. It had to be a madhouse out there. 'Aladdin, duty controller. Stand by . . .'

'This is Hardcastle, Annette.'

'Ian, I'm glad you called on the land line. The radios are a mess. I see on the status board that you're down, but where the hell are you? Are you okay?'

'We landed at Naples Municipal. The crew and the plane are safe. I heard the SCATANA warning. Can you give me the situation? Where do you need Lion Two-Nine?'

'I think the best place for you and the crew is back here at the Zoo,' Fields said. 'Hammerhead One was hit. Bad. Reports from some of the Sea Lion birds that made it off said that the platform was hit by two missiles launched from high-speed fighters. The platform was heavily damaged and on fire.'

Hardcastle was struck dumb by the horror of the news. He swallowed hard. 'Casualties?'

'No count yet.' The reply was wooden. Hardcastle could imagine what the answer was. 'Two Sea Lions made it off. Each had five on board. They're involved in rescue operations now.' What Hardcastle was expecting was left unsaid – the rescue crews had not recovered any survivors.

'I'll bring Two-Nine to the Zoo, drop off the crew and

head on over to Hammerhead One. How many Sea Lions does Hammerhead Two have available?'

'Four, plus two Dolphins. All their planes are airborne and ready.'

'They're all set in case of an attack,' Hardcastle said. 'The bird I've got is in shuttle configuration only – it's no good for rescue work. I'll go back to Aladdin with the crew, refuel, take out the seats and put on a winch, boats and a gun pod.'

'All right, I'll be expecting you. I'll have a maintenance crew standing by to configure your plane.'

'Any word from KEYSTONE or any marine units?'

'KEYSTONE and Hammerhead Two are still on the air,' Fields said. 'We're expecting attacks on them but the air traffic situation is a nightmare. We're trying to sort it out but – '

'You've got to keep aircraft away from those sites, Annette,' Hardcastle said. 'If they shut down NAPALM and KEYSTONE . . .'

'I know, I know. We'll be blind. But no one would be crazy enough to try to attack those two sites. KEYSTONE is on U.S. territory and Hammerhead Two is too far north.'

Hardcastle thought about Salazar trying to kidnap their 'Russian' fighter crew earlier that same day – hell, he'd try anything, especially if he felt threatened. 'Don't bet on it, Annette. What about the jets that attacked HIGHBAL? Are they headed toward KEYSTONE or Hammerhead Two?'

'KEYSTONE tracked the four jets that hit CARABAL and HIGHBAL heading south by southeast at high speed and low altitude. It looks like they're done for the day. We're trying to get a fix on their destination.'

'I can tell you what their damned destination is . . .' But Hardcastle paused. During his conversation a crowd had begun to gather around him, all wanting to know what was

499

happening. 'I'll see you in twenty minutes,' he said abruptly and hung up.

Over the Dry Tortugas, Eighty Miles South of the Hammerhead Two Platform

Even with weeks of planning, days of briefings and practice runs it would have been difficult for even the best-trained air crews to execute the two-pronged strike mission against the Hammerhead air-staging platforms precisely on time. Yet the Cuchillos were doing it with an outdated, untested plan, with a few hours of briefing and preparation and no practice runs. Having the two separate strike packages only ten minutes off was a minor miracle – a miracle that spoke well of the skills of the Cuchillo pilots and had an unexpected consequence.

The four Cuchillo jets striking CARABAL and Hammerhead One had to fly fourteen hundred miles, much of it at low altitude, to destroy both radar sites and return to Verrettes; it was easy for communications to break down, route timing to deteriorate, corrections not to be made. In the heat of battle, especially if under attack, force-timing and strike-package integrity were sacrificed to survive. If the plan was discovered it was important to get your plane over the target, evade the defenders and worry about coordination and timing later. These pilots would be flying right down the barrel of the gun, directly at the heart of the Border Security Force's center of operations.

The second group of strike aircraft, another group of two MiG-21 fighters and Mirage F1C fighter-bombers, had to fly almost eighteen hundred miles to complete their mission, all but twenty minutes of the flight flown in relative safety. The second-strike package had traveled from Haiti up along the north coast of Cuba, following established airways and talking with Cuban military flight controllers. With such routeing the planes attracted almost no attention from the Border Security Force, who routinely monitored all such flights. When the planes suddenly turned north-ward, the attack on the aerostat site on Grand Bahama Island had been completed and the attack on Hammerhead One was underway. The confusion factor was very great as all attention was focused on events to the east.

But the Cuchillo fighters were still several minutes from Cudjoe Key, the big island in the Florida Keys chain where the aerostat radar balloon was located; for obvious reasons – namely the Naval Air Station, Coast Guard and Border Security Force bases – the Hammerheads' base itself was not a target: only the balloon-tether site, located fifteen miles away, was to be destroyed.

But the first-strike package had hit early. The attacks on CARABAL and KEYSTONE were supposed to have been simultaneous; now American fighters were swarming over the skies even before the Hammerhead One platform had been hit, and the first target of the second group had still not been touched.

The leader of the second-strike group swore into his oxygen mask as the radio messages and warnings began. They were nearly ten minutes behind time when the radar site on Grand Bahama Island was struck – the second group was not yet in American airspace, let alone in position to launch their attack.

'Gold Group, this is Gold One,' the leader radioed to his group. 'Silver Group has apparently struck his first target. Warning messages have been transmitted on the emergency frequencies.'

'What will we do?' one of the other pilots asked in Spanish. They all had the same question, but only the youngest, the least disciplined, was scared enough to ask. The feeling was one of nakedness, helplessness. It was as if the whole world could see you, that every missile and every gun was pointed in your direction.

'First, we will *maintain radio silence*,' the leader replied angrily in English. Even though their transmissions were scrambled, it was an antiquated and easily broken mechanical scrambling routine. Non-tactical transmissions were supposed to be done in English in case of eaves-dropping – a lot of military talk in English would be less suspicious to eavesdroppers than a foreign tongue. 'Formation changes, fangs and claws, now.'

The formation was originally in their strike-and-cover arrangement – the fang, who was the leader in the MiG-21 paired with the Mirage on his left wing, and the claws, the air-cover MiG and Mirage fighters on the leader's right wing. At the leader's command the air-cover Mirage took spacing on the strike MiG by flying a few hundred yards to the leader's right; then the strike Mirage on the leader's left wing slowed and passed underneath his comrades, joining on the Mirage's right wing. The formation was now broken up into two formations of similar aircraft, with one strike and one air-cover fighter in each group.

'Leader's group will take the platform, the rest take the radar site. Gold Three, monitor the Border Security Force tactical channel. We will meet on the rendezvous channel in fifteen minutes to plan a join-up. Good luck.' The leader with his MiG-21 banked left to get on course for the platform. The other group banked right to clear the formation and began their attack run on the KEYSTONE radar site.

Border Security Force Headquarters Command Center, Aladdin City

On the radar displays of west and southwest Florida it was a

502

madhouse. Airplanes were everywhere. Airliners with hundreds of passengers were within a thousand feet, and sometimes within five hundred feet, of small single- and twin-engine planes; every pilot up there was calling in for instructions or clarification. The FAA controllers were overloaded with traffic-collision alerts as planes scrambled to find someplace to land before the shooting started. With radio navigation aids selectively blocked out by the Hammerheads, planes were reporting themselves lost or drifting out of their assigned corridors. Intruder as well as collision alerts were flashing on the boards.

And now the Air Force was entering the picture. F-16 interceptors from the 125th Fighter Interceptor Group at Homestead Air Force Base were responding to the air-defense warning; a few fighters from the 56th Tactical Training Wing at MacDill AFB, an F-16 replacement training base near Tampa, were flitting around the area itching to get in on some action. And now fighters from the 125th Fighter Interceptor Group at Jacksonville, the parent group of the Florida-based fighters, were moving in to reinforce their detachment at Homestead AFB. Every civilian plane in the sky began expressing their concern about being the target of an F-16 attack, and several reported seeing bombs going off, missiles being launched, explosions rocking the sky. Military controllers of the Air Force Southeast Air Defense Sector at Tyndall Air Force Base in northwest Florida wanted to take charge of the situation now that the F-16s were airborne – even after nearly three years of operation, no one yet completely trusted the Border Security Force with anything but their own aircraft. It was bedlam.

Annette Fields at the duty-controller's desk at the Aladdin City command center had a big job – to sort out the legitimate air traffic, find the real intruders and keep everyone away from the NAPALM, KEYSTONE and

ALADDIN radar sites. Each site had two major air-traffic corridors running across the aerostat's restricted airspace spots. Alpha-758 and Alpha-39 from the Yucatán Peninsula of Mexico to Miami ran just twenty miles south of Hammerhead Two and was widely travelled by Central American planes as well as planes from the west side of South America. Golf-448 ran from Venezuela to Marathon, Florida – the major north–south airway from the Caribbean and South America to the United States – and although it was thirty miles from the KEYSTONE site it was of real concern to Fields.

The worst security threat came on Bravo-646, the major east–west route from South and Central America to the Bahamas – this one used the Key West VORTAC radio navigation facility as a major checkpoint, which placed the route almost directly over KEYSTONE; the northern edge of Bravo-646's flight route corridor actually touched the edge of KEYSTONE's protective restricted airspace. Overflights and collision alerts with the big KEYSTONE balloon, which at fourteen thousand feet altitude placed it very close to most air traffic on Bravo-646, were common.

Fields' only option was to keep all air traffic south of Bravo-646 – that was the only way to insure that all aircraft would stay at least thirty miles from each site. Once clear of KEYSTONE, Miami Air Route Traffic Control Center would put them back on their flight plan routing or vector them for the approach into the Miami or Fort Lauderdale area. It sounded easy, but Fields' order was creating havoc. On top of all this the Hammerheads still had to make sure that no smugglers used this opportunity of confusion to sneak past the radar cordon. Even with the radar-detection systems operating at full capability it was sometimes easy for a small fast plane to fly very close to an airliner and merge their radar returns.

'Key West Approach, this is Aladdin, I need Mexicali

one-seven-niner charlie vectored clear of Bravo-646,'
Fields heard one of her controllers, Darrell Fjelmann, tell
the FAA air-traffic controllers. 'I don't care if he's not
following your vectors. I need it right now . . . do it
immediately or there might be an accident . . . I mean he
might get a missile up the kazoo, sir, and you've received
fair warning. Now clear that route.' Fjelmann pounded the
button to cut off the channel, then spun wearily in his chair
and rubbed his eyes.

'Hang in there, Darrell, hang in there,' Fields told him.

'Annette, Lion Two-Two is coming in from Hammerhead One,' another controller reported. 'They might have
a survivor.'

After that announcement the Hammerheads on duty
latched onto even the dimmest glimmer of hope out of that
evening's horror. 'Tell Two-Two to head directly to
Homestead,' Fields said. 'Request clearance from
Homestead for the AV-22 to land on the oval in front of the
base hospital.'

Suddenly Fjelmann cursed, and swung back to his
control board and mashed the channel button. 'Key West,
where's that Mexicali flight going? He's supposed to turn
right, not left . . . You think he's disoriented? I can see
that. If he continues the turn he's doing he's going to be
face-to-face with our aerostat . . . well, talk to him.
Convince this guy that unless he wants to spend the next
year in jail or worse he'd better turn right and get the hell
out of our airspace . . . no, *you* tell him. That's your job,
dammit.'

'Ease up, Darrell,' Fields told him. 'That's a scheduled
flight. We're not going to bust the pilot because he panics.
Keep them away from KEYSTONE as much as you can but
don't make threats, it won't help.'

'It's like these pilots just woke up or something,'
Fjelmann said irritably. 'They take a long time to adjust if

you suddenly bust them out of their routine. We give them a simple command and they all go to pieces. The only thing these guys seem to do right is turn the autopilot on.'

'Well, don't you go to pieces on *me* . . .'

'All right, all right, I'm just burning off steam.' Fjelmann took off his headset and rubbed his temples, trying to force away the pain growing in his skull behind his eyeballs. He put back his headset, swiveled his chair back to face his screen, took a deep breath and reconfigured his scope to monitor the errant Mexican airliner, which was drifting ever closer to the aerostat radar balloon suspended over Cudjoe Key. There was no stopping him now – he was going to cross into the aerostat's protected airspace for sure. 'Annette, I need to turn the lights on KEYSTONE. Otherwise this guy's gonna go nose-to-nose with it.'

Fields took a look at the monitor, nodded, then keyed her microphone: 'Security, give me strobes on KEY-STONE for sixty seconds,' she ordered.

Aboard the Lead Cuchillo Mirage F1C Fighter-Bomber

Cruising down Bravo-646 at six hundred nautical miles per hour, Gold Three and his wingman, aboard the two Cuchillo Mirage F1C fighter-bombers, were sixty miles from their target. The sky appeared to be ablaze with slow-moving comets – airliners coming in from all directions, flying around with their anti-collision and landing lights on in the dense, confused air-traffic environment. The risk of a midair collision was so great that everyone had their lights on. The two Mirages had adjusted their altitude until they were squarely in the middle of the bright pearls of light, figuring it would make it that much more difficult to be pursued by military interceptors if they remained in among the civilian planes.

Suddenly the pilot of Gold Three clicked his radio to get his wingman's attention. Far out toward the horizon they saw an astounding sight – a bright pillar of light, like a massive, shiny pin, had appeared from out of nowhere. The apparition began to blink once every two seconds. It was such an unearthly sight, grand and almost magical. It was as if God himself had used the Earth as His own pincushion, jabbing the globe with a celestial pin that shone like a beacon far into the distance. A truly awesome sight.

But the magic did not last long – it was soon replaced by happiness and a bit of relief that endured even after the unusual sight blinked into nothingness a few seconds later. The Cuchillo pilots knew that the heavenly object was KEYSTONE, their target, illuminated for a brief period undoubtedly because of all the air traffic swirling around it. They were right on course. In less than nine minutes, that stickpin from God should be a crushed and burned hulk in the ocean.

Border Security Force Air Command Center

'Key West Approach, that Mexicali flight looks clear of the aerostat,' Darrell Fjelmann said on the phone line to the FAA, 'but I want him south of Bravo-646. I need him back on that southerly heading for another two minutes . . . at *least* two minutes . . . thanks. I appreciate that. Yes, I see him turning now. Thanks for putting a bug in that guy's ear for me . . . yeah, things are still a mess. Thanks again.'

Fjelmann reconfigured his scope for longer ranges. Things were starting to calm down a bit, traffic alerts were getting resolved and air traffic seemed to be moving along . . . Another alert. This one looked like a fast-mover, maybe a bizjet or military toad trying to beat out the airliners into line for approaches into south Florida.

Fjelmann was about to reach for the channel button back to Key West Approach, but for once the FAA controller buzzed him first:

'I think you might have an intruder, Aladdin,' the FAA controller said without preamble. 'One of my Delta flights got a good look at the plane that passed close to him. He said it looked like a foreign jet to him. He said there might have been two of them. I don't have a squawk from this guy.'

'Annette, we got an unknown, forty-eight miles west of KEYSTONE and coming in at six hundred knots,' Fjelmann called over to her.

Fields was beside his left shoulder in an instant. 'What happened?'

'I missed him, that's all,' Fjelmann said. 'With all the traffic alerts I've seen in the past ten minutes I started tuning them out of my mind. These guys slipped in right in the middle of the divert planes going south for Bravo-646 while I was watching the guy around KEYSTONE. I'm only picking up one, but a pilot says he may have seen two foreign-looking jets – '

'Foreign-looking jets? That's the best ID they could come up with?' But Fields knew the answer to that one – at night, in all this confusion, they were lucky to get any kind of eyeball on anyone out there. 'Okay, we treat them like hostiles until we get a positive visual on them. If they're bad guys they'll break out of the airliners' pack and head right for KEYSTONE. Bring Homestead's two F-16 fighters in as soon as you can. You've got the intercept.'

But the miss really hurt Fjelmann. He could feel the stares of his buddies around him and felt he'd let them down. Fjelmann stared blankly at his screen and muttered. 'Maybe you should get someone else . . .'

'We don't have anyone else. You've got the intercept.' On interphone Fields announced: 'Listen up, everyone.

We got two intruders that are going to break out of the pack in a few seconds and try a run on KEYSTONE. Get on the horn to your approach controllers and move your planes away from the area.' To Fjelmann, Fields said, 'All right, get those F-16s in, and for God's sake don't miss.'

Aboard the Lead Cuchillo Mirage Attack Plane

It was pitch black outside, calm and warm. Off in the distance out the left side of the nose, a few lights could be seen on the horizon – the Florida Keys and Key West, just thirty miles away. A few stars were sprinkled in – the sky was so clear that the stars seemed to touch the horizon, and they felt so close that it seemed he could touch them all around him in the cockpit. A few airliners could still be seen off in the distance, but a lot of the confusion had subsided and the commercial jets were on their way, although several miles south of their original course.

The mission was going so smoothly . . . Where were the air-defense fighters? The target was right over there, seemingly within easy reach. Except for the airliners all around him, the skies were peaceful and serene. It was going too easy . . .

The pilot of the lead Mirage F1C fighter-bomber felt his plane start to turn right and climb. Had he actually drifted off to sleep? Lulled into complacency? He shook himself hard to get his blood flowing, then depressed his left rudder pedal and nudged his stick left to regain control.

Suddenly he heard 'Lead, get on your gauges,' on his radio and he quickly scanned his flight instruments, fighting off the sudden vertigo when he realized that what was happening in his brain really wasn't happening to his plane. The plane wasn't turning right – his gauges confirmed that. He was experiencing spatial disorientation, a sudden and sometimes uncontrollable loss of 'up' and 'down' where the brain would interpret what the eyes were seeing in a perverse way. The stars began to look like the lights of the Florida Keys, and those stars formed their own false horizon that made it look as if he was in a climbing right turn.

Easy, now, he coached himself. Light on the controls . . . roll back wings level . . . merge with the airliners again. Now stop staring out the windows and concentrate on the mission –

'Lead . . .'

'I'm okay,' he reported. 'Got a little lopsided,' he muttered to himself. Be careful or Salazar will make it permanent . . .

'We're right on course,' the wingman reported.

The lead pilot checked his heading with the airliners' they were following. They were heading farther south than before. Their distance to the target had already increased to over thirty miles even though they were heading eastbound at over eight miles a minute. Were the airliners being kicked out of the area? If so, that could only mean . . .

His suspicions were answered a moment later. A warning bleep on his threat-warning receiver, a high-tech radar detector that searched for signals from enemy fighters or ground-missile sites, told the real story – they had just been picked up by enemy attack-radar. The airliners were clearing out before the shootout.

The Cuchillo lead pilot turned left, got the heading direct to the target off the Doppler navigation set and fine-tuned his heading to put them on course to the aerostat radar site. He resisted the urge to push the power up any higher than eight hundred kilometers an hour – five hundred miles an hour, about the same speed as the airliners – and he resisted activating his EP-171 radar-jamming pod. A jamming strobe would tell the whole world they were military planes, and he didn't want to do that, not yet. Time to play the final games, the ones that would decide whether they made it into the target area or not.

The flight leader switched his radio to 121.5, the international emergency frequency. He took a deep breath, keyed the mike, and in his best American accent said, 'Mayday, mayday, mayday, Challenger five-six mike-mike on GUARD. Can anyone hear me?' The call sign was a last-minute inspiration from something he had seen on an American television show – it was the well-known call letters of one of the corporate jets of the Disney Corporation.

'Falcon five-six mike-mike, this is the United States Border Security Force. We read you loud and clear. Squawk emergency and go ahead.'

'Squawk emergency,' the pilot knew, meant switch his identification encoder to code 7700, which would pinpoint his location on the American's radar scopes. He made sure that his encoder could not transmit any altitude data by turning the mode C function of the encoder off, then set in the 7700 code and flicked it on. He let it run a few seconds, then flicked it off.

The Americans knew where they were now, but they would still need a few minutes to sort it all out before deciding on a course of action – and he and his pilots were now only three minutes away from their target.

Border Security Force Command Center

'We got him,' Fjelmann called out. 'He's reporting in now on GUARD. His call sign is Challenger five-six mike-mike. He . . . damn, I just lost his beacon.'

But Annette Fields was too keyed up to consider any

511

other possibility. 'Continue the intercept. Kick him out of our airspace and get him turned around.'

'He transmitted a mayday – '

'I don't care. I want him heading south until we get an ID on him.'

'But that call sign. Mike-mike. Mickey Mouse. . . ?'

'I said kick him out and continue the intercept.'

Fjelmann nodded, then switched to the F-16's fighter-intercept frequency. 'Trap Two flight, this is Aladdin. We have an intruder alert, one, possibly two jets now at your two o'clock, seventy miles, ten thousand feet. Come right heading two-five-zero, take angels twelve for intercept.'

There was a slight pause, then: 'Aladdin, this is Trap Two flight. We're talking with BUTCHER on this frequency. Stand by.' BUTCHER was the southeast military air-intercept controller.

'Trap flight, Border Security will handle the intercept. Turn right heading two-five-zero and take angels twelve.'

'I said stand by, Aladdin. We're coordinating with our command post.'

Fields had heard the interchange and was instantly on the phone to Homestead Air Force Base. The throbbing in Fjelmann's temples increased as he switched channels to talk to the unidentified intruder.

Lead Cuchillo Mirage Strike-Fighter

'Challenger five-six mike-mike, this is the United States Border Security Force, radar contact. We have lost your beacon, primary target only. Recycle your transponder, turn right and stay clear of Bravo-646 until further notice. SCATANA procedures are in effect. Acknowledge. Over.'

They weren't buying it, the lead pilot thought. Try once

more, then forget the ruse. 'I've got an engine on fire and smoke in the cockpit,' the Cuchillo called out over the radio. 'I need to land immediately, I'm heading toward Key West for emergency landing. Over.'

'Five-six mike-mike, unable your request. You must remain south of route Bravo-646 due to an air-defense emergency. Turn right immediately and clear the area. We will vector you to Marathon Airport for emergency landing.'

'I won't make it to Marathon. I am landing at Key West. I am declaring an emergency and I wish priority routeing. Over.'

'If you can make it to Key West from your present position you can make it to Marathon,' the Hammerheads controller told him. He was right – the two Mirage F1Cs were almost equidistant between Key West and Marathon. The ruse was over. 'Turn right immediately to heading one-two-zero. Over.'

'Key West has a longer runway and crash equipment, sir,' the Cuchillo pilot persisted. 'Marathon is unacceptable. I want to land in Key West. Get me your supervisor – '

'My supervisor is unavailable, five-six mike-mike. You are endangering yourself, your passengers and other air traffic on your present course. No flight plan is on file for you and identification has not been established. You are not authorized, repeat, not authorized to proceed. Turn right heading one-two-zero, vectors clear of restricted airspace. Acknowledge and comply. Over.'

Well, thought the lead Cuchillo pilot, at least they had bought a few precious minutes. He flashed his wingtip position-lights on and off, a signal for the wingman to take spacing. When the bomber moved out, he turned on the rotating beacon once, then off, then flashed the lights once again – the signal to jettison the external fuel tank and arm

513

weapons. He quickly safed all weapons, selected the centerline stores station, jettisoned the empty centerline ten-thousand-liter fuel tank, then reselected and rearmed all offensive weapons.

He could only assume that his wingman had done the same . . . he couldn't see the other plane in the darkness. He would have to assume everything else about his wingman for the next few minutes – assume he would stay on course, assume he would strike his target, assume he would get out safely – because from now on they were all on their own. The bomb-equipped Mirage would descend to less than a hundred meters above the water and start his target run, and the leader would try to destroy all attackers until he ran out of weapons and it was time to run.

He began to push the throttle up to full power, checked once again that his weapons were armed and ready, then activated his jamming pod and attack radar.

Another bleep on the warning receiver, this time longer and strong enough to trigger the automatic jamming pod – it meant the American planes were getting their final radar fixes before starting their attack . . .

Border Security Force Headquarters Command Center

'Challenger five-six mike-mike, acknowledge and comply. Over . . . Five-six mike-mike, you are in danger of coming under attack without further warning. Turn right immediately. Over.' Panic seized Fjelmann and he lunged for the interphone button, searching for the duty controller at the same time.

'That Challenger plane just started accelerating,' Fjelmann shouted out to anyone on interphone who would listen. 'He's up to Mach point eight.' The warning came unbidden and was unnecessary – he was controlling the

514

intercept. Others would report to him or keep silent. 'Trap two and three, this is Aladdin, vector to intercept, right turn heading one-niner-zero, altitude five hundred feet, range, mark, forty miles.'

'Aladdin, please stand by,' the lead pilot in the F-16 formation said. He was obviously confused too – he was itching to get into the fight but uncertain whether to take commands from a non-Air Force controller. 'Sir, we do not have authorization or authentication to take vectors from you. We're waiting for instructions.'

'Dammitall . . .' Fjelmann exploded but choked down his protest just in time. Fields rushed over to study the radar display. 'Trap flight, you had better make a decision right now or I'm going to clear you out of my airspace for Hammerhead aircraft to respond. Take the vectors or reverse course. Now!'

There was another pause, then: 'Aladdin, can you give me a data link to your target?'

'Do it,' Fields said. Fjelmann began furiously typing on his computer keyboard. A data link between the ground radar and the aircraft gave steering signals to the fighter. The F-16 pilot could, if he wanted, engage his autopilot and let the fighter fly itself to an intercept. But it also provided a quick way to test the authenticity of a controller's instructions, because only an authorized agency would have the equipment and expertise to use a data link. On the F-16 pilot's head-up display the data link would appear as a small circle with a channel number superimposed over it – in the Border Security Force's case, a circle with an 8 in the middle – where the target was.

Moments later, Fjelmann heard, 'Aladdin, we have your uplink. Trap Two flight of two in a right turn.' Seconds later: 'Trap Two contact, twelve o'clock, twenty-seven miles. Judy.' 'Judy' meaning that the F-16 pilot was using his own attack radar to intercept the target and that he was ready to take over on his own.

'Negative, Trap Two.' Sweat popped out on Fjelmann's forehead. 'Negative. Your bogey's at thirty-five miles, heading north at five hundred feet.' A spike of white streaked across the digital screen, and the message 'WARNING FREQ AGILE WAIT WAIT' appeared on the screen. Fjelmann cursed on interphone. 'That Mexicali flight is right in the goddamned way, and the bastard's jamming us – '

'Trap Two flight is negative contact . . . Trap flight has music.' The F-16 fighters were reporting that they had received jamming as well. 'Trap flight has radar contact, radar contact . . . stand by . . . stand by, Hammerhead.' The jamming would only get stronger as the F-16 got closer.

'Trap flight, your bogey's at twelve o'clock, twenty miles. Additional traffic moving to your ten o'clock, fifteen miles and high, use caution. Target at eighteen miles, twelve o'clock low, moving to eleven o'clock, call Judy.'

'Trap Two is popeye . . . dammitall . . . two, I think I'm knocked up, take the lead.' Like the Hammerhead's radar system, the F-16's attack radar could counter jamming by switching frequencies away from a jamming signal – but apparently the lead F-16's anti-jamming system wasn't working. The number-two plane would now have to take the lead and search for the target.

'Don't do that, don't do that,' Fjelmann muttered to himself. 'You don't have time . . .'

And, as if the F-16 pilots had heard him: 'Disregard, two. I'll stay in the lead. No room for a lead change. Hammerhead, sing out.'

'Roger, Trap flight. Eleven o'clock, eight miles, offset one half mile, low, target altitude now eight hundred feet, ten-thirty, seven miles, offset three-quarters of a mile . . .'

'Trap leader has a Judy, Aladdin. Judy. Ten-thirty, six miles.'

'That's your target, Trap flight. Ten seconds to feet wet.'

'How far from that civilian, Aladdin?'

'Seven miles at your nine-thirty position, offset seven miles.' Then, just as the F-16s crossed over the Keys: 'Feet wet, Trap flight. Cleared in hot. Caution, there might be two bogeys. Cleared in hot.'

Aboard the Lead Cuchillo Mirage F1C Fighter

The Mirage's threat-warning system was squawking so loud that the pilot finally turned it off. No use overstating the obvious – the fight was on for real.

The aggressor always has the advantage, at least so they had been taught by Colonel Salazar. No matter what the odds, no matter how great the deficiency in weapons or technology, a sudden, aggressive attacker always had the upper hand. It was time to put the colonel's idea to the test.

Aboard the Lead F-16 Fighter

The Hammerheads controller's last warning was met by the scream of the F-16's Threat Warning System, a radar detector that not only revealed the presence of enemy radar transmissions but could pinpoint the relative direction of the radar beam and determine if the signal was a search radar, a target tracking radar or a missile-guidance signal. This time, at such close range, the lead F-16 pilot got all three almost immediately – the radar signal started out as a search radar, quickly changed to a target-tracking signal as it acquired and locked onto the F-16s, then switched to missile-lock seconds later. A large 'LOCK' light flashed on the instrument panel, and the words 'MISSILE LAUNCH' appeared in the pilot's head-up display.

'Trap flight, breaking right,' the lead pilot called out. For the moment the attack was forgotten and the pilot's concentration was on saving himself and his plane. He hadn't expected the missile-launch signal at all – a reliable missile hit with two fighters heading directly toward each other was almost impossible unless the attacker had very sophisticated weapons . . .

Whatever the reason, a missile-launch warning was nothing to ignore. The lead F-16 pilot ejected chaff – radar decoys – from his left ejector and yanked his nose hard right and up in a hard, fast, six-G maneuver. After gaining over a thousand feet in seconds the pilot rolled his F-16 inverted with a quick snap and dove for the water, straining to execute the tightest possible turn without blacking out. Just before making the dive he ejected more chaff, hoping that the missile would lock onto the slow-drifting tinsel-like decoy instead of his fast-moving Falcon.

But the Cuchillo's Mirage fighter had not launched a missile. He had simulated a missile-launch indication, designed to force an enemy fighter prematurely to maneuver and go into a defensive posture – which was what the lead F-16 fighter did. When the lead Cuchillo pilot saw the F-16 go into a sharp snap-climb he immediately switched from his longer-range radar-guided missiles to his shorter-range heat-seeking missiles, accelerated and climbed right behind and up with the F-16. Now, instead of going head-to-head, the Cuchillo fighter had managed to slip behind the maneuvering F-16, getting into missile-firing position . . .

But the trick of using a false missile-launch indication was

518

an old one, and the two F-16s had made sure they used the proper defense – lagging the wingman behind a little farther when making a defensive maneuver with the enemy in front. When the lead F-16 made its sharp climb, his wingman waited two long, agonizing seconds – agonizing because there really *could* be a missile in the air heading for him – scanned the skies for another plane, then began a climb behind the attacker when he appeared. The maneuver worked. When the Mirage pulled in behind the lead F-16, the second F-16 was right behind him. When the lead F-16 began its dive, the less maneuverable Mirage could not follow as sharply or accelerate as quickly and remained vulnerable for the several seconds it took for the second F-16 to close within range of its multibarrel Vulcan cannon and open fire.

'Fox three, fox three!' the second F-16 pilot called over the phone as he squeezed the trigger on his control stick. 'There he is . . . I can't see who it is but it sure moves like a sonofabitch . . .'

Aboard the Attacking Mirage F1C Fighter

There was a moment when the F-16 was dead in his sights on the radar scope, *perfectly* dead-center, and he felt an almost overwhelming sense of victory – what some called the 'hunter's rush' or the 'hunter's hard-on.' He also knew it was the time he was the most vulnerable to mistakes. Carefully the Cuchillo pilot checked his instruments and warned himself this was no time to get sloppy.

He was too close for a missile shot but just outside good cannon range. Patience, patience, patience. The Cuchillo pilot knew that even though the F-16 had enough power to accelerate in a vertical climb, in this case it would probably eject chaff and flares to decoy any missile and descend to regain the airspeed lost in its emergency climb. The Cuchillo pilot therefore rolled inverted, waiting for the split-second when the F-16 would roll and pull over – its entire profile would be visible then, a perfect aspect to fire on. He couldn't see the F-16 roll on radar – it was pitch black outside except for the occasional glimpse of lights from the Keys that would catch and hold his attention – but the instant the radar blip headed downward or when he saw a decoy flare ejected he would pull downward as well, cut off the angle and start shooting. The F-16 would fly right through his stream of bullets.

Just as he expected the F-16 to make its move – as indicated by his own dramatic loss of airspeed in the pursuit climb – suddenly the Cuchillo pilot felt a sharp hammering reverberate through his plane. At first he thought he had stalled his fighter, but the engines were still running. Did he squeeze the trigger? It felt as if his guns were firing – maybe he had squeezed the trigger without realizing it. He checked the threat-warning receiver – it was silent. Not even a peep from stray emissions from the F-16 in front of him . . .

Which shouldn't be the case. With the F-16 in so close he should be picking up *something* from his radar . . .

Then he realized that he had shut off the threat-warning receiver. There was another F-16 at his six, shooting at him . . .

Still inverted, he pulled his nose down to the ground, rolled hard right, turned ninety degrees off heading, then reversed course – anything to get out of the F-16's radar beam and escape into the darkness. But he had overlooked another classic rule of engagement – don't focus in on one machine for too long. He had allowed the F-16's wingman to get behind him. He reactivated his threat-warning receiver but by now it was chirping continually and, unlike the F-16's version, the Mirage's threat-warning system could not tell from what direction the threat was coming.

Darkness, low altitude – the entire engagement with the F-16 had all taken place below one thousand meters – low speed, threat warnings everywhere, nothing on the radar scope, no wingman, no real situational awareness . . . it all meant only one thing. Time to bug out. Extend, escape and live to fight another day. He rolled wings-level, started a shallow descent to the relative safety of the dark sea and pushed the throttles all the way to full afterburner. Once established upright and heading south out to sea, he began searching the skies around him for any sign of the enemy . . .

. . . And he looked aft, behind his right wing, just in time to see an AIM-9L Sidewinder missile streak out of the darkness and crash into his tailpipe. He reached down to the ejection lever between his legs but the Mirage spun end-over-end and crashed into the sea long before he could pull the yellow-painted handle. He stayed alive long enough to feel the impact and experience the cool south Florida waters before they closed over him and crushed him to death.

Aboard the Lead F-16 Fighter

'Your tail's clear, lead,' the pilot heard his wingman call out. 'Splash one, Hammerheads. Hey, he came outta *nowhere*.'

The lead F-16 pilot rolled upright, then began a sharp climb when he realized he was only a hundred feet above the water. Another moment's hesitation and he'd have been dead.

'Trap flight, another target heading north, low altitude. Vector heading zero-three-zero, take angels one, target eight miles, velocity six hundred knots.'

The lead pilot climbed to one thousand feet, thankful to

be above the waves even if it was only a thousand feet – his Falcon fought much better at ten-thousand or twenty-thousand feet – and this time used the data-link signal from the Border Security Force to run the intercept. He rolled in behind the target and began increasing power to regain the speed he had lost escaping from the first attacker . . .

But he had put the power back in too slowly, recovered too slowly – after all the jinking he was *still* not fully caught up with his air machine. It took him several seconds of watching the airspeed meter slowly wind upward before realizing that his attack radar had locked onto the target. 'Trap two has a Judy,' he reported.

'Cleared in hot, Trap Two.'

He began a slight climb to get above the target – all medium- or long-range missiles, especially his AIM-7F, needed some altitude in order to glide in to the target so their sort-pulse rocket motors wouldn't be used just to maintain the missile's altitude. He got a flashing diamond on the head-up display that encircled the radar-target square, which told him that the Sparrow missile was in launch parameters and ready to fire. The word 'SHOOT' appeared just underneath the aiming reticle. As soon as he reached two thousand feet he rechecked his switch positions, called, 'Trap two, fox one, fox one,' on the radio to warn of the missile launches – and squeezed the launch button.

Aboard the Cuchillo Mirage F1C Strike Fighter-Bomber

The Mirage had no fancy lasers or radio beacons to guide the bomb, no inertial navigation set, no ring-laser gyros or satellite navigation system. The young twenty-year-old pilot, who had joined the Cuchillos only a few months after – unjustly, he felt – being washed out of a Cuban

Revolutionary Air Force fighter-bombing program, was tired, excited, and nervous all at once. This was his first time that he was flying alone, with no instructor, no leader, no wingmen, not even a ground controller watching over him.

But bombing was in his blood, and he was able to swallow his nervousness and use his excitement to help himself through this run. Being suddenly alone, without the comforting curses and grunts coming through from his lead pilot on their scrambled radio channel, at least made it easier for him to concentrate. For him, the whole world was condensed down to his cockpit, his controls, and the little yellow blips on his four-inch radar scope.

He would have to rely on dead reckoning, depending on simple time and heading, to get within twenty miles of the target until he could pick out any recognizable landmarks on the radar, find the target visually or by using those landmarks, adjust the aircraft's course so the track line on the radar lay across the target, then release the bomb sometime before flying over the target. If he acquired the target visually, at six hundred knots groundspeed and three hundred feet above ground, he would release the cluster-bomb unit when the end of the air-data computer probe on the nose touched the target. If he was using the radar only, he would release at one 500-meter tick on the radar back from the target for every hundred feet he was flying above ground. It was imprecise, but it still had a reliability to it, especially with a cluster-bomb unit that could wipe out nearly a square kilometer area in one pass.

The fear and nervousness washed over him once again when the threat-warning signal beeped insistently in his helmet – they had found him. Flying straight and level like this, he was an easy target for an advanced fighter-interceptor like the F-16. He knew he had only seconds to react. He couldn't see the target yet but he knew he was on track and very close. If he tried zigzagging to escape the fighters he'd be far off-course and would have to spend too much time getting back on track.

He pitched up hard, sending his Mirage fighter into a straight-up vertical climb. After gaining almost two thousand meters he rolled inverted and pulled his stick back, looping over the top and aiming his nose straight at the ground.

His abrupt maneuver had saved his life – the lead F-16's first two Sparrow missiles missed and were unable to reacquire the target before running out of power and self-destructing.

He still couldn't see the target, but what he could see was the entire shadowy bulk of Cudjoe Key against the dark, reflective background of the sea. The island was a little more than two kilometers long and a half-kilometer wide, with buildings and docks along the north side, a wide paved road running south, and the Border Security Force's aerostat unit in the center of the island along with four support trailers, a power generator and a helicopter landing pad all in a five-hundred-meter-square fenced-off area. He aimed the nose of his Mirage into the center of the island, made a few small corrections when he saw the lights of the docks on the north side – and made a final correction when he saw one tiny light, either from a porch or an open doorway, peek on. The aerostat unit was the only structure in the interior of the island. That had to be it . . .

He pickled off the cluster-bomb unit, then selected the Kingfisher anti-ship missile and launched it at the center of the island. With an F-16, maybe two, on his tail he didn't have the luxury of searching for targets of opportunity, and without the added drag factor of the bombs, he might just have a chance to escape. He leveled off at one hundred meters, selected full afterburner power and raced south toward the open sea.

The cluster-bomb unit, designed to be released from a high-speed horizontal laydown delivery pass, was not supposed to be driven down into the ground like a conventional bomb; the one hundred individual bomblets never had a chance to scatter, and so the devastating effect of the weapon was minimized. But the Cuchillo pilot's instincts about where his target was were right on. The cluster-bomb canister opened up at three hundred feet when the special sensors in the canister detected the sharp deceleration after release and the automatic timers wound down; the bomblets dispersed only slightly but most of them landed between the aerostat recovery area and the power-generator building. There was one large secondary explosion as several bomblets destroyed the generator and exploded its diesel fuel tank, the concussion and fire reaching the data-generation and transmission facility, which cut off communications between the aerostat radar and Border Security Force headquarters.

Border Security Force Headquarters, Aladdin City

'Contact lost with KEYSTONE, Annette,' Fjelmann said in a low voice. The command center at Aladdin City suddenly went very quiet – no tapping of keyboards, no low voices, no footsteps. Fjelmann pounded his desktop in frustration.

'Shake it off,' Fields said, trying to pump her voice with enthusiasm. 'Reconfigure and find those intruders. Those F-16s out there are waiting on you.'

'Switching to Navy Key West and air traffic control radar data,' he acknowledged, punching instructions to the computer to reconfigure his display to use FAA radar from Key West and Miami Center. His screen went blank as the computers raced to convert the data from the Navy and

FAA's radars; then, slowly, the computers began to redisplay air targets, flight-information data blocks, and even managed to draw in island outlines, obstruction data, airports and airport traffic patterns. The data on sea targets was missing completely – none of the radars in use could see ships as well as the aerostats – and all of the computer's sophisticated intercept, analysis, research and recording options reported 'UNAVAILABLE.'

The computers didn't remember which target was which anymore, but it wasn't hard to spot the intruder – he was heading south away from KEYSTONE at just over Mach one. 'Trap flight, this is Aladdin, vectors to your target, right turn heading one-niner-zero, take two thousand feet. Altitude readout unavailable. His airspeed is seven-niner-zero and accelerating, range twenty miles.'

Fields was monitoring the chase over the Straits of Florida when another call came in over her command network: 'Aladdin, this is NAPALM. We have a situation. We've picked up two high-speed aircraft heading north right toward us. We have one air defense F-16 on the way. We need some help. What's your situation?'

'Stand by, NAPALM,' Field replied over the net. 'We've got two F-16s involved in a pursuit. KEYSTONE is down.' If they got the Hammerhead Two platform, Fields thought, it would be total disaster for the Hammerheads – there were over ninety people on that platform. They hadn't defended the other three major Border Security Force aerostat units – she had to do everything she could to defend the last one.

On the fighter-interceptor's frequency Fields said, 'Trap Two flight, this is Aladdin. We've received notice of another attack on the Hammerhead Two platform. We anticipate another two-ship fighter attack. We've got Trap Four responding solo. Can one of you assist?'

The reply was immediate. 'Affirmative, Aladdin.

Designate Trap Three heading north to assist. Trap Two will continue the south intercept. Over.'

'Copy that, Trap Two. Trap Three, fly heading three-three-eight, range one hundred ten miles, vectors to intercept. Take angels fifteen. Trap Two, your target is at twelve o'clock, eighteen miles. Call Judy.'

But Trap Two, the former lead F-16, was still having trouble with his attack radar readjusting after an anti-jamming frequency shift. 'Trap Two is still popeye,' he reported. 'Should lock on any minute . . .'

'Dammitall,' Fjelmann muttered to Fields, 'he might lose this guy. We're not sure of the target's altitude and he could go out of range of Key West approach radar in a few minutes.'

'Then use Miami Center's radar and vector him in the best you can. These F-16 guys can find him if he's pointed in the right direction. Just keep feeding him – '

At that instant they heard, 'Trap Two, Judy. Twelve o'clock, fifteen miles. He's at two hundred feet and Mach one point two. Full burners and balls to the wall.'

Aboard the F-16 Fighter-Interceptor Trap Two

The moment he locked onto the target on radar he looked up and was able to see the bright yellow spot low on the horizon – the attacker was indeed in full afterburner, heading south as fast as his jet could carry him, staying low to the water in the hope that the radar-clutter from the sea would decoy a radar-guided missile. But using afterburner made it easy to spot the guy, and it was an invitation to destruction with a weapon like the Sidewinder – which was a good thing, because except for 500 rounds of twenty-millimeter ammunition the only weapons he had left were two heat-seeking Sidewinders on his wingtips. He had launched both AIM-7 Sparrow missiles on his first pass over Key Cudjoe and missed.

The range was slowly running down – now less than twelve miles. The AIM-9L had a max range of ten miles, but it was very accurate inside eight miles and deadly from one to six. He had to wait. He decided to jettison his two external fuel tanks, which would give him an extra boost of speed when he tried for the kill. After that it was head back to the barn as fast as possible – he was already extended pretty far and the situation was worsening with every mile he continued southbound. The chase better be over very soon . . .

The missile lock-on diamond appeared at nine-and-a-half miles, and the 'SHOOT' designation appeared just inside nine miles. The F-16 pilot waited, waited, waited until just inside eight miles before calling, 'Trap Two, fox two,' and launching a missile from his left wingtip. The smaller Sidewinder missile didn't rumble the air or blind the pilot like the hefty AIM-7F Sparrow missile did after launch – a smooth, silken *whoosh*, a sudden glare and the missile was gone. It had accelerated to Mach two before reaching one mile, and it was tracking dead on target.

The missile's motor winked out well before hitting the escaping fighter, so the F-16 pilot never saw exactly what happened. But he did see the afterburner on the enemy fighter extinguish, saw a quick flash of light, and nothing else. But a quick check of the radar told him the bad news – the enemy fighter was still flying. It was slowing, decelerating below the Mach very quickly, but it soon stabilized at about six hundred knots and stayed at low altitude. The Sidewinder had either missed or exploded too far away from the target to produce a lethal result.

This guy sure had nine lives, the F-16 pilot thought. He used his attack radar to get behind his target again and waited a few more seconds before launching his last missile.

He was going to wait until six miles to attack again. If the last Sidewinder didn't work, he would have enough gas for one, maybe two gun passes before he'd be forced to turn around and head for home.

Aboard the Mirage F1C Fighter-Bomber

The Cuchillo pilot peered at his instrument panel, trying to shake away the blurriness and dimness. His oxygen supply had been cut off and he had no choice but to drop his face mask. He felt shards of glass in his arms and shoulders, and he was moving the throttle with his shoulder more than his left hand because all feeling had drained from his left side. Even though the air outside was pleasant and warm, the pilot shivered.

Just before the Sidewinder missile exploded, the Cuchillo pilot had performed a clearing turn – a sharp high-banked turn in both directions so the pilot could see behind him for signs of pursuit – and it was the last-moment maneuver that saved his life. The heat-seeking missile missed the Mirage's hot exhaust, flew over the fuselage and across the left wing and exploded beside the cockpit. The canopy of his fighter had been all but blown away by the near-hit, sending pieces of the canopy driven by the eight-hundred-mile-per-hour windblast right into his upper body. The Mirage was still functioning, but the windblast and the wounds he had sustained were driving him to the edge of unconsciousness and he was forced to reduce speed to keep the windblast from snapping his neck.

Ejecting from his stricken fighter was not an option for the young pilot. The plane was still flying, he was still alive, and Colonel Salazar had told him he'd return to a hero's welcome if he accomplished his mission. Although he knew that the Colonel spoke like that often, and he also suspected that eventually he would have to eject, he would rather do it in Cuban or Haitian waters than in international or American waters.

For now, the only thing he thought about was how to protect himself from another attack, and the answer was . . . turn and fight. He had six hundred pounds of ammunition and two French Matra R-550 Magic heat-seeking missiles. It was time to use them. But it had to be fast and unexpected – he knew the American pilots and their F-16 fighters were nearly unstoppable in close-range dogfights.

In spite of his wounds and the fact that he had no canopy or protection from windblast except his helmet, the Mirage pilot pulled his nose skyward, completing a half-loop in just five seconds and five thousand feet. While inverted at the top of the loop, he set his radar to air-to-air mode, selected a missile, and scanned the sky in his wake for any attackers. Without waiting for the Matra Magic missile to signal a lock-on – unlike the AIM-9L Sidewinder it was not able to lock onto a target in head-to-head engagements – the Cuchillo pilot squeezed the trigger and launched the missile as soon as the radar picked up an air target.

Aboard the F-16 Fighting Falcon, Trap Two

The sudden maneuver that registered on the APG-66 attack radar was somewhat unexpected – no fighter pilot was going to let another pilot shoot missiles at him all night without fighting – but the sudden quick flash of light he saw caught him by surprise. A head-to-head missile engagement was low percentage, even with an advanced Sidewinder. But these guys weren't playing percentages – they were going for the kill, the missile had to be countered no matter how great the odds were against that missile hitting.

530

There was no 'MISSILE LAUNCH' signal from the threat-warning receiver, so it had to be either an unguided missile or a heat-seeker. The Falcon pilot rolled up onto his right wing and made sure he was in full power without any afterburners lighting up the sky behind him. Rolling up on one side presented the smallest and coolest profile to the missile's seeker-head. He watched as the missile's motor burned out, held the wing-high attitude for two seconds, rolled wings-level, then began a sharp climb. The Falcon pilot had to put as much cool metal between his hot tailpipe and the missile's seeker-head, or the missile might just track. He quickly lost sight of the missile as its solid-rocket motor burned out, but the missile had obviously not been tracking because it appeared to be passing well behind him, without any telltale wobbling in the motor glare that would indicate that it was tracking him.

Now, concentrate on the fighter itself. The enemy fighter was coming down right for him, but now he had the speed advantage. The speed at which the fighter had suddenly turned and the speed at which it was descending told the F-16 pilot that his attacker might still be inverted. One thing to do – turn hard, reverse course and avoid flying underneath the fighter, where his high position would give him a speed-and-angles advantage.

The F-16 quickly completed a 180-degree turn, and he found his threat-warning receiver quiet – if the attacker had not been inverted he would have been able to get behind the F-16 for another missile or gun attack. The American pilot used some pent-up speed to extend for several seconds, waited for the first hint of a search radar being aimed at him, then turned hard and reversed course again. Following the indications on his head-up display, he managed to use the Falcon's tight seven-G turn capability to line up with his adversary, who had managed to get turned around himself and was starting to come for him.

Checking to be sure he had selected his cannon, the F-16 pilot continued his hard right turn to lead his target before opening fire. The fire-control radar and attack-computer drew a line on the display, indicating the computer's best guess at the target's flight path – the F-16 pilot used that lead-computing line to position his aiming reticle before opening fire. The enemy plane – he still had no idea who it was or what kind of plane he was about to shoot at – had apparently realized that the F-16 had the angle and was turning into the F-16 and accelerating to decrease the time in the box, within the lethal cone of fire. The F-16 pilot opened fire when the range decreased to below one mile, keeping the aiming reticle of the display directly on the lead-computing indicator and tracking it in toward the radar-target square. He had time for five short squeezes of the trigger before the target zipped away and had to turn hard to pursue.

Now out the right side of his bubble canopy he saw small spurts of flame erupting from the side of the enemy fighter. 'Aladdin, this is Trap Two. My target is on fire. I am closing again to pursue. Over.'

No reply. The F-16 pilot checked his navigation display with his charts – he was over sixty miles south of Key West. With the KEYSTONE radar down and the air-traffic mess in south Florida he had probably drifted out of radio contact thirty miles ago. He wouldn't be able to pick up his Hammerhead controller unless he climbed back up to a higher altitude. He took a quick fuel check: he was only minutes away from his return point at this range and considering the traffic over south Florida he was probably beyond it – if he had to divert to MacDill or Jacksonville he was going to be running on fumes if he delayed any longer. He began a turn northward, started a gradual climb and opened his checklist to the performance section to look up the best range-speed for his aircraft weight and configuration.

He had just passed ten-thousand feet when the radio chatter began to increase again and he felt safer. 'Aladdin, this is Trap Two. I am RTB hot with nine thousand pounds, fifty south of Key West, code one. Over . . .'

'Trap Two, Trap Two, this is Aladdin. We've been trying to reach you. You have bogeys now at your six o'clock, nine miles. Six o'clock, nine miles and closing. We read three bogeys, repeat, three bogeys . . .'

Suddenly the hunter had become the hunted. The F-16 pilot selected full military power and started a steep but controlled descent. As he did the threat-warning receiver came to life, squawking and beeping the message that he already knew – he was probably too late.

The attackers were much smaller, much less capable, and much slower than the F-16 Fighting Falcon – the moment the F-16 pilot pushed his throttle up to military power he was flying one-hundred knots faster than his pursuers – but the tiny Albatros attack-trainers of Salazar's Cuchillos had the element of surprise, which meant disaster for the lone F-16. The Albatros jet trainers were airborne to provide terminal air cover for the returning strike fighters; each carried two 1,800-liter external fuel tanks, a single underbelly GSh-23 cannon and two Bofers RBS-70 heat-seeking missiles mounted in bulky single-missile pods on each wing. Like the Hammerheads' Sea Stinger missile, the RBS-70 was a modified man-portable anti-aircraft missile, adapted for use on aircraft and capable against air, sea and land targets.

One by one each Albatros launched missiles at the fleeing F-16. The range between the aircraft had decreased to five miles, just inside the lethal range of the tiny RBS-70 missiles, but the F-16's speed had jumped to nearly Mach one in military power. The first missile missed the F-16 by only a few meters, causing the pilot to begin a series of violent vertical and horizontal moves to break the lock of any other missiles fired at him. The other two missiles never had a chance to lock on – even at the missile's top speed of Mach two, they could not maneuver fast enough to keep up with the agile F-16 and quickly broke lock, self-destructing after fifteen seconds of flight.

But even without a kill, the Albatros attackers had done their job. The F-16 fighter, forced to waste more fuel escaping the surprise attack, did not have the fuel to turn and counterattack, and was forced to head for home.

A half-hour later the surviving Mirage fighter safely ejected just off the west coast of Haiti, within a hundred yards of a boat waiting to pick up the pilot.

The battle did not go as well for the Cuchillos attacking the Hammerhead Two platform. With the matchup now two-on-two instead of two-on-one, a third F-16 on the way and with a much less cluttered air-traffic scene, the battles were brief and decisive. The MiG carrying his load of cluster bombs and Kingfisher missiles was forced to jettison them overwater when he found himself jumped by the two F-16s – and even the added speed and maneuverability he gained by getting rid of the clumsy bombs could not make up for the superiority of the F-16 over the aged MiG-21. Both MiGs were destroyed by missiles – neither F-16 had to move closer than six miles to his target to destroy it.

But the damage had already been done . . .

On Board an Air Force C-20B Transport
Several Minutes Later

'Thank God,' Elliott said on board the transport, a modified Gulfstream III business jet fitted with special communications facilities, speeding to south Florida from Washington. 'NAPALM wasn't touched?'

'They didn't get within twenty minutes of the platform this time,' Hardcastle replied, speaking to him from the Border Security Force headquarters at Aladdin City. 'The F-16s got both planes trying to attack Hammerhead Two, and we think we got one of the group that attacked KEYSTONE. But the F-16 ran into three more planes flying up from Cuba and was forced to turn back.'

'Cuban planes?'

'Negative. The RAZORBACK ROTH unit tracked them flying out of central Haiti. We don't have an exact base of origin, but except for Port-au-Prince the only other hard-surface runway in Haiti that could have handled jets big enough to carry air-to-air missiles is Verrettes. Salazar staged an attack on the Hammerheads' radar units. I *still* don't believe it.'

'Stand by,' Elliott said, and stared out one of the tiny round windows in the back of the C-20 . . . The Border Security Force was in serious trouble. The overwhelming attack on Hammerhead One and CARABAL had wiped out half the Force's precision long-range detection capability, and the personnel loss on the Hammerhead One platform was devastating. The entire Caribbean basin would be newly open to air and sea smugglers unless an interim radar platform was set up . . . 'I'll get the contingency plan in effect as fast as I can,' Elliott radioed to Hardcastle. 'I think we can get the *Oriskany* in position within the week. The President's already authorized the Navy to assist in the Caribbean region. We might have F-14s flying chase missions with our Sea Lions.' Hardcastle's original proposal for a forward air base for the V-22 tilt-rotor interdiction plane included using aged, retired aircraft carriers as air-operations platforms. A Navy training or reserve aircraft carrier would be positioned in critical drug-trafficking routes; they already had several vessels lined up for possible use, most likely the retired USS

535

Coral Sea or the research and training Essex-class *Oriskany*, which had been repeatedly rescued from the scrapyards by various government agencies wanting a carrier to play with.

'I'm not interested in what we're going to do about sealing off the borders right now, Brad,' Hardcastle said. 'I want to know what we're going to do about Salazar and his outfit.'

'Well, if we want to get Salazar and his terrorists we've got to do it now. By this time tomorrow they could be long gone –'

'Then, damn it, get your F-111 back and bomb the hell out of Verrettes,' Hardcastle said. 'Or ask the President to send in the Rapid Deployment Force, or Delta Force, or the Special Forces. Brad, they killed over *forty* people on Hammerhead One. Michael Becker was on that platform –'

'I know, I know.' Hardcastle had rattled off options that Elliott was already considering, and he thought of some others too – his strike aircraft at Dreamland topping the list. Ever since organizing the Sukhoi-27 flight into Haiti, Elliott had put his second-in-command, John Ormack, and his staff to planning other reconnaissance and strike options against Verrettes, including aircraft not in any active Air Force operational squadron.

As if he could read Elliott's thoughts, Hardcastle asked, 'How long would it take the Air Force to come up with a plan to strike Verrettes, Brad?'

'All tactical fighter and Special Operations units have contingency plans for various regions of the world, pre-packaged and ready to be implemented – but I don't think Haiti is one of them. With computerized flight planning combined with the intelligence data we received from our own mission we could assemble a package in, say, four hours, brief it, get the aircraft and crews together and be airborne in six hours.'

536

'Then let's *do* it . . .'

'All that presumes we get a White House okay for a strike against Verrettes,' Elliott added quickly. 'Ian, you know as well as I do that the main bottleneck in any operation like this is getting the authorization. Most Air Force units can't load one bomb on a plane without permission from *someone* at least at the Secretary of the Air Force's level, and to execute a mission like this . . . it would probably need the President. He's been notified of the attack, of course, but he won't convene the Cabinet and the Joint Chiefs until morning – at least six hours from now.'

'But we can *start* to get the ball rolling before authorization.'

'We can draw up all the charts we want, gather intelligence, formulate options – but no wing commander is going to authorize the use of one of his crews, a plane or even one lousy iron bomb until he has permission from his boss. Air division won't approve it without permission from numbered air force. They won't approve it without permission from the major command. It goes up higher and higher and takes longer and longer – '

'Then we're going to lose Salazar. We're going to just let the guy go. Is that it?'

'I don't know,' he muttered as he let his finger off the TALK button and cursed into the air. He had to do something to protect his force. If he didn't act others might move in and take charge, or decide for him that they should disband. If there was one thing he had learned in ten years as a general officer it was that *everyone* expected the commander to take charge and *do* something. If he didn't do it someone else would.

His facts were still right – no military commander would authorize the use of his assets for a strike mission without approval from higher headquarters. But Elliott was a

537

commander – he could order his own troops to go anywhere within their capability. He was also the past commander of another flying organization – Dreamland, the High Technology Aerospace Weapon Center. He had weapons there, all highly classified, weapons that few in the world had even imagined let alone used in battle. John Ormack and the senior staff at Dreamland still consulted him on a regular basis – in effect he was still running things there too, although Ormack, now an Air Force one-star general, was in command.

Elliott went through his briefcase on the seat beside him, to Hardcastle's earlier facsimile transmission – the plan he and Patrick McLanahan had drawn up for an attack on Verrettes. He had had a chance to read it only briefly after it was received, and again briefly while being taken from Andrews to the White House earlier that day. 'Ian, this plan you and McLanahan drew up . . . you want to use the Seagull drones to draw out Salazar's air defenses – I read that much. Then what?'

'Use Sea Lions and Seagulls armed with rockets to take out the buildings and any targets of opportunity. After that . . . we'd have to land troops on Verrettes and capture Salazar and as many of his men as we could, but – '

'How many drones and Sea Lions are available right now?'

'Stand by, I'll check.' It took only a few moments for Hardcastle to call up the operational status of every air-breathing vehicle in the Hammerheads' inventory. As Elliott suspected, most of the available rotor-driven air machines were involved in search-and-rescue operations: 'We have twenty Seagulls, twelve Sky Lions and one Sea Lion here in Aladdin City. Five Sky Lions and four of our Sea Lions are involved in rescue operations. NAPALM has four Seagulls, five Sky Lions and one Sea Lion on board. Two of their Sea Lions are involved in rescue operations.

We have six other Sea Lions deployed in the Caribbean, Key West and along the Gulf, including two involved with recovery operations on Grand Bahama Island and two at the Cudjoe Key aerostat site – '

'All right.' The fixed-wing, speedy, well-armed Seagull drones were unsuitable for search-and-rescue operations so none were being used – that left the Seagull fleet available. 'Ian, I need to find out – '

'About the airborne drone-control system,' Hardcastle anticipated. 'I just buzzed McLanahan. Are we going to do this? Are we finally going to kick some ass around here?'

'I'm considering an authorized Border Security long-range search operation,' Elliott replied. 'We're not going out to kick any ass but with KEYSTONE, HIGHBAL and CARABAL down we're going to need some long-range eyes up there until we get our replacement picket-ships operating.'

'McLanahan here, General. You want to know the status of the airborne drone control system? If we can get our E-2 back from Mobile I can have the sensor software changed in about an hour. That'll put control of the drones in the hands of the senior radar controller – '

'I've already recalled the E-2 from Alabama,' Hardcastle said, referring to a sophisticated aircraft-carrier-based radar plane that could scan thousands of cubic miles of airspace at a time. Customs had acquired several of these planes for drug patrols and they were then turned over to the Hammerheads. With the aerostat sites in the southeast, the E-2 patrols were moved farther west, where aerostat coverage had not yet been established. 'His ETA is about thirty minutes. I was going to put him on patrol in the Santaren Channel to assist in recovery operations.'

'Do you need him for anything in particular?' Elliott asked.

'He was going to fill in the Caribbean radar picture for us

until we got the Navy ships on-line,' Hardcastle said, 'but I don't think we're going to see too many smugglers coming through here for a while, they'll be too worried they'll get their asses shot down by an F-16. I can kick him loose.'

'Good. Patrick, recover him in Aladdin City and begin the software change as soon as you can. Ian, get the Seagulls armed and ready to fly. We'll see if we can't put together a "patrol" with them tonight.'

Border Security Force Headquarters, Aladdin City, Florida
Two Hours Later

The ramp area of the Hammerheads' aircraft-parking area was ablaze with lights and bustling with activity as at least one AV-22 Sea Lion tilt-rotor landed or lifted off every three minutes. Fuel trucks scurried among the parked aircraft, refueling and servicing each plane minutes after it landed. There were ambulances parked near the head-quarters building with their rotating lights on but with no sirens – there was no need for hurry, no survivors had yet been found from Hammerhead One.

On the opposite side of the parking ramp the area was not as brightly lit and was more secluded but it was just as active with men pulling dark, bat-like shapes from storage hangars.

One by one the unusual-looking devices were prepared. A fuel truck serviced each of these aircraft, but the refueling operation took far less time than for the big tilt-rotor aircraft – more like putting gas into the family car at the corner service station, even to the extent of checking the engine oil and wiping the 'windshield,' in this case the bulbous six-inch-round glass sensor eye on the very nose of the Seagull long-range drone.

540

After refueling and the service check, armorers came out and fitted two fiberglass tubes onto the drones, one under each wing near the fuselage. Each tube was about three and a half inches in diameter and six feet long and weighed only forty pounds; two men could snap on a canister to a Seagull drone with ease. The canisters contained one Sea Stinger missile along with its remote-controlled firing system and a rocket-motor exhaust-deflection system to keep the missile's first-stage exhaust gases – which ejected the missile from the canister and far enough away from the drone to safely ignite the main rocket motor – from damaging the drone's propeller. Along with the six-missile Sea Stinger pod and the Chain Gun pod on the AV-22 Sea Lion aircraft that was going along on the mission, they would be carrying a total of forty-six deadly missiles.

While the aircraft were quickly, quietly fitted out, the crewmen were being briefed in one of the offices in the drone's maintenance hangar. Elliott had a map of the Caribbean on an easel – for an unauthorized, secret operation such as this, there were no sophisticated computer-generated graphics or presentations.

'The Hammerheads were dealt a blow tonight,' Elliott began. 'The latest word is thirty-five dead and five missing from the Hammerhead One platform. Three people, including two children, were killed at the CARABAL aerostat site during the attack. There were injuries sustained at the KEYSTONE site. One Air Force pilot is injured. Three of our four aerostats in the area have been destroyed or heavily damaged. The losses we sustained run into the billions.

'Earlier today I organized a mission into a remote Haitian airstrip called Verrettes, where we suspected a good deal of smuggling activity has been originating. Patrick McLanahan and one of my pilots from Nevada flew the mission. They landed, and the pilot actully spoke with the commander of the base, a Colonel Salazar. While at Verrettes, McLanahan and his partner observed several makes of sophisticated and heavily armed jets, including Russian MiG-21s, French Mirages, Aero Albatros attack planes and FMA Pucara ground-support aircraft. Salazar, an ex-Cuban Air Force officer, is supposedly a local militia commander, yet he commands an air force superior to that of any country in the Caribbean basin except Cuba itself.

'That was this morning. It is my strong suspicion that this Salazar organized an air strike against our aerostat stations in retaliation for our reconnaissance mission and to knock out our capability to interdict his drug-smuggling planes. The weapon load, flight characteristics, range and profile of the aircraft used in the air strikes all match those of the aircraft found at Verrettes, and match no other nation's air force except Cuba's, and we have no evidence to link Cuba with this act.

'We also now believe this Salazar and his group were responsible for attacks against the Coast Guard and Customs Service dating as far back as the Mahogany Hammock attack three years ago *and* the downing of a Coast Guard Falcon jet near Bimini, as well as the deliberate murder of children he carried in his smuggling planes in recent weeks. He may have been responsible for as much as fifty percent of the air-smuggling activities in the southeast in the last five years. He was for sure the man in charge of the air strikes tonight . . .

'So . . . by my authority as commander of the Border Security Force I am going to conduct a reconnaissance and surveillance mission into the Caribbean basin, specifically, against the Hispaniola–Cuba–Turks and Caicos area, with special emphasis on Haiti and the air base at Verrettes. Because of the possible threat from Salazar's forces I am directing that armed drones, controlled from our E-2 Hawkeye aircraft, precede the single AV-22 aircraft that

542

will conduct the mission. I am also directing that if any aircraft is attacked we will respond to protect our lives and insure the success of this mission.'

Elliott moved away from the front of the office and among the pilots, crewmembers and technicians involved in the mission, looking into the eyes of the heavily armed I-Team members and saying in a quiet matter-of-fact tone, 'What I've just told you is the official word, *my* official word, and you will use it if asked later on by competent authority. Otherwise this mission is strictly confidential . . . You all know, I think, the real objective behind this mission. We're going in to Verrettes to destroy Salazar's smuggling operation. If we see any aircraft on the ground at Verrettes, I will order McLanahan to attack them with the Seagull drones. I will also order him to attack any air-defense units, aircraft hangars, communications or maintenance facilities and aircraft shelters. If we don't encounter too much resistance I'll order the I-Team to move in and destroy any aircraft or key buildings remaining; otherwise the AV-22 will orbit the base and assess damage.

'We're going with twenty Seagull drones, each carrying two Sea Stinger missiles. I wish we had more but we can't get to them without stirring up too much suspicion. If the drones don't make it all the way into Verrettes because of heavy air defense, we abort the mission. I hope we'll take out a few of theirs on the way in.

'We'll have one AV-22 tilt-rotor, call-sign Lion Two-Nine. Rushell Masters will be the commander in Two-Nine. The mission commander will be myself, flying in Two-Nine's left seat. Two-Nine will carry a standard Sea Stinger pod and an M230 Chain Gun pod, with only one reload to save weight. We will carry an eight-man I-Team armed and armored, sidearms and rifles with M203 grenade launchers. I also wish we had heavier weapons but we don't have access to them. The AV-22 will have one RHIB on board.

'We'll have one E-2 Hawkeye radar plane, call-sign Lion Seven-One, which will be along primarily to control the drones from the air and secondarily to provide tactical warning for the package. Command of the drone package will be McLanahan aboard the E-2 Hawkeye.

'For support we'll have one V-22, Lion Three-Three, configured for inflight refueling for the AV-22 and the Hawkeye if necessary. He'll stay behind with the Hawkeye but he'll be armed with Sea Stingers and a Chain Gun pod and can assist in case anything happens at Verrettes. He'll carry an extra eight thousand pounds of fuel, which should be insurance for the manned aircraft in the package making the round trip.' Elliott looked at a dejected Hardcastle sitting in front of him. 'Sorry, Ian, but someone's got to hold down the fort.'

'Then let me do it.' The voice came in from the office door. Heads turned to see Sandra Geffar standing in the doorway wearing a flight suit and with her .45 in its shoulder rig. She wore a smile but it couldn't mask the pain she was feeling as she entered the office and, with Hardcastle's help, took a desk seat.

'What are you doing out of the hospital?'

'I was going to stay there with my platform destroyed and my crew dead? I'm all right. I haven't heard your whole briefing but I have a few suggestions – '

'You are *not* all right . . .'

'Okay, Dr Elliott, I'm not one hundred percent, I hurt like hell, but I don't belong in the hospital. I belong here.' She looked into Elliott's taut, exhausted face, scanned the other faces in the office. 'I've had a helluva lot more rest than any of you during the last forty-eight hours. You guys look worse than I feel. How much crew rest have *you* had?

Shall we start sending everyone home here that's not legally qualified to fly this mission?'

Elliott kept silent.

'All right, then. General Elliott, you shouldn't be in the AV-22 – you should be in the E-2 with McLanahan. You can't command a mission like this and act as copilot in an AV-22 at the same time. Move Ian into the AV-22 with Rush. I'll take command here with Annette.' She tried to cross her arms on her chest after finishing her pronouncement, thought better after the pain shot through her body, then sat quietly in the chair.

'All right. Recommendations accepted.' Who could argue? 'Ian, you're in Two-Nine with Rush.'

Elliott motioned to the map. 'We fly with approved flight plans along Alpha-39 to URSUS intersection, then south along Alpha-509. Our due-regard point at which we cease mandatory radio checkpoint reporting is over Great Inagua Island. The E-2 and the tanker V-22 will take up stations southeast of there. The rest of the aircraft will proceed south through the Windward Passage, turn inbound when we're halfway down the Gonave Gulf, go feet-dry south of the town of Saint-Marc and overland to Verrettes.

'Our major resistance will come from Verrettes. We'll cross within thirty miles of the Haitian naval base at Gonaives, but they have no anti-air capability. We may expect possible interference from Cuban aircraft – their closest air bases are at Holguin and Santiago de Cuba, about two hundred miles away – but at night, so far from Cuba, and on approved flight plans until just before overflight, I don't expect any trouble.

'Verrettes is defended by anti-aircraft artillery, fighters, and we can expect surface-to-air missiles similar to SA-7s or Stingers. Salazar commands at least two MiG-21s, two Mirage F1C fighters, two Aero Albatros and two FMA Pucara jets. Our Seagull drones will go in first and they'll plot the locations of any hostile air defense emplacements, map out the base in greater detail, and strike buildings, parked aircraft and other targets of opportunity. Rushell and I will move in after the drones check out the area for any additional reconnaissance information that remains . . . available.' In other words, he was thinking, they were the mop-up crew to hit anything the Seagulls missed.

'We'll withdraw and head back to Aladdin City for recovery. The mission is fourteen hundred miles with a planned duration of four hours enroute and no more than an hour over Verrettes. That leaves at least an hour for the Seagull drones in reserve. The E-2 has the legs for this mission but the AV-22 will have to refuel. There is no alternate recovery base for the Seagull drones except for Hammerhead Two. If we need to ditch a drone we can mark its position and have us or the Coast Guard retrieve it later. The E-2 and the tilt-rotors may recover in Puerto Rico or the Virgin Islands in case of emergency or if the AV-22 can't take on fuel. Other possibilities might be Guantanamo, Kew or Grand Turk in the Turks and Caicos Islands, any dry or shallow spot in the Bahamas, or Kingston in Jamaica.

'I've given you weather sheets, flight plans, orders of battle and Border Security Force landing and overflight authorization permits for the Bahamas and the Turks and Caicos Islands in your sortie kits. Stay well clear of Cuban airspace, and stay away from the Dominican Republic except in extreme emergency.' Elliott paused, looking at each crewmember carefully for signs of doubt, confusion or fear. He saw apprehension, nervousness and excitement – and grim determination. They might indeed be afraid of what they were about to do, but they were going in. He saw no heroes – but he did see guys ready to go up against the people that had struck so hard at their own. 'Questions?'

'What support can we expect from the Navy at Guantanamo Bay, sir?' one of the I-Team members asked.

'Very little. We have no authorization to land. If you need it, get on Navy Fleet Common or GUARD and ask for it, but don't expect it. Navassa Island, here, west of the Hotte Peninsula of Haiti, might be a good try in an emergency. The Navy has a radio communications facility there. As most of you know, we have confused political relations with Haiti, on-again, off-again, but the people are friendly . . .'

'Which means, take your green and take your plastic,' Rushell Masters said. 'These landing and overflight forms don't mean squat next to a good old American Express card.'

Elliott was thankful for Masters and his try at humor. 'We're not at war with Haiti or Cuba or anyone, remember that. We're going in to check out this Salazar and his terrorists in Verrettes. Any more questions? All right. We launch in thirty minutes.'

Elliott authorized the launch at 3:00 A.M., about five hours after the attack on the Hammerhead One platform began. The E-2 radar plane launched first from the Aladdin City runway in plain sight of reporters and onlookers surrounding the base – it would appear to be a normal part of the recovery operations.

With the E-2 heading southbound at slow speed, the Seagull drones began to launch. To avoid detection from onlookers the decision was made to launch the drones from an access road paralleling the taxiway opposite the main part of the Border Security Force complex. The drones needed only a few hundred feet for takeoff, and they would be flying away from the onlookers that crowded the main complex. An arresting net was set up at the end of the access road to catch any drones that had to abort their takeoff runs – and unfortunately two drones didn't make the launch; one hit the net hard enough to sustain damage, the other was stopped by McLanahan short of the net, serviced and launched minutes later.

As soon as the drones were launched, checked out for flyability and headed south along with the E-2, the two V-22 tilt-rotors made conventional heavyweight takeoffs from the main highway with the engine nacelles in full airplane rather than in helicopter mode – at their gross weight it would have taken more power, and so more fuel, to make the takeoff in helicopter mode. And they had to save every drop of fuel to insure they had enough while they were over such a heavily defended target as Verrettes. The two departing Sea Lions did cause some speculation as they made their takeoff runs, but only because all the others had made their more spectacular helicopter or hybrid airplane-helicopter takeoffs; in full airplane mode even a Sea Lion was not very unusual.

For the first hour the flight was very quiet. To be sure a fuel transfer could be made and to keep the tanks topped off while far from a major divert base, the E-2 and the AV-22 each filled up to full tanks from the tanker-modified V-22 when they were fifteen minutes from the orbit point. This meant that the drones had to be put on autopilot for several minutes during both the AV-22's and E-2's time on the hose-and-drogue refueling line, since any kind of strong radar emissions created a hazard with fuel vapors anywhere in the area.

The V-22 unreeled a long hose with a lighted padding-covered metal basket at the end. Once the basket or drogue was unreeled about a hundred feet from the back of the V-22, the E-2 and AV-22 in turn would fly behind the drogue, line up with it and insert a receptacle into the open side of the basket – magnetic clamps would then secure the receptacle to the drogue and fuel was pumped from the tanker V-22 to the receiver aircraft. The E-2 crew, more experienced at night air-refueling, got their unload quickly

548

and easily. Rushell Masters, who had practiced night refuelings only a few times in a simulator, took several minutes to make a contact.

'This is crazy,' he muttered after his third contact attempt. 'It's like trying to thread a needle at night on a roller coaster.'

'Just think about how far we have to swim back if you don't get this refueling,' Hardcastle told him.

'Hey, it's tough enough, all right?' Masters made contact on the next try and managed to stay in the basket for a few thousand pounds' worth of fuel then was forced to pull away on account of wild swings in the refueling envelope.

'I think you leaked more gas than you put in the tanks, Rush,' Hardcastle said, 'but I guess we got enough.' He referred to the computerized checklist on the center console display to finish the post-refueling checklist: 'Refueling valves closed, tanks to pressurize, fuel feed and quantity check.' He switched to the command radio: 'Two-Nine's in the green, eleven thousand pounds.' On interphone he ordered, 'Station check, crew. Check your gear, check the cabin, check your buddies.'

'Seven-One in the green, twelve thousand,' the E-2 pilot reported.

'Connectivity with all Seagulls reestablished,' McLanahan added. 'We might have a weapon problem with a coupla birds. I'm checking it out now.'

'Three-Three's in the green, fifteen thousand,' the pilot aboard the V-22 tanker replied. He carried six-thousand pounds extra fuel in fuselage ferry tanks. He would top off Lion Two-Nine once more after getting to the orbit point.

After reaching Great Inagua Island between Cuba and Haiti the E-2 took up a standard figure-eight orbit clear of national airspace boundaries. The two AV-22s and their gaggle of drones turned south and proceeded along the Windward Passage, the narrow strip of water between

Cuba and Haiti. As soon as they were established in the air corridor over the Windward Passage they set up for their last refueling before entering Haitian airspace.

Hardcastle made the first contact. 'You need to watch out for autogyration, Rush,' he said. 'When you fix on a small lighted object against a dark background the object will start to move on its own even though you're steady. If you try to chase it you'll be all over the sky. Concentrate on staying level with the tanker, and just guide the probe in toward the drogue. When you're in close you can tweak the probe in. Keep your eyes moving and use the tanker's profile to keep your horizon perspective.' As he talked Hardcastle gently glided the probe into the bushel-basket-size drogue. 'Two-Nine contact.'

'Three-Three contact, taking fuel.'

'Two-Nine.' Hardcastle took on a few hundred pounds of fuel, then ordered a disconnect and backed out. 'You got the airplane.'

'I've got it,' Masters acknowledged. With their target only a hundred miles away, Masters wasn't about to let anything go wrong – he plugged the AV-22's long boom receptacle into the extended drogue on the first try as if he had been doing it all his life.

'It's amazing how a little pucker-factor improves your air-refueling performance, Rush,' Hardcastle said.

'Damn straight,' Masters muttered, not taking his eyes off the lighted white ring in front of him. They completed their final air refueling hookup twenty miles outside the turnpoint and start-descent point, and the tanker-configured Sea Lion broke away and headed back to rejoin the E-2 Hawkeye over Great Inagua Island.

'You've got fifteen Seagulls on your tail,' McLanahan reported on the secure radio channel after they made their turn inbound toward Haiti. 'I aborted four on you – two because of connectivity faults with the Sea Stingers, one because of an engine problem, one because the data link seemed to get weaker at longer ranges. All the rest looked good, Admiral. You're clear to descend. I'll work the drones down behind you and keep them five hundred feet above you the whole time.'

'Thanks, people. Two-Nine's in the green with twelve thousand pounds,' Hardcastle replied. 'Talk to you in a few.' On interphone he said, 'Ready any time you are, Rush.'

'Go for it.'

'Roger. Autopilot is on, heading hold on, altitude hold off. Radar and radar altimeter.'

'On and checked,' Masters replied. 'Radar altimeter-alerter bug set to five hundred feet. Radar on terrain-avoidance mode, fault lights off, press-to-test good.'

'My left MFD set for TA, thirty-mile range,' Hardcastle said, setting his left-side nine-inch color computer monitor so it showed a wedge-shaped radar display with five-mile-range marks and flight-data information arranged along the edges. He set his second MFD to show engine and performance data, and the center MFD to show infrared scanner pictures. 'Checked and set.' He put his hands on the control stick and power control. 'I've got the airplane.'

'You've got the airplane,' Masters acknowledged, transferring control to Hardcastle so he could set up his own MFD configuration. He set his right MFD to show the radar data and the left main MFD to show engine peformance indicators in large numerals and graphic displays so he would immediately notice any engine malfunctions. 'My MFDs are checked and set. Let me test the IR picture first . . . if it's good I'll use it for landfall.'

Hardcastle punched the FLIR scanner controls on his control stick to ON, and the ten-inch nitrogen-cooled eye unstowed itself on the Sea Lion's nose and activated. They could easily see Haiti on the horizon ahead of them as a strip of white, with the coastal headlands looming cold and dark beyond. Masters lowered his helmet-targeting visor and activated the TADS/PNVS system, which slaved the scanner ball – and the Chain Gun pod when activated – to point at whatever he was looking at. The image projected clearly and without much distortion on the visor, still allowing him to see out the window and look at his MFDs and controls when he wanted. 'My sights look good.' He raised his targeting visor, glanced over at Hardcastle and put his hands on the controls once again. 'I've got the aircraft. Check out your sights and take another look around the cockpit. Make sure I've got the exterior lights off.'

'You've got the aircraft,' Hardcastle verified, placing his fingers on the light switches to double-check – there would be no use flying low to avoid detection if all the anticol-lision, strobes, position and running lights were still on. 'Exterior lights are off.'

On interphone Masters announced, 'Crew, prepare for low-level descent. Helmets, jackets, gloves, strapped in and secure.'

'Crew ready for descent,' the report from the I-Team commander came.

'Very good. Here we go.' On the command channel Masters called out, 'Two-Nine starting descent.'

'Roger, Two-Nine,' Elliott said on the radio. 'Good hunting. You've got the Seagull gaggle ready to go behind you.'

'Roger.' Masters gently pushed the control stick forward and the altitude slowly began to wind down. He trimmed the aircraft for a thousand-foot-per-minute descent rate and checked the radar altimeter to be sure it was respond-ing. 'Good radar altimeter, good radar. Nacelles still at zero.'

'Checks,' Hardcastle replied. He let his crosscheck cover

the cockpit, the instruments and out the windows as well. He could see a faint outline of the rugged coast ahead, but everything else was dark. Punching up the satellite-navigation system he double-checked the navigation data with three shore-based navigation radios. 'Looks like the satellite data's good. Right on course.' He made another scan.

'We would've heard something from Seven-One if we were off,' Masters said. 'Passing ten thousand feet for five hundred.'

'Checks,' Hardcastle replied.

Several minutes later the AV-22 leveled off at five hundred feet above the waters of the Golfe de la Gonave, thirty miles before reaching Haiti's west-central coast. Masters engaged the autopilot on hard-altitude hold and rechecked the radar altimeter, terrain-avoidance/terrain-following radar system and scanner system as the coastline approached. 'I've got a pretty good picture with the FLIR so I'll stick with that,' Masters announced. Hardcastle flipped the multimode radar to STANDBY so as to avoid detection by Haitian coastal defense units. They could hear a few isolated radio reports from airliners and small commercial planes heading into Port-au-Prince and Gonaives, but no alerts, either in Spanish, French or English, about the presence of the AV-22 or the drones.

'Feet dry for Two-Nine,' Hardcastle reported to Elliott as they crossed the coastline. He turned to his interphone: 'Ten minutes to target crossing, crew.'

'Here's where it starts hitting the fan,' Hardcastle muttered, tightening his lap and shoulder belts and rolling his sleeves back down. 'We should start seeing the drones move ahead of us.'

There were no messages from the E-2, no visual contact with the drones, no radio calls on any frequency. 'Six minutes,' Hardcastle announced. 'The drones should be approaching Verrettes soon.'

'Sure is quiet,' Masters said.

'I've got a feeling Salazar won't issue us any warning messages,' Hardcastle said, searching the sky all around them. 'If he finds us, he'll be right on our tail. McLanahan briefed that they didn't start getting challenged until they were relatively close to the base, and the drones are a lot smaller than a fighter.'

They waited another minute; by then, with only five minutes to go before the AV-22 arrived over Verrettes, they should have heard *something* – the attack couldn't be going this well . . . 'I can't stand it any longer,' Hardcastle said. 'I know I shouldn't break radio silence, but I gotta know what's going on.' He switched to the command frequency. 'Seven-One, this is Two-Nine. What's our status?' No reply. 'Seven-One, how copy?'

'Loud and clear, Two-Nine,' McLanahan replied.

'Where are the drones? What's going on? Are they engaging?'

A slight pause, then: 'Two-Nine, the drones are RTB at this time.'

'*What?* You're sending them back? *All* of them?'

'Affirmative.'

'Elliott, dammit, what the hell is going on? What are you doing? Are you sending us in there by ourselves? We don't have the firepower to do it by ourselves. What's going on? Are you under attack?'

'Negative, Two-Nine. We're in contact with you . . . and with Shadow One-One flight.'

'Shadow flight? Who are they?'

'Check out your two o'clock position, two miles.'

'What the hell . . . ?' Masters engaged the terrain-avoidance radar to help them stay above the rolling ground, engaged the autopilot, then used the infrared scanner to look out to his right. Hardcastle lowered his helmet-targeting visor and also looked out.

What they saw were two dark shapes that reminded Masters of two huge flying cockroaches. They had flat undercarriages, an unusually curved upper fuselage, stubby low-mounted wings and a very thin, steeply sloped aft section topped off with two thin, radically swept stubby vertical stabilizers. Unlike a normal aircraft's image in an infrared scanner, with a hot aft-end near the engine exhausts and a hot spot near the cockpit, this one appeared cool and dark all over with no telltale heat emissions to give itself away – its infrared signature was cooler than the surrounding countryside. Masters zoomed in on the two buglike aircraft, but even at high magnification he could make out little detail. The two planes slowly accelerated away from the AV-22 and were soon lost in the darkness – even looking at their aft end with the infrared seeker they could see no hot exhaust dots, no rear profile, not even an exhaust trail.

It had simply disappeared into the night. It was definitely out there, just a few miles away – easily within detection range of both the infrared scanner and the multimode radar – but none of their systems was picking them up.

'Did you *see* that?' Masters said. 'What were they?' He set the infrared scanner to full wide view – still nothing. 'I'm not picking them up on the FLIR. Did they go supersonic?'

'I don't think so,' Hardcastle replied. 'Stealth fighters don't go supersonic – '

'Stealth fighters? *Those* things were Stealth fighters? What are they doing here?'

'I think Elliott has just declared war on Salazar and the drug smugglers,' Hardcastle said in a low voice. 'He's not going to keep on using only Border Security assets to deal with those guys – he's brought in his own air force.'

'But . . . can he do that?' Masters asked, taking the AV-22 off hard autopilot and returning to manual flying with the scanner. 'I mean, how can he pretend this is a simple

Border Security Force reconnaissance run when he's got Stealth fighters flying around out here? Can Elliott order planes like that to – '

Masters paused, his mind racing as he realized what was happening. 'Elliott really *did* declare war on these guys,' Masters said cross-cockpit. 'He's going to bomb the bloody hell out of Verrettes . . .'

The town of Verrettes was located in the Artibonite River valley, a gently sloping fertile plane in the west-central part of Haiti. The F-117A Stealth fighters stayed at low altitude, less than five hundred feet above ground, hugging the crest of the hills and staying away from the road and railroad lines down toward the river. Unlike the AV-22 Sea Lion, the Stealth fighters did not use radar to search out the terrain – they employed a computerized navigation data-base to pick the minimum altitude along their route of flight, then used an infrared scanner to circumnavigate the occasional manmade obstructions not on the database.

The Stealth fighter was designed to avoid detection in several ways . . . Its multifaceted, bug-like shape did not allow radar energy to reflect directly back at enemy radar receivers, which reduced its radar signature. Its twin turbofan engines used a complex system of baffles to cool the engine exhaust to reduce the heat signature, making acquisition by passing heat detectors much more difficult. It used no radar transmitters for navigation, so it could not be detected by passive radar threat-warning receivers – it used infrared scanners, both forward- and downward-looking, for navigation and bombing. The Stealth carried no external weapons or fuel tanks – they had to bring a KC-135 tanker from their base in Tonopah, Nevada, all the way to the Great Inagua Island rendezvous point – a post-attack refueling was essential. All of the fighter's weapons were carried in semi-recessed fuselage wells in the belly, which reduced drag and radar signature. Although the F-117A could travel at supersonic speeds the sonic booms and shock waves would be a dead giveaway, so they stayed at a much more conservative, fuel-efficient speed of nine miles per minute as they sped toward Verrettes.

The Stealth's fighter crews were prepared for evasive maneuvers and even lower bomb-run altitudes but they received no indications of attack as they started their run. Instead of evading all the way to the runway, they were able to roll into their target and stabilize for several seconds, picking their aimpoints.

Each fighter-bomber carried two Durandal runway-cratering bombs and four infrared-imaging guided Maverick missiles. Taking ten-second separation between planes, the first Stealth fighter raced over the main runway, dropping the Durandal bombs along the runway centerline in two-thousand-foot intervals. The Durandal bombs had rocket-propelled warheads in them that dug several feet into the runway, then detonated with the shattering force of five hundred pounds of dynamite. The underground explosion heaved the steel reinforced concrete runway ten feet high out of a thirty-foot-wide crater, causing huge slabs of concrete to fly out of the hole like a deck of cards thrown into the wind. Because Verrettes had a wide parallel taxiway, the second Stealth fighter attacked that taxiway in the same way.

Within minutes the runway and main parallel taxiway at Verrettes were made completely unusable to fixed-wing jet aircraft – only a helicopter or light plane could safely avoid the craters.

The Stealth fighter crew had their eight Maverick missiles' targets very carefully laid out in advance. The fighter-bombers peeled off to the south of the base, executed several clearing turns to scan for pursuit or ground fire, then turned north back toward the base and lined up on their targets. Two missiles were immediately designated for the alert shelters at the end of the main runway; the rest were targeted against the larger hangars and fuel stubs where jet aircraft had been parked when McLanahan and Powell made their reconnaissance trip. One by one the Stealth crews searched out a target with their scanners, locked the image in their sights and launched the Maverick missile at a one- to two-mile range. The first F-117 would head in, fire a missile, clear the target, execute a clearing turn and turn in toward the next target while the second fighter made its attack. The two planes were like incessant insects, pouncing on a target, flying away out of reach, then zooming in again and again.

It did not take long to expend eight Maverick missiles. The Stealth fighters made one more pass over the base to examine the damage and consider reattacks on any targets that had only minor damage or for targets of opportunity. Each Stealth fighter also carried an internal twenty-millimeter gun with five hundred rounds of armor-piercing high-explosive ammunition, but no targets of opportunity seemed to be evident.

'Lion Seven-One, this is Shadow Flight. Off the target and clear. We will rendezvous and stand by for damage assessment by Lion Two-Nine. Over.'

'Seven-One copies. Clear of traffic.' The E-2 Hawkeye would continue to scan for any signs of pursuit as the Stealth fighters made their way out of Verrettes at treetop level and clear of Haiti. Once out over the Gulf of Gonave with no pursuit, they began a climb to a more fuel-efficient altitude and set up to refuel with the KC-135 tanker orbiting with the E-2.

Within two minutes the second raid of the F-117 Stealth fighter – the first had been against the Panamanian Defense Force in January of 1990 before the capture of Manuel Noriega – was successfully completed.

The AV-22 made its first pass over Verrettes at high speed – nearly five miles per minute – in case the base's air defense units had not been completely destroyed and had been reorganized after the Stealth fighters' attack. With the Sea Lion on hard autopilot, Hardcaste and Masters searched the base for signs of activity – the winking of anti-aircraft guns, scrambled taxi lights, even missiles being fired at them. Nothing. No lights on the base, none near the parking ramps, no sign of activity at all. The two switched between the FLIR scanner and regular visual checks – nothing.

Regardless, Masters performed a hard, sweeping combat break-and-clearing turn at the end of the runway in case they were pursued after their pass. He used the Sea Lion's prop-rotors and maneuverability to quickly change direction, swoop down to below treetop level and skim the ground at low altitude. He headed for a clear section of ground right behind the alert hangars – his first targets.

'Cannon and missile pods deployed,' Hardcastle called out. 'Pods armed and ready. TADS/PNVS to enable and COMBAT.'

Masters hovered twenty feet above ground behind the open backside of the alert shelters, searching for aircraft, soldiers, vehicles – nothing. The two Maverick missiles from the Stealth fighters had turned the insides of the shelters into burnt hulks of charred wood and twisted metal. The roof had collapsed, only small sections of the block walls were still standing. Masters searched hard and fast for a target – and found nothing.

'Time,' Hardcastle shouted. Masters poured the power on, sending his Sea Lion into a hard climb over the shelter. He quickly pivoted around at the top of the climb, pushed the nose down and zoomed back facing in the opposite direction, training the Chain Gun on the buildings and few trees behind the alert aircraft shelters. Again he searched for vehicles or troops that might have tried to get behind the AV-22 while it was in its hover – nothing.

'No aircraft in these shelters,' Masters called out. 'I see no vehicles, no troops, no bodies. The place looks deserted. This morning they had a jet-fighter squadron here – *we saw the pictures.* They must've had two dozen planes here, maybe two hundred men. How could they have packed up so fast?'

'They've got to be nearby,' Hardcastle said. 'Keep searching the buildings near the runway. We'll send out the I-Team if we find nothing else.'

Using unexpected severe cuts and maneuvers, Masters darted from building to building and from section to section, never being too predictable, never spending more than a few seconds on any spot before darting away. But after a few more minutes Hardcastle was convinced – the place was deserted.

Masters flew the AV-22 to the opposite side of the runway from the parking ramp and hangars and as close to a grove of trees as he could for seclusion and protection from shoulder-fired missiles. 'All right, I-Team,' Hardcastle said, 'we've swept the area and found nothing. We'll roll in across the runway between those two big hangars there, drop off the I-Team and get out again. You guys sweep the area for a few hundred yards. We'll orbit the periphery of the base and check for any soldiers that might be hiding and getting ready to move in on us. When the parking area's secure we'll come back and land.'

The AV-22 picked up about ten feet off the ground, then raced across the runway at almost a hundred miles an hour. Once he reached the parking area Masters pivoted the big tilt-rotor plane so his nose was facing out toward the runway and dropped quickly down to the pavement. The I-Team members scrambled out the rear cargo ramp, fanning out in different directions. They raised their rifles to any opening, rooftop or shadows they could find, ready to repel a sudden attack. When the last man was off, the AV-22 lifted straight up a hundred feet into the darkness, then turned and sped away.

The occupied part of the base was not very big, and it only took a few moments to cruise the perimeter. No sign of life. Off in the distance they detected a truck slowly heading toward the base, but it was several miles off and at its present speed and judging by the steep, twisting roads, would take a long time to reach them. Masters followed the main road from the front gate to the headquarters building, and although he did find a few abandoned vehicles with warm engine compartments he did not see one living being anywhere.

'I-Team, report,' Hardcastle said over the radio net. Masters cruised by the parking area again and set down in case any of the team needed support. But the I-Team had dispersed and there was no one else around – not even animals or birds.

'West sweep is negative,' the I-Team leader, Arturo Cordova, reported. 'I've checked all hangars in this direction. They obviously left in one helluva hurry.'

'North sweep is negative,' another member reported. 'I'm in the control tower. They left log books, notes, schedules, but no sign of soldiers or any recent activity.'

'Collect all the log books you can carry,' Hardcastle said. 'We'll make another sweep of the runway and perimeter and meet back between the hangars in ten minutes.'

'I-Team copies.' Cordova and his partner ran off toward the control tower to help with the search.

Masters lifted off and started another inspection of the trees and fence line. They found spots where towable anti-aircraft guns could have been placed, low-walked bunkers with separate ammunition bunkers nearby, but the pads and bunkers were empty. 'They booked, all right,'

Hardcastle said. 'They packed up this entire unit and bugged out in less than eighteen hours. That's pretty damn amazing.'

Just then, Elliott called on the command net: 'Two-Nine, this is Seven-One. Looks like you might have company. Judging by their speed, you could have a light fixed wing or chopper heading toward your position. His takeoff point looked like Port-au-Prince. He's got modes and codes – might be a Haitian military or police investigator. His ETA is one-three minutes. What's your status?'

'The place is deserted,' Hardcastle said. '*Nothing* here. We're picking up a few log books and records they left behind.'

'Okay. We need to start heading north with the drones to maintain contact so we need you airborne in ten minutes. Get FLIR videotapes of the base as you head out for damage assessment.'

'Copy that, Seven-One.' Hardcastle looked at Masters and shook his head. 'Elliott sounds like real calm, like attacking a deserted home base is par for the course for him.'

'He couldn't have known they'd bug out so fast. Still . . .'

'Still, it makes him, and us, look like idiots,' Hardcastle said. 'This was a well-planned, well-executed sortie. Only one goddamn little problem – the bad guys already got away.'

Aboard the E-2 Hawkeye Radar Plane, Lion Seven-One
Several Minutes Later

Elliott sat back in his seat between the radar operator and McLanahan's drone-control console. He was drained, could barely stand to look at the radar scopes any longer.

'Two-Nine's airborne,' the radar controller reported. 'That air target is still ten miles out, still heading for Verrettes. No other sign of pursuit.'

'Full connectivity with all drones,' McLanahan reported. 'Should be able to recover all of them back at Aladdin City.'

Elliott nodded, rubbing his eyes wearily. 'Send the Stealth fighters home,' he told the controller. 'We'll debrief once we get back on the ground. Tell them well done. Which is more than I can say for myself.'

'I still can't believe it,' McLanahan said. 'A US fighter base could probably pack up twenty planes and disperse them in eighteen hours, weapons and all, but they couldn't move all of its maintenance, administrative and operational assets in so short a time. These guys moved *everything*. Obviously they knew we were coming for them.' He paused, then added: 'You couldn't have known they would punch out so fast, general. Anyway, you *had* to go in there.'

'They must have planned to move their operation at the same time they planned to attack the aerostat units,' Elliott said. 'They figured we'd retaliate right away after such an attack – the strike aircraft were probably the last ones to leave Verrettes.'

'But where could they go?'

'Anywhere. They could be in Colombia – that's only six hundred miles away – or they could have gone a few miles further inland. Some of the cargo-class aircraft you saw could reach Mexico, or Venezuela, or even as far as Brazil.' He slapped a hand on an armrest. 'I *never* should have gone in without an intelligence update. My best bet was to keep them under constant surveillance when we figured out who they were. Instead I let them sneak away. Now they've mounted a successful attack on CARABAL, KEY-STONE, and HIGHBAL, *and* they got clean away.

We mount a big deal counteroffensive, and come up empty.'

Elliott was quiet for several moments, then, angry at himself, straightened up in his seat. 'All right, Patrick, we've still got work to do, and, I guess, be thankful that we're alive to fight another day . . . I need an update on the situation at Hammerhead One, KEYSTONE and CARABAL, plus a status report on our available units and mission capability. When you get a report from head-quarters we'll give the Secretary of Defense's office a call. That'll be no later than six A.M. – he should be awake but not yet at the Pentagon – and we should reach him before any reporters do in case this raid was somehow leaked to the press. I'll report what happened here tonight and ask to see the President in the morning. Our number-one priority has got to be reactivating the border security units in the affected areas. I'll suggest stationing sea-borne aerostat units in the Bimini Straits, the Straits of Florida off Key West and in Bahamian waters, and we'll get the carrier stationed near Hammerhead so we can reestablish airspace control.

'Once we've done that – we'll coordinate a search for this magician Salazar and his outfit. We can check radar records for flights out of Haiti and try to follow up any suspicious flights from Haiti to isolated parts of countries in the region. We should also get together with CIA and our DEA guys to figure out a way to draw Salazar out into the open – he'll go deep underground for a while.'

'There's one way to dig these guys out of hiding,' McLanahan said. 'Money. It can outweigh the fear of discovery . . .'

But when? How long? Elliott thought. He couldn't just sit and wait. He needed to smoke them out. Somehow . . .

* * *

The White House Oval Office
Two Hours Later

'Say that again, Tom,' the President said, staring at Secretary of Defense Preston. 'Elliott flew a mission to Haiti – an *attack* mission?'

'So he reported this to me a few minutes ago. His mission was – '

'*His* mission? I didn't order any mission to Haiti, especially not a damned attack mission. What did he do? What did he use? Another B-52?'

'Two Sea Lion tilt-rotor aircraft from his headquarters in Florida, one E-2 radar plane belonging to the Border Security Force, twenty armed Seagull drones and two F-117 Stealth fighters from the tactical fighter unit in Nevada.'

'Stealth fighters . . . he used *Stealth fighters* on this mission without my authorization? How can he do that? How can he even get his hands on those things without my permission?'

'Sir, General Elliott was in charge of the test unit at Tonopah for many years before it became a tactical fighter wing. He's still in virtual command of his unit at the weapons test center in Nevada even though he's not active there – '

'I should have that sonofabitch shot. What's he going to do next? Bomb Cuba? Bomb China? Bomb Washington if he doesn't get what he wants when he wants?'

'Sir, if I could offer an explanation . . . He was fully empowered to conduct this operation.' The President only stared at Preston. 'As a member of the US military, as a de facto military commander and general officer, he has authority to conduct security, defensive, counter-insurgency, search-and-destroy and reconnaissance operations in defense of his installations and in defense of the

United States. General Elliott followed the rules, sir. He conducted an authorized reconnaissance mission. He briefed you yesterday on his findings, on the threat posed to his command, his installations, to the security of the country and on appropriate responses. Four of his installations came under attack last night and he had every reason to believe that the attack came from that base in Haiti. He had no other option – he had to respond with force. There's no question – '

'Can the lecture, Tom. He acted without notifying anyone – not even you . . .'

'Commanders aren't required to immediately notify us when their bases or commands come under attack – '

'That's bull, Preston – '

'It's also the truth. If Russia had a change of heart and Soviet tanks started rolling across into West Germany, we'd expect our commanders there to execute their wartime responses, defend their installations and fight back – without notifying us immediately. If they saw a weakness that they felt they had to exploit, we would expect them to do it if it served to protect American lives and property. We expect our commanders to act, Mr President. General Elliott did just that.'

The President seemed to calm down as he turned to his Chief of Staff, Jack Pledgeman: 'I want Martindale, Chapman, Curtis and Mitchell in here. Quietly, Jack.' Pledgeman left to use the phone in the outer office.

'All right. Let's table whether he had authority to do what he did. What did he find over there? What happened?'

'The base had been evacuated,' Preston told him, and added the details.

'What about these drones, these Seagull things?'

'They weren't used in the attack. I think General Elliott had planned on using them if he couldn't obtain the Stealth fighters.'

'Everyone got out? No casualties?'

'General Elliott reported the loss of two drones enroute,' Preston said, 'apparently due to maintenance problems. They were parachuted to the ocean and will be recovered by a Border Security Force crew. Under the circumstances, I am impressed with the operation. General Elliott organized quite a mission in little time, in utter secrecy and with considerable firepower given his limited resources and the need for fast execution. If he had encountered resistance in Haiti he still would have had a very good chance for success with few or no casualties. He struck with speed, precision and restraint – '

'Yeah, I know. You love the guy, everybody goddamn loves the guy. But I don't want him running all over the Caribbean slinging bombs at every strip of land that looks like a smuggler's hideout. I don't want my commanders planning their own strikes against foreign nations without my explicit approval. I don't care what the book says his responsibility is. Defending American airspace is one thing – bombing another country is another, for God's sake!'

'I'll be sure to give that message to General Elliott,' Preston dead-panned. 'He's due here in about three hours. Would you like to see him?'

'Yes, I'd like to see him. I'd also like to strangle that four-star sonofabitch. No, maybe I'll demote him to lieutenant colonel and *then* strangle the sonofabitch.'

'I believe the people will be expecting an appropriate response to the attack, sir,' Preston pointed out. 'General Elliott's strike, as much as you disapprove of it, may fill the bill very well.' He paused, reading the smoldering doubt in the President's face. 'We may consider leaking it to the press tonight, or perhaps tomorrow. No details, of course – but it will be that much more believable because we will neither confirm nor deny it. If the press investigates and finds a bombed-out base in Haiti – well, we still deny it but

567

the public will have what it wants. People love secrets – especially when they discover them.'

'There's nothing I hate more than playing games like that. I don't want to be forced to accept Elliott's gunslinger act as part of my foreign policy and *then* have to play the informed-White-House-sources-leak game.'

'Are you certain, Mr President, that what General Elliott did was not what you really wanted?'

'What are you talking about. . . ?'

'I'm just suggesting that perhaps all you wanted was to be in control of the situation. You're not necessarily objecting to the mission per se, you object to not being informed and not directing the effort – '

'I don't need your two-bit psychoanalysis, Preston.' But the truth was, he silently admitted, Preston probably was right . . . 'I want you to brief the rest of the staff for me when they arrive – delay my scheduled news conference if you need to.' Pledgeman arrived back in the Oval Office, but before he could say anything the President snapped, 'They should be here by now, Jack.'

'Waiting on Director Mitchell, sir. He's down in the communications center.'

'We'll start without him. Send 'em in, Jack. I hope the hell they brought briefing notes for me.'

'Got them right here, sir,' Pledgeman said, holding up a stack of briefing sheets – he would condense and revise these so that the President could refer to them if he needed to during the press conference.

'I need them in five minutes.' The President got to his feet and moved away from the tall window to his right – the one that looked out over the White House lawn, the one through which reporters with long lenses could get pictures of the chief executive. He had always wanted to move his desk away from that window, but it had always been there and probably always would. It was a symbol of the presidency, an image of the man in charge, hard at work . . .

The man in charge . . . Sometimes it was nothing but a damn joke . . .

The White House Situation Room
Three Hours Later

The Vice President, two military aides and Brad Elliott were the only ones left in the Situation Room. The last hourly meeting with the President and his Cabinet had just broken up, and developments in the Caribbean were now being handled directly from the White House. Everyone was required to stay in touch, which meant stay in the White House. From the Situation Room most calls and messages did not have to go through the switchboard or the Chief of Staff's office, which allowed greater speed and responsiveness.

They were all watching the replay of the President's press conference – as expected, it had been no picnic – along with inserted pictures of the destroyed Hammerhead One platform surrounded by rescue ships. Off in the background the camera picked up the looming sight of the USS *Coral Sea*, now on station to provide border security and area-interdiction duties. The commentators were now interjecting their thoughts on the horror that had occurred in south Florida, but the Vice President had the sound turned down as he began: 'What a damned nightmare,' he muttered. 'Forced to use one of our carriers, even an old bitch like the *Coral Sea*, to protect our *own* shores. The press is having a field day.'

'Anything is better than leaving the area unprotected,' Elliott said. 'The aircraft carrier is our best option until we activate a new platform.'

569

'And how long will that be?'

'We can have a new platform in place in two weeks. Outfitting it for full-flight operations will take another one to two months. Getting an aerostat unit on board, another few months. In all, perhaps a year for a fully operational platform. The plan is to make the new platform less of a command center and more of a remote airbase – less personnel, less computers, less monitoring systems. All those functions can be done from headquarters . . .

'A better option would be to tow Hammerhead Two from west Florida to take over in this area, and move the *Coral Sea* to west Florida. From there it can cruise the Gulf and stage flight operations that could control the region. We can beef up the platform's defensive armament to protect it against attack, but with the F-16s at Homestead so close and with other Navy ships in the area I think smugglers will stay clear of the platform.'

The Vice President did not reply immediately but closed his eyes and nodded. 'Submit the pricetags for both proposals to me and I'll present them to the Old Man. But don't expect too much. He is plenty pissed off, and when you come to him asking for money he's likely to blow his top – '

The door to the Situation Room opened and the President along with Chief of Staff Pledgeman, Secretary of Defense Preston, Drug Control Advisor Massey and National Security Advisor Curtis entered. The President took his place at the head of the table, waited as Pledgeman arranged reports and papers around him, motioned to the stenographer, who was sitting patiently in a corner of the room, then looked at Elliott for the first time. 'Had a busy twenty-four hours, General?'

'Yes, sir.'

'I know Preston and Chapman and their staffs have debriefed you. I have their notes here,' the President said, motioning to the folders arranged in front of him. 'General Elliott, why the hell didn't you notify the White House of your intention to fly this mission to Haiti?'

'If we were to have any chance of stopping the terrorists responsible for the attack on our aerostats and air-staging platforms we had to act – '

'You're right, but not unilaterally. You don't have the authority to bomb another country. You could have caused a major embarrassment to this administration. We counted on you to lead the Border Security Force in time of a major disaster. I find you were out bombing some airstrip in Haiti – and with Stealth fighters, which you surely have no authority to employ.'

The President paused, staring at Elliott. Elliott stared back. 'We all know you're a resourceful, intelligent and effective commander, Brad – but dammit, you're an agent of the President of the United States, not an authority unto yourself.'

'I'm sure you realize, Mr President, that I believe that all my actions were based on what I thought was necessary and right for security and for the Border Security Force,' Elliott said. 'I do have a responsibility to defend the United States, and I did what I thought was necessary at the time to do that. I made a decision and acted.'

'So you did.' The President folded his hands, took a deep breath and said, 'All right, on consultation with the Cabinet – which was by no means unanimous – no action will be taken against you. We need to get through this and back on our feet. It's not an endorsement of what you did. I expect you to carry out the orders given you and to conduct operations within your specific area of responsibility, namely the border identification areas specified in the Border Security Force charter. All other operations require approval by me. Clear, General?'

'Yes, sir.'

571

'Brad, you're a hell of an officer, a man who can get things done, but if I can't trust you I'll replace you in a heartbeat. My meaning had better be crystal clear.'

'It is, sir.'

'Okay.' He opened the first folder in front of him, an agenda of items to consider in response to the attack. 'Let's talk about what we do next . . .'

'If I may, sir,' Elliott spoke up immediately. The President looked up from his notes, suppressed a sigh and acknowledged him with a slight nod.

'The first thing you need to do, Mr President, is fire me and deactivate the Hammerhead Two air-staging platform.'

'*What?* Elliott, what the hell are you talking about?'

'Sir, the smuggling outfit of Colonel Agusto Salazar has gone underground. We weren't able to get an accurate fix on his location when he made his escape from Haiti. He could be anywhere in Central or South America. I've got a plan that I think will help draw him out of hiding to attempt a large-scale drug shipment, but for it to be successful we have to convince him that the Hammerheads are being phased out and that it will be relatively safe for him to make another shipment . . .' He looked for a reaction, saw none and rushed on . . . 'For that to be believable you must announce that I will be forced to step down because of my bungling Border Security Force operations, and that the Hammerhead Two platform will be towed into shore for repairs and eventual replacement in the Straits of Florida, where Hammerhead One used to be.' Now he was getting reactions, mostly incredulous stares. 'You will announce that the carrier *Coral Sea* will be moved to west Florida to replace Hammerhead Two, but instead it will pull into port, at St Petersburg or Mobile, Alabama, and stay there because of budget constraints and Congressional opposition to the whole Border Security Force concept.'

'This may not be a pretend scenario, General,' the President said, 'if you keep on like this . . .'

'Sir, we can't allow Salazar's group the luxury of developing alternate smuggling routes and distribution networks across the Mexican border or in the west – the Hammerheads aren't set up yet for large-scale operations there. His networks are already well established in Florida and the southeast, and so are the Hammerheads. But if we make some macho pledge to blast every unknown vessel or aircraft in the region to hell, Salazar may well not risk sending his planes or ships into the area and decide to stay underground. If he does that it may take our intelligence network months to find him.'

'What makes you so sure he won't stay underground and bring his drugs in some other place, Brad?' Chairman of the Joint Chiefs Curtis asked. 'This Salazar guy's a rat but he's not stupid.'

'I have no guarantee that he won't ignore what is happening and continue operating someplace else. But all our information points to one significant fact – that the drug capital of the world is, and probably always will be, south Florida. We've noted that drugs that have been imported someplace other than Florida, as far away as California, are eventually *tracked back to Florida*, where they're put into the distribution pipeline. For example, the smugglers killed in the raid in Louisiana were members of a New York crime syndicate that operates out of Miami. We have every indication that the shipment brought in that night was headed for New York but back through Florida. There's no established pipeline for shipments this size from the deep south to the northeast – they all must go through Florida. The only reason that shipment *landed* in Louisiana was because we had the southeast locked up tight. I feel if we tell the world we will continue to secure the southeast, especially with heavy weapons, then Salazar will quietly explore entrees in other areas. But if he perceives what he thinks is a weakness in our operations in the southeast he might be bold enough and cocky enough to rush in, or at least surface. Then we have a chance of catching him.'

'If you have no platforms or radars watching the coast,' Vice President Martindale asked, 'how are you going to find the smugglers – *if* they're all that cooperative and try more drug runs?'

'With the ROTH radar in Arkansas, sir. The over-the-horizon backscatter radar can detect planes and vessels for hundreds of miles, from the North Carolina coast almost to California. That system can get our planes in close enough for them to use their on-board radars to complete the intercept.'

'I've seen the ROTH radar in action,' Drug Control Advisor Massey said, 'and it is a very impressive device. But you pointed out several serious deficiencies in the system – its lack of reliable altitude data, its atmospheric vulnerability, its experimental status. Can we count on this ROTH radar to stop Salazar when and if he tries another drug run?'

'I understand there are a lot of ifs here,' Elliott said. 'But I believe it's our best chance. We can rely on intelligence and informants to find Salazar, and hope by then that he hasn't busted the borders wide open and flooded the market with drugs before we nail him. Or we can try to lure him out by pretending to be weakened by his attack.

'Salazar feeds on weakness and is driven by greed. He'll return because the chances for big profits are better than ever before. *But* if we send in the Navy to secure the southeast he'll stay away and find another weak spot – and we have a lot of them, especially over the Mexican border. We've seen him move his operation westward faster than we can keep up with him, and we have to stop him before he establishes a major network there.'

The President turned to the others around him. 'Comments?'

'With respect, General Elliott,' Drug Advisor Samuel Massey said, 'I think this incident has shown us that we should rethink this entire Border Security Force concept. We may have called it the Border Security Force, and we may delude ourselves into thinking this is only a paramilitary organization, but in essence the Border Security Force, these Hammerheads, are fulfilling a military function, Brad. I give you and Admiral Hardcastle and Chief Inspector Geffar all the credit in the world. What you've done in the past couple of years has been outstanding. But now we have to keep an aircraft carrier in place out there, plus pay billions more to replace what was destroyed – not to mention the irreplaceable loss of life – and on top of all that we still need to insure that we have adequate military forces in the region to protect all these assets . . . I suggest we disband the Border Security Force for *real* and integrate the remaining assets into the standing military forces. We could use mothballed Navy ships on patrol in place of vulnerable oil platforms. These vessels can still launch and recover aircraft and drones, and drug-interdiction duties can be combined with other exercises or patrols . . .'

And you, Massey, you son of a bitch, can get rid of us, which you've wanted to do ever since Hardcastle came up with the Hammerheads idea, Elliott thought and almost said aloud. Fortunately the President made it unnecessary.

'Very good, Sam, draw up some notes for me, turn them over to the Vice President. For now, however, I want the Border Security Force to continue their operations as planned.'

He then turned to the Vice President: 'Kevin, I'm going to drop this one on your lap. Get together with General Elliott and Secretary Preston, draw up a plan of action, and brief me on it as soon as possible. It's an intriguing ploy, we'll give it a try.' To Elliott he said, 'Brad' – he paused, an exasperated-amused smile was on his face – 'Brad, you're like a damned cat – somehow you always manage to land on your feet. I was ready to string you up this morning, and here I am going along with your crazy idea. Which you better pray works . . .'

Jabbing a thumb at Elliott, he turned to the Vice President and said with a straight face, 'Okay, Kevin, fire that sonofabitch.'

Chapter Nine

Westchester, Florida
Two Weeks Later

Hardcastle surprised himself at how good he used to live. The house that his ex-wife Jennifer now lived in with Daniel was a lovely two-story Tudor-style home in a gated community southwest of Miami. As he parked his old station wagon out front, he reminded himself he was not here on a nostalgia trip. He was here to try to regain a son.

He saw a brand-new motorcycle parked beside the garage under the eaves. So this was Jennifer's solution to the trouble Daniel had gotten into when he 'borrowed' the motorcycle to see his father. His irritation quickly subsided when he realized that the incident had happened almost three years ago. And he had seen Daniel maybe a dozen times since then.

He noted another car in the driveway, a foreign job he didn't recognize. But he was sure it belonged to Jennifer's attorney and sometime companion – Hardcastle still couldn't imagine them as lovers – Vance Hargrove.

Hardcastle had come here right after another fifteen-hour day at Border Security Force headquarters. Too damn many hassles with the Navy, the DOD, the Coast Guard, everybody . . . Getting the *Coral Sea* moved to west Florida was bad enough, but now the state of Florida and the Coast Guard were having major problems moving the Hammerhead Two platform to the east side – they were afraid of toxic spills, terrorist acts, expenses, of their own damn shadows.

Jennifer had sounded upset enough to make him come right over from Aladdin City without changing out of his Hammerheads flight overalls with his SIG Sauer automatic in the belt holster – the old rule about Border Security Force members not wearing sidearms off-duty had been relaxed since the attacks on the aerostat units. At first he'd been annoyed, then realized it could be serious, and maybe it would give him a chance to get close to Daniel . . .

Jennifer answered the door, and skipped the niceties.

'Come in.' She said it like an order, not an invitation.

'What's wrong? You sounded upset over the phone.' In the foyer he wasn't surprised to see Vance in his six-hundred-dollar suit and silk tie, a crystal glass of something amber in his hand.

'He's upstairs,' she said coolly.

'What's he doing?'

'You tell me.'

'Come on, Jen, what's up?'

'What's up is I think he's doing drugs. He spends all his time in his room. He stays out until all hours. I'm *worried* about him.'

'Have you tried talking to him?'

'Of course. He says there's nothing to worry about, everything's fine. But, he just seems more and more . . . distant. I can't control him, I'm at a loss – '

'I can see that.' He nodded toward Hargrove. 'Why is *he* here?'

'He called this afternoon. I told him what I thought was happening and he came over . . .'

'He's your lawyer, not Danny's father. Never mind,' he said; he unbuckled his leather belt, removed his ammunition belt and holster.

Hardcastle could smell it before he reached the top of the stairs, the sweet but pungent odor of marijuana. Oddly enough, Hardcastle's first reaction wasn't anger towards

578

Daniel – it was anger towards his ex-wife. Cooking heroin? Jennifer was a bit protected all her life, but he assumed even she could recognize pot when she smelled it.

He went to Daniel's room and knocked on the door. 'Daniel?'

'Dad?' He noted a bit of surprise in his son's voice; he fully expected a long delay as Daniel tried to conceal the evidence, but the door opened right away. 'Hey, Dad, I didn't expect you.'

'Can I come in?'

Daniel seemed genuinely surprised at the question. 'Hey, it's your house . . .' Then, he grinned and added, 'Well, it used to be . . . I mean . . .'

'Forget it. I know what you mean.' He entered the room, and Daniel shoveled an armful of clothes off an armchair – one of the armchairs that used to be downstairs, one of *his* den chairs – and motioned his father to sit down.

'Fine, Dad, fine.' Daniel was trying hard to carry it off. 'Just up here studying for a test. How are things with you? Sounds like the Hammerheads are in some hot water.'

'We've had better days. Your mother's worried about you,' Hardcastle began. 'She thinks you're up here cooking heroin.'

'Heroin? Is she kidding . . . ?'

'No, she's very serious,' Hardcastle said. He looked around the room, then back at his son. 'She doesn't know – or chooses not to know – what marijuana smells like. She's scared, bud. I wish you'd straighten it out with her.'

'It wouldn't do any good . . .'

'You know that's not true, Daniel. She adores you. If you explain what you're doing, she'll listen.'

Daniel looked at his father with a puzzled expression. 'What about you? You're not mad at me? For doing grass up here?'

'You were expecting me to be angry . . . maybe hoping

I'd be. Listen, Daniel, I don't like it, you know that. Considering what I do for a living, it's not exactly what I'd hoped for. But, damn it, you're old enough to make up your own mind about some things. You want to do that stuff, it's your life, go ahead and do it. But I do care. I worry about you. I'm worried that you need pot to help yourself feel good, and I'm worried that you might be out driving that motorcycle after you've had a few hits of that stuff. I'm worried that if you keep on doing grass that it might lead to your doing hard drugs, and then your life will really be screwed up. But I know I can't run your life for you, Danny. Just think about why you're doing it before you do it. Think about going on the freeways with that motorcycle out there before doing that stuff – if you get into an accident on that thing . . . Remember, other people can get hurt.' He paused. 'Well, open up with your mother a bit more . . .'

'I don't think she'd understand, Dad. I think she'd go into hysterics. She'd throw me into a rehab clinic – or into jail.' He paused, smiled, then added, 'Or call my father on me. Is that what she did? Call the old man?'

Hardcastle wanted to smile at his son's intuitiveness, indulge in a little 'chip of the old block' self-gratification, but instead he shook his head. 'Never mind that. The bottom line is this: she was worried about you – terrified is more like it – and she wanted to talk with someone before she confronted you like an inquisitor. That's the kind of treatment you get when you're dishonest with someone.'

'With Mom, it's better to keep this kind of news away from her,' Daniel insisted. 'If I drank a bottle of wine at dinner every night, she'd think I was being sociable. If I took one hit on a joint in her presence she'd flip out.'

'Probably so. Most people would.'

'Sure. I get it. "Wine is fine but pot is not," right?'

'Christ,' Hardcastle said with a sardonic laugh, 'that's the same damned line we used back in the sixties, and I'm sorry we used it back then because it sounds pretty lame now. Neither is fine, and you know it.' Daniel shrugged and nodded.

'Just think about why you're doing it before you do it, that's all I ask. Remember it's just like drinking alcohol – it'll impair your driving, your reaction time, your motor skills. Think about going on the freeways with that motorcycle out there before doing that stuff – if you get into an accident on that thing, you're dead meat. Also, remember that the slightest reference to drugs these days will bring the wrath of God down on you – the cops are everywhere, the judges are under a lot of pressure to reduce drug use – and lines like "wine is fine but pot is not" won't get you anywhere with the law. If they catch you using, carrying, or buying that stuff in anything but tiny quantities, they'll hammer you, hammer me, hammer your mother. Do you understand what I'm saying? Vice is *not* a victimless crime, Daniel. Other people get hurt. I just want you to know that. Hey, I'm a great one to talk. Flying that Sea Lion after your victory dinner wasn't exactly a smart idea. Remember that?'

'How can I ever forget? I was shocked, scared, I guess I thought I'd die.' Daniel touched his head where bits of the pilot's helmet and his seat had cut him, blasted by the smuggler's bullets. Hardcastle shook his head . . . his son came so close to death . . . 'I lectured you that night you got pulled in by the sheriffs, and then I pulled a stunt like flying after drinking.'

Daniel couldn't quite believe what he was hearing, but he was liking it. 'Maybe messing up runs a little in this family,' Daniel said.

'And maybe I get a son who's got more sense than his old man. I think I better get to know him better . . .'

The two sat quietly now, savoring something neither had known for years . . . the sense of being father and son . . .

'So what about the Hammerheads?' Daniel asked. 'They say on the news you won't be around too much longer.'

Hardcastle shrugged. 'It's all up in the air, Daniel. Right now we're just trying to get back on our feet.'

'They went ahead and fired General Elliott?'

Hardcastle nodded.

'Why?'

Hardcastle couldn't talk about the secret mission to Haiti, couldn't talk about the ploy cooked up to try to lure the smugglers into the open. 'I don't understand it myself, except sometimes it shakes things up to fire the head honcho. Elliott's been there for almost three years, that's about par for the course.'

'I liked the guy,' Daniel said. 'He seems pretty cool on TV. Full of piss and vinegar.'

'I think the general would like that characterization,' Hardcastle said.

A beat of silence. Several of them. Finally, Daniel said, 'So maybe I should go down and talk to Mom, huh?'

'I think that's a good idea,' Hardcastle said. 'You may want to wait until after Hargrove leaves.'

'The man's a wimp,' Daniel said with a smile. 'He's over here every day sniffing after Mom.' At his father's disapproving glare, he added, 'Mom likes having him over, but she doesn't encourage him. Don't worry. I think the only meat Mom's getting from Greg is dinner at Aldo's.'

'Where the hell you learn how to talk like that?' Hardcastle said with a short laugh. 'Certainly not from your old man.'

'Nahhh . . .'

'You talk about getting high or getting stoned? Hargrove is down there right now drinking something or other, and he'll be off in his Beemer or Jag or whatever he's driving and be on the highways. But that's considered acceptable these days. True, the public tolerance for alcohol is tightening, but guys like Hargrove can get away wih driving with a snootful, even if he does get caught. Where's the lesson here? Some of my officers celebrate after they catch a big drug smuggler by going out and getting shit-faced at some sleazy Miami bars. That doesn't say much for our society when we reward ourselves with alcohol while trying to stop drugs.' He shrugged his shoulders and said, 'Lecture over.'

Hardcastle nodded, then let himself go and hugged his son. 'Well, I better be going.'

Downstairs he said a quick good-bye to Jennifer and went outside. He saw Hargrove leaning on his car hood and walked past him without saying a word. Hargrove and Jennifer exchanged a few words, followed by the sound of the car door closing. The big foreign-make engine revved up and Hargrove peeled down the driveway and out into the street with a roar.

Hardcastle got into his old station wagon and pulled out into traffic. Well, it had been quite a day – he had gotten his son back, managed to see Jennifer without doing battle . . . now to top it off, one more thing to do . . .

He pulled the portable radio out of its belt holster. 'Aladdin, this is Tiger.'

'Go ahead, Tiger.'

'Relay a message to Dade County for me. Ask them to look out for a silver Alfa Romeo, vanity license number hotel-golf-romeo-oscar-victor-echo-november-two, last seen heading eastbound on Taimiami Trail Boulevard. He seems to be weaving in traffic. Ask them to investigate. Over.'

'Copy all, Tiger.'

'Thanks. Tiger is ten-six. Out.'

The end of a damn near perfect day.

* * *

On a Yacht Off the Coast of Belize, Central America
Several Days Later

A motor launch pulled up alongside the gleaming white steel sides of Gachez's yacht and two figures disembarked and steeped up the boarding stairs. They were thoroughly searched after reaching the top of the stairs and escorted before decks into the main salon.

Agusto Salazar spotted Gachez seated behind an expensive walnut desk in the salon and opened his arms wide. 'My old friend,' Salazar said in a loud voice. 'Good to see you again. It was very kind of you to invite me on board.' He moved closer to the desk. Gachez had not gotten to his feet but continued puffing on a cigar. Salazar lowered his arms but not his fixed smile. Finally Gachez motioned Salazar to a leather chair in front of the desk. This time Salazar did the ignoring.

Gachez watched Salazar move around the salon. After a few moments he motioned to the man beside him. 'Leave us.'

Maxwell Van Nuys looked at both Salazar and Gachez. Ever since the incident at Sunrise Beach, Van Nuys had been under the protection, more or less, of Gachez and the Medellín Cartel, in return shuttling around the Caribbean, and even the United States on occasion, on errands. His latest was to escort Salazar to Gachez for this meeting. 'We're partners now, Gachez,' Van Nuys protested. 'If you're going to make a deal with this peacock, I want to be in on it.'

'This is personal, Van Nuys. You will be involved in any business discussions we might have.'

'I had better be. I'm taking the big risk here.' Still not satisfied but not wanting to start an argument in front of Salazar, Van Nuys left.

'I am impressed with your new errand boy, Luiz,' Salazar said. 'Impertinent, but that is true for all Americans.'

'Bypassing customs inspections in Belize is child's play,' Gachez said. 'But he seems to have the Mexican *federales* on his payroll as well. I used to have police helicopters circling my yacht in Mexico taking pictures – now I have *federales* calling me sir and flying me to the airport. He has managed to open up new shipment routes and distribution networks all across the region, including the southwest United States, and his holding companies, casinos, banks and real estate ventures make good investment vehicles for the Cartel. We have made new inroads into legitimate enterprises. But Van Nuys can't provide us with a way to move product in bulk.'

'Which is why you have called on me.'

'My associates and I would like to know if the Cuchillos are available for business,' Gachez said. 'You have been in hiding for days now. Can we count on you or not?'

'We are *not* out of the business. It has taken longer than I had anticipated to recruit replacement pilots and to procure airframes, but now those preparations have been accomplished. We can organize our first full shipment – '

'My associates will be pleased. Where is your base of operations now?'

'I must insist on secrecy, Señor Gachez,' Salazar said, 'even with you. We are still vulnerable . . . I know you will understand – '

'No. I understand the need for security, but I also insist on knowing all there is about those who work for me. As before, you will tell me the location of your base and allow an inspection by my deputies.'

'Not possible. Security was compromised and it cost the lives of several of my best pilots and the loss of nearly all my high-performance jet aircraft – '

'That was not *my* fault, Salazar. I did not order an attack against the Border Security Force. It was a suicide mission from the start. As for the breach of your security, it is an occupational hazard with an organization your size. You must have known you would be discovered sooner or later. You continued to fly your planes from the United States and the Caribbean directly back to Haiti instead of arranging decoy bases and covers – that was *your* mistake, not mine. I also don't understand why you keep jet aircraft in a smuggling organization. The jets carry no drugs, they protect nothing. They are your toys. So be it, but you are responsible for you own fate – '

'True, I *am* responsible for my own fate,' Salazar said. 'And it is my responsibility to protect my organization as we regroup and consolidate. That includes keeping our location, strength and assets secret – even from the Cartel.'

'Then the Cartel will not do business with you. You can't expect us to hand over millions of dollars worth of product to you without inspecting your facilities and verifying your base of operations – '

'I refuse.'

'You cannot extort the Cartel like this. We will shut down your operation. You must pay for those expensive toys you threw away in that raid on the American radar sites – you will find it impossible to pay if you find no customers to haul product for.'

'I have my aircraft, my unit is operational now. We are the flyers that beat the United States Air Force in their own front yard. You may head the Medellín Cartel, Gachez, but you do not own the entire hemisphere's trade. With American addicts paying almost a hundred thousand dollars a kilo for street cocaine you'll find more competition. The Cali and Bogotá cartels have already told me they are interested in my services. I believe Señor Sienca in Cali runs a very powerful Colombian drug cartel now, surpassing the Medellín – please, let me finish . . . The Mexico City and Guadalajara cartels grow stronger every day, and they export only by land. If they should have an air-delivery system as reliable as the Cuchillos they could force you out – '

Gachez shook his head. 'The Medellín cartel is richer and more powerful than ever.'

'Then the Mexicans' need of the Cuchillos is so great they will pay more, even make me a full partner . . .'

Always the same, Gachez thought. The same problems his brothers encountered years ago – he could trust no one from the outside, always someone wanted more. But Salazar was mistaken if he thought any Mexican cartel was or could be more powerful than the Colombian organizations. Still, their leadership could be threatened if the Mexicans moved product and the Colombians did not . . .

'I will make it easy for you, Señor Gachez, to avoid any prolonged, fruitless negotiations. The price to deliver a kilo of cocaine from Colombia to anywhere in the United States is thirty thousand dollars. I will receive half up front and the rest upon delivery . . .'

'That's *three times* the normal rate – '

'I beat the Hammerheads and the United States Air Force once, I will do it again. And *that* is why my terms are not only reasonable but generous – '

'My employees don't tell me how to do business – '

'*Bueno*, I am no longer one of your employees. It is your choice.' He turned and walked to the salon door.

'And it is also my choice that you be shark bait.' He buzzed for two of his soldiers, who burst into the salon, one from behind the desk, one from behind Salazar.

The attack, however, was over before it began. Before Gachez could get to his feet there was a knife slash across one soldier's stomach, the other was stuck in the left shoulder. Salazar had disarmed both men and taken one of the soldier's automatic pistols in hand. 'Call your guards and tell them to stay out of sight,' Salazar ordered. 'If I see one guard or one weapon, I'll kill you.'

587

To his surprise, Gachez, with practiced smoothness in the face of crisis, only smiled and faintly, derisively, applauded. 'Excellent, Colonel, *excellent*. Very good moves for an older man.' Gachez reached down to the intercom on his desk. 'José. Colonel Salazar is leaving. Keep all your men out of sight until he leaves. He will be carrying a gun. Make no moves against him.' Then to Salazar: 'I would be interested to learn how you managed to get those knives past my guards, Colonel.'

Salazar reached down to his right boot, extracted another knife, and hurled it into the leather chair behind the desk, inches from Gachez's left hip. Gachez yanked it out of the leather and inspected it. 'A gift for you, Señor Gachez. My knives are made of ceramic composites, lighter and stronger than steel and undetectable by conventional metal detectors. You should update your security.' He left then and made his way to the boarding ladder to his waiting motor launch.

Gachez's smile vanished as Salazar left the salon. He hit the intercom button. 'José, send two men in here.' He stood at his desk examining the knife as guards came in and helped the two stricken guards out. Chief of Security named José followed the guards in, a submachine gun drawn. Maxwell Van Nuys came after.

'What the hell happened?' Van Nuys asked. 'Where's Salazar?'

'Something you gringos would not understand,' Gachez said. 'We were playing a game for men.'

'A game for men? He cuts two of your men and uses you for target practice. That's real manly. Where is he? Is he going to take the job?'

'He asks for thirty thousand a kilo, with half up front.'

'So you said no and he threw a knife.'

The chief cartel leader walked quickly to the liquor cabinet and poured himself a glass of vodka.

'So much for your macho negotiation technique. We can continue to make shipments overland through Mexico, but it takes weeks to get a shipment across the border, and then we have to get it into the hands of the distributors in Florida and California – '

'Your job is not to worry about where or how the shipments are sent. Your job is to take care of foreign Customs and the money in your banks . . .'

Van Nuys shook his head. 'It might end up costing you a lot more if you don't go with Salazar and his Cuchillos. He gets the job done. It'll cost you ten thousand a kilo to get it into the United States overland, but then you have to see that it gets from New Mexico and Texas all the way to Florida or Los Angeles. Each shipment spends weeks on the road and you risk interception every day it's out of your hands. Even if a few shipments are lost or intercepted, you get more product delivered in less time with air deliveries, and you don't mess with Customs.'

'You are saying you can't handle your end of our bargain?'

'I can handle it but it's dangerous,' Van Nuys said. 'We can pay off these officials all we want, but one day someone's going to come with more money, more booze, a better-looking woman, *or* a bigger gun – and then these Customs agents belong to someone else . . . Read the newspapers. The Border Security Force is going down the drain. The government may make a big deal about having the military take over drug interdiction duties, but it's a lot more expensive to run an F-16 than a Sea Lion aircraft or a drone. If you ask me, you have no choice but to go with Salazar. They want people to think the smugglers are laying low, when the Air Force or the Navy can't find their butts with both hands. Salazar might be greedy, but he did the job. The borders are wide open.'

Gachez slowly turned Salazar's throwing knife over in his

hand, then returned to his desk with his glass of vodka. '*Bueno*. Then you will handle Colonel Salazar. You will accompany him to his base, inspect his facilities and report to me that he has the resources to do the job. I will decide whether to trust him enough for a major shipment.'

'*Me?* Why should I – ?'

'You are an experienced pilot, able to judge the value of his planes and the capabilities of his new facilities. You can chart his base's location and report on his organization. He will not tolerate one of my people to go along with him. You are less threatening, a compromise he can accept.'

'It's because of the leaks in your organization and your own handling of Salazar I was almost busted by the Hammerheads. I'm working with you until I can recoup my losses and then I'm retired.'

'You work for me now, Mr Van Nuys. I could have had you killed or turned you over to the authorities when I discovered your little smuggling operation. I did neither. You traded your life for a long-term employment contract with me. If you really hope to live until this fanciful retirement you speak of, you will do as I say. What I need from you is to verify that Salazar will not soak us, and will handle our business. The Cartel wishes the main shipment on its way as soon as possible, but not before I have Salazar checked out.'

Van Nuys hesitated. 'How big is this main shipment?'

'I want to know if Salazar can handle fifty thousand kilos,' Gachez said casually.

'Fifty . . . thousand . . . kilos? Of cocaine?'

'Maybe more. The Cartel has been shipping only one-tenth its normal volume for the past twelve months, but *production* has not slowed. We are backlogged with product. At a wholesale price of sixty thousand a kilo we can make a very great profit . . .'

'That's *three billion dollars* worth you want shipped? All at once?'

'Of course, all at once. The Americans are starving for cocaine. This is a major relief effort, like airlifting food to Ethiopia, or gas masks to Bhopal, or lead underwear to Chernobyl.' Gachez smiled at his own wit. 'Even paying Salazar his exorbitant fee, the Cartel will net over a billion dollars from wholesale and our portion of the retail sales – and all in a few days' work. As the leading producer for the Cartel, we will get the largest cut – over four hundred million dollars.'

Van Nuys considered the enormous figures. On the street the stuff was worth twice its wholesale value – over six billion dollars. Once cut and prepared it was enough cocaine to give every man, woman and child in the United States two 'lines.' And if it was processed into crack cocaine . . .

'And the shipment is ready to go immediately,' Gachez was saying. 'I want you on the plane with Salazar tonight, back to whatever hole he has dug for himself.'

The profit potential was huge, Van Nuys told himself. Three billion dollars . . .

'All right, all right. Just this once. But remember, I'm a lawyer, not one of your damned bean-counters – '

'You are a greedy bastard like everyone else,' Gachez said, downing the last of his vodka. 'You complain, but *you* came to *me*. No one cares who you were or what you did before this. Do as you're told and you get your money. And that makes you no different from the old woman who cleans my toilets every day. Follow Salazar every minute of every day, be ready to report in detail about where he's hiding and what equipment he has. That's it.'

After Van Nuys left, escorted by two soldiers, Gachez turned to Luiz Canseco, the youngster who had volunteered to test the Hammerheads' defenses and who was now a top lieutenant in Gachez's most trusted cadre. 'Luiz, you go with Van Nuys. Keep a close eye on him. Follow him – charter a plane, buy a boat, bribe local officials, do whatever you must, but follow him everywhere and report back to me. If he is even seen with an American agent or police, an official of any kind, execute him.'

Ciudad del Carmen, Mexico
The Next Morning

'*This* is your new operation?' Van Nuys said. They had touched down on a beautiful sun-drenched airport surrounded by a narrow inlet and a broad green-blue bay in southeastern Mexico. As they taxied back down the runway, Van Nuys saw palm trees, city buses plying the airport grounds, immaculately painted and maintained hangars and a modern, multi-story glass passenger terminal. The Lear jet carrying Salazar, Van Nuys, Canseco, and several soldiers and assistants taxied past the passenger terminal to a row of private hangars and maintenance buildings. They parked on a concrete ramp, complete with a red painted 'welcome' runner leading from the scrupulously clean ramp into the private offices nearby.

'A bit different from Verrettes, but every bit as functional, I assure you,' Salazar said as he parked the Lear and shut down the engines – Van Nuys quickly memorized the latitude and longitude coordinates on the LORAN navigation set before Salazar shut it off. 'In Haiti I was set up as a district military commander and given full use of a base and facilities, but that was when Gachez and the Medellín cartel financed my entire operation. They were content to have me live like a common soldier, no better than a peasant. But, I invested much of my own funds into this operation, and now, as you can see . . .'

A Mexican customs official met them, copied down the plane's tail number, made a few more scratches on a form

592

on a clipboard, saluted Salazar and departed – he made no effort to check the cargo compartments, when he would have found over one hundred million dollars in American, Mexican, West German and Colombian currency. 'They are very thorough and tough in the tourist passenger terminal,' Salazar commented, 'but out here they all belong to me. We can bring anything we wish into Ciudad del Carmen at any time as long as the local officials and the militia get their considerations.'

'Do you keep tabs on who comes and goes in this city?'

'Of course,' Salazar said. 'The Customs officials report all Americans coming into the area, especially any American government officials – they can be DEA or Border Security, although their passport says State Department. The militia reports any suspicious newcomers into the city, and we act accordingly.'

'Why this city?' Van Nuys asked. 'Ciudad del Carmen looks like a resort town. Your base of operations is on a major tourist airport, not two hundred meters from the main passenger terminal.'

'Ciudad del Carmen *is* a major resort city. Not as big or as fancy as Veracruz or Cancún but very popular with Europeans and Asians. The American tourists stopped coming here after the city was badly damaged by a hurricane. And why shouldn't we be located on the main airport? Carmen del Sol Airlines is the major tourist airline of the state of Campeche, with regular flights as far away as Boston and San Francisco. The tourists like flying here because it is much less expensive than Cancún, but then they drive, bike or sail around the Yucatán Peninsula to Cancún or down the coast to Veracruz. In a sense my pilots and I are also tourists . . .'

They exited the jet and began down the taxiway, inspecting whitewashed buildings with colorful murals and welcome signs on the hangars. Everyone working at

Carmen del Sol Airlines wore white short-sleeved coveralls with the company logo on the breast pocket – but Van Nuys also recognized the military-style haircuts and detected the bulges of concealed weapons on a few of the so-called mechanics.

'And the Cuchillos *are* Carmen del Sol Airlines?'

'Exactly. We are a regional and international carrier, and we run a charter service for oil companies and manufacturers in the neighboring provinces. We also hire out our mechanics and facilities to a variety of users, from United Airlines to Mexicali Airlines – including one very special customer.' Salazar motioned him to a closed hangar, where a guard checked them in and gave them ID badges.

When they entered the hangar Van Nuys could not believe what he saw – two Mexican Air Force F-5 fighters, complete with missiles and guns, being worked on by Cuchillo maintenance men.

'We contracted out to the Mexican government for engine-repair work and structural modification jobs,' Salazar said proudly. 'We easily undercut other bidders, and my men can do a better job than any government-trained person. We now have a legitimate, government-approved front, legitimate outlets for our funds and access to all manner of weapons and military equipment – no more need of black market suppliers. Of course, we have full authorization to test-fly these and any other aircraft we receive, and we require a great many test flights. Our other jets, the one remaining Mirage and the Aero Albatros bombers that survived the attack on the Border Security Force installations, are being repaired or modified in other locations.'

'Gachez should be pleased,' Van Nuys said, and meant it. Salazar had worked a minor miracle since the evacuation from Verrettes.

'Gachez is becoming an old woman,' Salazar said. 'He worries too much.'

'He also calls the shots. He wants a successful delivery and fast. Can you do it tomorrow night?'

'I can. Without the Hammerheads it will be much easier. There are scattered thunderstorms in the area – we will be able to hide between them . . . How big is this shipment that Señor Old Woman would like delivered?'

'Fifty thousand kilos. In one drop. Drop sites in the Bahamas, Florida and near Cuba.'

'Fifty thousand . . . impressive.'

'The job's not finished yet. What are you going to need?'

'It will require detailed planning,' Salazar said. 'I will need a breakdown of the drop points, the timing of each drop, the exact size of the shipment.'

'I'll get you everything you require,' Van Nuys said, 'but I will review your plan before Gachez will allow your planes to fly to Colombia to pick up the shipment. Frankly I don't see how you can pick up so much and deliver it tomorrow night, but if you think we can do it, we'll go ahead.'

'You are dealing with the new Cuchillos, Mr Van Nuys,' Salazar said. 'The job is as good as done.'

Mexican Customs Office, Ciudad del Carmen, Mexico

When the Mexican Customs official arrived back in his office he went immediately to his supervisor's office. 'Sir, Señor Salazar has returned,' he told his superior, Major Carlos Fiera, after being waved into the office. The senior officer extended his hand, and the inspector gave him his clipboard with the completed inspection form on it.

Fiera scanned the form. 'You indicate four other passengers on this flight. Who else was with Señor Salazar?'

'I did not inquire,' the inspector said, 'per your

instructions.' But he paused briefly as his supervisor's eyes grew darker, and added, 'Two were Salazar's men. One was a Cuban named Canseco. He was carrying a light pistol. The fourth was an American. His name was Maxwell Van Nuys. He was carrying a briefcase. That was all I could observe, sir.'

'Were they carrying anything else?' The inspector was silent as he tried to think of an appropriate response. 'Unofficially, what else did you observe?'

'Several bundles and suitcases were loaded into an armed car, sir.'

Cash, not drugs, Fiera concluded. Any movement of drugs meant trouble, but any amount of cash entering the country, especially this town where Salazar had such control, was business as usual. The Customs supervisor scribbled his signature on the inspection form in the required block and handed it back to the inspector. 'Tell no one else. Dismissed.'

As soon as the inspector left with the report, Fiera rose from his chair, stretched, and went to the far corner of his office to pour himself a cup of coffee. Through the shutters he watched the battered old taxis make their way up and down the cobblestone streets of downtown Ciudad del Carmen. He cast admiring glances at the middle-aged, still erotic-looking European women sifting through hats and souvenirs in the stores, and sneered at the growing numbers of Japanese that seemed to be filling the town's streets more every year – he appreciated their money but despised their monotonous appearance and their unintelligible chatter. He half-closed the louvered blinds and lowered them down the full length of the window.

That gesture was a rehearsed signal to an American contact who would ride past the Customs office a few times each day. By lunchtime he would look out the window again and check for a return signal. If there was a bicycle padlocked to a stop sign just outside the window, with its front wheel removed and the stop signpost placed within the front wheel fork, he would know that his signal had been removed and the meet was on.

Carlos Fiera had been so reporting unusual activities to the United States Drug Enforcement Administration for several years in every town he had worked during his tenure with the Mexican Customs Bureau. The DEA always paid well and kept relations with their informants confidential. Because Ciudad del Carmen was so small and because Salazar had such a tight grip on the town's officials, extraordinary steps had to be taken when communicating with the DEA – no phone calls, no visits, no correspondence through the mail. In fact, the Customs supervisor would report any official visits by the DEA or the Mexican government *to* Salazar.

The only safe methods of contact were blind drops, brief exchanges inside a store or a crowded restaurant, or car-to-car swaps on a deserted road late at night. He would pass a coded note with information, and the DEA agent would pass an envelope with cash – most of the time he never saw the American agent for longer than a few seconds. There were no interviews, no official reports exchanged, no cooperative efforts between the Mexican officials and the DEA.

The Customs supervisor's primary assignment from the DEA was to keep an eye on Salazar's new enterprise, Carmen del Sol Airlines. The DEA had been interested in any new enterprises being established, such as air cargo, truck lines or fishing ventures. The small airline had been under observation for months, but until recently it did not seem to catch anyone's attention. When the Mexican government contracted for work with the airline, the DEA all but ignored them.

But when Carmen del Sol Airlines had suddenly

quadrupled in size, using huge amounts of cash to buy silence and cooperation, the DEA was very interested; and when the military-style transports and crewmen arrived, right about the time of the attacks in the United States, interest quickly heated up. The DEA was paying a lot of money for information now, as was Salazar – a man could find himself very rich if he was smart and not too greedy.

Spying on someone as powerful and as influential as Salazar was not easy. He had been reporting on as much of Salazar's operation as he could, but it was difficult to chart the numerous comings and goings of all Carmen del Sol Airlines planes without risking discovery, so his reports on Salazar's activities were spotty. But this was a real discovery, one that the DEA would pay extra for.

The special request from the DEA came in just a few days earlier – be on the lookout for a man named Van Nuys, a tall dark American who might be traveling through Mexico alone or in the company of Salazar or his men.

The Mexican Customs supervisor returned to his desk until almost eleven o'clock, then looked outside again. Sure enough, the bicycle was there, with the front wheel missing and the fork stuck through the post.

When the rest of the office began filtering out to lunch, Fiera began preparing the coded message. It was a simple code, easily broken by an expert cryptographer, but to anyone who might glance at it if they picked it up off the street it would appear as a series of random numbers and letters. A message could be prepared in less than five minutes, without using a pencil and paper to draw a complicated encoding grid or keyword breakdown.

Moments later the message was done. Fiera folded the message up and stuck it in a pocket, then checked the blotter and any papers underneath for any signs that the message had been creased to anything else. He refolded the paper into a thin square about the size of a peso, told his secretary he was going to lunch, and left.

Several blocks from the office Fiera spotted a man with a jacket looped over his right arm. He headed toward him, trying not to stare at him or single him out with his eyes or his body. The man wore sunglasses and a pair of colorful Tour de France-style bicycle racing tights, which most of the tourist population of bicycle-crazy Ciudad del Carmen wore.

When Fiera got within a few steps of him the man took the jacket from his right arm and flipped it over his right shoulder. Fiera acknowledged the message by scuffing his right foot along the pavement as he walked past. The contact cleared his throat. Fiera continued on to find a restaurant for lunch.

On exiting the restaurant an hour later Fiera saw the man entering the restaurant just as he was going through the door. The contact had the jacket looped over his right arm once again. As they passed each other in the doorway, turning nearly chest to chest, the contact's left hand flicked out from under the jacket and plucked the note out of Fiera's hand.

Fiera thought nothing else about the incident all day. If the information he had passed was worthwhile, another meet would be arranged and Fiera would get his money. He would keep a few hundred pesos for himself, send most of it by courier to his grandchildren in Mexico City, use a little here and there for his own informants and spies, and, of course, give a little to his ladyfriends. He kept his bank balance low, his excesses in check, and a traveling bag packed – knowing that the government, Salazar and doubtless others kept tabs on the financial situations of all important officials – the peaceful little town of Ciudad del Carmen could turn ugly for him very quickly.

But later that afternoon, just a few minutes before his

normal quitting time, Fiera heard a knock on his office door. 'Excuse me, sir,' his assistant said, 'but there is someone here who wishes to lodge a complaint with you.'

'Take his report and tell him to come back tomorrow.'

'But sir – ' The aide was cut off and Fiera heard an American voice: 'Yeah, man, I want to complain about your inspectors at the airport.'

'We are closed . . .' Fiera looked up from his desk and saw a tall man in bicycle racing tights standing in front of him – his contact. Fiera quickly blanked his expression and finished his sentence with '. . . come back later.'

'Your men are trying to rip me off, General,' the man said. 'They're tryin' to take my tunes.'

'Your . . . what?'

'My tunes, man.' The agent swung a huge portable radio/tape player/compact disc player up onto Fiera's desk and pushed a button; immediately the heavy booming, guttural lines of rap music crashed in the air. 'You gotta listen to me, General, you *gotta*.'

His assistant took hold of the man's arms. 'Shall I escort this gentleman out, sir?'

Fiera held up a hand. 'It's all right, Lieutenant.' The assistant gave the American an angry look and departed. Fiera then said over the blare of the music, 'What the hell are you doing here?'

'Is it true about Van Nuys?' the DEA agent asked.

'I could be shot for talking to you like this. Salazar has this entire place wired, I'm sure of it . . .'

'The music will scramble his bugs. Answer me. Is it Van Nuys? Is he with Salazar here?'

'Yes. I have not seen him myself but one of my inspectors reported it.'

'Where is he staying? How long will he be here. . . ?'

'I did not ask, and neither did my man. I have as little contact as possible with Salazar. His men will slice me to ribbons if he suspects I am spying on him. You've got all the information you're going to get.' Fiera raised his voice over the heavy rhythm of the rap music. 'Now get out of here before I have you arrested for interfering with a police officer – '

'All right, all right.' But before he turned off the music, the agent said in a lowered voice, 'If Van Nuys and Salazar are here, the Hammerheads will be coming after them. They're not out of business. Clean up your records and get out of town. If they ever get Salazar, your government will be asking embarrassing questions. If the Hammerheads miss, Salazar will be after your ass. Now confiscate this radio. Your last paycheck's inside.'

'And you will leave that radio here until this matter is cleared up,' Fiera shouted, immediately taking his cue. 'Now shut that thing off!'

The DEA agent jabbed the OFF button. 'I'll be back as soon as I get the receipt, General. I swear it's not stolen, I'll have the receipt for you tomorrow morning, I promise . . .' The agent put on his sunglasses once again and hurried out. Through the side window Fiera could see him pedal off down the main street and into the crowd.

Fiera quickly opened the compartment in the back of the radio where the electrical cord was stored and found a tightly wrapped roll of one-hundred-dollar bills packed beneath a false bottom under the cord. He removed the money and replaced the cover just as his assistant knocked on the door. 'Everything all right, sir?'

'That American tried to make me believe this radio isn't stolen,' Fiera said casually. 'He claims he will be coming back for it in the morning. If he fails to return, which I believe will be the case, the radio is yours.'

His assistant's eyes lit up as he reached for the 'boom box.' 'I will put it in a safe place until tomorrow, sir.' The radio was going straight into his assistant's car trunk, of course. No better way to insure someone's discretion than making him an accomplice.

Fiera stayed a few minutes longer, collecting his personal copies of reports, logs and journals and packing them in a traveling case. The American was right – this beautiful little town would not be a safe place for him if the American Border Security Force was coming for Salazar. The Mexican government would make inquiries, wondering how a major smuggling ring could operate in Ciudad del Carmen right under the nose of a senior Customs officer.

But the head of the Medellín cartel would also be making inquiries. Fiera did not want to be around when they came for him.

Border Security Force Headquarters, Aladdin City, Florida
Three Hours Later

The Hammerheads were in the glassed-in, soundproof room overlooking the command center – Elliott, Hardcastle, Masters, McLanahan, members of the Hammerheads' I-Team, including the I-Team's new chief and Geffar's old deputy at Homestead, Curtis Long.

Elliott started off. 'Well, we have a solid lead on both Salazar and Van Nuys. They're in Mexico. But Salazar apparently has some serious juice now. The Mexican government won't even consider touching him without a federal grand-jury indictment.'

Geffar spoke what the rest were thinking. 'This was the man who put together the attack on our radar sites . . . killed *forty* persons . . . and the Mexican government won't help us nail him?'

Elliott nodded. 'Salazar apparently *works* for the Mexican government as a so-called military contractor, and the government protects contractors unless indicted by a Mexican federal grand jury or a military high tribunal – I doubt if an American grand jury would get him extradited. Van Nuys holds an American passport so we can get to him a little easier.'

'And Van Nuys is with Salazar in Mexico?' Long put in. 'I thought we had a warrant out for him. Why the hell wasn't he picked up when he *entered* Mexico? The Mexican government is supposed to cooperate – '

'Salazar,' Elliott told him, 'seems to own the Customs Bureau, the militia, the police – the works. He decides who comes and goes. My guess is that Van Nuys had been in Colombia with the Medellín Cartel up until now. He might well be working for them. State and Justice want to make an official request for help in getting Van Nuys but I asked them to hold off. If we march in with federal marshals to get Van Nuys, Salazar may dive deep underground again.'

Elliott called up a map of central America on the five-foot briefing screen. 'Salazar runs an air charter service in eastern Mexico called Carmen del Sol Airlines in the coastal town of Ciudad del Carmen. He's managed to bring in most of his aircraft from Haiti into Mexico, and he's got access to spare parts, fuel, weapons, even military hardware – he does contract work for the Mexican Air Force. Our source says Salazar's worked on everything from the presidential shuttle to fighter jets.'

'First the Haitians, now the Mexicans,' Hardcastle muttered.

'Salazar has the region wired for sound,' Elliott continued. 'He's got people that inform his organization about every move the Mexican government makes and every move our agents make. We've been getting intelligence on Salazar only because we've gotten down to stuff out of John Le Carré. But our source is no longer available. Now we have no solid intelligence on Salazar's and Van Nuys' *exact* location, we only know that they're both in Ciudad del Carmen. Our contact reports activity at Salazar's charter company . . . he thinks several of Salazar's *largest* planes may be taking off soon – '

'Which means he's planning a big delivery,' Geffar said. 'This is the delivery we've been waiting for. But we need more info on the specifics.'

'I can give you a plan to put a combined DEA and I-Team unit in Ciudad del Carmen to begin surveillance on Salazar and his charter air service,' Long said. 'We can't do anything *too* elaborate or Salazar will bolt. But we need enough manpower to stop his soldiers and planes if we turn up anything.'

'Or we can grab Van Nuys,' Geffar said. 'He's obviously involved in this. He might be able to give us the information we need to jump Salazar – '

'Can't trust Van Nuys,' Hardcastle said, looking at Geffar. 'He tried to kill you once, he'll do it again. He has nothing to lose now. And even if we do grab him we have no assurance that he'll tell us anything about Salazar's operation. I'd guess he's more afraid of Salazar and the Cartel than US justice.' He turned to Elliott. 'Why don't we just send the I-Team in and level Salazar's charter operation? Why don't we just go in and grab Salazar?'

'Not that easy,' Curtis Long put in. 'We either catch him out in the open, or we stand a good chance of missing.'

'And an I-Team raid on the charter operation is out for now,' Elliott said. 'We'd never get approval . . . Even if we got a grand-jury indictment against Salazar and then approval from Mexico to enforce it, it would be a *Mexican* operation, not a Hammerheads'. They won't even let an I-Team cross the border, let alone help their police or militia.'

'So what do we do?' McLanahan said impatiently. 'Just continue surveillance?'

'That's our only option right now. Reinforce the back-scatter radar with P-3 and E-2 flights off the Mexican coast. If, or when, Salazar tries this big delivery, we can hope to be ready and waiting . . . Meanwhile, Curt, I'd like a plan from you to take an I-Team into Ciudad del Carmen to arrest Van Nuys and Salazar . . .'

As the group filed out of the briefing center Geffar and Hardcastle stayed back. 'Brad,' Geffar said, 'nobody can stand this waiting. We all know tomorrow can be too late . . . send me into Ciudad del Carmen to find Van Nuys.'

'Out of the damn question. You'd be dead the minute you stepped on Mexican soil. Salazar has informants everywhere – Customs, the police, storekeepers, hotels. They target Americans for round-the-clock surveillance –

'And even if you did find him, what then?' Hardcastle said. 'You going to drag him by the locks back to Miami? With Salazar he'll be under heavy guard. Even if you did find him, he'd blow you away before he'd let you take him back to the States.'

'Listen,' Geffar said angrily, 'we're wasting time. We know some things now . . . we know the area where Salazar and Van Nuys are, we know they're planning a big operation, a major drug shipment, and we know that we need to get someone in to find out *specifics*. We can't send an I-Team, and we can't go through official channels – '

'If we did decide to send someone in it wouldn't be you,' Elliott said. 'You're still hurt, Van Nuys knows you, he no doubt told Salazar's men about you, they'll be on the lookout – '

'Forget all that. I think I can turn Van Nuys. I talked to him before Hokum shot me at Sunrise Beach. At the time he was more scared than anything else. He wants an out . . . He doesn't want to deal with Salazar but figures he has no choice. Salazar owns him, Van Nuys needs money. I tell you he was ready to deal when I found him out at Sunrise

Beach. He was ready to turn over Salazar and what he knows about the Medellín Cartel in exchange for his freedom. I think he'll still deal with me. I know he won't deal with anyone else. And even if he only pretends to go along, figuring he can handle any female, and so forth, I'm ready for that too . . .'

Elliott was shaking his head.

'General, I feel strong enough about this to request a leave of absence and fly down there myself.'

Elliott said, 'It's a suicide mission – '

'I disagree, but I'd like a little backup when I got down there. I'll do without, though, if that's how you want it.'

'If you really think Van Nuys can be turned, we'll send someone else – maybe use the DEA agent in place down there – '

'You know that won't work. The contact would be blown, Salazar would kill the contact and take off, and Van Nuys would disappear too. I'll have an advantage over anyone else you can think of.'

'And more disadvantages,' Elliott said. 'You'd be going in there with no support, your face is known, you're not a hundred percent fit – '

'General, like I said and you know, we lose our best opportunity to get Salazar if we pass this up. We can get a Sea Lion to fly me in tonight and I'll make my way to Ciudad del Carmen to Van Nuys. I'll either convince him to cooperate with us and take down Salazar . . . or I'll get out.'

Nobody said a word. It was the closest Elliott could come to saying yes.

* * *

606

Isla del Carmen, Mexico
Later That Evening

In an estate on the south-central side of Isla del Carmen, about five miles east to the city, the Cuchillos were presenting their mission plan to Salazar and Van Nuys. They were in a large office with a spectacular view of the Laguna de Terminos to the south and the lush green forests of the Candelaria River valley beyond, all still visible in the rapidly approaching twilight. The office was on the fifth floor of the mansion, surrounded by bulletproof glass. The estate itself was on top of a man-made hill that made Salazar's retreat the highest elevation of any spot in the state of Campeche. The twenty-acre compound was guarded by a small, well-equipped army of Cuchillo soldiers; the mansion itself was more like a medieval castle, complete with drawbridges and gates along the road leading to the house designed to slow advancing vehicles.

Major José Trujillo, the Cuchillos' senior pilot, was standing by the briefing board with a pointer. Just like his old military days – in full uniform, inspection-ready, with all ribbons and awards earned over fifteen years as a squadron commander in the Cuban Revolutionary Air Force. He was not only presenting a plan to his commander – he was presenting the Cuchillos as a united, strengthened force of top aviators ready to go to war again.

'The transports will begin launching in one hour for the flight to Valdivia, Colombia. Our plan is to begin launching aircraft one every ten or fifteen minutes, as close as possible to our normal departure scheduling and interspersing these departures with normal civilian traffic.

'The slower planes, the light twins and heavy singles, will move out first, followed by the light turboprops and then by the heavy turboprops and jets. The light aircraft have stops planned in San Salvador, San José and Panama City. Some

607

medium-range planes will make stops in Costa Rica and Bluefields in Nicaragua. The heavy transports can make it all the way on one refueling, but we have planned stops for them in Cartagena, Colombia, and David, Panama, to resemble our regularly scheduled flights as much as possible. All our flights will be on approved ICAO international aviation convention flight plans with Carmen del Sol Airlines call signs.'

Trujillo motioned to Van Nuys, who got to his feet. 'I've arranged for customs clearances for all our flights to Valdivia. All our flights have no-inspection clearances straight through. But since we can never count on those to hold up, each crewmember must be prepared for a full check in case of a no-notice inspection. That means current passports, current inoculations and all immigration papers in order. The planes have to be sanitized so as to not reveal the flight's actual destination in Colombia or any evidence of the deliveries into North America.

'If they find one scrap of evidence to suggest what we're carrying, they will confiscate it and arrest everyone on the spot. If one crewman opens his mouth and mentions one word about Valdivia, drugs or the Cartel to the wrong person it could ruin everything. Don't assume a man in a Customs uniform is a Customs officer – he could be a DEA agent or an informer or a spy. You keep your mouths shut and be alert for trouble.'

'Gachez told me you could guarantee safe passage for all my crewmembers, Van Nuys,' Salazar said angrily.

'I can't *guarantee* anything. I've put the Cartel's paid inspectors on duty in the proper time and place for each flight's arrival, but I have no control over what actually happens, especially in Panama, El Salvador and Costa Rica – the US has a lot of clout there. You know that Customs work in these countries is political, Colonel. I've set up everything, that's all I can do.'

'It had better work,' Salazar said. 'You are betting your life on it.'

In the silence that followed that exchange, Trujillo pressed on. 'All aircraft are due in Valdivia by tomorrow morning. They will begin loading immediately after servicing and refueling. The bulk of the cargo will be handled by the Antonov, Shorts and Douglas transports, with ten thousand kilos on board the Antonov-26, six thousand on the Shorts 440 and nine thousand for the Douglas DC-3. The remaining twenty-five thousand kilos will be divided among the other ten planes.'

Trujillo flipped charts on the briefing board. Instead of a series of lines leading overland from Mexico to Colombia, this chart had a series of lines going from Colombia overwater to several Caribbean islands. 'The return flights will be long and difficult. We will divide the planes into three groups. All aircraft will refuel in northern Colombia, either at Uribia or Cienaga. The smaller planes, the light twins and heavy singles, will fly to remote landing strips in Panama, Jamaica or Haiti, depending on fuel reserves and flight performances . . . you all have packages that describe the landing points, with LORAN coordinates and WET SNOW marker beacon-codes and frequencies – I have produced instrument letdown plates and instructions for each package in case you need to use the landing spot in bad weather.

'The planes heading westbound will refuel at remote strips in Nicaragua, Guatemala, and then here at Ciudad del Carmen. Our alternate for the Mexican planes is Valladolid in the northeastern part of the Yucatán Peninsula, where we have our improved recovery strip. These planes will proceed overwater to drop zones along the Cuban coastline, the Straits of Florida and into Bahamian waters. Flights going to Jamaica will proceed over Cuba for drops in the Florida Everglades. Flights refueling in Haiti will make drops in the Turks and Caicos Islands and the Bahamas.

'The larger aircraft, after refueling in northern Colombia, will either proceed north to drop points in the Bahamas, or fly here, refuel and then make drops in New Mexico, Texas, and Louisiana. These flights will be on approved American flight plans but will divert from their flight plans at the last moment to make their drops.

'Our intelligence informs us there has been no Border Security Force activity in this region or in Florida for some time,' Trujillo said. 'The Hammerhead Two platform has been towed into Key West for repairs before being moved to the Atlantic Ocean side of Florida, and the aircraft carrier that in the past has been used to stage interceptor flights in eastern Florida is now at anchor near Miami. Aircraft have been observed using it but our sources believe these are training flights only.

'Our greatest threat comes from US Air Force jet interceptors, but that threat is very limited. We will be saturating the area with over a dozen low slow-moving targets, only a few of which actually threaten the coast itself. As long as we stay low and close to normal airways we will not be intercepted. The Americans have not shown a willingness to use their air-defense aircraft for drug-interdiction duties. This gives us an advantage.

'The planes flying into the Everglades are under the greatest threat of interception. That is why I will be flying one of these planes, along with Captain Estevez and Captain Garzon, our most experienced pilots. We also will have the Mexican F-5 jets for air cover for the heavy transports heading into Texas and Louisiana – '

A knock on the door to Salazar's office, and a clerk hurried in with a note for Salazar. He read it, smiled, stood and took the podium from Trujillo.

'Thank you, Major Trujillo. Your plan is a masterwork

of deception, operational redundancy and attention to detail. I thank you and your staff.' To the assembled pilots: 'Well, the battle begins. I have just received an advisory from Mexican Customs. A United States Border Security AV-22 with eight crewmen has requested permission to fly into Veracruz the day after tomorrow, estimated time of arrival, eleven o'clock local. Our sources are checking out the nature of their visit, but it's fairly obvious they will be moving in on us very soon.' He turned to Trujillo. 'All flights will use the Valladolid alternate recovery base. Do not fly in Ciudad del Carmen until further notice. The Border Security Force will be too late,' Salazar went on. 'When the Hammerheads arrive in Ciudad del Carmen . . . I estimate no more than one hour after landing in Veracruz . . . our planes will have completed their missions and dispersed to locations for scrubdowns and records-updating before returning here. If we do our jobs right we can present proof to all inspectors about where our planes were at all times. There will be no evidence of the mission except for a group of happy, tired pilots. Of course, because of crew-rest regulations you will not be interviewed by anyone. I will see to that. We will annotate your log books to correspond to your assigned routes and schedules – their inspection will lead to nothing.'

He paced the front of the office, then said, 'We have already won a major victory. The US has denounced the Border Security Force for what it is – a terrorist organization that tried to dominate the entire hemisphere with their weapons. We taught them a lesson by attacking the Hammerheads' radar installations. Our actions were vindicated by the people and the Congress when they deactivated the Border Security Force. It took the dedication of all of you . . . and the lives of comrades.

'You are soldiers and you have a mission.' His voice rose slightly, its intensity deepened greatly. 'You fly because you are the best pilots in the world, and now you test your skills and courage against a huge, meddling superpower. Money is fine, and you deserve all you receive, but the mission is manhood, which you test in the night sky and against overwhelming odds. You are the Cuchillos. You will be victorious . . .'

Salazar waited as his young pilots erupted as planned and prepared by him. He let them carry on for a few moments longer, then raised his hand.

'I must also tell you that I will be aboard the Mirage F1C fighter to protect the Antonov transport as it makes its way into the United States. I will be the last line of defense for our flagship.' Which announcement brought forth a second outburst, followed, ironically, by the Cuban national anthem.

After the pilots had gone to the buses to be taken to the airport, Van Nuys had to compliment Salazar on his hold over the Cuchillo pilots. 'My only purpose is to make sure my crewmen believe in themselves and in what they are about to do.'

'Whatever you say,' Van Nuys said, 'but you seem to whip these guys up pretty easy. It's almost like they're on something themselves.'

'Not exactly. Their food and drink were . . . fortified with amphetamines, to keep them alert on their long trip.'

'You drugged your own pilots?'

'They keep their fighting edge better with a little stimulation. The same will be done in Valdivia before they depart for the United States and the drop sites. Don't worry about my pilots, Van Nuys. Worry about the Customs procedures and the money. If even one of my men has trouble with Customs anywhere, your services are terminated. Worry about that for a while.'

* * *

Carmen del Sol Airlines, Ciudad del Carmen, Mexico
Two Hours Later

The launch went off with military precision. The smallest plane of the group, a single-engine Cessna Caravan cargo plane, was the first to begin the fourteen-hundred-mile flight from Mexico to the Medellín Cartel's drug-distribution center at Valdivia; it would take the plane nearly ten hours to make the trip, including quick-turn refueling stops. One by one the twin-engine planes, the other Cessnas, Pipers and Aerospatiales leaped into the warm night sky to begin the largest single air-smuggling operation in history. They were followed by the higher-performance turboprops, commuter and business jets, and the smaller cargo planes, most sporting Carmen del Sol Airlines livery.

Finally the big boys rolled down the taxiway and took their place at the end of the runway for takeoff – the huge Soviet Antonov-26 Curl transport, modified and upgraded to boost its load-carrying capacity to 22,000 pounds; the boxy, droop-nosed Shorts 440, built in Northern Ireland and one of the most modern planes in the Cuchillos' fleet; and the venerable old Douglas DC-3 tail-dragger, spewing great volumes of black smoke as its engines were started and its huge silver props began to turn. All these planes had been modified to carry huge volumes of drugs – all creature comforts had been either pulled out or bolted in temporarily, able to be removed on very short notice, and the engine horsepower had been boosted well above safe limits to increase its load-carrying capacity.

All would be fitted with extended-range fuel bladders to boost their effective ranges by at least fifty percent; with the bladders on board and a full load of drugs, the Antonov-26 was able to fly for over two thousand miles without refueling, plenty of range to fly directly from Colombia to the United States, make its drops and return to Mexico or an alternate. The other planes would land and refuel at prearranged spots in the Bahamas, Cuba or Mexico; or they would be forced to ditch their planes near land and make their escape on their own.

In the Carmen del Sol Airlines traffic office Van Nuys, ordered there by Salazar, watched as the Cuchillos' controller logged the departure of each flight and began tracking their progress on a chart. They could communicate with each plane via high-frequency radio either directly or by relays through the country's international flight-following system. He was amazed at the precision of these men – it must be like this to stand in the War Room at the Pentagon.

After checking that all the flight plans were activated and flowing through the currents of international commercial air traffic, Van Nuys went back to the airline director's office and closed the door. It was going to be a long, long night. The Caravan would be stopping in five hours at its first refueling stop, a seldom-used airport outside San Salvador; because it was only a quick-turn refueling on a stopover flight plan, El Salvadorean Customs had already signed off the plane for landing and would probably not even show up at the airport. That was going to be the routine for most of the Cuchillos; but if it turned out differently there wasn't a hell of a lot he figured he could do about it except hope the Customs official could be bribed or scared over the phone. Van Nuys had a Learjet and a suitcase full of cash waiting, ready to speed out to some foreign airfield to bail a plane out, but he hoped like hell he wouldn't have to do that.

He was settled in the chair and beginning to doze off when there was a loud knock on the door and a clerk said in broken English, 'Señor, a man waits for you outside.'

'I'm not expecting anyone, tell him to go away.'

'He says give you this.' The clerk came in and presented Van Nuys a small dark .22 caliber automatic pistol – Salman's gun. It was a special, manufactured from advanced plastics and Kevlar that made it undetectable by metal detectors, which meant his ex-bodyguard, butler and secretary always had a gun no matter where he went. 'What is this man's name?' Van Nuys asked.

'He says his name is Salman.'

'Big guy? Tall? Big shoulders?'

'*Si, señor. Muy grande. Muy gordo.* Shall I bring him in?'

Van Nuys waved a hand at the clerk. 'No, I'll go out.' But before he did he caught up with the clerk and pulled out his sidearm, an all-steel Walther P38 that had to be at least twenty years old. He wasn't going out unarmed.

Salman was standing outside the airlines building in the alley between the rear entrance and the first set of hangars, guarded by a Cuchillo soldier. Van Nuys waved the guard away. 'Salman? How'd you get here?'

'I was released on bail a few days ago,' he replied in his customary monotone. 'I heard you were in Mexico so I came as fast as I could.'

Van Nuys was going to ask who put up bail but decided to table that question for now. The fact he had not done so would have teed off Salman . . . 'How did you find out I was here?'

'Why did you not come to my help?' was Salman's answer. 'I was in jail, you did not come to help . . .'

The big guy's tone of voice was as always, but coming from a man as big as Salman, the accusing words sounded like a physical threat. Van Nuys pulled out the Walther and aimed it at Salman's stomach. 'I asked you a question. How did you know I was here?'

'We told him, Max,' said a female voice – immediately preceded by a loud *snik* of a hammer being locked into place. Van Nuys glanced out of the corner of his eye. Beyond the muzzle of a .45 caliber Smith and Wesson he saw . . . Sandra Geffar.

With the .45 directed at Van Nuys' right eye, Geffar quickly reached over and plucked the Walther from Van Nuys' hand. 'Hello, Max. I've come for a visit, you left so abruptly last time. Straight ahead to the left of that hangar. Not a sound or Salman will remove your tongue through your ears. He's pretty well annoyed with you.' Salman reached over, put an arm on Van Nuys' shoulders and led him to the darkness of a small alleyway between two vacated aircraft hangars.

'What are you doing here, Sandra . . . ?' Van Nuys began, trying to recoup. Salman's hand moved to the back of his neck, his big fingers clamped down.

'I said not a sound, Max.' Geffar checked behind her, then hurried them between the hangars, stopping at the other end. Curt Long appeared from around the corner, dragging an unconscious guard. 'Curt, what happened?'

'Foot patrol. We're running out of time.' They heard a voice behind them near the airline offices calling for Van Nuys – the guard had come back. 'Scratch that. We've *run* out of time.'

'Can we make it off the airport?'

'No good. We saw armed police in the streets – the town wouldn't be safe for us.'

'Call the Huey in,' Geffar said. Long reached into a pocket, extracted a lighter-sized device and punched a button. A red light flashed on, followed by a green one. 'Message received. He's on the way.'

'Rushell Masters, no doubt,' Van Nuys said. 'So, the old Customs Service gang is here. The Hammerheads weren't supposed to show for another two days.'

'You're really well informed, Max . . . except this is a private party, just for you.'

A Jeep appeared about a hundred yards away on the other side of the fence that bordered the airport. It stopped just opposite the hangars, and a searchlight began moving across the ground, scanning the hangars and the alleyways. The three men and the woman between two of the hangars crouched down as low as they could as the beam swept over in their direction into the alleyway – and stopped. Soon they heard warning shouts coming from the men on the other side of the fence.

'Get back,' Geffar said. She fired at the searchlight, sending sparks flying from the Jeep's fender. The soldiers went for cover as Geffar lined up more carefully and knocked out the searchlight with the next shot.

Geffar turned and saw Salman, Van Nuys and Long climbing up a ladder bolted on the side of the hangar leading to the roof. She fired three more times at the Jeep to pin down the soldiers, then ran for the ladder, holstered her .45 and started climbing.

It was a long, hard one. The bruised muscles in her chest were throbbing after a few rungs. The last twenty feet of the six-story climb were agony – she was sure her fingers and arms would give out any moment. Her thighs burned and trembled. When she dared to look up to see how far she had to go, she couldn't even see the top – the ladder seemed to go on forever.

A shot rang out from somewhere behind her, and she stopped climbing and clung to the ladder. Long began returning fire from the roof, his shots close enough to get her moving again. A few feet from the top, arms lifted her up and onto the roof.

'Not much time,' Long said. 'They'll be up here any minute.' Long had set the tiny device in the center of the hangar roof. A radio transmitter and locator beacon, the device also had a small infrared rescue strobe, a bright flashing light that was invisible to the naked eye but could be seen for miles on an infrared scanner or night-vision goggles.

'What's the point, Sandra?' Van Nuys said as Long and Salman moved to cover the various ladders up to the roof. 'You've just about succeeded in getting us all killed – '

'We're taking you back. That's the point.'

'Like hell. This is Mexico, the Border Security Force has no jurisdiction here – '

'We can arrest an American citizen anyplace.' Well, it sounded good. 'Now, you are going to tell me about Salazar. He's planning a large drug delivery . . . where is he delivering the drugs?'

He shook his head. She moved the muzzle of the .45 away from the ladder and aimed it into his face. 'Max, you know me. If you don't cooperate I'll have to kill you. Now.'

'I don't believe that.'

God, what an ego, she thought. Even now. 'I can do better. I can leave you for Salazar, his knife . . . Would you prefer to take your chances with Salazar?' She could smell his fear. Dapper Max, scared shitless. 'I could let you go but he'd believe you talked and have you sliced into fish food.' She reached into a pocket and pulled out a handful of American bills. 'I'll knock you unconscious, put money and my card in your pocket. Smooth-talk your way out of that.' She reached over and stuffed the money into his pants. 'There you go, Max. You tell him you just don't know how that money got there – '

'All *right*, get me out of here and I'll make a deal – '

'First things first, Max. Talk to us now and we'll talk about getting you out. Don't talk and . . .'

'Okay, okay . . . Salazar has a huge drug shipment going on right now. His planes are flying to Colombia to make the pickup, they'll be delivered tomorrow night – '

'Where?'

'All over. Florida, Louisiana, Texas, the Bahamas – he's got fifty thousand kilos coming in . . .'

'*Fifty thousand?*'

'Yeah. Now get me the hell out of here.'

'Keep your head down and we might,' Geffar said. It would be good to get him back to the States, make an example of him – Just then an automatic rifle opened up, bullets whizzing through the air, pieces of tar ripping up the rooftop. Geffar rolled onto her stomach, took quick aim at the outline of a man on the roof of an adjacent hangar, fired twice. The man called out in pain and disappeared from sight. Geffar knew the muzzle blast from her own gun was a dead giveaway. She grabbed Van Nuys and pulled him to his knees. 'Move in, Max.' And half-dragged him away moments before more gunshots chewed into the tar at the spot where they had been.

The hangar they were on was the middle one of five hangars, and they could see soldiers on both adjacent hangars as well as on top of the airline offices building fifty yards away. 'We're going to be surrounded,' Long said. 'Where's that helicopter? It should be here . . .'

And suddenly the whole area was bathed in brilliant white light. The soldiers had turned on the ballpark lights, the large banks of lights on tall towers that usually lit up the aircraft parking ramps, and had turned them inward to illuminate the hangar rooftops. Geffar and Long saw that both adjacent hangars were lined with soldiers, three or four on each side, and more were coming up. Nowhere to find cover.

'As recuers you people make good gravediggers,' Van Nuys said, and started to get to his feet.

'Stay down,' Geffar said in a low voice.

Van Nuys shook her hand away. 'I'll just tell them you tried to kidnap me. They still need me for their operation, they won't do anything right away . . .' He got to his feet, arms raised high, and turned in a full circle to show that he was hiding nothing.

'It's me, Van Nuys, Colonel Salazar's assistant. They tried to kidnap me – '

A shot rang out. Van Nuys grabbed his shoulder and collapsed to the roof. Geffar crawled over to him. 'I told you to stay down. You are a total jerk.' She glanced over at Long. 'I think I hear the chopper coming.'

'Checks.' He opened his left hand to reveal a black-colored canister about the size of a soda can, with a rectangular top and a pull ring; another was in his other hand. 'Ready any time.'

Geffar produced two similar canisters from a small waistpack. 'Wait until the chopper comes closer.'

It did not take long. A few seconds later the heavy beating of rotors was clear. A few soldiers began to make the climb up to the roof where Geffar was trapped, but most were frozen, waiting for orders. Soon the helicopter zoomed overhead, less than ten feet above the rooftops, scattering soldiers across the rooftops.

'*Now*,' Geffar shouted. They threw canisters onto the adjacent rooftops, then buried their heads under their arms. The shock wave from the two concussion grenades erupted in their faces, sucking the air out of their lungs.

'Up,' Geffar called out. Van Nuys, stunned by the grenades, was rolling about the roof, disoriented and in pain. Salman was also shaken but was strong enough to fight off the pain and help carry/drag Van Nuys. Geffar could see soldiers still on their feet on the roofs around them, but they had hands over their ears. The concussion grenades were not altogether effective in the open, but with the soldiers clustered together on the rooftop the effect was devastating enough.

The helicopter made a tight pirouette over the taxiway in front of the airline terminal and headed back toward the row of hangars. Hearing rifle shots as the chopper approached, Long and Geffar tossed concussion grenades out over the front of the hangar as the green and blue UH-1 Huey helicopter swooped back over the hangars and settled into a close hover near the center hangar. Door gunners covered both sides of the chopper, sending bursts of gunfire over the heads of the troops on both adjacent rooftops to keep them from counterattacking. Seconds later everyone was aboard and the helicopter was speeding out of range of the tiny Mexican airport . . .

'You all right?' Masters shouted from the cockpit. 'Anyone hurt?'

'Van Nuys got hit in the shoulder,' Geffar called back. The copilot tossed her a first-aid kit, and she ripped off his jacket and shirt and dressed the wound. Wouldn't do to have fancy Max bleed to death before the courts got to him.

'How bad is it?' Van Nuys said, more lucid now.

'You'll live,' she said.

'We're off the airport?'

'We made it – no thanks to you, you sonofabitch,' Geffar said, deliberately pulling the bandages tighter. 'You almost got us all killed. Now listen up. Do as I say or we'll dump you off back in Ciudad del Carmen and you can tap dance in front of your buddy Salazar. Tell me about this drug shipment . . .'

Carmen del Sol Airlines, Ciudad del Carmen Airport, Mexico

Salazar's face was red as he chewed out his chief of security at the airline office, along with Major Trujillo's deputy chief pilot, Captain Garza, the security shift supervisor and the three squad leaders in charge of the airport security detail. 'Three unknowns, including a *woman* – infiltrate my base and kidnap Van Nuys out from under your noses?'

'It was a well-trained commando-style unit, sir,' the shift

621

supervisor tried. 'They used automatic weapons and concussion grenades. We had no way of defending – '

'I didn't ask for your excuses. Get out.' The security commanders left in a hurry, all except the chief of security.

'I have begun a search of the district, sir. I have ordered the chief of the militia, the local police and the Customs Bureau to report here at once and coordinate the search. I took the liberty of requisitioning six helicopters from operations – five are in the air conducting the search, the sixth is standing by for you in case they are found.'

'I am warning you, Captain,' Salazar said, barely able to control his temper, 'that if they are not found in an hour ... I can almost forgive lax security procedures at Verrettes when you faced an aerial bombardment, but stopping three persons? Get out of here and don't come back unless you find those intruders.' The chief of security retreated quickly, thankful he was leaving with all of his fingers and most of his bodily fluids and internal organs intact.

When they were alone, the deputy chief pilot, Garza, said, 'With Van Nuys missing, sir, the mission is in jeopardy – '

'I *know* that, Captain. Is that all you can offer?'

'Señor Gachez and Major Trujillo in Colombia must be notified, sir. If it *was* agents from the Border Security or the DEA that took Van Nuys, the shipment is at risk. We must assume that all our routes, the contacts, the distribution network – everything – has been compromised.'

'I know *that* too. But Gachez cannot be told.'

'Not tell Gachez? It will put his entire shipment at risk if he is not informed – '

'Garza, I don't care a rat's ass about his shipment. I care about finding a way to preserve the one and a half *billion* dollars we'll be paid for this job.'

Garza looked at his superior officer. 'But . . . but how

can that be done? We *must* assume that if Van Nuys is alive he will eventually talk . . .'

Salazar ignored him, going on as if talking to himself. 'If Gachez is told about Van Nuys' disappearance he will take his cocaine and head for the jungle. But if we don't tell him and the operation is permitted to continue we receive six hundred and fifty million dollars wired to our European and Caribbean accounts in non-refundable, non-traceable American dollars the minute our planes leave Valdivia, *plus* the one hundred million in cash we already have. If the shipment is intercepted enroute, that money will still be ours. And we can't be certain that Van Nuys will blab our plan . . . at least in time for the Hammerheads to stop us, and that means we make fifteen thousand dollars for every kilo of cocaine that is eventually delivered. We must keep silent until our planes can be loaded and launched out of Valdivia,' Salazar said, a smile appearing. 'Even if we lose every plane and every gram of cocaine, the three-quarters of a billion dollars is not too bad . . .'

'But . . . but what about our pilots? What about Major Trujillo? We know that the Border Security Force is after them, we have an obligation to inform our crewmen – '

'Garza, you are a good man but think . . . if we try to get a message to our crew now, Gachez will intercept it. It is much too risky. We can try to send a message to them after they clear Colombia and the money is safe in our hands – '

'But Colonel . . . those are your men out there. They are your Cuchillos. These men trust you – '

'They are *not* being abandoned, Captain Garza,' Salazar said almost casually, returning to his desk and swiveling around in his chair, a man at peace with himself. 'They are brave men, fighting men well aware of the risks. It is prudent to assume that Van Nuys will talk to the Hammerheads, but we are not *sure* of it – perhaps Gachez has a tighter hold on Van Nuys' tongue than one imagines.

623

We should not abort the mission because we merely *think* he will talk.' Garza did not look convinced.

'In any case, the Hammerheads are still weak, disorganized. They may not be capable of stopping my Cuchillos even if they have the necessary information. The Cuchillos know the procedures in case they are intercepted – avoid detection if possible, avoid pursuit if detected, avoid interception if pursued, avoid attack if intercepted, avoid capture if attacked, and keep silent if captured. We will not abandon them. I have confidence in our pilots to be sufficiently skillful to complete . . . to complete at least part of their missions.'

He stopped his swiveling and fixed Garza with a glare. 'You will brief the detachment here that they are to remain silent about the incident tonight. There will be no transmissions whatsoever about it. You will prepare alternate routes for our crews in case we receive word that our mission has been compromised. Above all, you and that useless worm of a security chief will insure that not a word is leaked to anyone outside this base. We can still profit from this disaster, Garza, but only if Gachez never finds out that Van Nuys is gone.'

Chapter Ten

The White House Oval Office, Washington, DC
The Next Morning

Vice President Martindale greeted the Mexican ambassador, Dr Lidia Pereira, at the door of the Oval Office and escorted her in. The President, Secretary of State Conrad Chapman, Chief of Staff Pledgeman, NSC Chairman Curtis, all got to their feet as the young ambassador from Mexico entered.

'How are you, Mr President?' Pereira needed no interpreter; her English had not a trace of accent.

'Very well, Dr Pereira, thank you.' The President, who at first had underestimated her, knew her now as a smart, tenacious firebrand, someone to be reckoned with.

Which was why she was in the White House this morning. Pereira carried a considerable influence in both the United States and Mexico and it was important to win her over early.

The President turned toward his advisors strategically arranged around the Oval Office. 'I believe you know everyone,' but he went through the introductions anyway. 'Dr Pereira,' the President said, 'I'm afraid we have an urgent matter to discuss.' He nodded to Vice President Martindale.

'Madame Ambassador, the United States Border Security Force has received information that a former Cuban military officer, a dual national of Haiti and Cuba, is operating a large-scale drug-smuggling operation out of Ciudad del Carmen,' Martindale said. 'An informant, a partner in a Colombian drug cartel, informs us that major shipments of cocaine will take place within the next few days, bound for the United States by air through central Mexico. As I'm sure you know, drug-smuggling activities through Mexico have sharply increased in recent years. Although the bulk of drug shipments still go through the Caribbean, and probably always will, we estimate that at least thirty to forty percent of illegal narcotics entering the United States now flow through Mexico.'

'I am *aware* of that,' Pereira said. 'It is not difficult to explain. We do not have the sophisticated air-traffic surveillance and police organization you do – police activities are almost nonexistent in the countryside. We also recognize that at times some of our government officials can be compromised by the enormous sums of money offered by the drug cartels in exchange for silence or non-interference. We are not alone in that. But we patrol our borders with you with all the resources and all the manpower we can possibly provide.'

'I know that, Madame Ambassador,' Martindale said. 'But along with stepped-up education, treatment and enforcement programs, we also have found that interdiction plays a *very* important part. Our Border Security Force has especially relied on cooperation with our neighbors to help stop the drug smugglers before they cross our borders . . . We need your help in a very special request to your government for a program that we would like to implement immediately.'

'My staff briefed me this morning when we received your call,' she said. 'I assume you are referring to a free-flight operation for your Border Security Force aircraft – your Hammerheads, I believe you call them. Am I correct?'

'Yes. Our proposal is simple: allow Border Security Force aircraft with Mexican justice department or federal police forces aboard to fly across the Mexican border in hot pursuit of aircraft not cleared to enter the United States, or aircraft that are flying a smuggler's profile typical of drug smugglers – low altitude, no identification beacons or radio broadcasts, no flight plan or official clearance. The program has been implemented in other Caribbean and Central American nations with success. The Bahamas, the Turks and Caicos, Anguilla, the Dominican Republic, Honduras – even Bolivia and Colombia use our aircraft and resources in their own fight against drug smugglers. We provide protection, transportation, advisors, money and training in exchange for the added security that stepped-up patrols in other countries provide. We do *not* interfere with enforcement matters not under our jurisdiction.

'Mexico has provided a great deal of support and cooperation in our drug interdiction, intelligence and surveillance operations, but more is needed. Mexico, I'm afraid, remains a safe haven for drug smugglers – '

'An unfair and exaggerated characterization – '

'Our aircraft are forbidden to cross the border without prior permission,' Martindale pressed on, not responding to her protest. 'Notification is usually unsuitable for such fast-breaking operations as confront us today, and is too easily exploited by the drug smugglers. Mexico is now the most vital link in our efforts to control drug smuggling into the United States. Will you help us, Dr Pereira?'

'Mexico already has such a program, Mr Vice President. We extend a great deal of support to your Drug Enforcement Administration agents, and we cooperate with your Customs Service, the Coast Guard, your Border Patrol *and* your local police departments.'

'True, Dr Pereira, but here's what we now face: unidentified aircraft crossing our border with Mexico know that Border Security Force aircraft are not permitted to cross the border, and they know that if they are discovered by us they can simply fly right back across the border into

627

Mexico to safety. An aircraft making drug drops anywhere near the border feels confident he can escape interception. If he's found he simply flies south to safety, lands, refuels and tries again later. If he makes a drop on the Mexico side of the border the drugs are dispersed and border crossings can be made on foot or by off-road vehicles, with a very good chance of safely moving the drugs north – '

'I believe all that is grossly overestimated,' Pereira said flatly. 'My government responds very well to requests by US Customs to such border intrusions, and we respond with all the enforcement assets we have. Our anti-drug task forces are the best-equipped and best-trained people in Mexico. I realize they may not be up to the standard of the Hammerheads . . .' She paused, a hint of derision in her tone, '. . . but my government believes our efforts are in proportion to the level of the drug problem that exists . . . for the *Mexican* people.'

'I take your point,' he said. 'There would be no drug-smuggling if the demand for drugs were not so high in our country. But the facts remain, a drug problem does exist in your country as well as ours. And your country has become a major pipeline for the flow of illegal drugs. We have the means to reduce substantially that flow, but we need your help – '

'What exactly do you propose?'

Pledgeman was on. He came forward with copies of a proposal in blue plastic folders, presented one to Dr Pereira and passed out copies to the others. 'This is an outline of the concept, Dr Pereira, but allow me to summarize it for you: Provide our Border Security Force with a contingent of one hundred enforcement officers. These officers will be stationed on American bases along the border. Two to four officers accompany each interdiction flight. Give our aircraft overflight and landing privileges throughout Mexico. If the suspect aircraft is in

Mexico, your officers have jurisdiction over the suspects and the evidence. If the suspects are in the United States we retain jurisdiction. The Border Security Force pilots retain command and control of their aircraft. We also ask for unlimited overflight and landing privileges for our unmanned surveillance and interception aircraft.'

'What about weapons?' Pereira asked. 'Will you begin shooting down Mexican citizens?'

'As with our collaborative operations in the Caribbean, officers will not use their weapons on foreign soil, except, of course, to protect themselves. This includes the use of air-to-air or air-to-surface weapons on some of our aircraft. They may assist in arrests and detention of prisoners but only on direction of the Mexican officer in charge. To insure safety, armed unmanned aircraft will not be allowed to overfly Mexico.'

Pereira looked at Air Force General Wilbur Curtis, then asked, 'And what about your Air Force or Army?'

Curtis said: 'This plan deals only with Border Security Force and Customs Service operations. Unless specifically authorized, we may not fly military aircraft into Mexico under this agreement. We must adhere to all national and international laws.'

She gave Curtis a skeptical look. 'But the Border Security Force is part of the military, is it not?'

'The Border Security Force is in effect a separate agency,' the Vice President said, 'and it will soon be official by act of Congress. In any case our proposal limits the specific aircraft allowed to cross the borders at will, and except for the unmanned aircraft, all of these aircraft must have Mexican enforcement agents on board.'

'What advantages does this proposal offer for Mexico? It gives your Border Security Force great powers in the use of Mexico's sovereign airspace, but what do we get in return?'

'We strengthen and modernize your border patrol units

629

and frontier military units,' the Vice President told her. 'Surveillance aircraft, access to surveillance radar and aerostat data, modern tactical and transport aircraft and helicopters, access to fuel and spare parts – it's a package worth well over a hundred million a year. In addition we have companies that are eager to help modernize many of your outlying and coastal airports and port facilities. Mainly, we will be building a greater bond between our two countries. Cooperation in border-security operations will certainly lead to cooperative ventures in many, many other areas – immigration, agriculture, jobs, industrial expansion . . .'

She got to her feet, picked up the blue plastic folder and tucked it under an arm. 'I believe we both have much to think about, Mr President, so I will ask to be excused. I look forward to our next meeting.' There was her radiant, disarming smile.

The Vice President was quickly on his feet. 'Dr Pereira, this issue can't wait. We have information that a major smuggling operation is underway right now. The Border Security Force needs permission now to conduct flight operations along the Mexican border and to pursue suspect aircraft across the border. We know your President can authorize these flight operations on his signature for as long as thirty days.' Martindale motioned to the phone on the coffee table in the center of the room. 'We have an open line and we have requested a conversation with your President. He has promised to stand by for our call. With your recommendation I believe he will give the approval we need.'

'This is not the way such negotiations are usually conducted, Mr Vice President.' She looked quickly at the President, then back at Martindale. 'Allow me to take your proposal back to my government. This can be in the President's hands by tomorrow via special courier. A synopsis with my recommendations will follow shortly after.'

'That may be too late, Dr Pereira,' Martindale said. 'We need aircraft in position, the shipments may have already begun . . .'

'I can't help that, Mr Vice President. Your proposal must go through channels. You ought to understand that.'

'Madame Ambassador, this is an important matter,' the President cut in. 'I understand the need for protocol, but I'm sure you can understand the need for action. We've made telephone requests of your government in the past – '

'Mr President, a request from a Coast Guard vessel to board a tramp steamer flying the flag of Mexico is one thing,' Pereira said. 'Overflight of Mexico by armed American aircraft is another. This is not a decision to be made hastily. The President must be properly briefed, the ministers of interior, justice and military should all be consulted, the opposition party leaders must also be notified – '

'Our surveillance aircraft are already in the air on both coasts of Mexico,' the Vice President said. 'We must have clearance to overfly – '

'You have *already* placed your aircraft off our coasts? Strike aircraft? Just what *have* you done, Mr Vice President?'

'The Border Security Force's radar surveillance planes, the E2C and P-3B,' Martindale said. '*Not* strike aircraft. They are off your Gulf and Pacific coasts, outside your national airspace and far from commercial flight paths – '

'My government wasn't told of this. It's certainly damned irregular – '

'The aircraft are in international airspace, Doctor,' the President said. 'No official notification is necessary – '

'With *respect*, Mr President, this's not the point. Any

631

such operation involving Mexico should naturally involve informing Mexico and getting our input. Launching spy planes to eavesdrop on my country, preparing to launch attack aircraft against planes operating in Mexican airspace, even directing one watt of energy across our borders without our knowledge . . . they are not the acts of a friendly neighbor. Sending spy planes against Cuba or the Soviet Union requires no notification – do you put the Republic of Mexico in the same category with them?'

'We're consulting with you now, Dr Pereira,' the President said irritably, 'and we're *asking* for your help. We'll do, however, what we feel is in our national interest. What our aircraft do in international airspace is our affair. And as for our radar energy crossing your borders, well, no nation has been very successful in regulating that. We'd prefer to conduct this operation with your government's cooperation, but we're capable of proceeding without it.'

The President paused, waiting for Pereira to answer. When all he got was silence he added: 'Our operation must begin immediately. I'm sorry, but we can't wait for you to deliver our proposal. We'll contact your President directly, without your assistance.'

'You cannot steamroll us like this, sir,' Pereira said, her dark eyes flashing. 'The President will consult with me on this matter and I will urge that he *carefully* study the written proposal you have given me.'

The President got to his feet, his fingertips resting on his desk as if anchoring himself there. 'Then it seems we have nothing else to talk about.'

'Except,' the Vice President put in, 'without Mexico's cooperation we will be forced to explain to the world the reason for our increased surveillance of the region. This includes the fact that a major international drug trafficker has not only illegally entered Mexico but has set up a business in the heart of Mexico, financed by illicit drug money and all under the auspices of the Mexican government – '

'That's a *lie*.'

Martindale ignored her lapse from diplomatic jargon, almost welcomed it . . . 'And he has obviously paid off government officials all across the country, leaving and entering the country at will with drugs, foreign currency and foreign criminals. I can tell you the Republic of Mexico even sends him warplanes to repair. He not only uses his contacts in the government to purchase spare parts, weapons and fuel for his drug shipments, he uses those warplanes as escort aircraft for his drug shipments – all courtesy of the Mexican government – '

'You would actually tell lies to get our cooperation, Mr President?'

'He's telling the truth, Madame Ambassador.'

'One of Gonzalez Gachez's henchmen, an American citizen wanted in this country for drug trafficking and conspiracy, was recently seized in Ciudad del Carmen,' the Vice President said. Pereira was about to protest that action as well but Martindale didn't give her the chance. 'He gave information for what he hoped would be immunity and protection. He told us about Colonel Agusto Salazar's operation in Mexico, where it has surfaced from Haiti. An American grand jury handed down an indictment against Salazar, based on his testimony and evidence collected in connection with the recent raids on Border Security Force installations. When Secretary Chapman contacted your foreign ministry for assistance in capturing Salazar in Ciudad del Carman we were told that Salazar was protected by the government *because he was a government defense contractor*.'

'Once again, Dr Pereira,' the President said, 'will you help us?'

Pereira paused, returning the powerful stare of the

President of the United States. She took a breath, averted her eyes and moved back to the sofa beside the telephone . . .

Over the Turks Island Passage, Turks and Caicos Islands, West Indies
That Evening

'Nassau Flight Following, Nassau Flight Following, this is Carmen del Sol Flight seven-seven-victor, over CABAL intersection, Alpha eight-six, at zero-four-one-one Zulu, altitude one-niner thousand feet, expecting point CROOK at zero-five-two zero Zulu. Weather report follows: IMC above and below, temperature forty degrees Fahrenheit uncorrected, estimated winds from the north at thirty gusting to forty-five, occasional light to moderate chop. Over.'

There was a long loud hiss on the high-frequency radio band when the pilot completed his mandatory overwater flight-following position report. Then a half-British, half-Jamaican-accented voice replied: 'Carmen del Sol Flight seven-seven victor, Nassau Flight Following copies all. You are still very weak but readable. Contact Nassau Centre on frequency one-two-four point seven at CROOK intersection. Have a safe flight.' The voice melted into the eerie hisses and pops of long-range radio.

'Roger, Nassau. Thank you. Out.' The pilot put the mike back in its holder – likely it was the last time he would use it for the entire trip. This was the big one. They carried one thousand kilograms of cocaine destined for the Turks and Caicos Islands, a small island nation north of Haiti, and the Bahamas. Their plane, a Cessna Caravan high-wing single-engine cargo plane, was not at nineteen thousand feet as they reported – it was at five hundred feet above the

634

water, and had been there now for the past thirty minutes. Which was the reason for the bad transmission quality – with the high-frequency radio antenna mounted on the plane's belly, they were firing most of the transmitter's energy right into the sea.

From the very beginning the pilots knew this flight would be a bitch. Each had gotten only a few hours' sleep during the last twenty-four hours, and they still had at least six hours of flying to go. The Caravan's autopilot was not working, which meant that the plane had to be hand-flown, and in the tricky winds and turbulence of a passing Caribbean storm, it was a nightmare come true.

They had stayed on flight plan course from Uribia, Colombia, across the Caribbean Sea up the Windward Passage between Cuba and Haiti into the Turks and Caicos Islands chain, with a planned stop in Nassau. But instead of going directly to Nassau from their present position they would detour under surveillance radars on Caicos Island and make two two-hundred-fifty-kilo drops along the ridge of tiny islands south of East Caicos Point. They would then head northwest, make another two-hundred-fifty-kilo drop south of Mayaguana Island in the Bahamas, head further west and pick up their flight plan near Crooked Island.

With seven hundred fifty kilograms of cocaine delivered, they would then divert to Arthurs Town on Cat Island in the Bahamas, claiming engine trouble, and land on a pre-selected road north of town. Waiting there was a heavily armed six-man crew that would secure the landing site, recover the plane, remove the last two hundred fifty kilos and the fuel bladders, scrub down the plane's cargo hold, spray it with a bovine hormone, phrenopherone, that was odorless to humans but concocted to desensitize a dog's sense of smell – in the Bahamas even traces of cocaine detectable only by trained drug dogs was enough to get a conviction – and load the plane up with a few hundred

635

pounds of Colombian coffee and a few 'passengers.' They would then call Bahamian Customs – if they hadn't already arrived by then – who would come out and inspect their 'disabled' aircraft. In a few minutes everything would appear perfectly normal.

That was the plan . . . but, being tossed around like a kite in a stiff March breeze only a few seconds from crashing into the Caribbean Sea, feeling strength sap from his body as fast as his precious fuel was diminishing, it seemed to the Caravan's pilot the ambitious plan could never work. He was also fighting off sleep as he watched the radar altimeter and monitored his plane's performance. He caught only five hours' sleep in Valdivia after an exhausting eleven-hour flight from Mexico to Colombia, had dinner and then was off once again. The short two-hour flight from Valdivia to Uribia in northern Colombia for refueling was better – for some reason he felt charged-up, wide awake and alert as a panther, and he thought the rest of the flight would be the same. Not so. After the third hour of flight, as they neared Haiti, he felt his body tremble and his skin alternate between ice cold and feverishly hot. He couldn't get to sleep and he couldn't stay awake.

Now he felt as if he was being dragged into a dark pit of sleep, and he was using every trick in the book to stay awake. The old fighter pilot's trick of tickling the roof of his mouth with his tongue wasn't working anymore. The heat had been turned off long ago. Cold water down the pants didn't seem to help. 'Take the controls for me, Jorge,' he told his copilot. It took a moment for the copilot to respond – obviously he was feeling the same exhaustion – but he soon felt the copilot's hands on the controls. The pilot got up to find some coffee and stretch his legs.

The starboard cargo door was open, and the drone of the Caravan's single four-hundred-horsepower engine was deafening. What the pilot saw in the back of the Caravan

636

sent him into a rage. The two crewmen were sound asleep, snoring loudly enough to hear over the windblast and engine noise. When the pilot gave the first man he reached a not-too-gentle side kick, he slumped over as if he was dead, hit his head on a fiberglass case full of cocaine and snapped awake as if a gun had been fired on him.

'Wake up, you idiot,' the pilot told him. 'We're only a few minutes from the drop.' The other crewman got to his feet as well, rubbing his face and windmilling his arms to try to get himself going. 'What the hell is wrong with you?'

'I'm sorry, sir,' the first crewman said. 'We were okay until just a few minutes ago. Now, we just . . . conked out. We'll be okay.'

'The time for napping is over. Stick your head out the cargo door or pinch yourself, but get ready or you'll go out the door with the dope.'

'Sorry, sir. It won't happen again. We were just – '

'I'm not interested in your excuses. Just get back on headsets and stand by.'

'You don't have to yell, sir,' the loadmaster retorted. 'We've been at this for nearly thirty hours. We would have responded on interphone if you – '

'Dammit, I said keep silent and do as you're told,' the pilot snapped. 'One more word out of you, and you're on report.' The two men faced each other, both refusing to back down, both ready for a fight. But at a sudden swerve and precipitous dip in the Caravan, the pilot took a firm hold on the cargo-bay roof and quickly made his way to the cockpit.

'What's wrong up here?' he asked the copilot.

'Sorry,' the copilot replied. 'I tried to engage the autopilot and I thought it was working again. We lost a few hundred feet. But I got it – '

'Like hell.' The pilot slipped into his seat, strapped in and took the controls. 'What is going *on* here? You knew we red X-ed the autopilot hours ago. We're acting like amateurs. Manuel and Lidio were sleeping in the back, and you – '

'I know. I'm just very tired, that's all.'

'Everyone's got an excuse tonight.'

The copilot did not continue the argument. He checked his navigation charts with the LORAN long-range navigation receiver. 'I show about ten minutes to go until the first drop.'

The pilot checked that the correct frequency was set in the WET SNOW radio beacon receiver mounted on his dashboard, then flicked on the coded attention-signal switch. He left it on for five seconds without receiving a reply, then flicked it off. 'No reply yet. Are you sure of our position?'

'The LORAN is running fine,' the copilot replied. He began dialing in several ADF ground-navigation stations and triangulating their position on a chart.

'Well?'

The copilot turned toward the pilot but thought better of saying anything. A few moments later he said, 'The LORAN is within two miles of our position. The pickup crew must be asleep.'

'More likely you turned us to the wrong heading,' the pilot said.

'Screw you.'

'What. . . ?'

'Look, I'm working my butt off here. I said we're on course and I goddamned *meant* it.'

Without warning, the pilot reached over with his right hand and grabbed the copilot by the throat. He was much smaller and weaker and was simply too tired to put up much of a fight. But a few moments later, the pilot withdrew his hand, shaking his head in puzzlement.

'What am I doing? What the hell is going on?' He put

both his hands back on the control wheel, rubbed his eyes and stared straight ahead into the darkness. 'If I didn't know better I'd say we were hypoxic. But we're only at five hundred damned feet.'

'I'm exhausted. We all are,' the copilot said.

'We've had longer and tougher missions than this before. The strain must be getting to us.' He shook his head once again, then clicked on the code-transmit switch once again. This time he received a green 'REPLY' light immediately. The WET SNOW receiver indicated the relative bearing to the beacon, and the pilot set the bearing in his directional gyro and flicked the code switch back to 'STANDBY.' 'Beacon received. Bearing is three-zero-zero, range thirty-two miles.'

'Roger,' the copilot acknowledged. On interphone he announced, 'Crew, ten minutes to first drop. Load canisters for drop one and stand by.' To the pilot he said, 'Inbound course for first drop is three-five-zero. We've got a five-canister drop coming up. Planned ripple is set for fifty feet at one-hundred-twenty knots groundspeed.'

'Turning to heading three-five zero, descending to one hundred feet, slowing to one-fifty,' the pilot responded. He slowly moved the control wheel right and pulled off a little throttle. 'We'll get an update on the bearing every five to six minutes, then every minute within ten miles, then continuously inside three miles.'

'Roger,' the copilot replied. 'I've got a stopwatch running. Groundspeed looks good. Cockpit check and fuel log . . .'

The pilot finally began to relax as the copilot ran through the pre-drop checklists. At last, everything sounded as if it was coming together.

The pilot flipped on his WET SNOW beacon receiver again and took another range-and-bearing reading. Unlike the Cuchillos' radar-equipped aircraft, he had only a bearing needle to guide him to the drop point. The crews who used radar with the WET SNOW system could usually. make a drop within a few meters of a target. He would be satisfied with being within one or two hundred meters. He flicked the switch off.

'Bearing set. Correcting for a few degrees drift . . . five miles to go.'

In the cargo department the load crew had arranged the first five canisters on the sled ready for the drop. The first one-hundred-kilo canister was set on the sled's rails, aimed out the right cargo door. At the drop signal the first canister would be released. The canisters were roped together with twenty meters of nylon rope. At the preplanned drop airspeed and altitude, the rope gave the drop crew just enough time to haul the next canister onto the sled before the preceding canister yanked it into the slipstream. This would continue until all five canisters were out. This way they could deliver the canisters with speed and precision without scattering drugs all over the drop zone.

'One minute to go.'

The pilot nodded and switched on the WET SNOW beacon, then left it on. Now he would make continuous corrections all the way to the drop point. He settled the big Cessna down to fifty feet on the radar altimeter and tried his best to peg one hundred twenty knots groundspeed – the occasional buffets of wind and up- and down-drafts made that practically impossible. 'Thirty seconds. Load crew, stand by.'

'Load crew ready.' The first canister was on the sled, and the two crewmen were holding the handles on the second, ready to lift it onto the sled's rails as soon as the first was released. They stood, tensed and ready to go, looking out through the cargo doors into the inky blackness beyond . . .

When suddenly a shape appeared out of the night sky

like a huge, dark specter. It was as menacing as a hornet with its long pointed tail and nose. Seconds later a brilliant beam of light emanated from the apparition's nose and hit the load-crew square in the face, temporarily blinding them.

'Ten seconds, load crew – '

'A *helicopter*,' one of the crewmen yelled. 'Off our right side, a chopper . . .'

The two pilots stared as the huge Black Hawk helicopter maneuvered even closer. Running and navigation lights popped on all over the chopper, revealing the words 'US CUSTOMS' painted in large black-and-gold letters. A large door was open on the left side of the Customs Service chopper, revealing two soldiers in life jackets and helmets, aiming M-16 rifles at the plane.

'Customs! Where the hell did they come from?'

'Never mind that. Drop,' the pilot ordered over the interphone. 'Drop *now*.'

One load crewman hit the foot lever to eject the first canister, ignoring the blinding NightSun searchlight that seemed to illuminate every corner of the Cessna's cargo hold. The first canister slid down the rails and disappeared, whipping the carefully coiled rope behind it. But just as the load crew was pulling the second canister up onto the rails, the soldiers in the Customs Service chopper opened fire, spraying the Cessna's cargo hold with bullets. One crewman was hit in the right shoulder and shoved back to the other side of the plane; the other dodged the hail of bullets and jumped back away from the door.

The second canister never made it out the cargo door. It hit the cargo deck sideways, skipped awkwardly over the sled's rails and wedged itself between the sled and the bulkhead. The first canister hit the water, but the nylon rope did not break and the canister was dragged through the water. The sudden drag pulled the Cessna Caravan's nose hard right and down, precariously close to the water.

'Pull up, pull up,' the copilot shouted, but the pilot was already struggling with the controls. Just as he regained control of the plane, another volley of gunfire ripped across the right cockpit windows, shattering the glass and killing the copilot. The sudden attack diverted the pilot's attention for a split-second, but it was enough when flying a fifteen-thousand-pound plane at slow speed only fifty feet above the sea – the Caravan nosed over, the nose lifted but the plane continued to lose altitude, crashing seconds later and flipping end-over-end for hundreds of feet across the warm Caribbean waters.

Border Security Force Headquarters, Aladdin City, Florida

'Lost contact with the target.'

The right-side situation-monitor on the front wall of the Command-Control-Communications-Intelligence Center at Border Security Force headquarters had zoomed in on the northeast sector of the Caribbean. Centered in the display was a single red box with a cross in the center – an unidentified radar target, designated by the controllers as an intercept target. Data readouts beside the box showed the target's speed, approximate altitude, heading and velocity changes – now all suddenly read zero.

Annette Fields was in the intelligence center of the Hammerheads C-3-I complex, manning the data console along with another technician. With her was Brad Elliott. 'ROTH has his airspeed at zero,' Fields said. 'Altitude data is unreliable but that reads zero too.'

'Message from Bat Seven,' the technician reported. 'The Turks constables opened fire on the target.'

'What?' from Elliott. 'Get a report from them.'

The technician listened intently, taking notes, then

acknowledged. To Elliott, he said, 'They hit the target with a searchlight and observed the target beginning a drop, sir. When the smugglers kicked out the first load, the Turks and Caicos constables opened fire. The crew lost control of the plane and it crashed.'

'No one ordered them to open fire,' Fields said. 'We should have gone after them ourselves.'

'The OPBAT team is better suited for this job than we are,' Elliott said. OPBAT stood for Operations Bahamas/Anguilla/Turks and Caicos, a US Customs operations unit that transported foreign police and military units to the scene of drug-smuggling drops where the United States did not have jurisdiction. OPBAT teams regularly made drug arrests all across the Caribbean by carrying foreign constables aboard Customs Service, Coast Guard and US Navy aircraft and surface vessels. It was one of the few drug-interdiction operations not turned over to the Hammerheads after the creation of the Border Security Force. This OPBAT operation used a Customs Service Black Hawk helicopter to carry constables from both the Turks and Caicos and the Bahamas.

'The Turks constables have every authority to do what they want – Customs is the taxi driver,' Elliott said. 'The Turks and Caicos government have always had a straight-forward altitude about drug trafficking – if they catch you, you're dead. Get someone else to monitor the rescue. Let's get the status of the other inbounds.'

Fields had expanded the scale of the radar display on the monitor to include the northern half of the Bahamas, Florida and northern Cuba. She highlighted a red square with an 'X' in the middle, a designated radar target moving east to west, roughly between Andros Island in the Bahamas and Key Largo, Florida. 'The other target is another twenty minutes to the Cay Sal Bank,' Fields reported. 'He's still at ten thousand feet, should be descending soon.' Directly behind that target was another square, this one in blue – an AV-22 Sea Lion tilt-rotor plane, Lion Three-Three, which had picked up the target coming across Andros Island and was now following a few miles behind and a few thousand feet above, waiting for the opportunity to pounce.

'Why didn't we bust this guy in Nassau?' Fields asked. 'Right now he looks legitimate – he's cleared Bahamian Customs, he's dead on course on Bravo-646 and he has a valid flight plan to Mexico. But we *know* the guy is carrying drugs – '

'He didn't actually *clear* Customs in Nassau,' Elliott corrected her. 'In fact, he didn't have to go through Customs at all. He's on a stopover flight plan from Jamaica to Cancún with no deliveries scheduled for any stop – only pickups and refueling. Bahamian customs doesn't have to inspect his plane unless they have probable cause.'

'But we *do* have probable cause. Van Nuys said this guy had five hundred kilos of cocaine on board. That should have been enough – '

'Wouldn't have made any difference. We couldn't convince Bahamian Customs to let us wire this guy or check his documents,' Elliott said. 'They told us we had to get a court order or go through their home secretary. As they say, the fix was already in.'

'If we busted this guy the word might get out that we're onto this operation,' Fields added. 'Besides, if Van Nuys' information is straight goods, this guy will make a drop somewhere along the Keys or in Florida Bay and we can get both the plane and the man on the ground if we wait.'

'*If* we can determine that the plane dropped drugs in US territory,' Elliott said. 'Congress, the White House doesn't want a repeat of the Lion Two-Two incident when that smuggler was shot down over the Gulf of Mexico. Even with all that's happened to the Hammerheads, the rules are tighter than ever – even tighter than the old rules for the use of deadly force. Which means we have to see the drop, find the drugs, determine that the recovered container was the thing that was thrown from the plane and then determine that the container contains cocaine or some other illegal substance. And we have to do all this before the guy leaves American airspace.' Elliott shook his head. 'I don't like this. We should do a standard intercept and turn him away. We're risking missing both the drop and the plane.'

'We've got McLanahan airborne in the E-2 with six Sky Lion drones to chase down the ground smugglers,' Fields said, 'and an AV-22 on this guy's tail. We're covered. So far Van Nuys has given us good information. I think we should take advantage of it.'

'Looks like he's descending,' Fields reported. 'The target's data block indicated the plane leaving ten thousand feet.' Although the altitude readout was erratic, the Hammerheads' Relocatable Over-the-Horizon Backscatter radar system could usually detect altitude changes and alert the operators. 'Groundspeed may have dropped off too . . . he's turning northwest. He's starting his inbound track. Sixty miles east of Marathon at this time. Lion Three-Three is turning, maintaining contact . . .'

Aboard the Inbound Smuggler's Plane

'Miami Center, Carmen del Sol Airline's flight nine-oh-niner Charlie, descending VFR on top to eight thousand five hundred. Over.'

'Del Sol nine-oh-niner Charlie, roger,' the air traffic controllers replied. 'Be advised, MEA in your area is eight thousand feet, limited radar coverage until within range of Key West Approach. Over.'

'Thanks for the advisory, Center, nine-oh-niner Charlie. Eight point five will be our final. We were getting some bad winds up there.' The controller replied with two clicks of his mike, then went on to talk to someone else.

The pilot of the Cuchillos' twin-engine Cheyenne turbo-prop, Major José Trujillo, reached up to a special device on his instrument panel and flicked it on. Normally, air traffic control radar interrogated a plane's IFF, its Identification Friend or Foe system, which would reply with the plane's assigned code and the altitude readout from the pressure altimeter. This device allowed the pilot to transmit any altitude data he wanted through the plane's mode-C encoder. With the device on, air traffic control would read the plane's altitude as eight thousand five hundred feet, although the plane could be at any altitude.

'Position?' Trujillo asked his copilot.

'Coming up in five miles,' the copilot replied. He had the WET SNOW beacon receiver on his side of the instrument panel, intermittently activating the system to get a bearing to the drop point, then flicking it off to prevent detection. He had been directing the pilot to steer toward the ground crew, who were arranged along Lower Matecumbe Key waiting for the five-hundred-kilo shipment.

The copilot took one long, last bearing – they were right on target. He tightened his seat and shoulder belts, looked back at the cargo crew – they had no seats but were holding on tight to whatever they could – nodded to Trujillo and said, 'Now.'

Trujillo pulled the throttles all the way back to idle, hauled the plane into a steep ninety-degree right-bank and knifed the nose down toward the dark waters below. The vertical-velocity indicator snapped down to two-thousand-feet-per-minute descent and pegged. In seconds the plane had descended from eight thousand to two thousand feet.

'Del Sol niner-zero-niner-Charlie, recycle your transponder and check code four-one-three-three. Over.'

Trujillo had to control his voice during the dizzying descent as he replied, 'Niner-zero-niner-Charlie, roger.' He hoped the controller wouldn't notice the tension in his voice as the altimeter unwound like a racing stopwatch gone wild.

'Niner-zero-niner-Charlie, recycle your transponder once again.'

'Pull *up*,' the copilot shouted cross-cockpit. They had shot through two thousand feet with the nose still ten degrees below the horizon and the plane still at ninety degrees bank, in an accelerated stall. Trujillo shoved the throttles back in to arrest the screaming descent, leveled the wings and pulled back on the control column. At six hundred feet the vertical-velocity indicator finally bounced off the dial and began to creep upward. They finally leveled off at three hundred feet . . .

Aboard Lion Three-Three, in Pursuit of Carmen Del Sol Nine-Zero-Nine Charlie

Through the Pilot's Night Vision Sensor goggles Ken Sherrey saw the suspect plane in front of him, a huge Cheyenne turboprop, do a high-G wingover and plummet toward the ocean like a rock. Sherrey pulled the left-power lever on his AV-22 Sea Lion tilt-rotor back to reduce power, ignored the computerized warnings to change nacelle angle and let the Sea Lion's nose drop to pursue.

'Aladdin, the suspect is doing a hard descent,' Sherrey reported. 'He's heading for the deck at five thousand feet a minute – that guy must have steel balls to do a wingover in a Cheyenne at night.'

'We copy, Three-Three,' Annette Fields replied. 'Can you maintain contact?'

'My I-Team guys are weightless in the back but I can still

647

see him okay. I can maintain contact. You better check with the Sky Lions, though.'

'Roger,' Field said. 'Break. Hawk Four-One, did you copy?'

'Roger that,' McLanahan replied aboard the E-2 Hawkeye radar plane orbiting forty miles away. 'The drones are descending too. I've got radar contact with both the suspect and the Three-Three. We also have IR contact on several surface targets near Lower Matecumbe Key . . . I think that's our drop. I've got two Sky Lions on auto-intercept on the confirmed surface targets.'

'Copy all, Four-One.'

'Three-Three copies all.' Sherrey let the speed increase as he continued his own hard descent. 'He better pull up soon,' Sherrey's copilot murmured.

'He's still nose low and wing high,' Sherrey said. 'Even if he does get level he might sink right down into the drink.'

But the suspect plane did not crash. Slowly, inexorably, the big turboprop leveled its wings. It seemed to hang motionless in the green-and-white infrared/night-vision video screen. Sherrey was still positive the plane would pancake in, but after several moments it was obvious that the smugglers made it.

'Pretty damned good flying,' Sherrey's copilot said.

'Luck of the devil,' Sherrey muttered. He kept the AV-22 coming down until he was at one thousand feet above the water, well above and behind the low-flying smuggler. 'Luck of the devil . . .'

The copilot had the WET SNOW beacon system on as soon as the plane leveled off and took a reading as soon as he was sure Trujillo had the big turboprop back under control. 'Five degrees left, ten seconds,' the copilot shouted. Trujillo's chest was heaving from the exertion, but he slapped the plane to the left and worked to inch the plane down to one hundred feet, one hundred twenty knots, the precalculated drop parameters. 'Drop crew, stand by . . . stand by . . . *now*.'

They had no fancy sled drop devices – two men in the back of the Cheyenne just started sliding the fifty-kilo canisters out the door as fast as they could. In thirty seconds they had slid all ten bullet-shaped canisters out the door. 'Drop completed. *Go*.'

'Cargo in the water,' Sherrey's copilot called out as he saw the canisters fly out the Cheyenne's cargo door.

'I got it, I got it,' Sherrey said, talking to himself more than anyone else. 'I'm breaking off from the Cheyenne. I-Team, stand by.'

Sherrey rotated the engine-nacelle switch up, which swung the Sea Lion's twin engines to the vertical position. As he did so the AV-22's controls changed from standard aircraft rudders and ailerons to helicopter cyclic and collectives. He quickly dropped down to just a few feet above the water and hovered yards away from three canisters he could see bobbing in the water.

'I've got a canister just ten yards on the right,' he said as he settled the big plane down for a gentle water landing. 'I-Team, out.' In the cargo bay of the AV-22 the five-man I-Team slid their rigid-hull inflatable boat off the rear cargo ramp and into the water. With the helmsman wearing a set of night-vision goggles he was able to pick out the canisters. Sherrey water-taxied the AV-22 clear so his rotor wash wouldn't capsize the RHIB, and the I-Team members threw a rope around the canister and lashed it to their boat.

Just as they pulled the floating canister to the side of the RHIB the helmsman announced from his helmet-mounted radio: 'I've got a boat at three o'clock, closing fast . . .'

'Get back aboard,' Sherrey shouted over the radio. But just as he called out the orders Sherrey could see winks of light coming from the approximate position of the newcomer – they were being fired on.

'Aladdin, this is Three-Three,' Sherrey radioed. 'We've got hostiles at our three o'clock. Shots fired. I-Team taking heavy fire. We're recovering the I-Team and can't lift off.' The copilot unbuckled and headed back to the cargo bay, ready to help the I-Team back in.

'Break. Three-Three, this is Four-One,' McLanahan suddenly cut in from the E-2 Hawkeye radar lane. 'Stand by, we're coming in.'

The helmsman standing up in the RHIB was the first to fall to the fusillade of bullets from the attackers. Several of the I-Team flattened themselves down and began to return fire with sidearms, while two others helped the wounded helmsman and began to steer the RHIB back to the cargo ramp. 'Four-One, get down here,' Sherrey shouted. 'We're taking heavy fire . . .'

And out in the darkness beyond the right engine nacelle Sherrey saw a brilliant flash of light and a yellow streak of fire race across the sky, heading to the surface. A moment later there was an explosion just fifty yards away. One of the Sea Lion drones following the surface ships it had detected with its infrared scanner had fired a Sea Stinger missile at the oncoming boat. Moments later a second missile plunged into the attacker's boat, creating a mushroom of fire rolling across the ocean. And the boat began to burn fiercely, lighting up the sky for hundreds of yards.

'Three-Three, I've got another Sky Lion moving in to your position,' McLanahan radioed from the E-2. 'Do you need further assistance?'

'Negative. Your wind-up toys did a nice job,' Sherrey said. 'Stand by.' He turned in his seat. 'How's Joe?'

The helmsman's right arm was covered with blood but he was sitting up, alert, and could wave back at Sherrey. 'I'm okay, get those sons of bitches.'

'You sure, Joe?' The helmsman waved again. 'The drones got the pickup boat. Crack that case open and let's see what we got.'

Steel bands were cut off the fiberglass canister, and after a quick check for explosives, triggering devices or other booby traps they opened the case – because the smuggler's pickup crew often had to open a case to disperse the load it was rarely booby-trapped, but it was a good idea to be sure. What they found was fifty one-kilo bricks of a grayish-white powder. One of the I-Team members brought out a test kit, and they cut into one brick and dumped a knifeful into a vial of cobalt cyanimide. 'Pure as my baby sister,' he called out.

'Secure that back ramp and get strapped in,' Sherrey ordered. He had already lifted off and was starting his pursuit before the copilot made it back into his seat.

Major José Trujillo aboard the Cheyenne shoved the throttles back to full power and started a steep climb after making the drop. As he passed through five thousand feet they started to hear snatches of radio transmissions from Miami Center: '. . . Charlie, if you can hear me, contact Miami Center on one-one-eight-point-two-five. Repeat, Del Sol niner-zero-niner-Charlie, come up this frequency immediately.'

'Miami Center, Del Sol niner-zero-niner-Charlie, we can hear you fine, sir,' the Cuchillo pilot said. 'I've been identing, can you see my beacon now?'

'Affirmative, niner-zero-niner-Charlie,' the controller said. The Cheyenne was now passing six thousand eight hundred feet. 'I show you level at eight thousand five hundred. You didn't acknowledge my calls.'

'I heard you fine,' Trujillo replied. 'I guess I was hitting the wrong button, sorry . . .'

'Copy.' A few moments later the Miami Center

651

controller got back on the radio: 'Del Sol nine-zero-niner-Charlie . . . ah, sir, you have traffic at your six o'clock, five miles.'

Trujillo hesitated – usually the air traffic controllers didn't report traffic behind you because they knew you probably couldn't see it, and in any case they usually reported the other aircraft's altitude and type of aircraft. Finally he said, 'Roger, Center. Can't see him.'

Another pause, longer than the first, ten: 'Del Sol nine-zero-niner-Charlie, switch to frequency one-one-two point five-five.'

The two Cuchillos pilots looked at each other. They knew what that frequency was – the Border Security Force's air-surface common channel. They had been discovered.

They worked without talking. Trujillo immediately turned south, pushed the throttles up to full power and pushed the nose down to lose altitude. Meanwhile the copilots shut off the IFF transponder and double-checked that all the exterior lights were off.

'Carmen Del Sol niner-zero-niner-Charlie, this is the Border Security Force,' Ken Sherrey radioed from his AV-22 on the international GUARD emergency channel. 'We show you exiting your flight corridor and assigned altitude. You are currently on the Marathon zero-niner-two-degree radial at twenty-five DME, heading south, currently at five thousand feet and descending. You are in violation of United States border security procedures. Maintain your present altitude and lower your landing gear. Contact me at VHF frequency one-one-two-point-five-five or on VHF GUARD one-two-one-point-five.'

One of the cargo crewmembers rushed up the cockpit. 'What's going on? What are you doing?'

'Shut up and sit down . . .' But just then a brilliant beam of light stabbed into the Cheyenne's cabin from the left side, flashing along the fuselage and wings before settling on the pilot.

'The Hammerheads, they've found us . . .' Looking out the windows on the left side, the crewman could see the flashing warning lights and the white spotlight very close behind. 'They're right behind us, seven o'clock, about a half mile. Can you outrun them?'

Trujillo pulled the sun visor around to his left to try to block out the bright NightSun spotlight. 'What do you think?' the pilot said. 'We head south and try to get out of US waters before they open fire.'

'It's no use to try to run,' the voice said on the radio. 'We got one of your canisters, we got the drugs, we saw you drop the canister – we even got your pickup boat.' The spotlight began to flash slowly, the beam swinging in and out of the cockpit and across the left wing. 'I can see faces in the windows, people, which means this warning message and my searchlight have been seen. Lower your landing gear and start a right turn now or we will open fire.'

'What are we going to do?' the Cheyenne's copilot said. 'They're going to shoot . . .'

'Quiet,' Trujillo said. 'Get on the short-wave radio and try to reach one of the other Cuchillos. Tell them we have been intercepted.' He pulled the throttles back to seventy-percent power, reached over to the center console and pulled the landing gear handle down. The 'GEAR UNSAFE WARNING' light came on briefly as the gear dropped into the slipstream, but it soon went out and was replaced by three green 'GEAR DOWN AND LOCKED' lights.

Trujillo switched his radio to the Hammerheads' common frequency. 'Carmen del Sol Airlines flight niner-zero-niner-Charlie has lowered its landing gear. We protest this unwarranted action and demand that the Border Security Force aircraft at our seven o'clock position move away and turn off that searchlight. We are cancelling our international flight plan and are exiting American airspace. We are no longer under your control. Move clear.'

'Zero-niner-Charlie, you have been intercepted by the United States Border Security Force. You are required to follow my directions and acknowledge all transmissions or you will be fired on. Traffic separation and obstacle clearance will be provided by me. Turn right to magnetic heading three-five-zero and prepare for a visual approach and landing at Taimiami Airport.'

Trujillo turned his head at the glare of the searchlight, then began a slow right turn to the heading he was given. As he did he reached up to the patch on his left breast pocket of his flight suit – a blue diamond with a set of gold hawk's wings, the symbol of the Cuchillos borrowed from the wings of the Cuban Revolutionary Air Force. He ripped the patch off his flight suit and tossed it away, a silent apology to the man who had betrayed him – Colonel Agusto Salazar.

Border Security Force Headquarters, Aladdin City, Florida

'Suspect is decelerating and turning northbound,' Fields said, her voice rising. 'Three-Three reports he has lowered his landing gear.'

A cheer from the main command center controller.

'We need Customs and the Coast Guard to pick up the other canisters and check out that pickup boat,' Elliott said. 'See if we can get another Sea Lion airborne to escort the Cheyenne back into Taimiami, and have Three-Three fly into Homestead to have his crewman dropped off at the base hospital.'

'Yes, *sir*,' Field said.

Elliott looked at Annette Fields. 'This is turning into a major bust, and we only got two of the twelve planes Van Nuys said would be on this operation.'

Cuidad del Carmen Airport, Mexico
Twenty Minutes Later

Agusto Salazar was just completing a walk-around inspection of one of the two F-5E fighters that would be going on the escort flight. The F-5, he had to admit, was a beautiful plane, as deadly looking as a stiletto even with two big fuel tanks on the wings and a big ground- and surface-attack rocket-pod on the belly. A far cry from his old MiGs, and sleeker and faster-looking than the French-built Mirage F1C. The Mexican government had purchased a lot of new equipment for these F-5s, so Salazar was going to fly them on this escort mission instead of the bigger but less capable Mirages.

His F-5 also carried two M39-A2 twenty-millimeter guns in the nose, each with 280 rounds of ammunition; two older Air Force AIM-9J Sidewinder missiles, the cheaper but less capable heat-seeking missiles that were useful only short-range stern chases, mounted on wingtip rails; and two ancient AIM-4 Genie radar-guided missiles linked to the F-5's upgraded AN/APQ-159 radar on wing hardpoints. The AIM-4 missiles were a last-minute experiment for this mission and had never been tested, but the missiles would 'talk' with the fire-control radar so he was going with the untested Genie missiles to retain a longer-range radar attack weapon. His wingman would be similarly equipped, except the other F-5 had only one twenty-millimeter cannon instead of two. Both fighters were still in their maintenance hangars, shielding their activities from curious onlookers – the Mexican Air Force would certainly not approve of their aircraft loaded up with missiles and ammunition on an unauthorized drug-smuggling escort flight.

The plan was to launch the F-5s as the Antonov and Douglas transport planes made their way north through Mexico toward the United States. The fighters would join with the transports over the Gulf of Mexico east of Tampico, outside of radar coverage of both Mexico and the United States, then fly in close formation with the transports as they made their drops.

With the extra fuel tanks and a bit of luck, the F-5s could fly for almost two thousand miles, which would allow the fighters to escort the transports well inside the United States to their drop points and well back into Mexico. They had refueling points set up for the returning planes all through central Mexico, at civilian airports as well as remote landing strips.

A clerk ran over to Salazar as he walked to the boarding ladder to finish his cockpit checks. 'Urgent message for you, sir,' the clerk said. Salazar read the note as his wingman, Captain Tony Vasquez, walked over to his side.

'Trouble, Colonel?'

'We received an HF message from nine-nine-Charlie. Trujillo was intercepted by the Hammerheads east of Marathon. The Hammerheads also got Gachez's pickup boat.' He crumpled up the note and threw it into the clerk's face. 'How are they finding our planes?' But of course he knew. Van Nuys . . .

'They must be using satellites or radar planes,' Vasquez said. 'We know they don't have one aerostat or carrier out there.' He paused. 'What about the other planes? What are we going to do – '

'We continue, of course,' Salazar said. 'The Hammerheads could have a dozen radar planes up there but they can't catch us if we're spread out over two thousand miles across the continent. Besides, we win every time one of those canisters leaves our planes. This is a war of numbers, Captain. We will win it.' Salazar chose not to mention that he would become that much richer if the mission continued. He turned to the clerk, who had stayed and waited for any orders. 'I want an update on the cargo planes headed to Texas, New Mexico and Louisiana,' he said.

'Right here, sir,' the clerk said, producing a clipboard. 'All three planes have landed safely in Valladolid and are refueling now. They should be airborne in fifteen minutes.'

Salazar checked his watch and made some fast mental calculations. 'We will launch as scheduled in one hour, and rendezvous in about two hours near Ciudad Victoria,' he said. 'We still have the upper hand. The Hammerheads are too late to stop us.'

Over North-Central Mexico, Near San Antonio de Bravo
Three Hours Later

The rendezvous had gone off without a hitch. Two hundred miles east of Tampico, on Mexico's east central coast, Salazar and his wingman in their F-5E fighters rendezvoused with the Antonov-26 and the Douglas DC-3 cargo planes. It was a textbook operation, using strict timing and course control with only occasional bursts of attack radar data from the F-5s to make the joinup. The two F-5s each sided with a cargo plane and tucked in close, nearly merging wingtips. By the time the flight of aircraft was within radar range of Mexican air-traffic controllers at Tampico, they looked precisely what their flight planes said they would be – two Carmen del Sol Airlines planes flying together. The planes were precisely on course and on time, and so they received immediate clearance to enter Mexican airspace. As the flight of aircraft reached a point one hundred miles east of Chihuahua, the DC-3 with its F-5 fighter continued northeast on its flight-plan route to Nogales, while the Antonov-26 headed north towards Ciudad Juarez, skirting the Rio Grande River.

The routing of this flight was critical. Unlike the DC-3, which would land in Nogales and offload its cargo on the ground, the Antonov-26 would make a drop along the US–Mexican border in spots between the towns of Ojinaga and Felix Gomez in an area that had restricted radar coverage. A Border Security Force aerostat unit was located in Eagle Pass, Texas, and another at Fort Huachuca, Arizona, and both sites were effective and well maintained. But two other sites at Deming, New Mexico, and Marfa, Texas, had suspended operations on account of budget constraints. So there was a significant gap in radar coverage that was only partially offset by air traffic control radars in El Paso and Juarez. Although Customs and Border Security Force patrols had been increased in the southwest Texas border area, there should be no way to track an aircraft at low altitude in this area . . . at least that was what Salazar believed as the Antonov-26 cleared off frequency with air traffic controllers in Chihuahua, waited a few minutes until safely off the controller's screens, then descended to a thousand feet to begin their drops.

Salazar's intelligence was correct: the aerostat radar balloons at Marfa and Deming were indeed impotent – they were flying as a show, the radars were not functional. But the ROTH radar site in north-central Arkansas scanned the border area constantly, and it had steered the Hammerheads' modified P-3 Orion radar plane and two AV-22 Sea Lion aircraft into the area. Another Border Security Force radar plane was carefully following the Douglas transport as it made its way to Nogales . . .

'Lion flight, this is Shark,' the controller aboard the P-3 called on the scrambled tactical frequency, 'your target has just begun a descent. He's at your ten o'clock, twenty miles. Descend to four thousand feet MSL, use caution, high terrain and power lines in your vicinity and within five hundred feet of your final altitude, El Paso altimeter, two-niner-niner-eight.'

'Lion Two-One flight of two, leaving ten thousand for four thousand,' Hardcastle replied. He was in the lead Sea Lion aircraft, with ex-army helicopter pilot Rachel Sanchez as his copilot; Rushell Masters and Sandra Geffar were in Lion Two-Two flying in formation with him. They were just on the U.S. side of the border paralleling Salazar's course. Hardcastle was using the PNVS goggles to locate terrain and other obstructions. 'Give me the MMR on "MW SEARCH," Rachel,' Hardcastle said as they passed eight thousand feet.

'You got it, Multi-mode radar to "OPR," mode set to millimeter-wave radar search, built-in test completed, and you've got a green light.' Sanchez had activated the Sea Lion's millimeter-wave radar system; the ten-inch-diameter radar would help detect small obstructions in the plane's flight path such as power lines and radio towers, dangerous features that were usually undetectable even with a high-quality night-vision system. The MMR impulses were transmitted to Hardcastle's night-vision goggles as a thin white line across his field of view; if an obstruction was detected the line would squiggle and jump in the area of the strongest radar reflections.

'I've got a good trace,' Hardcastle said. He continued his descent and leveled off at four thousand feet; the radar altimeter read about fifteen hundred feet. They were on the western edge of the Stockton Plateau of southern Texas – although the terrain was generally flat and rolling, the high desert terrain also showed a few cliffs and dangerous valleys with power lines strung across them that had very often trapped unwary pilots. 'MMR to standby.' Sanchez flipped off the radar for him; they were still high enough to clear all obstacles in the area.

'Target at your eleven o'clock, ten miles, altitude five hundred feet, speed two hundred knots,' Hardcastle said.

'He might as well be a thousand miles away,' Sanchez said irritably. 'We still can't touch him without clearance to cross into Mexican airspace.'

'Elliott said he'd get it, so he will,' Hardcastle said.

'And what if he doesn't? We're up here watching the biggest drug shipment in history go down right before our eyes.'

'Give it a rest, Rachel,' Hardcastle said. 'Everything that can be done is being done . . .' It sounded lame even to Hardcastle too. Sanchez was only saying what she was thinking. The only thing that kept the Hammerheads away from getting the Cuchillos was a line on a map. There was no such line out here in the dead of night, flying the nap of the earth. One push on the stick, one nudge of the power control, and he'd have this smuggler in his sights.

'Target now at two hundred feet AGL, airspeed one-fifty,' the controller aboard the P-3 Orion radar plane reported. 'Lion flight, recommend you maintain your altitude to insure terrain clearance. We show you at one thousand six hundred AGL at this time.'

'Checks, Shark,' Hardcastle replied, verifying the Orion's readout with the radar altitude. 'Shark, I know the target's making a drop. Are you *positive* he's in Mexico?'

'Affirmative, Two-One. Well south of the border, five miles south-west of San Antonio de Bravo. He's not taking any chances.'

'There's no runway for a hundred miles – he's sure as hell not getting ready to land,' Hardcastle said. 'It's pitch-black dark outside – he's sure as hell not sightseeing. You showing any other aircraft in this area?'

'Negative, Lion flight. Normal traffic in and around Juarez and El Paso, nothing in this area.'

'So the *federales* aren't here. Great. So much for support from the Mexicans. Where's our clearance? If they don't want to get this guy why not let us do it? Has any one of those bozos from Washington called yet?'

'Negative, Two-One. We'll notify you as soon as they do.'

If they do . . . Hardcastle thought. 'This is stupid, what a waste – '

'Lead, this is Two-Two,' Geffar radioed over to him. 'What are we going to do? Bore more holes in the sky?'

Hardcastle was tempted to ignore the P-3 controllers and conduct the intercept on his own – it would have been easy, if not legal, to say that in his opinion the suspects were in the United States. Instead he hit the mike button: 'Sit tight, Two-Two. We'll go when we get clearance.'

'Lion Two-One flight, this is Shark. I have two high-speed aircraft heading northeast-bound from Chihuahua, range seven-zero miles, speed one-three zero knots. I'm picking up Mexican Air Force modes and codes. Looks like your *federales* are on the way after all.'

'Are they heading for the target aircraft or the drop point?'

'Neither right now,' the controller replied. 'They're heading northeast towards Ojinaga, about fifty miles south of here. They may be heading for the border on a standard patrol sweep, or it may just be a liaison flight – cargo or passengers only. They may not know that a drop is in progress.'

'Or care,' Sanchez said cross-cockpit.

'Shark, is there any way to contact them?' Hardcastle asked. 'Can we find their tactical frequency? I don't want to alert the smugglers if I can help it.'

'I can contact Chihuahua Approach or Monterey Flight

Following on a land line and see if they'll give me that information. Stand by.'

A two-minute pause, then: 'Two-One, this is Shark. Negative on your request. Chihuahua has no air-traffic-control contact with that flight. They did verify that it was a Mexican Air Force border-patrol flight but they won't give me his tactical frequency. I have the phone number of the district border-patrol headquarters. I'll see if I can get anywhere with that. Chihuahua said that flight does monitor GUARD channel.'

The two Sea Lion interceptors had moved as close to the border as they could – they were directly overflying the center of the Rio Grande River. Off in the distance, a few miles south of the tiny village of San Antonio de Bravo, Hardcastle could see clusters of headlights spaced about a hundred feet apart, with vehicles racing from one group of lights to the other. With the PNVS zoomed to maximum magnification, Hardcastle could just make out a few trucks and vans encircling a small, tubular object.

'Shark, I see trucks and vans around what appears to be a cylindrical container. There are groups of trucks, each about a hundred feet apart. I think that plane made a drop just south of San Antonio de Bravo.' Hardcastle flipped up his night-vision sight system, reached over to the center multi-function display and entered the VHF GUARD emergency channel frequency into the number-two radio. Before Sanchez could ask what he was going to do, Hardcastle hit the mike button: 'Attention, Mexican Air Force helicopter on northeasterly heading, thirty miles west of Ojinaga, Mexico, this is the United States Border Security Force on GUARD. We are five miles south of San Antonio de Bravo over Rio Grande. We have observed a suspect drug drop in this vicinity and have suspects in view. We request you divert San Antonio de Bravo and contact us on VHF frequency one-one-two point five-five for further information. Please acknowledge. Over.'

Sanchez nodded to Hardcastle as he lowered his visor once again. 'I guess it was the only thing we could do,' she said. 'But the smugglers had to have heard that message . . . they're bound to run now.'

Hardcastle had transitioned to full helicopter mode and was flying gentle circles around the Rio Grande, just on the other side of the border from the suspected drop site – without a telescope night-vision system it was unlikely they could be spotted by the smugglers. 'I just hope the *federales* hightail it over here now.'

And then on the Hammerheads' common tactical frequency they heard, 'United States Border Security Force, this is Pajaro One-Seven-One flight of two on frequency one-one-two point five-five. We read you. Over.'

'Pajaro One-Seven-One, this is Lion Two-One Flight of two. Can you divert immediately to San Antonio de Bravo to investigate a suspected drug delivery? We are in pursuit of a suspect and believe he has made a drug drop in this area. Over.'

'Affirmative, Lion Two-One. We were notified of this by our headquarters. Hold your position. We are vectoring now.'

'Lion flight, that Mexican helicopter is turning toward you,' the P-3 reported. 'His ETE is fourteen minutes.'

'Shark, get on the phone again and call Aladdin,' Hardcastle said. 'In fourteen minutes these guys on the ground will be gone. We need permission to cross *now*.'

'Roger, Two-One. We'll rattle their cage again.' But a moment later: 'Lion flight, be advised, the target is descending once again and slowing. Looks like another drop. This one is twenty miles north of your position, right along the border.'

'Copy that. Two-Two, break off and catch up with that air target. Keep him under surveillance as long as you can.'

663

'Roger, Two-One,' Rushell Masters replied. 'Shark, Lion Two-Two is proceeding northward as a solo.'

'Roger, Two-Two. Squawk normal, fly heading three-five five, take eight thousand feet, your target is twenty miles. El Paso altimeter, two-niner-niner-eight.' Hardcastle turned and watched as the second AV-22, which had dropped into a hover just a few yards off Hardcastle's left wing, banked hard left and sped away.

But when Hardcastle looked back at the drop zone, he felt another wave of frustration wash over him. The trucks and vans that had clustered around the drop zone now began to pull away from the area, scattering in all directions. The smugglers were escaping . . . 'Pajaro One-Seven-One, this is Lion Two-One, the suspects on the ground are leaving the area. Two trucks seem to be heading in your direction. They're paralleling the river. Will you be able to spot them?'

'Affirmative, Two-One,' the Mexican helicopter pilot replied. 'We are night-vision-goggle equipped. Stand by.'

Hardcastle translated the AV-22 left so he could keep as many vehicles in view as possible, but he soon had to leave the larger group and focus in on the two large trucks that were speeding along the low hills and gullies of the Rio Grande. A few long minutes later, Hardcastle could see flashing lights and an occasional searchlight beam stab into the darkness and sweep across the ground. Soon the searchlight beam stopped its sweeping search-pattern and held steady on one of the retreating trucks. The second Mexican helicopter peeled off and hit the second truck with another searchlight.

On the scrambled tactical frequency Hardcastle reported, 'Shark, this is Two-One. It looks like those Pajaro choppers got – '

Suddenly a burst of fire erupted from one of the helicopters, and the searchlight beam began to swerve and jab in every direction. As the glare of the searchlight cut off, Hardcastle could see volleys of heavy automatic-weapons fire erupting from both trucks. 'They're under attack . . .'

Screaming in Spanish was heard on the Hammerheads' frequency. '*Ayuda, ayuda, Pájaro . . . ataque para fusil enemigo . . . ayuda . . .*'

'Pájaro One-Seven-One, this is Lion Two-One,' Hardcastle said over the flight common frequency. 'Can you hear me?'

The searchlight had gone out, but some of the lead helicopter's lights were still on. The pilot was apparently still in at least partial control of the chopper, trying to get out of range of the murderous guns on the truck and to autorotate his machine for landing. Through the PNVS visor Hardcastle could see smoke billow from the sides of the chopper, which was still being raked by gunfire. 'Pájaro One-Seven-One, acknowledge! Do you need assistance?'

'Lion . . . Lion Two-One . . . this is Pájaro flight . . . Mayday, Mayday, we are under attack . . . Mayday . . .'

'That's it,' Hardcastle said. He threw full power into his Sea Lion and raced forward across the Rio Grande toward the scene of the attack. 'Shark, this is Lion Two-One. I have received a Mayday call and I can observe an aircraft in distress. I am moving to investigate. Notify Mexican defense authorities that Pájaro One-Seven-One flight of two helicopters are under attack and that I am moving to render assistance.'

'Lion Two-One, roger, understand and acknowledge receipt of Mayday broadcast.'

The rules changed on receipt of a Mayday. But at this point Hardcastle probably couldn't have held off any longer. 'Get the lights on, set radar to terrain-avoidance and put fifty feet on the radar altimeter-warning bug, Rachel,' Hardcastle said. As Sanchez hurried to set up the cockpit Hardcastle pressed the interphone button and told Don Rice, commander of his I-Team: 'Stand by on the cargo ramp. We've got a Mexican helicopter under attack by heavy-weapons fire from the ground. Deploying weapons pods.' He activated the TADS targeting system, which automatically swung both the six-missile Sea Stinger and the Chain Gun pods into slipstream and activated them. Hardcastle selected the Sea Stinger aiming system and centered the aiming doughnut on the nearest truck.

The lead Mexican helicopter had meanwhile autorotated to a hard landing about fifty yards from the two trucks. 'The Pájaro bird's down,' Sanchez called out.. 'It's lying on its side, but I don't see any fire. Some soldiers are climbing out . . .'

Men on the first truck were still firing on the fallen helicopter with what looked like an M60 machine gun, poking through a rip in the canvas side of the truck and held in position by large brownish white packages – they were bracing the machine gun with bags of *cocaine*. 'They're still hosing the chopper.' Hardcastle deactivated his night-vision visor, retaining the TADS targeting system for the Sea Stingers, and turned on the NightSun searchlight. 'Come on, scumbags – you want someone to shoot at, take a poke at me.'

The searchlight had the effect Hardcastle wanted. Through his visor Hardcastle watched as men on the truck pointed at the searchlight beam. The M60 gun disappeared, only to reappear at the back of the truck, this time on a short metal pedestal. The men in the truck did not appear to have any night-vision equipment, so Hardcastle deactivated the searchlight. Seconds later Hardcastle could see the M60 open fire in his direction.

'Crew, we are under attack,' Hardcastle said. He clicked the radio onto the GUARD channel: 'United States Border Security Force, cease fire. Shark, Two-One is under attack and is returning fire.' He then armed the Sea Stinger pod, waited two seconds until he got a lock-on tone from a missile, flipped open the trigger guard, and fired one missile. Actually, he was not authorized to return fire unless fired on, and even then he was required to notify his command authority and issue a warning before attempting to defend his aircraft. Well, you couldn't always cross all the damn Ts . . .

At first the Sea Stinger had nothing to aim at but the residual warmth of the truck's rear, but with the M60 pumping out two hundred rounds per minute, the missile found more than enough heat energy to lock onto. The missile's motor was still running when the Sea Stinger plowed into the back end of the truck and exploded. As the truck erupted into flames, the fire mixed with the five hundred pounds of cocaine to form a black, burning caramel-like sludge that coated the gunmen in the truck with napalm-like liquid fire. Burning bodies dropped and crawled through the brush and sand until the fire found the truck's gas tank and exploded, quickly ending the screams.

Hardcastle now locked the targeting system onto the second truck. The second Mexican Air Force helicopter had landed about two hundred yards away and the soldiers had leapt out and were beginning to move in toward the last truck in the cover of darkness. When the first truck exploded, the second was not about to wait around – it dropped into low gear and sped south, a gunman in the back firing random bursts at anything that moved.

The Sea Stinger missile system indicated a solid lock-on after Hardcastle centered the doughnut on the fleeing truck. The missile went into the engine compartment near the left front wheel, ripping the front axle off the truck in the explosion of its warhead. The engine compartment began to burn fiercely, but several men jumped to safety and ran in every direction. Hardcastle pivoted the AV-22 around and deactivated the weapon system, stowing both weapons pods back into the cargo bay. Using the night-vision system, he maneuvered back to the stricken Mexican helicopter and set down about forty yards away.

'I-Team, the Mexican chopper is on the starboard side about fifteen yards away,' Hardcastle announced. 'Don, check out the occupants and ask the commander to come aboard.' With sidearms drawn, Don Rice and another member of the I-Team went through the starboard entry door after Hardcastle signaled that it was safe to exit. Two other I-Team members unslung M-16 rifles and covered them.

The Mexican Air Force soldiers were banged up, one badly injured, but all were able to travel. With one I-Team member ushering the soldiers away from the starboard engine nacelle's powerful exhaust, Rice escorted the Mexican soldiers carrying an injured man into the Sea Lion chopper. The soldiers set the man on a seat just to the right of the entry hatch. When Hardcastle came back to speak with them he noted that the injured man wore a flight suit and silver stars on his shoulders. 'Are you the pilot?' Hardcastle asked.

The man nodded. Rice brought a first-aid kid as the Mexican said, 'I am Colonel Geraldo Hidalgo of the Mexican Air Force. You . . . you are the commander of this aircraft?'

'Ian Hardcastle, United States Border Security Force.'

'Hardcastle? Admiral Hardcastle. Commander of the Hammerheads?'

'Yes and no. I'm just another pilot tonight. Are you hurt badly?'

'I can't move my left leg or wrist, but I don't think they're broken. What about my other helicopter? What about the smugglers?'

'Your men appear safe, their helicopter landed okay. We

got both trucks. Your men are rounding up the smugglers from the second truck. They won't have to bother with the ones from the first.'

'So I noticed,' Hidalgo said, managing a weak smile. 'Impressive firepower. I have always wanted to fly one of your Sea Lions . . .' He looked at his wrist, limp on his thigh, 'Now when I find myself aboard I cannot fly it.'

'No, but you can take command of her,' Hardcastle said. 'The plane that dropped these drugs is making multiple drops all along the Texas–Mexico border. We've been tracking him for hours but couldn't pursue him into Mexican airspace without authorization . . . But with *you* aboard in charge of the operation, we can do it . . .'

Hidalgo's face brightened. 'You mean we go after those *perros sucios* in this Sea Lion . . . and I am in command? *Sí*, Admiral Hardcastle. If all you require is my permission, I give it to you. Let me check on my wingman first, then we will see about these *desenmascarars*.'

It did not take long for Hidalgo to check on the rest of his men; four of the six smugglers were already being led toward the Sea Lion by Mexican troops, and those captured smugglers were carrying the bodies of two more smugglers. The commander of the second Mexican helicopter gave Hidalgo a report that was obviously favorable . . . Hidalgo clasped him firmly on the shoulder and ordered himself taken back to the AV-22.

Hidalgo found a headset and set it on his head. 'We have a job to do, Admiral Hardcastle. Let's begin.'

Near the Town of Felix U. Gomez, Seventy-five Miles Northwest of San Antonio de Bravo, Mexico

Salazar's largest cargo plane, the Antonov-26 that he was escorting near the US–Mexico border near El Paso, still had fifteen hundred kilos of cocaine on board when they heard Hardcastle's first warning on the emergency GUARD channel. The formation maintained radio silence, but Salazar had no trouble guessing what the crew of the Antonov was thinking – get as far away from the United States as possible. That was confirmed when the last transmission they heard on the Hammerheads' common frequency said that one of the AV-22's was responding to an emergency situation across the border. Gachez's people on the ground were heavily armed and may have been able to tear up the Mexican patrol that was in the area, but it would be a different story against an armed AV-22.

If they had only a few hundred kilos of cocaine left, he might have ordered the Antonov crew to abort the last few drops and get away from the border, from whatever long-range surveillance system was feeding the Hammerheads with such accurate intercept data. But they had fifteen hundred kilos on board – over three thousand pounds – and it was worth over twenty-two million dollars extra if they delivered it as planned. It didn't matter if the Mexican *federales* snatched it all up five minutes after the delivery – his part of the contract ended when the drugs were delivered to the spot designated by the ground crew.

The fact that the Hammerheads had closed in so fast made it obvious that Van Nuys had been taken by the Border Security Force and had spilled his guts right after his capture. Equally obvious, Carmen del Sol Airlines was history, and although he had several other front-companies established in other countries, including a few in the US itself, he was a man without a country or a base. He had his life, a few secret bank accounts, a few loyal soldiers to throw into battle, and for now he had a beautiful F-5E jet fighter with plenty of firepower aching to be released. It just might be enough.

But to survive this thing he needed every dime he could

670

scratch from Gachez and the rest of the Medellín Cartel before everything completely went to hell. Which once again meant making this last delivery and earning that last twenty-two million *no matter what*. One plus in all this was, for security reasons, the ground crews at each drop-point knew nothing about what was happening at another site and could not communicate with each other – so it was still possible for him to make this delivery and get his money, even though the whole thing was unraveling before his eyes.

Two more drops, and it would be all over . . .

Salazar now found himself pulling back on the F-5's throttle to maintain his position on the Antonov-26 cargo plane. He checked his watch and flight plan – five minutes until the next drop. The An-26 was slowing down for the drop, getting into the proper flight parameters – precise airspeed, altitude and drift correction – for a ballistically computed drop. For a safety margin, Salazar extended the flaps ten degrees to allow the F-5 to fly at the slower speed with better control, and increased his altitude so he could better watch all sides of the Antonov for signs of pursuit. At this new vantage point just a few meters above and behind the cargo plane's rudder, he could see the big vertical stabilizer oscillate back and forth as the pilot made small corrections to stay on course . . .

The beam of light lanced out of the night sky like a spear thrown from the Almighty. It hit the pilot's side of the cockpit like a thunderbolt, the glare so bright, so sudden that the An-26's pilot had to fight to maintain control – it was even too bright in Salazar's F-5's cockpit, where it wasn't even aimed. The An-26's pilot was so badly startled he almost lost control of the plane, and Salazar finally had to peel off to the right, take spacing and put in more power to stay with him. At less than one hundred feet above the ground there was no room for error.

The An-26 pilot did somehow get back control, but the drop was blown – they had already moved several hundred meters closer to the Rio Grande River than they should be. Salazar gained more altitude and saw it: less than a mile behind them, a silver bullet illuminated like a Christmas tree from hell – a Hammerheads AV-22 Sea Lion tilt-rotor interceptor with its flashing warning lights, the steerable NightSun searchlight. Salazar could even see the 'FOLLOW ME' sign in huge electroluminescent letters on its fuselage. *What was an AV-22 doing in Mexican airspace?*

'Break radio silence,' Salazar radioed to the Antonov-26. 'Get back on course and make the drop. Ignore the aircraft off your left wing . . .'

'Attention cargo plane, attention fighter plane, this is the Air Force of the Republic of Mexico,' a voice cut in on the emergency GUARD channel. 'You are in violation of Mexican air-navigation and national-security laws. Lower your landing gear and follow me. If you do not comply you will be forced to land or be attacked. I am authorized by the Republic of Mexico to use deadly force if necessary.' The message began to be repeated in Spanish.

'Continue the drop,' Salazar ordered over the command radio.

'We've lost the WET SNOW beacon, colonel,' the An-26 pilot replied. 'Repeat, we've lost the beacon . . .'

'Damn them . . .' Salazar meant the ground crew that had obviously spotted the AV-22's lights and run off. 'Proceed on backup timing and flight plan route. *Make the drop.*'

The AV-22 had moved closer, almost abeam the pilot's left side and now less than a quarter-mile away. The NightSun searchlight was boring into the Antonov's cockpit – Salazar's eyes almost hurt thinking of what the pilots were experiencing. 'Make the drop,' he called out again. And then realized that the An-26 had lost several dozen

672

feet and a good deal of airspeed – the pilot probably couldn't see the instrument panel any more. 'Get your nose up, get back on course . . .'

As the pilot panicked when he saw that his altitude had deteriorated, the An-26 heeled sharply left and up with the engines at full power. A few canisters of cocaine dropped out of the big cargo doors on the left and right sides, but the crew had abandoned the drop as well.

'Lower your landing gear and follow me or you will be fired on,' the Spanish-accented voice said again on GUARD. 'This is your final warning.'

Salazar now threw full afterburner power on the twin turbojets and accelerated above and past the Antonov-26. When clear of the cargo plane he punched off the two nearly empty fuel tanks and armed his AIM-4 and AIM-9 missiles as well as the twenty-millimeter cannons. He climbed to five thousand feet in twenty seconds, rolled hard left, and searched for the AV-22.

Nothing. The AV-22 crew had extinguished the searchlight and the warning lights as soon as his F-5 broke formation . . .

Aboard the AV-22 Sea Lion Two-One

'Two-One, target two is climbing rapidly at your twelve to one o'clock position, now four miles,' the P-3 Orion controller's warning blared on the scrambled channel. 'Target two is level at five thousand feet, moving to your eleven o'clock, airspeed three hundred knots and accelerating. He's turning in front of you.'

Hardcastle shut down the searchlight the moment he saw the F-5's afterburners ignite. 'Set the MMR to air-search mode,' he ordered. He pushed in full power, set the AV-22's engine nacelles to forty-five degrees for maximum velocity and vertical-lift authority and began a slow, nose-high climb. 'Get the lights off, crew, we're under attack.'

Sanchez quickly shut off all the exterior lights and dimmed the cockpit lights, but while she set the multi-mode to air-target search mode she said, 'What are you doing, you can't dogfight this guy – '

'We can't outrun him, either,' Hardcastle said. 'We've got to hold on until – '

The center multi-function display on Hardcastle's instrument panel flared to life. The Sea Lion's phased-array radar, which sent out a cone of radar energy that swept thirty degrees in every direction around the nose, picked up an air target and locked on. Hardcastle switched the targeting system to slave to the radar, which locked the infrared scanner onto the fast-moving fighter. Hardcastle tried to turn fast enough to keep the radar aimed at the fighter, but the radar quickly broke lock. The fighter was racing in a tight circle around the Sea Lion.

'Two-One, target two has moved around to your eight o'clock position, three miles, airspeed three-fifty,' the Orion controller reported. 'Descend and maintain one hundred feet AGL, turn to heading one-zero-five, vector to the border. You can use the terrain along the river banks to hide from him.'

'It's no use,' Hardcastle said. 'He's moving too fast. Hang on.'

Leaving the throttles at full power, Hardcastle moved the engine nacelles to full vertical position, then did a tight pivot to face the F-5 fighter head-on and translated into a hover just out of ground effect at three-hundred feet, adjusting the throttles to hold the Sea Lion's altitude steady. The radar locked on as the nose swept around. 'There he is,' Sanchez called out. 'We're head-to-head. His airspeed's up to four hundred knots, range two miles . . .'

Hardcastle shoved the throttles back to full power. With

the engine nacelles full vertical, the Sea Lion darted straight up at six hundred feet per minute. Just as he started to climb, he could see tongues of flame and bright winks of light erupt from the point in the darkness ahead where the F-5 was – he was firing on them . . . Hardcastle quickly switched to the M230 cannon, slaved the cannon pod's aiming system to the multi-mode radar and pulled the trigger when the fighter was within one mile.

But the M230 cannon pod wasn't designed for high-speed dogfights – it was made for attacking surface vessels and aircraft flying less than half the speed of Salazar's F-5. Hardcastle caught a glimpse of the F-5 as it sped less than a hundred feet under the hovering Sea Lion, wheeled left and tried to turn the Sea Lion fast enough for the M230 pod to keep track, but he had no chance with the Chain Gun pod . . .

Quickly he selected the Sea Stinger missile pod, then pivoted further to align on the retreating F-5 fighter as he waited for the aiming doughnut to appear. But the instant it popped onto his field of view he made a small correction to center it on the radar-tracking signal, got a lock-on beep from one of the Sea Stinger missiles – and fired.

He knew the game was over moments after the missile left the pod. It tracked dead on the hot tailpipe of the F-5E fighter – until Salazar made a hard climbing right turn to line up again on the AV-22. The small Sea Stinger missile made a sharp but erratic bob to try to keep up, immediately lost the heat signal, and exploded moments later. Like the Chain Gun pod, the Sea Stinger, Hardcastle knew, was just not designed to kill fast-moving jets, especially one as small and maneuverable as an F-5.

Now he dialed the engine nacelles down to begin moving forward – the closer he could get toward the oncoming F-5, the less time Salazar would have to aim and fire. But with the F-5 now traveling seven miles a minute, the AV-22 appeared as if it was in a constant hover. Hardcastle switched back to the Chain Gun pod, raised the nose and held the trigger down as the F-5 bore in for the kill. Firing ten high-explosive rounds per second and already partially depleted from the earlier attacks, the Chain Gun ran out of ammunition in a few seconds, well before the F-5 fighter opened fire. In a last-ditch effort to save them, Hardcastle chopped the power and dumped the nose, throwing the AV-22 toward the earth.

The sudden maneuver may have kept Salazar in the F-5 from concentrating a sustained burst on the Sea Lion but it wasn't enough to keep Hardcastle's plane from getting hit. Twenty-millimeter shells plowed into the center-wing area, rupturing fuel-transfer lines and causing a fire in the hydraulic and fuel systems. The F-5 used a little right rudder and walked the murderous gunfire straight down the left wing, chewing great holes in the wing and splitting open the left-engine nacelle. The Sea Lion heeled sharply over into the free-rotating left rotor, and the aircraft plummeted to the ground.

Because Hardcastle had almost landed the plane before the attack the drop was only thirty feet. The left engine nacelle and wing hit first, collapsed into a ball of flames and burst apart. The destroyed wing tore free of the weakened center-wing pivot, and the fuselage was thrown another two hundred feet along the desert and scrub brush before nosing over an embankment and skidding down into the Rio Grande.

Although smoke filled the cockpit, Hardcastle found his harness-release switch, unstrapped and climbed out of his seat. The left side cockpit windows were smashed in, clouds of smoke and debris flowing inside and waves of searing heat enveloping Sanchez. Fueled by a rush of adrenaline, Hardcastle unstrapped her from the seat and carried her from the plane, cradling her bleeding head on his shoulder.

Nearly ankle-deep in fuel-soaked sand, Hardcastle ran into the Rio Grande, waded in thigh-deep water until his legs gave out, then half-floated, half-crawled to the shore, a hundred yards downstream from the crash site. The Sea Lion lay crumpled on its right side, the right-engine nacelle bent awkwardly and nearly snapped off the wing and the right rotor blades stuck deep into the side of the embankment. It looked like a mangled bird, with its huge cockpit windows a blank death's stare, imploring for help. A fire had started in the area of the sheared left wing, and quickly spread to the right wing.

'Rice!' Hardcastle shouted. 'Hidalgo!' He tried to crawl up to his feet but his legs were too weak. Cursing his body, Hardcastle made sure Rachel Sanchez was safely out of the water and breathing, then began crawling through the sand up the embankment.

Suddenly, the sound of burning fuel and popping metal was replaced by the smooth, rattlesnake-like hissing of a jet fighter passing overhead – the F-5 fighter screaming less than fifty feet overhead. He was coming around for one last pass . . .

In the glow of the stricken Sea Lion aircraft Salazar saw him – none other than Admiral Hardcastle, crawling up the side of the riverbank. Someone was with him, still lying near the water's edge. Salazar checked his fuel – less than forty minutes' worth – but he had made up his mind as soon as he saw Hardcastle crawling like a dried-up old turtle on the water's edge. It didn't matter if he was only running on fumes. He was going to kill Admiral Hardcastle. He started a thirty-degree-bank turn to the right, circling over the crash site and using the burning Sea Lion as a landmark. He used the tight turn to bleed off airspeed, slowing to one hundred eight knots – the slowest he dared go at such a low altitude – and racetracked around to line up for one last strafing run on the beach. The F-5E had no true ground-attack mode for the twin cannons, but the reticle was accurate enough to smear bullets in the area.

Rolling out of his final turn, he saw Hardcastle trying to drag his comrade out of the water and into the shadow of a few bushes near the top of the embankment. It was thoughtful of them to move closer together. As he moved within cannon range, he saw that Hardcastle had taken out his sidearm and appeared to be firing . . . at *him*. The ultimate futile gesture, like a mouse pissing on an eagle just before the end –

'Yo. Colonel Salazar. This is your old friend Viktor Charbakov. I'm a'comin' for you, old buddy.'

'Who? What?' The strange voice on the emergency GUARD channel was immediately followed by the scream of the F-5's Threat Warning Receiver and a blinking red air-to-air radar threat-warning indicator. At first Salazar was distracted by the man's voice on the radio, then by the warning light. He quickly looked around for any sign of pursuit – pointless, really, since except for the burning AV-22 below it was totally black outside. By the time he faced around to check his alignment on Hardcastle, the aiming reticle had just passed over him. He did get a half-second burst off before flying overhead. But who. . . ?

'You remember me, Colonel. Flight Kepten Viktor Peytorvich Charbakov?' It was, Salazar now realized, the young pilot that had flown the Sukhoi-29 into Verrettes!

Powell had been alerted by Elliott once the details of Salazar's plan were known, and since the Border Security Force and the Mexican government had finally made a cooperative border security agreement, he had been standing by with a two-seat F-15E fighter from nearby Luke Air Force Base, with the representative of the Mexican Air Force flying in the backseat, to chase down Agusto Salazar.

'You threw one of your pig-stickers into my arm,

Colonel. I wanted to get you so bad I joined the U.S. Air Force to get a shot at you. Now it's just you and me.'

Salazar put in full power. No afterburners . . . that would have been an easy giveaway . . . climbed to only two hundred feet and turned northwest. With an enemy somewhere nearby, pitch black outside, a threat-warning receiver that didn't give bearings to the source of the enemy radar, he had no choice against a pursuer except to run – and the best place to run was the city of Juarez, with El Paso right across the river. The ground clutter might disrupt their radar, giving him a better chance to escape.

'Colonel Agusto Salazar,' another voice, an older, Latino voice, came on the channel, 'this is General Tomas Rodriguez Fuentes of the Monterrey District Head-quarters of the Mexican Air Forces. You are ordered to reverse course and lower your landing gear immediately.'

Salazar was only ten miles outside Juarez – already overflying outlying villages and communities. He had to delay his pursuers for just a few moments longer – then, so close to the city, they would not dare open fire on him . . . 'General, I would not do that,' Salazar said on the GUARD emergency channel. 'My men have your family . . .'

There was a long pause. The lights of the city were getting closer – Juarez was just six miles away, the outlying lights almost touching the air-data probe on the needle-nose of the F-5. Just a few more . . .

Salazar reached between his legs and pulled the yellow ejection ring moments before the Mexican general hit the launch button and sent two Sidewinder missiles from Powell's F-15E fighter into the F-5. Both missiles hit dead on target, and the fighter blew apart like a ripe melon hit full force by a sledgehammer, pieces scattering for miles across the Rio Grande and sending debris over both sides of the border . . .

Salazar was jarred by a huge slap of jet-hot wind followed by a driving, pounding noise. His helmet was ripped from his head, breaking his nose and temporarily blinding him. His parachute opened in time to give him one swing in a fully opened chute before he slammed into the hard-packed earth, head and shoulders first.

Dazed, bleeding, his left shoulder in a vise-tight jaw of pain, Salazar untangled his feet from the parachute risers and painfully unclipped himself from the parachute harness. There was a shack about a half-mile away on fire, and beyond that it seemed the entire desert was ablaze. He dragged himself to a tree nearby and drew his sidearm, a Soviet-made Tokarev ten-millimeter automatic pistol with a nine-round clip.

It now appeared to Salazar that he had landed just a few hundred meters outside a small farm. He could see buildings and a pyramid-shaped grain silo, highlighted by the glow of the fires. Just ten meters to his left he saw a pickup truck and decided to make his way to it. But as he did he heard a sound overhead – another Sea Lion aircraft was hovering only a few hundred meters away, searching near the area where he had landed. He couldn't stay around here – the Hammerheads were closing in . . .

Ignoring the pain in his shoulder, Salazar crawled to his feet and ran to the pickup, crashing, exhausted, into the passenger door. He pulled open the door and crawled inside just as the NightSun searchlight flared through the darkness and the heavy, rhythmic beat of the Sea Lion's rotors got louder and louder –

The driver's door now swung open, Salazar raised his pistol and aimed at the head of . . . an old women who had come out to see what all the late-night commotion was about. What she confronted, and froze her, was a mangled, bloody face.

As the searchlight beam came closer Salazar managed to

get out in Spanish, 'Wave at the plane, old woman. Wave pretty . . .'

The NightSun beam swept across the side of the farmhouse and rested just in front of the pickup truck. Salazar slumped to the floor of the truck, as far into the shadows as he could. '*Wave*.' The old woman looked into the bright light and waved at the Sea Lion crew. The beam swept around the yard, searching the tree that Salazar had just hidden near, then moved away . . .

He had made it . . . the Hammerheads had missed the dark, camouflaged parachute in the plowed-up field, missed the tracks he had made in the dirt.

He hauled himself up off the floor and into the passenger side of the truck. 'Get in, old woman,' he ordered. 'You will drive me into Juarez.'

Too frightened to protest, the woman finally slid into the driver's seat and started the engine.

'Take a back road,' Salazar told her as she pulled out onto the main road. 'If we are caught by the police, you will be shot.'

'*No, señor, por favor* . . .'

'Just do as I say and you will be safe . . .' They began moving down the chip-and-seal road toward the distant glow of the city of Juarez. The woman was hunched over the steering wheel, her lips moving but not making a sound. 'Turn your damned headlights on,' Salazar shouted at her. 'Drive normally.'

The woman gasped, reached down and turned the headlight switch on . . .

And there, illuminated in the dull glow of the headlights, was a person standing in the middle of the road leading a donkey by the reins.

'*¡Jesus Cristo, el burro mio!*' the woman wailed. Salazar got a glimpse of a woman in a pair of bright-colored overalls just before the old woman slammed on the brakes. Unable to hold himself steady with his left arm, Salazar pitched forward and crashed against the dashboard.

'*¡Vaya! ¡Vaya! ¡Al abrigo!*' someone was shouting. With remarkable speed the old woman threw open her door and scrambled out. Salazar fired once out the driver's door but the woman had disappeared. He climbed behind the steering wheel, put the Tokarev automatic pistol on the seat beside him, and was about to put the pickup truck into gear when a blinding white light hit him in the face.

And rising out of the darkness, like some mythic, fire-breathing dragon, the AV-22 Sea Lion hovered in ground effect just a few dozen yards directly in front of the truck. The aircraft had been hiding behind a lush tree line on one side of the highway and had, seemingly, popped up out of nowhere. Salazar could see the Chain Gun pod deployed and aimed at him – in fact, he was close enough to see the pilot in the right seat with the targeting visor lowered. Soldiers in dark helmets carrying M-16 rifles were running down both sides of the road, moving to surround him . . .

He reached for the pistol . . .

'*¡Pare!*' a woman's voice sounded over the roar of the Sea Lion's rotors. 'Don't move, Salazar,' she said in English. Salazar looked to his right and saw Geffar, who had left the AV-22 when Masters landed it to unload the I-Team, aiming a huge automatic pistol directly into his bloody face. She wore a Hammerheads orange flight suit and an I-Team communications helmet. Her eyes were directly on his, as unwavering as the automatic.

The fingers of his good right hand were inches from the gun. He tried to inch it down . . .

'Go ahead,' Sandra Geffar said. 'I need to kill you. Give me a reason.'

Salazar straightened his fingers, carefully lifted them clear of the pistol.

'Hands behind your head – slow.' Salazar raised his right

hand to the back of his head, his left arm as high as he could – his dislocated shoulder was obvious. 'Don't move.' Geffar stepped away from the truck door and reached up to her helmet to draw the communications microphone closer to her lips. The Hammerheads I-Team and *federales* were closing in. 'Got him . . . Salazar,' Geffar radioed to them. 'Looks like he's hurt. Better get ground transportation out here – '

In a flash – desperation helped – Salazar's right hand moved down to the special sling behind his neck, his fingers found the leather-wrapped butt-end of a throwing knife, the knife was slipped out of the sling and Salazar aimed –

Fast as he was, his old lightning speed had been leeched by the injury, which, along with Van Nuys' tip, gave Geffar her chance . . . and as he aimed to let fly she dropped into a shooter's crouch and fired, all in a single motion. The first .45-caliber slug, the one that counted, that made the difference, went through his right eye, into the back of his skull, scattering brain tissue over the cab of the truck. The remaining rounds were redundant, but necessary. They were for too many good people, dead and still to die, thanks to the late Colonel Agusto Salazar.

Epilogue

The White House Press Room, Washington, DC
Two Days Later

The senior officers of the Border Security Force were standing in a line on the stage, hands behind their backs, fidgeting uncomfortably under the hot lights: Curtis Long, Rushell Masters, Sandra Geffar and Ian Hardcastle on one side of the President; the Mexican ambassador Lidia Pereira, Vice President Martindale and Drug Control Policy Advisor Samuel T. Massey on the other.

'I did not want to make a public statement about the events of the past few days,' the President began, 'without recognizing the people on this platform today. It was because of their remarkable efforts that a major multi-billion-dollar drug shipment was stopped and the principal smugglers arrested or killed. It has been a crippling, if not fatal, blow to the cartel. My special thanks go to the people and the government of Mexico, who have had the courage and conviction to enter into an unprecedented cooperative border security and anti-smuggling task force with us, one in which we will fly, sail and fight together to secure our common borders. I would especially like to thank the ambassador from Mexico, Dr Lidia Pereira, for her . . . role in securing this historic agreement.' Pereira nodded her thanks to the President, maintaining her famous smile in spite of the qualifying pause in the President's accolade. She caught it, as he intended.

'The real warriors are represented by these men and women here. They are the ones who directed the Border

Security Force aircraft, vessels and surveillance forces against a well-organized and remarkably strong paramilitary organization. My thanks to Curtis Long, director of the Hammerheads' Investigating Team; Rushell Masters, chief pilot; and especially Inspector Sandra Geffar and Admiral Ian Hardcastle, the heart, the soul of the organization. They may not consider it a reward, but I'm grounding both of them effective immediately – Ian Hardcastle will take command of the new western division of the Border Security Force, where he will be in charge of establishing detection and interception facilities and procedures for the Mexican border and against the growing California smuggling trade. Sandra Geffar will command the eastern division, including the expanded Hammerhead facilities along the Atlantic seaboard.

'I anticipate that Congress will very soon pass the law elevating the Border Security Force, the Hammerheads, to Cabinet level under civilian command. At that time my current drug control advisor, Samuel Massey, will be nominated to be the first Secretary of Border Security Forces. Further, under pending legislation, the Border Security Forces will soon officially include the Coast Guard and Customs Service under one roof so to speak, thereby uniting all federal agencies concerned with traffic across America's borders . . .'

Hardcastle, listening to the President's intention to name Massey, had to wince inwardly, remembering as he did Massey's early opposition to the notion of the Hammerheads to protect his turf. Still, maybe it was a good sign that a bureaucrat with a fierce protective instinct about his territory would be the nominal head of Hammerheads. And he suspected, thinking on it, that the President had the same idea in mind . . .

'Finally,' the President went on, 'I'd like to recognize the efforts of the Vice President in behalf of the Border

Security Force. As director of national drug control and enforcement, Kevin Martindale has taken the lead in insuring that our country remains effective in controlling our borders and stopping the spread of illegal drugs in our society. At the risk of sounding too much like a campaign speech, let me suggest America should be proud to have a man of such strength and firmness of conviction as its Vice President . . .'

Brad Elliott, Patrick McLanahan and Roland (J.C.) Powell got to their feet as the President entered the Oval Office several minutes later. The President immediately loosened his tie and sat down on the sofa, motioning for the others to join him. 'Ah, press conferences.' He sighed. 'A royal pain in the butt.'

Jack Pledgeman poured coffee for all three of them. Automatically, the President reached for the little china pot with the blue ribbon tied around its handle. Just before he poured, he stopped and looked at the little white pot with a scowl.

'What a hypocrite I am,' he muttered. 'Here I am, on my high horse preaching against drugs, and I keep this crap around my office. What the hell is the difference between this stuff and marijuana? Where the hell do I draw the line? If I put some marijuana in a china pot and tied a blue ribbon around it, would it be OK then?' He looked at the three puzzled faces seated around him, none of whom knew about the Irish cream. 'This is how we kill off society, gents – not with guns and bullets, but with tired old men with narrow minds, china pots, and blue ribbons tied to them.' He handed the pot to Pledgeman. 'Take that out of my sight and clean out every drop of it you find in my offices. Do it right now.'

The others were afraid to touch their coffee cups until the President picked his up. He looked at Elliott and smiled.

'Sorry I had to fire you for real this time, Brad. No offense, General, but I just don't think you're cut out for public life.'

'I say you're right, Mr President.'

'I'm glad you agree. Because I'm sending you and Patrick and Roland – '

'J.C., sir.'

'What?'

Elliott and McLanahan winced, knowing what was coming.

'J.C., sir. The name's J.C. No one calls me Roland except my mom.'

The President shook his head, looking at Elliott as if to ask, Where do you find these guys, General? Instead the President was heard muttering, 'Jesus Christ . . .'

'Thank you, Mr President,' J.C. deadpanned.

'As I was *saying*, General,' the President continued, giving Powell a bemused look, 'I'm sending you back to Dreamland. It would be too difficult to explain how you can be fired and promoted at the same time, so I'm sending you jokers out to the desert, where I don't have to deal with you. I know it would be too much to ask you to stay out of trouble, so I'll just say good luck and watch yourselves at all times.'

'Thank you, Mr President,' Elliott said. 'I think you've made a wise decision. We have some stuff cooking at HAWC that I think will really knock you out . . .'

'Oh God,' the President muttered, 'tell me no more . . .'

Medellín, Colombia
That Same Day

'Our losses are impossible to calculate,' Jorge Luiz Peña, one of the senior Cartel members, was saying. He and ten other directors of the Medellín drug cartel were meeting at Gonzales Rodriguez Gachez's offices in downtown Medellín going over the catastrophe that had just occurred. 'You say only five billion dollars, Gachez. *Only* five billion dollars? You are able to sit there and smile and pretend nothing has happened?'

Gachez was not really smiling, but he also was not whining like the pudgy Peña. The news of Salazar's death and the interception of the three main drug shipments was bad, very bad. They had had losses before, but never in such devastating quantities. Still, he must be careful not to appear devastated. To show weakness would be fatal with these men.

'You complain too much,' Gachez said calmly. 'You lost less product than most of us, Peña. I personally lost over two billion dollars. Escalante' – he nodded to the man – 'lost almost a billion.'

'I say to hell with you, Gachez. You and your fancy education. They sure didn't teach you much . . .' Peña's voice was rising. 'I may not have lost much compared to you, but I lost *everything*. You can start making more cocaine and be back in production in weeks. I have no way of recouping any losses. Because of *you*.'

'*I* did not lose our product,' Gachez said. 'Salazar was too confident, too cocky . . . too greedy. He actually believed he had wiped out the whole Border Security Force. He compromised all of us with his delusional behavior – '

'What about Van Nuys?' Pablo Escalante said quietly. 'You took on Van Nuys. You sent him to Mexico with Salazar . . .'

'Van Nuys had arranged things. Van Nuys was a valuable asset. It was a traitor in the Mexican Customs Bureau that turned Van Nuys in to the Hammerheads. I guarantee I will personally take care of the Customs Bureau Chief – '

'It is too late for that. He is long gone,' Escalante said. Gachez stared at Escalante. Normally animated and genial, he had been unusually quiet all during the briefing and the strategy meetings. Escalante did not have the seniority that was a traditional qualification for taking control of the Cartel, but he was rich and powerful enough to command attention when he spoke. How much had he been speaking to the others . . . ?

'Never mind, he can never get far enough away to escape me,' Gachez said with more earnestness in his voice than he intended. 'Now listen, all of you, it does us no good to point fingers at one another. We are here to discuss the future. All members will be supported through our ample contingency fund until we can resume our stockpiles and began active shipments again. No one will suffer. We must and we will find a way to break through the Border Security Force's new structure. They get tough, we get tough too. I propose – '

The doors to the conference room opened and Colombian national police officers rushed into the office with rifles at the ready. Gachez instantly was on his feet as the soldiers surrounded the Cartel officers. 'What is this? Are you crazy?'

No one said a word. No one else had gotten to their feet, or protested. In fact, it seemed he was the only one in the room that was surprised by the raid.

A senior police officer entered the room. Gachez turned to Escalante, who returned his look with a shrug.

The police officer announced, 'You are all under arrest on suspicion of trafficking cocaine. If you have any weapons, declare them immediately and surrender – '

Gachez could no longer stand it. 'You are on *my* payroll. All of you are on my payroll. I give the orders here.'

Escalante now slowly rose to his feet, and the police chief moved beside him. Gachez understood without believing. '*You?* You, Pablo? You think they will follow you? You don't have the guts or brains to run this organization. It takes strength, the willingness and ability to use it . . .'

As if in reply, Escalante reached into a coat pocket and withdrew a small semi-automatic pistol. 'You make too many threats, Gonzales. You are history, the past. You are a failure. You hired failures like Salazar, who was also a traitor and a thief.'

Escalante slid the pistol across the table to Gachez, who did not look at it. He raised his hands and smiled. 'You want to take over, Pablo? Fine. We shall see how well you do. I predict you all will come begging me to return – '

'I don't think so, Gonzales.'

The police chief raised his pistol at Gachez. 'Put down the gun, señor, or I will be forced to shoot.'

Gachez stumbled back away from the table, his hands still raised as three shots rang out. Gachez was tossed backward and landed back against the wall, blood running from his wounds for several long moments.

'Gonzales Rodriguez Gachez was wanted for questioning,' the police chief intoned. He withdrew a warrant from a tunic pocket. 'Here is the warrant. He resisted arrest, tried to flee, and fired at officers of the law, who had no choice but to return fire.'

Pablo Escalante nodded. The police chief saluted and left the office, closing the two solid oak doors behind him. Escalante returned to his seat, settled back. 'Now, gentlemen, let us get down to the business at hand. A cooperative agreement has been proposed between ourselves and the government to control the violence and . . . the excesses of our past activity, including foolish and self-defeating challenges to the American Border Security Force. At least for the time being. In return, the government will suspend its prosecutions and oppose further extraditions of our officers.' He motioned to the body on the floor. 'Gonzales Rodriguez Gachez votes in favor of the proposal. What say you, gentlemen?'

Storming Heaven

Dale Brown

The USA is under siege. With chilling ruthlessness terrorist Henri Cazaux has demonstrated the vulnerability of the USA's air defences by using large commercial aircraft to drop bombs on unsuspecting major airports. When he hits San Francisco Airport the destruction of life and property is enormous. The national panic that ensues reaches all the way to the White House.

Only one man can end the chaos: Rear Admiral Ian Hardcastle. Charged by the President with re-establishing security in the skies, Hardcastle must take drastic action to control the emergency – and quickly. But then Cazaux sets his sights on the biggest target of all – the nation's capital . . .

Storming Heaven is ex-pilot Dale Brown's most relentlessly action-packed novel yet, filled with the spectacular flying scenes, technological detail and astonishing realism that have won him his place at the leading edge of modern military thriller writing.

'Aviation ace Dale Brown has firmly established his high-tech credentials in seven bestselling aviation thrillers – *Storming Heaven*, his new, edge-of-the-cockpit novel, should rocket him out to the Van Allen belt.'

New York Daily News

'Suspenseful flying scenes – high drama in the skies.'

Today

'Cazaux is a fascinating monster; *Storming Heaven* is an explosive success.' *Booklist*

ISBN 0 00 649357 2